Elizabeth's unborn child needs a father.

Daniel's bratty ten-year-old needs a mother.

And the wailing bundle in Chandra's barn needs all the help he can get.

Elizabeth, Daniel and Chandra. They were parents without partners...but look what they've fallen into!

Suddenly, they're on the family plan....

DALLAS SCHULZE
loves books, old movies, her husband and her cat,
not necessarily in that order. She is a sucker for a
happy ending. Dallas' writing has given her an outlet
for her imagination—and she hopes that readers have
half as much fun with her books as she does!

LISA JACKSON
has written over forty books for Silhouette. Married
and the mother of two sons, Ms. Jackson also writes
mainstream fiction for Zebra Books and historical
romances for Pocket Books under the name
Susan Crose.

KASEY MICHAELS
is a *New York Times* bestselling author who has
written more than two dozen books and divides
her creative time between writing contemporary
romances and Regency novels. Ms. Michaels, who
is married and the mother of four, is the recipient of
the Romance Writers of America Golden Medallion
Award and the *Romantic Times* Best Regency Trophy.

The Parent Trap

Dallas Schulze
Lisa Jackson
Kasey Michaels

Published by Silhouette Books
America's Publisher of Contemporary Romance

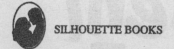 SILHOUETTE BOOKS

by Request

THE PARENT TRAP

Copyright © 1996 by Harlequin Books S.A.

ISBN 0-373-20122-2

The publisher acknowledges the copyright holders of the individual works as follows:

DONOVAN'S PROMISE
Copyright © 1988 by Dallas Schulze

MILLION DOLLAR BABY
Copyright © 1992 by Lisa Jackson

HIS CHARIOT AWAITS
Copyright © 1990 by Kasey Michaels

Printed in U.S.A.

CONTENTS

A Note from Dallas Schulze

Dear Reader,

There's one question that most writers dread hearing: Where do you get your ideas? We shuffle our feet and mumble something about ideas being everywhere and gosh, we just don't know exactly where they come from. It's a less than satisfactory response. But the truth is that ideas come from everywhere and nowhere and it's often impossible to point to a specific moment as the inspiration for a story.

I'm relieved to be able to say that *Donovan's Promise* is an exception to that rule. For once, when my editor called and asked me to write a letter saying what had inspired me to write a book, I didn't have to whine about not knowing what my inspiration had been.

The idea for *Donovan's Promise* came to me after watching Madonna's video for *"Papa Don't Preach."* The song is about a girl who finds herself pregnant by a boy of whom her father doesn't approve. The young couple are in love and she's determined to keep the baby, which is the whole theme of the song. I was watching it one day and found myself wondering what might happen to them as the years passed.

So, I crafted the story of Beth and Donovan Sinclair, who start out in love, weather life's storms and then find out that love, like all living things, needs to be nurtured to stay alive. Of all the books I've done, this remains one of my favorites. I hope you enjoy it.

Best,

Dallas Schulze

DONOVAN'S PROMISE

Dallas Schulze

Prologue

"I want a divorce."

The words were spoken without fanfare. The tone was even, emotionless. She could just as well have asked for the sugar bowl or commented that it looked as though it might rain.

But Elizabeth Sinclair had just requested an end to her marriage of eighteen years.

Having shattered her world, she pulled her gaze away from the window and looked at the man seated across the table. For a few, tense moments, there was no reaction. He didn't lift his head from the stack of papers he'd been studying during breakfast, he didn't gasp or choke or sputter. When he set his coffee cup down, his hand wasn't trembling.

If she hadn't known him so well, she might have thought he hadn't heard her. But she knew Donovan as well as it was possible to know another human being. He was digesting what she'd said.

She looked at him, feeling as if she was seeing him from a great distance. At thirty-eight he was a strikingly good-looking man—even more attractive than he'd been when they'd met. The gray that painted silver streaks at his temples only emphasized the inky blackness of his hair. His features were still even, but now they carried the added weight of maturity—hardening his jaw, leaving creases around his eyes.

He looked like exactly what he was: a successful man who was approaching forty without fears, who was tanned, fit, sure of himself and his life. There had been a time when Elizabeth had felt herself a part of that life. But that time was gone, drifting away so quietly she wasn't even sure when it had disappeared.

He lifted his head slowly, his gaze meeting hers. Donovan's eyes had always reflected his emotions. They'd turn warm green when he was happy and almost pure gold when he was angry. Now, they were blank.

"What?"

Elizabeth felt vaguely guilty. Even though she hadn't planned on saying anything at that particular moment, she'd had some time to form a decision, to brace herself to say the words. To Donovan, it must have seemed as if they were coming out of the blue.

"If this is a joke, it's not very funny." Irritation rumbled in the husky words.

"I'm not joking. I want a divorce, Donovan."

Panic flickered in his eyes. "What brought this on? If it's because I forgot to pick up the dry cleaning, I think you're overreacting a bit." His smile wavered uncertainly.

"It's got nothing to do with the dry cleaning."

"Then what the hell is this about?"

She ignored the snap in his words, knowing fear more than anger had put it there.

"I'm not happy." She said the words simply.

Donovan stared at her, clearly at a loss. "You're not happy. What do you mean? Why aren't you happy? And why haven't you said something or done something?"

She picked up her teacup and stared into the amber liquid. It was easier than looking into his eyes. His eyes demanded answers that she couldn't give. She couldn't even answer her own questions. How could she explain that somewhere along the line she'd lost herself. She'd lost her identity.

"What should I have said or done?"

"Why didn't you tell me you weren't happy?"

"Why should I? It wasn't your problem."

"Not my problem? Elizabeth, you're my wife. You've just announced that you want a divorce because you're not happy. I think that makes it my problem."

"Not really." She set her teacup down, but she still couldn't look at him.

He ran his fingers through his hair, tousling it into heavy, black waves. "Elizabeth, what's wrong? Is it something I've done? Something I've said? Do you think I'm having an affair or embezzling money or something?"

"Of course not!"

"Then what is it? You don't end eighteen years of marriage over nothing."

"Donovan, it hasn't anything to do with you. I'm just not happy."

She needed to do something so she got up and started to clear the table. She'd known this wasn't going to be easy, but somehow she hadn't expected his pain to hurt her.

She set the plates in the sink. When she turned, he was standing in front of her. She leaned against the counter, tilting her head back until she could meet his eyes. It was a mistake. The turmoil she saw there almost made her change her mind, almost made her tell him that she hadn't meant a word she'd said. Almost.

"Elizabeth. Beth. Talk to me."

The old diminutive gave her an unexpected stab of pain. It had been so long since he'd called her Beth. She drew in a deep breath and stared over his shoulder.

"We've grown apart, Donovan. We don't have anything to say to each other anymore. We hardly even see each other."

"What are you talking about? I'm home every night. We have breakfast together most mornings."

"But you're not here *with* me. You come home at night and you work in the study. In the morning you've always got a stack of papers beside you."

"If you didn't like my working at home, why didn't you just say so?"

"It's not just your working at home, Donovan. We've grown apart. Maybe you haven't noticed, but I have."

He again thrust his fingers through his hair, frustrated. "Why is it that women think you have to spend every minute of every day together to be close? I can't run a business without spending time at it."

"I know that."

"Then what's the big problem? You're not making any sense."

She stared at him, trying to think of a way to make him see what she was trying to say. "Donovan, what was the last thing that you and I did together? Just the two of us. Something that didn't revolve around Michael?"

The silence stretched out while he stared at her. Elizabeth waited for a minute and then edged by him to pick up the drinking glasses left on the table. He didn't move to stop her. He just continued to stand next to the counter, his expression hard and tight. She set the glasses in the sink.

"All right, so maybe we haven't been spending a lot of time together, but that could be changed."

"I don't think so."

"Stop saying that!" His hand closed around her upper arm, jerking her around to face him. "You can't just throw eighteen years of marriage out the window because we haven't been spending enough time together. What about Michael? How are you going to explain this to him?"

"Michael is old enough to understand."

"Understand? How the hell do you expect an eighteen-year-old kid to understand when it doesn't make any sense to me?"

"Donovan—"

"What the hell are you thinking of, Beth? You can't do this."

"Donovan, I don't want to hurt you. That's the last thing I want."

"Well, you're doing a damn fine job of it." His fingers dug into her arm, but she knew he wasn't even aware of the pressure. She could feel her nerves stretching tighter. In a minute she was going to start screaming, and she was afraid she'd never stop.

"Donovan, when was the last time we made love? Can you remember?"

He stared at her, stunned. His fingers loosened, and she knew he was trying to remember, appalled by the time that had slipped by unnoticed.

He drew a quick, hard breath, his hand again tightening on her arm, pulling her closer. "If that's what this is about, it's easily remedied."

Elizabeth tried to draw back, but he held her in place, his free hand cupping the back of her neck, tilting her head. She didn't struggle as his mouth came down on hers. She knew he wouldn't hurt her—at least not physically. The pain she felt was lodged deep inside.

She could taste his desperation, could feel it in the taut muscles of his body. But that was all she felt. She could remember a time when just the touch of his mouth had lit a fire inside her where now she felt nothing but emptiness and regret.

The fire was gone. Not even an ember remained. Only a pile of cold ashes, gray and worn, without life.

She remained passive in his hold, sensing that this would convince him as perhaps nothing else could. A tear slipped from beneath her closed lids, losing itself in the golden-blond hair at her temple.

Donovan raised his head slowly and took his hands away from her, but not before she felt the tremor in his fingers. His breathing was harsh in the quiet room. She opened her eyes, seeing him through a blur of tears. Was it possible for a person to age in a matter of minutes? He suddenly looked every one of his thirty-eight years.

"I'm sorry, Donovan. I just don't love you anymore."

Chapter 1

Then - nineteen years ago

"**I** love you, Donovan. I'll love you forever." Beth's voice shook with the force of her emotions. At sixteen, she was sure of her feelings. Nothing would ever change the way she felt about the young man who lay next to her.

Donovan smoothed golden-blond hair back off her forehead and smiled. With only two more years behind him he was immeasurably older than the girl lying beside him.

"I love you too, Beth, but we've got to be sensible."

"I don't want to be sensible." She walked her fingers up his chest, feeling the way his heartbeat accelerated beneath the light touch. "I'm sixteen. That's old enough to make up my own mind."

Donovan caught her fingers in his. "Beth, we can't get married now. You're too young. And even if you weren't, your father would never give us permission. He doesn't like me. I've seen the way he looks at me."

"Daddy just doesn't know you, that's all. He thinks you're bad for me, but if he got to know you, he'd see how wonderful you are."

His mouth twisted. "I doubt it. And he's right. You deserve someone a lot better than I am. You could date any guy in school." She tugged her fingers loose and put them over his mouth.

"Stop it. I don't want to date any guy in school. I love you, Donovan. I love you so much."

"I can't offer you anything. A beat-up motorcycle, a job in a garage..."

"You're going to be an architect. The best architect in the whole world. Someday, you'll be rich and famous."

He felt her belief in him like a gentle hand stroking across his soul. In all his life, no one had ever had such complete faith, such boundless belief, in him. Looking into her clear blue eyes, he could almost see his dreams reflected there, whole and shining, polished by the light of her love.

"Oh, Beth. What did I ever do without you?"

"Much worse, I'm sure." Her fingers slid into the thick blackness of his hair. It fell in waves to just past his shoulders. Beth thought it made him look like a young Greek god, but she'd never have said so to Donovan. She was old enough to know the compliment would embarrass him.

Donovan leaned over her, his palm resting against her waist, left bare by low hip-huggers and a shirt tied under her breasts. Beth shivered beneath the look in his eyes. They'd been lovers for almost three months, but she didn't think she'd ever get used to the way he made her feel. She knew that after three months or thirty years, Donovan Sinclair would always be able to melt her bones with a look.

She closed her eyes against the intensity of his look, her mouth softening in anticipation of his kiss. His mouth was firm and warm, coaxing her lips to open to his. His hand slid around her waist, his fingers splayed against her spine, arching her into his body. Beth's hands tightened against his shoulders, clinging to him as his tongue explored her mouth.

A hot September sun blazed down around them, denying that summer was over. The grass smelled sweet and green with memories of summer. In the distance a group of small children were playing, but their shouts and laughter seemed very far away.

All that mattered was Beth and Donovan, lying beneath a huge, old willow in the warm, sweet grass. The dying summer didn't matter. Her father's disapproval didn't matter. All that mattered was Donovan's mouth on hers, his hands warm on her bare back.

He dragged his mouth away from hers, his breathing ragged. She could feel the pressure of his arousal against her thigh. She slipped her hands inside his chambray shirt, feeling his sweat-dampened skin. It excited her to know that he wanted her so much. Her fingers explored the hard muscles under the light dusting of hair that covered his chest.

Donovan was not like the boys she went to school with. At eighteen he was hard and firm, muscled from years of working after school and on weekends. When she'd first met him, all her girlfriends had warned her about him. He was older, he rode a motorcycle, he wore a black leather jacket. Everything about him spelled Danger.

Everyone in Remembrance, Indiana, knew about Donovan Sinclair. Boys like him never came to any good. His father was a drunk who'd never done an honest day's labor in his life. His mother had been a good woman who'd worked herself to death trying to support her husband and her son. Donovan himself was clearly destined for no good. No one could explain why this was so clear—maybe it was the way he looked. He was too handsome, too tough, too sure of himself. Maybe it was the way he dressed. Rebellion might have become a symbol of youth in the rest of the country, but in Remembrance there were still only two kinds of kids: good ones and bad ones.

The good ones played football or were cheerleaders, according to their sex. The bad ones wore black leather jackets, jeans that were a little too tight and hair that was a little too long. There were a few people who took note of the fact that Donovan Sinclair had never been known to take a drink and had held a steady job since he was sixteen. But most folks saw the insolent twist of his mouth and the way his eyes could seem to look right through a person, and they knew exactly what to label him.

Trouble.

Beth Martin had known Donovan most of her life—or, at least, she'd known *of* him. In a town as small as Remembrance, everybody knew just about everybody else, at least by sight. She'd never thought much about him one way or another until six months ago. She'd had a fight with her boyfriend, and Donovan had offered her a ride home on his motorcycle. Ordinarily she would have refused, but she was just mad enough at Brad to accept the offer.

During the course of that ride her entire world had changed. There was an electricity between the two of them that couldn't be denied. She knew Donovan felt it, too. Brad and the other boys on the football team suddenly seemed callow and boring. But Donovan knew what it would do to a girl's reputation to be seen with him, and he'd dropped her off at her house without saying a word about seeing her again.

For the first time in her life, Beth was the one doing the pursuing. It had taken her almost a month to wear down Donovan's resistance and convince him that she wasn't going to go away.

"Stop it, Beth." Donovan's voice dragged her out of her thoughts. His hand caught hers, pressing her palm flat against his chest, halting her sensuous exploration. She lifted her gaze to his and then looked away quickly. It still half frightened her to see how much he wanted her.

Donovan saw her uncertainty and his eyes softened. Sometimes he felt aeons older than Beth. She'd lived such a sheltered life. She'd never had to wonder where her next meal was coming from, never had to worry about having enough heat in the winter. Her mother had died when she was just a baby, but her father had done everything he could to see that his only child never lacked for anything, whether it was love or material things.

Donovan ran his fingers through her silky hair, contrasting its golden blond with his own tanned, work-roughened hands. She was so full of light, both inside and out. Everybody said he was no good, and he more than half believed it himself. How could she possibly love someone like him? But she did love him, impossible though it seemed, and Donovan was careful to do nothing that would frighten her, nothing that would show her just how unworthy he was of that love.

"You're so beautiful, Beth. What did I ever do to deserve you?" Beth smiled up at him, unaware of the underlying ache in his voice.

"I guess you just got lucky."

"I guess I did." His mouth touched hers again, feeling her body arch into his. He groaned low in his throat, rolling to press his full length against hers. The sweet scent of crushed grass rose around them. His hand slid upward, easing beneath the edge of her shirt to cup her breast. Beth stiffened for a moment and then seemed to melt beneath him.

Somewhere in the distance a dog barked, reminding Donovan that they were hardly alone. The hanging branches of the old willow provided a fragile privacy at best. He dragged his hand away from temptation and slowly broke the kiss, ignoring her murmur of protest.

"Beth, in a minute we're going to get arrested for indecent exposure."

"So what?" Her hands slipped reluctantly off his shoulders as he sat up.

"So I don't think you'd like jail, and I don't think your father would like bailing you out. I know he's not all that happy that you're seeing me anyway."

Beth felt the color rise in her cheeks, and she was glad that his back was to her. "Guilt" must be written in scarlet letters across her forehead.

"Daddy trusts my judgment. Besides, I'm sixteen, not six. He knows he can't tell me what to do anymore."

She hoped she sounded more confident than she felt. Less than a week ago, her father had strictly forbidden her to see Donovan again. He said people were beginning to talk. Beth didn't care what people said. She loved Donovan, and nothing was going to keep her from him. Not even her father.

Donovan stood up. "I'd better get you home. I'm due at work in an hour, and you've probably got homework to finish before school tomorrow."

Beth let him pull her up, sliding her arms around his waist and leaning into the lean strength of his body. "You work too hard."

"If I'm going to start college in January, I need all the money I can get. I won't be able to work as many hours."

"You'll probably have even less time for me then."

He slid his fingers into her long hair, cupping the back of her head and tilting her face upward. "I'll always have time for you."

Her mock pout faded into a smile that made his heart pound. Sometimes he wondered if Beth knew just how she affected him. She was so beautiful. He bent his head to taste her smile, as if he could drink in her warmth and light and banish some of the dark corners in his soul.

"How's Donovan?"

Beth swirled the straw in her glass of iced tea and glanced across the table at her companion. Carol Montgomery had been her best friend since kindergarten. They'd shared every big moment in each other's lives, from first boyfriends to bras. Looking into Carol's curious face, Beth found herself oddly reluctant to discuss Donovan. It wasn't that she was afraid Carol couldn't keep a secret, because in all their years of friendship, neither had ever betrayed a confidence.

Beth couldn't put her finger on what it was. Somehow, her relationship with Donovan was private. It was something she didn't want to share with anyone—not even her best friend.

She shrugged. "He's fine."

"Does your dad know you're still seeing him?"

"No. And Donovan doesn't know Daddy told me not to see him anymore."

Carol reached for another pack of sugar and stirred it into her tea. She was blessed with a metabolism that allowed her to eat anything and never gain an ounce. For once Beth didn't feel envious of her friend's genetic luck. The tea tasted funny. In fact, she was sorry they'd come to Danny's at all. The smell of baking pizza made her feel vaguely queasy. On the jukebox the Rolling Stones were screaming "Jumpin' Jack Flash," and the sound intensified the headache that had been plaguing her all day.

"What are you going to do if your father finds out you're still seeing Donovan?"

Beth pushed her tea away. "I don't know. I don't understand why Daddy's being so unreasonable about this. Donovan's never been in trouble."

"It's because he looks like he has been or will be at any minute." Carol leaned back as the waiter set their pizza in the middle of the table. "Boy, does that look terrific." Beth swallowed hard and closed her eyes against the smell of cheese and tomato sauce. "Aren't you going to have some?"

She opened her eyes and smiled at Carol. "In a minute." The queasiness was fading.

Carol bit into a slice of pizza oozing cheese, her expression indicative of absolute bliss. "The thing you've got to remember is that all parents automatically dislike anyone their children like." Carol delivered this piece of philosophy between bites.

"Daddy's never been like that."

"That makes it worse. All that pent-up feeling is just now coming out. He'll be adamant about Donovan. When you argue he'll say things like, 'Beth, I've never been unreasonable about your friends, have I? You'll just have to trust my judgment on this one.' "

Despite the seriousness of the situation, Carol's accurate imitation of her father's words drew a halfhearted laugh out of Beth. She reached for the smallest slice of pizza and set it on her plate.

"I'm *not* going to trust his judgment on this one. I love Donovan and he loves me, and I'm not going to give him up—not for anything in the world."

"Good for you. Personally, I think Donovan Sinclair is gorgeous."

"He is, isn't he?" Beth pushed a mushroom around the rim of her plate, the expression in her eyes dreamy.

Carol looked at her friend, her thin features envious. "Beth, I'm your best friend, aren't I?"

Beth looked up, dragging her mind away from Donovan. "Of course. Why do you ask?"

"What's it like when you and Donovan...when you...you know?"

Beth did know, and she felt the color come up in her cheeks until she was sure they were as red as the vinyl booth. "It's none of your business."

Carol sat back in her seat, her face as flushed as Beth's. "I'm sorry, Beth. I shouldn't have asked. It's just that you and Donovan look so happy together. I just wondered."

"It's okay." Beth looked anywhere but at her friend.

Carol reached for another slice of pizza. "I just hope you know what you're doing. I mean, I hope you're being careful."

"Careful about what?"

"Babies." Carol bit into her pizza, leaving Beth to flush even darker.

"Donovan takes care of that."

Carol nodded sagely. "That's what Betty Durbin's boyfriend told her, and she had to leave school."

"Donovan is very careful!" The words came out with more of a snap than she'd intended, and she looked around the big room, hoping that no one was close enough to hear what they were saying. Trust Carol to start a conversation like this in public.

She shifted, uneasy with the topic. Staring down at her pizza, she remembered one time when they hadn't been careful and how angry Donovan had been with himself. Still, one time couldn't be dangerous. Could it?

"Beth, you're going to be late for school." In answer to her father's call, Beth took one last look in the mirror and snatched up her books before hurrying out of her bedroom. She rushed downstairs, where her father was waiting impatiently by the door. His expression softened, as it always did when looking at his daughter.

Patrick Martin still found it hard to believe that this beautiful, vital young woman was his little girl. It seemed like such a short time ago that he'd been struggling to take care of a baby, juggling his work and fatherhood.

"Isn't that skirt a little short?"

Beth glanced down at the white denim miniskirt that ended several inches above her knee and then gave her father the exasperated look that all teenagers perfect early on.

"This is longer than the skirts a lot of the girls are wearing, Daddy."

"I'm not worried about a lot of the girls." But he didn't press the issue. He had to admit that the style suited her. How had those pudgy toddler's legs slimmed into this?

He picked up his hard hat and briefcase and followed his daughter out the door, giving a cursory check to the lock. There was no crime to speak of in Remembrance. Locks were more of a token gesture than a necessity.

Father and daughter climbed into the Chevy pickup that sat in the driveway. By a long-standing agreement, the radio stayed off. Since Beth wanted to listen to rock and roll and her father wanted to listen to the morning business report, they'd agreed that they wouldn't listen to anything at all.

Patrick started the truck and backed out of the driveway. "If they've fixed the light on Main Street, I should be able to get you to school before the first bell."

Beth nodded. The silence continued for several blocks. Patrick glanced at his daughter but her eyes were turned to the front, her expression pensive.

"Beth? Something wrong?"

She glanced at him and shook her head. "No."

The silence went on.

"Are you still upset with me over the Sinclair boy? I know you think I'm being unreasonable, but I haven't forbidden you much over the years. You'll just have to trust my judgment on this one, honey."

"I was just thinking about what kind of dress I want for the Homecoming Dance. Carol and I are going shopping tomorrow."

If he had been watching his daughter instead of watching the road, Patrick might have seen the guilty flush in her cheeks and the way her fingers clenched around the books in her lap. He might also have thought it was a little odd that she'd argued so passionately when he forbade her to see Donovan and now she seemed to have accepted his decision. But he wasn't looking at her, and he was relieved that she seemed to be taking it so well so he didn't probe.

"Who are you going with this year?"

Beth shrugged, not looking at him. "I don't know yet."

He slowed the truck for the turn into the school and pulled to a stop near the main entrance. "Well, I'm sure you'll have all kinds of offers."

Beth scrambled out of the truck without answering.

"See you tonight."

Beth lifted her hand in answer to his wave. The dark blue truck pulled into traffic, passing several parents who were getting their progeny to school even later than Beth.

Beth watched him go, blinking back tears. She'd never expected to feel so guilty about lying to her father. Since her mother's death when she was a few months old, it had always been her and her father against the world. He'd been her friend as well as her parent.

How could she tell him that she knew exactly who she was going to the Homecoming Dance with? Donovan had promised to take her more than a month ago. Her father would find out, she couldn't hide her relationship with Donovan forever. Once he understood how much she loved Donovan, he'd see how wrong he'd been.

The final bell rang, startling her out of her thoughts. She turned and sprinted for the entrance. She was going to be late for homeroom, after all.

"I don't think this is such a good idea, Beth. Your father wouldn't like the idea of your having me in the house when he's not home."

"Daddy will never know. He's not going to be back from Indianapolis until tomorrow afternoon at the earliest. Come on, Donovan. I want you to see my dress." Beth pulled on his hand, tugging him over the threshold into her bedroom.

Donovan stepped onto the thick, shag carpeting, hoping he didn't have any grease from the garage on his shoes. The carpet was the palest of pinks. It matched the ruffled curtains and bedspread. The furniture was painted with white enamel. Shelves along one wall held stuffed toys and books.

Everything about the room was feminine and spoke of comfort.

Donovan felt as out of place as a buffalo at a wedding. He shoved his hands into the pockets of his jeans. He didn't belong in this room. This room spoke of too many things he'd never known: home, family, money.

"Don't you think it's beautiful?"

Donovan looked at the dress Beth held up, but he couldn't have said anything about it. About all that registered was that it was peach colored. What caught his eye was the excitement in Beth's face. She was so beautiful. What could she possibly see in him?

"It's... really nice." He hoped he'd said the right thing. Beth seemed content. She hung the dress back up and shut the closet door.

"I can't wait till the dance. I bet you look gorgeous in a suit." She sat on the bed and patted the spot next to her.

"I'll bet I look like an idiot." Donovan reluctantly took the place beside her. Beth snuggled against his side and he put his arm around her shoulders. "Don't you think we should leave now?"

She put her hand on his chest, working it inside the open front of his shirt, feeling the catch in his breathing when she touched him.

"Don't you like my room?"

"It's... it's beautiful." He slid his hand into her hair, tilting her head back until their eyes met. "You're beautiful. I just don't want to get you in trouble." His mouth touched hers, lingering in a slow kiss.

"I told you, Daddy won't be home until tomorrow."

His hand slid inside the neck of her peasant blouse, feeling the satiny skin of her shoulders, tracing the delicate line of her collarbone.

"What about the neighbors?"

"They aren't home." She lifted her mouth to his, feeling her bones melt like butter left out in the sun. He was everything she'd ever dreamed of, everything she'd ever want. His hands slid across her back as he leaned forward, lowering her slowly.

The mattress yielded beneath their combined weight. Donovan pushed the loose neckline down and let his lips trace the satiny skin of her shoulders. Beth closed her eyes, shutting out the familiar bedroom walls, shutting out everything but the feel of him against her.

He felt so right.

"Do you love me, Donovan?"

"Always." The word ghosted out against her breast. Beth's fingers slid into the silky, black hair at the nape of his neck, pulling him closer. "I'll love you always, Beth."

And she didn't doubt that it was true.

The late-September sun blazed down, but there was a melancholy feeling in the air that bespoke the end of summer. The leaves on the maple trees were turning colors, the brilliant green fading. It wouldn't be long until winter.

Beth felt as if winter had already arrived. There was a cold, heavy lump in her chest. She shut the door of Dr. Morrison's office behind her with a careful click and turned to walk blindly down the street.

At ten o'clock in the morning on a weekday, Remembrance was quiet. Inside the brick and wood buildings, people were doing business, but the streets were quiet. Beth wouldn't have noticed if a parade had been marching down Main. She walked without thought, her mind a blank.

It wasn't until she stumbled over a curb that she noticed her surroundings. The park was completely empty, the wrought-iron benches gathering the last of summer's sun as if preparing for winter's onslaught. Beth sat down. Her eyes were focused on the lake, but she wasn't seeing the cool water.

Pregnant. The word echoed in her mind. Pregnant. She couldn't get beyond that single fact. She was carrying Donovan's baby. She wrapped her arms around her waist, closing her eyes. It just didn't seem real. She couldn't be pregnant. Not from just one mistake. They'd always been so careful.

What was Donovan going to say? And her father? Oh God, how could she tell her father? She bit her lip to stop a whimper.

What was she going to do?

She stood up. She couldn't stay here. There was too much chance of seeing someone she knew. There would be questions to answer, and she couldn't deal with questions.

She turned toward home but stopped after taking a few steps. She couldn't go home. Her father wouldn't be there, but if one of the neighbors saw her they would want to know what was wrong. They'd ask if she was sick. A hysterical laugh threatened to escape. Sick? If only it was that simple.

She turned in the opposite direction, her feet moving automatically. She would go to Donovan's. He would be at work, but he'd shown her a way to climb in the window of his rented room.

It took her ten minutes to reach the little back street and Donovan's worn-down building. She slipped off her shoes and jammed them in her suede purse. The tree was just where it had always been, and it was the work of only a few minutes to climb to the branch that reached Donovan's window. She slid onto the warped floorboards, feeling as if she'd reached a sanctuary.

Donovan had only brought her here twice. He'd never said as much but Beth knew that he was ashamed of the place. She stood in the middle of the room for a long moment, just breathing. No one would find her here. No one was expecting her anywhere until after the school day ended, and she'd told her father she might be going home with Carol, so that gave her even more time.

And she needed the time. She needed every second. She set her purse down in the corner. Today Donovan worked until midafternoon. That gave her a few hours until he'd be home. She'd have a little time to decide what she was going to say to him.

What could she say? She was pregnant. Right now she couldn't get beyond that one, blinding fact. She was going to have Donovan's baby. She sat down on the bed, feeling the mattress sag beneath her. They'd never talked about children. She loved Donovan, she wanted to marry him. In her world, love and marriage generally added up to children. But not like this. Never like this.

This kind of thing happened to other girls. Girls no one talked about. This didn't happen to Beth Martin. It just didn't. She wrapped her arms around her stomach and leaned forward, closing her eyes. It didn't matter how hard she tried, she couldn't make it real.

Tears welled up. She tried to blink them back, but they wouldn't be denied. The dingy, little room swam in front of her, and a harsh sob escaped. What was Donovan going to say? Would he hate her? She could bear anything but that.

She lay down, her arms still wrapped around herself, her face buried in Donovan's pillow. Donovan would know what to do. He always knew what to do for her. She had to believe that this time wouldn't be any different.

Chapter 2

It was late afternoon when Beth heard Donovan's footsteps on the stairs. She sat up, brushing trembling hands
over her hair, rubbing her fingers under her eyes, hoping she
didn't have mascara streaking down her face. She hadn't
spent a lot of time on tears. The situation seemed to have
gone beyond that.

Her heartbeat picked up speed with every second that
passed. What was he going to say when he saw her? How
was she going to tell him? It had been foolish to come here.
Their lives would be changed forever. She wasn't ready to
see him yet. She couldn't tell him.

She was halfway to the window with some half-baked idea
of escape, when he opened the door. She froze, then turned
toward him. She couldn't tell him. Not now. Not yet. She
pinned a smile on her face. She would just pretend that
nothing was wrong and leave as soon as possible.

Donovan shoved open the door, his eyes on the mail that
Mrs. Hill had given him. Junk, as usual. She always gave
him anything addressed to "occupant." Maybe she thought

it made him feel more at home. He caught a whiff of Beth's scent. He'd given her that perfume for the one-month anniversary of their first date, and she always wore it. She said it made her feel close to him even when they weren't together.

His head jerked up. She was standing between the window and the bed, her stockinged feet poised as if to run, her slim body tense. His eyes fell on her face. Her smile was bright and beautiful, but her face was pale and her eyes were filled with a frightening mixture of despair and panic.

The envelopes scattered to the floor with soft, whispering sounds, and he stepped toward her, his arms opening.

"My God, Beth, what's wrong?"

Beth saw the loving concern in Donovan's face, the strong arms held out to her. With a sob she rushed forward, burying her face in his chest, her arms locking around his waist. It was a safe haven after hours of emotional pain. Donovan was here for her. He'd always be here.

Donovan kicked the door shut and lifted Beth in his arms, carrying her to the bed and sitting down with her in his lap. She was shaking but not crying, her slim body trembling against him. He stroked her hair, his mind racing with each disastrous possibility.

"What's wrong, Beth? Is it your father? Has something happened to him? Something at school? Did someone say something to upset you? Something about us?"

She shook her head to each possibility, her face buried in his shirt. Donovan held her, reining in his fears, waiting for the trembling to ease. When she pushed away, he eased his arms from around her, letting her get up. She backed away without looking at him, her eyes on the scuffed floor. Donovan stood up, bracing himself.

"I've got to tell you something." Her voice was hardly more than a whisper.

"You can tell me anything, Beth. You know that." He
waited, barely breathing. What if she said she didn't want
to see him anymore? How could he bear it if he lost her?

"I . . . I went to the doctor this morning. I'm pregnant."

The words came out louder than she'd intended. They
seemed to echo in the small room, growing louder and
louder until they almost shouted back at them from the
chipped wallpaper. Pregnant. Pregnant.

Donovan felt the words slam into him, knocking the
breath from his lungs, leaving him gasping. Pregnant. A
baby. Beth was carrying his baby. No! It wasn't fair. It just
wasn't fair. There had only been that one time. One stinking time. It couldn't happen.

"Are you sure?" His voice sounded strange—hoarse. Not
his at all.

She nodded without lifting her head. "Dr. Morrison says
there's no doubt. I'm going to have a baby." Her voice
broke on the last word.

"It's all right." Donovan spoke automatically. "It's going to be all right, Beth. Don't worry." He reached out,
taking hold of her shoulders and pulling her into his arms.
She was stiff in his hold for a moment, and then she went
limp, letting him support her weight.

"What are we going to do, Donovan? It's all my fault.
I'm so sorry."

"Stop it!" He shook her slightly, cutting off the flow of
words. "It's not your fault. We got carried away and I
should have known better. I *did* know better." There was a
wealth of self-anger in the words.

"What are we going to do? I've thought and I've thought
and I don't know what to do. I can't have an . . . I can't get
rid of it. I don't even know how to find someone who'd . . .
I just can't do that. I'm sorry. I can't, I can't."

Donovan shook her again, harder this time, breaking off
the hysteria that threatened in her voice. He held her away

from him until she met his eyes. "Stop it, Beth. I don't want you to get rid of this baby. Don't even think about it."

Beth blinked, responding to the authority in his tone. "What are we going to do?"

"It's going to be fine." Donovan pushed his own panic aside. "We didn't plan it this way, but we'll work it out. We'll just get married right away. I'm making pretty good money at the garage, and I've got some money put aside. We'll get by. I'll take care of the baby. I'll take care of you."

Beth leaned into him, drawing on his strength, feeling the panic leave her. If Donovan said he'd take care of her, she believed him. The room was silent while each of them tried to come to grips with the momentous changes a baby was going to make in their lives. In the end, it was too much to grasp.

"When is the baby due?" Donovan had to clear his throat to get the question out. It made it seem almost real. Permanent.

"The end of April, I guess. I'm sorry, Donovan." Her voice shattered on the words, his name leaving her on a sob. He eased her down on the bed and she began to cry—not the quiet tears she'd shed earlier, but harsh, sobbing tears that left her choked and breathless. "I'm so sorry."

"Stop it, Beth." Donovan closed his arms around her, drawing her against his chest and holding her tightly, telling her over and over again that it was going to be all right. Above her golden head, his eyes were bleak. He could reassure Beth, but the words rang hollow in his ears.

He let her cry out all her fears, her tears soaking his worn shirt. His hand stroked her hair, offering comfort and reassurance. When the tears at last faded into an occasional choked breath, he eased her back down on the pillows and stood up. Beth was too exhausted to protest, though her hand clutched at his shirttail.

"I'm just going to get a wet cloth." He was back in a moment with a damp washcloth, and Beth lay passive as he wiped the cool fabric over her hot face.

"I'm sorry, Donovan." A convulsive sob broke his name in half.

"Stop saying that. It was my responsibility."

"What are we going to do?" Her eyes looked up at him with such faith that Donovan felt a momentary flash of panic. She shouldn't depend on him so. Hadn't he already proved that he wasn't worthy of her trust? She wouldn't be in this mess if he hadn't let things get out of control. He swallowed hard and forced a half smile, his eyes showing more confidence than he felt.

"We'll get married, and I'll take care of you and the baby."

"I'll have to quit school, won't I?"

"I...probably." Donovan took her hands and wiped the cloth over them. It hurt him to see her in pain. She was so young. This was his fault and his alone. It wasn't fair that she should suffer, too.

"What will we do for money?"

"Don't worry about it. I'm making pretty good money at the garage, and I think Dave will give me more hours if I ask him to. And I've got some money saved up."

"But that's your college money. You're going to be an architect."

Donovan's mouth twisted. He'd long ago learned the pain of broken dreams. He wouldn't have thought it would still hurt. All chances for getting his education were fading rapidly into the distance. But along with broken dreams, he'd also learned that you took responsibility for your own actions without whining about it. Beth needed him to be strong for her.

"I'll go to college later. Lots of people do."

Beth's eyes searched his, but she was too frightened herself to question his strength. She needed it too much.

"I'm scared, Donovan." In that moment, she looked so young and vulnerable that his heart ached.

"I know. But I'll take care of you. I promise. I love you, Beth. I won't let anything hurt you."

"I love you, too." She sat up and put her arms around his neck, resting her face against his shoulder. "I love you so much. At least we'll be together."

Donovan stroked her back, letting himself believe that everything would work out.

They held each other for a long time, not saying anything, not thinking anything—drawing strength from being together. Donovan had no idea how much time had passed until he heard the big clock in the hall downstairs start to chime. He counted each strike of the hammer. Five o'clock—and he'd left the garage at four. His whole life had changed in the space of an hour. Irrevocably altered. Never to be the same.

"Beth?" Her arms tightened around him, and he knew she was resisting a return to reality. "Beth, it's getting late. Your father will be worried about you." He felt the shudder that ran up her spine. "I know, love, I know. But he's got to be told. I think we should get married as soon as possible."

She let her arms slip away reluctantly, her eyes downcast. Donovan cupped her face in his hands, tilting it upward until her eyes met his. "I said I'd take care of you, Beth, and I meant it."

"I know. It's just that my father is going to be so angry."

"We'll face him together. He loves you. Let me change out of this greasy shirt, and we'll go see him."

Beth watched as he stripped his shirt off, her mind still only half functioning. She felt as though she was in the middle of some terrible nightmare. Any minute now she would wake up and find out that none of this was real, that her world hadn't tilted on its axis.

"I think I should talk to Daddy alone." She wasn't aware of thinking the words until they were said. Donovan turned from the tiny closet in one corner of the room, halfway into a clean shirt.

"I don't think that's such a good idea, Beth. We should face him together."

She shook her head. "I'll go alone. I didn't tell you that he forbid me to see you. I think I need to pave the way a bit before I tell him about the . . . about my . . . about me."

Beth stood up, smoothing her hands over her miniskirt and tugging the neckline of her peasant blouse into place. She ran her fingers through her long, straight hair.

"I think I should go with you."

"No. Really. It will be better if I do it alone. I'll call you and tell you what happened."

Donovan wanted to argue further, but he could see that her mind was made up. He didn't know Patrick Martin. Maybe Beth was right, maybe he would take it better this way.

"Let me at least give you a ride home."

"No, I'll walk." Her smile was strained. "I need some time to think."

He opened the door for her, his hand on her arm holding her for a moment. "Just remember that I love you."

Beth swallowed hard. "I know. I love you."

"Don't look so scared. Everything's going to be fine. We'll work it out."

Donovan shut the door and leaned back against it, listening to her footsteps on the stairs. His shoulders slumped. Now that she was gone, his confident facade crumbled.

He ran his hand over his face, aware that his fingers were shaking. For the first time in his life he wanted a drink. All the years he'd watched his old man drink himself into oblivion, he'd never understood why he didn't fight instead of hiding in a bottle. Now he had at least a partial understanding.

He pushed himself from the door and stumbled over to the bed, feeling centuries older than his eighteen years. The bed creaked beneath his weight, the sound loud in the quiet room. He didn't know how long he sat there, staring at nothing, letting everything sink in, trying not to think too much. Outside, people went about their business. Husbands were coming home from work, sitting down to dinner. Everything went on just as if disaster hadn't struck.

Beth was going to have his baby. He buried his head in his hands, swallowing hard on the sob that threatened to escape. It wasn't fair. It just wasn't fair. Like an echo he heard his mother's hoarse voice, cracked by hard work and too many cigarettes. "Who the hell ever told you that life was supposed to be fair, boy? You roll with the punches and hope the good Lord don't deal you nothin' you can't handle."

"I don't know if I can handle this, Mom. I don't know if I can," he said out loud.

But he knew he had to. For Beth's sake—and the baby's—he had to be strong. He loved her too much to let her down. Beth was the best thing to ever happen to him. He had to take care of her, and it had to start now. He should never have let her go home alone. He should be there when she talked to her father.

"Daddy? I'm sorry." Beth swallowed hard against the lump that threatened to choke her. She hadn't expected it to hurt so much when she told her father. There hadn't been time to think beyond what this was going to do to her life and Donovan's. "I'm sorry, Daddy."

Patrick Martin slumped in the big easy chair, his eyes focused on nothing in particular, his face old and worn. Silence stretched between them until Beth thought she'd break out screaming. The pain in her father's face hurt her, frightened her. What would she do if he threw her out? Her father had been the center of her life, someone she could always depend on to be there for her.

She knelt by his chair, her face white. "Daddy, I love you. I'm sorry. I'm sorry."

Patrick's eyes slowly refocused on her pale features, and he saw the panic in her eyes. Beth had been his life since her mother died. He couldn't remember a time when he hadn't worried about her, fussed over her, loved her. He'd watched her grow from a chubby toddler to a graceful young woman who sometimes seemed frighteningly adult. He'd wanted so much for her, had so many dreams. Now they were all in pieces. But she still needed him.

"It's okay, pumpkin." His hand was shaking as he lifted it to smooth her hair. With a sob, Beth bent and put her forehead against his knee. For a moment, she was a child again, able to believe that her father could make everything right.

"I'm so scared, Daddy."

"I know, Beth, I know. But I'll take care of you. Don't cry, honey. Come on, sit over here. We need to talk, and tears aren't going to do any good."

Beth sat on the hassock in front of him, wiping her eyes with the back of her hand. Patrick handed her a handkerchief, and she blew her nose. They sat in silence for a few minutes—father and daughter—not looking at each other, not speaking, each aware that nothing could ever be the same again. Patrick cleared his throat.

"Did Dr. Morrison say anything about your health? Are you okay?"

Beth nodded, twisting the handkerchief in her fingers. "I'm fine."

"Good. Good." The silence stretched again. "I don't want you to worry about anything, Beth. I'll take care of you, just like I always have. There's room for a baby here, probably liven the place up a bit. I don't want this to be the end of your life, either. You'll have to drop out of school now, but we'll get you into night school or a correspondence course or something. You're still going to get your education. We'll find someone who can take care of the baby while you're studying. You'll see. Everything will work out.''

"Donovan and I want to get married."

Patrick shifted abruptly in his chair, just the mention of Donovan's name enough to remind him of how impossible the situation was.

"I don't think so, pumpkin. You shouldn't compound one mistake by making another. You're too young to get married."

"Donovan wants to take care of me and the baby."

It was an effort to keep his voice level. "Donovan is just a boy. How could he possibly take care of a wife and a baby? The two of you would just be making a bigger mistake than you already have."

"I don't want my child to grow up without a father, Mr. Martin."

Patrick's head jerked toward the door, angry color rising in his face. He opened his mouth to order Donovan out, to harangue him for what he'd done to Beth.

"Donovan!" Beth was in Donovan's arms before Patrick could stand up. Donovan's dark head bent over Beth's fair hair as his arms closed around her.

"I shouldn't have let you come alone, Beth. I should have been with you."

Patrick wanted to rush across the room and tear Beth away from the boy. How dare he come here to this house? Hadn't he done enough damage already? But Beth clung to him, her arms around his waist, her face buried in his shoulder, holding him as if he were the most important thing in the world.

Patrick looked away, swallowing his paternal rage, trying to think calmly. No matter how much it hurt, he had to face the fact that this situation was also Beth's doing. He looked back at the young couple. They were so young.

Donovan lifted his head and looked at her father. His eyes met Patrick's without flinching, his expression calm and too old for his years.

"You'd better come in and sit down, both of you."

Donovan kept his arm around Beth as they sat on the sofa opposite her father.

"This must have been a shock to you, Mr. Martin. I'm very sorry."

"I think it's been a bit of a shock to all of us."

"I want to marry Beth, Mr. Martin."

Patrick tried to gather his thoughts. How did he explain to this serious young man that marriage was going to be just the beginning of their problems?

"Marriage is a serious commitment. You're both very young—"

Beth interrupted. "We're old enough to know that we love each other, Daddy. I wanted to marry Donovan even before... this happened." Beth's hands tightened around Donovan's arm as if she were afraid her father would try to drag them apart. Patrick looked at her helplessly. She was his little girl, his baby. He had always tried to protect her, to shield her from hurt.

"Mr. Martin." Donovan's quiet voice drew Patrick's attention to him. "I know this isn't what you wanted for Beth. It isn't what I wanted, either. But it's happened, and we can't change that. If Beth and I get married, it will at least give the baby a name. I love Beth. I'd take care of her and the baby. I'd do my best to make her happy."

"Just how do you plan to support a wife and child?" Patrick saw the boy's jaw tighten, and he regretted his sarcastic tone.

"I have a good job at Sam's garage. I know they'd give me more hours if I asked. I also have some money saved. I had . . . other plans for it, but they can wait. It's not much, but it would get Beth and me started.''

"Please, Daddy. Please say yes." Beth's mouth quivered with the intensity of the plea. Donovan put his arm around her, holding her protectively.

Patrick leaned back in his chair; suddenly he felt incredibly old. They were so pathetically young and so much in love. They didn't have any idea of what they were facing. Patrick studied Donovan's face, the eyes too old for his years and the jaw that already spoke of determination and will. The boy knew what they were up against, which made it all the more commendable that he wanted to take responsibility.

But that wasn't going to make it any easier. And Beth. His lovely Beth. She couldn't possibly understand what she was facing by undertaking motherhood and marriage. Either was a difficult adjustment, but to take on both at once . . . He loved his daughter, but he didn't know if she was up to the challenge.

On the other hand, if he refused to let them marry it would mean that his first grandchild would be illegitimate. While the rest of the country might be stirring and changing and saying "love child" instead of "bastard," Remembrance wasn't going to change anytime soon. A child born out of wedlock was going to have a rough time.

He closed his eyes, shutting out the young couple across from him. The burden of their future weighed on him. The decision he made now would affect both their lives as well as the baby's. It was important that he make the right choice.

He opened his eyes slowly and looked at them. Beth's face was pressed against Donovan's shoulder, her hands wrapped around his arm. Donovan bent over her, his hand stroking her hair, his expression tender. Patrick swallowed against a sudden pain in his chest. Beth wasn't his little girl anymore. She had other loyalties, other loves.

"I won't stand in the way of your marriage—on one condition."

Beth and Donovan looked at him, Beth's eyes bright with relief, Donovan's wary. He'd learned a long time ago that "conditions" were rarely pleasant.

"I think you'll agree that it's going to be very difficult for you to make ends meet on your salary alone."

"We'll manage."

"Beth is pregnant. That's not a good time to 'manage.' You can marry my daughter, but I want the two of you to agree to live in the apartment over our garage. We could have it cleaned out and fixed up in less than a week. It would save you rent money and let me keep an eye on Beth."

"Once Beth and I are married, she'll be my responsibility. I can take care of her." Pride bristled in the words.

"Swallow your pride, boy." Patrick felt unutterably weary. "It's going to be hard enough to manage all the expenses that go with a family. Beth is going to need some extra pampering now and, once the baby is here, you're going to need help with that. Think of what's best for Beth."

Donovan stared at him, stubbornness in the set of his jaw, his eyes flaring. Beth said nothing. It was clear to her that the decision lay between the two males.

After a long moment, Donovan nodded, the movement stiff, as if it hurt to make it. "Fine. Thank you, Mr. Martin. I only want what's best for Beth."

A week later, Beth and Donovan were married in a quiet ceremony in a judge's office on the outskirts of town. The proper words were said, and Donovan slipped a narrow gold band on her finger. Beth knew that the ring had belonged to his mother, the only thing she'd given him except her stubborn determination. The only guests were Beth's father and the judge's wife.

Afterward, Patrick drove them to a neighboring town for a wedding supper so they didn't have to worry about the sideways looks and whispered comments that were already beginning to follow them in Remembrance. Beth had dropped out of school, and no one had to ask why. There was only one reason why a girl left school. The fact that Donovan was the boy involved only added to the juiciness of the story. Everyone was able to say how they had always known that Donovan Sinclair was no good. His father had been no good, and blood will tell. It was just too bad that he'd ruined sweet, little Beth Martin.

It was a quiet supper. Beth picked at her food, speaking only when spoken to. Donovan ate with dogged determination, as if to prove that nothing was bothering him. Patrick barely noticed what he was putting in his mouth. The one question that ran over and over in his mind was, Had he done the right thing in letting them marry?

The drive back to Remembrance was short and silent. Beth sat between her father and Donovan, twisting the wedding band on her finger. Donovan stared out the side window, his shoulders rigid. Patrick concentrated on his driving as if they were on a four-lane highway instead of a two-lane country road.

When the truck was stopped in front of the Martin home, no one moved for a long moment. They stared at the garage in front of them, all thinking about the pleasant little apartment above it. Each knew that their lives were forever changed. Donovan opened his door first, stepping out of the truck and onto the gravel driveway before turning back to lift Beth down.

Patrick got out, and the three of them met in front of the shiny hood. It was almost dark. Beth's hair caught the last of the sunlight, seeming to glow with a life of its own. She stood next to Donovan, his arm around her waist. Patrick swallowed hard. A few hours ago, he'd given her in marriage, but he felt as if this was the real parting. She was a married woman now and soon to be a mother.

He leaned down to drop a kiss on her forehead, glad the light was too dim to show the dampness in his eyes. "Be happy, pumpkin."

"I will, Daddy."

Donovan and Beth watched as the older man turned and walked into the house, shutting the door behind him without looking back. They silently walked up the flight of stairs that led to their new home. Donovan pulled out the key and unlocked the door. Then they stood on the small landing, not quite looking at each other, not quite looking at anything else.

After a long moment, Donovan pushed open the door and then looked at Beth. "Welcome home, Mrs. Sinclair."

He lifted her in his arms and stepped across the threshold with her. They'd left a light on, so the room was bathed in a soft glow. During the past week, Donovan had spent every moment he wasn't working or sleeping in fixing the apartment up. Beth's father contributed some furniture, and Beth hung curtains. It wasn't fancy, but it was cheerful and clean—not an altogether bad place in which to start married life.

Donovan set her down on the worn, wooden floor. Beth said nothing, but she continued to twist her wedding band.

Donovan cleared his throat. "It's pretty late. I guess we ought to get to bed. I ... I'm sorry I couldn't take time off to give you a honeymoon, Beth. We're going to need all the money I can scrape together before the ... in the next few months." It was funny how difficult it was to say the word. As if actually saying "baby" would make the situation real.

Beth shrugged. "It's okay. A honeymoon seems a little silly anyway."

"If you'd like to use the bathroom first, I'll just watch the news or something."

"Fine." She moved away without looking at him, and Donovan watched her go. She was so young. The bathroom door shut behind her, and he thrust his fingers through his hair, letting his calm facade slip. He had to be strong for her sake. He knew that he couldn't let Beth down, but it didn't seem to still the aching pressure in his gut.

He realized far better than she did just how rough life could get. Beth had never wanted for anything. His salary could provide the necessities, but there would be nothing left over for the things that Beth didn't even think of as luxuries. Much as it hurt his pride, he admitted to himself that being able to live rent-free was going to make life a lot easier.

He heard the bathroom door open and he turned, his face reflecting none of his tortured thinking. Whatever problems lay ahead, he would keep them away from Beth as much as possible. It was his fault she was in this situation; the burdens would be his.

All thoughts of burdens and future problems flew out the window when he saw his bride. He'd never seen her look so beautiful. She stopped, obviously wanting his approval, but Donovan couldn't find the words. The pure white negligee draped and flowed to the floor, hinting at curves, suggesting bare skin, without revealing anything at all. A pale peach lace ruffle decorated the bottom of the sleeves, the hem and stood up in a ruff around her neck. When she moved, the front of the negligee parted to show a matching white nightgown with an Empire waist.

She looked pure and innocent. Provocative and sensual. She was every dream he'd ever had. With her hair brushed out and flowing over her shoulders, he thought that surely she was the most beautiful woman in the world.

"Beth." Her name was all he could manage.

She turned her head away, and she smoothed her hand over the front of the negligee, her fingers shaking. "Do you like it?"

"Like it? Oh, Beth, you look . . . you look beautiful. I've never seen anybody as beautiful as you." His voice shook, and it was only through willpower that he prevented it from breaking, something it hadn't done since he was fifteen.

"Thank you."

Donovan stepped toward her, his hands touching her shoulders gently as if he expected her to disappear like a princess in a fairy tale.

"It's going to be okay, Beth. I'll take care of you. I promise."

She buried her face in her hands, her slim shoulders shaking with sobs. "Nothing is going to be the same again. None of my friends will speak to me. You can't go to college. We have to live in this stupid, little apartment. I'm going to get fat and ugly. You'll hate me sooner or later. I know you will. I don't want a baby." The words ended on a wail, her voice shattered into sobs.

Donovan pulled her into his arms, his chest aching. "Beth, listen to me. It *is* going to work. You'll see. It may take a while for your friends to come around, but they will. This place isn't so bad. We'll fix it up some more, and it'll be real nice. I'll go to school one of these days." He stopped, swallowing hard. He knew better than she ever could how unlikely that was. When he continued, his voice reflected nothing but optimism and reassurance. "And you're not going to be fat and ugly. My mom always said that a woman was most beautiful when she was pregnant."

Her sobs continued and he cupped one hand under her chin and lifted her head until she was forced to look him in his eyes. "You could never be ugly to me, Beth. Never. And I could never hate you. I love you. I'll love you always."

Her eyes clung to his, her mouth quivering. "Promise?"

"I promise. Nothing in the world could make me stop loving you."

He reached around her to pull a tissue out of the box on the tiny breakfast bar and wiped her tears away. "It's late and you need to get your rest."

He picked her up and she lay against his chest trustingly. If Donovan said he would love her forever, she'd believe him. Right now, she desperately needed to believe him. He carried her into the apartment's bedroom and set her on the bed, easing down beside her.

"I'll stay with you until you go to sleep."

"Don't you...shouldn't we... It's our wedding night..." She trailed off, her face flushed with embarrassment.

"We've got the rest of our lives." He brushed the hair back from her damp forehead. "Go to sleep."

She closed her eyes, her head resting on his shoulder. Donovan lay still, listening to her breathing gradually deepen and slow. The light spilled in from the living room and he stared at the bright path it left on the floor. He felt as if the weight of the world rested on his shoulders.

He rested his head against the headboard as he let the full burden of his responsibilities sink in. He squeezed his eyes together, but nothing could stop the slow tears that crept out, winding down his lean cheeks. With a shaky breath, he bent to lay his cheek against Beth's hair.

Chapter 3

The following two weeks were a confusing and difficult time for the newlyweds. There was so much they had to come to terms with, so many adjustments to be made. Marriage itself was difficult enough, but there was also the problem of Beth's pregnancy, which made its presence known with a vengeance.

Donovan held her while she was sick, held her while she cried, and held her sanity together. Beth didn't know which was worse, the morning sickness or the long hours when there was nothing to do but think. Donovan took on extra hours at the garage and, for the first time in her life, Beth found herself with only her own company day in and day out.

At first it was a novel experience. She was young enough to enjoy the vaguely sinful feeling of being at home when everyone else was at school or work. The novelty wore off quickly, and she found herself thinking about where she'd be if she was still in school, and wondering what her former classmates were doing.

Desperation drove her to find something to fill her time. There was an old, treadle sewing machine in one corner of the apartment. It had belonged to her grandmother and, out of curiosity, Beth opened it up, dusted it off and found that it still worked quite well. With some fabric she bought on sale, she made a new set of curtains for her father's kitchen. Donovan was duly impressed when she showed him her creation. Her father proudly hung the blue-and-white check fabric across the windows and then went out and bought her the new sewing machine, which was the cause of her first fight with Donovan.

"Dammit, Beth, if you wanted a sewing machine, why didn't you tell *me*? I'm your husband. It's my responsibility to take care of you." Donovan thrust his fingers through his dark hair, his mouth tight with anger.

"I didn't ask Daddy for a sewing machine. He was worried about me using that old treadle machine so he bought me a new one."

"Give it back to him."

"What?"

"I said, give it back to him."

"No."

They glared at each other, the little room seemed to quiver with tension. Anger filled Beth's eyes. She'd been so excited by the present, and he was ruining everything.

Donovan's chin set in a hard line. She was his wife, he would buy her anything she needed.

"We don't need your father's charity. I can take care of *my* wife."

"It's not charity. It's a present."

"Same difference. If you want a sewing machine, I'll buy you one."

"Fine." She bit the word off. "You can give my father two hundred dollars to pay for this one."

"Two hundred dollars? For that?" He pointed at the blue-and-white case that sat on the table.

"Two hundred dollars. You're so determined to buy it for me. Go ahead." She crossed her arms and glared at him.

He jammed his hands into his pockets, staring at the offending case. Pride roiled in his gut. He could take care of his own family. He *had* to take care of Beth and the baby. They had the money, and pride demanded that he march over to the big house and write her father a check. But practicality told him how impossible that was. They were going to need that money—that and every dime he could earn. Sometimes he allowed himself to wonder if it would be enough.

"Well, you're so all fired set on getting it for me. Go ahead."

He dug his hands deeper into his pockets. "No." The one word held a wealth of pain and brought Beth up short. His face was angled away from her as he looked at the sewing machine, but she could see the way the muscle ticked in his jaw, the hard set of his chin.

Her own anger and hurt faded as she realized that this was something that was important to him. He wasn't just asserting his rights as a husband.

"It's only a sewing machine. No big deal." Her voice softened unconsciously, pleading with him to understand, to see it the way she did. For a moment she thought he wasn't going to say anything.

"It isn't the damn sewing machine." His voice was raw with pride. "*I* should have thought of it. And *I* should be able to buy it for you. But I can't."

Beth struggled to understand, to comfort when she *didn't* fully understand. "It's not that big a deal. Daddy likes to buy me things. He always has. If it bothers you that much, I'll tell him I don't want it, after all."

The stiffness left Donovan's shoulders, and he reached out, pulling her close in a convulsive movement. "Oh God. What did I ever do to deserve you? I don't want you to give the stupid thing back to your father. I'm sorry I made such a fuss about it. It was a rough day. I guess I took it out on you. I'm sorry."

Beth wrapped her arms around his waist, holding him just as he was holding her. "It's okay. I understand." She didn't understand at all, but the important thing was that Donovan was holding her close. "I love you."

"I love you, too."

Beth didn't entirely comprehend Donovan's anger over the gift, but she did know that it galled him to accept help. After the sewing machine incident, she was very careful about accepting gifts from her father. If it was important to Donovan, she would try to do what would make him happy.

While Beth coped with the changes in her body and the pressures of having to grow up all at once, Donovan was trying to deal with a hundred different emotions, none of them comfortable, all of them demanding.

Guilt clutched at him every time he saw Beth. She was so young. The fact that he was only two years older didn't occur to him. He'd had to grow up quickly. Watching his parents' ruined lives made him realize at an early age that he was going to have to take care of himself. He'd accepted it the same way he accepted his parents' deaths, the same way he accepted the way people in Remembrance looked at him, expecting him to go bad.

But Beth . . . Beth was different. She was special. Her life should have overflowed with golden promises, all fulfilled. It was his fault that it hadn't been that way. Every morning he held her head while she was sick, and every morning his guilt was renewed, as was his determination.

Beth would have everything she deserved. He was going to make sure of that.

"Beth? Are you home?"

It had been three days since the argument over the sewing machine. Not another word had been said about it. Today was their three-week anniversary, and Donovan's hand tightened over the small bouquet of flowers he'd bought. Beth had been quiet, almost sad the past couple of days. If their fight was still bothering her, he hoped the flowers would ease the way to forgetting.

"Beth?"

"I'll be right out." The words sounded muffled, as if she were speaking through a pillow, and Donovan frowned, wondering if she was catching cold. Was it dangerous to catch a cold while you were pregnant? He heard the closet door shut and he followed the sound into the bedroom.

Beth was smoothing the already-smooth bedspread, her head bent forward so that her hair hid her face from him.

"Are you sick?"

She jumped at the sound of his voice, but she didn't look at him. "I'm fine. You're home early. I haven't done anything about dinner or anything yet."

Donovan frowned. "I told you not to worry about cooking. You should be resting and taking care of yourself."

"If I rest anymore I'm going to go into a coma." She laughed but the sound had little humor.

"I brought you some flowers. It's our third anniversary. They aren't much, but I thought they might brighten the place up some...." He trailed off and stared at the bouquet a moment, feeling silly. It was really such a small bouquet. It should have been a dozen red roses not a few simple flowers. "I wish I could give you more." He cleared his throat of huskiness and held the flowers toward her.

Beth took them from him, her hands shaking. "Oh, Donovan, they're beautiful. Thank you." Tears filled her voice as she smoothed the petals of a white daisy.

Donovan reached out, catching her chin when she would have turned away again. She kept her eyes lowered, but the blotchy redness around them spoke for itself. "You've been crying. What's wrong?"

She shook her head, forcing a smile that quivered around the edges. "It was nothing."

"It's not nothing when it makes you cry. Did someone say something to you?" Anger filtered through the words, boding ill for anyone who dared to upset her.

"Nobody said anything. I haven't seen anyone. I guess they're all afraid that pregnancy might be catching." There was a catch in her voice, but she swallowed hard. "I'd better go put these flowers in water." She edged by his taut figure and hurried out of the room.

Donovan could hear water running in the kitchen as she filled a vase. It hurt to think that Beth was unhappy, but there didn't seem to be much he could do. No one could have prepared her for the way her friends forgot her existence. He forced his clenched fists to unfurl. The only thing he could do was to make sure that Beth knew how much he cared. He turned to leave the room, but a flash of color caught his eye. Something was stuck in the closet door.

Opening the door, he started to tuck the scrap of fabric back inside, but his fingers froze on the peach-colored skirt. Moving slowly, he drew the garment out and hung it on the top of the closet door. It was the dress Beth had bought for the Homecoming Dance. He stared at it, remembering how excited she'd been. That was the day they'd made love in her bedroom.

It seemed so long ago. Years. Before they found out about the baby, before they got married, and when both of them still had all the normal dreams and ambitions. Their existence had been so different before reality crashed in on their heads. He fingered the soft fabric, seeing Beth's excited face when she'd shown the dress to him. She'd really been looking forward to that dance.

The puzzle pieces clicked slowly into place. She'd had the dress out, and she'd been crying. The dance was tomorrow night. Had she been thinking about how things might have been—how they *should* have been?

He turned when he heard Beth come into the room. Her eyes widened when she saw the dress.

"You were crying because of the dance, weren't you?"

"I told you, I was just being silly."

"You really want to go to this thing, don't you?"

She shook her head. "We can't so there's no sense in even thinking about it." But he saw the way her eyes shifted to the dress.

Rage swept through him. Beth hadn't done anything wrong. Her only mistake had been to fall in love with him. It was his fault. She'd done nothing wrong, but she was being treated as if she had the plague. It wasn't fair that she should lose her youth because of one mistake.

"We're going to the dance."

She stared at him, her mouth dropping slightly open when she read the determination in his eyes. "We can't."

"Like hell we can't."

"It wouldn't be right."

"Why not?" he asked coolly. "We haven't committed any major crimes. We didn't do anything to be ashamed of."

"What would people say?"

"Who gives a damn? They're already talking about us. Let's go to this dance and show them what we think of their opinions."

Beneath her uncertainty, Beth felt a glow of excitement. Donovan sounded so sure, so determined. What harm could it do? He was right, people *were* talking about them. It didn't matter whether they went to the dance or not, it wasn't going to change anyone's opinion.

"We can't." But the words had lost their conviction.

"Sure we can."

"You think so?" Maybe if they went, she could pretend for a little while that things hadn't changed. She could forget that nothing could ever be the same again. She'd had such high hopes for this dance. So many dreams had been wrapped up in that dress. She reached out and fingered the skirt, an abstract expression in her eyes. Maybe, just maybe...

The next evening she wasn't so sure there was any "maybe" about it. The whole idea was nuts. They couldn't go to the dance. It just wouldn't be right. She twisted her arms to reach the zipper on her dress, sucking in her breath as it hesitated at the waist and then slid the rest of the way up. Her hand was shaking as she smoothed it over her stomach. She was putting on weight. It wasn't obvious yet, but it wouldn't be long now. The realization added to her doubts. It was going to be a disaster.

She'd have told him so, but he wasn't there to tell. He'd made it a point that they dress separately, saying that he'd pick her up just as if it were a real date, which was why she was dressing in her old bedroom and Donovan was in the little apartment over the garage. She looked at the room through the mirror, wondering if it was the room that had changed or only the way she saw it. It felt strange, not quite right. Everything looked so young, so soft and frilly. She looked away, uneasy with the new perspective.

Downstairs, she heard the doorbell ring and her heart began to pound. That would be Donovan. She'd tell him that they couldn't go. It was crazy. She picked up her purse and took one last look in the mirror. The person who looked back at her was someone she wasn't quite comfortable with. She wasn't the girl who'd grown up in this room, but she wasn't quite a woman, either. She was somewhere betwixt and between.

She turned away from her reflection. Running her hand over her hair, she felt a sudden spurt of defiance. Donovan was right. They hadn't done anything wrong. Why shouldn't they go to this dance?

Donovan was waiting in the hall as she came downstairs. The look on his face banished the last of her doubts—or at least pushed them aside. He looked as if he'd never seen anything quite so beautiful in his life.

"Beth." He didn't say anything else, just her name was enough. With that one word, she knew how he felt. Her smile shook with nerves.

"Donovan." The intensity in his eyes was too much to bear for long, and she turned to her father, her smile hesitant. His own smile was wide, and there was a suspicious glitter in his eyes.

"I've never seen you look prettier, baby. You're going to knock all their socks off."

"Thank you, Daddy."

He hugged her, his arms tightening convulsively for a moment. "You keep your chin up, Beth."

"I will, Daddy." She turned to Donovan, her fingers clenched over her purse.

"I got this for you." Donovan stepped forward and held out a corsage of ivory rosebuds and baby's breath. "Shall I pin it on for you?"

"Please." Beth stood still as he slid his fingers inside the neck of her dress and pinned the corsage to her shoulder. Donovan could feel his hand trembling and hoped that Beth wouldn't notice. It was silly to be so nervous. This whole thing had been his idea.

The short drive passed in silence. There didn't seem to be anything to say. Donovan had borrowed her father's truck, since a motorcycle was hardly appropriate transportation. They were arriving late so they had to park almost a block away from the school.

Walking down the dark sidewalk, they could hear the music from the gym growing gradually louder. Beth's heartbeat speeded up. If she could have found her voice, she would have told Donovan that she didn't want to go. But she couldn't seem to do anything but cling to his arm and keep walking.

Donovan pulled open the door and stepped into a short, wide hall. Ahead of them they could see the big doors opening into the gym. Music poured out on a wave. There was a table set up near the door, and Donovan confidently walked up to it. Beth could only go along, her heart in her throat. The two girls sitting at the table had been staring rather forlornly at the dancers inside. The dark-haired girl turned her head slowly, her hand reaching out to take their tickets.

Under other circumstances, her expression might have been funny. Her hand froze, half extended, her jaw dropped slightly open and her eyes glazed over with shock.

"Beth!" The name came out on a squeak, drawing the attention of her companion, whose reaction was much the same.

Beth hoped her smile didn't look as ghastly as it felt. "Hello, Ann. Hi, Mary."

Donovan handed Ann the tickets and she took them automatically, staring at the couple in front of her as if they were ghosts.

"Nobody expected to see you," Ann choked out. "I mean, what a surprise."

Donovan took the ticket stubs and drew Beth's hand through his arm, pinning it firmly to his elbow as he pulled her toward the door. Beth forgot about the two girls at the table. Their reaction was nothing compared to what she would face inside. She didn't want to go in there. She tugged on her hand, her tongue glued to the roof of her mouth, but Donovan ignored her.

They stepped through the doors just as the last notes of "Born to be Wild" faded away. The gym was brightly lighted. Streamers hung from the ceiling and balloons decorated the walls. To Beth's frightened eyes, it seemed as if the room was packed with people. The ripple started near the door as people saw them. She heard the shocked whispers and saw the eyes that couldn't believe what they were seeing. Information flowed across the room as everyone became aware that something was going on. In a matter of seconds, she and Donovan were the center of attention.

It was only Donovan's firm grip that kept Beth from collapsing in a terrified heap and crawling out the door. A space cleared around them as if by magic. For several slow heartbeats, the gym was dead silent. No one said a word. Donovan looked slowly around the room, his mouth set in an arrogant sneer, his eyes daring anyone to say a word.

The silence stretched until Beth was certain that the strain was going to kill her, and then there was a ripple of movement to one side as someone pushed forward. Beth held her breath as Carol ducked into the small circle that had grown between them and the rest of the school. She hadn't seen Carol since she left school. Her friend's parents had forbidden all contact. They'd talked once on the phone, but it had been a furtive, hurried call that left her wondering if she'd lost her best friend along with everything else that was lost.

Carol's eyes met hers, but it was impossible to tell what she was thinking. Was Carol going to snub her in front of the entire school? She felt Donovan's arm tense beneath her fingers and knew he was wondering the same thing.

Carol's thin face broke out in a wide grin. "Beth! It's great to see you." Her voice carried easily in the cavernous room and Beth felt her knees weaken as Carol hurried across the short distance between them. She had to blink back tears as she returned her friend's hug.

"It's nice to see you, too."

Carol linked her arm with Beth's so that she and Donovan flanked her. Carol's wide smile challenged the room, flicking over the other students, her look as much a dare as Donovan's was a warning. There was a mutter to the left of them, and Jane Masterson stepped forward, her face flushed.

"I'm glad you came, Beth. What a cool dress."

Someone put a record on, several people came forward to say hello. The tension was broken. Donovan's muscles eased, and Beth started to breathe again. It was going to be okay.

The dance was both nothing like she'd dreamed and more than she'd expected. Her dreams had been nebulous, unformed things in which she walked in with Donovan and everyone who saw them instantly recognized that they belonged together. Her father would then see how wrong he'd been and she and Donovan could be together without hiding their feelings.

Her life had shifted 180 degrees since then. The dream had become irrelevant, her expectations had become more realistic, her new hopes a little more hesitant.

Nice girls did not get pregnant and drop out of school to get married. But even Remembrance had to change with the times. Sluggishly, reluctantly, but it did change. There was room now for forgiveness, especially for a girl who did the right thing and got married, even if it was to Donovan Sinclair.

Her friends seemed genuinely glad to see her. No one mentioned the reason she'd left school, no one asked awkward questions. They all pretended nothing had happened. If there were whispers skating around the room, no one was rude enough to allow Beth to hear them—or perhaps no one wanted to chance the cool threat in Donovan's eyes.

It should have been wonderful, and in some ways, it was. But underneath the relief and pleasure, Beth was conscious of a vague sadness. She'd changed. She wasn't the same girl who'd started the new school year a few short weeks ago. She had a new life, new responsibilities. Gradually she realized that she could never go back and be that girl. The realization broke over her on a wave of melancholy.

The music changed before the sadness could get too firm a hold. The smooth sound of "In the Midnight Hour" poured out of the speakers, and she turned to Donovan. That song had been playing the night she'd met him, and it had been on the radio again the first time he kissed her.

Their eyes met and she saw the memory in his. Without speaking, he held out his hand and led her onto the dance floor. The lights had been dimmed for the slow tune, and couples filled the floor, swaying to the rhythm. As far as Beth and Donovan were concerned, they could have been alone. With Donovan's hands resting on the small of her back, his dark head bent close to hers, Beth felt as if she'd come home. He was holding her as though he'd never let her go. She leaned her forehead against his chest, linking her arms around his neck, letting the music flow over them.

"I love you, Beth." The words whispered against her hair, blending with the music.

"Oh, Donovan." There didn't seem to be any need to say more.

Driving home, Beth leaned her head against Donovan's shoulder. Her father's house was dark when they pulled into the driveway. Donovan's shoes crunched in the gravel as he stepped out, the sound strangely loud in the still night. Beth slid under the steering wheel, bracing her hands on his shoulders, letting him lift her out of the truck. The gravel felt rough beneath her stockinged feet, and she remembered that her shoes were still clutched in her hand.

"Thank you for taking me to the dance, Mr. Sinclair."

"The pleasure was mine, Mrs. Sinclair." The name sounded so right when he said it. Beth smiled at him, feeling truly happy for the first time since Dr. Morrison had told her she was pregnant.

Donovan wondered if she had any idea how beautiful she looked standing there in the moonlight. There was a full harvest moon in the sky and its soft light caught in her hair, turning it to pure silver. Her eyes were dark, mysterious pools and her mouth had never looked more kissable. Desire stirred.

They hadn't made love since they'd found out about the baby. The few short weeks had seemed like aeons. Lying next to her in bed at night, Donovan sometimes thought he'd go mad with wanting her, and then he'd be ashamed of himself. She was pregnant, her life had been torn apart. He'd give her all the time she wanted. All the time in the world, if that's what it took.

But she stood there in the cool light of an autumn moon looking so desirable. Almost too beautiful to touch—yet he had to touch her. His head dipped slowly, his eyes on hers. It was impossible to read her expression, but he could taste the softness of her mouth. The kiss deepened and her arms lifted to circle his shoulders, her shoes bumping against his back.

He angled his head to deepen the kiss, his arms tightening around her. Beth sighed, her lips opening, one hand slipping up to burrow into his hair, drawing him closer. With a groan Donovan bent and caught her up in his arms, catching her soft gasp in his mouth. Beth lay against him trustingly, her softness cradled in his arms as he carried her up the stairs and into the small apartment that was their home.

Chapter 4

"Donovan? Donovan, wake up. I think I'm in labor."
Beth's voice shook, its note of panic bringing Donovan to
attention even more than her words. He was offering reas-
surances almost before his eyes were open.

"I'm here, Beth. Don't be scared." He sat up, running his
hand over his face and blinking the sleep away. He snapped
on the bedside lamp.

"How far apart are the pains?"

"I don't know. It hurts."

"I know, sweetheart. Just breathe and ride the pain. We
didn't drive all the way to Indianapolis for those classes for
nothing, did we?"

He was tucking pillows behind her as he spoke, easing her
into a more comfortable position. He brushed the hair back
from her forehead, seeing the fright in her eyes and hoping
that he looked calm and reassuring. Her hand came up to
clutch his.

"I'm scared." Her voice broke and he had to force a
smile.

"I'm right here and I'm not going to let anything happen to you. I promised to take care of you, didn't I?"

She nodded. "What if something goes wrong? What if..." Her fingers tightened over his as a contraction took hold.

Donovan laid his free hand over the taut mound of her belly, feeling the muscles ripple beneath his fingers. He swallowed his own panic. She was so young. What if something went wrong? How could he bear it if something happened to Beth—or to the baby who'd be his son or daughter? The contraction eased and he looked at the clock, automatically noting the time.

"Just relax and save your strength. Remember what the doctor said. It's probably going to be a while before it's even time to take you to the hospital."

"Don't leave me alone. I don't want to be alone."

"I'm not going anywhere. We've got plenty of time."

But the baby's idea of plenty of time was different than Donovan's. In less than three hours, Beth's contractions were coming five minutes apart. Donovan helped her down the stairs, afraid to carry her. Patrick was waiting to take them to the hospital, his face white and drawn in the dawn light.

Donovan held Beth during the short drive, brushing the hair back from her face, murmuring softly, promising her that everything was going to be all right, bottling up the terror that rose in his throat every time a contraction hit. Patrick pulled the truck up in front of the hospital entrance and Donovan lifted Beth down. A light spring rain was falling, and he eased her carefully up the concrete steps, supporting her swollen body as much as possible.

Once inside, the smell of antiseptic and the quiet bustle of the emergency room enfolded them. Donovan signed papers as they were thrust at him, holding those necessary for Beth to put her shaky signature on. Someone had found a wheelchair, and Beth sat in it, looking so small and fragile that Donovan felt fear engulf him.

When the last paper was signed, a nurse came to wheel Beth away, directing Donovan to the waiting room. Beth sobbed, her fingers closing around his wrist with bruising strength.

"Don't leave me. Please, please. You promised. You promised." Hysteria wrapped the words.

"Really, Mrs. Sinclair, having a baby is a perfectly natural thing. We don't need your husband—"

"I'm going with her." Donovan's calm statement cut through the woman's professional condescension.

"I'm afraid we don't allow that, Mr. Sinclair. Fathers have to wait in the waiting room. You'll have plenty of company."

"I'm going with my wife. We already discussed this with Dr. Grant."

The nurse sniffed, thus stating her opinion of Dr. Grant. "Then you'll just have to wait until she arrives. In the meantime, you can wait with the other fathers."

"You promised." Beth dug her fingers into his arm, her other hand pressed against her stomach as another contraction gripped her, her eyes hazy with pain. "You promised."

Donovan looked from her frightened face to that of the nurse, who was standing ramrod stiff beside the wheelchair, her expression filled with disapproval. "I'm staying with her."

"I can't allow that."

Donovan drew himself up to his full six-foot-two height, his frame muscular from hard work. "Do you want to stop me?"

The nurse stared at him, reading the determination in his eyes. He was less than half her age. By all rights, he should have been intimidated by her authority. *She* was the one in charge. But staring into those hazel eyes, she decided that this was one time she'd cut her losses. If she called security, it was going to cause a major scene. Looking at the boy's looming presence, she wasn't sure security would win anyway. He was damned determined. With a furious sniff, she capitulated.

"I'm going to discuss this with Dr. Grant the moment she arrives."

Donovan was no longer listening. He pried Beth's fingers loose from his arm so that he could take her hand, bending down to look into her pale face.

"It's all right, sweetheart."

"You're not going to leave me, are you? You promised you'd stay. You promised."

"You're not going anywhere without me. I'll stay right here."

He ignored the stunned disapproval of the nurses who prepared Beth for giving birth. He ignored the whispered consultations as to what to do with a father who planned on staying through delivery. He didn't care about anything but Beth. Each contraction seemed to drain more of her strength. He held her hand, whispering encouragement and wiping the sweat from her forehead.

When the doctor arrived, Donovan was vaguely aware of the hushed argument going on between her and the nurses. He assumed it was about his presence in the delivery room, but it didn't seem relevant. He was staying with Beth. That was the end of it as far as he was concerned.

"How are you doing, Beth?" Dr. Grant studied Beth's chart, her plain features reassuringly calm.

"I want to go home. It hurts."

"I know it does. Remember, the two of you decided that you wanted natural childbirth. This is part of bringing a beautiful child into the world. You're doing just fine."

"I'm not fine." Beth spit the words out on a wave of exhausted rage. What did this woman know about how she was? She was dying. Nothing else could hurt this much.

They'd told her that having a baby was going to be a wonderful, glorious experience. There was nothing wonderful or glorious about this.

"I want to go home. Donovan, take me home." She struggled up on her elbows, her chin set.

"Beth, you can't go home now." Donovan pressed her back down, casting a panicked look at the doctor who looked as if this was all perfectly natural.

"I want to—" The words choked off as another contraction grabbed her. Her neck arched, her nails dug holes in his arm.

"Don't worry, Beth. You're doing fine." Beth wanted to scream at the doctor to stop lying. She wasn't fine. She was in agony. Her entire body felt as if it belonged to someone else, someone who was torturing her. She felt Donovan's arm beneath her hand and opened her eyes to focus on his face. As long as she focused on his face, she could get through this. He was the only thing linking her to the real world, the world she'd been a part of before this horrible creature took over.

"The head's coming now, Beth. Push. You can push now."

Stupid woman, Beth thought. I can't push. I don't have the strength. But somehow, she was pushing. Her breath came out in sobbing puffs, but she was pushing. There was a tremendous pressure and then a sudden emptiness.

"Good girl. You've got a beautiful little boy." The doctor's words came to her through a haze.

"A boy. Let me see." She'd never have believed it a few minutes ago, but she felt a tingle of excitement.

"Just a minute. Let the nurse clean him up a bit. And we're not quite through with you yet."

Beth's face tightened as she felt another contraction, but it was nothing like the earlier ones. She knew it must be the afterbirth. They'd been told about that at the classes. There was a quick tug and then the doctor was smiling up at her.

"You did a good job, Beth." Dr. Grant took a tiny bundle from the nurse. "I think you should introduce your wife and son, Donovan."

Donovan's hands were shaking as he took the baby from the doctor's arms and turned toward Beth. Beth pushed herself up on her elbows, oblivious to the quiet bustle going on around them or to the nurse who propped pillows behind her back.

Donovan carefully laid the baby in her outstretched arms, tugging back the soft blanket. Beth stared down at the wiggling red creature.

"He's beautiful," Beth said. She saw him through a haze of tears, but she knew he was perfect. From the thick, dark hair that covered his head to all ten of his tiny little toes, she'd never seen anything more perfect in her life.

Donovan reached out and nudged a flailing hand with his finger. Instantly the tiny fingers closed around his thumb. Beth's laugh ended on a half sob. She looked up at Donovan, and she wasn't surprised to see him wiping self-consciously at the dampness in his eyes.

"He's beautiful."

"Almost as beautiful as his mother." The husky words held a wealth of love, and Beth felt new tears fill her eyes.

"You need to let Beth get some rest now, Donovan." Dr. Grant bent to lift the baby from Beth's arms.

"I'm not tired." But even as she said the words, Beth felt exhaustion sweep over her. She barely felt the kiss Donovan brushed across her forehead.

Michael Patrick Sinclair arrived home on a spring day full of sunshine. The weather might have been celebrating his arrival. His grandfather carried him up the stairs to his first home while Donovan carried Beth. Beth protested that she was capable of walking on her own, but Donovan ignored her. She looked so fragile and felt so light in his arms.

"I think he smiled at me." Donovan set Beth on the sofa and glanced over his shoulder at his father-in-law. Patrick's face was bent over the small bundle that was his grandson. Donovan couldn't help but grin at the fatuous expression on Patrick's face. The fact that Beth had come through the pregnancy and birth as well as she had seemed to have eased the tension between the two men. In the long run, Donovan supposed that they had a strong common bond. They both loved Beth and now there was Michael.

"Are you sure you don't want to go to bed?" He smoothed the hair back from Beth's forehead, his eyes worried.

"Donovan, I've spent the past three days in bed. I'll let you know if I get to feeling too tired. I promise."

He smiled but the worry didn't leave his eyes. It wouldn't until she had the color back in her cheeks. Guilt washed over him again. It was his fault she'd gone through all this. Beth swore that it hadn't been so bad, at least not now that she had the baby, but Donovan's memories were too vivid, too frightening. Never again did he want to see Beth so frightened or in such pain. He'd promised to take care of her.

During the next few months, he kept that promise so well that Beth never suspected the tremendous toll it was taking on him. All her time and energy was taken up with the baby. She'd never realized how demanding an infant could be. There was more to motherhood than just an occasional feeding or diaper change. Michael needed to be held and talked to and played with. All the baby books she'd read said that it was important for a baby to live in an environment full of stimuli, and she worked hard to provide that.

During the summer months, Carol spent a lot of time amusing the baby, giving Beth a few much-needed hours to relax. Carol thought it was great fun to be Michael's "aunt"; Beth was just grateful to have a friend. The town had gradually accepted her marriage and child. She no longer felt as if she were wearing a scarlet "A" on her chest every time she took Michael to the store, but Carol was the only friend who'd managed to make the transition gracefully. Beth knew it hadn't been easy, but Carol had remained her friend without ever speaking a word of reproach.

The expenses that came with a baby were surprising, too. Donovan had to take on extra hours at the garage to make ends meet. Beth learned how to budget, sometimes shedding tears of frustration because the money never seemed to go as far as she hoped. But her eyes were always dried before Donovan got home. She knew instinctively that he would feel as if her tears were a symbol of some failure on his part.

Donovan took an active role as a father. During the first few months, he got up with Michael as often as Beth did. His hands, so much larger than Beth's, were just as competent when it came to warming a bottle or cuddling a fussy baby. Michael would stop crying for Donovan as easily as for Beth.

If Beth occasionally mentioned the lines of strain around her husband's mouth, he told her it was her imagination. She was too busy with Michael and the pressures of being a wife and mother before her eighteenth birthday to pursue the issue. Donovan was always there—she could always depend on him. Always.

Beth woke one night, about six months after Michael's birth. Next to her, the bed was empty and she leaned on one elbow, searching the room with sleepy eyes. She crawled out of bed, yawning as she reached for her robe. Michael's crib stood in the corner, but Michael wasn't in it. Maybe the baby had started to fuss and Donovan had been afraid he would wake her.

She wandered into the living room, tugging her hair from beneath the collar of her robe as she went. There was a light on in the kitchen, and it cast soft shadows in the living room. Donovan was sitting on the sofa, Michael asleep against his chest, his tiny body sprawled out across his father's much-larger frame. Beth stopped in the doorway, her face soft with love for both of them.

In the strange hours between midnight and dawn, she felt as if she was seeing Donovan for the first time in months. Caught up in the day-to-day pressures of living, it had been a long time since she'd really looked at him. He was wearing jeans and a heavy, flannel shirt that he hadn't bothered to button. His body was taut from hours of hard work. One broad hand lay across Michael's back, holding him secure, and Beth winced at the scrapes and bruises that marked his knuckles.

Donovan's twentieth birthday was just a few weeks away, but he looked much older—too much older. Somehow the dim light emphasized the lines of strain that framed his mouth. He looked drawn and worn, like a man who was reaching the end of his rope. Beth put her hand to her throat, trying to swallow the tightness there as she moved closer, her slippered feet silent on the worn, wooden floor.

Donovan was strong and tough. He'd always been there for her. From the moment he'd offered her that first ride home, through her pregnancy and the pressures of being a parent, Donovan had been strong. He'd offered her a shoulder to lean on, a hand to smooth the way across any rough patches. Now he looked vulnerable and tired. His lashes lay against his cheeks in dark crescents, emphasizing the pallor of his skin.

He wasn't aware of her presence until she sat next to him, the old sofa dipping beneath her weight. His eyes flew open, and he immediately turned his head away, running his hand over his face as if he had been asleep. But Beth had seen the dampness on his cheeks.

"Donovan? What's wrong?"

"Nothing. I guess Michael and I fell asleep." He didn't look at her, occupying himself with the baby.

"You were crying." Her voice shook.

"Don't be silly, Beth. You must be half asleep. Why don't you go back to bed, and I'll put Michael in the crib and join you." He still hadn't looked at her.

Beth put her hand on his arm, feeling the tautness of his muscles. "Donovan, don't lie to me. Please. If something is wrong, I want to know about it."

He didn't say anything. He stared down at Michael sleeping peacefully in his arms, confident that his small world was safe and secure. Beth saw Donovan draw a deep breath, his shoulders sagging slightly as if weighed down. For a moment, she thought he was going to refuse to talk about whatever was bothering him, and she felt the knot in her stomach tighten.

"Please, Donovan. I love you."

The whispered words seemed to break down some barrier held tight within him. His breath left him on a sound that was perilously close to a sob. He lifted his free hand to pinch the bridge of his nose, his eyes pressed shut.

"Sometimes I'm so tired, Beth. So damned tired. I'm afraid that one morning I'll just be too tired to get up." Exhaustion threaded through his every word.

"You've been working too hard. You shouldn't have taken on so many extra hours." Beth felt a wave of relief. This was something simple, something she could deal with.

"We need the money, Beth. But it doesn't really matter because I'll have to cut back my hours anyway. Things always slow down in the winter." He stood up abruptly, lifting Michael with him. "I'm going to put the baby to bed."

Beth didn't move. She watched him leave the room, trying to pin down the uneasiness nibbling at the back of her mind. There was something more here than just temporary exhaustion. She was ashamed that she hadn't noticed how tired he was, but she knew that wasn't the whole story.

When Donovan came back, he didn't sit down again. He moved around the dim room restlessly, and Beth could feel the tension building. Finally, she ended the silence herself.

"Are we broke?"

Donovan turned to look at her, his face shadowed. "We can get by. I suppose even if my hours are cut, we can survive. We've got this place rent-free, thanks to your father." His words were laced with suppressed anger.

Beth waited for him to go on, to explain what was bothering him, but he didn't say anything more. He stood next to the kitchen table, his fingers shifting restlessly over its edge. She moved over to him, taking his hand in hers, stilling the aimless movement.

"Donovan, what is it? What's bothering you? You said we could get by."

Donovan's gaze met hers. The light was at his back, his face all in shadow, but Beth could read the blaze of emotion, could feel it in the way his hand turned to grip hers.

"I don't want to 'get by.' I don't want that for you or Michael, and I don't want it for myself. You want to know what's bothering me, Beth? You really want to know?"

She nodded, half frightened by the intensity that shimmered around him.

"I'm scared. I'm scared half to death sometimes."

"Scared? Scared of what?" She swallowed the quiver in her voice. Her whole world was trembling. Donovan was her rock. He was always there, always strong.

"Sometimes, I look at our future and it scares me."

Beth drew a sharp breath as pain stabbed in her chest. She jerked her hand from his and stepped back, instinctively moving away from the light. He didn't love her anymore. All she wanted in the world was a future with Donovan, but he was saying that wasn't what he wanted.

He reached out and caught her hands. Ignoring her resistance, he pulled her toward him. Beth kept her face turned away. She couldn't bear to see the look in his eyes. She didn't want to see how he looked when he told her he was leaving.

"Beth, no. That's not what I meant. I love you." He took hold of her shoulders, shaking her gently, coaxing her to meet his eyes. "I'll always love you."

Beth lifted her eyes, seeing the truth in his face. With a muffled sob, she relaxed against his chest, letting him support her, her fingers clutching at the edges of his shirt.

"Then why did you say that a future with me looked frightening?" She sounded like just what she was. Very young, very frightened and in desperate need of reassurance.

Donovan stroked the back of her head, his long fingers offering wordless comfort. "I didn't mean that a future with you frightened me. I don't know what I'd do without you, Beth."

"What did you mean?"

"Do you ever look ahead, Beth? I mean really look ahead and wonder where we'll be a few years from now?"

"Michael will be in school, I suppose."

"I don't mean that kind of thing. I mean the future." The way he said it put the word in capital letters, and Beth drew back, staring at him.

"What do you mean?" There was a note in his voice that made her uneasy. It said her world wasn't safe yet and might not be safe again for a long time. "What kind of 'future'?"

"That's exactly what I'm talking about. Do you look ahead five or ten or fifteen years and see us still living here, taking charity from your father—me working in the garage and you keeping house?"

"I . . . I hadn't thought about it all that much. I guess I thought maybe we'd have another baby eventually, maybe even two or three. Aren't you happy?"

He stared at her, his expression unreadable. He seemed to be weighing something in his mind, and Beth held her breath, sensing that his answer might hurt.

"No. No, I'm not happy." He caught her hands before she could pull away. "I'm happy with you. You know that. I love you. I love Michael. Maybe that should be enough, but it isn't. Beth, I don't want to work in a garage for the rest of my life. I don't want you to be a housewife unless that's what you want to do. I want us to have some choices."

"We do have choices."

"What? Whether we should have hamburger or splurge on a chicken for dinner? Whether to buy you a winter coat or buy Michael new shoes? Whether we're going to have to ask your father for another loan to pay our bills?"

"Daddy doesn't mind—"

"*I* mind! Dammit, Beth, I don't want to live like this. I don't want it for me, I don't want it for you, and I sure as hell don't want it for our son. I want him to have choices, too. I want him to be able to go to college. *I* want to go to college. I'm twenty years old. You're barely eighteen. I don't want to give up all our dreams."

"If I hadn't gotten pregnant, we could have done a lot of things. But I did get pregnant." Her voice was thick with tears, and Donovan softened his tone, trying to get her to see what he was saying without making her feel as though she was being accused of something.

"Beth, you're talking like we have to be punished for what we did. We made a mistake. *I* made a mistake. But I love Michael, I wouldn't wish him away if I could. We didn't do anything wrong, and I don't see why we should have to give up all our dreams because of it."

She stared at him, her eyes bright with unshed tears. "I love you. I just want to be with you."

"God, Beth, I want that, too." He drew her close, feeling the dampness of her tears against his chest, feeling her pain as if it were his own. "I want that more than anything in the world. But I want to be able to give you all the things you should have. A nice house, a car. I want those things for you. I want to be able to buy Michael a bicycle when he's old enough, and I don't want to have to scrimp and save for months to do it."

They were silent for a long time. Around them, the little apartment was quiet. Michael slept securely in the next room. Beth had no such security. She felt as if she were standing on a patch of ice that was threatening to throw her off balance.

It had taken her a long time to adjust to all the changes in her life, but she'd adjusted and she'd worked hard at it. If she sometimes had twinges of discontent or wondered if this was all there was to life, then she suppressed them. One thing her father had taught her was that when you made your bed, you had to lie in it.

Now, Donovan was throwing all her careful thinking out of whack. Everyone knew that children took priority. Parents didn't have dreams except for their children's futures. She'd been living day to day, not really looking at anything but the present. His words made it impossible to go on that way.

She stepped back, wiping her eyes with her hands. "I could get a job. We could get someone to baby-sit Michael, and I could go to work. If we saved carefully, we could get a house and—"

Donovan laughed. "Beth, that's not going to do it. It would take years to save enough money for a house. And you going to work isn't going to do any good because anything you earned would have to go right in to paying whoever was taking care of Michael."

"Well, then I don't see what we can do. We can't turn the clock back."

"I don't want to turn it back, but I'm not willing to give up our dreams, Beth. Remember the way we always talked about our future together? I want those dreams. Dammit! We're going to have those dreams."

"What are you going to do?"

Donovan stared at her, his eyes old far beyond his years, deep lines tightening his mouth. "I'm going to join the marines, Beth."

Beth forgot how to breathe. Her gaze clung to his, pleading with him to say that this was all a bad dream. She read the pain in his eyes, but there was iron determination in the set of his jaw.

"No. There must be some other way."

"There is no other way. I can spend a couple of years in the marines, and when I get out, I can go to school on the GI bill. Money will still be tight, but once I've got a degree, I'll be able to start earning a good salary."

"If you come back." The words were out before she could stop them, and she pressed her hands to her mouth, staring at him as if she'd never seen him before. If he loved her he wouldn't even consider doing this to her.

The war in Vietnam had been nothing more than a frightening but distant news story. Parts of the nation might be protesting and boiling with discontent, but Remembrance went peacefully about its business. She knew a few girls at school who had older brothers in Vietnam, but none of them were her close friends. It was something that had no relevance to her own life. With one sentence, Donovan changed all that. Suddenly the fighting was very real. Those men she'd seen on the television all had Donovan's face.

A sob escaped her and she pressed her hands tighter against her mouth. But she couldn't do anything about the tears that welled up in her eyes and spilled onto her cheeks.

"Oh, Beth, don't cry." Donovan took her in his arms, holding her close.

"What if you get killed? Please don't do this." The pleas came out between ragged sobs, her face pressed tightly to his chest.

"I have to, sweetheart. If I don't volunteer, I might be drafted. At least this way I have some choice about it. Nothing is going to happen to me. Didn't I promise I'd take care of you? I can't do that if I let myself get shot. Come on, sweetheart, don't cry like that. You'll make yourself sick."

Beneath the loving concern lay determination, and Beth knew she'd lost the war before the first battle was ever fought. Donovan was going to do what he felt was right, and there was nothing she could do but learn to live with it.

Two days after Michael's first Christmas, Donovan caught a bus to Indianapolis. From there he would take a plane to South Carolina and start boot camp. Beth didn't cry when he left. She'd already shed all her tears, and she swore she would send him off without them. But she stood in the bus station long after his bus was gone, unable to break the last link and move from the spot where he'd kissed her goodbye.

He had to come home safely. He'd promised. And Donovan never broke his promises.

Never.

Chapter 5

Dear Donovan,

I hope this letter finds you well and drier than you were when you last wrote. The weather here has been unusually warm. We're having a hot summer—not much rain.

Michael is starting to walk. He's really starting to fall down, I suppose. He does pretty well if he's got something to hold on to, and I know he'll get the hang of it soon. He's talking now, enough to get across what he wants.

I've started the night school I told you about in my last letter. Carol or Daddy take care of Michael the nights I'm in school. Carol will be starting college this fall. I feel a little stupid trying to get my high school diploma, but I guess it's a good idea. Anyway, it fills some time.

I'm enclosing pictures of Michael. He's grown so much since you left. I wish you were here to see him, but I've taken a lot of pictures so that you'll be able to see those when you get home.

When will you be home? I promised myself I wouldn't ask, but I can't help it. I miss you so much. Michael tries but he can't fill the gap his daddy left. Our home feels empty without you. I feel empty without you.

We hear so many frightening things on the news. I dread turning on the TV for fear I'll see your face, maybe lying in the road somewhere hurt or dying. I probably shouldn't tell you how frightened I am. I don't want you to worry about me. I want you to think about yourself.

Remember you promised to come home to me.

I love you.

                                                    Beth

Donovan folded the letter and carefully slipped it back into the envelope before picking up the pictures. His fingers were trembling as he sorted through the half-dozen photos. They were all of Michael, and he felt an ache in his chest as he realized how much his son had grown. He looked happy and healthy, his smile proudly showing off his first few teeth.

Beth was holding him in one picture, and Donovan stared at that one the longest. It had been taken outside and the sunlight poured over her, turning her hair to pure gold. She was smiling at the camera, her arms wrapped around Michael's sturdy little body.

"Letter from your wife?"

He dragged his eyes away from the photo. "Yeah. She sent pictures."

"Pictures, huh? Of her and the kid?"

"Mostly Michael, but one of her."

Smitty sat up, swinging his feet off the cot. "Let me see. I want to see if she's as pretty as you said she was."

Donovan grinned and handed the photos across the short space that separated them. Lowell Smith—Smitty, if you didn't want to carry your teeth in your hand—fancied himself a connoisseur of women. In the months Donovan had known him, he'd discovered that Smitty had opinions about everything, from the proper way to chew tobacco to the proper way to hold a rifle. He didn't really expect anyone to follow his suggestions, but he made damn sure everyone knew what he thought.

Smitty shuffled through the pictures until he found the photo of Beth. Donovan leaned back on his cot, already knowing what the Southerner's comment was going to be.

"Ooooeee! That's one powerful pretty woman. I bet her mother was from the South. The prettiest women—"

"Grow in the South." Donovan finished the comment for him. "Beth's mother was born and raised in Indiana."

Smitty shrugged, not in the least disturbed. "Might'a been her grandma, then. But I can tell she's got southern blood in her."

Donovan shook his head, reaching out to take the photos back. Smitty handed them over, his thin face wistful. "That's a nice little boy you got there, too. You're a lucky man, Dono. A lucky, lucky man."

"You hear from your girl?"

"No. But I reckon Sue Ann is pretty busy with college and all. She's going to be a doctor. That takes a lot of work."

"Yeah, I guess it does." Donovan slipped the photos back inside the letter and put both under his pillow. In the months they'd trained together and then shipped out, Smitty had received two letters from Sue Ann.

Outside, the rain poured down without showing any signs of stopping. Donovan lay back on his cot, hearing the soft crackle of Beth's letter beneath his head. It made him feel closer to her. If he closed his eyes, he could almost imagine that the endless sound of the rain was the dusty rustle of a cornfield, the silks no brighter than Beth's hair.

"We're heading farther in tomorrow."

"So I heard."

"Don't you ever lose your cool, Dono?"

"I might if you don't stop calling me Dono." Donovan's voice was lazy. It was an old argument, one they'd had since boot camp.

"I mean it. You always look like you expect to go home in one piece. Don't you ever worry, ever think that some of us ain't gonna make it?"

Donovan opened his eyes, turning his head to look at his friend. "I don't think about it. I'm going home. I've got a wife and kid to take care of."

"You think the VC care? A lot of guys got wives and kids. They ain't all going home."

"I promised Beth."

"Dammit! Don't it ever occur to you, you might not keep that promise?"

Smitty's voice held a ragged edge, and Donovan sat up, clasping his hands between his knees. He stared at the canvas floor.

"Don't you ever get scared?" Smitty's question was quiet, blending with the rain.

"Yeah, I get scared. We're all scared. This is supposed to be a war. I'd be nuts if I wasn't scared. But it doesn't do any good to think about it. I try to think about Beth and Michael and how much they need me."

"Must be nice to have someone need you that much."

Donovan looked at Smitty and then looked away. There was too much vulnerability there, too much pain. No man wanted another to see him like that.

"Sue Ann needs you." Whatever his personal thoughts on Smitty's girlfriend, he knew how much it meant to know that someone was waiting for you, that someone cared about you coming back.

"Hell, she don't care none. That last letter I got a month ago? It didn't say how much she missed me, like I told y'all.

It said that she thinks we got no business being over here, and it wouldn't be moral of her to keep writing to me. She said I should refuse to fight, even if they send me to jail for it."

Donovan stared at his hands. He didn't need to see the naked pain on Smitty's face, it was in his voice. Somewhere in the distance, they could hear a staccato burst of gunfire, too far away to be a threat, too close to ignore. Someone was dying out there. Someone would never go home. In both their minds was the thought that tomorrow it might be one of them.

The firing died away and Smitty spoke again. "I wrote her a letter. I tried to explain what it was like over here. The jungle and the rice paddies and how you never know when a sniper is going to pick you off. You just don't refuse to fight because of some moral issue. How else am I going to stay alive? I guess I don't think much about the politics of it. I just want to keep me and my buddies in one piece."

"That's about all any of us do. We're just trying to stay alive. There's nothing wrong with that."

Smitty rubbed his hand over his face, his angular features twisting in a smile that held so much pain, Donovan felt an ache in his gut. "I suppose. I never sent the letter. I reckon she ain't going to change her opinion none."

"She probably doesn't really mean it. I bet in a few weeks you'll get a letter saying how sorry she is. She's young, Smitty."

"I used to think I was pretty young. I guess maybe I won't never be young again. None of us will."

Donovan stared at him, the words echoing in his mind. He opened his mouth and then closed it again. There didn't seem to be anything to say.

"Incoming! Incoming! Hit the dirt! Hit the dirt!"

Donovan dove for the floor, hearing the whine of the rockets endless seconds before they hit. Time was suspended between life and death as he and Smitty braced for the impact, wondering where the ammo would land, wondering if these were their last seconds alive.

The explosion rocked the ground. The gunfire must have hit one of the few solid buildings in the camp. Boards smashed against the tent, ripping the walls apart. Debris scattered over them. The light went out. Donovan put his hands over his head, his cheek pressed to the thin, canvas floor, feeling the hard dirt underneath. The second rocket hit nearby, the sound shattering around them. The tent collapsed like a badly stacked deck of cards, smothering them in damp canvas.

"Come on, we've got to get out of here." He groped for Smitty, finding his arm in the darkness and tugging. There was no response, and Donovan edged to his knees, fighting the layer of canvas, finding Smitty's shoulders and dragging him toward where the entrance had been. Two more rockets slammed into the ground, and he heard the sound of answering fire, knew that their gunners were trying to get a fix on the enemy's location. He didn't think about any of that. All he thought about was getting the two of them out. Smitty was a deadweight, knocked unconscious in the blast.

Donovan edged backward, groping for the opening, finding it at last and backing out into the rain, dragging Smitty with him. The rain fell steadily, not the gentle rain that fell on Indiana cornfields but a heavy curtain that seemed smotheringly thick. Donovan wiped his hand over his eyes, casting a quick look around the camp, seeing the scurry of activity, then hearing the heavy boom of a rocket launcher. All of that was secondary to his concern for Smitty. He wiped the rain out of his eyes again and reached for his buddy. The medic was across the camp. He was halfway to his knees, Smitty cradled against him, when he realized that there was no rush.

There wasn't anything a medic could do for him.

It must have been the first rocket that did it. From the looks of it, a board must have caught him, breaking his neck and killing him instantly. Donovan laid him down gently. He reached out to close his friend's eyes, vaguely disturbed by that blank stare. He knelt there for a long time... until someone came along and took him by the shoulders, lifting him to his feet and pulling him away from the body. He didn't say anything while the medics dabbed antiseptic on his numerous cuts, cuts he hadn't even been aware of. They released him, going back to the more seriously wounded.

Donovan walked back to the remains of the tent. Smitty's body was gone, but there had been no time to do anything about the collapsed tent. There were more important priorities. But not to Donovan. He shifted through the debris to find Beth's letter. It was wet but it would be all right once it dried out. He tucked it in his pocket and then went through Smitty's belongings methodically, packing them up to be shipped home to his folks.

He found the letter Smitty had written to his girlfriend. Without thinking about it, he tucked it in his pocket. The next day, it was on its way back to the States, exactly as Smitty had written it but with a simple postscript written by Donovan.

"He's dead."

Dear Beth,

I wish I could be there for Thanksgiving dinner. I know you'll be having turkey and all the trimmings. Eat some for me, would you?

I know I said I might be able to make it home for Christmas but, as it turns out, that won't be possible. If everyone who wanted Christmas leave got it, there wouldn't be a war during the month of December because no one would be here to fight it. I'll be home in January, though. Save some Christmas ham for me.

I can't wait to see you, Beth. I miss you so much. It's like an ache in my gut every minute. I don't know what

I'd do if I didn't have you to think about. You and Michael are what keeps me going.

I didn't tell you before because I didn't want to worry you, but Smitty was killed a few weeks ago. I guess I mentioned him in some of my letters. He was a great guy. I don't want you to worry about me, though. I've been really lucky. Nothing but a few cuts and scrapes.

There doesn't seem to be any real sense to anything that happens over here. Who lives and who dies seems to be a matter of luck sometimes. Or being in the wrong place at the wrong time. I'm doing my best to be in the right places at the right times.

I miss you and I love you. I'll send you all the dates for January just as soon as everything is cleared. Kiss Michael for me. I wish I was there to do it myself.

                                        Love, Donovan

"Do I look okay? Do you think this dress is too wild? Or too uptight? What about my hair? Maybe I should have cut it."

"Beth, you look just fine. Donovan is going to be dazzled. Besides, it's a little late to start worrying about that now. Your plane takes off in twenty minutes. Did you tell him you were going to meet him in San Francisco?"

"No, I wanted to surprise him." She stared at the open gate. Passengers were filing onto the plane, but she couldn't seem to move. "What if he doesn't recognize me, Daddy? What if he's changed and he doesn't love me anymore?"

"Don't be silly, muffin. That boy loves you enough to find you in the dark."

"What about Michael? Are you sure you can take care of him?" She fussed with the fringes on her suede purse, her eyes anxious.

"Stop stalling. I didn't buy you a ticket just to wait here at the airport while you missed the flight. I raised *you* okay. I think I can take care of my grandson for two days." He picked up her small case and handed it to her, edging her toward the gate. At the last minute, Beth turned and threw her arms around him, giving him a fierce hug.

"Thank you, Daddy."

"Just have a good time, muffin."

The flight to San Francisco was endless. Beth felt as if she could have walked to California in less time than it was taking the plane to get there. Her flight was supposed to get into San Francisco two hours before Donovan's arrived from Honolulu.

Despite the way time crawled, she was soon standing in the terminal, watching Donovan's plane taxi up to the building. She smoothed her hair again, hoping the upswept style made her look older and more mature. She wanted Donovan to see how she'd grown up in his absence. She'd coped without him, dealt with being a single parent, and she wanted him to be able to see it all.

Her heart started to pound with slow, heavy thumps as the first passengers exited. She watched anxiously, her thoughts scattered in a million different directions. There were several men in uniform, but she knew Donovan the minute he stepped off the plane even though his head was bent, and his cap shielded his face.

She opened her mouth to call his name, but nothing came out. Her voice was caught somewhere in her throat, and she could only stand and stare at him, her eyes filling with foolish tears. He seemed to feel her gaze, because he suddenly looked up and looked directly at her.

She wanted to run forward, but her feet were frozen. Time was frozen as they stared at each other. She'd never seen anything more wonderful in her life.

She wasn't sure which of them moved first. But all that mattered was that she was in his arms, feeling them tight and warm around her. He was holding her so close that she couldn't breathe, but that didn't matter, either.

"Oh God, Beth. Are you really here? I'm not dreaming you?"

"Donovan, Donovan." She couldn't seem to get out more than his name. His hand cupped the back of her head, destroying her carefully pinned hair as he tilted her face back until he could look at her. She knocked his cap off, oblivious to everything around them as his mouth found hers. It was only a kiss, but it held a solid year of loneliness—twelve months of being apart and a lifetime of worry.

She had no idea how long they stood in the middle of the terminal kissing. People bumped into them, but she didn't care. She didn't care about anything but the feel of Donovan's mouth on hers.

"Sir? I think you dropped this."

It took a bit for the voice to penetrate. Donovan lifted his head, his eyes locked on Beth's.

"Sir?" the voice prodded again.

Donovan dragged his gaze away, lowering Beth to her feet. His arms slid away as he took his cap from the stewardess dusting it off on his sleeve and setting it back on his head. He bent to pick up his case, throwing his other arm around his wife.

"We'd better hurry if we're going to catch our flight. You're flying with me?"

"I canceled your reservations. We've got reservations at a hotel, and we've got two days together before we go home. It was a Christmas present from Daddy. He's taking care of Michael. Please don't get mad. I didn't let him get me anything else. I didn't even let him buy me a birthday present, so this isn't like taking charity from him or anything."

"I don't care what it is. All I care about is that you're here. I guess even my pride has its limits. Do you have a bag?"

The ride to the hotel was short and full of news. Donovan wanted to hear everything Beth had done and everything Michael had learned in the past year. It seemed as if there was so much to tell him, and he was hungry for every little detail.

A light drizzle was falling when they got to the hotel. San Francisco was damp and gray, and a shadowy fog blanketed the bay. The tall, narrow buildings and famous hills might have been flat desert and wooden shacks for all Donovan and Beth cared.

It wasn't until the door to their room was shut and they were completely alone that Beth felt a wave of uncertainty. In the warm lamplight, Donovan looked different. He looked harder, older. She was suddenly out of things to say. She glanced at him and then looked away, moving to the window to stare out at the rain.

It had been a year. They'd both changed.

She felt him come up behind her, but she didn't turn. What if he didn't love her anymore? He laid his hands on her shoulders, and Beth felt a shiver run up her spine. It had been so long. She responded to the gentle pressure he applied and leaned back against him, letting the broad strength of his chest support her.

"I missed you so much, Beth."

"I missed you, too."

He slid his arms around her waist and rested his cheek on the top of her head, staring out the window with her.

"Nervous?" His breath whispered against her hair.

She nodded, vividly aware of his arms around her.

"So am I. All I could think about was getting back to you. It's what kept me going, kept me alive. Now that I've got you, I'm afraid you're going to disappear. I'm afraid I'll wake up and find out that you're not here at all."

Beth felt some of the tension slip away. He was as nervous as she was. His arms loosened as she turned. She laid her hands on his chest and looked up at him, her eyes searching his face. Yes, there were changes there, but his eyes were the same—green gold and warm with love.

"I love you, Donovan."

''Oh, Beth. I love you so much.'' The last word was a caress against her mouth. Beth closed her eyes, her hands sliding upward as he pulled her closer. The kiss was full of love, full of healing.

Gradually, the texture of the moment changed. Desire slowly edged in. Donovan's mouth firmed over hers, his tongue tracing the edge of her lips. With a sigh Beth opened her mouth to him and his tongue slid within, tracing the ridge of her teeth before moving on to softer territory. He relearned the velvety softness of her mouth, their tongues tangling, twining.

He broke the kiss slowly, easing away. Beth's eyelids felt weighted as she forced them to lift. His gaze was on hers, heating to gold, half asking, half demanding. She let her eyes drift shut again, her hands sliding upward into the thickness of his hair, giving him an answer without words.

He kissed her again, this time more a demand—less a question. A year of hunger lay dammed up in both of them. A year of nights alone, days of worry. Passion lay simmering near the surface. It took only a kiss to set it free.

Donovan's fingers fumbled with the zipper at the back of her dress, finding the tab and sliding it downward. Goose bumps came up on Beth's back as the zipper opened, but it wasn't because the room was cool. Her bones seemed to melt with every inch.

Donovan flattened his palm against the small of her back, pressing her closer, letting her feel the heat of his arousal. Beth moaned, a soft plea muffled by the pressure of his mouth, and suddenly desire was an urgent presence in the room.

She tugged at his uniform, anxious to feel his skin against hers. Donovan gave a choked laugh as he dragged his mouth from hers and stepped back. Beth would have protested, but she saw his hands on the buttons of his jacket, his fingers shaking with urgency, his eyes never leaving her face. She shrugged out of her dress, letting it drop to the floor.

The afternoon sunlight filtered through the sheer drapes, filling the room with soft, gray light. The last of Donovan's clothes hit the floor, and he was reaching for her. Beth went into his arms, knowing it was the only place in the world she wanted to be.

Her breath left her in a sob as he lifted her, cradling her to his chest as he crossed the few feet to the bed. He tossed the covers back impatiently and set her on the cool, linen sheets. Beth reached up to pull him down to her but he held back, catching her hands and pressing them against the pillow, holding her a gentle captive.

"Let me look at you. Do you know how many nights I dreamed that you were lying next to me? I can't quite believe you're here, really here."

She tugged her hands free, reaching up to cup his face in her palms. "I was always there. Always. There wasn't a moment when I wasn't thinking of you, praying for you. A part of me will always be with you."

"You are so beautiful."

Beth's smile was shaky. "Kiss me. Love me."

"Always, Beth. Always." The promise was whispered against her lips.

She moaned as he lowered his weight onto the bed. He lay half over her, half beside her, his chest gently crushing her breasts, one thigh resting across her hips. She was captured, a willing prisoner. Her hands slid over his shoulders, testing new muscles, feeling the feverish heat of him.

His mouth slid down her neck, his tongue tasting the frantic pulse that beat at the base of her throat. Her short nails dug into his shoulders as his mouth sought softer territory, his tongue swirling across one pink nipple before taking it inside and suckling deeply.

A year's separation had only made the fire burn hotter between them. Beth arched against the pressure of his leg across her thighs and Donovan shifted, allowing her to draw one knee up so that she cradled his hard thigh between her own. The pressure was tantalizing, but not enough. She could feel his arousal burning against her, the pressure urgent, but no less urgent than the pressure building inside her.

He switched his attentions to her other breast, painting it with quick strokes of his tongue, building the fire higher and higher until Beth was sure that she would be consumed in the blaze of need.

"Please, please." She wasn't even aware of the breathless repetition, but Donovan heard it. He lifted his head from her breast, capturing her mouth in a hard kiss, his body shifting.

Beth drew her knees up, cradling his body. She could feel him against her, hot and hard. She arched, her body quivering, but he drew back. She whimpered as he caught her head in his hands.

"Look at me, Beth. Open your eyes, baby." Her lashes lifted slowly, weighted down with passion. His eyes were pure gold, reflecting her hunger, burning with her need. "I've spent a year dreaming about this. Show me, Beth. Show me."

Their eyes never shifted as she reached between them, her slim fingers closing over him. His breath caught, his lashes flickering at the feel of her cool hand on his heated flesh. She drew him to her, leading him home, her fingers sliding away to rest against his hip.

He thrust forward slowly, ever so slowly, giving her body time to adjust. At last he was sheathed in the velvet warmth of her. He rested against her for a moment, their eyes still locked, each savoring the feel of his warmth within her. He shifted and her lashes dropped, her body arching hungrily.

"Beth." Her name was a mere breath as he lowered his weight, his chest gently crushing her breasts. Beth swallowed a moan as he began to move, a slow, undulating movement that quickened, gaining power, hurtling them both along the path to fulfillment. Pressure built, wonderful, delicious pressure, demanding release, promising pleasure.

"Donovan." His name broke from her on a whimper as the pressure exploded into satisfaction. Her nails dug into his shoulders, her body arching beneath his. Donovan groaned, feeling the delicate contractions tighten around him, holding him, caressing him. With a sound that was almost a sob, he released the tight control he'd held. Beth held him, her hands clutching his shoulders as the shock waves raced through them, tossing them both high and leaving them to float down to earth on a cloud of contentment.

It was a long time before Donovan moved. He shifted to one side, ignoring her whispered protest.

"I'll mash you."

"I wouldn't mind."

He chuckled, his breath stirring the fine hair at her temples as he pulled her close. "I would. I like you too much the way you are."

She snuggled up to his side, her fingers sifting through the light dusting of hair on his chest. "I missed you."

"All I thought about was you."

"I don't want you to go again. I don't think I can stand saying goodbye again."

"Shh." He lifted her until she lay along his body, feeling the strength of the muscles supporting her. He reached up to tuck her hair back, his eyes tender. "Don't think about it now, Beth. I'm home now. Don't think about anything else. I'll always come home to you."

"Promise?" Her voice broke on a sob, and she buried her face in his shoulder, ashamed of her tears. His hand stroked the back of her head.

"I promise. Hey, don't I always keep my promises?" She nodded against his shoulder.

"Sometimes I get so scared."

"I know, baby. But it's going to be all right. I'm not going to let anything happen to me. I've got too much to come home to. Now, stop crying and kiss me. Tell me you love me. I've got a year to make up for.''

She lifted her head and his hands cupped her face, his thumbs stroking away the tears, his smile coaxing her. She smiled. It was shaky around the edges, but it was still a smile.

"I love you, I love you, I love you, I—" His mouth stopped the rest of her words. He rolled, pinning her beneath him, making her forget all her fears. Making her forget everything but Donovan. For now, he was home. That would have to be enough.

Chapter 6

When Beth had time to think, she was amazed by how
quickly time passed in some respects and how slowly it
seemed to go in others. Now Donovan was home for good,
but when they'd been apart time had seemed to be deliberately holding back. Every endless day he was away was time
to wonder if he'd been wounded, if he was cold or wet or
hungry.

Then she'd look at Michael and time was running on
winged feet. He'd changed so quickly, moving from infant
to toddler to little boy. One minute he was learning to walk,
the next he was riding a trike.

And her own life seemed to be spinning by so quickly.
When Donovan was gone, Beth had grown up in a hurry.
After night school the next logical step was to get a job.

When a new shopping mall had opened on the outskirts
of Remembrance, she'd gathered up all her courage and
applied for a job in a department store. When they'd asked
if she had any special skills, she stretched the truth so thin
she was afraid they would be able to see the holes in it. She'd

told them she had some experience in decorating, which wasn't exactly a lie. She *had* done the decorating in the tiny apartment over the garage, and everyone agreed it was exceptionally nice.

She'd gotten a job in the furniture department. Her age was a mark against her, but she learned to style her hair so she'd look older and introduced herself as Elizabeth Sinclair, since that sounded more mature than Beth.

While the girls she'd gone to school with were going to college—some marching in protests, some looking for a man to take care of them—Beth was raising her son, working a job and praying for Donovan's return.

Now Donovan was home—older, harder, toughened by things she couldn't imagine, things he wouldn't discuss. She'd always thought that if he just came back safe and sound everything else would fall into place. She was still young enough to believe in happily ever after. What she discovered was that happily ever after didn't come without a lot of work.

The afternoon was still and quiet. Beth set down the small shirt she was attempting to mend and leaned her head against the sofa back. Summer had barely arrived, but summer's heat was here early. Rain had been threatening for two days, but so far all that had arrived were low clouds that held the heat next to the earth, promising relief but never delivering.

Outside, Donovan sat on the tiny landing, a book in his lap, a notebook set next to him. When she'd thought of having him home, she'd never gone beyond having his arms around her again, keeping her safe, loving her. She hadn't thought about things like having him go back to school and get a job.

She picked up the shirt. She shouldn't complain. At least he'd made it home, and he was only working so hard because he wanted a better life for her and Michael.

"Dammit, Michael! I told you no!" The words were punctuated by a terrifying crash as something bumped down the wooden stairs. Beth was halfway across the apartment when Michael began to scream, heartrending sobs of anguish that brought her mothering instincts to full alert. She nearly crashed into Donovan as he stalked into the living room, Michael's arm clutched firmly in his hand.

"Mommy!" Michael's face crumpled in anguish as only a four-year-old's could. Tears streamed down his flushed cheeks. He reached toward her, and Beth's arms opened automatically, only to drop to her side at Donovan's stern voice.

"No. Michael, go to your room. You're not hurt so you can stop the crying."

Beth's hands clenched. Every instinct was screaming for her to go to her son and comfort him. But it would not be a good idea to contradict Donovan's order. With his father's gentle push giving him a start, Michael dragged toward the tiny storage room that had been converted into his bedroom. Heartbreaking sobs trailed behind him, telling of permanent psychological damage being done.

Beth barely contained herself until the door shut behind him. "How could you be so cruel? Can't you see how upset he is?"

A muscle ticked in his jaw, but Donovan kept his voice level. "There's nothing wrong with him except that he got a good swat on the butt. He's more startled than hurt."

"You *hit* him?" She couldn't have sounded more appalled if he'd just confessed to beating the child. "I've never hit him. No wonder he's so upset."

"No wonder he's so damned spoiled," Donovan shot back.

"Spoiled? He's not spoiled. He's a normal four-year-old who's been treated with love and kindness, not brutality."

"Brutality? For crying out loud, I didn't tear him limb from limb. Most children survive an occasional swat without permanent damage."

"I've never found it necessary."

His eyes glittered with anger. "It hasn't even occurred to you to ask why I felt it necessary."

Beth glared at him. "He was probably trying to get some of your attention. God knows that's in short supply these days. The least you could do was have a little patience with him. He hardly knows you. You can't expect to come home and step right into being his father again."

The words spilled out without plan. She hadn't even been aware of thinking most of them until she heard herself. Donovan paled.

"I don't think that's fair, Beth. I spend as much time with him as I can. Part of being a father is disciplining when it's necessary. I'm not going to apologize for that."

"So, what horrible crime did he commit?"

"He wanted to ride his trike down the stairs and, when I refused to let him do that, he pushed it down the stairs. Next time, he might have been on it."

Beth looked away. "I'm sorry. I should have asked before I jumped all over you."

The silence stretched, and she thought he was going to ignore her apology. "I suppose it's difficult for you to get used to having someone else help you with Michael."

"It is. It was just the two of us for quite a while. I'm sorry."

"Don't worry. This weather has everybody on edge."

He ran his hand around the back of his neck, offering her a smile that said that everything was back to normal. Beth smiled back but she didn't feel very happy. Everything wasn't back to normal. She was beginning to wonder if this funny tension that lay beneath every moment they were together was going to become part of their lives.

* * *

"So, how's the happiest couple in Remembrance?" Carol's voice turned heads, and Beth found herself wishing there was something to hide behind besides Donovan's bulk.

"Fine." She hugged her friend as Carol edged through the crowd of graduates and families. "Congratulations. You look great."

"Sure. Black is my best color, and don't you love the cool tassle?" She grinned, her mild sarcasm a shield for her obvious excitement. "Well, Donovan, I'm glad to see you made it back in one piece. I told Beth you were too stubborn to get killed."

Donovan smiled, the first relaxed smile Beth had seen in weeks. She swallowed a twinge of jealousy when he hugged Carol. "Congratulations."

"Thanks. I can't wait to see you in one of these horrible robes."

Donovan looked at the stage that had recently held the graduates, and Beth had no trouble reading the hunger in his eyes. "It'll be a while, but I'll get there."

"So, what did you do with the curtain climber?"

"Michael is staying with my dad for the night. We thought we might make an evening of it. Dinner, maybe a movie."

"A cheap motel in the anonymous big city?" Carol waggled her eyebrows suggestively.

Beth laughed and then wondered if it sounded as strained to her companions as it did to her. They talked with Carol for a few minutes. But Beth didn't feel like laughing and smiling. She felt like standing in a corner somewhere and screaming over and over again. She wanted to scream and scream and beat her fists against something nice and solid—like Donovan. That thought slipped in unwanted, and she shoved it aside, not wanting to face it.

She had no reason to be angry at Donovan. She loved him. He hadn't done anything to deserve her anger. He'd come home just as he'd promised. He was working very hard between his job and school. She was proud of him.

"Beth? We're home." She looked up, startled. She hadn't realized how long she'd been silent, thinking. Her father had left the porch light on for them. In the thin illumination, Donovan's face was questioning. She looked away, not wanting to see the questions, knowing she didn't have the answers.

"I really enjoyed dinner. It was nice to get out of the house. I hope Daddy didn't have any trouble with Michael. Carol looked so nice. Her parents are really proud of her for getting her degree, though I don't know what she's going to do with a degree in botany. I don't think she does, either."

She was aware of Donovan following her up the stairs. For some reason she felt she should keep talking, as if a moment's silence might be fatal. Donovan reached around her to unlock the door. She flipped on the light as they walked in.

"Feels funny without Michael here, doesn't it? I hope Daddy didn't have any problems with him."

"You said that already." Donovan's voice was level, and Beth felt a spurt of rage, quick and uncontrollable.

"Excuse me for repeating myself." She shrugged out of her jacket and dropped it on the sofa.

"Beth, what's wrong?"

"Nothing's wrong." She snapped the answer out without looking at him.

"Something's bothering you. You've been uptight for weeks."

"I'm not uptight."

"I've been walking on eggs around you and so has Michael."

"Michael? What do you know about how he feels? Has he told you?" She turned to look at him, her eyes full of

anger. Donovan struggled with his irritation, his expression
carefully calm.

"I can see the way he watches you. I'm not criticizing
you. I just want to know what's wrong."

"You're not criticizing me? Well, isn't that nice of you.
You'd damn well better not criticize me! Who the hell do
you think you are? Telling me what my son thinks."

"He's my son, too." Anger threaded through his quiet
words, but Beth was too angry to care.

"Your son? *Your* son? I wonder if he knows that. You've
been gone most of his life. You're home a few weeks and
you're already beating him."

"Beating him! I swatted him once, more than a week ago.
I don't think that qualifies as a beating."

"If you don't like the way I raised him, maybe you should
have stayed home to help me."

"Do you think I wanted to leave you? Do you think I
chose to spend that time away from both of you?"

"Didn't you? You volunteered. You decided it was the
best thing for both of us."

"It was the only way out for us. Don't tell me you want
to live in this place for the rest of our lives."

"There were other ways. My father would have helped
us."

Donovan gestured sharply, his hands cutting through her
words. "Your father has already helped us enough. I
wouldn't have gone to him to ask for more."

"No, of course not. You'd rather go off and get shot at.
You went off to your stupid war and left me with all the
pieces. *I* had to take care of our son. *I* had to cope with
faucets that leaked and cars that wouldn't start. *I* had to
wonder every minute of every day if you were still alive or
if someone had put a bullet through your head."

Tears blurred her vision and her voice shook but she
didn't slow down. She was only just now realizing the rage
that had been building inside for years, dammed up by

conventions that taught her that a woman endured without resentment.

"*I* was the one who stayed up with Michael when he had the measles. *I* was the one who watched the news, wondering if I was going to see your body lying in a ditch somewhere. Every time someone knocked on the door, I had to wonder if it was going to be a telegram telling me you were dead."

"Beth, I—"

But she didn't give him time to say anything. "Do you know what I felt today, watching Carol get her diploma? I thought, that could have been me. I could have been up there. My father could have been sitting with the other parents, proud of me."

"Your father is proud of you." If she hadn't been so upset, Beth might have heard the unaccustomed tightness in Donovan's voice, the way his eyes glittered with emotion.

"Oh sure, he's really proud of me. For what? I haven't done anything to be proud of. You want to know what I was upset about today? I'll tell you. I gave up everything to marry you. Everything. I had to grow up in a matter of months. And then you went off to play soldier and left me with the pieces. I—"

The crash of Donovan's fist going through the wall stopped her words in midsentence. Beth gasped, her eyes widening as he spun to face her. For just an instant, she wondered if he was going to hit her, but he didn't move from where he stood. She was too shocked for tears, too frightened for words. This wasn't the Donovan she knew. This was someone else, a man capable of violence.

His eyes glittered with a rage that dwarfed hers, his hands were clenched into fists. Blood oozed from the hand he'd put through the wall, but he didn't seem to notice. Beth couldn't drag her gaze from his face.

"*You* gave up everything? What about what I gave up? You watched the news and wondered if I was alive or dead?

Well, I woke up every day and wondered if I'd be alive long enough to go to sleep again. I watched my buddies get killed and wondered why it wasn't me, why I was the one surviving. I learned to carry a machine gun and I learned to kill people. I learned to kill because it was them or me and I had to stay alive. I had to stay alive because I had you and Michael to come home to, because you needed me.

"Ha! You needed me. I get home to find that you've done just fine without me, thank you, and you don't much want interference. I feel like a visitor here, I feel like a visitor in my son's life. And I feel like a visitor in our bed.

"Why don't we compare notes and see just who the hell gave up the most? And you know what the most ridiculous thing is?" He crossed the distance between them so quickly that Beth didn't have time to move. Not that she was sure she could have moved. Her feet seemed rooted to the floor.

"Do you know what the stupidest part of this whole damn mess is?"

She shook her head, mesmerized by the glitter of his eyes.

"The stupid part is—I still love you." There was so much pain and anger in the words that it took a minute for Beth to realize what he'd said.

They stared at each other, tension humming between them. Years of pain and anger both separated and drew them together. She wasn't sure just when Donovan had taken hold of her shoulders, anymore than she knew just how her hands had come to rest on his chest.

"I love you, too." His mouth caught the sob that ended the vow. Beth's hands slid up, her arms circling his neck, her fingers sliding into the thick, dark hair at his nape.

"Beth, Beth." His mouth slid down her throat, her name a prayer.

The tension that had lain between them since he returned home now lay exposed, its power shifted from anger to passion in the blink of an eye. In the aftermath of harsh words and harsher feelings, each needed reassurance that they still loved each other.

Donovan's hands were rough on her dress. She heard the fabric tear, but she didn't protest. Nothing mattered except that his hands were on her bare skin. She struggled with the buttons on his shirt, popping two of them off, but then her palms were flattened against hard muscle and crisp hair and nothing else was important.

Donovan's laugh held an undercurrent of pain as she fought with his belt. He stripped the ruined dress from her, and seconds later she was naked but for a pair of panties. His belt gave way before her determined assault, and he kicked his jeans aside before crushing her against his body.

Beth gasped, feeling the feverish heat of him warming every inch of her body. Her nails bit into his shoulders as he lifted her, holding her easily, her toes off the ground as his mouth found her breast, suckling and licking until she thought she'd surely go mad with need.

He set her down, his mouth devouring hers. Never before had passion been so quick to fire, nor had the fire ever burned quite this hot, consuming all the pain and anger, leaving nothing but need behind.

He lifted her again, his mouth locked on hers as he cradled her against his chest and carried her into the bedroom. It was dim and cool, illuminated only by the light that spilled in from the living room. But they didn't need light. Donovan's image was burned into her soul, a part of her, never to be forgotten, never to be left behind.

He set her on the bed, stripping the last of their clothing, leaving nothing between them. Beth lay back, opening herself to him, body and soul, heart and mind. With a groan Donovan lay over her, his weight braced on his arms.

"I don't think I can wait, Beth. I want you so much."

"Now. Please now." Beth's whisper echoed in the small room. Her body arched, her nails biting into his shoulders as he thrust home, his heat finding the deep core of her, making them one.

Their passion burned too hot, too fiery for it to last long. Each rocking movement, each whispered word seemed to meld them closer together until Beth and Donovan ceased to exist as individuals and became one being, their love the glue that bound them to each other.

The climax, when it came, was stunning, as explosive as the passion that built up to it. Beth's whimper was drowned in Donovan's guttural moan. He collapsed against her. She took his weight willingly, her arms circling his back, holding him even closer, feeling complete for the first time since he'd come home.

The silence lasted a long time. After a while, Donovan lifted himself from her with a mutter of apology. He rolled to the side, pulling her with him. Beth tucked her head on his shoulder, curling into his warmth, needing the feel of him against her.

"I love you, Beth."

"I love you, too. I'm sorry I threw a fit."

"I'm not." His breath stirred her hair and his arm tightened around her. "I think we've been building up to this for a long time. I'm sorry I yelled at you."

"It's okay." She rubbed her fingers through the hair on his chest. "Did I really make you feel like I didn't need you?"

"A little. I guess maybe a part of me wanted to believe that you couldn't live without me. When I got back, you'd done so well without me, it kind of hurt. You had a job, you'd gotten your diploma. You took care of Michael."

"But I did it because I knew I had to hold things together for you. I wanted you to be proud of me."

"I am proud of you. I was always proud of you. I know you gave up a lot because we had to get married."

She put her fingers over his mouth, stopping the difficult words, tilting her head back to look into his eyes.

"We both gave up quite a bit, but I think maybe we got even more in the bargain. I love you, Donovan. Being with you is the most important thing in the world to me."

"I don't know what I'd do without you, Beth. You're everything to me. You always will be."

"We'll always be together. No matter what, we'll always have each other."

"Always." Donovan's kiss sealed the promise.

Chapter 7

The present

Michael Sinclair tightened his grip on his backpack and pushed open the front door. Stepping into the wide entry, he dropped the pack and stretched.

"Mom, I'm home." Dead silence greeted his call. He shrugged. She was probably at some committee meeting or something. He straightened and then almost dropped the pack. His father was standing in the door to the study, his face tight, his body rigid.

"Dad! What are you doing home? Where's Mom? Is something wrong?"

"Not unless you count sheer insanity as something wrong." The words were snapped off, each one distinct.

"What?"

"Your mother is upstairs packing."

"Packing? Where's she going?"

"She's going to 'find herself.'" Donovan turned and stalked into the study, leaving his son staring after him.

"Find herself? What do you mean?"

Donovan picked up a glass of Scotch, his fingers grasping the heavy crystal. Michael's eyes widened. He'd *never* seen his father drink in the middle of the day. It wasn't something that he talked about, but Michael was aware that Donovan's father drank himself to death. He'd always assumed that was why Donovan didn't drink. To see him with a drink in his hand and the sun shining outside was enough to punch home just how serious the situation must be.

"What's wrong with Mom?"

Donovan took a swallow of the Scotch, grimacing in distaste before he set the glass down. "Damn stuff tastes like battery acid," he muttered. His gaze slid to his son and then away. He stared at the pine-paneled wall opposite, his college degree neatly framed in the middle of it. When he spoke, it was clear that he was trying to be calm for Michael's sake.

"Your mother is moving out."

"Moving out? You mean *moving out*?" Michael couldn't quite grasp the concept. "What for?"

"To find herself. She needs an identity apart from me. I'm not offering her enough support."

"I didn't say anything of the kind, Donovan." Michael turned with relief. His mother could explain this mess.

"Mom. I don't understand what's going on."

"That makes two of us," Donovan muttered.

Elizabeth ignored her husband's comment and moved into the room, hugging her son. "How was Colorado?"

"The trip was fine. I want to know what's been going on here while I've been gone. Jeez, I leave the two of you alone for a week and you get all messed up." The attempt at humor fell flat, and Michael swallowed hard. Whatever was going on here was major.

Elizabeth linked her hands together, her gaze skittering over Donovan's looming figure to focus on her son.

"I'm moving out. I'm putting the last of my stuff into the station wagon right now. It has nothing to do with you. I don't want you to think for even a minute that it does."

"Why? What happened?" Michael suddenly felt very young and confused.

"Ha! If you can get her to explain that one, you're doing better than I did."

Elizabeth glanced at her husband and then looked back at Michael. "It's nothing specific, Michael. It's just that your father and I don't have much in common anymore."

"Just eighteen years of marriage."

"And we don't talk much."

"Only every morning and every evening."

"It's just time to end it now, while we still care about each other."

"A great way to show how much you care." Donovan didn't look at her. His eyes were focused on the Scotch glass, watching the patterns of light in the amber liquid.

Michael thrust his fingers through his hair, feeling his world crack and then resettle. He searched for some surprise and didn't find it. On some level, he'd been aware that this was coming for a long time. It wasn't something he'd ever dwelled on, but now that it was here, he didn't feel as shocked as he should have.

"So, how come you're the one moving out?"

"Because it's what I want." She twisted her fingers together, her eyes pleading with him to understand. "I've been a wife and mother for so long that I'm not sure who else I am. I want to find out if I am something more."

"Of course you're more than a wife and mother. Don't be an idiot."

Elizabeth looked at Donovan, her eyes full of pain. "What else am I, Donovan? You tell me."

He frowned. "You're Elizabeth. Beth. Yourself. What more do you need to be?"

"Don't you understand? I've got to find out who that is. I don't know anymore."

They stared at each other across an abyss of pain, Elizabeth's eyes pleading with him to understand. Donovan looked at her for a moment and then snorted in contempt.

"Sounds like a lot of pop psychology. You are who you are and tearing your life apart doesn't change that."

He slammed the glass down on the desk, splashing the liquid up over the side. He stalked from the room without another word, but not before Michael saw the loss in his eyes.

There was silence until the front door slammed and they could both hear the sound of an engine starting up. Donovan's car roared down the street and Elizabeth sighed, looking up at her son.

"I'm sorry, Michael. I know it's not a very good homecoming this time."

"It's okay, Mom. I think I understand what's going on."

"God, I wish I did." She moved to the desk, picking up the abused glass and using her shirttail to mop up the alcohol before it could damage the finish. "I'm not asking you to choose between your father and me, but it would mean a lot if you could accept what I'm doing and wish me luck." She set the glass on a coaster and turned to look at him.

Michael stared at her, for the first time seeing the vulnerability she'd been working so hard to conceal. "I do, Mom. Really I do. I just wish it didn't have to be so hard on Dad."

"I wish it didn't, either. I didn't think it would be." She stared at the door Donovan had stalked through. "I didn't want to hurt him."

"I know, Mom."

She forced a smile and moved away from the desk, giving her son a tight hug. "I love you, Michael Patrick Sinclair. And your father loves you. Don't you forget it."

Michael's arms circled her awkwardly. "I love you, too, Mom. I . . . hope you find what you need. And I know Dad wants to see you happy, too."

Elizabeth blinked back tears, the first she'd shed in the three days since she'd asked Donovan for a divorce. She had to have done something right to have a son like Michael.

Donovan scraped the remains of his supper into the garbage disposal. Michael joined him, and two charred pork chops joined overcooked peas and undercooked potatoes.

"We could send out for a pizza." Donovan glanced over his shoulder, his mouth twisting in a smile.

"Go ahead. At this rate, we're both going to either starve to death or die of cholesterol overdose from all the pizza we've been eating."

"I'd rather risk the cholesterol. I'm starved." Donovan rinsed the dishes and set them in the dishwasher, vaguely aware of Michael's voice in the background ordering an extra-large pizza with the works. He shut the dishwasher and stared at the panel of buttons. Sooner or later he was going to have to dig up the instructions on the damn thing and figure out how to run it. Eventually, either they were going to run out of dishes or the dishwasher was going to burst.

Funny, it wasn't until somebody left that you realized all the little things they'd done in your life. The kitchen was immaculate, if you didn't count the rapidly filling dishwasher. Some people might have expected him to let the place fall to pieces now that he and Michael were living alone, but he wasn't going to fall into that stupid trap.

"Danny's says they'll have the pizza here in thirty minutes, tops."

"That means it will be at least forty-five. I don't think they've delivered a pizza on time in the last twenty years."

"You and Mom used to go there, didn't you?"

Donovan could feel his muscles tighten at the memories the simple question evoked. "That was a long time ago." He opened the refrigerator door and made a production out of looking inside. "You want a soda or something?"

"Sure." Michael took the can his father handed him and popped the tab. Aside from the hushed fizz of the soda, the kitchen was silent. Donovan sprawled in one of the kitchen chairs, his long legs out in front of him.

Outside, the autumn night was chill with the promise of winter's cold. Remembrance was already settling down and bracing for snow. Donovan stared out the window at the darkness. Funny. They'd lived in this house for almost twelve years. He could remember how excited Beth had been to move in.

Michael had been just six, and he'd been beside himself with the idea of a room of his own. He'd boasted about how he was going to sleep all by himself and that no one was to come into his room without knocking first. They'd promised to respect his privacy, which was a big thing to Michael at age six.

Half an hour after the lights were out and Donovan and Elizabeth were snuggled in their new bed, Michael had come scooting into their room, his eyes wide in the dim light. He'd skidded to a halt at the side of the bed, panting from the sprint between the rooms. Elizabeth had asked him what was wrong, and he'd gathered all his six years of dignity about him and announced that he thought they might like some company.

Donovan's mouth softened, his eyes distant as he remembered lifting that sturdy little body into bed and tucking him under the covers. His eyes had met Elizabeth's and... He frowned, cutting the memory off and reaching for his cola. That was all a very long time ago.

Michael looked at his father. It wasn't hard to see the pain he was going through. It was almost a week since his mother moved out, but not once had Donovan mentioned Elizabeth's name. He seemed to be trying to pretend that noth-

ing had happened, as if she were on a vacation or
something.

"I saw Mom today."

Donovan's eyes jerked toward his son and then away.
"Oh?" The question was flat, as if he weren't really interested.

"She moved the last of her stuff into her new apartment.
It's pretty nice. It's in that new development over on Bush."

"Cracker boxes. The guy who designed those places
ought to apologize for calling himself an architect."

"Well, it's certainly not a Sinclair design, but the apart-
ments are pretty nice inside."

Donovan grunted and took another swallow. Michael
decided that it was encouraging that he hadn't tried to
change the subject.

"She's got a nice, little one-bedroom place on the second
floor. Aunt Carol was over all afternoon. She's going to fill
the place up with plants."

"At the rate Carol gives plants away, it's a wonder that
nursery of hers didn't go belly-up a long time ago."

"I thought you gave her a lot of the work on your projects."

"I didn't say she wasn't good with plants. She's just not
much of a businesswoman."

"She seems happy enough."

"Meaning I don't? I suppose you agree with your mother
and think I haven't spent enough time at home."

Michael said nothing, disconcerted by this sudden flare of
temper. The silence was full, pulsing with tension. Donovan stared at the table for a minute and then looked at his
son, his mouth twisting in a half smile of apology.

"I'm sorry, Michael. I shouldn't have snapped. It's not
your fault."

"That's okay." Michael shrugged awkwardly and took a
swallow of cola. "It's not Mom's fault, either, you know."

"Well, it's sure as hell not mine. I'm not the one who came home one day and announced that I had to go 'find myself.' Hell, I didn't even know you could lose yourself. I don't understand her at all."

"Maybe that's part of the problem." Michael didn't look at his father as he spoke. His finger traced the distinctive pattern on the soda can.

Donovan stared at the table, his expression brooding. "If she was unhappy, why didn't she come to me? I would have done something. Anything."

Michael looked at him and then looked away. "You know, Dad, you aren't really home all that much. And a lot of times you bring blueprints or schedules or whatever with you. Maybe she felt you didn't have time for her."

"I've always had time for her." Donovan winced at the defensiveness he heard in his own voice. "Maybe I have been pretty busy lately, but a business doesn't run itself. Somebody's got to take care of it."

"I guess maybe you could say the same thing about a marriage." Michael's words were punctuated by the mellow chimes of the doorbell. "Great! Food at last." He loped out of the kitchen, leaving his father to stare after him, his eyes stunned.

"You realize, of course, that I think you're completely bananas. Only a mental case would give up a man like Donovan Sinclair." Carol raised her voice to be heard over the roar of the vacuum. "And I don't know why you're vacuuming when you don't have everything unpacked. You're just going to have to do it again."

Elizabeth shut off the vacuum, trying not to wince at the sudden silence. She'd hoped that the noise would keep Carol from harassing her, but she might have known her ploy wouldn't work. A little thing like a vacuum cleaner wouldn't have made Carol hesitate to state her opinion when they were young, and nothing had changed with age. Elizabeth looped the cord around the handle, aware of her friend watching her, her blue eyes bright with curiosity.

"Well?"

"Well what?" Playing dumb wasn't going to do much good, but it was a stalling tactic.

"Why did you do it?"

"Vaccum before the packing was through? I don't know. It seemed like the thing to do."

"Don't be an idiot. You and I both know that I'm not going to leave you alone until you tell me what on earth drove you to leave a gorgeous man like Donovan."

Elizabeth shrugged. "I don't know." The answer sounded weak to her own ears, and she knew it would never be enough to satisfy Carol. She was right.

"You don't know? You just up and dump him and you don't know why? Beth, my dear, you've gone over the edge. It's mid-thirties delirium."

"Beth. That's part of it."

Carol cocked her head to one side. "You are sick. My name is Carol, remember? How many fingers am I holding up?"

"No, that's not what I meant. He calls me Elizabeth."

"*Everyone* calls you Elizabeth."

"You don't."

"That's because you can't teach an old dog new tricks. In my case, you couldn't teach me tricks even before I was an old dog." Carol reached for a doughnut, part of her house-warming present to Elizabeth. She took a bite, leaving a line of chocolate frosting on her upper lip. "Let me get this straight. You left Donovan because he called you Elizabeth, just like everybody else does. I thought you *wanted* to be called Elizabeth. You've been Elizabeth to most of the town for years. Seems to me like it would have been easier to ask him to call you something else."

Elizabeth reached for a doughnut. She didn't want one. She didn't even particularly like them. But she needed something to do with her hands.

"I didn't leave him because of that. It's just part of everything else that was wrong. He hasn't called me Beth in years. Beth was someone young and pretty that he was in love with. Elizabeth was an adult, mature and responsible and not very interesting. I know I'm the one who wanted to be Elizabeth because I wanted to seem older than I was, but couldn't I have still been Beth sometimes, too?"

Carol stared at her. "I don't know. I get the feeling I'm talking to several different people here. You wanted to be Elizabeth but you wanted to be Beth, too, only Elizabeth and Beth are the same person but different."

Elizabeth took a bite of her doughnut, scattering powdered sugar over the front of her sweatshirt. "I suppose it does sound kind of ridiculous."

"No. I think it casts serious doubts on my sanity, but I understand what you're saying."

"He didn't even seem to miss Beth. It was like she never existed. Somehow I got all caught up in being Elizabeth, wife of a successful architect, mother of a terrific son, member of every charitable committee in Indiana. Only where was Beth in all that? I had dreams, too, you know."

"I know you did." Carol licked the chocolate from her fingers. "You've got to take some responsibility for that yourself, you know. I don't think Donovan expected you to give up your dreams for his or for Michael's."

"Maybe he didn't expect it. But he let me do it."

"What did you expect him to do? Sit you down and insist that you take time out for what you wanted to do? Maybe he thought you were already doing what you wanted to do."

"I think it's been years since he's even wondered what I wanted to do. He just accepted that I was there."

"He does have some workaholic tendencies."

"I know you think Donovan is perfect, but he's got his flaws, too." She sounded like a four-year-old and she knew it. The problem was that she felt like a four-year-old at the moment.

"I've never thought he was perfect." Carol reached for another doughnut and bit into it thoughtfully. "I just think he's about the best thing I've seen in men. And I think what you two have together is pretty special, and it's not going to be easy to replace."

"What we *had*. *Had* is the operative word. Somewhere along the line we lost it. He got all caught up in being the world's greatest architect and I got all caught up in playing suburban wife and we drifted apart. You know, we'd always planned to have more kids. But we always put it off until 'things' were more settled. We haven't even talked about it in years. We haven't talked about *anything* in years."

"Maybe that's all the two of you need. Just a chance to talk."

Elizabeth shook her head. "No. It's too late for that. After a while, love dies if it isn't fed."

"Has your father called since you moved out?"

Two years ago Patrick had remarried, and he and his new wife had decided to travel around the country. He called once a week from whatever state they happened to be in.

Elizabeth's voice softened. "Donovan gave him my new number when he called the house. Dad was pretty confused, but he said that I had to do what I thought was best. All he wants is for me to be happy. He also said I shouldn't throw away anything I might want back. Only there's not much to throw away anymore."

Carol swallowed the last of her doughnut, her eyes thoughtful. "I just can't believe that a love like the two of you had can die that easily."

"It wasn't easy. It was a long, slow process, but it's dead."

"Maybe."

Carol's stubborn determination to believe what she wanted drew a short laugh from Elizabeth. "You're a closet romantic, that's all. Life doesn't offer a lot of happily ever afters, Carol. Donovan and I had some good years together, and we've got a wonderful son. That's more than a lot of people ever have."

"I think you're fooling yourself, but it's certainly none of my business." Her features took on a saintly cast, and Elizabeth laughed again.

"The day when you can keep your nose out of someone else's business will be the day they bury you."

"I'm the soul of discretion."

"I didn't say you weren't discreet. I said you were nosy." Elizabeth looked at the clock that was stuck haphazardly on top of a crate. "You'd better get going. It's late and you've got a business to run. And tomorrow, I start job hunting."

Carol stood up, reaching for a third doughnut. "I'll need something to keep me awake on the drive home."

"Most people consider driving reason enough to keep their eyes open."

"In Remembrance? You've got to be kidding. The streets are as dull as the rest of the place. Food is the only thing that keeps me breathing."

"If I ate like you do, I'd look like a blimp."

"Yes, but you'd be a much prettier blimp than I would be." Carol hesitated in the doorway, her blue eyes unusually serious. "Are you going to be all right? You know, you'd be welcome to stay at my place as long as you wanted. It's kind of nice to have someone to talk to besides the plants."

Elizabeth hugged her friend, her eyes stinging. "I'll be fine. I've got a brand-new apartment to play in, and tomorrow I'm going to find a terrific job."

Carol looked doubtful, but she didn't argue any further. If Beth wanted to pretend that she was happy as a clam, Carol wouldn't be the one to burst her bubble.

Elizabeth shut the door behind Carol and let her smile fade. She stared around her new apartment, still full of boxes, the furniture stuck wherever was convenient. It didn't look like a home yet, but it would soon.

She clasped her hands over her upper arms and rubbed. The chill she felt had little to do with the temperature. She was alone, really alone, for the first time in her life. Nobody was going to come in the door unless she invited them.

She hadn't realized how much it was going to hurt to break the ties with Donovan. She'd moved out a week ago, and she hadn't seen him in all that time. Surprising how much you could miss somebody. She told herself that it wasn't love causing this ache in her gut, but Donovan had been a part of her life for a long time. His absence left a big gap.

But she was going to fill that gap with new experiences and growth. She had this big, roomy place all to herself. She could do anything at all she wanted with it. She didn't have to consult anybody's taste but her own.

She had a sudden image of the cramped, little rooms over her father's garage where she and Donovan had started their married life. They'd worked so hard to make them seem like home. It had been the beginning for them.

She blinked, clearing the image away. This was a beginning for her. And she was just as happy as she had been then. She could do anything she wanted, anything at all. And that was exciting and wonderful.

Which explained why she was sitting on a packing crate full of dishes in the middle of her wonderful, new apartment crying her eyes out.

Chapter 8

SIX MONTHS LATER

What did you buy for a young man about to turn nineteen? Elizabeth stared at a display of action figures without seeing them. She'd wandered into the toy store more out of nostalgia than anything else. It had been a few years since she'd been able to shop for Michael in one. He'd outgrown such presents a long time ago.

Sometimes it seemed like just yesterday when he'd been clamoring for the latest toys touted by his cartoon friends. And sometimes it seemed as if centuries had gone by.

Moving down the aisle, she paused in front of a shelf full of Legos. The bright, primary colors brought a surge of memories. The hours she'd spent putting those things together. She must have built enough houses to create a small town. And anything she hadn't built, Donovan had. He'd been good at the more-exotic things like cars and rocket ships. During the months after he got back from 'Nam, Legos had been one of his strongest links to Michael.

He had made up for his absence. He'd been a good father. Loving, but not afraid to be firm.

"Daddy, look!" The shrill voice shook her out of her memories and Elizabeth moved aside just in time to avoid being run over by a little girl in pink overalls. The child skidded to a halt in front of a display of bright puzzles.

"Please, Daddy. Please could we get a puzzle?" The words held a wealth of longing.

"You've got lots of puzzles, Bethany." Bethany's father stopped next to his daughter and stared at the boxes. "I don't know which ones you've got."

"*I* know."

Elizabeth bit her lip to control a smile. The scorn in the little girl's voice would have done justice to a duchess ten times her age.

Her father glanced at Elizabeth, sharing her amusement. He looked as though he was about thirty-two or thirty-three, not that much younger than Elizabeth. Somehow, watching him, she felt centuries older. Michael had been a teenager by the time she was this man's age.

She moved away, leaving father and daughter to hash out the question of how many puzzles they should buy. He was standing firm on two, but Bethany was bargaining for a jillion. Elizabeth wouldn't have laid bets on who would win.

She wandered down the aisle and turned a corner. Dolls. She stopped next to a display of baby dolls, her face softening. The toys she'd played with as a little girl had mostly disappeared, relegated to the ranks of collectibles. But baby dolls never changed. She reached out to touch the smooth, vinyl skin on a plump infant that promised to do nothing but be soft in a little girl's arms.

Elizabeth didn't have to close her eyes to picture a little girl cuddling the doll. She had Donovan's hair, inky black and as soft as silk, and maybe his eyes, too. Her father would teach her to ride a bicycle, but he'd also be willing to play dolls with her or baseball. She'd definitely be Daddy's girl, but she would be close to her mother, too.

She blinked and the picture vanished. She pulled her hand away from the doll. It was foolish to hope for something that would never happen.

After six months she still envisioned Donovan as a father. She shrugged uneasily. There was nothing significant in that. They'd been married a long time. There had never been another man in her life. The little fantasy had nothing to do with the hollow feeling she sometimes had when she thought about Donovan.

She turned away from the dolls, shoving her hands into her jeans' pockets. It was only natural that she was feeling a bit nostalgic. Shopping for Michael's gifts was something she and Donovan had always done together. Even in the past few years, when they did so little as a couple, that was one tradition that had survived. This was the first time since Donovan returned from the war that she'd had to shop for Michael's gift alone.

Nostalgia was all this empty feeling was. It had nothing to do with regrets, because she didn't regret leaving Donovan. She'd done the right thing. It was just that, sometimes, she felt a little hollow. She was free to do as she pleased, but there was no one to care that she did.

Donovan ducked out of sight behind a display of stuffed dinosaurs, feeling like a fool. He had to be nuts, hiding from his own wife behind a purple stegosaurus, but he wasn't ready for her to see him yet. He wasn't sure he'd ever be ready.

It felt like centuries since he'd seen her. He'd almost managed to forget the softness of her skin and the way her hair caught the light. In slim-fitting jeans and a bright blue sweatshirt, she looked young and vibrant and stunningly beautiful.

He'd been watching her ever since she entered the store, dogging her down the aisles, ducking out of sight to avoid being seen. He'd gotten some funny looks from a couple of kids but, so far, no one had called the cops. More likely, they'd call the men in white coats. He was acting like a demented teenager, not like a mature man of thirty-eight.

He edged farther behind the stegosaurus as Elizabeth wandered toward the front of the store. When had he stopped noticing how beautiful she was? How long had it been since he'd really looked at her?

She stopped next to a rack of children's books. The harsh, fluorescent lighting gilded her hair. She looked so young—not that much different than when they'd first met. God, that seemed like so long ago. She glanced up and Donovan squatted down, turning his face away as if vitally interested in the toys displayed on the lower shelf.

"Are you playing hide-and-seek?" The voice was solemn and unusually deep considering its owner was under three feet tall.

Donovan's startled eyes met those of the little boy who must have been standing right behind him. Serious brown eyes studied him. Donovan felt a flush slowly creep up from his neck. He cleared his throat, searching for the authority that was supposed to go with being an adult. Only he didn't feel much like an adult at the moment.

"I . . . ah . . . I'm trying to find a present for someone."

"For who?" The child looked prepared to wait as long as it took to get his answer.

Donovan glanced over his shoulder. Elizabeth was still scanning the books. He turned back to his inquisitor. "For my son."

Brown eyes studied him, considering that answer. "How old is he?"

"He's going to be nineteen."

"I like these."

"I . . . ah . . . Michael probably does, too."

"I don't have the leader yet, but Mom says I might get it for my birthday."

"I don't think Michael has it, either. Maybe I'll get him that."

"They're at the front."

Donovan glanced over his shoulder to see Elizabeth leaving the store. "At the front. Thanks."

"You're welcome."

Donovan was just in time to see Elizabeth wander down the mall. He waited a few seconds and then followed her, feeling like a second-rate James Bond. Did spies feel this stupid following someone?

She stopped to look in the window of a clothing store and he turned, staring intently at a display of copper cookware. This was ridiculous. He'd been married to the woman for eighteen years. They were *still* married if it came right down to it. He had no reason to be lurking behind her—no reason except the knot in his gut that threatened to climb into his throat and choke him.

Elizabeth felt him behind her an instant before his hand touched her shoulder. She forced herself to turn slowly, keeping her expression utterly calm.

"Hello, Elizabeth."

"Hello, Donovan." She'd almost managed to forget his height and the width of his shoulders. He was wearing a blue plaid, flannel shirt tucked into a pair of brown corduroys. He looked fit and trim and amazingly handsome. His hair was still inky black, with just a touch of gray at the temples. His eyes were still that wonderful green-gold shade, impossible to read, impossible to ignore.

"How have you been?" It was a simple question. Why was it that she couldn't find a simple answer? Did she tell him how hard it had been to make the break; how she'd cried herself to sleep more than once? Or did she tell him about her job and how much she loved it? Did she mention the sense of pride she felt when she came home to an apartment that she paid for herself?

"I'm fine. You?"

"Fine. You look...well." What had he been going to say? Had he been going to tell her that she looked pretty? Did he still think she was pretty? She tugged at the bottom of her sweatshirt, unaware of the way it molded the fabric to her breasts.

"So do you."

Silence stretched between them. Each of them avoided looking at the other, but neither of them could think about anything else. Around them the mall bustled with people. They could have been all alone for all the awareness they had of anyone else.

"I—"

"Well—"

Each started to speak and then stopped abruptly. Their eyes met.

"You go ahead," he offered.

"I was just going to ask if you were shopping for Michael's birthday present."

"What else would drag me to a mall?"

Elizabeth smiled, a quick expression gone immediately. "You designed this place. I don't see how you can hate it so much."

"Too many people in too small an area."

"I suppose. I was shopping for Michael, too."

"I know. I've been following you."

Her eyes jerked back to his face in time to see him flush. "You've been following me?"

He shrugged. "Sounds dumb, I know. But I saw you in the toy store and I couldn't quite get up the nerve to say anything, so I sort of followed you."

"You were watching me?"

"Well, not exactly watching. Just sort of...following..." He trailed off and shrugged again. "I said it was dumb. You should have seen the funny looks some of the kids in there gave me. One little guy even gave me advice on what to get Michael.''

Elizabeth's mouth twitched, picturing Donovan lurking around the toy store. She supposed she should be angry. At another time, maybe she would have been. But, somehow, at this moment, she just couldn't find the anger.

"Why didn't you just come up and say hello?"

"Well, it's been quite a while. And we didn't exactly part on the best of terms."

"I suppose." Her smile faded, reminded of just how they'd parted. She stared past him at the people who hurried back and forth in the mall. The silence stretched.

Donovan cleared his throat. "You know, since we're both here and we're both shopping for Michael, maybe we should talk about what we're going to get him. That way we could avoid duplicating anything. We could have a cup of coffee."

There wasn't any real need to discuss what they were going to buy for Michael. She'd say no, of course. This encounter had been awkward enough already, and who knew how much worse it might get if they spent more time together. Donovan was part of her past, and she was quite content to keep him that way. There wasn't any reason to renew any old ties.

"It *would* be awkward if we both ended up getting him the same thing."

Five minutes later they were seated across a table from each other. Coffee steamed in front of them. The bustle of the mall was muted in the restaurant. It was too late for the lunch crowd and too early for the dinner crowd.

Elizabeth stared at her coffee and listened to the silence stretch. She'd been an idiot to agree to this. Donovan was undoubtedly regretting the impulse that had made him suggest it. The whole point of her leaving him was that they hadn't any more to say to each other. So why was she sitting here, pretending there was something to talk about now?

"Michael tells me you've got a nice place."

Elizabeth shrugged. "It's small but it's comfortable. I don't really want a lot of room."

"I know what you mean. With Michael in school most of the time, I rattle around in that house. I've been half thinking of selling it."

"You *can't*." Donovan's head jerked up at her vehement denial, and she tried to soften the words. "I mean, isn't the real estate market soft or hard or something? It probably wouldn't be a good time to sell." She stared at the table.

"I wouldn't do anything drastic without talking to you. It's your house, too."

It had been their dream house—one of the first projects Donovan designed. Once they'd had the money to buy the lot, they'd still had to put a lot of their own labor into the place in order to afford to build the house itself. A lot of sweat and a few tears were built into that house. Funny how she didn't want to live there, but it still hurt to think of it being sold.

"I wish you'd let me give you at least some of the value of it. I feel guilty about living in the place."

"That's okay. I don't need the money right now. If you...if you sell it, then we can talk about it."

Silence hung over the table again, a third party to the conversation. Again, it was Donovan who broke it.

"So, Michael tells me that you really like your job."

"I do. I'm working at Mason's. They needed an interior decorator, and they didn't insist that I have a certificate or a degree. It's a great place to work."

Donovan looked away. It hurt to hear her sound so happy. It hurt to realize how long it had been since he'd seen her face light up. How long had she been unhappy, and why hadn't he seen it?

"You always did have a flair for decorating. It's great that you found something you liked."

"I was pleased." If the conversation got any more stilted, it was going to require medical attention just to revive it. She took a swallow of coffee and searched for something to say. Funny how they were both being so careful not to talk about what was really on their minds. They'd talked around her leaving, but neither of them had said anything definite. They avoided words like *separation* and *divorce*.

She looked out the window that opened into the mall in time to see a young couple walk by, arm in arm and obviously very much in love.

"That guy looks just like Brad Mossman."

Elizabeth glanced across the table to see Donovan's eyes following the same couple. "He doesn't look anything like Brad."

"Sure he does. Same I'm-adorable chin, same you're-lucky-to-be-with-me-baby walk."

She laughed, the naturalness of it surprising. "You never did like Brad. Looking back on it, I think you did your best to intimidate the poor guy every chance you got."

"Hell, yes. That guy had a personality that would make the Pope want to punch him in the lip."

"Careful. You're talking about my first real boyfriend. I wore his ring for two whole weeks."

"Until you got in a fight with him and I gave you a ride home."

"On the back of that scruffy motorcycle. All the girls thought you looked really sexy riding that thing, and they all wanted to know if you'd tried anything."

"On the back of a moving motorcycle? I think that would have discouraged even Casanova. I wanted to, though. You looked so sexy in those tight, little hip-huggers and that green shirt. I didn't dare get off the bike when I got to your house."

Elizabeth flushed at the memory. She could remember that short ride as if it were yesterday. The wind streaming by them, Donovan's hard body in front of her. She'd felt so safe.

"So what did you tell all your girlfriends when they wanted to know if I'd made a pass?"

"I told them you'd been a perfect gentleman, of course."

"Liar."

Her head jerked up. He took a swallow of his coffee, his eyes on hers over the rim of the cup. Mischief danced in his gaze.

"What do you mean? I'm not a liar."

"Yes, you are. Carol told me the truth years ago. You told all the girls that I kissed you thoroughly when I took you home. As I recall you went into fairly vivid detail. I think I put my hand—"

"All right. All right." Elizabeth waved her hand in surrender. Her face felt as if it were on fire. "Remind me to murder Carol next time I see her. Every girl in town had the hots for you, whether they'd admit it or not. You could hardly expect me to go back to school after leaving Danny's with the infamous Donovan Sinclair and tell them you really had been a gentleman."

"Every girl in town?" He laughed. "I think you're exaggerating my appeal."

"Every girl. You looked so dangerous, so adult. And of course, any parent would have had apoplexy if their daughter went out with you. That was icing on the cake."

"I had no idea I was so popular. No one ever spoke to me."

"Of course no one spoke to you. You were too sexy to talk to. Besides, you had such an aura of mystery and danger, we were all too scared."

"*You* weren't too scared. I couldn't believe you'd actually come to the garage to see me."

"I wanted to thank you for giving me a ride home."

"Four times in one week?"

"I wanted to be sure you knew how much I appreciated the ride."

"Sure you did. You were so beautiful. You know, the first time I kissed you, I expected you to dissolve because I knew it had to be a dream. You couldn't really be there in my arms."

Elizabeth couldn't pull her gaze away from his. She felt flushed all over, remembering the feel of him against her, remembering the way his slightest touch had made her skin heat.

They stared at each other, a wealth of memories between them, the present almost forgotten. They'd shared so much. Their surroundings faded away. For a moment there was only the two of them, all alone.

"Beth, I—"

She jerked her eyes away and made a point of looking at her watch. "Good heavens, look at the time. I'd better get going."

Donovan stared at her and, for a moment, she was afraid he was going to insist on finishing whatever he'd started to say. She didn't want him to finish. She didn't want to hear it. She'd made her decisions and she didn't regret them. She didn't.

She fumbled with her purse, aware of him watching every move she made. After a long moment, he slid out of his seat and stood next to the table, waiting for her.

She stood up, conscious of his size, aware of the way her body wanted to lean into his. Her skin tingled with his nearness. All those memories had served to remind her of so many things she wanted to forget—was afraid to remember.

"I'll walk you to your car."

"That's really not necessary. I'm not parked all that far away."

"I'd feel better if I saw you to your car."

She glanced at the stubborn set of his jaw and shrugged. It wasn't worth arguing over. In a few minutes, she'd be gone. Neither of them spoke as they left the mall and stepped into the softly lit parking lot. A light rain was falling, not enough to require an umbrella. The rain somehow created a feeling of intimacy, as if it were just the two of them.

She unlocked her car and turned to him. Silhouetted in the lamplight, he looked bigger than ever—safe and warm and secure. But the uneven rhythm of her pulse had nothing to do with safety.

"It was nice to see you." God, she talked as if he were a casual acquaintance. How did you say goodbye to someone who'd once been your entire life?

"Maybe we could have dinner some night. There's a new steak house on the north end of Main."

Elizabeth wanted to say yes. She wanted to say it so badly it hurt. The very intensity of the feeling frightened her. She stared up at him, blinking against the sudden burning in her eyes.

"I...don't think that would be such a good idea." Could he hear how hard it was to say the words?

The light was behind him, making it impossible to read his expression. His shoulders seemed a little stiff, as if held too tight. The silence stretched, building until Elizabeth could stand no more. It hurt too much.

"Goodbye, Donovan." She slid into the car, shutting the door on the rain, shutting him outside. There were tears on her face. It was only the rain. That's all it was.

Donovan watched as she backed out of the parking place and drove down the aisle, tires hissing on the wet pavement. He didn't move until her taillights turned out of the parking lot and disappeared in the traffic.

Rain soaked his hair, seeping through his shirt. He shoved his hands into his pockets, hunching his shoulders against the dampness as he turned toward his own car.

Was it always going to hurt this much to say goodbye?

Chapter 9

"**Y**ou can't hibernate forever, Beth. You're hardly old enough to take up celibacy as a hobby." Carol waved a Danish for emphasis.

"I'm not planning on hibernating forever. It hasn't been that long. It's only been a few months, and I'm just not ready to start dating. And I'm definitely not ready to sleep with anyone."

"I didn't say you had to go to bed with a guy on the first date. That may be the rule in some parts of the country but here in Remembrance, we expect our womenfolk to have more discretion than that.

"All I'm saying is that if you don't want to spend the rest of your life alone, you'd better start looking around now. There aren't that many great guys lying around waiting to be found. Look at me, I haven't found one yet."

"That's because you're so finicky."

"I know. I always insist on a man who can walk and chew gum at the same time. And in this town that's a rarity. Donovan is one of the few good ones, and you're crazy to have turned him loose. If I managed to get hold of a man like that..." A sigh completed the thought, and Elizabeth forced herself to smile.

Carol pulled herself away from her daydream. "Anyway, you'd better start looking around. We ain't getting any younger, you know."

"I know. It's just that it's only been a few months, and Donovan and I were together for so long." She pushed a crumb across the table with the tip of her finger.

In the bright warmth of her kitchen, it was almost possible to forget that meeting with Donovan a week ago. Until then, she'd been proud of the way she was putting her life together. She was proving that she could make it on her own, and she was happy. Somehow seeing him again had made it all seem so hollow, as if it was just a facade and he'd shown her the emptiness underneath.

"Beth, I know it's not going to be easy for you to see other men. But unless you want to spend your life alone, you ought to start looking around. Take my word for it, living by yourself isn't all it's cracked up to be. Right now it seems okay, but wait until you've done it a few more years. Sure, there's nobody to tell you what time to get home, but there's nobody to care if you don't make it home at all. It can get damned lonely. It's okay for me. I'm used to it, and I've gotten pretty set in my ways over the years, but you aren't used to it, and I don't think you'll like it."

Elizabeth reached out to squeeze Carol's hand, knowing that anything more concrete by way of sympathy would be dismissed with a laugh and a joke. The picture Carol drew was not inviting. She loved her job, but it wasn't enough to fill her life.

"Even if I wanted to date—and I'm not saying I do—I don't know how to go about meeting men. If there's a singles' bar in town, I don't know where it is."

"Not to worry." Carol set down her Danish and leaned across the table to pat her friend's hand. "Just let Matchmaker Carol take care of everything. I have a guy in mind."

"Wait a minute. What kind of a guy?"

Carol grinned. "A male kind of a guy. Two legs, two arms, two eyes, one—"

"I can fill in the rest. I mean what does he do for a living? Do I have anything in common with him? What makes you think he'd even want to go out with me?"

"Beth, Beth. Don't be an idiot. Have you looked in a mirror lately? You're gorgeous."

"I thought I wasn't getting any younger."

"You're not but some things age well. Believe me, George will be more than happy to pay for dinner just for the chance to drool at you from across the table." She waved a hand, cutting off Elizabeth's next objection. "Trust me. Would I lie to you?"

Three days later Elizabeth was still debating the answer to that question. It wasn't that she thought Carol would actually lie. But she'd been known to poke the truth into a shape that fit her wishes.

She smoothed her hands over her hips, turning to check the fit of the pale aqua silk dress. She felt a little reassured by the reflection in the mirror. She wasn't sixteen anymore, but she didn't look half-bad. Maybe Carol was right, perhaps she had improved with age. The dress was new and very flattering if she did say so herself. She'd bought it just the day before, and the fitted top and flared skirt suited her.

Would Donovan like it? He'd always liked her in anything blue. She traced her fingers over the scooped neckline. He'd definitely approve of the fit. She stared in the mirror. With her eyes half closed, she could almost imagine him coming into the room, could see his reflection in the mirror. He'd pause when he saw her, his eyes flaring for an instant. Then he'd come up behind her, and his hands would slide around her waist, pulling her back to rest against his chest. He'd hold her, and then maybe he'd reach up to pull the pins out of her hair because he always preferred it down. Her hair would spill over his fingers, and he'd brush it aside to kiss her ear. She'd turn and—

Her eyes snapped open, and Elizabeth stared in the mirror, horrified by the direction her thoughts were taking. She hadn't put this dress on for Donovan. She didn't dress for him anymore. She had to get it through her head that he wasn't the center of her life. Not now, not ever again. It was her choice and it was the right choice.

She tucked a strand of hair into place and reached for her earrings. Donovan Sinclair had no business intruding into her daydreams. He was part of her past, and she wanted him to stay that way. The immediate future belonged to George Bonner.

Her hands were shaking as she slipped her shoes on and took one last look in the mirror before going into the living room to await the arrival of her date. *Her date*. The words sounded funny even in her head. She hadn't had a date in almost twenty years. What was she supposed to say to him? What did a man expect on a date these days? Would he expect her to be full of witty conversation?

As it turned out, she didn't have to worry much about what to say to George Bonner. George didn't need outside help with the conversation—he carried it quite efficiently by himself.

Seated across the table from him at the Haufbrau, Remembrance's one genuinely fancy restaurant, Elizabeth was able to carry her end of the conversation with little more than an occasional yes or a mumbled sound of agreement. He didn't seem to need anything more than a periodic indication that she was still conscious.

He ordered for her, a gesture that Donovan would have made seem courtly. George made it seem officious. She smiled and said nothing. This was her first date in twenty years; she was going to enjoy it if it killed her.

Staring at him, she couldn't help but make a few comparisons. George was about the same age as Donovan, give or take a year, but he had none of Donovan's hard strength. He was shorter, wider, softer, paler and duller.

She reached for her wineglass and took a sip of the California Chenin Blanc he'd ordered. He hadn't consulted her, but he had informed her that it was a very modest little wine with no pretensions to greatness. Too bad the same couldn't be said of George. The wine tasted rather thin to her, but she smiled and made polite noises about it. Donovan had always allowed her to order the wine, admitting quite bluntly that it all tasted alike to him. Too bad George didn't know he had a cork for a palate.

"Carol tells me you're an interior decorator." Elizabeth looked at him, hardly able to believe her ears. Good heavens, was the man going to let her talk? Was he actually expressing an interest in something she might have done?

"Yes, I am."

"You wouldn't believe how important some people think interior decorating is. It can make or break a house sale. I've had clients refuse to buy a house because they didn't like the decoration. Slap on a little paint, I tell them, but they don't listen. Just last week I had a place that was done in lime green, and I told the owners, I said—"

Elizabeth tuned him out. She could imagine what George had told the owners. It was amazing but, after only an hour or so in his company, she had the feeling that she could imagine what George would say in just about any situation.

Suddenly, she realized that hadn't been the case with Donovan. She'd known him as well as it was possible to know another human being, and yet he'd always managed to surprise her. She took another sip of her wine. What was Donovan doing tonight? Was he at home? Was he thinking about her at all?

Actually, at that moment, Donovan was about twenty feet away, sitting at a table just around the corner from Elizabeth. He smiled at his dinner companion and hoped that the glazed feeling in his brain didn't extend to a glaze in his eyes.

This date had been a major mistake. He should have known better. It was too soon to start dating. In fact, it might never be the right time if tonight was any indication.

"You know, they've done studies that prove that a woman in my age group has a better chance of being struck by lightning than she does of getting married."

Donovan resisted the urge to look hopefully upward. There hadn't been a cloud in the sky when they drove here. Lightning was unlikely.

"I'm sure that's not true."

"It was in the paper." She stared at him, the expression in her eyes solemn. Clearly, if it was in the paper, there was no arguing with it. He thought of pointing out that it was possible to skew statistics to prove just about anything, and then he decided against it.

"Well, I'm sure any woman who truly wants to get married can find a like-minded man."

He took a sip of his wine, wondering if it tasted as much like lamp fuel to her as it did to him.

She shook her head, her mouth pursed. "It's not that simple. You see, statistically speaking, there aren't as many men as there are women, and then you have to figure in the necessity of finding someone with like interests. Oh, and someone who wants children. Not all men want children, you know."

He could have said the same about a lot of women, but he didn't. He'd already learned that it was simpler to say nothing at all. He took another sip of his wine and then reached for the water glass. It was going to be a long evening.

Seeing Elizabeth last week had made him realize that he'd only been marking time since she left. He'd been living in limbo, not thinking about the future, trying not to think about the past. It couldn't go on forever.

Jane Bartholomew was a sales rep for a firm he'd dealt with for several years. They'd talked at the office, and she'd always seemed to be intelligent and interesting. When she walked into the office on Monday, he'd found himself asking her if she'd like to have dinner with him on Friday. He hadn't thought long and hard, hadn't analyzed the decision to ask her out. He'd just decided that it was time he started giving up the past and this was as good a way as any to start.

Unfortunately, Jane didn't see it quite that simply. Donovan leaned back as the waiter brought their food. He smiled across the table at Jane and wondered why he'd never noticed the hungry gleam in her eyes that had nothing to do with the trout almondine the waiter set in front of her.

It wasn't that he didn't sympathize with her. She was thirty-seven and clearly feeling the pinch of the biological time clock. She wanted a husband and a baby and she wanted them now. The minute he asked her out, she'd refiled him in her mind from unavailable to available, and the change in her attitude toward him was nothing short of stunning.

Donovan cut into his steak, trying not to notice the way she watched him. He now knew how a stallion must feel when it was being considered for stud. Any minute now he expected her to lunge across the table and pry open his mouth to study his teeth.

It wasn't that he didn't like Jane. He did, despite her not-too-subtle hints about marriage and children and time running out. She was a nice woman, and he wished her the best of luck. But he wasn't interested.

He speared a mushroom and stared at it glumly. The problem was he wasn't interested in any woman except Elizabeth, and he'd been stupid enough to lose her. Asking Jane out had been a foolish attempt to pretend that he was going to get over Beth. It hadn't worked. She was deep in his soul. It was only now that she was gone that he realized just how much he needed her.

The past six months had been gray and barren, an empty wasteland without her. She was probably perfectly happy without him. After all, she hadn't lost that much. She'd been right, he *had* let their marriage drift away while he pursued his work. He'd thought somehow that it would simply maintain itself, without any effort on his part. He knew now that it was too late.

He took another bite of steak, forcing himself to smile. It was too bad he wasn't a drinking man. Right now the idea of being stinking, filthy drunk had a definite appeal—if only to help him forget what he'd lost.

The date wasn't a raging success, but it wasn't a total disaster. Eventually Jane did allow him to turn the conversation away from marriage. When the small band began to play in the bar, he forced himself to do the gentlemanly thing and ask Jane if she'd like to dance.

She was light on her feet and, if their steps didn't match quite like his and Elizabeth's had, Donovan didn't allow himself to think about it. The music was slow and mellow, and they moved around the dance floor in reasonable harmony. At least she didn't feel as if she had to carry on a conversation while dancing.

He casually gazed over her head, looking at the other couples. He nodded to one or two acquaintances. In a town the size of Remembrance, it was impossible to go out without running into someone you knew. There was Jase Bower, who owned the local feed store, out with his wife, who was pregnant again, and Levar Davis who was the closest thing to a celebrity Remembrance could boast. He'd been on *Jeopardy* three times and had actually won some money. Levar was with his wife. George Bonner, the local real estate agent, was dancing with—

Donovan mumbled an apology as his foot came down on Jane's toe. *Elizabeth.* He wasn't imagining things. She was actually here dancing with George Bonner, that annoying pip-squeak. She looked up and her gaze fell on him. George seemed to stumble, as if confused by the sudden rigidity of his partner. Then Elizabeth dragged her gaze away from Donovan's and stared fixedly downward, her feet moving automatically to the music.

Donovan turned Jane so that his back was to the other couple. He hadn't expected to feel the absolute, blinding rage that gripped him. If he'd thought about it, he would have expected Elizabeth to be dating. After all, she was the one who'd left him, so it made sense that she would be ready to see other men. How long had she been dating George, and what did she see in the little twerp?

Had George kissed her? Were they sleeping together? Jane squeaked in protest as his hand tightened on hers.

"Sorry." But the muttered apology was automatic. Even though his back was to her, Donovan was aware of Elizabeth with every fiber. She had no right to be going out with other men. She was his: his wife, his woman. She had been since the moment they met.

He turned Jane again. Now Elizabeth's back was to him, and Donovan scowled at the way George was holding her. His hand was too low on her hips. He was too close. They were making a spectacle of themselves.

The music came to a halt, but Donovan wasn't aware of it until he realized that no one else was moving. George started to lead Elizabeth off the dance floor. Without thinking, Donovan moved forward, pulling Jane with him.

"Elizabeth, George. How nice to see you." Elizabeth stiffened before turning slowly toward him. George turned, and Donovan was maliciously pleased to see a twinge of uneasiness in the smaller man's eyes.

"Sinclair. Nice to see you."

"Have you met Jane? Jane, this is George Bonner, our local real estate whiz kid, and this is Elizabeth Sinclair—my wife."

''That's not quite accurate.'' Elizabeth kept the smile on her face, but Donovan could see her annoyance.

Jane murmured hello, clearly uncomfortable. Donovan barely noticed. The band had started playing again, and his smile became even more sharklike. ''George, would you mind if I danced with Elizabeth. This used to be our song, didn't it, Beth? Why don't you and Jane dance? I bet the two of you have a lot in common.''

It was rude. It was ruthless. But he didn't care. He pushed Jane's hand toward George and reached around her to take Elizabeth's arm. Without creating a scene, there was nothing anyone could do but go along with the arrangements he'd so cavalierly made.

Elizabeth was stiff as he led her onto the floor and pulled her into his arms. Her steps matched his automatically even as she tried to avoid letting him draw her close.

''I hope you're proud of yourself. That was quite a performance.''

''I don't know what you're talking about. I just wanted to dance with my wife.''

''I'm not your wife,'' she spat out, but the words lacked impact. It felt remarkably nice to be in Donovan's arms. ''And this isn't our song. I don't even know what song this is.''

''Neither do I. Who cares?''

''You were very rude.''

''I know.''

''George probably thinks you're nuts and so does Janet.''

''Jane.''

Beth's perfume was just as evocative as ever. Soft and floral, it always made him think of wildflowers and bedrooms. He drew her a little closer, liking the way her breasts pressed against his chest.

''I wish you wouldn't hold me so close.''

''You didn't object when George held you like this.''

"He wasn't holding me this tight. Besides, George is my date."

"Do you let all your dates hold you like this?"

"No. Yes. It's none of your business. Besides, this is the first date I've been on." She could have bitten her tongue out the minute the words were said. She could actually feel the pleasure they gave him.

"So, is George showing you a rollicking good time? I bet you could qualify for a real estate license by now."

Elizabeth bit her lip against a smile. Obviously Donovan had spent a little time with George. His hand tightened on her back, shifting her still closer. Not even a whisper could have worked its way between them. It was foolish. She'd regret it. But, for just a moment, she allowed herself to savor the hard length of his body against hers.

"I suppose Janine is a barrel of laughs."

"Jane. Actually, Jane is looking for a stud."

"What?"

Donovan ignored the pressure of her hands on his chest and kept her close. "She's looking for a husband and a baby, and she wants them immediately."

"And she thinks you're a good candidate?" A confusing mixture of emotions churned inside, angering her.

"She seems to think I qualify." He sounded so smug it made her want to hit him. Hard.

"Tell her to talk to me first. She doesn't realize what she'd be getting into. A man who's married to his career first and his wife second, a man who's never home. And when he does come home, he brings the office with him." She was aware that her words were taking on an hysterical edge, but she couldn't seem to stop them. "And as far as having a baby is concerned, she'd have a hard time getting pregnant. A rabbit couldn't have gotten pregnant with our sex life the past few years. The music has stopped. Would you please let me go?"

She didn't look at him as he let his arms drop. Without a word, she turned and left the dance floor, searching blindly for her date. She found him on the edge of the floor, holding an animated conversation with Janine or Janet or whatever her name was.

"I'm sorry, George, I've got an awful headache. Would you mind if we went home now?" She directed a vague smile toward the other woman, wondering quite viciously what bottle she'd found her hair color in. She was acutely aware of Donovan standing just behind her, but she didn't look at him. She couldn't.

George might have wondered that she'd developed a headache immediately after dancing with her semi-ex-husband, but he was gentleman enough not to question. He took her arm, murmuring solicitously as he led her away. Elizabeth could feel Donovan's eyes on her until she and George turned a corner.

George had the good sense to remain relatively quiet on the way home. Elizabeth struggled to find answers to his polite comments regarding how pleasant he'd found the evening. He left her at her door without trying to kiss her good-night, which raised him a couple of notches in her estimation. He might be a bore, but he wasn't totally insensitive.

She shut the door and leaned against it, staring at her apartment. She had gone to so much trouble to turn it into a home. It *was* her home. Why was it that a chance meeting with Donovan should suddenly make the place feel empty? She closed her eyes against burning tears. He'd been part of her life for so long, she'd been a fool to think that it wouldn't hurt to cut him out of it.

A tear escaped to slide down her cheek. He'd put his career ahead of their marriage for so long. She'd waited and waited, and was devastated when she finally realized that nothing was going to change because he wasn't unhappy with the way things were. She didn't love him anymore. *She didn't.* It shouldn't hurt so much to see him again.

Outside, the street was dark. Most of the small town slept. Donovan hunched his shoulders inside his leather jacket, staring up at the angular building. He knew she was in there crying as surely as if he were standing next to her. It hurt to know that she was in pain and that he was the cause of it. He hadn't meant to hurt her, but he couldn't help but feel a small flicker of satisfaction. If she didn't care, she wouldn't be hurt.

Elizabeth might not be ready to acknowledge it, but she did still care about him. She couldn't cut him out of her life so easily.

He pulled his collar up and shoved his hands into his pockets. The spring air was cold late at night. He should go home. He was acting like a lovesick teenager. He'd never told her about the nights he'd spent standing outside her bedroom twenty years ago. Sometimes, he'd walk to her house late at night and just stand outside her window, imagining her asleep in her ruffled bed.

He'd always felt so unworthy and he'd never been able to believe that she really loved him. She could have had anyone, and she'd chosen him. Maybe that was part of what went wrong. He'd spent too much time trying to prove he was good enough for her, and in doing so he let his ambitions take precedence over their marriage.

A chill breeze wove its way down the street and he shivered, staring at the building another long minute before turning to get in his car. He'd lost so much.

Michael's birthday party was only two weeks away. Maybe that was long enough for tonight's wounds to fade and for him to remember how to court his wife again. She hadn't filed for divorce, hadn't even asked for a formal separation. That had to mean something.

Chapter 10

The party to celebrate Michael's nineteenth birthday was a small gathering for family and friends. In a stilted phone conversation, Elizabeth had offered to come over and help with the preparations. Donovan had been very casual about refusing her offer, telling her that he had everything under control. The caterers dropped everything off the afternoon of the party along with written instructions spelling out oven temperatures and serving times.

Donovan spent the day cleaning the house. Michael, who had a few days off from college, watched his father whirl around the house like a maniac. He didn't ask why. He might be only nineteen but he understood exactly what his father was doing. Donovan didn't want any evidence that the house wasn't running as smoothly as it had when Elizabeth was in charge. The fact that several of the closets could have been registered as lethal weapons and that he finally had to spray oven cleaner on the bathtubs to get them clean were things that no one needed to know.

So Michael offered an occasional hand and was tactful enough to swallow his amusement. As the day wore on, Donovan's expression became more harried, his hair stood on end and his jeans looked like the place where dirt came to die. He'd never realized how much work went into cleaning a house.

When the first guests arrived at seven, the place was, if not immaculate, at least presentable. Donovan's hair was still damp from his shower, and he had the nagging feeling that he'd forgotten a hundred things, but none of that showed in his face. He was the very picture of masculine calm.

It might have consoled him to know that Elizabeth was at least as nervous as he was. She was bringing the cake, and no one but her and the ficus in her kitchen would know that the cake she brought was her third attempt. The other two resided in the trash can.

It felt very strange to be parking her car on the street and walking up the familiar brick walkway. She reached for the doorknob and then stopped herself. She had to remember that she was a guest here now. This wasn't her home anymore, and she didn't regret that choice, she reminded herself fiercely.

Ringing the bell, she stared at the closed door and swallowed nervously. She hadn't seen Donovan since that disastrous evening two weeks ago. She should never have let him see that he was capable of upsetting her. She should have remained cool and calm. Tonight would be different. She was going to make it clear that she didn't regret her decisions.

Her heart bumped when the door swung open, and she felt almost weak-kneed with relief when she saw that it was Michael.

"Hi, Mom. I hope that's chocolate." The casual normalcy of his greeting put her at ease. He reached out to take the plate from her.

"Is there any other flavor?" She stepped into the hallway and hugged her son, feeling a rush of foolish tears. He was so tall, as tall as his father and already broadening out. He wasn't a little boy anymore.

He returned her hug with one arm, balancing the cake on his other hand. "This smells great."

She drew back, smiling, hoping he wouldn't notice that her eyes were a little too bright. "Don't sound so surprised. My cakes always smell great."

"They taste great, too." She stiffened at Donovan's quiet voice, frozen for an instant before she forced herself to turn, hoping she looked more casual than she felt.

"Hello, Elizabeth." He was standing at the bottom of the stairs wearing a pair of crisp jeans and a green cashmere sweater. He looked relaxed, at home and so intensely masculine that, for a moment, it was a little hard to breathe.

"Hello, Donovan." She was acutely aware of the way his eyes went over her, taking in the soft, cotton dress with the full skirt that swirled just above her ankles. His eyes told her that he liked what he saw—not that she cared whether he liked her clothes or not.

Michael looked from one parent to the other, sensing the tension between them, wondering at its cause. "I'll put this in the kitchen. You should see the great spread the caterers left, Mom. Shrimp and mushroom and all kinds of great stuff."

Elizabeth dragged her gaze from Donovan. "I'll go with you, just to make sure you don't sample the frosting."

"Would I do that?" His face was the very picture of innocence.

She laughed. "I'll just make sure temptation doesn't get the best of you."

Donovan shoved his hands into his pockets, watching the two of them disappear into the kitchen. He hadn't realized how hungry he'd been for the sight of her until she was on his doorstep, or how possessive he'd feel once she was back in this house. This was her home, it was where she belonged.

The party was apparently a success, though neither Donovan nor Elizabeth could have said exactly what happened during the evening. Though they spoke directly to each other only a few times, there wasn't a moment when they weren't intensely aware of each other.

Everyone had a wonderful time, Michael was thrilled with his gifts, the party was pronounced great fun. All Elizabeth knew was that she felt breathless, almost hunted. Donovan didn't say anything to her. He didn't watch her every move, but she was intensely aware of him. Even when her back was to him, she knew where he was.

It felt so natural to be back in this house, playing hostess to their friends, celebrating their son's birthday. When everyone began to leave, it felt natural to start cleaning up. Michael yawned and reached for a plate, and she took it from him, shooing him off to bed. As the birthday boy he wasn't expected to help with the dishes.

He trailed off upstairs, and Elizabeth felt the sting of tears. It seemed as if he'd grown up in such a short time.

"Hard to believe he's nineteen. Seems like just a couple of years ago we were worrying about him riding his bike to school." Elizabeth's words were quiet, fitting with the slight melancholy of the late hour.

"I was just thinking the same thing. I guess children always grow up too fast to suit their parents." She moved back into the living room and lifted a stack of plates. They worked in companionable silence for a few minutes.

Without speaking, Donovan filled the sink with water and began to wash the crystal. Elizabeth hesitated, loath to give up the quiet intimacy that had settled between them, knowing she should go home. She moved forward and picked up a towel.

"I think everyone had a good time."

"They seemed to." His arm brushed hers as he rinsed a fragile glass and set it in the drainer. She picked it up and dried it automatically. He was so close, she could smell the woodsy scent of his after-shave. The scent brought back so many memories.

"How is the job going?"

"Really well. I'm redoing some of the store displays. Next week I'm supposed to go out and see Mrs. Buckman about redecorating her house."

"Mrs. Buckman? She hasn't changed a thing in that place in the past thirty years."

"I know but her sister is coming to visit and I think she wants an updated image."

"She must have been impressed with you."

"Well, she hasn't let me do anything yet. We're just at the talking stage."

"You'll get the job."

His confidence in her lit a small glow. She'd almost forgotten that Donovan had always believed in her, no matter what she wanted to do. It had been so long since they'd talked about dreams and hopes for the future.

He seemed to be taking a long time washing the last goblet. With the sleeves of his sweater shoved up above his elbows and his forearms disappearing into mounds of fluffy suds, he looked distractingly attractive. She should have gone home as soon as Michael went to bed.

"I'm thinking about buying another motorcycle."

"What for?"

He shrugged. "I don't know. Maybe to recapture my lost youth. I seem to have gotten a bit stuck in the mud lately."

"They're dangerous." The protest was automatic. She could sense that the idea excited him.

"You didn't seem to mind that when we met."

"I was sixteen. Sixteen-year-old girls don't really think about things like motorcycle wrecks. All I knew was that you looked sexy in a black leather jacket and it was exciting to feel the wind in my hair.''

"Did you think I looked sexy in a black leather jacket?'' The look he slanted her was dangerous. Its effect wasn't lessened by the suds that coated his forearms. She took the last goblet from him.

"Of course I thought you looked sexy. Every girl in school thought you looked sexy.''

She was grateful when he didn't pursue the question. She set the sparkling crystal on the counter and folded the towel, her movements precise, matching the corners perfectly, smoothing the damp cotton into perfect folds. She was disturbingly conscious of Donovan draining and rinsing out the sink.

"You know, there's going to be a reunion concert of some of the sixties groups in the city this weekend.''

"Oh, really?'' She put another fold in the towel, not looking at Donovan.

"I . . . I've got a couple of tickets.'' His tone was elaborately casual, his attention all for the sink. It was apparently important that every trace of suds be rinsed away.

"You do?''

"Yeah. It's supposed to be a great concert.'' He named some of the popular groups from that decade.

"Sounds interesting.'' She folded the towel again, making sure the corners met precisely.

"Do you . . . Would you be interested in going?''

"It sounds like fun.'' She was cautious, not sure if he was asking her to go with him or suggesting that he could let her have the tickets.

"I could pick you up Saturday afternoon. We could go into Indianapolis and get something to eat before the concert starts. Make a day of it.''

"I'd like that.'' She didn't look at him, staring at the towel in her hands.

"Would one o'clock be too early?''

"No, that would be fine."

"Great. It should be fun."

"Yes." Elizabeth set the towel on the counter. She'd folded it to a size only slightly larger than a postage stamp. What on earth was she thinking? She'd just agreed to go on a date with Donovan. They were practically divorced and she was going to a concert with him. It was crazy.

"Michael, have you seen that dark green shirt of mine?"

"Have you checked the closet?" Michael leaned in the doorway of the bedroom his parents had shared.

Donovan straightened from looking under the bed. "No. I know I wore it three days ago, and I didn't hang it up."

"The laundry delivered everything yesterday afternoon while you were at work. I hung a bunch of stuff in your closet, and I think I saw that shirt." He took a bite out of the apple he held, his eyes curious.

Donovan hurried to the closet, stumbling over a pair of shoes. They were only one of several pairs stacked haphazardly at the foot of the bed. The bed itself held half a dozen pairs of jeans and a handful of shirts.

"You cleaning out your closet? 'Cause if you are, can I have that gold shirt? My girlfriend likes the way I look in gold."

"Take it." Donovan's muffled voice came out of the depths of the walk-in closet. Michael took another bite of apple.

"How about the gray slacks? They'd look great with some of my shirts."

"Sure."

"You know, I've always liked this bedspread. It would be terrific on the wall of the dorm."

"Okay."

Michael crunched some more apple. "Dad? I need a loan. Could you spare ten thousand or so? I was thinking of taking a trip to Europe instead of finishing out this quarter.

Maybe joining a gang in Paris or Rome or something. I thought I might break into the Louvre and steal the *Mona Lisa*. And then I could smuggle it back to the States and we could hang it in the bathroom. Of course, we'd have to change the towels. I don't think that color would go."

"Fine. Have you seen my black boots?"

"They're out here on the floor." Michael finished his apple and measured the core between thumb and forefinger, eyeing the wastebasket across the room. The core hit it with satisfying precision just as Donovan came out of the closet, the green shirt dangling from one arm, his expression distracted. He sorted through the tangle of shoes to find his boots. With them in hand, he looked at his son, apparently truly aware of him for the first time.

"Don't you have a date tonight?"

"Not tonight. Sara went home to her parents for the weekend. Are you nervous about having a date with Mom?"

"It's not a date."

"I thought you two were going to get something to eat and then go to a concert with a bunch of old guys." He dodged the shoe Donovan threw at him, his grin full of mischief. "Seems to me that qualifies as a date."

"Your mother and I are just getting together for a casual meal and a concert."

"What's the difference between that and a date?"

Donovan ignored the question, pulling on the short, black boots. "When you and Sara go out, what do you do?"

"We get together and we go somewhere. Pizza. A movie. Sometimes a concert."

Donovan stood up, stomping his feet to settle the boots into place. "No. I mean, do you buy flowers or candy or anything like that?" His tone was elaborately casual. Too casual. His son's eyes narrowed.

"Are you asking me for pointers on how to date?"

"Of course not. I was just curious." Donovan shrugged into his shirt, his head bent to conceal the flush in his cheekbones.

Michael reached into his back pocket and pulled out a banana, peeling it with careful movements. Donovan waited a few moments and then prompted him.

"Well?"

"Well what?" Michael glanced up, his expression all innocence. His father clamped his teeth together and thought longingly of the time when his son had been too young to speak.

"Do you buy her flowers or something?"

Michael took a bite of the banana and chewed slowly. "Sara is allergic to flowers and she hates candy."

"Oh."

"Now, if you were asking me if I thought you should get Mom some flowers for this nondate, that would be a different story."

"It would?"

"Sure. Mom loves flowers. Of course, since this isn't really a date, then flowers would probably be kind of silly." He peeled the banana another careful inch.

"I should have beaten you more often when you were little. It's your mother's fault that you've turned out this way."

Michael grinned and didn't shift his comfortable position slouched in the doorway. Donovan buttoned his shirt, aware of the way he had to concentrate to get the buttons through the proper holes. He hadn't been this nervous in years.

"Are you trying to get Mom back?"

His hands stilled and he angled a glance at his son. Damn, when had he grown up?

"Do you think I should?"

"Do you still love her?"

This was no conversation to be having with his son. He was sure any psychology book would tell him that.

"I . . . yes, I do."

Michael nodded, folding the banana peel neatly and tucking it back in his pocket. "I thought so."

"You did, huh?"

"Sure. Mom's terrific. How could you not love her?"

The simplistic answer was impossible to argue with, especially since Donovan felt much the same. He finished buttoning his shirt and unsnapped his jeans to tuck the tails in.

"It's not going to be easy to get her back, you know. You better not take it for granted that she's just going to fall back into your arms."

"I'm not."

"She's dating again, I think."

Donovan's jaw set, remembering the one date he'd been witness to. If he had his way, there wouldn't be any more. Elizabeth belonged with him. All he had to do was convince her of that.

"Well, here I am to help you prepare for the big night." Carol's cheery greeting drew a distracted smile. Elizabeth shut the door behind her friend.

"It's not that big a deal. Donovan just happened to have tickets for this concert and he thought I might enjoy it. That's all."

"Is that why you look like you're facing a firing squad at dusk?" Carol's sharp eyes skimmed over Elizabeth, taking in the pale features, the half-done makeup, the rumpled bathrobe clutched in a white-knuckled grip at the throat.

"I'm just a little nervous, that's all."

"So was Marie Antoinette just before they chopped off her head, and I bet she didn't look as nervous as you do. What are you planning on wearing?"

"I don't know." The question appeared to cause Elizabeth some distress.

"Show me what your choices are."

"Well, I've tried on a few things, and everything makes me look too fat or too old. I should have gone out and bought something new, but it's too late now." She led the way into her bedroom as she spoke. "I just couldn't find anything that looked right." She ran her fingers through her hair and gave Carol a helpless look.

Carol stared at the bedroom solemnly. Clothes were draped over every possible surface except the vanity table, which was covered with opened bottles and eye-shadow cases. Shoes were piled here and there in forlorn little heaps.

"I can see your problem. Have you tried all this stuff on?"

"Most of it. I just can't find anything that looks right. What do you wear to a concert these days?"

"Well, I'm no authority, but it seems to me that something in between the blue terry-cloth rompers and the black silk sheath would probably hit about the right note."

Elizabeth stared at her friend blankly and then looked around the room, seeing the mess for the first time, really looking at all the things she'd tried on.

"Oh, Lord."

"I don't think divine intervention is called for. Why don't you finish your makeup while I sort out a few things that seem reasonable. Maybe if you don't have so many choices, it'll be easier to make a decision."

A few minutes of Carol's sensible company and Elizabeth could feel her nervousness subsiding to a manageable level. She forced herself to concentrate on her makeup, trying not to jam a mascara wand in her eye. Behind her, Carol sorted through her clothes, finally setting aside a few things and then sitting on the edge of the bed to watch her.

"You love him, don't you?"

Elizabeth muttered a curse as her lipstick pencil swerved and, instead of outlining her mouth, she created a new and impossible lip line. Her hand was shaking as she reached for a tissue to repair the damage.

"I don't know what you're talking about. I'm just a little worried about this, that's all."

"You weren't this worked up about going out with George."

"George wasn't this important." The words were out before she thought about them. Her hand stilled on her face. Her eyes met Carol's in the mirror, and then she pulled her gaze away.

"There's nothing wrong with loving Donovan, you know. I've always thought he was a pretty terrific guy."

"He is. I never said he wasn't." She stirred a finger through some spilled powder. "I don't know how I feel anymore. I always thought I'd love him forever, that nothing could ever make me change my feelings for him. And then, these past few years, we just didn't have anything to say to each other anymore. I began to feel lost, like I didn't have any identity of my own. I just stopped loving him."

"Did you really?"

Elizabeth shrugged without looking at her friend. "I don't know. I thought I did. Then I moved out and a whole new world opened up to me. Only there was this hole where Donovan had always been. We've shared so much of our lives, Carol. I've been with him since I was sixteen. We raised a son together. You can't break those ties."

"Do you really think that's all that holds you two together? Look at yourself. If it was just old ties that bind, you wouldn't be so upset by a simple date. It really would be 'no big deal.'"

"I don't know. No one else has ever made me feel like Donovan does. I just don't know if we can recapture what we had. I don't even know if I want to recapture it—or if he does. But I'm not settling for anything less. I'd rather live alone than go back to what it was the past few years."

"I think the two of you were meant for each other, and I think you're going to get back together, stronger than ever."

"Maybe." Elizabeth stood up. "Okay, show me what you think I should wear."

Half an hour later she was suitably attired in a pair of snug, black jeans with white pinstriping and a bright blue blouse that made her eyes seem bluer than ever. Her hair reached her shoulders in a soft fall of golden blond. She felt like she was sixteen again, waiting for Donovan's knock, wildly excited and scared.

"You look terrific. You're going to knock his socks off. I'll clean up the mess here after you've gone and let myself out."

"You don't have to do that. I can clean it up tonight or in the morning."

"It's the least I can do to aid the cause. You don't want to come home to a place that looks like a tornado went through it."

"Thanks." Elizabeth hugged her friend, blinking back tears. "I don't know what I'd do without you."

"A lot worse." But Carol's hug was equally fierce.

Elizabeth took one last look in the mirror, jumping when the doorbell rang. Her eyes met Carol's, panic flickering in their depths.

"I think I'm going to throw up."

"No, you're not. You're a grown woman, and you're going to handle this date with the sophistication that comes only with maturity. Donovan will be stunned by your beauty, impressed by your wit, and left speechless by your suavity."

"Suavity? I'm not even sure that's a word, let alone something to impress someone with."

Carol shrugged, pushing Elizabeth toward the door. "Who cares? You get the idea. You look dynamite. Go knock 'em dead."

Elizabeth wiped her hands down the sides of her jeans and took a deep breath, trying to still the foolish pounding of her heart. Carol was right. This was just a simple evening out, nothing to panic about. It was only Donovan waiting on the other side of the door. It was only the one man she'd ever loved, the one man who could still reduce her to a puddle of quivering mush with just a look. No big deal at all.

She reached for the doorknob and took a deep breath, feeling as if fate waited on the other side.

And perhaps it did.

Chapter 11

"It's nothing fancy, but steak and lobster didn't seem like a good prelude to a rock concert."

"This is perfect." Elizabeth picked up a barbecued rib and bit into it with delicate greed. She'd been too nervous to eat all day, and the hot and spicy ribs tasted wonderful.

The small restaurant was crowded. Families, couples and groups of friends filled every table, and a line waited outside. Best Ribs in Indianapolis announced the sign outside. Elizabeth wouldn't have sworn to that, but they were certainly superb. And it was impossible to remain nervous with a snowy-white napkin tucked into the top of your blouse like a bib and your fingers covered in barbecue sauce.

Besides, there'd been nothing to be nervous about in the first place. True, Donovan did look devastatingly attractive, and he had presented her with flowers, but he'd also been comfortably casual about the whole thing.

A family with a little girl was seated at the table next to them, and Elizabeth glanced over, holding back the urge to laugh out loud. Her parents watched in helpless wonderment as the child managed to dress herself completely in barbecue sauce, all in the course of eating one rib. Elizabeth glanced at Donovan, her eyes alight with laughter.

He'd been watching her. In the instant before his gaze shifted away, she read a hunger that had nothing to do with the food in front of them. Her laughter faded and she stared at the table, feeling a nervous jump in her stomach that wasn't caused by the spicy food.

"I looked at motorcycles yesterday. I think I'm definitely going to buy one. Probably in the next week or so." He picked up another rib and bit into it, and she wondered if she'd imagined what she'd seen a moment ago. He didn't look as if he had anything more on his mind than food and motorcycles.

"What are you going to do with it? Ride it to the office?"

"Maybe. I could strap my briefcase onto the back, or I might get one of those enormous bikes with the saddle bags."

"I still think they're too dangerous."

"If you're careful, they're not that bad. Besides, you only live once."

"That doesn't mean you have to try and get yourself killed."

"I'm not going to get myself killed. I'm just going to have a little fun. Come on, admit it. Don't you think I'd look great sitting on a Harley in a black leather jacket? I could do my hair in a DA and get a pair of really cool shades and wait outside Mason's for you to get off work."

"There's only one problem with that scenario. I wear skirts to work, and I'm not climbing on a motorcycle in a skirt. Besides, my boss would probably call the police as soon as she saw you lurking outside the store."

"Lurking? I wouldn't be lurking. I'd be sitting there looking tough and cool."

She reached for a French fry. "I don't think Mrs. Tancredi would recognize 'tough and cool' as a good thing. She might decide that you were casing the joint. She watches a lot of television, and she's got a vivid imagination."

"You're taking all the fun out of it." He sounded so disgruntled that Elizabeth grinned. Seeing that, Donovan leaned across the table, his expression coaxing. "Come on, wouldn't it be exciting to go whizzing down the highway on the back of my bike?"

She set her mouth very primly, her eyes dancing. "I think you're trying to capture a piece of your lost youth."

Donovan stared at her, and that hungry look was back in his eyes. "Would that be so bad? It seems to me that our lost youth was pretty good."

She looked at him, the noisy restaurant fading away, a thousand memories tangling with the present. He was right, but a past together didn't make up to a future.

Donovan leaned back, deliberately breaking the tension that had crept between them. "The problem with you, Beth, is that you're too practical. You wait till I get my bike. You're gonna love it. You done?"

She nodded, dipping her hands in the battered stainless steel bowl of water in the middle of the table and drying them on her napkin. He kept throwing her off balance. One minute they might have been casual friends and the next he was reminding her of all they'd shared in the past.

Donovan dug into his pocket and threw some bills on the table. "Let's get out of here. I bet the arena is going to be packed."

The arena *was* packed, but no one seemed to mind. The crowd swayed back and forth and clapped their hands and lost themselves in the cheerful rhythms of twenty years ago. Memories seemed to float on the air. Every song brought new cheers, and it was impossible not to have a good time.

Donovan's arm around her shoulders seemed perfectly natural, and Elizabeth leaned into him, letting him shield her from occasional jostles, enjoying the feel of his muscular body against hers.

For just a little while, it was almost possible to pretend that it really *was* twenty years ago. She felt young and excited, the whole world opening up in front of her. With Donovan's arm around her, she could do anything.

The concert ended at last with a rollicking chorus in which the entire crowd joined. There was a lot of good-natured jostling and laughter as people began to make their way out of the stadium. Elizabeth allowed the fantasy to stretch as they walked across the parking lot. There was no need for Donovan to keep his arm around her, but it felt so right there.

"We could go out for a late supper, if you'd like."

Somewhere, a small voice cautioned her that she was letting things drift along and she might regret it later, but she ignored the warning. There was magic in the air, and she was going to savor every minute of it.

"I'd like that."

He took her to a small restaurant, full of dimly lit tables and quiet conversations. Looking at the menu, she was surprised to find that she was hungry. It didn't seem possible after all the ribs she'd consumed.

"I think music must burn up a lot of calories." Donovan's comment fit her own thinking so exactly that he might have read her mind. It was a pleasant thought.

"Why don't we split the seafood platter?" she suggested. Her mouth watered at the thought and he laughed at her eager nod.

Once the order was given to the waiter, Donovan leaned back and looked at her, his fingers toying with his silverware. "Did you enjoy yourself?"

"Couldn't you tell? I must have sung fifty-four choruses of every song. Thank you for inviting me. I wouldn't have missed it for the world."

"The pleaure was all mine." The quiet sincerity in his voice brought a flush to her cheeks, and she looked away, feeling very young and deliciously vulnerable. "It brought back a lot of memories."

"I think it did that for just about everyone there."

"A lot of good memories."

Elizabeth looked across the table, her eyes soft. "A lot of good memories."

Their eyes held for a long moment, all the good times they'd had together lying between them like a thick, warm quilt. The waiter was a welcome interruption, at least as far as Elizabeth was concerned. Too much seemed to lay unspoken, things she wasn't sure she wanted to hear.

The meal passed in uncomplicated pleasure. The seafood platter was beautifully prepared and definitely enough for two. She and Donovan squabbled amicably over who ate more than their share. Donovan graciously allowed her to have the last shrimp, she returned the favor by insisting he take the last oyster.

On the road home, Elizabeth felt wonderfully relaxed. It had been so long since the two of them had simply gone out and had fun together. Whenever they went out, there was an underlying purpose to it—something at Michael's school or dining with a client Donovan was designing a building for.

She'd almost forgotten how much fun they'd always had together. She leaned her head back against the smooth leather of the car seat. Outside the fields rushed by in a blur of open spaces. A full moon hung overhead, ghosting the land with pale light. It was nearly summer, but the late-night air was cold. Donovan had turned the heater on low, just enough to make Elizabeth feel pleasantly cosseted. The radio was set to a station playing classical music, and smooth cellos and horns added to the feeling.

She closed her eyes, letting herself imagine—just for a moment—that everything was still perfect between them. They'd never grown apart, love hadn't faded. They were going home to the house they'd built together, full of memories and dreams.

The fantasy was so pleasant that, when Donovan stopped the car, she was surprised to find herself in front of her apartment building.

"You looked very content. What were you thinking?" Donovan's voice was quiet.

Elizabeth hoped that the light from the streetlamp wasn't enough to reveal the flush in her cheeks. "Nothing in particular. I was just thinking how much fun I had this evening. Thank you."

"Maybe we could do it again."

"Maybe." She reached for her purse. "Well, good night."

"I'll walk you to your door."

"That's really not necessary." But the words went unheard. Donovan was already out of the car and walking around to the passenger side. He opened the door and she slid out, murmuring another thank-you.

"You really don't have to do this. It's a very quiet neighborhood."

"It's no problem."

The street was silent. In the late-night hours, everyone was in bed, the lights out. Even the dogs were quiet. Elizabeth walked across the street beside Donovan, his presence looming next to her. Where had all those relaxed feelings gone? Tension crept over her with each step.

They walked upstairs to her apartment and she pulled the keys out of her purse. Donovan took them from her, turning the lock but not opening the door. Elizabeth didn't move. She stared at the door, feeling the tension stretched taut as a wire between them.

Slowly, feeling as if she was fighting herself, she looked at him, her gaze traveling across the broad width of his chest, pausing on the stubborn strength of his chin and the masculine molding of his mouth. When her eyes at last met his, her heart was bumping against her chest and she felt breathless.

His eyes were a warm, liquid gold that looked deep into her soul, pulling out needs she didn't want to know existed. When his hand curled around the back of her neck, she closed her eyes, her palms coming up to rest on his chest but not to push him away. Some dim, half-heard voice said that she was taking too many chances, but the warning was smothered by the feel of Donovan's mouth on hers.

At the first touch of his lips, she felt her knees weaken. It had been so long since she'd felt this way. She leaned into Donovan, opening her mouth to the hard pressure of his. His hand tightened on the back of her neck, tilting her head to his, his other arm circling her waist, lifting her onto her toes, her breasts crushed against his chest.

His mouth was warm and hard, demanding and receiving total surrender. His tongue traced the ridge of her teeth before sliding past to explore the softness of her mouth. Elizabeth moaned, her body melding to his, her arms circling his neck, her fingers burrowing into the silky blackness of his hair.

His tongue fenced with hers—touching, withdrawing, only to touch again. It was an ancient duel without winner or loser. His tongue stabbed deep into her mouth and then withdrew, only to return. The suggestive rhythm pulsed through her body, like waves breaking in the pit of her stomach.

She was breathless, half fainting when his mouth left hers. The day-old beard that stubbled his chin rasped gently over her face as he kissed his way to her ear. His tongue traced its contours, making every nerve in her body quiver.

"Beth. Let me stay with you."

The words shivered across her skin, tempting her. Her body screamed at her to say yes. She didn't want him to leave. She didn't want to go in to her empty apartment and her lonely bed. She wanted to feel his hands on her, his hardness against her softness. She ached with the wanting. His tongue swirled against the pulse that beat so heavily at the base of her throat. Another minute, another second and she'd be lost.

"Donovan. No." The word was not particularly loud. She could barely force it out past the need to say yes, the need to let him stay.

His mouth stilled against her. For a moment, neither of them moved. She wasn't sure of her answer, and they both knew it. If he ignored her words, held her closer, let his mouth coax her, she'd say yes. He wouldn't be leaving, she wouldn't be sleeping alone tonight. His arms tightened around her and Elizabeth held her breath, half hoping he'd take the decision out of her hands.

"All right." His hands slid reluctantly away, lowering her to stand on her own two feet. Elizabeth's fingers left the softness of his hair reluctantly. She leaned back against the door, uncertain about her knees' ability to hold her. Donovan's eyes simmered gold, stealing what little breath she had left.

"Thank you."

He shrugged, his mouth twisting. "Think nothing of it. I'm insane, of course, but think nothing of it."

"It's too soon. I'm not ready for... for this."

His hand came up to cup her chin, his thumb stroking her soft cheek. "Cold showers are good for my circulation."

Elizabeth turned her face into his hand, leaning against that strength for an instant.

"I'm sorry. I—"

His thumb pressed across her lips, silencing her apology. "Hush. You've got nothing to apologize for. I shouldn't have pushed it. I swore I wouldn't, but you looked so delicious and you tasted even better." He grinned. "The devil made me do it."

Her smile was shaky, but the tension was reduced to a bearable level. Nobody but Donovan had ever been able to spark her emotions so quickly with so little effort. He could take her from passion to laughter in a matter of seconds, leaving her breathless from the ride.

"When can I see you again? Can you make dinner Wednesday night?" It was phrased as a request, but his eyes spoke a demand. Elizabeth ignored the small voice that warned her things were moving too quickly.

"I'd like that." His relief told her he hadn't been as sure of her answer as he'd seemed.

He reached behind her to open the door, easing her inside. "I'll pick you up at seven." He dropped a quick, hard kiss on her mouth that left her tingling, and then pulled the door shut, closing her inside.

Elizabeth leaned against the door, listening to the sound of his footsteps disappearing in the quiet night. She lifted her hand to her mouth, aware of the way her fingers trembled.

She hadn't felt so alive, so wonderfully, marvelously alive in months, years maybe. It was frightening, it was fabulous. She felt like a teenager, with everything life had to offer all spread out in front of her. And all the frightening, wonderful feelings that boiled inside were because Donovan was back in her life.

She closed her eyes, pushing aside the thought. She wasn't going to think about it now. For now, it was enough that she was happy, that life was exciting. She would think about the whys and wherefores another time. Right now, all she wanted to do was go to bed and dream about the day just past.

Wednesday night seemed aeons away.

Wednesday night eventually came, as did Friday night and Saturday and Sunday and the next Tuesday. And every one of those days, Donovan filled her life with picnics and dinners and movies. On the days she didn't see him, Elizabeth thought about him and looked forward to the next time they'd be together.

He courted her with beautiful flowers and wonderful late-spring days. Even without Carol's blunt summation of the situation—"The man obviously wants you back, dummy"—Elizabeth could hardly doubt his intentions.

He cared for her, she knew that and she cared for him. In her weak moments she might even admit that she might be falling in love with him again. But only in a weak moment and only to herself.

Nearly two weeks after their first date, Elizabeth was putting her notes together for a redecorating project. It was near the end of the day and she was looking forward to getting home. Her tiny office was stuffy and the warm sun had been trying to coax her outside all day.

Donovan had said he might come by this evening. He'd been very mysterious, promising that he'd have something to show her. Her mouth softened and her pencil slowed. Donovan. In a couple of weeks, he'd somehow become central to her life again, and she wasn't even sure what she wanted out of a relationship with him. After all, he was practically her *ex*-husband.

"Elizabeth." Mrs. Tancredi's voice interrupted Elizabeth's thinking. She looked up to find her manager's short, stout figure standing in the doorway, her plump features set in an expression of stern disapproval.

"There's a man here who says you're expecting him."

"A man?"

Mrs. Tancredi sniffed. "I nearly called security but, on the off chance that you do know him, I decided to wait."

Elizabeth stood up and edged her way around the desk. Donovan? He hadn't said anything about picking her up at work. Besides, if it was Donovan, why on earth would Mrs. Tancredi consider calling security? He was a respected businessman. He looked respectable if you didn't notice the wild streak that sometimes sparkled in his eyes. He was—

She came to a screeching halt between a sofa covered in green-and-blue plaid and a chair covered in brown tufted tweed. He was standing a few feet away staring at an abstract print. From the way his head was tilted, he seemed to be considering the possibility that it was upside-down. It was Donovan all right, but not a Donovan she'd ever seen before.

Her astonished eyes started at his feet and worked their way up. Size twelve feet were encased in black boots decorated with gold chains. Worn blue jeans disappeared into their tops. The jeans fit as if they'd been molded to him, outlining the muscles in his long thighs. A black leather belt cinched his waist, and a black T-shirt disappeared into the waistband. His shoulders looked enormous in a leather jacket. The jacket could only be described as "bad boy black." If the clothes weren't enough, he'd combed his thick hair back off his forehead. Not only combed it back—he'd greased it so that every heavy wave caught the light.

He turned, meeting her stunned eyes. Elizabeth was aware of Mrs. Tancredi standing behind her. She wondered vaguely if the other woman was depending on her for protection.

"Hi, Babe."

Babe? "Donovan?"

His eyes held a wicked spark that caused a convulsive bump in her chest. He should have looked ridiculous. He *did* look ridiculous. Why did he have to look so sexy, too?

"You ready to blow this joint? I've got my new wheels." He pulled out a pair of wraparound sunglasses and slid them on his nose.

"New—wheels?" she said weakly.

"Yeah? You ready? This place is like a tomb." He looked around him, his mouth set contemptuously. Elizabeth bit her lip to hold back a giggle.

"Have you gone nuts?"

"If you don't know this man, Elizabeth, I really think it would be best to call security." Mrs. Tancredi's hurried whisper brought another choked giggle out of Elizabeth.

"I know him, Mrs. Tancredi. Or at least, I think I know him. I don't think it will be necessary to call security."

"Hey, Babe. I don't want to hang around this place too long. It's not good for my image, ya know what I mean?" He hunched his shoulders inside the jacket, giving the impression that he might be allergic to the conservative tastes that surrounded him.

"I know what you mean. Let me get my purse."

She ignored her manager's muttered protest and hurried back to her office. Her notes were only half finished, but she didn't give them a glance. She grabbed her purse and hurried out.

Neither Donovan nor Mrs. Tancredi had moved during the few minutes she'd been gone. Donovan still wore the sunglasses, his mouth was still molded into an expression of insolent contempt. Mrs. Tancredi was still watching him as if expecting him to whip out a switchblade at any moment and start slashing the stock. It was all Elizabeth could do to keep from laughing.

"I'm ready."

Donovan hunched his shoulders again. "Let's make tracks."

He slung an arm over her shoulders and pulled her close. "All this respectability is makin' me itch."

Elizabeth waved to Mrs. Tancredi, pretending not to see her completely scandalized expression. As soon as they'd turned a corner and were out of sight, Donovan reached up to take off the sunglasses.

"Couldn't see a thing," he muttered.

Elizabeth collapsed against him, giggling. "You idiot. What is all this in aid of?"

He looked hurt. "Don't you think I look tough?" He guided her wavering footsteps toward the exit. "I was hoping to impress you with my macho image."

"Well, you certainly impressed my boss."

"Was that your boss?"

"*Was* may be the operative word. After this, she may decide I'm too wild to risk having me in the store."

"You can always tell her that you only went with me to protect the store's image. She looks like the type to love a little noble sacrifice."

"Maybe. What are you doing here? I thought you were going to come by my house later tonight."

"I couldn't wait to show you."

"Show me what?" But she had a sinking sensation that she knew what.

Donovan's grin was appealingly boyish, his eyes excited as he ushered her through the door. Parked illegally at the curb was a shiny, new motorcycle. Bright red with black trim, it looked enormous, fast and dangerous.

"Isn't it great? I just picked it up."

"It's very—red." She hoped she sounded enthused enough.

"I thought I could follow you home and wait while you changed, and then maybe we could go for a ride. I bought you a helmet." His expression was coaxing. He was well aware of her doubts about two-wheeled transportation.

She looked at him and then looked at the bike. It *did* look reassuringly large. Besides, Donovan was an adult. He wasn't going to be doing crazy things on the highway. And, though she was reluctant to admit it, there was something exciting about whizzing along with the wind in your face.

An hour later she climbed gingerly onto the back of the motorcycle. The helmet that covered her head made her feel like an extra in a science fiction movie, and once on the bike, it seemed an amazingly long way to the ground. Donovan had clearly bought the machine with his measurements in mind, not hers.

On the road, she was grateful for the solidity of the machine between her legs and even more grateful for the hard strength of Donovan's body in front of her. The countryside flashed by, the wind roaring in her ears. She'd expected to be nervous. She hadn't been on a motorcycle since Donovan had sold his right after they got married. She'd underestimated her confidence in the man who controlled the machine.

"Like it?" He had to shout to be heard, and she caught just the edge of his grin as he turned his head.

It had been years since she'd seen him so excited about something that didn't have to do with his profession. That alone made this expensive toy acceptable.

"It's great."

Late spring turned to early summer, and the weather remained bright and perfect. Elizabeth couldn't remember the last time she'd felt so happy and alive. She tried not to analyze what was happening or ask herself what the future might hold. For now, it was enough that Donovan was in her life, a large, warm presence that somehow completed something vital to her happiness.

Michael watched his parents without comment. Carol was not so tactful, and expressed her opinion anytime the subject came up. Clearly, Elizabeth and Donovan were destined to be together, and Elizabeth was a fool if she didn't just face the fact and accept her fate. Elizabeth wasn't quite ready to admit any such thing, but she couldn't deny that she was happier than she'd been in a long time.

Chapter 12

"Would you like some coffee?" The moment the invitation was spoken, Elizabeth wondered why she'd made it.

"Thanks."

She smiled, hoping her nervousness didn't show, and opened the door wide. Donovan stepped into the living room, bringing all the tension in with him.

"I'll just go put it on. It won't take a minute." She escaped to the kitchen, wishing there was a door to shut between them. Her hands shook as she opened cupboards and got out cups.

She'd been nuts to invite him in on tonight of all nights. In the six weeks they'd been dating, she'd avoided having him in her apartment, and she'd flatly refused his invitations to have dinner at their old home. There were too many memories there and there was too much intimacy here. She wasn't sure where their relationship was going, but she wasn't going to rush. Whatever happened, this time around she was going to give it a lot of thought. She would be thirty-seven on her next birthday. A mature woman by anybody's standards.

She put water on to heat and leaned against the counter, taking deep breaths. She couldn't see Donovan from here, but she could feel him. He was only a few feet away, and the tension that had been building between them reached out to catch her in its web.

It was that stupid movie. She'd been crazy to suggest that they go see a film billed as a passionate love story. The love scenes had been enough to make the screen threaten to melt. She'd sat through them, her arms held against her side, avoiding any contact with Donovan's muscular shoulder.

It wasn't as if there hadn't been sexual tension between them right along. She knew Donovan wanted her, and physically, she wanted him. But she wasn't jumping into anything, and he'd respected that wish. When he kissed her good-night, she could feel his tension and she knew it would take only a word from her to change everything.

Tonight, she wanted to say that word. But she wasn't going to give in to temporary desire sparked by a sensuous movie. She was going to remain rational and calm. If and when she slept with Donovan it was going to be after they'd discussed their relationship and clarified just what each of them wanted from it. That was the adult, sensible way to handle things.

She was so absorbed in her thoughts that she wasn't aware she was no longer alone until Donovan's mouth settled on the nape of her neck, which had been left bare by her chignon. A shiver ran through her, leaving her knees weak. Her logical thoughts scattered in a thousand directions as his lips moved against her tender skin, finding every nerve ending and bringing it to life.

"Donovan." She'd intended his name to be a protest, but it came out as more of a whimper.

"Hmm?" His teeth nibbled gently at the curve where her neck and shoulder met, one hand tugging aside the neckline of her blouse to give him more room.

"Donovan. I want you—" She forgot what she was saying when his mouth found her ear. His tongue traced every curve, his teeth nipped at her earlobe. If it hadn't been for the counter in front of her and the length of his body behind her, Elizabeth would have melted to the floor.

"I want you, too." His kisses moved down the side of her neck. One of his hands found its way to her waist, sliding upward to cup the weight of her breast, his thumb brushing across the tip, bringing it singing to life. The thin cotton of her blouse was no protection.

"I mean I—" What did she mean? She couldn't think.

He slid his other hand downward, boldly cupping the warmth between her legs, drawing her backward until she was pressed against him. She drew in a quick, hard breath. His arousal pressed against her was a potent call for her to abandon logic and caution. How could she think when his hands held her so close, reminding her of how long it had been since he'd touched her like this.

She didn't protest as he turned her into his arms, his hands sliding across her back. Her head tilted back, her eyes closed. Her hands came up to press against his chest, somehow losing their impetus and sliding up to his shoulders.

"Beth."

No, don't say anything. Kiss me. Make me stop thinking.

"Beth, look at me." His voice was husky and she could feel his tension.

He wanted her. She could feel the proof of that like a hot brand against her stomach.

"Beth, open your eyes."

Her lashes fluttered and then slowly lifted. She wanted him to kiss her, to make her forget all her logic and caution. His eyes blazed down at her, hunger and need mixing in a potent combination.

"Is this what you want?"

Why was he making her decide? Didn't he know that all he had to do was kiss her and she'd melt? She didn't want to think about what she was doing.

"Beth, I ache with wanting you. But, if this isn't what you want, I'll walk out of here right now."

Her hands tightened on his shoulders. He wasn't going to let her pretend that she didn't know what was happening. He was going to make her face her choice head-on. If she said she wanted him to stay, he would make love to her. Their relationship would change, and there would be no going back to the quasi-safety of the past weeks.

"Are you going to stand there all night, or are you going to kiss me?" She could hardly get the words past the nervous lump in her throat. The golden flare of his eyes made her pulse jump, and the reckless grin that slashed his face stole her breath.

He bent, sweeping her off her feet to cradle her against his chest, his mouth capturing hers. With her last remnant of sanity, Beth reached out to shut the stove off. Somehow, she didn't think they'd be wanting any coffee.

He carried her through the apartment, his long strides covering the short distance to her dark, cool bedroom. He set her down. His hands cupped her face, and he kissed her over and over again until she was breathless.

The desire that had been building between them during the past weeks bubbled up, full and rich, a driving force that would not be denied. She fumbled with the buttons of his shirt, sighing with pleasure when her palms were at last able to press against his skin. Crisp, black curls covered hard muscles.

Donovan tugged at the shirt impatiently, his attention on Elizabeth's blouse. She reluctantly let him pull the blouse over her head. Her bra was quickly removed, tossed into some corner of the room.

A sob caught in the back of her throat as he drew her toward him again. The crisp, curling hair brushed against her swollen nipples, teasing, building the fire higher. She would have melted onto his chest but he held her away, tantalizing, moving her so that her nipples were barely touching him.

"Damn you." The words left her on a moan, and she heard him laugh just before he gave her what she wanted. She sobbed as he pushed her back onto the bed, lying over her, his chest crushing her breasts with delicious weight.

His mouth found hers, his tongue stabbing inside, tasting her, making her his. His fingers fumbled with the side fastening on her skirt, stripping the garment away. He slid his hand beneath her bottom, cupping her through the fragile silk of her panties, arching her upward as his jean-clad thigh slid between her legs.

It was too much and it wasn't nearly enough. Elizabeth was filled with need. Only Donovan had touched her like this. Surely no other man would ever know just the way to set her on fire. His head bent and his mouth captured the swollen peak of one breast, his teeth nibbling at the tender flesh. His thigh pressed upward, giving her a tantalizing glimpse of what she really wanted.

Her fingers clenched around his shoulders, her breath leaving her on soft moans. He held her helpless, leaving her no choice but to feel everything he was doing, every demand he was making. She pushed at his shoulders, her movements weak. She didn't want him to stop the delicious assault, but she wanted more—needed more—had to have it.

Donovan dragged his mouth from her breast, his breathing as ragged as hers. Elizabeth's fingers found the waist of his jeans. The snap gave easily, and her hand slid inside.

Donovan shuddered as her fingers closed around him, cool against the fiery heat of his arousal.

The jeans hit the floor with a soft thud. Elizabeth's panties followed, a whisper of light without sound. His legs slid between hers, his skin fiery hot. But no hotter than the passion he'd created inside her. She felt him against her, hot and hard, and she forgot how to breathe.

"Look at me, Beth." His voice seemed to rasp in his throat.

Elizabeth dragged her eyes open to stare into the green gold depths of his. The passion she read there only stoked the flames higher. No one had ever wanted her the way Donovan did. Body and soul, every inch of her belonging to him. No one would ever want her like that again.

"Donovan." The name was a whisper, a breath. It said everything and told him nothing.

His eyes holding hers, he slid forward, possessing and being possessed. Elizabeth arched, her breath leaving her on a sob as he filled the aching emptiness within. It had been so long. She'd almost convinced herself that it hadn't been this wonderful, this right. After the first, heavy thrust, he rested against her a moment, giving her body time to adjust, drawing on all his control.

He started to move, bracing his weight on his hands, his eyes never leaving her face. She could feel herself spinning out of control. Her hands slid up and down his back, seeking something to cling to, something to slow the spinning madness that beckoned her. There was nothing but Donovan's sweat-dampened skin, the muscles rippling beneath her fingers.

She wanted it to last forever. It had to end soon or she'd fly into a million pieces, never to be put back together again. Her head turned back and forth, scattering golden-blond hair across the pale blue bedspread. She couldn't breathe, couldn't think. All she could do was feel. Tension coiled low in her belly, each thrusting motion tightening the coil until she was begging him to end it.

"Please, please, please."

And he gave her what she sought.

He thrust deeply, seeming to reach to the very core of her, and the coil sprang apart, shattering the tension that held her together. Donovan's mouth caught her cry, swallowing it, absorbing it into himself, just as he seemed to have absorbed her into himself. Elizabeth's nails dug into his shoulders, her body tightening around him, demanding that he follow her into the spinning maelstrom that threatened to swallow her and drown her in pleasure. She tasted his groan of surrender, felt his shudder of completion and was filled with a purely feminine pleasure. In the taking, he had been taken. In the giving, he had received.

For a long time, there was no sound in the room beyond the ragged rhythm of their breathing. She murmured a protest when he shifted, lifting his weight from her. If he moved, she might have to acknowledge that the rest of the world existed. Right now, she didn't want to think of anything beyond this room, beyond this night.

"I'll squash you." He kissed her softly and lifted himself away.

"What a nice way to go." The words came out on a yawn, and she sensed more than saw his grin. She didn't open her eyes as the bed shook with his movements. He pulled down the covers and then bent to scoop her up and lay her against the sheets, her head on the pillow. She frowned but, before she could voice her protest, Donovan slid beneath the covers, his long body a warm contrast to the cool cotton sheets.

Elizabeth hadn't realized how the tension had been building until it was finally broken. She hadn't wanted to acknowledge the strong pull that lay between them. She snuggled against Donovan's side, more relaxed than she had been in months—years.

There were things that needed to be said, but right now, she couldn't think what they were. This changed everything, but she didn't want to think about the changes. She didn't want to think about anything except the delicious peace that filled her and the warmth of Donovan next to her. She drifted to sleep, aware of Donovan shifting her into a more comfortable position, his hand stroking the tangled hair back off her forehead.

She couldn't remember the last time she'd felt so safe and protected. Perhaps it had been the last time she'd gone to sleep in Donovan's arms.

It was not long past dawn when Donovan awoke. Sunlight streamed in through the lightweight curtains, spilling across the bed, promising a beautiful day. He didn't have to wonder why the sunlight was coming in at the wrong angle. Elizabeth's body was a warm, welcome weight along him. He knew exactly where he was.

For the first time in months, he was home. If Elizabeth was in his arms, that was home. It didn't matter in whose bed. It wouldn't matter if it was another state, another country or another planet. She snuggled closer to his side, one leg thrown across his thighs, one arm sprawled over his chest.

His smile held an element of pain. It had been so long. How could he have been such a fool to let this slip through his fingers, even for an instant? Having come so close to losing her forever, he'd never lose sight of just how precious she was. Without her, his life was only half-complete. She was what made everything worthwhile. His arms tightened around her. Now that he had her back, he'd never let go.

She'd been so sweetly responsive last night, demanding and giving, taking everything he had to offer and returning it to him ten times over. He nuzzled his face into her hair, inhaling all the remembered scents, refreshing his memory, savoring the peace of the moment.

These past few months had been miserable. But it was going to be all right now. They belonged together, and last night had shown that they both knew it. He kissed her forehead, kissing his way across each delicate eyebrow.

Elizabeth stirred. Donovan planted soft kisses down her nose before settling on her mouth. Her lips were soft and sleepy. She came awake under his mouth, her fingers flexing against his chest, reminding him of a cat kneading its paws with contentment. He pulled her closer, feeling himself growing hard beneath the weight of her leg. She felt it too, shifting her thigh to rub against him.

Their lovemaking was slow. Last night's driving pressure had been eased, and they took their time rediscovering each other. The pleasure was no less intense, but it was not the shattering force of the night before. Afterward, they lay silent for a while, savoring the delight in not waking up alone.

Donovan dropped a kiss on her temple, tasting the gentle pulse that beat there. "Let's go home. I want you back in our bed, in our home." He murmured the words against her ear, his contentment so deep that it took him a moment to sense her sudden stiffening.

He went still, feeling all the contentment drain away. Elizabeth pushed against him and he released her, watching as she sat up, the sheet drawn over her breasts. His heart was beating a little too hard and a little too fast. He had the sinking feeling that things were not going quite as he'd thought.

"Beth? What is it? You're coming back to me, aren't you?"

She looked away, but he'd seen the answer in her eyes. He swung his legs to the floor, sitting on the edge of the bed with his back to her, not wanting her to see the shattered look that must be in his eyes. Behind him, he felt her get out of bed, heard her open her closet door and knew she was putting something on.

"Donovan?" Her voice was hesitant, and he winced at the concern he heard. He wanted and needed her, but he was damned if he'd beg for her. He didn't want her pity. He stood up and walked around the bed, magnificently naked. He stooped to pick up his jeans, and stepped into them, keeping his expression rigidly under control.

"Donovan, don't be angry with me. Please."

He jerked the zipper up and shrugged. "I'm not angry. I shouldn't have assumed that last night meant you'd be coming back. I suppose these days, a night in bed together is no big deal." He reached for his shirt, but she got to it before he did, holding on to it when he would have pulled it away.

"Please. I don't want you to think it didn't mean anything to me. It's just too soon."

The catch in her voice made him look at her face, even though he only wanted to take his hurt and walk away. He wanted to go somewhere and beat his fists against a wall until that pain took away the ache in his chest.

But there was pain in her eyes, too, and he couldn't just walk away. With an effort, he shrugged, forcing a half smile.

"Don't worry about it. I assumed too much. You've probably got things to do, so if you'll give me my shirt, I'll get out of your way."

She shook her head, and his ache intensified. Did she know how gorgeous she was? Standing there in a peacock blue silk robe, her hair like a tangled, golden curtain on her shoulders, his shirt clutched to her breasts.

"I don't want you to leave until we've talked this out."

"What's to talk about? We made love, I made some assumptions."

"Don't be so damned pigheaded!" Anger flashed in her eyes. "Talk to me. I don't want to hear all this macho claptrap. I want you to talk to me, and I want you to listen to what I have to say. This is exactly the garbage that got us in trouble in the first place. If you won't talk to me, how can I know what you're feeling?''

"If I have to tell you what I'm feeling, then what's the sense? If two people are close enough, they should know what the other feels.''

"It doesn't always work that way. If it did, you would have realized a long time ago how unhappy I was.''

He stared at her, his gut full of turmoil. He couldn't answer her because she was right. He should have known and have done something, changed something, become something else. Only he'd been blind to her needs—so blind that he'd lost her.

"What do you want me to say?'' If the question was sullen, he couldn't help it. A man didn't go around laying his soul bare, not even to the woman he loved more than life itself.

She took a deep breath, and her fingers tightened around his shirt. "I don't want you to say anything. I just want you to listen. Last night meant a great deal to me. But I'm not ready to just pack up and move back in with you. I've never lived alone. If I give this all up and move back in with you, I'll never know if I can make it on my own.''

He threw his hand out in an impatient gesture. "Don't give me that stuff about finding yourself.''

"It's not 'stuff.' It's something that's very important to me. If you care about me, then you'll want me to do this.''

She stood there, dignified despite her tangled hair and bare feet. Her eyes met his evenly, demanding his support.

Donovan stared at her for a long time without saying anything. If he had any hopes of winning her back to him, he had to give her this chance—not grudgingly as if he were doing her a favor but openly and generously. He had to give her honest support in finding her dreams. Perhaps if he did that, she'd realize that *he* was one of her dreams.

"All right." He reached out to touch her cheek. "I really want you to be happy, Beth. I guess I'm just not sure where we go from here."

Her smile was shaky, but she leaned her face into his hand. "Couldn't we just go on as we have been? Dating and things."

"After last night, I don't think I could go back to leaving you at your door at night. There isn't enough cold water in the whole state of Indiana to keep me cool enough."

She flushed. "I didn't mean to go back to being platonic."

He widened his eyes, his expression shocked. "Are you suggesting that we have an affair, Ms. Sinclair? How thoroughly risqué of you."

"Wouldn't you like to have an affair with me? We haven't had one in twenty years." Her eyes coaxed him, and Donovan felt himself melting. His hand slid from her cheek to the back of her neck, pulling her closer until her bare feet were tucked between his, the silk of her robe brushing his jeans.

"I can't imagine anything that would give me more pleasure."

If all their problems weren't solved by their talk, at least some of them were eased. The summer days spun by in a haze of Indiana heat. The farmers talked about it being one of the best summers they'd had in years, but Elizabeth and Donovan wouldn't have noticed if a tornado had flattened every cornfield in a hundred-mile radius.

Michael spent his time going to or returning from camping trips, but when he was home, he seemed pleased with the direction his parents were heading. Elizabeth hadn't been sure how he'd feel about the two of them being together yet not together, but he seemed to take it in stride. He was more concerned with how often he could talk his father into letting him borrow the motorcycle.

That motorcycle was another worry of Elizabeth's. She acknowledged the exhilarating thrill of riding down the highway with the wind in your face, but she was still uneasy with the idea of Donovan riding it, let alone their son. She also knew it would be foolish to forbid Michael. He was nineteen, and there was nothing more natural in the world than that he should be excited by such a nifty toy. She had to trust in helmets, good sense and luck to keep both her men safe.

Luck, at least, seemed to be running on her side these days. She was doing so well with the interior decorating service at Mason's that the owner had moved her into a bigger office, increased her salary, and was giving her a percentage of the sales she made. Remembrance was growing. There were several small developments going up on the edge of town. Donovan had designed three of them, and he freely admitted to pulling some strings to get her hired to decorate the model homes.

At first, Elizabeth was uneasy with the idea of Donovan using his influence to get her work, but he pointed out that she still had to prove herself. If she did a lousy job, the blame would fall on her head. He laughed when she slugged him with a pillow and announced that she never did a lousy job. The resulting pillow fight ended with her pinned deliciously beneath him, paying a forfeit in kisses, a penalty she didn't mind a bit.

That was the best part of summer. If there were still subjects that she and Donovan didn't discuss, there were a million others to talk about. The recent past was taboo, as was the more distant future. Neither one of them wanted to rock the careful balance they'd achieved.

She and Donovan spent time together three or four times a week. Sometimes he took her out; sometimes she cooked dinner at her apartment. Once or twice he insisted on cooking dinner for her at their old home, but there were too many memories there for either of them to be entirely comfortable. Everything had changed too much. By unspoken consent, they didn't make love in their old bed. Elizabeth couldn't have said why, but it just didn't feel right.

As far as she was concerned, things were going well. She had her job, her son and her relationship with Donovan was getting stronger.

But the one constant in life is change, and nothing stays the same for long. While Elizabeth was enjoying her life, Donovan was marking time, waiting for the moment when they could get on with the real business of living. It was inevitable that their two goals were on a collision course.

Chapter 13

Donovan paced across the apartment, his movements restless, the expression in his eyes abstract. Elizabeth sat cross-legged on the sofa, a small pile of mending on her lap, her fingers weaving the needle through a button, stitching it onto a blue chambray shirt.

"I told you the laundry would do that." There was an edge to his voice, and he took a deep breath before going on. "There's no reason for you to mend my shirt."

"I don't mind. I have to do some of my own things, anyway, and this is lousy weather for a picnic but great weather for mending." She glanced out the window at the rain and shrugged.

"Yeah." Donovan moved to the window and stared out. A distance away, lightning cracked. On the street below, the rain washed the pavement clean and made even the oldest car look shiny and new. Behind him, the small living room was the picture of tranquillity. When the rain had made a picnic in the country impossible, they'd spread a sheet on Beth's floor and eaten their picnic there.

He hadn't minded, because any time spent with Elizabeth was time well spent. After the meal, they sat on the floor and talked—about a new project he was designing, about a house she was decorating, about Michael's second year at college, which lay just around the corner. He'd felt well fed and content. So why was he so restless now?

He didn't have to look far for the answer. Glancing at Elizabeth, he could feel the tension tightening in the pit of his stomach. She sat with his shirt spread across her lap, cheerfully sewing a button on. She looked the very picture of wifely devotion. It was infuriating.

He didn't want her to play at being wife. He didn't care if she mended or cooked or cleaned house—he could hire someone to do any or all of those things. He wanted her back in his home—*their* home, dammit! He didn't want to pick her up for dates and then come back to her place for wonderful, semi-illicit sex.

He was kicking forty in the teeth, and he was too old for these games. He wanted a home again, a wife, and the support and love that went with commitment. He'd made a lot of mistakes before, but he wouldn't repeat them. From now on his marriage came first.

The words hadn't been spoken but there could be no doubt that they loved each other. Maybe their love would be even stronger than before. He'd tried his best to be supportive—he wanted Elizabeth to be happy, he was proud of her career. She certainly didn't have to give it up if she moved back where she belonged. They'd hire a housekeeper, a cook, anything. He just wanted her home again.

"Is something wrong?" The quiet question made him realize how long he'd been staring out at the rain. He turned and looked at her.

She'd finished his shirt, and it lay neatly across the arm of the sofa. A silk negligee lay across her lap, the needle suspended over a delicate strap, torn loose from the bodice. He'd done that when she'd been in a teasing mood. She'd tantalized him, stripping off his clothes and then letting her fingers stroke his heated skin until he thought he'd go mad. He had a dim memory of reaching for her, of hearing the fragile silk tear, but then she'd been sprawled across the bed and he'd been over her, within her.

She'd played the mistress that night, driving him wild with need. Now she sat there playing wife, her fingers deft with the needle, her concern for how he was feeling. He was tired of playing at marriage. He wanted a real marriage, a commitment, promises.

"Donovan?" She looked at him, sensing his mood but uncertain of the cause.

The thought that if he pressed the issue he might lose her slipped in, but he pushed it away. They couldn't keep straddling the fence. *He* couldn't straddle the fence anymore. One of them had to take the first step.

"You've been staring out that window for the past twenty minutes. Are you watching for floodwaters?" He didn't even hear her mild joke. Shoving his hands in his pockets, he leaned back against the wall.

"Do you ever think about what we're doing?"

"At the moment, we're not doing much of anything. I'm mending and you're staring. Not much to think about." Her attention returned to the negligee.

"I don't mean right this minute." His tone was impatient and he saw her fingers still as if she was beginning to realize that something was truly wrong. "Do you ever think about what we're doing overall?"

"Well, I'm not sure we're making great contributions to history, if that's what you mean."

He pulled his hands out of his pockets and strode across the room to sit next to her. She didn't look at him as he set aside her mending before taking her hands.

"Beth, look at me." Her eyes came to his reluctantly, and it didn't take a genius to read the wariness in her face. "Do you ever think about our relationship? Where it's been, where it's going?"

"Of course I do. It's going very well, don't you think?" Her eyes pleaded with him to agree. *Don't rock the boat.*

"No." Hurt flared in her eyes and he sought to soften the blunt denial. "It isn't that I don't love spending time with you, Beth. You know I do. But I want something more. We can't just drift along like this forever."

"I never said anything about forever."

"How long, Beth? We've been playing this game for two months. How much longer?"

"I don't know." She turned her head away, tugging on her hands, but he refused to release her. "I can't give you a schedule!" The quick flare of anger faded as quickly as it had come, and she looked at him, her eyes pleading.

His fingers tightened over hers, trying to convey how important this was to him. "I want a commitment. We're married, we've got a grown son. I don't want to play at having an affair anymore. I want to have you in my home, in my bed. Our home. Our bed. I want your clothes next to mine in the closet and your underwear drying in the shower. I want to live with you again. I want a marriage again."

"Let's give it some more time."

"I don't want to give it some more time. I've been without you for almost a year. I don't want to live without you another day. Dammit, Beth! You love me. I know you do. Why are you so reluctant to come home again?"

She pulled her hands away and twisted them together in her lap, staring down at them. "I'm afraid that if I move back in, things might go back to what they were, with you gone all the time and me filling my days with committees and tea parties. I don't want that again."

"Neither do I, and I promise it won't be that way. I admit I lost track of priorities for a while. I *wasn't* spending enough time at home. But I wouldn't risk losing you again. Don't you want a home with me? Maybe...maybe even another child? We're not too old to think about it. We used to talk about having another baby."

"We always decided to wait until everything was right before having another child." Her voice was thick with tears.

"That was another mistake, but it's not too late to change things now. If you want, we could try. And if you don't want another baby, that's okay, too. *You're* the most important thing. Please, Beth, say you'll come home with me."

He stared at her down-bent head, feeling each beat of his heart, hearing every drop of rain that fell outside. Everything depended on her answer. She *had* to come home. Anything else was unbearable. The silence stretched, and Donovan's nerves stretched along with it. Why didn't she say something?

"I can't." A solitary tear fell onto her clasped hands.

Donovan stared at her, feeling the world rock beneath him. Hurt and rage stirred inside, but he swallowed hard, reminding himself that anger never did any good.

"Why not?" Despite his best efforts, the question sounded cold and angry.

Beth lifted her head, tears sparkling on her cheeks as she reached out to him, laying her palm on his arm, feeling the iron-hard muscles there.

"I'm just not ready, Donovan."

"I see." The anger in his eyes told her that he didn't see at all. "Moving back in with me would entail sacrificing too much, is that it?"

"No."

"That's what you're implying."

"No, it isn't!" She stopped and drew a deep breath, trying to find the words to describe the confusion she felt when she thought about being his wife again. "I met you when I was sixteen. By the time I turned seventeen, we were married and I was expecting Michael. Even when you were in Vietnam, I wasn't alone because there was Michael depending on me and I had to hold things together for him and for you. You came home and I didn't have to be strong anymore. I quit work and devoted myself to being a wife and mother. I'm not ashamed of that, but now I've got something different. I'm really living alone. No one depends on me for anything.''

"The problem with that is that no one is there to care if you don't come home some night. And there's no one to take care of you if you hurt yourself and no one to be excited for you if you get a big job. There's no one, Beth. Is that really what you want?''

The picture he painted was bleak, and she felt anger flare up, putting her on the defensive. "There's also no one to tell me what to do, or to read the paper at the breakfast table or to expect me to pick up dry cleaning without even thanking me. I can do what I want, when I want, without answering to anyone else.''

He stood up and she followed suit, unwilling to let him tower over her. Not that he didn't tower quite a bit even when she was on her feet, but she felt a little less overwhelmed. His eyes were cold.

"Fine. You stay here, without any responsibilities to anyone but yourself. I hope you'll be happy. But I can't play that game anymore. I want a commitment, Beth. I want a wife and a family, someone to share things with. If you change your mind, you know where to find me.''

She watched in shock as he pulled on his jacket and picked up his gloves and helmet.

"Where are you going?''

"Home. I can't play anymore.''

"I'm not playing.''

"No?'' He shrugged, drawing on his gloves, not looking at her. "Call it what you want. I want you to be happy, but I can't live on the fringes of your life. If this is what you need to be happy, I wish you luck. Count me out.''

"You're not going to bully me into making a decision like this."

"I'm not trying to. Goodbye, Elizabeth."

The door shut behind him. The quiet snick of the latch sounded more final than if he'd slammed it. *Elizabeth*. He'd called her Elizabeth. For the past few weeks she'd been Beth again. But just now he'd called her Elizabeth. *Goodbye, Elizabeth.* As if Beth wasn't someone he'd say goodbye to.

Outside, she heard the faint roar of the motorcycle engine and then it faded away, leaving only the rain. She turned slowly, feeling very old, and walked to the window. She saw shiny trees, shiny street, shiny cars, but he was gone. She let the curtain fall and crossed to the sofa, reaching down to pick up his shirt. It felt soft and supple in her hands. If she drew a deep breath, she could catch a whiff of his after-shave. She blinked against the tears that threatened to fall.

"Bull pucky." Carol spooned sugar into her cup of tea and stirred it vigorously.

Elizabeth blinked, startled by her friend's emphatic opinion. "Well, that's succinct. Would you mind telling me what you mean? What, precisely, do you think is bull pucky?"

"All of it." Carol set her spoon down with a thump. "Your whole line of reasoning."

"You think I'm wrong to want a little more time alone?" Elizabeth's voice was stiff. She'd been so sure that Carol would understand.

"I didn't say you were wrong. I said your reasoning was—"

"Yes, I know. Bull pucky." She rubbed her forehead, fighting the urge to put her head on the table and cry like a baby. It had been almost two weeks since Donovan had walked so quietly out of her apartment and out of her life. The first few days, she'd been angry, then she'd been hurt.

Now, the anger and the hurt were all tangled up together in a big ball that had settled at the bottom of her stomach.

"I didn't think I was asking for all that much. A few more months, maybe. Is that so bad?"

"With some men and some relationships that would be just fine, but Donovan isn't some men. You're asking for more than he can give."

"If he loves me, he should be able to understand. I'm so afraid he'll take me for granted again—that things will go back to the way they were."

"If *you* love *him*, you should be able to understand what he needs. Loving somebody doesn't automatically make a person omniscient."

"I know that. But after all these years, you'd think he could trust me, that he'd know I wanted this time because it was important."

"Beth, almost a year ago, you walked out on him. Even if he understands why now, even if he's willing to admit that you had good cause, it's bound to shake a man's faith a little."

"But—"

"But nothing. You expect too much of him, Beth. Donovan may be the best thing I've seen in pants in the past twenty years, but he's human. You don't make many allowances for that."

"What do you mean? I don't expect him to be more than human."

Carol took a swallow of her tea, her thin face calm despite Elizabeth's anger. "Don't you?"

"No. I just expect him to be fair."

"Right away you're asking more than most people ever get. Life isn't always fair, and both you and I know it. If life was fair, you'd have my metabolism so you could eat another cookie without looking like the Goodyear blimp, and I'd have your looks." Carol crunched into a cookie to emphasize her point.

"This has got nothing to do with metabolism or looks. This has to do with loving someone and wanting what's best for them."

"Donovan does love you. The problem here is that you think you need something he can't give you: the time you need. But he *needs* a commitment from you. He needs to know you love him enough to be his wife again. Quite frankly, I don't see what the problem is. Do you think he's going to ask you to give up your job?"

"No, he wouldn't do that. He knows how much I enjoy it."

"Is it the house? You don't want to live in the old place again?"

"No. Besides, I'm sure he wouldn't mind selling it if it bothered me."

"Then what's the big deal?"

Elizabeth ran the tip of her finger through some spilled sugar, creating small pathways and then destroying them. What *was* the big deal?

"Don't try and tell me you don't love him. I've seen the way you look at him," Carol continued.

"I love him. It's just that he's so strong. I guess I'm afraid of getting lost in that strength again—of forgetting to be someone besides his wife." She swept her hand across the table, scattering the fine grains of sugar. "It sounds stupid."

"No, it doesn't, but you're stronger than you give yourself credit for, Beth. I watched you when you found out you were pregnant. You were scared but you coped. And when Donovan went to 'Nam and left you alone with Michael, you became Supermom before anyone knew what the term meant."

"And as soon as Donovan came home, I let him take over. I *wanted* him to take over."

"So what's wrong with that? You were tired. You'd been going it alone for quite a while, and Donovan needed to know that he was needed at home. He needed to know that he had something to offer you."

"So I wimped out and he played Mr. Macho."

"It wasn't like that. I was there, remember?" Carol's voice was gentle, but there was no getting away from the truth in what she was saying. "You were hardly a wimp. You helped put Donovan through college. You were one hell of a mom to Michael. When Donovan got his degree and started trying to get clients, you stretched money and worked like a dog to help him in every way possible. Don't be ashamed of that, Beth."

"I'm not ashamed of it. But, somewhere along the way, I forgot to look at *my* dreams."

"So, you got off the track. You're still young. You're working for your dreams now. Donovan has been supportive, hasn't he? He's helped get you some great jobs, hasn't he?"

"Yes. But, what if I went back with him and then decided to give it all up?"

"That's your *choice*, Beth. Dreams don't get handed to you on a silver platter. You've got to work to make them come true. If you want your career bad enough, you'll stick with it, and you know Donovan will do everything he can to help you."

Elizabeth rubbed her fingers across her forehead. The headache that had been lurking behind her eyes all day had become a reality, but the throbbing pain was nothing compared to the ache in her heart.

"I just get scared. It wasn't easy to walk out, and I'm so afraid I'll have to do it again."

"You won't have to. If things get bad, you'll talk to him this time. Donovan would lay down his life for you."

"Then why can't he give me more time?"

"He needs you." Carol's mouth twisted, her eyes half-wistful. "I'd give just about anything to have what the two of you have. You two almost make me believe in destiny."

She didn't have to say anything more. Elizabeth had more than enough to think about. The idea of Donovan needing her stuck in her mind. She'd always thought of it as the other way around. He'd been the one to take care of her, he'd been the strong one. She'd never doubted that he loved her, but she'd never thought of him as needing her.

She loved him. She didn't deny that, not to Carol, not to herself. But, if she went back to him, would she let herself get swallowed up in his strength again? The past year had taught her the value of independence. It had also taught her something of its loneliness. Donovan had hit the nail on the head when he pointed out that there was no one to care whether she came home at all.

If she kept saying it loud enough and often enough that she liked living alone, it might sound completely sincere. She missed hearing someone else stirring around. She missed— She missed Donovan. And Michael.

She'd deliberately avoided thinking about Donovan's suggestion that they might have another baby. Now, the thought slipped in, surprisingly appealing. It had been a long time since she'd had a child to cuddle. Michael had grown out of the cuddly stage early. A baby. Donovan's baby. Yes, the idea had definite appeal.

As Elizabeth crawled into bed that night she decided that Carol was right. Maybe she was crazy to worry about anything beyond the fact that she and Donovan loved each other. Surely they'd learned from their mistakes. It would be a risk, but if she didn't make a commitment now, it might be too late.

The thought sent a shiver up her spine. *Too late.* Awful words. She turned over in bed and stared at the moonlight pouring in through a crack in the curtains. It couldn't be too late for her and Donovan. She'd go to him first thing in the morning and tell him she loved him and wanted to be with him.

The thought brought a wave of contentment. Morning couldn't come soon enough.

It seemed as if she'd just closed her eyes when the alarm went off. Moaning, she groped for the clock, her face still buried in the pillow. She pushed the alarm button but the ringing didn't stop. Groggy, she opened her eyes and stared at the clock. The first thing that registered was that it said two o'clock in the morning. The second thing was that the room was dark. And the third and most frightening was that it wasn't the alarm making that awful noise, it was the phone.

She stumbled out of bed, her feet half tangled in the covers. By the time she'd covered the few short feet to the living room, the ringing seemed to have gotten ten times louder. She found the phone by instinct, snatching the receiver, her heart pounding so hard she could hardly breathe. Phone calls at two in the morning were one of two things: wrong numbers or emergencies. She prayed it was someone looking for an all-night pizza parlor.

"Hello?"

"Mom?" She forgot how to breathe at the sound of Michael's voice.

"Michael? What's wrong? Are you all right?" *Please God, let him be all right.* "Where are you?"

"I'm at the hospital."

The hospital. A thousand nightmares flashed through her mind. "Are you badly hurt?" Amazing how calm her voice sounded. You couldn't even hear the panic that was screaming inside her.

"I'm fine, just a few scrapes and some bruises."

"Thank God." She swallowed tears, knowing he wouldn't welcome hearing her sob over the phone. "What happened? Never mind. You can tell me about it later. I'll be down as soon as I get some clothes on."

"It was the motorcycle. I think it's totaled. This car came from out of nowhere."

His voice was shaky. He was not at all the calm, young man who sometimes seemed too adult to have ever been a child.

"Don't worry about the motorcycle. As long as you're okay."

"I'm fine."

"I'm going to call your father and we'll both be there as soon as we can."

"Mom?"

Elizabeth's fingers knotted over the receiver, hearing the fear in his voice. There was more. "What is it, Michael?"

"Dad was with me. He tried to avoid the car, but the guy came out of nowhere. There was nothing he could do."

Elizabeth stared at the dark room, feeling the bottom of her stomach dissolve. She swallowed hard, fighting to stay calm.

"Is he . . . is he badly hurt?"

"I don't know. They won't tell me anything. He . . . he looked awful when they put him in the ambulance. They just keep telling me not to worry, but no one will tell me what's going on. He was bleeding a lot. I'm scared, Mom." His voice cracked.

"Stay calm, darling. He's strong. You stay right there and don't worry about anything. I'll be there in twenty minutes."

She set down the phone, making a conscious effort to uncurl her fingers from the receiver. In all the years they'd been together, she'd never seen Donovan seriously ill or hurt. He'd always been so strong, so invincible. Maybe Michael was wrong. Maybe he wasn't that badly hurt. After all, a lot of blood didn't have to be serious. Everyone knew that head wounds always bled out of proportion to their seriousness.

Head wounds. Oh God, what if he hadn't been wearing his helmet? She swallowed the bile that threatened to choke her. Donovan always wore his helmet. He was adamant about it. There was no sense in giving herself nightmares until she knew there was something to worry about. She wasn't going to worry about anything until she got to the hospital.

Chapter 14

The hospital smelled of antiseptic and fear. The lights seemed far too bright for two-thirty in the morning. Elizabeth forced herself to look calm and controlled as she approached the desk in the emergency room.

"Excuse me. I'm Elizabeth Sinclair. My son just called me. He and his father were in an accident."

The nurse looked up, her expression professionally sympathetic. "The motorcycle-car collision."

Elizabeth shuddered at the description. "Could you tell me how they are? My son said he was all right, but he didn't know about my husband."

"I'm afraid you'll have to speak to a doctor for an official report, but I can tell you that your son seems to be just fine. Very stubborn. He's refused to allow us to sedate him. He won't even lie down."

"I'd like to see him, please."

"Go right through that door and turn right. A nurse will direct you from there."

Elizabeth followed her instructions, but she didn't need anyone to direct her once through the doors. Michael was huddled on a plastic chair in the hallway. His face was pale in the revealing light, dark bruises showing up here and there. He was wearing torn and dirty jeans and a denim jacket in much the same condition.

Elizabeth paused, assessing the damage. He looked young, frightened and a bit battered but otherwise whole. She swallowed a sob, offering up a prayer of thanks.

"Michael."

"Mom!" He stood up, wavering a bit, and then she had her arms around him. She held him close, savoring the feel of his strong, young body, miraculously whole. He hugged her, burying his face against her neck, not an adult but a boy again, frightened and in need of comfort.

"It's going to be all right. I'm here now." She offered him the assurance, as mothers have since the beginning of time. It was senseless. He was old enough to know that she couldn't make everything all right with a wave of some maternal wand, but the old ritual was a comfort to them both. They stood there for a few minutes, holding each other, drawing strength for whatever was to come.

After a moment Elizabeth drew back, easing Michael down into a chair and sitting next to him, keeping hold of his hand. She reached up to brush a lock of hair off his forehead.

"You shouldn't be out here. The nurse says you wouldn't let them do anything for you."

"It's Dad I'm worried about. No one will tell me anything."

"They're probably still examining him. You know how cautious doctors are. Any minute now he'll probably walk through those doors with nothing more than a few bruises. He was . . . he was wearing his helmet, wasn't he?"

"We both were."

Elizabeth closed her eyes for a moment, letting the images of hideous head injuries fade back into the land of nightmares.

"The car just came right at us. There was nothing Dad could do." Michael's hands clenched into fists. "Dad swerved and the bike went out of control. I was thrown clear when it went over, but Dad's leg was caught under it. I couldn't do anything. The bike just slid and slid, dragging him with it. I could hear the metal screaming on the pavement. At first I thought it was Dad screaming. It kept sliding. I thought it was going to go on forever. I ran to him. The bike had stopped, but he was still trapped under it. I started to lift it, but he stopped me."

"He was conscious?"

"Yes, and his face was all white and funny. He told me to set up flares and flag down a car. I asked him what was wrong, and he said his leg was trapped but that he was going to be all right. I wasn't to worry. And then he passed out."

"Did he regain consciousness?"

"He was in and out. He was awake when the ambulance guys came. I heard him say something about his leg to them."

He stared at the opposite wall, his face white and set and looking too worn for his nineteen years. "The damn bike just wouldn't stop sliding."

Elizabeth knew he was seeing the accident again in his mind. She'd have given anything to be able to wipe the memory clean.

"Your father is very strong. I'm sure he's going to be fine."

"There was so much blood. And no one would tell me anything. They kept wanting to poke and prod at me. I told them it was Dad I was worried about."

"I know. But as soon as we find out your Dad is okay, you're going to let the doctors examine you."

He might have argued with her but the door of the examining room opened just then. Michael and Elizabeth were both on their feet before the doctor was halfway through the door. With his grizzled gray hair and lean face wrinkled by too many years squinting into the sun he looked the very picture of a country doctor. His white coat might have looked reassuring if it hadn't been for the blood—Donovan's blood—streaked across it. Elizabeth swallowed hard. He stopped, seeing their anxious faces.

"I see you haven't let anyone take a look at you yet." His eyes skimmed over Michael's dusty clothes and bruised face. "Could have a concussion, you know, or a cracked rib or two. Be a miracle if you came off completely scot-free." He didn't wait for a reply, turning his attention to Elizabeth. "Are you Mrs. Sinclair? You look too young."

"How is he?"

His eyes were as gray as his hair, shrewd and not unkind. "He's a strong man. I think he'll pull through this."

"You think?" Elizabeth clutched at Michael's arm, not sure who was steadying whom. "You think?"

The doctor frowned at her from under bushy gray eyebrows. "Come into the lounge, the both of you. I could use some coffee, and I'm sure you could, too."

Elizabeth followed him dazedly. He *thought* Donovan would pull through? He had to pull through. It wasn't possible to imagine the world without him.

Dr. Carson, as he introduced himself, set cups of coffee on the plastic surface of the table, settling wearily into a chair across from Elizabeth and Michael.

"I'm going to be as straight with you as I can—partly because you look strong enough to take it and partly because I'm too damn tired to remember all the medicalese that doctors like to use to confuse people."

"What's wrong with my husband?"

"He's been pretty badly banged up. That's the bad news. The good news is that he's damned lucky to be alive. And you're even luckier, son."

Dr. Carson took another swallow of coffee, gathering his thoughts. "Mr. Sinclair sustained some bad bruising. Several ribs are broken. Luckily, none of them punctured a lung. He was wearing a leather jacket, which saved him from a lot of upper-body injuries. From the description I've been given of the accident, the jacket kept the pavement from removing half his skin. The helmet undoubtedly saved his life. Even with it, he's bound to have a pretty nasty concussion."

Elizabeth allowed herself to breathe. From the sounds of it, Donovan was hurt, but it was nothing that wouldn't heal. "So he's going to pull through?"

"Don't get ahead of me. That takes care of his simple injuries. From what you told us, son, your dad was trapped under the bike, and it slid quite a ways with him."

Michael nodded. "I couldn't get to him before it stopped. I tried to lift the bike off of him, but he said to leave it."

The doctor nodded. "Probably kept him alive. The leg that was trapped under the bike is badly damaged. An artery was cut, and the weight of the bike kept enough pressure on it to keep your dad from bleeding to death."

Elizabeth felt herself grow pale, and she clenched her fingers on the edge of the table, forcing herself to breathe steadily. "How bad is it?"

"We stitched up the artery. He's lost a lot of blood, but transfusions should help that situation." He stared down at his coffee, his eyebrows hooked together in a bushy frown. "That leg is in bad shape." He paused and then drew a deep breath before looking up, his eyes meeting hers. "He may lose it."

Elizabeth heard the words from a long way away. She stared at him, unable to absorb their meaning. "Lose it?"

"I'm sorry. I don't want to frighten you unnecessarily. We're doing everything we can to save it. We're arranging for a helicopter to fly him to Indianapolis, their facilities are more sophisticated than ours. Medicine can still work miracles sometimes."

Elizabeth barely listened. Her fingers locked with Michael's, offering comfort when she had none to give herself. "Will he live?"

"Barring any complications. He's a strong, healthy man. Even if... even if he does lose the leg, there's no reason he shouldn't have a fine, productive life. I know that may not be much consolation if it comes to that."

"All that matters is that he's alive. We'll deal with whatever else comes along. Can we see him?"

"We're readying him for the move. I think it might be better if you and your son had a friend drive you to the city. I'll give you the name of the hospital."

It had started to rain—a cool, late-summer rain that carried a promise of fall. Carol's big station wagon swished down the highway, unperturbed by a little moisture. Inside, no one had much to say. Elizabeth had given Carol the bare facts when she called from the hospital and Carol, who knew when to ask questions and when to stay silent, hadn't asked for any details. Michael sat next to the door, his face white in the occasional passing headlights. In the east, there was the faintest hint of gray, promising daylight.

"It's my fault." Michael's voice was raw with pain.

Elizabeth looked at him, dragging her mind from Donovan. She put her hand on his arm, feeling the rigid muscles there, reminding her that he wasn't a little boy anymore to be distracted and coaxed out of his fears.

"It's not your fault. You weren't driving the car or the bike. There was nothing you could do."

"Dad wouldn't have been out tonight at all if my stupid car hadn't broken down. I called him and he came out to pick me up."

"It's not your fault your car broke down."

"Yes, it is. I should have taken better care of it. Dad warned me. He said I couldn't expect it to be dependable if I didn't take care of it."

"Michael, you can't blame something like this on your car. Your father shouldn't have come to pick you up on the motorcycle. Are you going to blame it on that?"

"His car is in the shop. I should have just spent the night in my car and then called in the morning. It's my fault."

"Michael, sometimes things just happen and no one's to blame. The only person at fault here is whoever was driving the car that almost hit you."

"What happened to the car?" Carol asked the question quietly.

Michael's face tightened, looking eerily like his father in anger. "They didn't even bother to stop. They just drove off and left Dad lying there in the road."

"Seems to me like your mom is right. The blame lies with them. Your dad doesn't need your guilt right now. It's not going to do him any good."

"Maybe."

Elizabeth glanced helplessly at Carol, who shrugged. Michael was going to have to work through his feelings. All she could do was be there for him. She couldn't lift the burden entirely, no matter how much she wanted to.

Carol pulled the car to a stop outside the hospital. The sun had come up enough to cast a gloomy light on the big building. The rain still fell, a soft drizzle that did nothing to lift the spirits.

Michael opened his door and stepped out into the rain, hunching his shoulders a bit as he waited for his mother. Elizabeth gave him a worried look. She wanted to take his pain away. It hurt her that she couldn't.

"Are you sure you don't want me to wait with you?"

"No, that's okay. You've got a business to run. If you wouldn't mind calling Mrs. Tancredi for me, and you'd better call Donovan's office and—"

"I know who to call, Beth. Don't worry about anything. I'll bring you some clothes tonight and something for Michael. I suppose you two are going to stay around here for a few days. Have you got money?"

"Money?" Elizabeth hadn't thought of anything yet beyond her family's welfare.

"You know, the green, crinkly stuff. You'll need it to buy food, etc." Carol reached into the pocket of her jacket and pulled out a wad of bills. "I robbed the register at the nursery."

"Oh Carol, you shouldn't have."

"Don't be an idiot, Beth. You can pay me back when everything is straightened out. I've got an exact tally of every dollar. I'll also figure the going interest rate, if it'll make you feel better."

"Thank you." Elizabeth blinked back tears, knowing Carol hadn't the least idea of how much money she'd handed her. "I'll call you as soon as there's any news."

"You do that. He's going to be fine, Beth. Donovan is too tough to do anything else."

"I know." Her hands were shaking as she stuffed the money into her purse. "I . . . I was going to tell him I loved him."

"You're still going to tell him. He's going to make it, Beth. You've got to believe it."

"I do."

"You'd better get out of here before Michael melts." Carol hugged her, her slim arms offering comfort. "You call me if you need anything. Anything at all."

"I will."

She slid out of the car and walked over to Michael. When she set her hand on his arm, he jumped. She wondered if he'd even been aware that he was standing in the rain. She had to tilt her head to see his face as they walked toward the hospital. He looked so much like his father. She looked away, blinking back tears. Donovan was going to be all right. He just had to be.

It was almost thirty-six hours before she was allowed to see her husband. Every hour seemed like ten. The nurses were kind and gave her what information they could. She knew when he went into surgery and she knew when he came out. Those were the worst hours. She and Michael could only sit and wonder if they would be able to save his leg. She told herself it didn't matter. As long as he was alive, anything else was secondary. But she knew it did matter. Nothing could change the way she felt about him, but it would matter to Donovan, and it frightened her to think how it might change him.

When the doctor at last came out of surgery, he told them they hadn't removed the leg. That wasn't a guarantee that they wouldn't have to yet, but he was cautiously optimistic. The damage had been extensive, but they'd managed to put things back in more or less the right order. Now, everything depended on Donovan's recuperative powers—whether or not the bones and blood vessels would knit themselves back together.

Michael's grasp left bruises on her forearm, but Elizabeth barely noticed. Donovan was alive and he wasn't going to lose his leg. She refused to believe anything else. She wasn't going to lose him. Once the doctor left, she put her arms around her son's waist and wept with relief.

After that, it was still almost another full day before they let anyone in to see Donovan. By then, the doctor's cautious optimism had been upgraded to not-so-cautious optimism. Things seemed to be going well. They weren't making any promises, but Elizabeth didn't care. All she wanted now was to see Donovan.

They warned her that he looked worse than he actually was, and she braced herself. But nothing could have prepared her for seeing him lying there, almost as pale as the sheets. Tubes ran everywhere, like some hideous, modern art sculpture. She bit her lip, hesitating in the doorway.

She'd never seen him so helpless. Donovan had always been larger than life, full of strength. This didn't even look like him. She crept closer, swallowing hard. Seeing him like this made her realize that she'd almost lost him. She grasped the side railings that fenced him into the bed and stared down at him. Reaching down, she brushed a lock of thick, black hair off his forehead, her fingers trembling.

"I love you, Donovan Sinclair." Her hushed voice was almost drowned in the quiet hum of the machinery they had him attached to. His eyelids fluttered. She held her breath as he opened his eyes slowly.

He stared up at her, his eyes a muddy green. "Beth." Her name formed on his lips though no sound came out.

"Don't try to talk, love. You're in the hospital but you're all right. Everything is going to be all right."

"Michael?" This time the name was distinguishable.

"He's fine. A few bruises and a scrape or two, but that's all."

"Worried." He closed his eyes as if the small effort had exhausted him.

"You don't have to worry about anything but getting better." She stroked her fingers over his cheek, feeling the faint rasp of stubble. She thought he'd gone back to sleep, but his lashes lifted again. This time his eyes were a little brighter, a little more urgent.

"My leg? Heard talking. Ambulance."

"Your leg is fine. It's going to be just as good as new," she promised recklessly.

Some of the urgency faded from his eyes. His hand lifted an inch or so and then fell back against the covers. Beth took his fingers in hers. "Go back to sleep, love. I'll stay with you."

"Don' worry." The words were slurred, his lashes already dropping against his cheeks. Beth sat until the nurse came and insisted she leave. They told her that they didn't need another patient on their hands, which was exactly what she'd be if she didn't get some rest.

From then on, Donovan progressed faster than the doctors had dared to hope. Elizabeth spent as much time with him as the hospital would allow. Neither of them spoke of the future or of what had happened between them before the accident. Future and past had been put on hold for now, but it couldn't be left that way forever.

"I want to know exactly what condition my leg is in. I'm tired of all this tap dancing around the subject."

Dr. Marin studied her patient over the top of her glasses. His impatience was easy to read. Overall, he'd been a good patient, better than most strong, healthy men ever were. She was well pleased with his recovery, but she had a feeling he might not quite share her enthusiasm when he knew the full truth.

"What, exactly, do you want to know?"

Donovan glared at her. "I want to know exactly what condition my leg is in." He spoke each word distinctly.

"Medically speaking, you're lucky you have a leg at all. Ten, even five years ago, damage like that would have resulted in amputation."

"I know that and I'm grateful. Believe me, I'm grateful." Gratitude, however, was hardly the emotion that filled his voice. "Now, I want to know the extent of the damage."

"You'll walk, if that's what's worrying you. You'll have a limp, but you'll walk."

"How much of a limp?" His tone was even, but she could see the lump his fist made under the sheet.

"Probably a fairly extensive one."

"Fairly extensive. What's fairly extensive? Am I going to be dragging my leg behind me like Quasimodo?"

"It shouldn't be that bad." She caught the rising irritation in his eyes. "Mr. Sinclair, I'm not trying to be difficult, though I know it sounds that way. The truth is I can't tell you just how much you will or won't limp. The damage your knee sustained was, quite frankly, horrendous. The joint is never going to work like it did before the accident. That's putting it as bluntly as I know how. You'll limp. You'll have pain if you overextend. You'll be on crutches for quite a while, but there's no reason to think you'll have to be on them permanently.

"As for running or going one-on-one on a basketball court, to a certain extent that will depend on you. You're certainly never going to have the speed you may have had in the past, and the knee is going to be prone to injury. You'll tire more quickly and you'll have to learn to gauge yourself."

"In other words, I'm never going to be normal again."

"That's a harsh way to put it. *Normal* is a relative term."

"It doesn't seem relative when it doesn't apply to you anymore. Don't worry, Doctor. I'm aware of how lucky I am. I could have lost my leg. I could have been killed. I'm grateful. Really I am. I just need to start preparing for what my life is going to be like once you guys turn me loose."

Elizabeth hurried down the corridor. The quiet bustle of the hospital had become familiar during the past few weeks. She smiled at a nurse whose name she didn't know but whose face was part of the daily routine. She should have been here when the doctor had told Donovan the extent of the damage to his leg. She didn't care whether he'd ever run a four-minute mile—all that mattered was that he was alive and going to stay that way. But she knew that Donovan wasn't going to feel the same. For a man who'd never been ill a day in his life, limited mobility was going to be a painful and difficult reality.

She stopped outside his door and smoothed her hands over the full skirt of her pale blue dress. Donovan liked her in blue, and he liked her in dresses. He'd always said it was a crime to cover legs like hers. She wasn't sure she agreed, but it was a small thing, a simple effort to cheer him.

She pushed open the door and stepped into the room. It was always a shock to see him lying in the hospital bed, though most of the tubes and machinery were gone now.

"Hi."

He'd been staring at the wall opposite the door but, at her soft greeting, he rolled his head to look at her. For just an instant, she thought she saw pain in his eyes, but then the expression was gone so quickly she might have imagined it.

"Hi. Nice dress." His smile seemed a little tight at the edges, and the lines in his face appeared a little deeper.

"That's what you said last time I wore it." She bent to kiss him and wondered if it was her imagination that made his response seem lukewarm.

"At least you know I wasn't lying."

"True." She sat in the chair beside his bed, her eyes betraying a touch of anxiety.

"How's Michael?"

"Fine. School starts next week. He said to tell you he'd be in this weekend."

"The doctors said I might be able to come home by then." His tone didn't indicate any excitement about this major step in his recovery.

"That would be wonderful! We'll have to do something to celebrate."

"No!" Elizabeth's eyes widened at the harsh refusal, and Donovan seemed to realize he'd been too strong. His smile was strained but coaxing. "I don't want any fuss. I just want to come home and settle in without having to be polite to people for a while. I'll probably be beat, anyway."

"Of course. I should have thought of that. Well, we'll have a celebration later, when you're feeling up to it."

"Fine." Silence settled between them. Elizabeth looked at him, trying to read his expression, but there was nothing there. He stared absently at the foot of his bed.

"Dr. Marin said she talked with you today. About your leg."

"Yeah. It was sort of a good news-bad news situation."

She waited, but he didn't seem inclined to say anything more. "I'm sorry. I know you must be pretty upset." *Talk to me Donovan. Tell me what you're feeling. Let me comfort you.*

"I don't know. It isn't that bad." His smile was twisted. "I could have lost the leg. Basically, I'm pretty lucky."

He didn't sound like he felt lucky, but the tone put up walls saying he didn't want her sympathy and didn't want her getting too close right now. Elizabeth swallowed her hurt. He had to deal with this in his own way. Maybe he needed some time to come to terms with his injury before he could talk about it.

"Well then, I'll go by the house and get it cleaned up and stock up on food for your homecoming. I have a feeling that's not really Michael's forte."

"You don't have to do that." Again, the tone put walls between them, shutting him on one side with his pain and closing her out. She wanted to scream and demand that he let her inside, but she couldn't.

"It's no problem. Is there anything I can—" She broke off as he stirred restlessly.

"Look, I hate to be rude, but I'm really beat. I'd like to get some sleep. The way this place is run, they get you up at dawn to take blood samples and poke needles in you." His mouth smiled but he didn't look at her, and his words made the dismissal clear. Polite, gentle but still a dismissal.

Elizabeth stared at him a moment and then got up. She didn't believe for a minute that he was going to go to sleep, but she didn't say anything. If he needed time alone, she'd give it to him.

"I'll come back this evening."

"Sure, that'll be great. I'm sorry I'm so exhausted."

"That's okay." She hesitated. She usually kissed him goodbye when she left, but he didn't look at her and didn't give any indication that a kiss would be welcome. She hovered awkwardly for a moment and then turned away. It was silly to feel hurt. He just needed a little time.

Donovan watched her leave, his hands clenched into fists, the knuckles aching with the pressure. His chest hurt, a burning ache that threatened to eat right through him and leave him bleeding. The door shut behind her, and the room seemed suddenly darker.

He wanted to call her back. He wanted to feel her arms around him and smell the sweet scent of her perfume. But he couldn't do that. Not now. Maybe not ever.

Chapter 15

"I swear, these potholes are life threatening. Are you sure they're not bothering your leg too much?" Elizabeth glanced anxiously at Donovan.

"I'm fine. If my leg was that fragile, they wouldn't have let me out of the hospital." The tightness of his smile reminded her not to fuss, and she quelled her concern. She had to keep in mind that Donovan wasn't going to welcome too much fussing. She was almost surprised he hadn't insisted on trying to drive himself home.

Neither of them said anything more until she pulled the car into the driveway. It could have been a comfortable silence, but it wasn't. It seemed as if there were things that no one was saying. Donovan was shutting her out as clearly as if he'd slammed a door in her face. He was pushing away her concern, telling her without words that he didn't need her help. Not hers, not anybody's.

"Well, here we are."

"Here we are." Donovan's agreement held no enthusiasm.

Elizabeth opened her door and circled the front of the car to his side. He was already halfway out the door, maneuvering crutches and a heavily bandaged leg.

"Here, let me help." Her move forward was checked by the ferocity of the look he threw her.

"I don't need any help." The words were accompanied by a smile that would have made a strong man cower. She stood back, her hands at her sides as she watched him struggle to get the crutches solidly under him.

When he was at last upright and more or less on his own two feet, he looked at her again, his smile less threatening but still cool. "I didn't mean to snap at you, but I've got to learn to manage things on my own."

"I understand." She didn't understand at all. Why did he keep her at arm's length? Why did he treat her as if she were a distant relation, someone he didn't know very well and didn't want to know any better?

The front door opened as Donovan reached the bottom of the steps, and Michael rushed out.

"Dad!" Donovan loosened his grip on one crutch enough to return his son's hug. Elizabeth swallowed hard. It hurt to see the warmth of his smile. She loved Donovan, too. Why was he pushing her away?

"How are you feeling?"

"Not bad. It's good to be home."

"It's great to have you back. Here, let me help you up the stairs."

"Thanks." Michael wrapped one arm around his father's waist. Elizabeth trailed behind them, knowing that if she'd made the same offer, Donovan would have thrown it back in her teeth. She couldn't even convince herself that it was because she didn't have the physical strength Michael did.

They made it into the house without incident, though Elizabeth held her breath with every step Donovan took. She didn't even want to think about the kind of damage a fall might do to his knee. Once inside, Donovan leaned on his crutches and drew in a deep breath.

"God, it's nice not to smell antiseptic."

"I made it a point not to clean anything. I figured a little dirt would be a nice change for you."

"Thanks, Michael." Donovan grinned at his son, and Elizabeth fought back her tears. He hadn't smiled at her like that in days. In fact, he'd barely even looked at her.

"Hi, Mom. I didn't mean to ignore you." Elizabeth smiled and returned Michael's hug.

"That's okay."

"You look tired."

"Thanks, Michael. I know I can always depend on you for an ego boost." She smoothed her hand over her hair, aware of Donovan looking at her, his eyes cool and watchful.

"Is there a reason we're all standing in the hall? I don't think it's a good idea for you to be on your feet for too long."

"Are you staying? I thought you'd probably want to get home right away. After spending all that time in the city, you must have a lot of things to catch up on."

Elizabeth stared at Donovan, wondering if it was possible to feel your heart actually break. The words weren't rude. The tone was light, even friendly. But the intent was clear. He didn't want her here. How could she tell him that her apartment wasn't home? *He* was home. She was aware of Michael drawing in a quick breath and knew that he'd caught his father's meaning as clearly as she had.

"I thought you might need some help with dinner and things...." Her voice trailed off, her eyes pleading with him. *I love you. Please, don't push me away.* If Donovan saw the plea, he chose to ignore it.

"I think Michael and I can manage okay. We did before."

"Of course. Silly of me." She smiled, hoping the light was dim enough to conceal the glint of tears in her eyes. "I'll give you a call tomorrow—maybe."

"Don't worry about me, Elizabeth. I'm fine. I really appreciate all the time you've spent on me. I hope it hasn't caused you too many problems."

"No problem. No problem at all." She backed toward the door, hoping he'd change his mind. "I'll see you both later, I guess."

"Sure, Mom. I'll come by tomorrow." Michael hugged her, and she wondered if it was her imagination that his arms held her a little tighter than usual. Maybe he sensed his father's coldness and was trying to make up for it. She blinked rapidly and managed a tight smile.

"Bye." She lifted her hand, hardly able to see Donovan through her tears, and slipped out the door, closing it quietly behind her.

Donovan watched her go without moving, his expression blank. Only the muscle that twitched in his jaw gave any indication of his feeling. He wanted to run after her and take her in his arms and tell her that he hadn't meant to hurt her. His fingers tightened around the crutches. He wasn't going to be running after anyone. Not now, not ever.

"You could have asked her to stay for dinner."

Donovan blinked and looked at Michael. It wasn't hard to see the disapproval in his son's eyes. "I'm sure your mother has a lot of things to do." He turned and thumped his way into the living room, lowering himself into a chair, painfully aware of the awkwardness of his movements.

"She was practically in tears." Michael stood in the doorway, his jaw tight.

"Probably tears of relief that she can get home again." Donovan kept his voice light.

"I don't think that was it. I think you hurt her."

"Well, I didn't mean to."

"I think you did."

Donovan's eyes jerked upward to meet Michael's angry gaze. "Leave it alone, Michael."

"Why?"

"This is between your mother and me. If I hurt her, then I'm sorry, and I'll tell her so myself."

"I don't understand you two at all. You love each other. Any idiot can see that. I thought you were going to get back together. I thought—"

"Drop it!" Donovan swallowed hard, aware that the words had been too loud, too harsh. "There are a lot of things between your mother and me that you can't possibly understand. I said that if I hurt her feelings, then I'll apologize. Satisfied?"

Michael looked far from satisfied, but he knew when to stop pushing. He didn't mention Elizabeth again that evening. It was a pity that Donovan's mind couldn't drop the subject as neatly. He knew that he'd hurt her. It hadn't been his intention, but it had been the result anyway.

Donovan stirred restlessly, the sheets rustling beneath him. His knee ached with a steady, throbbing pain that was beginning to seem almost normal. The doctors had warned him to expect that. It wasn't the pain in his knee that was keeping him awake. It was the gnawing feeling of loss eating into his gut that made sleep impossible.

He hadn't hurt this bad when she left him. Then, he'd had anger and righteous indignation to smother the pain. Now he had nothing. He stirred again, drawing a stabbing pain from his knee that warned him not to forget it was there— as if he could forget.

He didn't have to close his eyes to see the car bearing down on them, the headlights blinding him. He remembered swerving, trying desperately to keep the bike upright and then feeling it going over and knowing there was nothing he could do. And then he'd been sliding down the road, the weight of the bike pinning his leg to the unforgiving macadam even as it dragged him along.

He shuddered, staring up at the dark ceiling, beads of sweat coating his forehead. He didn't need the doctors to tell him he was lucky to be alive. He'd known it from the moment he opened his eyes to see Michael's terrified face staring down at him. And he knew he was lucky he hadn't lost his leg. He was truly grateful for that.

But it didn't change anything. He still had his leg, but it would never be right again. The doctors could talk about him living a full, healthy life, but they weren't the ones with a bent and twisted joint that would never be right again.

And there was nothing in the world he wanted more than to have Beth with him right now, but he didn't want her pity. He didn't need anyone's pity. If she could have come to him out of love, it would have made his world whole again. But he'd rather do without her forever than know that she'd only come back because she felt sorry for him.

He closed his eyes, forcing her image from his mind, willing his body to relax. Sleep. In sleep, he didn't have to think about what had happened or how things might have been.

Elizabeth took a deep breath and tightened her grip on the bag in her left hand. The door in front of her was familiar, but she couldn't have been more nervous if she'd been facing a firing squad. Her hand was shaking so badly that she had to try twice before she could get her finger on the doorbell. She could hear the quiet chime ringing inside the house.

The early October weather was blustery, hinting at winter cold. The chill she felt had nothing to do with the weather. It had to do with what lay behind the door. It felt strange to be standing on the doorstep, a visitor to a house that had been her home for more than ten years.

She heard the quiet thump of Donovan's crutches and shoved her hands into the pockets of her jacket, crossing her fingers in a childish prayer for luck. It had been almost two weeks since she'd brought him home. Two weeks that she'd forced herself to stay away. If he needed time to adjust, she'd given it to him.

None of her silent self-encouragement helped when the door swung open and she was face-to-face with Donovan. Her gaze met his, and all her carefully rehearsed, cheerful speeches flew out the window. She could only stare at him, drinking him in. He looked well. He'd lost some of the hospital pallor and gained a few pounds. His hair fell in a heavy, black wave onto his forehead, giving his face a boyishness that softened the strength of his chin. He was wearing a flannel shirt and a pair of worn jeans, the leg cut open at the seam to make room for the bulk of his cast. The lines around his mouth were too deep and his eyes were too tired, but he'd never looked better to her.

"Elizabeth." If he felt any emotion on seeing her, she couldn't tell. His expression revealed nothing.

"Hi. I thought you might be able to use a good cook. What with Michael in school and all and I know cooking isn't your favorite thing to do and I didn't have any plans for tonight. They had some great steaks at the market and it seemed a pity to waste them. Steak just doesn't taste right if you eat it alone."

She stopped, looking at him with what she hoped was a casually friendly expression. Donovan seemed to hesitate, as if weighing her words, his eyes searching her face.

"Can I come in?"

"Sure. Sorry. I didn't mean to keep you standing on the doorstep." He backed away, the crutches making his movements awkward. She looked away. It hurt to see him shackled. She didn't have to close her eyes to remember the graceful, swinging stride she'd always loved.

Donovan saw her look away and his jaw tightened. He shut the door with more force than was necessary and turned toward the kitchen. He felt clumsy and gawky on the crutches, but he'd grown accustomed to them and had actually begun to take some pride in his ability to maneuver. Seeing them through someone else's eyes, however, made him realize how awkward they must look.

"I was hoping you wouldn't mind if I just dropped in. I brought some wine and I thought maybe I'd throw some potatoes in to bake and we could relax over some wine until it was time to start the steaks." She set the sack on the counter and began to unload it, not looking at Donovan, talking too much.

"That sounds fine." He sounded doubtful, but she pretended not to hear it. She'd determined to make this a wonderful evening, and she was going to do just that, even if she had to drag him along with her.

"I bought a cabernet. I thought it would be nice with the steaks." She set the bottle on the counter and threw him a quick smile.

"Great. You know me. I don't know a cabernet from a Chardonnay." He opened a drawer and took out a corkscrew. Balancing on the crutches, he reached for the bottle. Elizabeth turned away from the oven and saw him preparing to twist the corkscrew into the cork.

"Here. Let me do that." She reached for the bottle, but Donovan's hand tightened, refusing to release the bottle.

"I can do it." The words were quiet but held anger firmly in check. Her eyes jerked to his face. "It's my leg that's crippled, not my hands."

She stepped back, flushing. "I'm sorry. I guess I just got used to worrying about you while you were in the hospital. I guess a wine bottle isn't a real threat, is it?"

"Not unless I drop it on my good foot." His smile was tight, the humor not reaching his eyes.

She turned away, cursing herself. She had to remember that he could manage and he didn't need her to fuss over him.

She scrubbed the potatoes more vigorously than was really necessary. Behind her, there was a subdued pop as the cork left the bottle. She deliberately didn't move to get the wineglasses or offer to pour the wine. Donovan wasn't helpless, and she had to make sure he knew that she realized that. Once the potatoes were in the oven, she turned to him. The wine was sitting on the counter, catching the light and refracting it into deep red patterns on the countertop.

"If you'd bring the wine, we can go into the living room." It obviously galled him to have to ask even that much, but there was no way he could carry a glass of wine and manage his crutches at the same time. Once in the living room, the silence threatened to grow awkward.

"How have you been managing?" She made the question casual, one any friend might ask.

"Fine."

"Have you been into the office?"

"Only once, but Donna brings work out to me."

He was really doing his part to keep up the conversation. How was she going to lead around to the subject of their relationship when he was acting as though they'd never had one?

Donovan swirled his wine, staring down into it. Did she have any idea how beautiful she looked? She was wearing a bright blue sweater that made her skin look milky white. Her hair was caught back in a loose twist, a few strands falling free around her face. He'd never seen her look more beautiful, more desirable. He took a swallow of his wine and glanced at her again. Why was she here?

"How are things at the store? You didn't have any problems because of all the time you spent at the hospital, did you?"

"No, they were very understanding."

"Good."

The room was so quiet they could hear the wind stirring the leaves outside.

"How's your leg?"

"I can't complain. It aches once in a while but nothing major. I'd rather have it there and aching than not there at all."

"We were so scared that you were going to lose it."

He stirred restlessly. "It's all over and done now, so you don't have to worry."

"I can't help but worry about you. A person always worries about someone they care about." *Great.* She sounded like a high school grammar book. *A person.* Why didn't she just come right out and say that she'd been worried about him? She stole a look at his face and then looked away. He didn't look as if he'd welcome her concern.

"That's nice of you, Elizabeth, but I'm fine."

His tone was so cool, pushing her away. She blinked against tears. "You know, for a while there, you called me Beth again."

"I did? Sorry."

"I . . . kind of liked it. It made me feel like I did when we were kids, when Michael was just a baby."

He stirred restlessly, and she knew it was only the weight of his cast that kept him from getting up and pacing the floor.

"That was a long time ago, Elizabeth."

He used the name deliberately, pushing her away.

"Not all that long." He didn't say anything, and she swallowed hard. "Do you know what day this is?"

Donovan threw her a quick look from under his lashes, his jaw tightening. Did she think he could forget?

"I have no idea." His voice was cool, as if whatever it was, it couldn't possibly be important.

"It's our anniversary."

"I don't think divorced people celebrate anniversaries."

She drew a quick, hurt breath. "We're not divorced."

"Only a matter of time." He took a swallow of his wine, not looking at her.

"Is that what you want? A divorce?"

"Seems the logical step. When two people don't live together anymore, there doesn't seem to be much reason to stay married."

"Donovan, before the accident, you said you wanted me to move back in with you."

"That was before the accident." The icy tone of his words might have stopped her, but she'd come too close to losing him forever to stop now.

"Why should that change the way you feel?"

"When you come that close to dying, it makes you think about a lot of things."

"Don't you . . . don't you want me anymore?"

He swallowed the last of his wine, wishing it was whiskey so that it might burn away some of his pain. She sat there looking like a dream come true and asked if he still wanted her. It was like asking a man dying of thirst. But he wanted her on his terms, not because she thought he needed her.

"Look, you've built a life you like. I've got a life of my own."

"We could combine the two. You thought we could."

"That was before the accident."

"I don't see why that changes anything. I . . . I want to move back in."

The stem of his wineglass snapped. Beth was beside him in an instant, reaching for his hand, but he jerked it away from her, the movement so full of rage that she couldn't move. She knelt next to his chair, staring up at him, watching the cool facade melt into seething anger.

"I don't need your help. I don't need anyone's help. I don't need you."

She sucked in a breath, her eyes shimmering with tears. There was deliberate cruelty in his words. He'd never been deliberately cruel to her.

"Donovan, please. I love you."

He outstretched his uninjured hand as if physically pushing her away. "Stop it. I'm not a fool. It's my leg that's crippled, not my brain. You think I can't manage on my own. That's pity, Beth. Not love. I don't need your pity."

A small kernel of healthy anger stirred beneath her hurt. "I was going to tell you before the accident. In fact, I made up my mind the night it happened. I was going to call you the next morning."

"Bull. I appreciate what you're trying to do, but no thanks. I can manage just fine. I don't want your damned pity."

The anger grew. She had just laid her soul bare to him.

She stood up, dashing her hand impatiently over the tears on her cheeks. "Fine. You don't want my pity, you don't have it. Why should I bother to pity you? You're doing a fine job of feeling sorry for yourself. You just go ahead and sit there and think of yourself as a cripple, but it's not your leg that's keeping you there. It's your thinking. I love you, Donovan Sinclair, and I think you love me. You almost let me go once and you're a damned fool if you let me go again."

She was almost to the door when she heard him call her name.

"Elizabeth." She hesitated. "Beth." She stopped but didn't turn. The tears that flooded her eyes blurred the hallway.

"What?"

"Don't go." She didn't turn, still poised for flight. "I can't chase you." The words held pain, and she turned to find him struggling out of the chair, half balanced on his good leg. His face was white but, looking into his eyes, she knew it wasn't pain. It was fear. Fear of losing her?

"What?" *Please. Please say that you love me.*

"Beth, I...are you..." He stopped and looked at her, and she felt some of the chill fade. "Are you sure it's not just pity?" His eyes showed his fears, his vulnerability.

She swallowed hard, taking a step toward him. "I'm sure."

"I don't know if I believe you but, God, I want to."

"Donovan." She crossed the short distance and put her arms around him. He wavered and then found his balance, his arms coming around her, holding her tightly, his face buried in her hair.

"God, I love you. I love you, but I can't stand it if it's pity."

She drew away, easing him back into the chair and kneeling in front of him. "Don't be an idiot. Who could pity you? You're too stubborn to pity."

His hands cupped her face, drinking in the love in her eyes. "Be sure, Beth. I can watch you leave now, but I don't know if I could later. Don't stay if you aren't sure."

"I'm sure. I've been sure for a long time. I'd have told you sooner, but you had to go and have this stupid accident. And then I thought I was going to lose you."

His thumbs brushed the tears from her cheeks, feeling their healing power. She was crying for him. Not because she felt sorry for him but because she'd almost lost him. The hard knot that had lain in his chest began to dissolve. She loved him. The knowledge held more healing power than all the medicine in the world.

"You're never going to lose me, Beth. I lost you once but never again. I'll never lose sight of the most important thing in the world. You are my world, and without you, everything is gray."

He leaned forward, kissing the dampness from her cheeks. His mouth settled on hers in a kiss full of promise, full of love.

"I love you, Donovan. I'll love you forever."

And he knew it was true.

* * * * *

A Note from Lisa Jackson

Dear Reader,

Once in a while an inspiration for a book comes along that just works. Such is the case with All But Guilty (duke). From the moment of the concept of the book— what would a woman with a secret past do if the lover to free a child under threat ——the story took off and my writer was absorbed.

I had imagined a couple falling about for years, but didn't realize what it started to write this particular book, how negative feelings of motherhood would be affecting, how much I would care about baby I.D.

I had written Chandra Hill and her attempts from the beginning and fell in love with Dallas O'Rourke; the character from the moment he stepped onto the page. These two people, at odds over what to do about the tiny, cut baby, yet attracted to each other, reached me as they did and others. They both were willing to give up everything they held dear, including their homes, for the sake of the baby. They couldn't help but fall in love not only with the adorable child but with each other as well, as if I knew...

I hope you enjoy reading All But Guilty (Dallas Jackson). I loved writing Dallas and Chandra's story.

A Note from Lisa Jackson

Dear Reader,

Once in a while an inspiration for a book comes along
that just works. Such is the case with *Million Dollar
Baby*. From the moment of the concept of the book—
what would a woman with a secret past do if she were
to find a baby on her doorstep?—the story took off and
strong characters emerged.

I'd read articles concerning abandoned infants, but
didn't realize when I started to write this particular
book how my own feelings of motherhood would be
affected, how much I would care about Baby J.D.

I felt akin to Chandra Hill and her dilemma from the
beginning and fell in love with Dallas O'Rourke, the
ER doctor, from the moment he stepped onto the page.
These two people, at odds over what to do about the
innocent baby yet attracted to each other, touched me
as they did each other. They both were willing to give
up everything they held dear, including their hearts, for
the sake of the baby. They couldn't help but fall in love
not only with the motherless child but with each other
as well.

I hope you enjoy reading *Million Dollar Baby*, because
I loved writing Dallas and Chandra's story.

Lisa Jackson

MILLION DOLLAR BABY

Lisa Jackson

Chapter One

The dog stuck his wet nose in Chandra's face. He whined and nuzzled her jaw.

"Go 'way," Chandra grumbled, squeezing her eyes shut. She burrowed deeper into the pillows, hoping Sam would get the message, but Sam didn't give up. The persistent retriever clawed at her covers and barked loudly enough to wake the neighbors ten miles down the road. "Knock it off, Sam!" Irritated, she yanked a pillow over her head and rolled over. But she was awake now and couldn't ignore Sam's whining and pacing along the rail of the loft; the metal licenses hanging from his collar rattled noisily.

When she didn't respond, he snorted loudly and padded quickly down the stairs, whereupon he barked again.

So he had to go out. "You should've thought of this earlier." Reluctantly, Chandra pulled herself into a sitting position and shoved a handful of hair from her eyes. She shivered a little and, yawning, rubbed her arms.

Sam barked excitedly, and she considered letting him out and leaving him on the porch. As Indian summer faded into autumn, the nighttime temperature in the Rocky Mountain foothills had begun to dip toward freezing. "It would serve you right," she said ungraciously as she glanced at the clock on the table near the bed. One forty-three. Still plenty of time to fall asleep again before the alarm clock was set to go off.

Grumbling under her breath, she had leaned over and was reaching under the bed, feeling around for her boots, when she heard it: the sound that had filtered through her dreams and pierced her subconscious over Sam's insistent barking. The noise, a distant wail, reminded Chandra of the hungry cry of a baby or the noise a Siamese cat would make if it were in pain. Chandra's skin crawled.

You're imagining things! she told herself. She was miles from civilization....

The cry, distant and muffled, broke the silence again. Chandra sat bolt upright in bed. Her heart knocked crazily. Clutching the quilt around her shoulders, she swung her feet to the floor and crossed the worn wood planks to the railing, where she could look down and survey the first floor of the cabin.

Moonlight streamed through the windows, and a few embers glowed behind the glass doors of the wood stove. Otherwise the cabin was cloaked in the darkness that night brought to this isolated stretch of woods.

She could barely see Sam. His whiskey-colored coat blended into the shadows as he paced beside the door, alternately whining and growling as he scratched on the threshold.

"So now you're Lassie, is that it?" she asked. "Telling me that there's something out there."

He yelped back.

"This is nuts. Hush, Sam," Chandra commanded, her skin prickling as her eyes adjusted to the shadows. Straining to listen, she reached for the pair of old jeans she'd tossed carelessly across the foot of the bed hours earlier. The familiar noises in this little cabin in the foothills hadn't changed. From the ticking of the grandfather clock to the murmur of the wind rushing through the boughs of the pine and aspen that surrounded the cabin, the sounds of the Colorado night were as comforting as they had always been. The wind chimes on her porch tinkled softly, and the leaky faucet in the bathroom dripped a steady tattoo.

The cry came again. A chill raced up Chandra's spine. Was it a baby? No way. Not up here in these steep hills. Her mind was playing tricks on her. Most likely some small beast had been wounded and was in pain—a cat who had strayed or a wounded raccoon . . . maybe even a bear cub separated from its mother. . . .

Snarling, Sam started back up the stairs toward her.

"Hold on, hold on." Chandra yanked on her jeans and stuffed the end of her flannel nightshirt into the waistband. She slid her feet into wool socks and, after another quick search under the bed, crammed her feet into her boots.

Her father's old .22 was tucked into a corner of the closet. She hesitated, grabbed her down jacket, then curled her fingers over the barrel of the Winchester. Better safe than sorry. Maybe the beast was too far gone and she'd have to put it out of its misery. Maybe it was rabid.

And maybe it's not a beast at all.

By the time she and the retriever crept back downstairs, Sam was nearly out of his mind, barking and growling, ready to take on the world. "Slow down," Chandra ordered, reaching into the pocket of her jacket, feeling the smooth shells for her .22. She slipped two cartridges into the rifle's cold chamber.

"Okay, now don't do anything stupid," she said to the dog. She considered leaving Sam in the house, for fear that he might be hurt by the wounded, desperate beast, but then again, she felt better with the old dog by her side. If she did stumble upon a lost bear cub, the mother might not be far away or in the best of moods.

As she opened the door, a blast of cool mountain air rushed into the room, billowing curtains and causing the fire to glow brightly. The night wind seemed to have forgotten the warm breath of summer that still lingered during the days.

Clouds drifted across the moon like solitary ghosts, casting shadows on the darkened landscape. The crying hadn't let up. Punctuated by gasps or hiccups, it grew louder as Chandra marched across the gravel and ignored the fear that stiffened her spine. She headed straight for the barn, to the source of the noise.

The wailing sounded human. But that was insane. She hadn't heard a baby cry in years... and there were no children for miles. Her dreams must have confused her... and yet...

She opened the latch, slid the barn door open and followed an anxious Sam inside. A horse whinnied, and the smells of dust and saddle soap and dry hay filled her nostrils. Snapping on the lights with one hand, she clutched the barrel of the gun with the other.

The horses were nervous. They rustled the straw on the floor of their boxes, snorting and pawing, tossing their dark heads and rolling their eyes as if they, too, were spooked. "It's all right," Chandra told them, though she knew that something in the barn was very, very wrong. The crying became louder and fiercer.

Her throat dry, her rifle held ready, Chandra walked carefully to the end stall, the only empty box. "What the devil...?" Chandra whispered as she spied a shock of black fur—no, *hair*—a baby's downy cap of hair! Chandra's heart nearly stopped, but she flew into action, laying down the gun, unlatching the stall and kneeling beside the small, swaddled bundle of newborn infant.

The tiny child was bound in a ratty yellow blanket and covered by a tattered army jacket. "Oh, God," Chandra whispered, picking up the small bundle only to have the piercing screams resume at a higher pitch. Blue-black eyes blinked at the harsh overhead lights, and the infant's little face was contorted and red from crying. One little fist had been freed from the blankets and now waved in agitation near its cheek. "Oh, God, oh, God." The baby, all lungs from the sound of it, squealed loudly.

"Oh, sweetheart, don't cry," Chandra murmured, plucking pieces of straw from the child's hair and holding him close to her breast, trying to be soothing. She scanned the rest of the barn, searching for the mother. "Hey—is anyone here?" Her sweat seemed to freeze on her skin as she listened for a response. "Hey? Anyone? Please, answer me!"

The only noises in the barn were the horses snorting, the baby hiccupping and crying, Sam's intermittent growls and Chandra's own thudding heart. "Shh...shh..." she said, as if the tiny infant could understand her. "We'll fix you up."

A mouse scurried across the floor, slipping into a crack in the barn wall, and Chandra, already nervous, had to bite back her own scream. "Come on," she whispered to the baby, as she realized the child had probably been abandoned. But who would leave this precious baby all alone? The infant howled more loudly as Chandra tucked it close to her. "Oh, baby, baby," Chandra murmured. Maternal emotions spurred her to kiss the downy little head while she secretly cursed the woman who had left this beautiful child alone and forsaken. "Who are you?" she whispered against the baby's dark crown. "And where's your mama?"

Wrapping the infant in her own jacket, she glanced around the dusty corners of the barn again, eyeing the hayloft, kicking open the door to the tack room, scanning the corners behind the feed barrels, searching for any signs of the mother. Sam, yelping and jumping at the baby, was no help in locating the woman's trail. "Hello? Are you here?" she called to anyone listening, but her own voice echoed back from the rafters.

"Look, if you're here, come on into the house. Don't be afraid. Just come in and we'll talk, okay?"

No answer.

"Please, if you can hear me, please come inside!"

Again, nothing. Just the sigh of the wind outside.

Great. Well, she'd tried. Whoever had brought the child here was on his or her own. Right now, the most pressing problem was taking proper care of the baby; anything else would have to wait. "Come on, you," she whispered to the infant again, tightening her hold on the squirming bundle. Ignoring the fretting horses, she slapped off the lights and closed the barn door behind her.

Once she was back in the cabin, Chandra cradled the child against her while she tossed fresh logs into the wood stove. "We'll get you warm," she promised, reaching for the phone and holding the receiver to her ear with her shoulder. She dialed 911, praying that the call would be answered quickly.

"Emergency," a dispatcher answered.

"Yes, this is Chandra Hill, I live on Flaming Moss Road," she said quickly, then rattled off her address over the baby's cries. "I discovered an infant in my barn. Newborn, dehydrated possibly, certainly hungry, with a chance of exposure. I—I don't know who it belongs to...or why it's here."

"We can send an ambulance."

"I live twenty miles from town. It'll be quicker if I meet the ambulance at Alder's Corner, where the highway intersects Flaming Moss."

"Just a minute." The dispatcher mumbled something to someone else and then was back on the line. "That's fine. The ambulance will meet you there."

"Good. Now, please contact the emergency room of the hospital...." Mechanically, she began to move and think in a way she hadn't done in years. Placing the child on the couch next to her, she carefully unwrapped the howling infant. Furious and hungry, the baby cried more loudly, his skinny little legs kicking. "It's a boy...probably two or three days old," she said, noticing the stump of the umbilical cord. How many infants so like this one had she examined during her short career as a physician? Hundreds. Refusing to let her mind wander into that forbidden territory, she concentrated on the wriggling child and carefully ran her fingers over his thin body. "He's Caucasian, very hungry, with no visible marks...." Her hands moved expertly over the smooth skin of the newborn, checking muscles and bones, small fingers and toes, legs, neck, spine, buttocks, head.... "Wait a minute..." She flipped the switch of a brighter light and noticed the yellow pallor of the whites of the baby's eyes. "He appears jaundiced and—" she touched the downy hair again, carefully prodding "—there's some swelling on the back of his head. Maybe caput succedaneum or cephalhematoma...yes, there's a slight bleeding from the scalp, and it appears only on the right side of his head. I don't think it's serious. The swelling isn't too large, but you'd better have a pediatrician look him over the minute he gets there." She continued to examine the infant as if he were her patient, her gaze practiced and sure. "I can't find anything else, at least not here without medical equipment. Did you get everything?"

"Every word," the dispatcher replied. "You're being recorded."

"Good." Chandra shone her flashlight in the baby's eyes, and he blinked and twisted his head away from the light. "Notify the sheriff's office that apparently the child's been abandoned."

"You don't know the mother?" the dispatcher questioned.

Chandra shook her head, though the woman on the other end of the line couldn't see her. "No. I have no idea whom this guy belongs to. So someone from the sheriff's office should come out here and look through my barn again and check the woods. I called out and looked around for the mother, but I didn't have much time. I was more concerned with the child." She glanced to the windows and the cold night beyond. "My guess is she isn't far off. You've got the address."

Chandra didn't wait for a response, but hung up. She pulled a blanket from her closet and rewrapped the tiny newborn. He was beautiful, she thought, with a shock of downy black hair that stood straight off his scalp and a voice that would wake the dead. But why had he been abandoned? Had the mother, perhaps homeless, left him in the relative comfort of the barn as she searched for food? But why not stop at the cabin? Why leave him in the barn where there was a chance he would go unnoticed, maybe even die? Chandra shuddered at the thought. No, any responsible mother would have knocked on the door and would never, *never* have abandoned her child. "Come on, you," she said to the baby, "we've got work to do. You can't just lie there and scream."

But scream he did until she swaddled him more tightly and held him in her arms again. Only then did his cries become pitiful little mews. Chandra clutched him even tighter; the sooner she got him to the hospital the better.

Sam was sitting at attention near the couch. She looked in his direction, and the big dog swept the floor with his tail. "You," she said, motioning to the retriever, "stick around. In case the mother wanders back or the police show up."

As if the dog could do anything, she thought with a wry smile.

She found more blankets and tucked the child into a wicker laundry basket which, along with several bungee cords and the baby, she carried to her suburban. After securing the basket by the safety belt in the back seat, she crisscrossed the bungee cords over the baby, hoping to hold him as tightly and safely as possible.

"Hang on," she said to the infant as she hauled herself into the driver's seat, slammed the door shut and switched on the ignition. She rammed the monstrous rig into gear. The beams of the headlights washed across the side of the barn, and Chandra half expected a woman to come running from the shadows. But no one appeared, and Chandra tromped on the accelerator, spewing gravel.

"Dr. O'Rourke. Dr. Dallas O'Rourke. Please call E.R."

Dallas O'Rourke was writing out instructions for a third-floor patient named William Aimes when the page sounded. He scowled menacingly, then strode to the nearest house phone and punched out the number for the main desk of Riverbend Hospital. Checking the clock at the nurse's station, he realized he'd been on duty for the past twenty-two hours. His back ached and his shoulders were stiff, and he felt gritty from lack of sleep. He probably looked worse than he felt, he thought grimly as the receiver of the phone rubbed against the stubble of beard on his chin.

A voice answered, and he cut in. "This is Dr. O'Rourke. I was just paged."

"That's right. I'll connect you to E.R."

The telephone clicked and a familiar voice answered quickly. "Emergency. Nurse Pratt."

"O'Rourke." Leaning a stiff shoulder against the wall, he scribbled his signature across Aimes's chart, then rubbed his burning eyes. How long had it been since he'd eaten? Six hours? Seven?

"You'd better hustle your bones down here," Shannon Pratt advised. "We're swamped, and we've got a live one coming in. The switchboard just took the call. Something about an abandoned baby, a newborn with possible exposure, dehydration, jaundice and cephalhematoma."

Dallas scowled to himself. What was the old saying? Something about no rest for the wicked? The adage seemed to apply. "I'll be down in a few minutes." God, what he wouldn't do for a hot shower, hotter cup of coffee, and about ten hours in the rack.

He only took the time to leave the chart in the patient's room and give the third-floor nurses' station some instructions about Bill Aimes's medication. "And make sure he takes it," Dallas warned. "It seems Mr. Aimes thinks he can self-diagnose."

"He won't fool us," Lenore Newell replied, and Dallas was satisfied. Lenore had twenty years of nursing experience under her belt, and she'd seen it all. If anyone could get Bill Aimes to swallow his medication, Dallas decided, Nurse Newell could.

Unwilling to wait for the elevator, he took the stairs to the first floor and shoved open the door. The bright lights and frenetic activity of the emergency room greeted him. Several doctors were treating patients, and there was a crowd in the waiting room.

Shannon Pratt, a slim, dark-haired woman and, in Dallas's opinion, the most efficient nurse on staff, gave the doctor a quick smile. "They're on their way. Mike just called. They'll be here in about five minutes."

Mike Rodgers was one of the regular paramedics who drove ambulance for Riverbend Hospital.

"How's the patient?"

Shannon glanced at the notes she'd attached to a clipboard that she cradled with one arm. "Looks like the information we received from the first call was right on. The paramedics confirmed what the woman who called in already told us. The baby—only a couple of days old—has some signs of exposure as well as possible jaundice and slight swelling on one side of the head—the, uh, right," she said, rechecking her notes. "No other visible problems. Vital signs are within the normal range."

"Good. Order a bilirubin and get the child under U.V. as soon as I finish examining him. Also, I want as much information from the mother as possible, especially her RH factor. If she doesn't know it, we'll take blood from her—"

Shannon touched Dallas lightly on the arm. "Hold on a minute, Doctor. The mother's not involved."

Dallas stopped. He glanced swiftly at Nurse Pratt—to see if she was putting him on. She wasn't. Her face was as stone sober as it always was in an emergency. "Not involved? Then how the hell—"

Pratt held up a hand. "The woman who found the child—"

"The woman who *found* the child?" Dallas repeated as they passed the admitting desk, where Nurse Lindquist, a drill sergeant of a woman, presided. Over the noise of rattling gurneys and wheelchairs, conversation, paging and computer terminals humming, Dallas heard the distant wail of a siren.

Pratt continued, "The mother isn't bringing him in. This is a case of abandonment, or so the woman who called—" she glanced down at her notes on her clipboard again "—Chandra Hill, claims. Apparently she's saying that she discovered the baby in her barn."

"Her *barn?*"

"Mmm. Doesn't know how he got there." Shannon rolled her large brown eyes and lifted one slim shoulder. "I guess we'll find out soon enough."

Dallas swore silently. "If she's not the mother, how can we do anything with—"

"We're already working on consent forms," Pratt cut in, ahead of him, as she usually was in a case like this. "The police are involved, and someone's looking up a judge to sign the waiver so we can admit the kid as a Baby John Doe."

"Wonderful," Dallas growled under his breath. With his luck, the kid's mother would show up, demand custody and file a complaint against the hospital. Or worse yet, not show up at all, and the child would have to be cared for by the state. "Just damned wonderful." What a way to end a shift!

The siren's wail increased to a glass-shattering scream that drowned out all conversation. Lights flashing, the white-and-orange rig ground to a stop near the double glass doors of the emergency room. Two men Dallas recognized hopped out of the cab and raced to the back of the emergency van.

"Okay, listen up," Dallas ordered Pratt. "I'll need that bilirubin A.S.A.P., and we'll need to test the child—drugs, HIV, white count, everything," he said, thinking of all the reasons a person might abandon a child. Maybe the woman couldn't afford proper medical attention for herself and the baby; maybe the child needed expensive care. "And get ready with an IV or a bottle..." God, what a mess!

The paramedics shoved open the back doors of the ambulance. Pulling out a small stretcher and carrying it between them, Mike Rodgers and Joe Klinger ran across the short covered span near the doors. A tiny baby, insulated by a thermal blanket, was strapped to the stretcher and was screaming bloody murder.

"Okay, Doc, looks like it's show time," Shannon observed as Dallas caught a glimpse of another vehicle, a huge red van of some sort, as it sped into the lot and skidded into a parking space.

The doors to the emergency room flew open. The paramedics, carrying the small stretcher, strode quickly inside.

"Room two," Nurse Pratt ordered.

Under the glare of fluorescent lights, Mike, a burly red-headed man with serious, oversize features and thick glasses, nodded curtly and headed down the hall without breaking stride. "As I said, it looks like exposure and dehydration, heart rate and b.p. are okay, but—"

Mike rattled off the child's vital signs as Joe unstrapped the child and placed him on the examining table. Dallas was listening, but had already reached for his penlight and snapped his stethoscope around his neck. He touched the child carefully. The right side of the infant's head was a little bit swollen, but there wasn't much evidence of bleeding. A good sign. The tiny boy's skin was tinged yellow, but again, not extremely noticeable. Whoever the woman was who found the child, she knew more than a little about medicine.

Dallas glanced over at the paramedic. "This woman who called in—Ms. Hill?—I want to talk to her. Do you have her number?"

"Don't need to," Mike said. "She followed us here. Drove that damned red van like a bat outta hell. . . ."

The red van. Of course. Good. Dallas wasn't convinced that she wasn't the mother just trying to get some free medical attention for her child. So how did she know about the child's condition? Either she'd diagnosed the baby herself or someone else had . . . someone who understood pediatric medicine. One way or another, Dallas thought, flashing the beam of his penlight into the baby's dark eyes, he needed to talk to Ms. Hill.

"When she shows up," he said, glancing at Nurse Pratt, "I want to see her."

Riverbend Hospital sprawled across five acres of hills. The building was either five floors, four or three, depending upon the terrain. Painted stark white, it seemed to grow from the very ground on which it was built.

It resembled a hundred other hospitals on the outside and inside, Chandra thought; it was a nondescript medical institution. She'd been here before, but now, as she got the runaround from a heavyset nurse at the emergency room desk, Chandra was rapidly losing her temper. "But I have to see the child, I'm the one who found him!" she said, with as much patience as she could muster.

The admitting nurse, whose name tag read Alma Lindquist, R.N., didn't budge. An expression of authority that brooked no argument was fixed on features too small for her fleshy face.

Chandra refused to be put off by Nurse Lindquist. She'd dealt with more than her share of authority figures in her lifetime—especially those in the medical profession. One more wouldn't stop her, though Nurse Lindquist did seem to guard the admittance gate to the emergency room of Riverbend Hospital as if it were the portal to heaven itself and Chandra was a sinner intent on sneaking past.

"If you're not the mother or the nearest living relative," Nurse Lindquist was saying in patient, long-suffering tones, "then you cannot be allowed—"

"I'm the responsible party." Chandra, barely holding on to her patience, leaned across the desk. She offered the woman a professional smile. "I found the boy. There's a chance I can help."

"Humph," the heavyset nurse snorted, obviously unconvinced that the staff needed Chandra's help, or opinion for that matter. Alma Lindquist lifted her reddish brows imperiously and turned back to the stack of admittance forms beside a humming computer terminal. "I'm sure Dr. O'Rourke will come out and let you know how the infant's doing as soon as the baby has been examined. Now, if you'll just take a chair in the waiting area . . ." She motioned a plump hand toward an alcove where olive green couches were grouped around Formica tables strewn with worn magazines. Lamps offered pools of light over the dog-eared copies of *Hunter's Digest, Women's Daily, Your Health,* and the like.

Chandra wasn't interested in the lounge or hospital routine or the precious domain of a woman on an authority trip. Not until she was satisfied that everything humanly possible was being done for the baby. "If you don't mind, I think I'll just see for myself," she said swiftly. Lifting her chin and creating her own aura of authority, Chandra marched through the gate separating the examining area from the waiting room as if she'd done it a million times.

"Hey! Hey—you can't go in there!" the nurse called after her, surprised that anyone would dare disregard her rules. "It's against all procedure! Hey, ma'am! Ms. Hill!" When Chandra's steps didn't falter, Nurse Lindquist shouted, "Stop that woman!"

"Hang procedure," Chandra muttered under her breath. She'd been in enough emergency rooms to know her way around. She quickly walked past prescription carts, the X-ray lab and a patient in a wheelchair, hurrying down the tiled corridors toward the distinctive sound of a baby's cry. She recognized another voice as well, the deep baritone belonging to the redheaded paramedic who had hustled the baby into the ambulance, Mike something-or-other.

She nearly ran into the paramedics as they left the examination room. "Is he all right?" she asked anxiously. "The baby?"

"He will be." Mike touched her lightly on the shoulder, as a kindly father would touch a worried child. "Believe me, he's in the best hands around these parts. Dr. O'Rourke'll take care of the boy."

The other paramedic—Joe—nodded and offered a gap-toothed smile. "Don't you worry none."

But she was worried. About a child she'd never seen before tonight, a child she felt responsible for, a child who, because she'd found him, had become, at least temporarily, a part of her life. Abandoned by his own mother, this baby needed someone championing his cause.

The baby's cries drifted through the partially opened door. Without a thought to "procedure," Chandra slipped into the room and watched as a scruffy-looking doctor bent over a table where the tiny infant lay.

The physician was a tall, lanky man in a rumpled lab coat. A stethoscope swung from his neck as he listened to the baby's heartbeat. Chandra guessed his age as being somewhere between thirty-five and forty. His black hair was cut long and looked as if it hadn't seen a comb in some time, his jaw was shaded with more than a day's growth of beard, and the whites of his eyes were close to bloodshot.

The man is dead on his feet. This was the doctor on whom she was supposed to depend? she thought angrily as her maternal instincts took charge of her emotions. He had no right to be examining the baby. Yet he touched the child gently, despite his gruff looks. Chandra took a step forward as he said to the nurse, "I want him on an IV immediately, and get that bilirubin. We'll need a pediatrician— Dr. Williams, if you can reach him." The physician's gaze centered on the squirming child. "In the meantime, have a special crib made up for him in the pediatric ward, but keep him isolated and under ultraviolet. We don't know much about him. See if he'll take some water from a bottle, but keep track of the intake. He could have anything. I want blood work and an urinalysis."

"A catheter?" Nurse Pratt asked.

"No!" Chandra said emphatically, though she understood the nurse's reasoning. But somehow it seemed cruel to subject this tiny lump of unwanted human flesh, this small person, to the rigors of twentieth-century hospital technology. *But that's why you brought him here, isn't it? So that he could get the best medical attention available?* Belatedly, she held her tongue.

But not before the doctor's head whipped around and Chandra was suddenly caught in the uncompromising glare of Dr. Dallas O'Rourke. She felt trapped, like a specimen under a microscope, and fought against the uncharacteristic need to swallow against a suddenly dry throat.

His eyes were harsh and cold, a vibrant shade of angry blue, his black eyebrows bushy and arched, his skin swarthy and tanned as it stretched tight across the harsh angles of his cheekbones and a nose that hooked slightly. Black Irish, she thought silently.

"You are . . . ?" he demanded.

"Chandra Hill." She tilted her chin and unconsciously squared her shoulders, as she'd done a hundred times before in a hospital not unlike this one.

"The woman who found the child." Dr. O'Rourke crossed his arms over his chest, his lab coat stretching at the shoulder seams, his lips compressed into a line as thin as paper, his stethoscope momentarily forgotten. "Ms. Hill, I'm glad you're here. I want to talk to you—"

Before he could finish, the door to the examining room flew open and banged against the wall. Chandra jumped, the baby squealed and O'Rourke swore under his breath.

Nurse Lindquist, red-faced and huffing, marched stiffly into the room. Her furious gaze landed on Chandra. "I knew it!" Turning her attention to the doctor, she said, "Dr. O'Rourke, I'm sorry. This woman—" she shook an accusing finger in Chandra's face "—refused to listen to me. I told her you'd talk to her after examining the child, but she barged in with complete disregard to hospital rules."

"I just wanted to see that the baby was safe and taken care of," Chandra interceded, facing O'Rourke squarely. "As I explained to the nurse, I've had medical training. I could help."

"Are you a doctor licensed in Colorado?"

"No, but I've worked at—"

"I knew it!" Nurse Lindquist cut in, her tiny mouth pursing even further.

"It's all right, Alma," O'Rourke replied over the baby's cries. "I'll handle Ms. Hill. Right now, we have a patient to deal with."

Nurse Lindquist's mouth dropped open, then snapped shut. Though her normal pallor had returned, two high spots of color remained on her cheeks. She shot Chandra a furious glare before striding, stiff backed, out of the room.

"You're not making any points here," the doctor stated, his hard jaw sliding to the side a little, as if he were actually amused at the display.

"That's not why I'm here." *Arrogant bastard,* Chandra thought. She'd seen the type before. Men of medicine who thought they were gods here on earth. Well, if Dr. O'Rourke thought he could dismiss her, he had another think coming. But to her surprise, he didn't ask her to leave. Instead, he turned his attention back to the baby and ran experienced hands over the infant's skin. "Okay, that should do it."

Chandra didn't wait. She picked up the tiny little boy, soothing the child as best she could, rocking him gently.

"Let's get him up to pediatrics," Dr. O'Rourke ordered.

"I'll take him." Nurse Pratt, after sending Chandra a quizzical glance, took the child from Chandra's unwilling arms and bustled out of the room.

The doctor waited until they were alone, then leaned a hip against the examining table. Closing his eyes for a second, he rubbed his temples, as if warding off a headache. Long, dark lashes swept his cheek for just an instant before his eyelids opened again. "Why don't you tell me everything you know about the baby," he suggested.

"I have," Chandra said simply. "I woke up and found him in my barn."

"Alone?"

"*I* was alone, and as far as I could tell, the baby was left."

He rubbed the back of his neck and winced, but some of the tension left his face. He almost smiled. "Come on, let's go down to the cafeteria. I'll buy you a cup of coffee. God knows I could use one."

Chandra was taken aback. Though his voice was gentle, practiced, his eyes were still harsh and assessing. "Why?"

"Why what?"

"The coffee. I don't think—"

"Humor me, Ms. Hill. I just have a few questions for you."

With a shrug, she agreed. After all, she only wanted what was best for the child. And, for the time being, this hard-edged doctor was her link to the baby. He held the door open for her, and she started instinctively toward the elevators. She glanced down a hallway, hoping to catch a glimpse of Nurse Pratt and the child.

Dr. O'Rourke, as if reading her mind, said, "The pediatric wing is on two and the nursery is on the other side, in maternity."

They reached the elevators and he pushed the call button. Crossing his arms over his chest and leaning a shoulder against the wall, he said, his voice slightly kinder, "Let's get back to the baby. You don't know whom he belongs to, right?"

"That's right."

"So he wasn't left by a relative or friend, someone who wasn't interested in keeping him?"

"No." Chandra felt a tide of color wash up her cheeks. "Look, Dr. O'Rourke, I've told you everything I know about him. My only concern is for the child. I'd like to stay here with him as long as possible."

"Why?" The doctor's gaze had lost its hard edge, but there were a thousand questions in his eyes. He was a handsome man, she realized, surprised that she noticed. And had it not been for the hours of sleeplessness that honed his features, he might even be appealing. But not to her, she reminded herself.

The elevator bell chimed softly and the doors whispered open. "You've done your duty—"

"It's more than duty, okay?" she cut in, unable to sever the fragile connection between her and the baby. Her feelings were pointless, she knew, but she couldn't just drive away from the hospital, leaving that small, abandoned infant. Not yet. Not until she was assured the child would be cared for. Dr. O'Rourke was holding the door open, so she stepped into the elevator.

"Dr. O'Rourke. Dr. Dallas O'Rourke..."

The doctor's shoulders slumped at the sound of the page. "I guess we'll have to take a rain check on the coffee." He seemed as if he were actually disappointed, but that was ridiculous. Though, to be honest, he looked as though he could use a quart of coffee.

As for Chandra, she was relieved that she didn't have to deal with him right now. He was unsettling somehow, and she'd already suffered through a very unsettling night. Pressing the Door Open button so that an elderly man could enter, she watched O'Rourke stride down the hall. She was grateful to be away from his hard, assessing gaze, though she suspected he wasn't as harsh as he outwardly appeared. She wondered if his sharp tongue was practiced, his guarded looks calculated....

"There she is! In there! Stop! Hold the elevator!"

Chandra felt a sinking sensation as she recognized the distinctive whine of Nurse Lindquist's voice. No doubt she'd called security and was going to have Chandra thrown off the hospital grounds. Footsteps clattered down the hall. Chandra glanced back to O'Rourke, whom she suddenly viewed as her savior, but he'd already disappeared around the corner at the far end of the corridor. As she looked in the other direction, she found the huge nurse, flanked by two deputies from the Sheriff's Department, moving with surprising speed toward her. Chandra's hand froze on the elevator's Door Open button, although her every instinct told her to flee.

One of the deputies, the shorter one with a flat face and salt-and-pepper hair, was staring straight at her. He didn't bother with a smile. "Chandra Hill?"

"Yes?"

He stiff-armed the elevator, holding the doors open, as if to ensure that she wouldn't escape. "I'm Deputy Bodine, and this is Deputy White." He motioned with his head toward the other man in uniform. "If you don't mind, we'd like to ask you a few questions about the child you found on your property."

Chapter Two

"So I followed the ambulance here," Chandra said, finishing her story as the two officers listened, alternately exchanging glances and sipping their coffee as she explained how she discovered the abandoned child.

Deputy Stan Bodine, the man who was asking the questions, slid his cafeteria chair closer to the table. "And you have no idea who the mother might be?"

"Not a clue," Chandra replied, tired of repeatedly answering the same questions. "I know it's strange, but that's what happened. Someone just left the baby in my barn." What was it about everyone in the hospital? Why were they so damned disbelieving? Aware of the curious glances cast her way by a few members of the staff who had come down to the cafeteria for their breaks, Chandra leaned across the table and met the deputy's direct gaze. "Why would I lie?"

"We didn't say—"

"I know, but I can tell you don't believe me."

Deputy White, the younger of the two, stopped writing in his notepad. With thin blond hair, narrow features and a slight build, he wasn't the least bit intimidating. In fact, he seemed almost friendly. Here, at least, was one man who seemed to trust that she was telling the truth.

Deputy Bodine was another story. As bulky as the younger man was slim, Bodine carried with him a cynical attitude honed by years with the Sheriff's Department. His expression was cautiously neutral, but suspicion radiated from him in invisible waves. As he swilled the bitter coffee and chewed on a day-old Danish he'd purchased at the counter, Chandra squirmed in her chair.

"No one said we didn't believe you," Bodine answered patiently. "But it's kind of an outrageous story, don't you think?"

"It's the truth."

"And we've seen lots of cases where someone has . . . changed the facts a little to protect someone."

"I'm *not* protecting anyone!" Chandra's patience hung by a fragile thread. She'd brought the baby to the hospital to get the poor child medical attention, and this cynic from the Sheriff's Department, as well as the good Dr. O'Rourke, were acting as if she were some kind of criminal. Only Deputy White seemed to trust her. "Look, if you don't believe me, you're welcome to check out all my acquaintances and relatives. I just found the baby. That's all. Someone apparently left him in the barn. I don't know why. There was no trace of the mother—or anyone else for that matter." To keep her hands busy, she rolled her cup in her fingers, and a thought struck her. "The only clue as to who the child might be could come from his swaddling. He was wrapped in a blanket—not the one I brought him here in—and an old army jacket."

Bodine perked up a bit. "Where's the jacket?"

"Back at my cabin."

"We'll pick it up in the morning. And don't disturb anything in that stall where you found the kid . . . or the rest of the barn for that matter." He took another bite of his Danish and washed it down with a swallow of coffee. Several crumbs fell onto the white table. He crumpled his cup. Without getting up from his chair, he tossed the wadded cup high into the air and watched as it bounced off the rim of a trash container.

The younger man clucked his tongue and tucked his notepad into his pocket. "I don't think the Nuggets will be drafting you this season," he joked. He shoved out his chair and picked up the discarded cup to arc it perfectly into the trash can.

"Lucky shot," Bodine grumbled.

Chandra was just grateful they were leaving. As Bodine scraped his chair back, Dr. O'Rourke strode into the room. He was as rumpled as before, though obviously his shift was over. His lab coat was missing, and he was wearing worn jeans, an off-white flannel shirt and a sheepskin jacket.

"Just the man we wanted to see," Bodine said, settling back in his chair. Chandra's hopes died. She wanted this interrogation over with.

"So I heard." O'Rourke paid for a cup of coffee and joined the group. "Nurse Pratt said you needed some information on Baby Doe. I've left a copy of the admittance forms at the E.R. desk, and I'll send you a complete physical description of the child, as well as that of his condition, as soon as it's transcribed, probably by the afternoon. I can mail it or—"

"We'll pick it up," Bodine cut in, kicking back his chair a little so that he could view both Chandra and O'Rourke in one glance. "Save us all some time. Anything specific we should know right now?"

"Just that the baby is jaundiced, with a swelling on the right side of his head, probably from a difficult birth. Other than that, he looks pretty healthy. We're keeping him iso lated, and we're still running tests, but he's eating and giving all the nurses a bad time."

Chandra swallowed a smile. So O'Rourke did have a sense of humor after all.

The doctor continued. "A pediatrician will examine him as soon as he gets here, and we'll give you a full report."

"Anything else?" White asked, scribbling quickly in his notepad again. He was standing now, but writing as quickly as before.

"Just one thing," O'Rourke replied, his gaze sliding to Chandra before returning to the two deputies. "The umbilical cord wasn't severed neatly or clamped properly."

Bodine dusted his hands. "Meaning?"

"Meaning that the baby probably wasn't born in a hospital. I'd guess that the child was delivered without any medical expertise at all. The mother probably just went into labor about three days ago, experienced some difficulty, and when the baby finally arrived, used a pair of scissors or a dull knife to cut the cord."

Chandra sucked in her breath and O'Rourke's gaze swung to her. She cringed at the thought of the baby being born in anything less than sterile surroundings, though, of course, she knew it happened often enough.

"What do you think?" O'Rourke asked, blue eyes drilling into hers.

"I don't know. I didn't really look at the cord, only to see that it wasn't bleeding." Why would he ask her opinion?

"You examined the infant, didn't you?"

Chandra's response died on her tongue. Dr. O'Rourke didn't know anything about her, she assumed, especially her past, and she intended to keep it that way. She'd come to this part of the country for the express purpose of burying her past, and she wasn't about to unearth it now. She fiddled with her coffee cup. "Yes, I examined him."

"And you were right on with your diagnosis."

No reason to explain. Not here. The Sheriff's Department and Dr. O'Rourke—and the rest of the world, for that matter—might find out all about her eventually, but not tonight. "I've had medical training," she replied, the wheels turning in her mind. "I work as a white-water and camping guide. We're required to know basic first aid, and I figure the more I know, the better I can handle any situation. So, yes, I've taken every medical course I could."

O'Rourke seemed satisfied; his gaze seemed less suspicious and his eyes turned a warmer shade of blue.

Bodine stood and hiked up his pants. "Well, even if you don't think the baby was delivered in a hospital, it won't hurt to check and find out if anyone's missing a boy."

"Missing from a hospital?" Chandra asked.

O'Rourke lifted a dark eyebrow. "What better place to steal a newborn?"

"Steal?" she repeated.

Squaring his hat on his head, Deputy Bodine said, "The black-market baby business is booming these days."

"You think someone *stole* this baby then left him in my barn? That's crazy—"

Bodine smiled his first genuine smile of the night. "Sounds a little farfetched, I admit, but we have to consider every angle. Could be that whoever took Baby Doe could have holed up in your barn for the night and something went wrong. Or they left him there while they went searching for food or more permanent shelter."

"Or you could've scared 'em off," Deputy White added.

Chandra shook her head. "There was no one in the barn. And I live nearly ten miles from the nearest store."

"We'll check out all the possibilities in the morning," Bodine assured her. Turning his gaze to O'Rourke, he said, "Thanks, Doctor. Ms. Hill."

The deputies left, and Chandra, not even realizing how tense she'd become, felt her shoulders slowly relax.

"So how's he doing?" she asked, surprised at her own anxiety, as if she and that tiny baby were somehow connected, though they weren't, of course. The child belonged to someone else. And probably, within the next few hours, Bodine and White would discover the true identity of Baby Doe and to whom he belonged. Chandra only hoped that the parents had one hell of an explanation for abandoning their child.

"The boy'll be fine," O'Rourke predicted, stretching his long legs in front of him. He sipped from his cup, scowled at the bitter taste and set the cup on the table, content to let the steam rise to his face in a dissipating cloud. Chandra noticed the lines of strain around the edges of his mouth, the droop at the corners of his eyelids.

"Can I see him?" she asked.

"In the morning."

"It *is* the morning."

His gaze locked with hers and the warmth she'd noticed earlier suddenly fled. "Look, Ms. Hill, I think you and the kid both need some rest. I know *I* do." As if to drive home his point, he rubbed a kink from his shoulders. "You can see him around ten."

"But he *is* eating." She'd heard him say so before, of course, but she couldn't stem the question or the concern she felt for the child.

A whisper of a smile crossed the doctor's thin lips. "Nurse Pratt can barely keep up with him." O'Rourke took another swallow of his coffee, his unsettling eyes regarding Chandra over the rim of his cup. She felt nervous and flustered, though she forced herself to remain outwardly calm. "So who do you think left him in your barn?" he asked.

"I don't know."

"No pregnant friends who needed help?"

Her lips twisted wryly. "I already told the deputies, if I had friends who needed help, I wouldn't suggest they use one of my stalls as a birthing room. They could've come into the house or I would've driven them to the hospital. I think, somehow, we would've found 'room at the inn,' so to speak.''

O'Rourke arched a thick eyebrow, and his lips twitched, as if he were suppressing a smile. "Look, there's no reason to get defensive. I'm just looking for some answers.''

"I gave all of mine to the deputies," she replied, tired of the unspoken innuendoes. She leaned forward, and her hair fell in front of her shoulders. "Now *you* look, *Doctor* O'Rourke, if I knew anything about that baby—anything at all—I'd pass that information along.''

He didn't speak, but his relentless stare continued to bother her. The man was so damn intimidating, used to getting his way—a handsome, arrogant son of a gun who was used to calling the shots. She could see he was tired, irritated, but a little amused at her quick temper. "You know," she said, "I expected the third degree from the police, but not from you.''

He lifted a shoulder. "The more I know about the child, the better able I am to take care of him. I just don't want to make any mistakes.''

She was about to retort, but the words didn't pass her lips. Chandra knew far too well about making mistakes as a physician. Her throat closed at the sudden burst of memories, and it was all she could do to keep her hands from shaking. She took a quick drink of coffee, then licked her lips. When she looked up at O'Rourke again, she found him staring at her so intently that she was certain he could see past the web of lies she'd so carefully woven around her life here in Ranger, Colorado. Did he know? Could he guess that she, too, had once been a physician?

But no one knew about her past, and that's the way she intended to keep it.

The silence stretched between them, and she shuffled her feet as if to rise. It was late, and she wanted to get some sleep before she returned later in the morning, and yet there was something mesmerizing about Dr. O'Rourke that kept her glued to her chair. He was good-looking in a sensual way that unnerved her, but she'd been around lots of good-looking men, none of whom had gotten under her skin the way O'Rourke had. Maybe it was because he was a doctor, or maybe it was because she was anxious about the baby, or maybe he was just so damned irresistible that even she, a woman who'd sworn off men, and most specifically men with medical degrees, was fascinated. She nearly choked on her coffee.

As if sensing she was about to flee, he finished his coffee and cleared his throat. "You know," he said, tenting his hands under his chin, "you'd better get used to answering questions, because the minute the press gets wind of this story, you're going to be asked to explain a helluva lot more than you have tonight."

The press. Her heart dropped like a stone and memories rushed over her—painful memories of dealing with reporters, photographers, cameramen. Oh, God, she couldn't face them again. She wasn't ready for the press. What if some hotshot reporter saw fit to dig into her background, through her personal life? Her hands grew suddenly damp. She slid her arms through the sleeves of the jacket she'd tossed over the back of her chair. "I think I can handle a few reporters," she lied, hoping she sounded far more confident than she felt.

"It'll be more than a few. Think about it. This could be the story of the year. Christmas is only a few months away, and the press just loves this kind of gut-wrenching drama."

"You could be wrong."

O'Rourke shook his head and stifled a yawn. "Nope. An abandoned baby, a complicated, unexplained birth, perhaps a missing mother, the mystery child swaddled only in an old army jacket—could it be the father's?—it all makes interesting copy." Rubbing a hand around his neck, he added, "You'll have a couple of reporters from the *Ban-*

ner, maybe someone from Denver. Not to mention the local television stations. My guess is that this story will go regional at least.'' He lifted his eyebrows speculatively, as if he believed he were far more informed than she. Typical. ''And once the story hits the news services, I'll bet that neither one of us is gonna get a moment's rest.'' He crossed one battered running shoe over the other and rested his heels on the seat of the chair Deputy White had recently vacated.

''Are you trying to scare me?'' Chandra asked.

''Just preparing you for the inevitable.''

''I can handle it,'' she assured him, while wondering what it was about this man that made her bristle. One minute she wanted to argue with him, the next she wanted to trust him with her very life. Good Lord, she must be more tired than she'd guessed. She'd instinctively come to depend on him because he was a doctor—the one man who could keep her in contact with the baby. After all, he could stop her from seeing the child.

Deep down, though, she knew her anger wasn't really directed at Dr. O'Rourke specifically. In fact, her wrath wasn't really aimed at doctors in general; just at a few doctors she'd known in her past, especially a particularly egotistical plastic surgeon to whom she'd once been married: Douglas Patrick Pendleton, M.D., P.C., and all-around jerk.

Now she couldn't afford to have Dr. O'Rourke against her. Not only was he her link to the child, there was a chance he might help her with the press and the Sheriff's Department—not that she needed any help, she reminded herself. But Dr. O'Rourke did seem fair and was probably sometimes kind, even though he appeared ragged and cynical around the edges.

''I guess I am tired,'' she finally said, as half an apology. Dr. O'Rourke wasn't the least bit like Doug. No, this man with his rugged good looks, beat-up running shoes and worn jacket looked more like a mountain climber than an emergency-room physician. She couldn't imagine him reading medical journals or prescribing blood-pressure medicine or attending medical conferences in Chicago or New York.

And yet it did seem possible that he could care for an abandoned infant. On that score, Chandra was comfortable. O'Rourke, she sensed, was a good doctor, the kind of man who had dedicated himself to people in need rather than to the almighty dollar. Unless the unshaven jaw, worn clothes and fatigue were all part of an act.

She didn't think so. His gaze was too honest. Cutting, yes. Intense, certainly. But honest.

Scraping back her chair, she stood and thrust her hand across the table. "Thanks for all the help."

He clasped her palm with his big hand, and she forced a smile, though Dr. O'Rourke didn't return the favor. As his fingers surrounded hers, the doctor stared at her with those electric blue eyes that could look straight into her soul, and her face suddenly felt hot.

Quickly, Chandra yanked back her hand and stuffed it into the pocket of her jeans. Her voice nearly failed her. "I'll be back later," she assured him as she turned and marched out of the cafeteria, hoping he didn't guess that she'd reacted to his touch. She was tired, that was all. Tired and nervous about the infant. God, what a night!

Dallas watched Chandra Hill retreat. A fascinating woman, he thought grudgingly as he swirled the dregs of coffee in his cup. There was something about her that didn't quite click, an attitude that didn't fit with the rest of her.

Still, she intrigued him. The feel of her hand in his had caused his heart to race a second, and she'd reacted, too— he'd seen the startled look in her eyes as she'd drawn back. He laughed inwardly. If she only knew how safe she was with him. He'd sworn off beautiful women long ago, and despite her uncombed hair, hastily donned clothes and face devoid of makeup, Chandra Hill was gorgeous.

And trouble. One hundred fifteen pounds of trouble packed onto a lithe frame. She obviously bucked authority: Nurse Lindquist would testify to that. At the thought of Alma Lindquist's agitated expression, Dallas grinned. Yes, he imagined Chandra with her sharp tongue and high-handed attitude could get under anyone's skin.

Fortunately, Dallas didn't have time for a woman in his profession. Not any woman. And especially not a firecracker like Ms. Hill. He rubbed his eyes and blinked several times, trying to dispel her image.

He was off duty. One last look at the Baby John Doe and then he'd go home and sleep for twelve hours. Maybe longer. But first, he might stop by the sheriff's office and listen to the recording of Chandra Hill's call to the emergency dispatcher. If he heard the tape, perhaps he'd get a better perspective on what condition the child was in when she found him. Oh, hell, it probably wouldn't do any good. In fact, he decided, he was just curious about the lady. And he hadn't been curious about a woman in a long, long time.

Squashing his cup with one hand, he shoved himself upright and glanced at the corridor down which Chandra had disappeared.

Who was this tiny woman with her unlikely knowledge of medicine? Jaundice was one thing, the layman could spot that. And a lay person might notice the swelling on the baby's head. But to come up with the medical term after a few first aid courses? Unlikely.

Nope. For some reason, Chandra Hill was deliberately holding back. His eyes narrowed at the thought.

Obviously the child wasn't hers. He'd checked out her trim figure and quick step. No, she wasn't the least bit postpartum, and she was far too young to have a daughter who'd gotten pregnant. But a sister? Or a friend?

Could the baby be stolen? Could Chandra have taken the child from its home, then realized it needed medical attention, concocted this story and brought him in? Dallas didn't think so. A dozen questions about Chandra Hill swam through his tired mind, but he couldn't come up with an answer.

Drawing in a long breath, he was surprised that the scent of her—a clean soapy scent unaffected by perfume—lingered in the stale air of the cafeteria, a fresh breeze in this desert of white walls, polished chrome, chipped Formica and the ever-present smell of antiseptic.

She was definitely a mystery, he decided as he shoved back his chair, but a mystery he was too damned tired to unravel.

Chapter Three

Sam was waiting for Chandra. As she opened the door, he jumped up, yipping excitedly, his tail wagging with unbridled enthusiasm. "Oh, come off it," Chandra said, smiling despite the yawn that crept up on her. "I wasn't gone that long."

But the big dog couldn't get enough attention. He bounded back and forth from his empty dish to her as she started for the stairs. "Don't get too anxious, Sam. Breakfast isn't for another three hours." In the loft, she nudged off one boot with the toe of the other. "What a night! Do you believe it? The police and even the doctor seem to think I had something to do with stealing the baby or kidnapping the kid or God only knows what! And that Dr. O'Rourke, you should meet him..." She shook her head, as if she could physically shake out her own thoughts of the doctor. Handsome, arrogant and sexy, he was a man to steer well clear of. But she couldn't. Not if she wanted to see the baby again. "Believe me, this is one mess," she told the dog, who was still pacing in the kitchen.

She thought about checking the barn one last time, but was too exhausted. Tossing off her jacket, she dropped onto the unmade bed, discarded her jeans and sought solace under the eiderdown quilt she'd inherited from her grandmother.

With a disgruntled sigh, Sam swept up the stairs and parked in his favorite spot on the floor near the end of the bed. Chandra heard his toes click on the old pine boards as he circled three times before dropping to the floor. She sighed to herself and hoped sleep would quickly overcome her weary body as it seemed to have done for the old dog.

Three days after moving into this place a couple of years before, Chandra had discovered Sam, so thin his ribs showed beneath his matted, dusty coat, his eyes without spark and a wound that stretched from one end of his belly to the other. He'd snarled at her approach, his white teeth flashing defensively as she'd tried to touch him. But she'd brought him water and food, and the listless dog had slowly begun to trust her. She'd eventually cleaned the wound, the mark of a cornered wild animal, she'd guessed, and brought Sam into the house. He'd been with her ever since, a permanent and loving fixture in her life.

But a far cry from a man or a child.

She smiled sadly and pulled the covers closer around her neck. Just because she'd found an abandoned infant was no reason to start dreaming old dreams that she'd discarded long ago. But though her body was fatigued, her mind was spinning with images of the wailing, red-faced infant, the sterile hospital room and the unsettling visage of Dr. Dallas O'Rourke. Even with her eyes closed, she could picture him—jet black hair, eyes as blue as a mountain lake and lips that could thin in anger or gentle into the hint of a smile.

Good Lord, what was wrong with her? In frustration, she pounded her pillow with her fist. In less than four hours, she had to get up and lead a white-water expedition of inexperienced rafters down the south fork of the Rattlesnake River. She didn't have time for complications, especially complications involving a man.

She glared at the clock one more second before squeezing her eyes closed and thinking how she would dearly love someday to have a baby of her very own.

Dallas washed the grit from his eyes and let the spray of the shower pour over him. He leaned one arm against the slippery tiles of the stall and closed his eyes as the jets of hot water soothed the ache of overly tired muscles.

The past thirty-six hours had been rough, one case after another. A twelve-year-old with a broken arm, a messy automobile accident with one fatality and two critically injured passengers flown by helicopter to Denver, a drug overdose, two severe strep cases, an elderly woman who had fallen and not only broken her hip, but fractured her pelvis, and, of course, the abandoned baby.

And it was the thoughts of the infant and the woman who'd found him that continued to rattle around in Dallas's tired mind. Probably because he was overworked. Overly tired. His emotions already strung tight because of the phone call....

He twisted off the faucets and pulled down a towel from the top of the glass shower doors, rubbing his body dry, hoping to infuse a little energy through his bloodstream.

He should eat, but he couldn't face an empty refrigerator. The joys of being a bachelor, he thought fatalistically, because he knew, from the experience of a brief, painful marriage, that he would never tie himself down to one woman again. No, medicine was his mistress, and a demanding mistress she was. She exacted far more attention than any woman would. Even the woman to whom he'd been married, Jennifer Smythe O'Rourke Duncan.

The bitch. He still couldn't think of her without the bitter taste of her betrayal rising like bile in his throat. How could he have been duped by her, when all along, she'd been more of a slave to her precious profession than he had to his?

He didn't bother shaving, that he could do in the morning, but walked through the connecting door to the bedroom and flopped, stark naked, onto the king-size bed. He dropped the towel onto the floor. He'd pick up it and his discarded clothes in the morning.

Muttering oaths he saved for the memory of his marriage, he noticed the red light flashing on his phone recorder, though he hadn't been paged. A personal call. Great. He didn't have to guess who the caller was. He rewound the tape and, settling back on the pillows, listened as his half brother's voice filled the room.

"Hey, Dal. How's it goin'? I just thought I'd touch base before I drop by tomorrow. You remember, don't ya?"

How could he forget, Dallas thought grimly. His half brother, Brian, was here in the waning weeks before college started, not because he was working, but because he'd spent the summer camping and rafting in the wilderness. Only now, with less than two weeks until he left for school, did Brian think about the more practical side of education.

"Hey, man, I really hate to bug you about this and I'll pay you back every dime, you know I will, but I just need a little something to keep me goin' until my money gets here."

Right. Brian's money was scholarship dollars and not nearly enough of them to pay for the tuition, books and a carefree life-style.

The machine clicked off, and Dallas scowled. He shouldn't loan Brian another nickel. Already the kid was into him for nearly ten thousand. But his mother's other children, Brian, Brian's twin sister, Brenda, and their older sister, Joanna, were the only family Dallas had ever known.

However, the loans to Brian were starting to bother Dallas, and he wondered, not for the first time, if he should be writing checks directly to University of Southern California rather than to the kid himself.

He'd find out this afternoon. After he felt refreshed and after he made rounds at the hospital, checking on his patients. The image of the newborn flitted through his mind again, and Dallas wondered if he'd run into Chandra Hill. Now there was a woman who was interesting, a woman who knew her own mind, a woman with a presence of authority that was uncommon, a woman who, even in old boots, jeans and a nightshirt, her hair wild, her face free of makeup, was the most attractive woman he'd seen in a long, long time.

He rolled under the covers, switched off the light and decided, as he drifted off, that chances were he might just see her again. And that thought wasn't all that unpleasant.

Chandra pulled her hair into a ponytail when she heard the hum of an engine and the crunch of tires against the gravel drive. She pulled back the curtains to discover a tan cruiser from the Sheriff's Department rolling to a stop near the barn. Sam, vigilant as ever, began to bark and growl.

"You haven't had this much excitement in a long while, have you?" Chandra asked the retriever as she yanked open the door. Two deputies, the same men she'd met in the hospital, climbed out of the car.

She met them on the porch.

"Sorry to bother you so early," Deputy White apologized, "but we're about to go off duty and would like to check over the barn and house."

"Just to see if there's anything you might have missed," Bodine added.

"I hope there is," Chandra replied, feeling more gracious this morning than she had last night. She thought again, as she had for the past four hours, of the dark-haired infant. She'd called the hospital the minute she'd awakened, but had been unable to prod much information from the nurse who had taken her call. "Doing as well as can be expected. Resting comfortably... in no apparent distress...."

When Chandra had mentioned that she'd brought the baby in, the nurse had warmed a bit. "Oh, Miss Hill, yes. Dr. O'Rourke said you'd probably call." Chandra's heart had nearly stopped. "But there's nothing new on the baby's condition."

So Chandra had been given stock answers that told her nothing. *Nothing!* Except that O'Rourke had had the decency to advise the staff that she would be inquiring. Surprised that he'd bothered at all, she again decided she'd have to make a friend of O'Rourke, even if it killed her.

She hadn't been this frustrated since she'd lived in Tennessee.... With a start, she pulled herself away from the painful thought of her past and her short-lived marriage, noticing that the deputies looked beyond fatigued. "How about a cup of coffee before you get started?" she asked, and the weary men, seeming much less belligerent in the soft morning light, smiled in response.

"I wouldn't want to trouble you," White said.

"No trouble at all. I was just about to pour myself a cup."

"In that case, you're on," Bodine cut in, obviously not wanting the younger man to talk them out of a quick break.

They followed her inside. Sam, ever watchful, growled deep in his throat as they crossed the threshold, but the men seemed unintimidated by the old retriever.

Chandra reached for two mugs from the shelf near the kitchen window and couldn't help asking, "Have you learned anything else?"

"About the baby?" Bodine asked, and taking off his hat, he shook his head. "Not yet. We thought maybe we could find something here. You got that jacket?"

"The what...? Oh! Just a minute." She poured them each a mug of coffee from the glass pot warming on the burner of the coffee maker. From the closet, she retrieved the ratty old army jacket and tattered blanket that had swaddled the newborn. Smudges of dirt, a few wisps of straw and several patches of a dark, dried substance that looked like blood discolored the dull green jacket. Faded black letters stated: U S ARMY, but no other lettering was visible.

"Anyone could pick up something like this in a local G.I. surplus store," Bodine grumbled to himself as he searched the jacket's pockets and discovered nothing more exciting than lint. He focused his attention on the blanket. It offered few clues to the identity of the newborn, fewer than the jacket. Frowning, he pulled a couple of plastic bags from his pocket and wrapped the blanket and jacket separately, then accepted a cup of coffee. Motioning toward his plastic-encased bundles, he added, "We'll see if the lab can come up with any clues from these."

"But don't hold your breath," White added. "Despite what Sheriff Newell thinks, the lab guys aren't gods. There's just not too much here to go on." He flashed a hint of a smile as Chandra handed him a steaming cup. "Thanks."

"Our best hope is for someone to step forward and claim the kid."

"Is it?" Chandra asked, surprised by her own sense of dread of some relative appearing. "But what if whoever tries to claim the child is a fraud?"

"We won't let that happen." Nonetheless, Bodine's eyebrows drew together and a deep cleft appeared on his forehead. He was worried. He studied the hot black liquid in his mug, as if he could find the answers he was searching for in the coffee. "Why don't you go over your story one more time." He held up a couple of fingers when he caught Chandra's look of distress. "Since we're here, talk us through it again and show us what you did last night."

Chandra wasn't all that eager to repeat the story, but she knew that was the only way to gain the deputies' confidence. And after all, they were all on the same side, weren't they? Didn't Chandra, the police and the hospital staff only want what was best for the tiny, motherless infant?

"Okay," she said with a forced smile. "It's just exactly what I said last night." As they sipped their coffee, Chandra pointed to the loft. "I was sleeping up there when Sam—" the big dog perked up his ears and his tail dusted the floor at the sound of his name "—started barking his fool head off. Wouldn't let up. And that's when I heard the sound."

"The baby crying," White cut in.

"Yes, but I didn't know that it was a baby at first." She continued while they finished their coffee, then led them back outside as Sam tagged along.

The sun was climbing across the morning sky, but frost still glazed the gravel of the parking lot. Sam nosed around the base of a blue spruce where, hidden in the thick needles, a squirrel scolded him. Deputy White tossed the jacket and blanket onto the front seat of the car.

"The noise was coming from the barn." Chandra followed her footsteps of the night before and shoved open the barn door. Shafts of sunlight pierced the dark interior, and the warm smell of horses and musty hay greeted her. The horses nickered softly as dust motes swirled in the air, reflecting the morning light.

"The baby was in the end stall." She pointed to the far wall while petting two velvety noses thrust over the stall doors.

As the officers began their search, Chandra winked at Cayenne, her favorite gelding. "I bet you want to go out," she said, patting his sleek neck. In response, the sorrel tossed his head and stamped. "I'll take that as a yes." Cayenne shoved his big head against her blouse and she chuckled. "Grouchy after you missed a night's sleep, aren't you?" She walked through the first stall and yanked open the back door. One by one, she opened the connecting gates of the other stalls and the horses trotted eagerly outside to kick up their heels and run, bucking and rearing, their tails unfurling like silky banners behind them.

Chandra couldn't help but smile at the small herd as she stood in the doorway. Life had become so uncomplicated since she'd moved to Ranger, and she loved her new existence. Well, life had been uncomplicated until last night. She rubbed her hand against the rough wood of the door and considered the baby, who only a few hours before had woken her and, no doubt, changed the course of her quiet life forever.

Inside the barn, Deputy Bodine examined the end stall while Deputy White poked and prodded the barrels of oats and mash, checked the bridles and tack hanging from the ceiling and then clambered up the ladder to the hayloft. A mouse scurried into a crack in the wall, and cobwebs, undisturbed for years, hung heavy with dust.

"This yours?" Bodine asked, holding up Chandra's father's .22, which she'd left in the barn upon discovering the infant.

Heat crept up her neck. "I must've dropped it here when I found the baby. I was so concerned about him, I didn't think of much else."

Bodine grunted as he checked the chamber.

"Nothing up here," Deputy White called down from the loft.

"I could've guessed," Bodine muttered under his breath as he turned his attention back to the stall, instructing Chandra to reconstruct the scene. She pointed out the position of the baby and answered all the questions he asked. Deputy White climbed down the ladder from the loft and, after observing the stall, asked a few more questions that Chandra couldn't answer.

The deputies didn't say as much, but Chandra read in their expressions that they'd come up against a dead end. Outside, they walked through the paddocks and fields, and even followed a couple of trails into the nearby woods. But they found nothing.

"Well, that's about all we can do for now," Bodine said as they walked across the yard. He brushed the dust from his hands.

"What about the baby?" Chandra asked, hoping for just a little more information on the infant. "What happens to him?"

"Don't worry about him. He's in good hands at the hospital. The way I hear it, Dr. O'Rourke is the best E.R. doctor in the county, and he'll link the kid up to a good pediatrician."

"I see."

Bodine actually offered her a smile. "I'm sure O'Rourke will let you look in on the kid, if you want. In the meantime, we'll keep looking for the baby's ma." He opened the passenger side of the cruiser while Deputy White slid behind the wheel. "If we find her, she's got a whole lotta questions to answer before she gets her kid back."

"And if you don't find her?"

"The baby becomes a ward of the state until we can locate a parent, grandparent or other relative."

Chandra's heart wrenched at the thought. "He'll be put in an institution?"

"Probably a foster home—whatever Social Services decides. But we'll cross that bridge when we come to it. Right now, we have to find the mother or next of kin. We'll keep you posted," he said, as if reading the worry in her eyes for the very first time.

Bodine slid into his seat, and Deputy White put the car into gear. Chandra waited until the car had disappeared around the bend in the drive before returning to the house with the rifle.

So what happens next? she wondered. If nothing else, the baby was certainly a part of her life.

As she walked into the house, she heard the phone ringing. She dashed to the kitchen. "Hello?"

"Miss Hill?"

She froze as she recognized Dr. O'Rourke's voice. "Hello, doctor," she said automatically, though her throat was dry. Something was wrong with the baby. Why else would he phone her?

"I thought you'd like to know that the baby's doing well," he said, and her knees nearly gave out on her. Tears of relief sprang to her eyes. O'Rourke chuckled, and the sound was throaty. "He's got the nurses working double time, but he's eating, and his vital signs are normal."

"Thank God."

"Anytime you want to check on him, just call," Dallas said.

"Thanks for calling."

There was a long pause before O'Rourke replied. "You seemed concerned last night and...since the boy has no family that we know of..."

"I appreciate the call."

As Dallas hung up the phone in his office at the hospital, he wondered what the devil had gotten into him. Calling Chandra Hill? All night long he'd remembered the worry in her eyes and, though he wasn't scheduled to work for hours, he'd gotten up and gone directly to the hospital, where he'd examined the baby again.

There was something about the boy that touched a part of him he'd thought was long buried, though he assumed his emotions were tangled up in the circumstances. The baby had been abandoned. Dallas's emotional reaction to the infant was because he knew that baby had no one to love him. No wonder he had felt the unlikely tug on his heartstrings when he'd examined the baby and the infant had blinked up at him with trusting eyes.

"This is crazy," Dallas muttered, and headed back to the parking lot. He would drive over to the club and swim out his frustrations before grabbing some breakfast.

Riverbend Hospital appeared larger in daylight. The whitewashed walls sprawled upward and outward, seeming to grow along the hillside, spawning several clinics connected by wide breezeways. The Rocky Mountains towered behind one facility, and below it, within view, flowed the Rattlesnake River. The town of Ranger was three miles away.

Chandra parked her truck in the visitors lot and prepared herself for a confrontation with another nurse on an authority trip. She wouldn't have to pass anywhere near the emergency room, so in all probability, she wouldn't run into Nurse Lindquist again. Or Dr. O'Rourke. He'd appeared dead on his feet last night, surely by now he was sleeping the morning away.

Probably with his wife.

Chandra's eyebrows pulled together, and above her nose a groove deepened—the worry line, Doug used to call it. The thought that Dr. O'Rourke was married shouldn't have been unpleasant. Good Lord, he deserved a normal life with a wife and kids... yet...

"Oh, stop it!" she grumbled, walking under the flat roof of a breezeway leading to the main entrance of the hospital. The doors opened automatically and she walked through.

The reception area was carpeted in an industrial-strength weave of forest green. The walls were gray-white and adorned with framed wildlife posters hung exactly ten feet apart.

A pert nurse with a cap of dark curls, a dash of freckles strewn upon an upturned nose and a genuine smile greeted Chandra from behind the information desk. "May I help you?"

Chandra returned the woman's infectious grin. "I hope
so. I'm Chandra Hill. I brought in the baby—"

The nurse, Jane Winthrop, laughed. "I *heard* about you
and the baby," she said, her dark eyes flashing merrily. "I
guess I should transfer to the night shift in E.R. That's
where all the action is."

"Is it?" Chandra replied.

"Oh, yeah. But a lot of it's not too pretty, y'know. Car
accidents—there was a bad one last night, not too long before you brought in the baby." Her smile faded and her
pretty dark eyes grew serious. "Anyway, what can I do for
you?"

Jane Winthrop was a refreshing change from Alma
Lindquist.

"I'd like to see the baby, see how he's doing."

"No problem. He's in pediatrics, on two. Take the elevator up one floor and turn to your left. Through the double doors and you're there. The admitting nurse, Shannon
Pratt, is still with him, I think. She'd just started her shift
when they brought the baby in."

Chandra didn't waste any time. She followed Jane's directions and stopped by the nurse's station in the pediatric
wing on the second floor. Chandra recognized Nurse Pratt,
the slim brunette, but hadn't met the other woman, plump,
apple cheeked, with platinum blond hair, a tanning-booth
shade to her skin and pale blue eyes rimmed with eyelashes
that were thick with mascara.

"You're back," Shannon said, looking up from some
paperwork on the desk. "I thought you would be." She
touched the eraser end of a pencil to her lips as she smiled
and winked. "And I bet you're looking for one spunky little guy, right?" Before Chandra could answer, Shannon
waved toward one of the long corridors. She leaned closer
to the other nurse. "I'll be back in a minute. This is the
woman who brought in the Baby Doe."

The blond nurse, whose nameplate read Leslie Nelson, R.N., smiled and a dimple creased one of her rosy cheeks. "He's already won over the entire staff—including Alma Lindquist!" She caught a warning glance from Shannon, but continued blithely on. "You know, there's something special about that little guy—" The phone jangled and Leslie rolled her huge, mascara-laden eyes as she picked up the receiver. "Pediatrics. Nurse Nelson."

"She's right about that," Shannon agreed as she led Chandra down the hallway. "Your little friend has wormed his way into the coldest hearts around. Even Dr. O'Rourke isn't immune to him."

"Is that right?" Chandra asked, lifting an eyebrow. She was surprised to hear Dr. O'Rourke's name, and even more surprised to glean a little bit about the man. Not that she cared. He was just a doctor, someone she'd have to deal with while visiting the baby.

"One of the nurses caught him holding the baby this morning. And he was actually smiling."

So there was a more human side to the gruff doctor. Chandra glanced down the hallway, half expecting to see him, and she was surprised at her feeling of disappointment when he didn't appear.

Shannon clucked her tongue and shook her head. "You know, I didn't think anyone could touch that man, but apparently I was wrong." She slid Chandra a glance. "Maybe there's hope for him yet. Here you go. This little guy's still isolated until we get the results of his tests. But my guess is, he'll be fine."

They stood behind a glass partition. On the other side of the clear wall, the dark-haired infant slept, his face serene as an ultraviolet light warmed him. There were other newborns as well, three sleeping infants, who, separated by the wall of glass, snoozed in the other room. Nearby, a nurse was weighing an unhappy infant who was showing off his lungs by screaming loudly.

"We're busy down here," Nurse Pratt said.

"Looks that way." Chandra focused her attention back on the isolated baby, and her heart tugged. So perfect. So beautiful. So precious. The fact that he was separated from the rest of the infants only made his plight seem more pitiful. Unwanted and unloved, living in a sterile hospital with only nurses and doctors—faces, hands and smells that changed every eight hours—to care for him.

A lump formed in her throat—a lump way out of proportion to the situation. She'd been a physician, for God's sake, a *pediatrician*. She was supposed to handle any given situation and keep her emotions in check. But this time, with this child, she was hopelessly ensnared in the trap of caring too much. Involuntarily her hand touched the cool glass. If only she could pick him up and hold him close....

Chandra felt Shannon's gaze resting on her, and she wondered just how much of her emotions played upon her face. "It looks as if he'll be okay once we get the jaundice under control," Shannon said softly.

"And his caput—"

"Nothing serious, according to Dr. O'Rourke, and he's the best E.R. physician I've ever met."

"And the pediatrician?"

"Dr. Spangler was on duty and looked him over last night. Agreed with O'Rourke right down the line. Dr. Williams will check the baby later this morning."

Chandra felt a sense of overwhelming relief. She stared at the perfect round cheeks and the dark sweep of lashes that caressed the infant's skin, watched as his tiny lips moved ever so slightly, as if he were sucking in his dream. On whose breast did he subconsciously nurse?

Chandra's heart wrenched again and she felt rooted to the spot. Though she'd seen hundreds of babies, they had all come with mothers firmly attached, and she'd never once experienced a pang of devotion so deep. The feeling seemed to spring from an inner well of love she'd never known existed.

True, she had been married, had hoped to bear her own children, and so, perhaps, all her motherly instincts had been turned inward. But now, years later, divorced and having no steady man in her life, her nurturing urges seemed stronger than ever, especially where this tiny baby was concerned.

"Uh-oh." Nurse Pratt exhaled softly. "Trouble."

"What?" Chandra turned and discovered two men striding toward her. Both were of medium height, one with curly black hair, the other straight brown. They wore slacks and sweaters, no hospital ID or lab coats.

"Make that double trouble," Shannon corrected.

"Miss Hill?" the man with the straight hair and hard eyes asked. "Bob Fillmore with the *Ranger Banner*."

Chandra's heart sank as the curly-haired man added, "Sid Levine." He held out his hand as if expecting Chandra to clasp it. "Photographer."

She felt Sid's fingers curl over her hand, but she could barely breathe. Reporters. Already. She wasn't yet ready to deal with the press. "But how did you know—"

"Have you got permission to be here?" Nurse Pratt cut in, obviously displeased.

Fillmore ignored her. "I heard you found an infant in the woods near your home. Abandoned, is that right?"

"I don't think this is the place to conduct an interview," Nurse Pratt insisted. Behind the glass, the baby started making noise, soft mewing sounds that erupted into the hard cries Chandra had heard the night before. Chandra whipped her head around and the sight of the infant, *her* baby—no, of course he wasn't hers, but he *was* in distress and she wanted desperately to run to him and pick him up.

"Is that the kid?" Fillmore asked. "Any idea who he belongs to? It is a he, right?" He looked to Chandra for verification as he withdrew a small pad and pen from the inner

pocket of his jacket. He'd also unearthed a small tape recorder from his voluminous pockets and switched on the
machine.

The baby cried louder, and Chandra felt her back stiffen.
"Look, I'm not ready to give you an interview, okay? Yes,
I found the baby—in my barn, not the woods—but since
this is a case the police are investigating, I think you'd better go to the sheriff's office to get your facts straight."

"But why your property?" Fillmore insisted, his tape recorder in his outstretched hand. Memories, painful as razors, cut through Chandra's mind as she remembered the
last time she'd had microphones and recorders waved in her
face, how she'd been forced to reveal information to the
press.

"I don't know. Now, if you'll excuse me—"

"Just a few more questions."

Obviously the man wasn't about to give up. Chandra
glanced at Nurse Pratt and, without thinking about proto-
col, ordered, "Call security."

Fillmore was outraged. "Hey—wait—you can't start
barking orders—"

"If she doesn't, I will." Dr. O'Rourke, who could have
heard only the last of the exchange, strode down the hall.
Dressed in jeans, a long-sleeved T-shirt and down vest, he
nonetheless oozed authority as he glared at the reporter and
photographer with a stare that would have turned the fainthearted to stone. He motioned to Shannon. "Do as Ms. Hill
suggests. Call security." Nurse Pratt walked to the nearest
telephone extension and dialed.

"Why all the secrecy?" Fillmore demanded, apparently
not fainthearted and not the least bit concerned about
O'Rourke's stature, anger or command of the situation.
"We could help you on this, y'know. A couple of pictures
of the baby and an article describing how he was found, and
maybe, just maybe, the kid's folks will reconsider and come
back. Who knows what happened to them? Or to him? For

all anyone knows, this kid—" he hooked a thumb toward the glass "—could've been stolen or kidnapped. Right now some distraught mother might be anxious to have him back again, and you guys are impeding us."

He's right, Chandra thought, disliking the reporter intensely as she noticed a flicker of doubt cross Dr. O'Rourke's strong features.

"In due time," the doctor replied, his gaze landing on Chandra for a heart-stopping second. A glimmer of understanding passed between them, as if she and the doctor were on the same side. Quickly, O'Rourke turned back to the reporters. "My first concern is for the child's health."

"The kid got problems?" Fillmore persisted, his eyes lighting with the idea of a new twist to an already newsworthy story.

"We're running tests." O'Rourke, in a sweeping glance, took in the two men and Chandra, and once again she felt a bond with him, though she told herself she imagined it. She had nothing, save the baby, in common with the man.

O'Rourke wasn't about to be pushed around. "Now, if you'll excuse me, I have a patient I have to see. If you want to continue with this interview, do it somewhere else." He turned just as two security guards, hands on holsters, entered the pediatric wing.

"Okay, what's going on here?" the first one, a man with a thick waist and a face scarred by acne, demanded. His partner stood two feet behind him, as if he expected the reporters to draw weapons.

"Just lookin' for a story," Fillmore said.

"Well, look somewhere else."

Levine threw up his hands, but Fillmore stood his ground and eyed the doctor. "What is it with you, O'Rourke? Why do you always see us as the bad guys?"

"Not bad guys, just guys without much dignity." Dr. O'Rourke stepped closer to Fillmore and scrutinized the reporter with his uncompromising gaze. "You tend to sensationalize things, try to stir up trouble, and that bothers me. Now if you'll excuse me, and even if you won't, I've got a patient to examine."

Summarily dismissing both men, O'Rourke stepped into the nursery to examine the baby. With a nudge from the guards, both reporter and photographer, muttering under their collective breath, headed out of the wing. "You, too," the heavier guard said, motioning toward Chandra.

"She can stay." O'Rourke, though on the other side of the window, pointed toward Chandra before focusing his attention on the crying infant. Chandra had to swallow a smile as she stared at the vest stretched taut across O'Rourke's back.

The guard shrugged and followed his partner through the double doors while Chandra stood dumbstruck. She didn't know what she expected of O'Rourke, but she suspected he wasn't a particularly tolerant man. His demeanor was on the edge of being harsh, and she was certain that just under his facade of civility, he was as explosive as a volcano.

On the other hand, he touched the infant carefully, tenderly, as he gently rolled the screaming baby from front to back, fingers expertly examining the child. It was all Chandra could do to keep from racing into the room and cradling the baby herself, holding the infant close and rocking him.

This has got to stop, Chandra, she told herself. *He's not yours—he's not!* If she had any brains at all, she'd tear herself away from the viewing window, walk out of Riverbend Hospital and never look back. Let the proper authorities take care of the child. If they could locate the parents or next of kin, so be it. If not, the Social Services would see that he was placed with a carefully-screened couple who desperately wanted a child, or in a foster home...

Quit torturing yourself!

But she stayed. Compelled by the child and fascinated by the doctor examining him, Chandra Hill watched from the other side of the glass.

Why she felt a special bond with the child and the doctor, she didn't know. And yet, as if catching a glimmer of the future in a crystal ball, she felt as if they, all three, were inextricably bound to each other.

Chapter Four

Dr. O'Rourke was quick and efficient. His examination
took no longer than five minutes, after which he gave Nurse
Pratt a few instructions before emerging from the glassed-in
room. "I think he'll be out of isolation tomorrow," he said,
joining Chandra.

"That's good."

"Know any more about him?"

She shook her head and began walking with him, wondering why she was even conversing with him. She thought
she caught an envious look from Shannon as they left the
nursery, but she chided herself afterward. Envious? Of
what?

"The Sheriff's Department show up at your place?" he
asked as they walked. His tone wasn't friendly, just curious. Chandra chalked his questions up to professional interest.

"This morning at the crack of dawn. The same two deputies." She stuffed her hands into her pockets. "They poked around the barn and the grounds. Didn't find much."

O'Rourke pushed the button for the elevator, and the doors opened immediately. "Parking lot?"

"Yes." She eyed him for a second, and as the car descended, said, "I'm surprised to see you here this early. Last night you looked like you could sleep for twenty years."

"Thirty," he corrected, then allowed her just the hint of a grin, and she was shocked by the sensual gleam of white teeth against his dark skin. His jaw was freshly shaven, and the scent of soap and leather clung to him, overpowering the antiseptic odor that had filtered through the hospital corridors and into the elevator. "But I've learned to survive on catnaps. Five hours and it's all over for me." He studied her with that intense gaze that made her throat grow tight, but she held her ground as a bell announced they'd landed at ground level. "What about you?"

"Eight—at least. I'm running on empty now."

He cocked a dubious eyebrow as they walked past the reception area and outside, where the sunlight was bright enough to hurt the eyes. Chandra reached into her purse for her sunglasses and noticed that O'Rourke squinted. The lines near his eyes deepened, adding a rugged edge to his profile. The man was handsome, she'd give him that. Dealing with him would be easier if he were less attractive, she thought.

"That reporter will be back," he predicted. "He smells a story and isn't about to leave it alone. You might be careful what you say."

Though she knew the answer from personal experience, she wanted to hear his side of the story. "Why?"

His lips twisted into a thin line of disapproval and his eyes turned cold. "Words can be misconstrued, taken out of context, turned around."

"Sounds like the voice of experience talking."

"Just a warning. For your own good."

He acted as if he were about to turn away, and Chandra impulsively grabbed the crook of his arm, restraining him. He turned sharply and his gaze landed on her with a force that made her catch her breath. She swallowed against the dryness in her throat and forced the words past her lips. "When can I see the baby? I mean, really see him—hold him."

She didn't remove her fingers and was aware of the tensing of his muscles beneath the sleeves of his shirt and jacket. "You want to hold him?"

"Oh, yes!" she cried, her emotion controlling her tongue.

"You feel something special for the child, some sort of bond?" he guessed.

"I..." She crumbled under the intensity of his gaze. "I guess I feel responsible."

When he waited, for what she knew was further elaboration, she couldn't help but ramble on. "I mean he was found on *my* property, in my barn. I can't help but think that someone wanted me to find him."

"That you were chosen?" He sounded as if he didn't believe her, yet he didn't draw his arm away.

"Yes. No. I mean—I don't know." She'd never been so confused in her life. Always she'd been a take-charge kind of individual, afraid of nothing, ready for any challenge. But one tiny newborn and one very intimidating man seemed to have turned her mind to mush. "Look, Doctor, I just want to hold the baby, if it's okay with you."

He hesitated, and his voice was a little kinder. "I don't know if it's a good idea."

"What?" She couldn't believe he would dissuade her now, after he'd called her to tell her the child had improved and then had let her stick around. But that warming trend had suddenly been reversed.

"Until the Sheriff's Department sets this matter straight, I think it's best for you and the child if you stayed away from the hospital until everything's settled."

Her hopes, which she had naively pinned on this man, collapsed. "But I thought—"

"I know what you thought," O'Rourke said. "You thought that since I rescued you from those vultures, loosely called reporters, that I was on your side, that you could get at the kid through me. Well, unfortunately, it doesn't work that way. Either you're a relative of the child or you're not. And I don't like being used."

"You called me," she reminded him, and watched his lips tighten.

"I've had second thoughts."

"To hell with your second thoughts!" Her temper, quickly rising, captured her tongue. "I'm not going to hurt the baby. I'm just someone who cares, Doctor. Someone who would like to offer that poor, abandoned child a little bit of love."

"Or someone who enjoys all the attention she's getting?"

"If that was the case, I wouldn't have tried to throw the reporters out of the hospital, now, would I?"

That stopped him, and whatever he was about to say was kept inside. He stared at her a few minutes, his gaze fairly raking over her, as if he were examining her for flaws. She almost expected a sneer to curl his lip, but he was a little too civilized for outward disdain. "I'm just being straight with you. There's a lot I don't know about that baby who's up in pediatrics, Ms. Hill. And a lot more I don't know about you. If it were up to me, I'd let you hang around. Based on first impressions, I'm guessing that you do care something for the infant. But I don't know that, the hospital administration doesn't know that and Social Services doesn't know that."

He turned then, and left her standing in the middle of the parking lot, her mouth nearly dropping open.

He didn't understand why he'd come to her rescue in the hospital, only to shoot her down a peg or two.

Instinctively, Dallas knew that she was a different kind of woman than those he'd met. There was something about her that attracted him as well as caused him to be suspicious. She seemed at once strong willed and yet innocent, able to take care of herself and needing something—a man?—to lean upon occasionally.

There had been a desperation in her eyes, a pleading that he hadn't been able to refuse in the hospital, but here, out in the light of day, she'd looked far from innocent—in fact, he suspected that Ms. Hill could handle herself in just about any situation.

Dallas felt himself drawn to her, like a fly buzzing around a spider's web. He didn't know a thing about her, and he was smart enough to realize that she was only interested in him because he was her link to the baby. Yet his stupid male pride fantasized that she might be interested in him—as a man.

"Fool," he muttered to himself, kicking at a fragment of loose gravel on the asphalt. The sharp-sided rock skidded across the lot, hitting the tire of a low-slung Porche, Dr. Prescott's latest toy.

He must be getting soft, Dallas decided. Why else would he let a woman get under his skin? Especially a woman who wasn't being entirely honest with him.

He slid behind the wheel of his truck and flipped on the ignition. What was it about Chandra Hill that had him saying one thing while meaning another? He didn't want to keep her from the child, and yet he had an obligation to protect the baby's interests. Hospital policy was very strict about visitors who weren't relatives.

But the baby needed someone to care about him, and Chandra was willing. If her motives were pure. He couldn't believe that she was lying, not completely, and yet there was a wariness to her, and she sometimes picked her words carefully, especially when the questions became too personal. But that wasn't a sin. She was entitled to her private life.

Yet he felt Chandra Hill was holding back, keeping information that he needed to herself. It was a feeling that kept nagging at him whenever he was around her; not that she said anything dishonest. No, it was her omissions that bothered him.

He crammed his truck into gear and watched Chandra haul herself into the cab of a huge red Chevrolet Suburban, the truck that last night he'd thought was a van. Her jeans stretched across taut buttocks and athletic thighs. Her skin was tanned, her straight blond hair streaked by the sun. She looked healthy and vibrant and forthright, and yet she was hiding something. He could feel it.

"All in your mind, O'Rourke," he told himself as he drove out of the parking lot and toward the center of town. He had hours before his meeting with Brian, so he decided that a stop at the sheriff's office might clear up a few questions he had about Chandra Hill and her abandoned baby.

Chandra drove into Ranger, her thoughts racing a mile a minute. Automatically, she adjusted her foot on the throttle, managing to stay under the speed limit. She stopped for a single red light and turned right on Coyote Avenue. Without thinking, she pulled into a dusty parking lot and slid into one of a dozen available spaces, her mind focused on the infant. Baby John Doe. Already she'd started thinking of him as J.D. Kind of a bad joke, but the child deserved a name.

Lord, who did he belong to?

And that damned Dr. O'Rourke, telling her she shouldn't "hang around" the hospital. That man—kind one minute, cruel the next—set her teeth on edge! Well, the less she thought of him, the better.

Flicking off the ignition, she grabbed her jacket and climbed from the cab onto the sun-baked asphalt. A few blades of grass and dandelions sprouted through the cracks in the pockmarked tarmac, but the neglect seemed only to add to the casual allure of this tourist town. Most of the buildings, including the gas stations, coin laundry, banks and restaurants, sported a Western motif, complete with false facades, long wooden porches and, at the veterinary clinic, a hitching post.

Years before, the city fathers had decided to mine whatever gold was left in Ranger—not in the surrounding hills, but in the pockets of the visitors who drove through this quaint village in the foothills of the Rocky Mountains. Those same far-thinking civic leaders had persuaded the town to adopt a Wild West atmosphere, and the mayor had encouraged renovating existing buildings to adopt the appearance of the grange hall, livery stable and old hotel, the only remaining structures built before the turn of the century, and therefore, authentically from the eighteen hundreds.

In the past twenty years, all the businesses facing Main Street and a few more on the side streets reeked of the Old West. Wild West Expeditions had willingly embraced the idea.

Situated near the livery, on the second floor of a building constructed in 1987 and made to look a hundred years older, Wild West Expeditions, owned by once-upon-a-time hippie Rick Benson, was Chandra's place of employment.

She climbed the exterior stairs, noticing a soft wind rush through the boughs of a birch tree, spinning the leaves so that they glittered a silver-green.

The door was propped open. The sign above, painted red and yellow, swung and creaked in the breeze.

"Hey—I heard a rumor about you!" Rick greeted her with a toothy smile. He was a big man, six-two with an extra twenty pounds around his middle. His hair was extremely thin on top and had turned to gray, but he still wore his meager locks in a pony tail that snaked halfway down his back. He had a flushed face, an easy smile and no enemy in the world. Not even the mother of his children, who, in the seventies, he hadn't bothered to marry, and ten years later hadn't needed to divorce when she took the kids and packed them back to "civilization" in St. Louis.

"A rumor, eh?" Chandra hung her jacket on a peg near the door. The interior of the establishment was as rustic as the rest of the town. Rough-hewn cedar walls, camping equipment, including ancient snowshoes and leather pouches, hanging from wooden pegs, a potbellied stove and a long counter that served as the reception desk. "Only good things, I hope."

"Something about an abandoned kid. Found by your mutt down near the creek. I heard the kid would've drowned if Sam hadn't led you to him."

"Well, that's not quite the truth, but close," Chandra said, thinking how quickly a story could be exaggerated in the gossip-riddled coffee shops and streets of Ranger. She gave Rick a quick rundown of what really happened, and he listened, all the while adding receipts on a very modern-looking adding machine, swilling coffee and answering the phone.

"Why'd'ya s'pose the kid was left in your barn?" he asked once she'd finished with her tale.

She poured herself a cup of coffee. "Beats me. That seems to be the million-dollar question."

"Must be a reason."

"Maybe, maybe not."

"The army jacket a clue?"

Chandra sighed and blew across her cup. "I don't know. The deputies took it and the blanket, but it seemed to me they think nothing will come back from the lab."

Rick pushed up the sleeves of his plaid shirt, which he wore as a jacket over a river boatman's collarless shirt, usually cream colored and decorated by a string of beads that surrounded his neck. "Well, whatever happens with the kid, the press will be all over you." He scowled, his beefy face creased. "Bob Fillmore has already called."

"We've met," Chandra said dryly.

"Watch him. He's a shark," Rick warned, his light brown gaze meeting hers. He never probed into her private life. Not even when, two years before, she'd shown up on this doorstep and applied for a job as a white-water and camping guide. He hadn't lifted an eyebrow at the holes in her résumé, nor had he mentioned the fact that she was a woman, and a small one at that. He'd just taken her down to a series of rapids known as Devil's Falls in the Rattlesnake River and said, "Do your stuff." When she'd expertly guided the rubber raft through the treacherous waters, he'd hired her on the spot, only insisting she learn basic first aid and the lay of the land so that she would become one of his "expert" guides. She'd passed with flying colors. As far as she knew, Rick had no knowledge of her past life and didn't seem interested. She doubted that he knew that she'd been married or had been a pediatrician. He didn't care about the past— only the here and now.

Rick rubbed his chin. "Fillmore wants you to call him back and set up an interview."

"And you don't think I should."

Lifting a big shoulder, Rick shook his head. "Up to you. Just don't let that piece of slime inside here, okay?"

"You don't like him."

"No." He didn't say why, but Chandra remembered hearing that Fillmore had once written a piece about Wild West Tours. The crux of the article had been a cynical evaluation of Rick's alternative life-style, his "sixties values" in the late eighties.

"What've we got going today?" she asked. "There's a group coming in—when?"

"Soon, but I've changed things around a little," Rick replied, glancing at his schedule. "That group of six from the Hastings Ranch want a medium-thrill ride. I thought the south fork of the river would work for them. But I've got one lone ranger who wants to play daredevil...let's see...the name's McGee. Brian McGee. Young guy. Twenty, maybe twenty-two. He wants, and I quote, 'the ultimate thrill—the biggest rush' we can give him before he heads back to college. You think you want to deal with him?"

With pleasure, Chandra thought, recalling the so-called he-men she went to college with. The boys who didn't think she'd cut it in medical school. "Grizzly Loop?" she asked.

"If you think *he* can handle it. I know you can, but who knows what kind of a nut this bozo is. If he wants to play macho man and doesn't know beans about rafting, you could be in a pile of trouble."

"I'll check it out."

"Good. He'll be in at eleven."

"And the other group?"

"Randy and Jake'll handle them. Unless you'd rather—"

"Oh, no," Chandra replied crisply, noticing the teasing lift of Rick's brow. "Bring on Mr. Macho." Maybe she just needed to throw herself into her work to forget about the baby and, most especially, Dr. O'Rourke.

The Sheriff's Department had ignored the Western motif of the other buildings in town. A single-story brick building, there wasn't the hint of pretension about the place. Inside, the walls were paneled in yellowed birch, and the floor was a mottled green-and-white tile that was worn near the front desk and door.

The receptionist recognized Dallas as he walked through the door. He'd helped deliver her second child two years earlier. With a grin, she slid one of the glass panels to the side. "Dr. O'Rourke!"

"Hi, Angie." He leaned one arm on the counter. "How're the boys?"

"Hell on wheels," she said with a heartfelt sigh. Behind her desk, officers in uniform or dressed in civilian clothes sat at desks and pushed paper, drank coffee, smoked and cradled phones to their ears as they filled out reports. "But you didn't come here to discuss the kids," Angie said. "What's up?"

"I'd like to talk to the dispatcher on duty early this morning, around one-thirty or two o'clock. A call came in about an abandoned baby."

"Let me check the log." Angie's fingers moved quickly over a computer keyboard, and she squinted into the blue light of a terminal. "Let's see... Here it is—1:57. Marla was on duty, but she won't be in until ten tonight."

"But the call was recorded?"

"They all are. You want to listen to the tape?"

"If it's all right."

Angie winked. "I've got connections around this place," she said. "Come on in." As Dallas walked through a door to the offices, he heard Angie ask another woman officer to cover for her, but his mind wasn't on the conversation. He was, as he had been ever since meeting her last night, contemplating Chandra Hill.

"So, you've got an abandoned kid on your hands," Angie said, snapping him out of his thoughts. She opened a door to an interrogation room. "Who would leave a baby alone like that?"

"I wish I knew."

"So do I. I'd personally wring her neck," Angie said fiercely. "Here, just pull up a chair. I'll get a copy of the tape. It'll be just a minute."

The room was windowless, with a long table, four folding chairs and little else. Just the basics. The faint scent of stale cigarette smoke hung in the air, and the two ashtrays on the table had been emptied, but not wiped clean.

He waited less than ten minutes for Angie to return, as promised, with a tape, a player and a cup of coffee, "compliments of the department."

"Thanks." He accepted the cup as she slipped the tape into the player.

"All the comforts of home," she teased, her dark eyes sparkling as she glanced at the bare walls and uncomfortable chairs. "Let me know if you need anything else."

"Will do."

She closed the door behind her as she left, and Dallas played the tape. Chandra's voice, at first frantic, calmed as she described the condition of the child. Cool and professional. And the medical terminology was used precisely—hardly typical of a first-aid class graduate. No, Chandra sounded very much like a physician.

Dallas sipped some of the coffee—stronger and more bitter than coffee served at the hospital—and rocked back in the chair. Chandra Hill. Beautiful and slightly mysterious. Sure, she came on strong and she seemed forthright, but there was more to her than what she said.

So what if she's a physician? Big deal. Maybe she just wants a little privacy. And, really, O'Rourke, it's none of your damned business. She brought you a patient, and you've got an obligation to care for him—and not for her.

Yet, as he heard her take-charge voice on the tape, he smiled. What, he wondered, would it be like to kiss a woman like that? Would she bite his lips and kick him in the groin, or would she melt against him, growing supple and compliant? The thought of pressing his mouth to hers caused an unwanted stirring between his legs.

"Damn," he muttered, angry at the turn of his thoughts. What the hell was he thinking?

Scowling darkly, he rewound the tape and listened to it again, his eyes narrowing through the steam rising from his cup. The tape gave him no more clues to the baby's parentage or to Chandra Hill. In fact, he thought sourly, he had more questions about her than ever.

"You're the guide?" Brian McGee couldn't swallow his surprised grin. He was handsome in a boyish way, with oversize features, large green eyes and a smile that was dazzlingly white. And he was shocked to his socks as he stared down at Chandra.

"I'm the guide," she quipped.

Brian glanced from Chandra to the counter, where Rick was busily working on the wording of a new brochure.

"I, uh, expected someone more—"

"Male?" she asked, tilting her chin upward and meeting his quizzical, amused gaze with her own steady eyes.

"Well, yeah, I was. I mean, not that you're not capable—"

"She's the best riverwoman I've got," Rick put in, never looking up from his work.

"But—"

"Come on, Mr. McGee. It'll be fun," Chandra assured him, though she was beginning to doubt her own words. This young buck definitely had ideas about male-female relationships on all levels. She grabbed a couple of life vests and a first-aid kit. "Believe it or not, you don't need extra testosterone to paddle a canoe."

He gulped. "Is anyone else going on this trip?"

"Nope. Just you and me."

McGee glanced back at Rick. "And this is a serious ride?"

Rick slid him a glance. "I guarantee you'll get the biggest rush of your life," he mocked, chuckling softly.

"That's what I want," McGee replied with a grin.

"Good." Chandra was already at the door. "The raft's tied to my rig. You follow me in yours, and we'll drop your car off at the south fork. Then you climb in my Suburban with me and we'll continue up the river. It'll only take about an hour to get there." She eyed him over her shoulder. "You have rafted before, haven't you?"

"Absolutely."

"Then let's get going."

While McGee paid for the excursion and signed the release forms, Chandra packed the truck. Within ten minutes, she was on the road, McGee following her in a beat-up Pontiac. They dropped his car off at Junction Park, and he climbed into the Suburban. Mentally crossing her fingers, Chandra hoped that Brian McGee wouldn't be too much trouble on the trip. She glanced at his profile as she put the truck into gear. For a second, she thought she was looking at Dallas O'Rourke. The profile, though much more boyish, was similar, the clear green eyes intense . . . but that was crazy. Calling herself every kind of fool, she snapped her sunglasses onto the bridge of her nose and vowed she wouldn't think of Dallas O'Rourke for the rest of the day!

She must really be losing it. To think that this . . . college boy resembled O'Rourke was ludicrous. And why Dr. O'Rourke wouldn't leave her mind alone was too obnoxious to contemplate.

"Somethin' wrong?" McGee asked, and she shook her head, as if to clear out a nest of cobwebs.

"Nope. You just..." She laughed. "You reminded me of someone I know."

His grin was enchanting. Boyish, but enchanting. "Someone you like?" he asked, his voice smooth as silk.

"I'm not sure," she said, and decided to end the conversation by turning on the radio. She wasn't interested in a college boy, or any man, for that matter.

McGee seemed to take the hint. He reached into his pocket for a pack of cigarettes and, rolling down the window, lit up. Tapping his foot to the sultry beat of an old Roy Orbison song, he seemed lost in his own world, which was fine with Chandra. She coveted her own thoughts, and they had nothing to do with the boy next to her.

Instead, her mind was crowded with images of a tiny baby and the doctor who cared for him. The baby, she understood. She'd wanted a child for a long, long time. But why Dr. O'Rourke? He was the baby's physician. And a man who was much too complicated for her—not that she wanted a simple man. She didn't want a man at all, thank you very much. And especially not a man like Dallas O'Rourke.

She gripped the wheel more tightly and realized that her palms were sweating as they drove upward, on a gravel road that twisted and turned along the forested banks of the Rattlesnake River.

Late, again. Dallas glanced at his watch and scowled. Brian had suggested they meet here, at the Rocky Horror Pub, at six. It was now 6:40, and Dallas had nursed one beer in the smoky interior. The after-work crowd had gathered. Pool balls clicked in the corner, a lively game of darts had begun, and the tables, as well as the bar itself, were packed with the regulars who always enjoyed a couple beers before heading home.

Five more minutes. That's all he'd give his irresponsible brother, then Brian could go borrow money at a bank, like a normal person.

Dallas finished his beer just as the saloon-type doors swung open and Brian, all one-hundred-eighty-five pounds of cockiness, strode in. Dressed in dusty jeans, a cowboy shirt and Stetson, Brian glanced around, spotted Dallas and waved.

"Sorry I'm late," he announced, plopping down on a chair at Dallas's table. He waved to the waitress and pointed at Dallas's empty. "Two more of those . . . wait a minute. Is that a *light?* Forget it. I want the real thing. Whatever you got on tap."

"And you?" the waitress asked, her eyebrows lifting at Dallas. "Do you want the 'real thing,' too?"

"Nothing," Dallas replied, glancing at his brother. "Better watch out, Brian. You could end up with a Coke."

"Bring this guy the same thing I'm having," Brian insisted, and the waitress, rolling her eyes, left them.

Settling back in his chair, Brian took off his hat and hung it on a hook near the table. His thick hair was unruly, springy and slightly damp. "I've just had the experience of a lifetime, let me tell you."

The waitress deposited the two glasses on the table and, surprisingly, Brian paid for them both. Reaching for a handful of peanuts and shaking his head, Brian asked, "Ever shot the rapids at Grizzly Loop?"

"No," Dallas replied.

"Hell, man, you should. It was incredible."

"Sounds dangerous." Dallas waited as Brian tossed peanuts into his mouth. Sooner or later, he would get to the point, which was, of course, how much.

"It was. But the woman who was in charge, man, could she shoot those rapids. Scared the living hell out of me!"

"Woman?"

"Yeah." Brian hooked his thumb toward the windows. "She works over at Wild West Expeditions. Chandra something-or-other. Just a little thing, but, boy, does she know how to ride a river."

"Does she?" Dallas asked dryly. He took a swallow of the beer he didn't want. What were the chances of there being more than one woman named Chandra in a town this size?

"Believe me, I was skeptical. This little thing, couldn't be more than five-three or four, drives a huge red rig, carries a backpack that's half her size and shoots rapids like some damned Indian guide!"

"She blond?" Dallas couldn't resist asking.

"And gorgeous." Brian smiled slyly and winked at his older brother. "Built a little on the slim side for my tastes, but good-lookin'." Dallas felt his back stiffen. "With women like that," Brian continued as he lifted his glass to his lips, "maybe I'll just hang around for a while. I could go back to school after Christmas."

"Like hell!" Dallas replied in a loud whisper. A few heads turned in his direction, and he immediately put a clamp on his runaway emotions. What the hell was wrong with him? Brian was only kidding around, anyone could see that. Yet Dallas's temper had flared white-hot, probably because he was guilty of the same thoughts himself.

"Hey, man, I was only—"

"I know." Dallas waved off his explanation. "Maybe we should get down to business."

Brian's smile left his face, and for the first time that Dallas could remember, the younger man seemed genuinely sincere. "Look, I hate to ask you again, but I do need a few bucks to get through the next couple of terms."

"How much?" Dallas asked, taking a swallow from his "real thing."

Brian turned his glass uneasily. "I don't know. Four—" he glanced up to see how far he was getting "—maybe five grand could get me through to spring."

He wasn't asking a lot, Dallas knew. Though part of Brian's tuition and books were paid by his scholarship, his room and board were not. Brian's dad helped him a little, but the monthly checks didn't stretch far enough. And living expenses alone would mount up to more than he was asking for. However, Dallas couldn't get over the fact that Brian hadn't bothered to earn one red cent all summer. It wasn't loaning Brian the money that bothered Dallas so much as wondering if the kid would ever get enough gumption to actually get a job and become self-reliant.

"I looked for a roommate," Brian added, and Dallas's head snapped up.

"I thought you had two roommates."

"They dropped out."

"So you're living alone?"

"It's only temporary. I'll hook up with someone once school starts. There's always guys looking for a place to stay, and I'm not too far from campus...."

Without roommates to share the expense of a Southern California apartment, Brian would go through five thousand dollars quickly.

Dallas frowned and rubbed the back of his head. "I'll send you the money once you get back to L.A.," he said, eyeing his half brother and wondering why, with the same mother, they were so unlike each other. Dallas had never shied from work; in fact, he'd been accused of having no emotions, no room for anything in his life but his profession. He'd put himself through school with a little help from a small inheritance from his grandmother. When that had run out, he'd borrowed money from the government. School had been a grind—long hours, no money, no room for anything but classes, studying and sleeping. And it had taken him years to pay off the debt. However, he didn't wish what he'd gone through on anyone, especially his younger brother.

Brian looked straight at Dallas. "I was kinda hoping you'd, uh, give me the check now." He licked his lips nervously, and Dallas noticed a tightening around the corners of his half brother's mouth.

"Are you in some kind of trouble?"

"Nah! Nothing serious," Brian said quickly, his mouth twisting into a boyish grin again. "It's just that I've got a temporary cash-flow problem and I thought...well, I was hoping..."

Dallas reached into his jacket pocket and pulled out his check book. "How much?"

"Just a couple of hundred..."

Wondering if he was doing more damage than good, Dallas wrote a check for three hundred dollars and handed it to his brother.

With obvious relief, Brian stuffed the check into his wallet. "I don't know how to thank you."

"Finish school."

"No worry about that. Oh, by the way, I bought you something."

"You *bought* me something?"

"Yeah, well, I couldn't resist."

"But I thought you were broke."

"I am. But I've got a bank card and . . . I guess I was in a generous mood."

Dallas was about to protest. No wonder the kid couldn't stretch a buck, but Brian withdrew some sort of coupon from his wallet and slid it across the table. It was a pass for a white-water camping trip from Wild West Expeditions.

"You need to lighten up," Brian said. "I thought you should do something besides hang around the hospital all the time."

"This must've cost you—"

"Relax, will ya. Think of it as your money. Have Chandra take you up to Grizzly Loop—I told the old man who runs the place you're to specifically ask for her. You'll never be the same, I guarantee it." He reached into his shirt pocket, grabbed a pen and, clicking it, scratched Chandra's name on the coupon. "There ya go! The experience of a lifetime!"

"If you say so," Dallas said, his lips twisting at the thought of spending a day alone with Ms. Hill. It could be interesting.

And dangerous. He didn't know anything about her, and her story about the baby didn't ring quite true. No, he was still convinced she was hiding something—something she didn't want him to find out about her. What it had to do with the abandoned infant, he didn't understand. But he would. In time, he'd figure it out and, he thought bitterly, he probably wouldn't like what he found.

Except that she was interesting, far more interesting than any woman he'd met in a long, long while. He considered her tanned skin and gray-green eyes. A day or two alone with Chandra Hill could spell more than trouble. His emotions were already on edge whenever he thought of the woman—which was too damned often. But the idea of being close to her, seeing her without all her attention centered on that baby, was far too appealing to turn down. And, even if she were trouble, he decided he was willing to take that chance. He slipped the pass into his wallet.

Chapter Five

A couple of days later, Dallas had his first weekend off in two months. Seated in his pickup, he stared through the glass at the rustic building where Chandra worked.

Baby Doe was doing well. Just yesterday, Dr. Williams had allowed the infant to be put in the general nursery with the others. Had the child a parent, he would be released soon. However, no one as yet had claimed the baby, despite the front-page story in this morning's *Banner*. Dallas glanced to the passenger seat, where the paper still lay open. "Mystery Baby Abandoned in Barn." Fortunately there were no photographs of the child. Chandra had only been quoted once, and it seemed that Bob Fillmore, a man Dallas didn't trust an inch, had gotten most of his information from the Sheriff's Department.

However, the first story in the *Banner* was unlikely the last. The press would keep sniffing around, Dallas thought, his gaze returning to the rough-finished building where Chandra worked. Fillmore, like the proverbial dog after the bone, wouldn't stop until he'd dug through every corner of Chandra's life. Things could get ugly.

Retrieving the coupon from his wallet, Dallas reached for the door handle and wondered, not for the first time, what the devil he was doing here. He was afraid his reasons had more to do with Chandra than with relaxing in the mountains. Yes, he was curious about her, but logic told him he was making a big mistake by taking up his brother's offer. Long ago, Dallas had decided he didn't need any complications in his life. Hadn't he had enough of complex relationships in L.A.? Weren't difficulties in his life in southern California the express reason he had retreated to this sleepy little mountain town? To his way of thinking, women always spelled trouble—with a capital *T*.

Chandra Hill would be no different—perhaps she was the most complex of all the women he'd ever met. Certainly she was fascinating. And she was crazy for that little boy. He'd checked with the nurses in pediatrics. It seemed Chandra was more often in the pediatrics wing of Riverbend Hospital than not. In two days, she'd visited the child five times— drawn inexplicably to the baby, as if she were the infant's mother or, at least, were nurturing some maternal bond.

He started up the steps leading to Wild West Expeditions. It wouldn't hurt to find out a little bit about the mysterious Ms. Hill, he decided. After all, he did have some stake in Baby Doe's future, in so far as he was the admitting physician. And the child had no one to fight his battles for him. Unless Dr. Dallas O'Rourke stepped in. His mouth twisted at the irony of it all—he'd never considered himself a hero of any kind. And here he was, deluding himself, making excuses just so he could spend a little time with Chandra Hill. Just like a schoolboy in the throes of lust. He hadn't felt this way in years.

"You're a case, O'Rourke," he muttered under his breath as he leaned on the door at the top of the stairs. It opened easily, and a brass bell jangled as he crossed the threshold.

Chandra was inside. Alone. She was seated at a make-shift desk, and glanced in his direction. Her fingers froze above the keyboard of a calculator, and surprise and anxiety registered in her even features. "Dr. O'Rourke," she said quietly. Standing, she yanked her glasses from her face and folded them into a case. As she approached the counter separating them, she asked. "Is . . . is anything wrong? The baby—is he—"

"He's fine," Dallas said, cutting in, and noticed relief ease the tension from her shoulders.

"Thank God. When I saw you here. . .well, I assumed the worst."

She blew her bangs from her eyes in a sigh of relief, and Dallas couldn't take his eyes from her face as he crossed the room and slapped his coupon onto the desk. "Actually, I'm here to cash this in."

Chandra picked up the voucher and eyed it carefully. "You want a white-water trip?"

"Overnight camp-out, I think it says."

"When?" She seemed ill at ease, drumming her fingers as she read the damned coupon again.

"As soon as possible. I've got three days off and thought we could get started whenever your schedule allows." He watched her and wondered if she'd try to beg out, try to palm him off on someone else—a man probably. He didn't blame her and, considering his fantasies of late, she would probably be right. Nonetheless, more than anything, Dallas wanted to spend the next couple of days alone with her.

"This coupon has my name on it," she said, glancing up at him with assessing hazel eyes. "Did you request me?"

"It was a gift. From my brother."

"Your brother?" She pulled her eyebrows together, and a deep line formed on her forehead.

"Half brother really. Brian McGee."

"McGee? Oh!" A smile of recognition lighted her eyes. "Mr. Macho."

"Was he?" Dallas wasn't certain he liked this twist in the conversation. Obviously Chandra had noticed Brian's dubious charms, and Dallas had hoped that she would be a little more selective. He saw her as a cut above the women Brian usually dated.

"He wasn't too thrilled to have a woman guide," she explained with a soft chuckle that struck a chord deep within Dallas. "But he changed his mind."

"Whatever you did, he sang your praises for two hours."

She laughed, and the sound was deep and throaty. "I scared him."

"You what?" Dallas couldn't help the grin that tugged at his lips. The thought of this little woman besting his brother was music to his ears.

"I scared the living tar right out of him." She glanced to the coupon and back to Dallas, and the laughter died in her eyes. "Am I supposed to do the same for you?"

"Do you think you can?"

"Without a doubt," she said, arching one fine eyebrow.

Was she teasing him? Women rarely had the nerve to joke with him; he'd heard his nickname, Dr. Ice, muttered angrily behind his back more than once. The name and the reputation suited him just fine. Kept things simple.

"Well, Ms. Hill, you're on."

"In that case, call me Chandra—I'll try to forget that you're a doctor." She flashed him a cool smile of even, white teeth that made him want to return her grin.

"Will that be possible?"

"Absolutely. But I think we should get some things clear before we set out—in case you want to back out." She leaned over the counter that separated them. "When we're in the boat, *Dallas,* I'm in charge. And that goes for the rest of the trip, as well. It was hard enough to convince your brother of that fact, so I hope I don't get any guff from you. Understood?"

For a little thing, he thought, she certainly could lay down the law. He couldn't help feeling slightly amused. "What time?"

"Let's see what we've got available." She turned, picked up a clipboard with several charts attached to it and ran her fingers along the top page. Scowling, as if she was disappointed to find she wasn't booked up, she said, "Be back here at ten-thirty today. I'll have everything ready by then."

"What do I need to bring?"

"Besides your nerve?" she asked, and slid a list of supplies across the desk. One column listed the equipment and food that would be provided, the other suggested items he might bring along. "Just remember we travel light."

"Aye, aye, captain," he said mockingly, and started for the door.

"One more thing," she called. He stopped short, turning to catch a glimpse of what—worry?—on her small features. "Will you be coming alone—the coupon is only for one. Or is anyone from your family...your wife, anyone, coming along?"

At that he snorted. "My wife?" he asked, and thought of Jennifer. Though they'd been divorced for years, she was the only woman who had become missus to his mister. "Nope. Just me." With that, he strode through the door.

Chandra let out her breath. If Rick was here right now, she'd personally strangle him. What did he mean to do, hooking her up with O'Rourke? And what about the cryptic comment from O'Rourke about his wife? Was he married or not? Already, Chandra was getting mixed signals from the man, and not knowing his marital status made things difficult. Not that his marital status mattered, of course. Dallas O'Rourke was nothing more than the doctor who had admitted the baby.

Nonetheless, Rick Benson had a lot of explaining to do! Putting her name down on the form!

Within ten minutes, her boss waltzed through the door. "What's gotten into you?" she demanded.

"Hey—what's wrong?"

"Everything." She threw up her hands in disgust. "You signed me up for an overnight with Dr. O'Rourke. Remember him? The guy who's about as friendly as a starving lion and as calm as a raftload of TNT going over the falls!"

"Hey, slow down. What's all this about?" Rick asked before spying the coupon on the desk. "Oh."

"'Oh' is right."

"Don't blame me. That college kid insisted that you give his brother the ride of his life."

Chandra's eyes narrowed suspiciously.

"The kid even paid for an overnight, but if you don't want to do it, I'm sure that Randy would—"

"No!" Chandra cut in, feeling cornered. "I already said I'd meet him today. I can't back down now."

"Sure you could. Get a headache or claim you have P.M.S. or—"

"Just like a man!" she said, throwing up her hands and glaring at him. "I swear, Rick, sometimes I think you're on *their* side."

"On whose side? Men's? No way, Chan, I'm just walking a thin line between the sexes." He looked up, trying to swallow a smile. "I hired you, didn't I? You should have heard all the flack I took about that."

"I know, I know," Chandra said, though she still felt betrayed. It wasn't that she didn't want to be with Dr. O'Rourke, she told herself; the man was interesting, even if his temper was a little on the rough side. But the thought of spending a day *and* a night with him...

"Hey—isn't he the guy who took care of the baby at the hospital?" Rick asked as he walked into the back room. He returned with a gross of pocket knives, which he put on display in the glass case near the door.

"Just the admitting doctor."

"Well, he works at the hospital, doesn't he? Maybe you could get a little more information on the kid. I know that you've been eatin' yourself up over it."

"Is it that obvious?"

"And then some." Rick opened one pocket knife to display the blades, then locked the case. He moved back to the desk, where Chandra had tried to resume tallying yesterday's receipts. "If you ask me, you're getting yourself too caught up with that little tyke."

"I don't remember asking." She took her glasses out of their case, then slid them onto her nose.

Rick pushed the sale button on the cash register and withdrew a five-dollar bill. A small smile played upon his lips. "This trip with the doc might be the best thing that happened to you in a long time."

O'Rourke was prompt, she'd give him that. At ten-thirty, his truck rounded the corner and pulled into the lot. He guided his pickup into the empty slot next to Chandra's Suburban. "Ready?" he asked as he hopped down from his truck.

"As I'll ever be," Chandra muttered under her breath, forcing a smile. "You bet." Dr. O'Rourke—no, Dallas—was as intimidating outside the hospital as he was in. Though he was dressed down in faded jeans, beat-up running shoes, a T-shirt and worn leather jacket, he still stood erect, his shoulders wide, his head cocked at an angle of authority. *What am I doing?* Chandra wondered as she, balancing on the running board of the Suburban, tightened a strap holding the inflated raft onto the top of her rig.

"Need help?"

"Not yet." She yanked hard, tied off the strap quickly and hopped to the ground. Dusting her hands, she said, "Just give me a hand with your gear and we'll get going. You follow me in your truck. You can park at the camp. We'll take my rig up the river."

"Sounds fair enough," he said, though he couldn't hide the skepticism in his voice.

Within minutes, they were ready—or as ready as Chandra would ever be—and the Suburban was breezing along the country road, which wound upward through the surrounding hills. Behind her, Dallas drove his truck, and she couldn't help glancing in the rearview to watch him. There was something about the man that was damned unsettling, and though she told herself differently, she knew her attraction to him—for that's what it was, whether she wanted to admit to it or not—had nothing to do with Baby J.D.

The drive took nearly two hours, and in that time the smooth asphalt of the country road deteriorated as they turned onto a gravel lane that twisted and turned up the mountains.

Tall pines and aspen grew in abundance along the roadside, their branches dancing in the wind and casting galloping shadows across the twin ruts of the sharp rock. Through the forest, flashes of silver water, the Rattlesnake River, glinted and sparkled in the trees.

Chandra pulled off at a widening in the road, just to the south of Grizzly Loop. Dust was still billowing from beneath her tires as Dallas's rig ground to a stop. Through the surrounding stands of trees, the river rushed in a deafening roar and the dank smell of water permeated the air.

Dallas cut the engine and shoved open the door of his truck. "I must be out of my mind," he said as he hopped to the ground. "Why I ever let Brian talk me into this . . ." He shook his head, and sunlight danced in his jet-black hair.

"So it wasn't your idea?"

"No way."

Chandra opened the back door of the Suburban and started pulling out crates of supplies. "Let me guess. You didn't really want to come today but your male pride got in your way, right? Since your brother—"

"Half brother," Dallas clarified gruffly.

"Whatever. Since he made the trip, your ego was on the line. You had to prove you were man enough to challenge the river." She smiled as she said the words, but Dallas got the distinct impression that she wasn't just teasing him. No, she was testing his mettle.

"Maybe I couldn't resist spending time with you," he said smoothly, then cringed at the sound of his own words. Good Lord, that corny line could've come straight out of an old black-and-white movie.

"I figured as much," she tossed back, but a dimple in her cheeks creased, and her hazel eyes seemed to catch the rays of the sun. Her eyes sparkled the same gray-green as the river that he glimpsed through the trees. "Well, are you going to give me a hand or what?"

"I thought you were the guide."

"On my trips, everyone pitches in." She reached into the truck again, withdrew some tent poles and tossed them to him. "I think we should set up camp at the edge of the forest."

"Whatever you say. You're the boss," he mocked, carrying tent poles, tarp and a heavy crate down a dusty path through the trees. Branches from the surrounding brush slapped at his thighs, and a bird, squawking at his intrusion, soared upward past the leafy branches to the blue sky.

For the first time, Dallas didn't doubt the wisdom of this little adventure. Though he hated to admit it, he decided that Brian might have been right about one thing—he did need a break from his sterile routine. For the past three years, he'd had no social life, contenting himself with work and sleep. He swam daily in the pool of a local athletic club, taking out his frustrations by swimming lap after tiring lap, and he skied in the winter.... Well, he hadn't last winter or the winter before that. He'd been too busy....

"This should do."

He hadn't even been aware that Chandra had joined him or that the path had ended at a solitary stretch of sand and rock. Chandra strapped on a tool belt and took the tent stakes from his hands. "Put the rest of the equipment right there and unload the back of the Suburban. But don't bring down the first-aid kit, life preservers or anything else you think we might need on the trip—including the small cooler." When he didn't move, she smiled sweetly and added, "Please."

Dallas wasn't used to taking orders. Especially not from some tiny woman puffed up on her own authority. And yet, she'd been straight with him from the beginning, so despite his natural tendency to rebel, he dropped the things he was carrying and, turning, started back up the path.

When he returned, Chandra was bent over her work. The stakes were driven into the earth, and the ropes were strung tight. She leaned her back into her efforts as she stretched the nylon tarp over the poles.

She'd tied a handkerchief around her forehead and had begun to sweat; shiny drops beaded over her eyebrows and along the gentle ridge of her spine where her blouse separated from her shorts. He wondered about the texture of her skin, so firm and supple, then closed his mind to that particular topic. What was coming over him? Since he'd moved to Ranger, more than his share of women had shown interest in him. Patients, nurses, even fellow doctors had been bold enough to try to get to know him, but he'd held firm. No woman, no matter how beautiful, no matter how interesting, was allowed past a certain point. He had made the mistake of putting his faith in a gorgeous woman once before, and he wasn't about to suffer that fate again.

Even if, as he was beginning to suspect, Chandra Hill was the most exciting female he'd met since stepping foot on Colorado soil.

Ignoring the obvious curve of her behind, he dropped the rest of their supplies. "Here, let me give you a hand with that."

"You know how?" she asked skeptically.

"Mmm."

"Don't tell me, you're an Eagle Scout in disguise," she joked sarcastically, but took the sting off her words by offering him that sexy smile again.

"Nope. The military."

"You were in the service?" she asked, turning all her attention his way. Her face, touched by the sunlight, seemed younger and more innocent than he'd first thought, and yet there was a trace of sadness in her eyes, a flickering shadow that darkened her gaze momentarily.

"My father was," he clarified, wondering why he was giving her any information about himself. "Career military doctor."

She rocked back on her heels and wiped her palms on her shorts. "And you decided to follow in his footsteps?"

"Something like that," he admitted, though the subject, as far as he was concerned, was closed. He'd come on this trip with the firm intention of gaining some insight on Ms. Hill, not the other way around.

They finished setting up camp, and Chandra, swinging a rope over a tall tree branch, hoisted a nylon bag of food twenty feet into the air. "Bears," she explained when she caught his questioning gaze. "They're as hungry as Yogi and twice as clever. So let's not leave any 'pic-i-nic baskets' around. Even this—" she hooked a thumb toward the tree "—might not be effective."

"No one mentioned bears on this trip."

"Don't worry, I'll protect you," she said, and laughed. That husky sound continually surprised him. Checking her watch, she said, "Come on, let's go. We want to get back here before dark."

He had no choice but to follow her back up the path, and though he tried to train his eyes on the steep curving trail, his gaze wandered continually to the movement of her tanned legs and the sway of her hips beneath khaki-colored shorts.

Her clothing, an aqua T-shirt and shorts, wasn't innately sexy, but there was something about her, some emotions simmering just beneath the surface of her calm smile, that hinted at a slumbering sexuality ready to awaken. His thoughts leapt ahead to a vivid picture of her lying naked on that sandy beach, hair wild and free, water from the river still clinging to her skin. Her arms were outstretched, her legs, beneath an apex of blond curls, demurely crossed, but her dark-tipped breasts pointing upward, beckoning—

"Ready?"

His heart slammed against his chest as he started from his fantasy and found her staring up at him. They had emerged from the forest, and the sunlight seemed harsh after the filtered shadows of the woods.

"Anytime you are," Dallas replied, his voice lower than usual as he shook the inviting image of her bare body from his mind with difficulty.

"Good." Crawling into the cab of her truck, Chandra added, "Hop in." She fired the engine and threw the big rig into gear. Dallas had barely settled into his seat and closed the door when she tromped on the accelerator and they were off to God-only-knew-where.

Dr. O'Rourke wasn't exactly as Chandra had expected him to be. He was quiet—too damned quiet. She never knew what he was thinking, and now, bumping over the lane to the start of Grizzly Loop, she wished she'd never agreed to be his guide. His brooding silence made her nervous, and the directness of his gaze made it impossible for her to relax. And that didn't even begin to touch his sexuality, which, now that she was alone with him in the wilderness, seemed more potent than ever.

She switched on the radio, hoping that music would dull the edge of tension that seemed to emanate from the man beside her. A Kris Kristofferson ballad drifted from the speakers.

"Where, exactly, are we going?" the doctor finally asked.

"To a point known as Fool's Bluff."

"Appropriate," he muttered, and slipped a pair of mirrored sunglasses onto the bridge of his hawkish nose.

She let that one slide. But as the gravel of the lane gave way to rocky ruts, she hazarded a glance at this man who was to be her companion for the next thirty-six hours. He was handsome, no doubt of that, and his profile, made more mysterious by the dark glasses, was potently virile and male. His features were hard, his hair wavy and willful, for the black strands appeared to lie as they wanted, refusing to be tamed by any civilized comb or brush.

He seemed to fill up the interior of her truck, the smell of him pure male and soap scents. His long legs were cramped, even in the roomy interior.

She knew that he was watching her from the corner of his eye, and she felt self-conscious. Never before had she needed to rack her brain for conversation; her clients had always, through anxiety or their outgoing personalities, managed to keep up a steady stream of small talk.

But not Dr. O'Rourke. No way.

The noon sun was intense, and the sky offered no traces of clouds. Chandra drove along the winding road that followed the twisted course of the river. Through the passing trees, flashes of gray-green water sped by. "Okay, let's go over a few safety rules," she said as she fished a pair of sunglasses from the glove box and slid them onto her nose. "First, as I told you before—I'm in charge. I'll let you guide the raft, but if we're getting into trouble, you've got to trust me to take over."

O'Rourke snorted, but inclined his head slightly.

"Secondly, you wear your life vest and helmet at all times."

"I read all the rules," he said, rolling down his window and propping his elbow on the ledge. Cool mountain air, smelling of fresh water and dust, rushed through the rig's interior, catching in Chandra's hair and caressing the back of her neck.

She rattled off a few more pieces of information about raft safety, but Dallas was way ahead of her, so she fell silent, watching the road as the Suburban jarred and bumped up the hillside. Shafts of sunlight pierced through the pines and aspen that clustered between the road and the river. Nearby, the mountains rose like stony sentinels, sharp-peaked and silent.

The road began to lose its definition, becoming nothing more than a pair of tire tracks between which grass, weeds and wildflowers grew.

"This part of the river is known as Grizzly Loop," Chandra said, glancing over at Dallas.

"So, there are really bears up here. I thought you hauled our provisions into the trees just to scare me."

"Did I...scare you?"

His smile was arrogant and mocking. "I was terrified."

"Right," she said sarcastically. "As for grizzlies, you'll see about as many as you see rattlesnakes. The river and parts of it were named a long time ago. I suppose there were a lot of bears here once, and there could be rattlesnakes, but I've never seen either, nor has anyone I know. Disappointed?"

"Relieved."

The radio, playing a mixture of soft pop and country, finally faded in a crackle of static, and the grass strip between the tire ruts grew wider. Long, sun-dried blades brushed the underbelly of the truck. Chandra fiddled with the dial, found no discernible signal and flipped off the radio. "I guess we'll have to settle for brilliant conversation."

"Suits me." He leaned against the passenger window and studied her more closely. "What do you want to talk about?"

"Baby Doe," she said automatically. No reason to beat around the bush, and that way she could avoid discussing her life.

"What about him?"

"Has anyone tried to claim him?"

Dallas shook his head, and Chandra felt a release of anxiety, like the rush of water from a burgeoning dam. Ever since she'd found the small child, crying and red faced in her barn, a tiny idea had sprouted in her mind, an idea that had grown and formed until she could recognize it for what it was. She wanted the baby, and though she'd argued with herself a million times, she knew that she was on a path to requesting guardianship. It was time she became a parent. She needed the baby, and, oh, Lord, the baby needed the kind of loving mother she could well become.

They drove a few more miles until they reached Fool's Bluff, which was situated some forty feet above the river. The rocky ledge provided a view of the curving Rattlesnake as it sliced through a canyon in the mountains. "That's where we'll be going," Chandra said, parking the truck and climbing out to point south, toward the wayward path of wild, white water.

"It looks pretty tame from up here," Dallas observed.

Chandra laughed. "Don't you know that looks can be deceiving?"

"I'm beginning to," he said, and he sent her an assessing glance that caused her heart to trip-hammer for a second as their gazes touched then moved away. Quickly, she turned back to the truck, and balancing on the running board, began to unleash the raft.

Dallas worked on the other side of the Suburban, and soon they were packing the raft and a few supplies along the narrow trail leading through the undergrowth and pines surrounding the river. "You're sure this is safe?" he asked, a smile nudging the corner of his mouth.

"You're insured, aren't you?"

He snorted. "To the max. I'm a doctor, remember? Insurance is a way of life."

"Then relax. You've got nothing to worry about," Chandra mocked, her eyes seeming to dance.

But Dallas wasn't convinced. With the single-minded perception he'd built a reputation upon, he realized that the next hours, while he was alone with Chandra in the forested hills, might prove to be his fateful undoing.

Chapter Six

Like an awakening serpent, the river bucked and reared,
rolling in a vast torrent of icy water that slashed furiously
through the terrain. Chandra propelled the raft through the
rapids, concentrating on the current, guiding the craft away
from rocks and fallen trees.

The raft hit a snag and spun.

Adrenaline surged through Chandra's blood as the raft
tilted, taking on water. *Hold on,* she told herself. Freezing
spray splashed in her face, and water drenched her shirt and
shorts as she tried to concentrate on the idiosyncrasies of the
river. The raft pitched and rolled as the Rattlesnake twisted
back upon itself. "Hang on," she yelled, putting her shoulders into the task of balancing the inflatable boat.

Blinking against the spray of water, she was aware of
Dallas shifting the position of his oars, of his body moving
with the flow of the current as easily as if he, too, were a
river guide.

The raft hit a submerged rock and bounced upward, landing back on the water with a slap and a curl, spinning out of control for a heart-stopping second before Chandra found the channel again.

Dallas, his black hair wet and shining, his face red where the water had slapped him, paddled with the current, helping Chandra keep on course.

"You lied. You *were* a Boy Scout," she screamed over the roar of wild water.

His laugh filtered back to her. "No. But I was taught to be prepared for anything."

"By your father?"

He didn't answer, but threw his back into his oar, and the craft whipped past a slick boulder that protruded from the frigid depths.

They shot past the final series of ripples, and finally, as the Rattlesnake's strength gave out, their craft slowed in the shallows to drift lazily in the ebbing current.

Chandra let out her breath in relief. Though she was always eager to challenge the river, she was also relieved when the most difficult part of the journey was over.

"You do this every day?" Dallas asked, settling back against the stern of the raft to look at her.

"No, thank God! Sometimes I guide trail rides or supervise camp-outs or rock climbs. In the winter, I work on the ski patrol and give lessons."

"The outdoorswoman who does it all."

"Not everything," she countered, shoving her wet hair from her face. "I don't hunt."

"No?"

She narrowed her eyes against the lowering sun and paddled slowly, anticipating the next series of rapids. Though smaller than the last, they were still treacherous. "I'm afraid that if meat didn't come wrapped in plastic on little trays in the store, I'd become a vegetarian."

He smiled at that, and his grin, honest in the outdoors, touched her.

"Show time," she said as the river picked up speed again, and together they slid through the rapids, following the Rattlesnake's thrashing course until, half an hour later, they glided around a final bend to the beach beneath Fool's Bluff, where their camp was waiting.

"Home sweet home," Chandra quipped, and Dallas couldn't help thinking she was right. The faded tents and supplies stacked nearby, the bag of food swinging twenty feet in the air, the tall pines and rocky shore all did seem as much home to him as anyplace he'd ever lived.

Skimming her paddles through the water, Chandra guided the boat to the bank. Near the beach, she hopped into the icy water. Dallas, sucking in his breath, followed suit, and soon they'd pulled the raft onto the beach, leaving it upside down to drain.

"Now what?" Dallas asked.

"Well, you can change into some dry clothes, or you can leave those on, they'll dry soon enough. We'll get started on dinner. Then, once it's dark, we'll tell ghost stories around the campfire and scare ourselves out of our minds," she deadpanned.

Dallas laughed, and Chandra couldn't help but grin. Beneath his hard facade, Dallas O'Rourke was a man with a sense of humor, and here in the mountains, he seemed less formidable, more carefree. What else was he hiding beneath his surgical mask and professional demeanor? she wondered before closing her mind to a subject that was strictly off-limits. He was the client, and she was the guide. Nothing more. And yet, as the time she shared with him passed, she found her thoughts drifting to him as she wondered what kind of a lover he would be. What kind of husband? What kind of father?

Before twilight descended, they drove upriver in his truck to retrieve the Suburban. By the time they returned, the sun was behind the mountains and long shadows stretched across the beach. Dinner consisted of sandwiches, fruit and cookies that Rick always purchased from a bakery on the first floor of the building housing Wild West Expeditions.

"Not exactly Maxim's," he remarked, leaning his back against a large boulder and stretching his legs in front of him.

"You complaining?"

"Me? Never."

"You could have bought the deluxe trail ride and rafting trip," she said. "The one with caviar, champagne, Thoroughbreds and a yacht."

His mouth lifted at the corner and he said lazily, "My brother's too cheap."

"Are you two close?" she asked, and was rewarded with silence. Only the swish of water and drone of insects disturbed the silence. The sky, as if painted by an invisible brush, was layered in bands of pink and lavender. Above the darkening peaks, the boldest stars glimmered seductively.

Chandra, leaning against a log, drew her legs to her chin and wrapped her arms around her shins. "It's gorgeous up here, don't you think? The first time I saw this place, I *knew* this was where I had to stay."

"Where're you from?" he asked. She turned to find him watching her so closely that her breath stopped for a second. For the first time since the river run, she realized that she'd be spending the night with this man—all alone in the wilderness. Though it wasn't a new experience—she'd led more than her share of trail rides and camping excursions—she could feel in the air that this night would be different. Because of Dallas. There was something that set him apart from the other men she'd guided along the river—or was there? She edged her toe in the sand, unwilling to admit any attraction for a man she'd met so recently, a man who could, for all she knew, be married.

The scent of water filled her nostrils and the night seemed clearer than usual. The evening air was warm, its breath laden with the scents of spruce and pine.

"I take it you're not a native," he pressed, those inscrutable eyes still staring at her.

"No, I'm originally from Idaho," she admitted. "Grew up there. My dad was a real outdoorsman, and since he had no sons and I was the oldest daughter, he spent a lot of time showing me the ropes of canoeing, horseback riding, swimming, rafting and mountain climbing."

"And you made it a profession?"

Picking up a stick, she nudged over a rock, exposing a beetle that quickly scurried for cover. "With some stops along the way," she admitted. "Why are you so interested?"

He looked at her long and hard. "Because I've never met a woman who, with a few first-aid courses, could so quickly and accurately diagnose a patient as you did. You were right on target, Ms. Hill."

"Chandra. Remember?" she said, and considered telling him the truth. He deserved that much, she supposed. "And you're right," she admitted, though she couldn't confide in him, not completely. There was too much emotional scarring that she wouldn't reveal, at least not yet. So she hedged. "I've had more training than basic first aid. I was in medical school for a while, but I dropped out."

"Why?" he asked. The word seemed to hang between them in the night air. The moon had risen, and dusk, like a familiar warm cloak, closed them off from the rest of the world. The river rippled by, shimmering with the silvery light of the moon. The mountains, craggy and black, loomed toward the twilight sky.

"I didn't think it was right for me," she lied, cringing inwardly. Why not tell him the truth and get it over with? But, though she tried, the words wouldn't pass her tongue. Standing, she dusted her palms on her shorts. She felt a chill, though the air still held warmth from the afternoon, and she didn't know how much she should tell Dallas.

He was leaning forward, hands clasped, watching her every move, but when she didn't explain any further, he stood and walked toward her, his gaze still fastened on her face. He stopped just short of her, and she was all too aware that he was standing inches from her, his sleeve, still damp, brushing the crook of her arm. She tried not to notice how close he was, how intimate the night had become. Dry leaves fluttered in the wind, rustling and whispering as the breeze moved along the course of the river.

Lifting her head, she focused on the straight line of his chin, his square jaw, the way his hair ruffled in the wind. As if he understood her pain, he didn't ask another question, just took her in his arms and held her. Her throat burned with his sudden gentleness, and tears threatened her eyes. She didn't try to break away, just let his arms and the sounds of the river envelop her. How long had it been since someone had held her?

His breath whispered across her crown, and his body was warm, a soothing balm for all the old wounds. Her arms wrapped around his as if of their own accord, and he groaned. "Chandra," he whispered, and his voice had grown husky.

Good Lord, what was she doing, embracing this . . . this stranger, for crying out loud? And why did she feel the need to tell him her life story? This was all wrong. Even if his arms felt right, he was a client, a doctor, for God's sake, not a man she could get involved with. He could be married, for all she knew! She tried to break away, but his arms, strong as hemp, wouldn't budge. "I think . . . this isn't right. . . . I don't know anything about you." She gazed up at him steadily. "Look, Dallas, I don't fool around. Especially with married men."

"Then you're safe."

"You're not married?"

The muscles surrounding her tensed. "Not anymore."

"Oh." She didn't know what to say.

She tried to slip out of his arms, but his grip tightened. "I still don't think this is very smart."

"I know it isn't."

"I don't get involved with *any* men," she clarified, her voice unusually low, her pulse beginning to race wildly. They were talking about a very serious subject, and yet she felt that there was an undercurrent in their conversation, and she couldn't concentrate on much more than the feel of his hard body pressed so close to hers.

Embracing him was crazy! Downright insane. She didn't even know the man—not really. All she had were impressions of an honest, overworked physician, who at times could be cuttingly harsh and other times as textured and smooth as velvet.

"I know you were right on the money with the baby," he said, his breath fanning across the top of her head. "I've seen you handle Alma Lindquist and Bob Fillmore. I know for a fact that I couldn't put you off when you demanded to know about the infant's condition. And I've seen you navigate one helluva river. My guess is that you do whatever you set your mind to, Ms. Hill."

"Chandra," she reminded him again, but the words strangled in her throat as his night-darkened gaze locked with hers for a heart-stopping instant. She knew in that flash of brilliance that he was going to kiss her and that she was unable to stop him. He dropped his head then, and his mouth molded intimately over hers.

It's been so long . . . she thought as a river of emotions carried her away. The smell of him was everywhere—earthy, sensual, divine. And the feel of his hands, so supple against her skin, caused tiny goose bumps to rise on her flesh. He locked one of his hands around the back of her neck and gently pulled her hair as his tongue traced the rim of her mouth.

Her breath was stilled, her heart beginning to pound a cadence as wild as the river rushing through this dusky canyon.

This is a mistake! she told herself, but didn't listen. She heard only the drumming of her heart and the answering cadence of his. Warm, hard, primal, he provoked a passion so long dormant, it awoke with a fury, creating desire that knew no bounds. He shifted his weight, drawing her down, and her knees gave way as he pressed her slowly, intimately, to the beach.

Cool sand touched her back, and he half lay across her, the weight of his chest welcome, the feel of his body divine. She didn't protest when his mouth moved from her lips to the slope of her chin and lower, against her neck. She was conscious only of the feel of the coming night, the cool sand against her back, the whisper of his lips against her skin, the firm placement of his hand across her abdomen, as if through her clothes he could feel the gentle pulsing at her very core.

He moved slightly, and his hand shifted, climbing upward to feel the weight of her breast. Chandra moaned as her nipple, in anticipation, grew taut and desire caused her breast to ache.

Dear Lord, this is madness! she thought, but couldn't stop. She gripped his shoulders and sighed when she felt him push aside the soft cotton of the T-shirt until his flesh was nearly touching hers and only the simple barrier of white lace kept skin from skin.

"Chandra," he groaned, as if in agony, against her ear. "Oh, God..." He tugged off her T-shirt then, as the first pale glow from the moon filtered through the forest. He stared at her, swallowing hard as his gaze centered on the dark nipple protruding against filmy lace.

Chandra shivered, but not from the coolness of the night so much as from that critical gaze that seemed to caress the border of tan and white flesh across her breast, below which the white skin, opalescent and veined with blue lines, rounded to a pert, dark crest.

Dallas closed his eyes, as if to steady himself, but when he looked at her again, none of his passion was gone. "This is crazy," he whispered, and she couldn't reply; her mouth was dry, her words unformed. But she felt him reach forward again, slowly push down the strap of her bra, peel away the gossamer fabric and allow her breast to spill free.

"You're beautiful," he said, and then, as if he knew the words were too often spoken in haste, looked her straight in the eyes. "It's probably as much a curse as a blessing."

Beautiful? She wasn't blind and knew she was pretty, but beautiful? Never. She felt herself blush and hoped the night hid the telltale scarlet stain creeping up her neck. "You don't have to say anything," she replied in a voice that sounded as if it had been filtered by dry leaves.

His arms surrounded her, and he drew her close, his mouth finding hers in a kiss that drew the very breath from her lungs. No longer tenuous, he pressed his tongue into her mouth and explored the wet lining, one hand surrounding her back, the other softly kneading her breast.

Chandra melted inside. Heat as intense as a fire burning out of control swirled inside her, through her blood and into her brain. She wrapped a leg around him and arched upward. He slid lower, then snapped the fastening of her bra, letting both breasts swing free. He captured one nipple in his teeth and sucked as if from hunger, his tongue flicking and massaging the soft underside of her skin.

Her passion igniting, Chandra cupped his head and pulled him closer, crying out in bittersweet agony when, as he breathed, his hot breath fanned her wet nipple.

"Please," she whispered, caught in this hot whirlpool of desire and unable to swim free. "Please."

He found the fastening on her shorts, and his fingers brushed against her abdomen and lower still.

Somewhere in the trees high above, an owl hooted softly, breaking the stillness of the night. Dallas's lips stopped their tender exploration, but the breath from his nostrils still seared her sensitive skin. He jerked his head away. "This is a mistake," he muttered, swiping a hand impatiently through his hair, as if in so doing, he could release the tension that was coiling his muscles. He rolled away from her. "Damn it all to hell, Chandra, I don't know what got into me."

Embarrassment crept up Chandra's spine at his rejection. Silently calling herself a fool, she scrambled for her clothes.

"Look, I'm sorry—"

"Don't apologize," she interrupted. "There's nothing to apologize for. Things just got out of hand, that's all." She wished she felt as calm as she sounded, but inside, her heart was pounding, and she wanted to die of mortification. She'd never played loose and fast. Never!

She'd been the butt of cruel jokes while in medical school. Doug's friends had wondered aloud and within her earshot if it were possible to light a fire in her or if she, so conscientious with her studies, were frigid. Doug had stood up for her, if feebly, and they had married, but she'd never forgotten how wretched those remarks had made her feel.

Nonetheless, she didn't see herself in the role of femme fatale, and this little escapade with Dallas was certainly out of character.

"This doesn't happen to me," he said.

"And you think it does to me?"

His lips compressed into a hard line, and Chandra nearly laughed. What did he think of her? She should be incensed, but she found his confusion amusing. She smothered a smile as she pulled her T-shirt over her head. "Well, what just happened between us is usually not part of the expedition, not even the most expensive trips," she teased, hoping to lighten the tension. Dallas wasn't in the mood for jokes. "Don't worry about it," she said, though she could think of nothing but the touch of his hands on her skin, the smell of him so close, the taste of his lips on hers. She turned back to the campsite. "Come on. We should start dinner, and if you think just because I'm a woman that I'm going to do it all myself you've got— Oh!"

He caught hold of her wrist and spun her around. She nearly tripped on a rock, and he caught her before she fell. Strong arms surrounded her, and his face, not smiling, but as intense as the night closing in on them, was pressed to hers. "I just want you to know," he said so quietly she could barely hear him above the wind soughing through the pines, "I don't play games."

She gulped. "I wouldn't think so."

"So when something like this…happens, I can't just take it lightly and shrug it off like you do."

"It's easier that way," she said, lying.

In the darkness, his eyes narrowed. "Just what kind of woman are you?"

She sucked in her breath, ragged though it was. "What kind of woman am I?" she repeated, incredulous. "I'm a woman who doesn't stand around waiting for a man to trip all over himself to open her car door, a woman who doesn't believe in love at first sight, a woman who would someday like a child but doesn't necessarily need a man, and a woman who expects any man she meets to pull his own weight," she managed to spit out, though she was all too aware of the feel of his hands against her skin and the tantalizing passion flaring in his eyes.

His grin slashed white in the darkness, and his hand was tight over her wrist. A chuckle deep and rumbling erupted from him. "Are you really so tough?"

"Tough enough," she replied, tilting her chin defiantly, though inside, she quivered. Not that she'd let him know. She didn't want Dallas to suspect any weakness. She twisted in his arms, afraid that if he saw into her eyes, he'd read her hesitation. Together, while the river flowed on in bright glimmers of silver moonlight, they stared at the water, and Chandra couldn't help feeling as if they were the only man and woman on earth.

"Come on," she finally said, afraid this intimacy would only make spending the night together more difficult. She drew her hand from his and, reluctantly, he let her go. "I'm starved."

They barbecued steaks and warmed bread, boiled potatoes and stir-fried fresh vegetables. Conversation was minimal. After dinner, they sat near the tents, the lanterns glowing in the wilderness and attracting insects. The smell and sound of the river filled the night, and Chandra felt more at peace than she had in a long, long while. There was something comforting about being with Dallas, something warm and homelike. And yet, there was another side to him, as well, the volatile, passionate side that kept her on edge. They drank coffee slowly, sitting apart, not daring to touch.

She wrapped her arms around her knees and stared at the man, whom she'd met as a doctor for J.D., but now knew as... well, not a friend... but more than an acquaintance. *And possibly a lover?* her mind teased, but she steadfastly shoved that absurd thought into a corner of her mind. Though she wanted to think of him as a man, she forced herself back to the issue at hand. She had more important things to think about.

"How long will Social Services wait until they place the baby?" she asked, sipping from her cup.

"As soon as we release him from the hospital. Probably in a day or two."

"That soon?" Chandra's heart took a nosedive. She'd have to work fast.

"He can't stay in the hospital forever." Dallas reached for the coffeepot, still warm on the camp stove, and, holding the enamel pot aloft, silently asked if she'd like more.

Shaking her head, Chandra bit her lower lip, her mind racing in circles. If no one claimed the baby, she'd try to adopt him. Why not? Tomorrow, when she returned home, she'd call her lawyer, have all the necessary applications filled out, do whatever she had to do, but, damn it, she intended to make a bid for the baby....

As if he saw the wheels turning in her mind, Dallas said, "What's on your mind, Chandra? You've been bringing up the baby all day." He stretched out on a sleeping bag and levered up on one elbow while his eyes, cast silver by the soft shafts of light from the moon, centered on her.

Could she trust him? She needed a friend, an ally, but Dr. O'Rourke was an unlikely choice. Licking her lip nervously, she decided to gamble. "I hope to adopt him," she admitted, holding his gaze.

"If no one claims him."

"If J.D.'s—" she saw the doctor's bushy eyebrows elevate a notch "—that's what I call him. You know, for John Doe." When he nodded, she continued. "If J.D.'s mother shows up, she'll have to prove to me that she's fit. What kind of woman would leave a baby in a barn?"

"A desperate one?"

"But why not stick around? Or knock on my door? I would've helped her, taken her and the child to the hospital," Chandra said, shaking her head and turning her attention back to the few swallows of coffee left in her cup. "Oh, no, there's no reason, no good reason, to leave a baby to die."

Dallas finished his coffee. "The baby didn't die," he pointed out. "Maybe the mother was in an abusive situation. Maybe she was trying to protect the child. The reason she didn't show her face is that she doesn't want her husband or boyfriend or whoever to show up, claim the baby, then perhaps hurt him or her. She could be on the run for a good reason."

"There are agencies—"

"Not enough."

Chandra glanced up at Dallas and noticed the serious lines deepening along his eyes and mouth. So there was a humanitarian side to Dr. O'Rourke. The man had many layers, Chandra decided, and she would all too willingly unravel each and every one to get a glimpse of the real man hidden beneath his cold, professional facade.

"I work in E.R. We see a lot of 'accidents' to children and women," he added, his voice deep and grim. "You don't know that the boy's mother wasn't a woman who, given her fear and limited knowledge, did the best she could."

"Leaving a baby alone and defenseless is never the best. That woman—whoever she is—had other options. She didn't have to take the coward's way out. She could have taken that baby with her wherever she was running."

"And what if she had a couple of other kids?" He sighed and threw the dregs of his coffee into the woods. "There's no reason to argue this. We don't know the woman's motives, but I think there's a chance the mother will surface, and when she does, she'll want her baby back."

Chandra knew he was right, and when her gaze met his eyes, she noticed a trace of sadness in their steely depths. Her heart grew suddenly cold.

"Just don't get too attached to... J.D.... Don't be giving him names and thinking about swaddling him in blankets and knitting little blue booties. You could get hurt."

"It's a chance I'll have to take."

Dallas drew one knee up and leaned over it. His face, illuminated by the fire, was serious as he studied the crackling flames. "There are other ways to become a mother—easier ways. Ways that will ensure that no one takes the child away from you."

She snorted. "Most of those ways involve a man." She stared boldly across the short space separating them, and asked, "Are you applying for the job?"

He returned her gaze for a long, tense moment, and Chandra wished she could call back the words, said too quickly. He probably thought she was seriously propositioning him.

"I just thought you could use some friendly advice," he finally said.

Chandra felt a rush of warmth for the man. "Thanks."

"You're still going to go through with it, aren't you?" When she didn't reply, he continued, "You know, you might still need a man. The system still likes to place children in homes where there is a role model for each parent. And, no, since you asked a little earlier, I don't go around fathering children." An emotion akin to anger pinched the corners of his mouth. "Call me old-fashioned, but I think it's a father's duty, responsibility and privilege to help raise his child."

"Well—" she stood and dusted her hands "—now we know where we stand."

"Almost." He tossed down his cup and stood, closing the distance between them. He grabbed both her shoulders in big, hard hands. "Be careful, Chandra. If you don't watch out, you and the baby and God-only-knows who else might be hurt by this."

"It's my business," she said simply, unmoving.

"It's my business, too, like it or not. We're both involved." He dropped his hands, and Chandra took the opportunity to step back a pace, to keep some distance from him. Her crazy heart was thundering. What was wrong with her? She'd been with dozens of men on trips like this. A few had even made the mistake of making a pass at her. But until tonight, resisting a man's advances had come easy.

To make herself look busy, she rinsed her cup in the warm water simmering on the stove. "I'd better get this food back in the bag and hang it from the tree, then we can turn in." She wished she'd never gotten close to O'Rourke. He'd only reinforced her fears that adopting the baby would be difficult, even painful, and might not work. But then he didn't know her, did he? He couldn't understand that once she'd set her mind on something, it would take the very devil himself to dissuade her.

Later, tucked snugly in her sleeping bag, she thought about the night stretching ahead of her, of the starlit sky, the mist rising off the river, the man who slept only a few feet away. Kissing him had seemed natural and safe. She touched her lips and quietly called herself a fool. Dallas O'Rourke was a doctor, for crying out loud, a man married to his job, a man who might stand in her way in her efforts to adopt J.D., a man of whom she knew very little. She'd had a physical response to him, that was all. It was no big deal. She hadn't been with a man since her divorce, and in those few years, she hadn't so much as let another man kiss her, though more than a few had tried.

It wasn't that she was a prude; her response to Dallas was evidence to the contrary. She just didn't want an involvement with any man, including Dr. O'Rourke.

Chapter Seven

Chandra was up at the crack of dawn and insisted they break camp early.

"That's it? We're finished?" Dallas asked, his chin dark with the shadow of a beard, his eyes a midnight blue as he stretched and yawned. A few clouds hovered in the sky, but the temperature was cool, the mountain air crisp with the promise of autumn.

"Not quite. We still have one run before you can return to civilization. We'll eat, take down the tents, check the supplies and make sure we haven't sprung any leaks in the raft. Then we'll shoot the lower flats."

"Lower flats? Calmer than Grizzly Loop, I hope."

"Different," she replied as she retrieved the supply sack. Fortunately, no bears had disturbed the food, though once before, on a camping trip in the mountains, she'd awakened to see her fat supply sack flapping in the breeze. It had been slashed at the bottom, the contents long gone, with only scraps of carton and paper and the wide tracks of a bear visible the next morning. That trip, they'd relied on the fish they'd caught and a few berries for the day. Fortunately, this time she wasn't embarrassed by a persistent and clever bear making a mockery of her precautions.

After a quick breakfast of muffins, fruit and coffee, they made preparations to break camp. Before she folded up her tent, Chandra changed into a swimsuit, shorts and blouse. She tied her hair away from her face, ignored any thoughts of makeup and yanked on a nylon parka.

Dallas, who hadn't bothered shaving, wore a khaki-colored pair of shorts and blue pullover. "You know, we could call it quits here," he said as he loosened a rope and his tent gave way.

"Your brother paid for a specific excursion," Chandra replied. "I wouldn't want to disappoint him."

"He'll never know."

Bending over her own flattened tent, she smiled at him over her shoulder. "Cold feet, Dr. O'Rourke?"

"I just thought I'd save you some trouble, that's all." His blue eyes gleamed with a devilish spark.

"No trouble at all."

Dallas didn't argue any further. Chandra could sure change a man's mind, he thought as he watched her move expertly through the campsite, packing gear, bending over without even realizing she was offering him a view of her rounded buttocks and tapered legs.

"Well?" she asked, turning to cast him an inquiring look. Her rope of tawny hair fell over one shoulder.

"You're the boss." He slapped his knees, and as he stood, he looked younger, more boyish, as if he were really enjoying himself.

She chuckled. "Now we're making progress." They packed the remaining gear and carried it up the shaded path to the strip of road where their trucks were parked.

Dallas pumped the throttle and flicked the ignition switch of his truck. The engine revved loudly, and despite his reservations, he felt a surge of excitement at the coming raft trip. Being alone with Chandra in the wilderness was more than a little appealing, and he remembered their embrace vividly, more vividly than he remembered caressing or kissing any other woman in a long, long while.

He forced his thoughts away from the impending rafting trip and the possibilities of kissing her again, of the silken feel of her skin against his, of the proud lift of her breasts, pale in the moonlight.

"Stop it," he muttered to himself, grinding the gears as he shifted down and wrenched on the wheel in an effort to follow her Suburban onto the flat rise of dry grass. She parked in the shade of some aspens that bordered the field. He stopped and willed his suddenly overactive sex drive into low gear.

The river curled close to the shore, cutting through the dry land in a shimmering swath that reminded him of a silvery snake.

Chandra cut the engine, hopped to the ground, locked the door, then climbed into the passenger side of Dallas's truck. She shoved her sunglasses onto the bridge of her nose and pretended she didn't notice the handsome thrust of his chin or the way his eyes crinkled near the corners as he squinted against the sun. She didn't let the masculine scent of him get to her, either.

He was just a man, she told herself firmly, forcing her gaze through the windshield to the rutted lane that wound through pools of sunlight and shadow. But he was her link to the baby—that was why she was attracted to him, she thought.

Deep in her heart, though, she knew she was kidding herself. Dallas was different, a man who touched a special chord deep within her, a chord that she didn't dare let him play.

She drummed her fingers on the armrest, and the hairs on the back of her neck lifted slightly when she felt him glance in her direction.

"Nervous?" he asked.

She shook her head. "Anxious to get back," she said evasively. Just being around Dallas was difficult; she felt she was always walking an emotional tightrope.

"Already she wants to get rid of me," he mocked.

Chandra laughed a little. "It's the baby. I wonder how he's doing," she replied, though the infant was only part of the reason. She needed to find her equilibrium again, something that proved impossible when she was with Dallas.

"I'll bet he's screaming for breakfast, or—" he made a big show of checking his watch "—or lunch. Demanding food seems to be what he does best."

Chandra glanced at the doctor, caught the sparkle in his eyes and was forced to smile. She relaxed a little, her spirits lifting with the morning sun as it rose higher in the sky.

Once they'd parked near the river, they checked the equipment one last time, shoved the raft into the frigid water and hopped in. The current was lazy near the shore, but as the craft drifted to the middle of the river, the stream picked up speed, narrowing as the current turned upon itself and the surge of white water filled the canyon.

The raft plunged into the first set of rapids, and the river became a torrent that curled around rocks and the shore. Chandra, jaw set, narrowed her eyes on the familiar stretch of water, shifting her weight and using her paddles against the primal force of the river.

Over the deafening roar of the water, Chandra shouted orders to Dallas, who responded quickly, expertly, his shoulders bunched, his eyes glued to the frothy water and rocks stretching before them.

He moved as they approached a rock, and they skidded past the slick, dark surface. Chandra bit her lower lip.

Downstream, Ridgeback Ripples foamed in furious waves, and Chandra braced herself for the pitch and roll that would occur as they rounded the dead tree that had fallen into the river.

She managed to steer clear of the fallen pine, avoiding the part of the stream that swirled near the blackened, dead branches. The water was clear, the rocks below shimmering gold and black. She shoved in her paddle, intending to move into deeper water.

"Watch out!" Dallas yelled.

Too late! The raft hit a snag in the water and responded by spinning, faster and faster, out of control. Water thrashed over the side. Chandra paddled more firmly.

The raft plunged deep, then bobbed up again, bucking wildly, out of control.

Hang in there, she told herself, refusing to lose her calm. They rammed a large rock and pitched forward. Chandra fell against the inflated side. Before she could get up on her knees again, the raft, still spinning, hit a shoal and buckled, flipping over.

"Hold on!" Chandra screamed as she was pitched overboard. Roaring ice-cold water poured over her in a deluge, forcing its way down her throat. Sputtering, she couldn't see, but reached out instinctively, grabbing hold of the capsized raft.

Dallas! Where was he? Oh, God! She surfaced, pulled by the drag of the current as it whisked the overturned raft downriver. Water rushed everywhere. "Dallas!" she yelled, coughing and looking around her as she tried vainly to tread water. Trees along the bank flashed by, and the sun, still bright, spangled the water, the light harsh against her eyes.

She didn't see him.

Come on, Dallas, come on. Show yourself. She looked upriver and down, searching for some sign of him as she was carried along with the current. "Dallas!" she screamed. Oh, Lord, was he trapped beneath the raft? Trying to grab on to a rock with her free hand, she scraped her arm. If she could only stop and look for him! Her heart pumped. She gasped in lungfuls of air and water. Adrenaline surged through her blood, bringing with it fear for the man she'd only recently met. *Where was he?*

If she'd inadvertently hurt him . . .

"Dallas!" she screamed again, just as the rapids rounded a bend and dumped into a relatively calm pool. She flipped the raft over, half expecting him to be caught beneath the yellow rubber.

Nothing.

Oh, God. Please don't let him drown! She couldn't lose someone in her care again . . . someone who had trusted her with his life . . . someone she'd begun to care about. "Dallas!" she screamed, her voice growing hoarse as she shouted over the roar of the river. "Oh, God, Dallas!" Her heart dived, and she struggled until she found a toehold where she could stand and scan the river as it roared by in fierce torrents. Coughing, her teeth chattering, she prayed she'd see him, his lifejacket keeping him afloat, his helmet preventing a head injury. "Come on, Dallas . . . please!" The river flowed past in swift retribution. "Dallas!" she yelled again, her voice catching in fear. *Think, Chandra, think! You know what to do!* She wouldn't just stand here. She'd had survival training, and she'd find him. He had to be alive— he had to! But fear kept her rooted to the spot, drew her eyes to the dark and suddenly evil-looking river.

She forced her legs to move with the current, knowing that he would have been swept downstream—

"Hey! Chandra!"

His voice boomed, and she turned to find him waving his arms on the shore at a bend in the river. He was the most beautiful sight she'd ever seen. Wet, bedraggled but grinning, he shouted her name again. Relief brought tears to her eyes, and she nearly fell on her knees and wept openly. Instead, she sent up a silent prayer of thanks. To think that he might have drowned . . . oh, God.

Still dragging the raft, she sloshed through the shallow water near the shore, wading toward him, and he, grinning sheepishly, slogged upstream. They met in waist-deep water, their lips blue, water running from the helmets and down their necks. Without thinking, Chandra flung her arms around him, wanting to feel his heartbeat, the strength of his body.

His arms, as sturdy as steel, surrounded her, drawing her close, and for a second in the frigid water, they forgot all propriety. She wanted to laugh and cry, scream in frustration and kiss him, all at the same time. Relief poured through her. Her senses, already charged by the fear that had stolen into her heart, filled with him. He smelled of the river, but his touch was warm and electric. He smoothed a strand of hair from her cheek, as if he, too, were savoring this moment when they were both alive. Her heart wrenched and her throat clogged. She pounded a fist against his chest. "You scared me half to death," she said, drawing her head back to stare up at him.

"It was my fault."

"Yours?" Shaking her head, she wouldn't let him take the blame. "No way. I was in charge. I shouldn't have let her capsize."

"But I steered the raft into the snag—"

"The current did that. It was my job to avoid the situation." Suddenly weak, she sighed and, ripping off her helmet, tossed the hair from her eyes, spraying his chest with icy pellets of water. "I'm just glad you're in one piece." His arms tightened a little, and when she glanced up at him again, her breath caught in her throat. His gaze, blue and intense, drilled deeply into hers. He, too, removed his helmet and cast it beside hers on the rocks of the shore.

"I'm glad you're in one piece, too," he said, his breath warm against her chilled skin. He lowered his head and kissed her, his cold lips molding to hers, his hands drawing her so close, she could scarcely breathe.

His tongue pressed lightly against her teeth and she responded, her heart soaring that they'd both survived the accident. Her mind, usually calm and rational, was now fuzzy with emotions she didn't want to dissect. She lost herself in his touch and the smell of his clean, wet skin. Clinging to him, her breasts flattened against the hard wall of his chest, she thought of nothing save his touch and the tingling of her skin whenever their bodies pressed close against each other.

He slid his hands across her back, and through her wet shirt she felt the warmth of him. He scaled her ribs with gentle fingers and slowly eased a palm over her breast.

She gasped, and he kissed her harder, his tongue plunging deep as his fingers moved insistently beneath the top of her swim suit, to her nipple, stroking the already hard peak until her entire breast ached.

The cold seeped away. The water rushing past their knees and slapping their thighs didn't exist. Chandra was only aware of Dallas, his kiss and the expert touch of his hands on her flesh.

She shivered deep inside as desire crept through her blood. Moaning, she wound her arms around his neck, her own tongue searching and tasting, delving and flicking.

He groaned in response and slid downward, moving his hands slowly to her buttocks, kissing the column of her throat.

Chandra sucked in her breath and he pressed his warm face against her abdomen before he pulled down her vest and suit and then rimmed her nipple with his tongue.

"Oooh," she whispered over the rush of wild water. Her fingers twisted in his hair as he suckled. Between the cold air and the warmth of his body, Chandra was suspended in tingling emotions that wouldn't lie still. She knew she should stop this madness, but couldn't. His body, hard and anxious, demanded exactly what hers wanted so desperately.

When he drew his mouth from hers, he gazed up at her and shook his head. "What're we going to do about this?" he wondered aloud, obviously as perplexed with the situation as she was.

"I don't know."

He slowly covered her breasts and stood, his arms still surrounding her. "Overused phrases like 'take it slow' or 'one step at a time' seem the appropriate thing to say, but I'm not sure slow is possible with you. And I'm sure it isn't with me." He sighed loudly in frustration. "You turn me inside out, Ms. Hill," he admitted, "and I don't think this is the time in my life for that kind of imbalance."

"Imbalance?" she repeated, shivering. "I'm causing you an imbalance?" Shaking her head, she turned back to the raft. "Well, we certainly wouldn't want to mess around with your well-ordered life, Dr. O'Rourke," she said, her anger rising. "It's not like I planned this, either, you know. It just happened!"

She was suddenly angry, and wondered if her fury was aimed mostly at herself. "Let's just forget this happened and get on with the trip."

"I don't know if I can."

She'd been reaching for the rope when his voice arrested her. Turning, she found him still standing in the river, his features thoughtful, almost disbelieving, as if something were happening to him that he couldn't control.

She cleared her throat. "We only have about a mile of river left, then we can pack up. You can go your way and I can go mine. And trust me, I won't try to imbalance your life again. Just make sure your brother doesn't buy you another expedition, okay?"

She grabbed his helmet off the beach and tossed it to him, then strapped hers on. "Let's get this over with."

"You're the boss."

"Right. So get in and we'll shove off!"

They both climbed into the raft, and Chandra, determined to be professional, guided them downstream. They didn't say another word, though a few blistering phrases leapt to Chandra's mind. She'd love to tell Dr. O'Rourke what she really thought of his attitude.

She didn't like being played with, and yet, every time he kissed her, she hadn't stopped him—hadn't been able to. Her traitorous body seemed to tingle with anticipation at his touch, and that thought alone disgusted her.

He was just a man! How many times did she have to remind herself of that one simple fact? She hazarded a glance in his direction and took comfort in the fact that he seemed as irritated and out of sorts as she was. And she consoled herself that he wasn't immune to her.

The raft glided around the final bend in the river. Chandra, feeling a mixture of relief and sadness, spied her truck parked beneath the tree. Soon, this wretched, lovely trip would be over.

Dallas saw the play of emotions on Chandra's face. She barked orders at him as he helped her drag the raft out of the water and lash it across the top of her rig. Silently, still wondering what the hell he was going to do with her, he admired how quickly and efficiently she worked, her arms tanned and strong, her fingers sure as she tied square knots and half hitches, and stored the gear in the back of her Suburban.

She moved with the natural grace and assuredness of an athlete, and yet her femininity was impossible to ignore. Her legs were supple and tanned, her buttocks round and firm, and her breasts, hidden beneath several layers, were soft, fleshy mounds that fit so perfectly in his palms.

But more intriguingly feminine than her obvious physical attributes was the sparkle of green in her gray eyes, the lift of her lips when she smiled, the arrogant toss of her hair over her shoulders. Chandra Hill was used to dealing out authority, probably from her year or two in medical school. He wondered how she could have ever given up medicine. Maybe she hadn't been able to afford the schooling. She claimed that she'd found out once she'd enrolled that she wasn't cut out to be a doctor, but he doubted that story. Chandra Hill seemed to be a woman who set goals for herself and then went about attaining them, no matter what the odds.

Somehow, guiding the idle rich down a dangerous stretch of water paled when compared with the ecstasy of saving a life. There were downsides to being a doctor, and tragedies that were impossible to ignore, but he'd learned to live with those, and he couldn't imagine giving up his livelihood as a physician. He'd rather cut off his right arm.

"That's it," she said, opening the driver's side of her truck. Dallas slid into the sunbaked interior and rolled down his window. He propped his elbow on the window frame as she started the truck and headed up the mountain road in a plume of dust. Reaching into the compartment between the two bucket seats, Chandra found a pair of sunglasses—ostensibly to replace those she lost during the rafting excursion—and set the shaded lenses across her nose. "Well, what d'ya think? Ready to go out again?"

"Maybe," he said, and she cast him a quick glance.

"Even after that spill?"

"Does it happen often?"

"This is only the second time," she said, a frown puckering her brow as she braked and the Suburban hugged a sharp turn in the road and slid to a stop. "Shh—look." She pointed to the undergrowth where a doe stared at them with huge, liquid eyes. A fawn pranced behind its mother until it saw the truck and froze, unmoving, blending into the background of dry grass, brush and trees.

"You love your job, don't you?" he asked.

Lifting a shoulder, Chandra shoved the rig into first and appeared to concentrate once again on the road that wound through the forest.

"And you're never going back to finish studying medicine," he predicted.

She flashed him a dark look. "I don't think so," she said, unhinged by his sudden display of compassion. "I-um—the trip's over. I really have to get back," she said, though a part of her wanted this trip to last forever.

"Someone waiting for you?"

She smiled slightly. "Oh, yes," she admitted, thinking of Sam. The old dog would be looking for his dinner. She'd fed him early yesterday morning, leaving enough food for two days along with several gallons of water, but by this time, he'd be starved. And lonely.

"There is?"

"Mmm. And he's very jealous."

Dallas cocked a thick eyebrow, his expression neutral, though his eyes had darkened a shade.

"His name is Sam and he lives with me," she clarified, smiling inwardly when she caught a gleam of jealousy in Dallas's eyes. Did he really think she would let him kiss her when she was seeing someone else? "He wanted to come along, but I told him that he'd just be in the way."

"Is that so? And how'd he like that?"

"Not at all. In fact he growled at me all night long."

The doctor's eyes narrowed, and all of his friendliness, so visible earlier, disappeared from his features. "You're *involved* with someone? And he lives with you?"

"Has since I moved in," she teased, waiting as Dallas opened the door. "He's become very possessive. In fact, he's been known to bite intruders."

A slow smile spread across Dallas's chin and Chandra couldn't help but chuckle. "Tell your 'friend' that I'm not afraid of him," he said with a laugh as he slammed the door shut.

"He'll be disappointed."

"I'll bring him a steak bone. Will that solve the problem?"

"He'll be forever in your debt," she said, ramming the Suburban into reverse and roaring off, her laughter hanging on the air as Dallas fished his keys from his pockets.

What was wrong with him? He'd almost acted as if he were planning to see her again. And he wasn't. If he'd learned anything from this fiasco of a trip, it was that he had to keep his distance from Chandra Hill. The woman was just too damned attractive for her own good. Or his.

But the thought of not seeing her again bothered him, and he took heart with the realization that, as long as Baby Doe—or J.D., as she insisted upon calling him—was a patient at Riverbend Hospital, Chandra Hill would be underfoot. She could very well pretend interest in Dallas just to get close to the baby. In fact, her interest in the infant explained why a strong-willed woman like Chandra could so easily be seduced.

He believed her when she said she didn't get involved with her clients—so why him? A physical attraction she couldn't deny? He scoffed at the idea, though his passion for her was something he could barely control. But, no, he suspected that Chandra was just using him to get close to the baby. Still, he couldn't just forget her. She was an impossible woman to forget.

He opened the door of his truck and sighed. Damned if you do and damned if you don't, he decided, pushing the key into his ignition. He didn't want to see Chandra again— well, at least he told himself that he didn't—and yet, he couldn't imagine not ever looking into her eyes again or catching the glimpse of her smile.

He hadn't felt this way since Jennifer. That realization was more shocking than a plunge in the icy depths of the Rattlesnake. He'd fallen hard once before, and, after more emotional pain than he'd ever thought existed, he'd proclaimed that he'd never fall again.

Since the divorce, he'd clung to his vow as if to life itself. He'd made sure that he had no time for a woman in his life, no time for anything but his work. And he'd been happy, or so he'd told himself.

Chapter Eight

Chandra, one hand pressed against the glass, stared at the baby. He was awake, his eyes bright, his face relaxed as he lay in the bassinet in the nursery with the other infants. There was a group of six small bodies wrapped in warm blankets, sleeping or blinking or yawning. Nurse Nelson was changing a squalling, tiny red baby without a trace of hair.

"Hi," she said from the other side of the glass that separated the nursery from the hallway where Chandra stood. "Would you like to hold him?" Leslie finished with the diaper, then motioned to J.D.

"Are you serious?" Chandra asked in a voice loud enough to be heard through the glass.

"Why not?" Opening the door a crack, Leslie flashed her dimples and tucked a blanket around the baby she'd been changing. "All these other guys—" she gestured to the bassinets with their squirming bundles "—get more than their share of attention. Of course, they're lucky. They have mothers." She disposed of the dirty diaper, then walked to

J.D.'s bassinet and wrapped his blanket tightly around him. "Come on, you," she said as she carried him through the double doors and placed him in Chandra's waiting arms.

Chandra's heart felt as if it might break. The baby cooed and shifted, nuzzling her chest. Emotions tore at her soul. Tears gathered behind her eyes, and her throat closed as she gazed down at this precious child with the perfectly arched eyebrows, pudgy round cheeks and loud voice. Any lingering doubts she had concerning this baby were quickly washed away. She had to adopt him. She had to! She had no other choice. She thought of all her reservations, but she couldn't help herself. Who cared if the baby's natural mother showed up? This child needed her. And she needed him. Desperately. To make her life complete. Or would it be? Even with J.D., her life might still be missing something vital, the third part of a perfect family—the husband and father.

She rocked gently back and forth, ignoring her disturbing thoughts, whispering to the infant, touching his downy hair, unaware that Dallas was watching her as Leslie Nelson returned to the nursery. On rounds, Dallas had worked his way through the second floor and ended up at the nurses' station, where he'd stopped when he'd spied Chandra cradling the infant.

A smile toyed with the corner of her lips, and her eyes were downcast, focused on the bundle in her arms. Dark lashes, looking slightly damp, swept her cheek as she, dressed in denim skirt, white sweater and suede vest, held the baby. She was talking to the infant, maybe singing to him. Dallas could only hear a word or two, but the scene resurrected an old dream of his—the dream of one day being a husband and a father. Now this woman—this woman he barely knew, with her blond hair and mischievous gray-green eyes—awakened feelings in him he'd hoped he'd long since destroyed. An unfamiliar tightness bound his chest, and he couldn't for the life of him drag his eyes away from Chandra and the child.

He folded his arms across his chest and wondered if Chandra's love for this child—for she obviously already did care for the baby as if it were her own—would cause her any heartbreak.

"Hush, little baby, don't say a word,
Mama's gonna buy you a mockingbird..."

Dallas felt an unlikely tug on his heart.

"And if that mockingbird don't sing,
Mama's gonna buy you a diamond ring..."

He cleared his throat, and she jumped, her head snapping up, her eyes focusing on him. "Looks like I've got some competition," he said, sauntering slowly up to her.

She blanched, as if she felt guilty for being caught with the child. "Com—competition?"

"For your affection."

"I didn't know it was a contest," she replied, turning her gaze back to the swaddled child in her arms. "And neither does he—do you, J.D.?"

"So, you're still calling him J.D.?"

A wonderful, soft shade of pink crawled up the back of her neck and stained her cheeks. "It sounds so much more..." She blinked as if she truly were embarrassed. "So much more personal than Baby John Doe."

"You can call him whatever you like," Dallas said, wondering if she were setting herself up for an emotional fall from which she'd never recover. She was building her dreams on this child, he could see that hope shining in her eyes, and it broke his heart. The child had only been here a few days. The mother—or some other relative—could still turn up. If not, the baby would end up with Social Services, a foster home, then be adopted. "Can I buy you a cup of coffee?"

One eyebrow lifted, and he could see that she was surprised by his offer. Surprised but pleased. "Thanks, I'd like that—but I have an appointment. Maybe some other time."

"Later today?" What was wrong with him? Why couldn't he just leave her alone? She'd been on his mind, in his thoughts, ever since she'd left him at the river just yesterday. Last night had been pure hell. Her vision had followed him into bed and never left him even as he'd dozed in the final hours before dawn. He'd awoken fully aroused, hoping his dream had been real. "I know we didn't part on the best of terms."

"I thought that's the way you wanted it."

He wished it were that simple. "To be honest, when it comes to you, I don't really know what I want," he admitted, baring his soul for the first time in years.

"That's what I like," she said sarcastically, "a man who knows his own mind."

He reached for her arm, wanting to shake some sense into her. Couldn't she see that this was hard for him? But he didn't touch her as she was holding the infant—the only person, it appeared, she truly cared for. "I'm trying to be big about this," he insisted, knowing emotion registered in his eyes. "It's not easy for me. All I'm asking is for a little of your time."

She eyed him speculatively, chewing on the corner of her mouth while she chased away what appeared to be indecision. So she was as wary of him as he was of her. "Sure. Coffee would be good," she finally said, her gaze lingering for a second too long in his. Beyond that, she didn't commit, just checked her watch, frowned and reluctantly handed the baby back to Nurse Nelson. "But not today. I've really got to run," she said as she clipped down the hall to wait for the elevator. Dallas watched her disappear through the parted doors.

He knew where she lived—she'd given her address to the dispatcher when she'd called 911—someplace on Flaming Moss Road, clear out of town.

"Dr. O'Rourke. Dr. Dallas O'Rourke." The page brought him out of his thoughts, but he decided he'd call on Chandra. To hell with the fact that he didn't need any complications. She definitely was a complication, but like it or not, she was already a part of his life. At least until the identity of the baby was discovered. After that...well, he didn't want to project that far into the future. Soon the baby would be released from the hospital and, no doubt, Ms. Hill would lose interest in him.

Dallas plucked a pen from his pocket and clicked it several times before writing instructions on a patient's chart. But as he started down the corridor toward the maternity wing, he passed the elevators and smelled the clean scent of Chandra, the whisper of her perfume still clinging to the air.

What was he doing thinking about her? he wondered angrily. He couldn't start fantasizing about her while he was working. He had a job to do, a job that required complete concentration. A job that was his whole life!

He stopped by a phone to pick up his page, and while the operator connected him to Dr. Spangler, Dallas rubbed his chin. He couldn't afford to get involved with a woman; he knew the price he'd have to pay. Closing his eyes briefly, he muttered irritably, "Come on, come on," hoping the operator would put him through to Spangler and get his mind off Chandra.

But her image wouldn't leave him alone. As he waited, his damned thoughts drifted to her again. He decided he was handling the situation all wrong. As long as she was distant, she would always be the forbidden fruit and her allure would never diminish. Before he got caught up in something he couldn't control, he needed to know more about her. He'd trusted a woman at face value once, and she'd proved far from the woman he'd thought he'd married. As for Chandra, what would it hurt to check out her story before he or the hospital was duped? She seemed sincere, and yet her tale about finding a baby and not knowing the mother was hard to believe.

He had a friend in Denver, a guy he'd gone to school with, a private detective who made a decent living out of poking into other people's lives. Guilt stiffened the back of his neck; he knew that Chandra was a private person and she'd be furious if she had any idea he was checking her out. But if he were going to see her again, it only made sense—

"Dallas?" Spangler's voice broke him out of his thoughts. "Would you mind looking in on a patient in 107? Eleanor Mills. Fractured tibia…" Dallas's mind jerked back to the present, but he knew he wasn't finished with Chandra Hill.

Roy Arnette stared at Chandra as if she were certifiably insane. "You want to adopt the kid you found in the barn?" he repeated, eyeing her over the tops of his wire-rimmed glasses. Roy had been her attorney ever since she'd landed in Ranger, and he was as straitlaced as a Victorian corset and just as inflexible. At sixty-three, he sported a thick shock of white hair, dark eyebrows and a quick smile. He was tall, six-two or three, and dressed the part of a Texan, with his gleaming lizard-skin cowboy boots and string tie. Even his office had a Southwestern motif, which fit right into the town's Western look. Cacti sat in clay pots in the corner, pictures of coyotes and adobe Indian villages graced the walls, and a Native American rug in hues of rust, blue and gray was spread over a bleached plank floor.

"That's right," Chandra said. "I want you to draw up the necessary papers and file whatever petitions are necessary. I want that child for my own."

Roy shook his head. "Whoa, darlin', aren't you gettin' the cart before the horse? You don't even know that baby won't be claimed. Hell, it's only been a few days."

"And any mother worth her salt would never have left J.D. in the first place."

"J.D.? You've already got a name for him?"

"Yes," she said firmly. She was on her feet, pacing in front of Roy's red-oak desk, a bundle of restless energy.

"As your lawyer, I'd advise you to take this slow," he drawled, licking his lips and staring up at her with worried eyes.

"I don't want to take it slow. In fact, the sooner we can get the child, the better."

"It's not that easy. You're not dealing with a private adoption, you know. The state's gonna have to get involved. Social Services. And there may be other people—the child's kin or just some couples anxious for a child of their own—who might want him."

"Who? If the boy had any family, surely they would've come forward."

"If they knew about him. And even if not..." He reached behind him to a stack of newspapers, unfolded one and searched until he'd found the section he wanted. With a rustle of paper, he snapped the page open, pressed the newsprint onto his desk and pointed a long finger at the personals column. "Take a look-see."

Chandra swept her gaze over the advertisements:

ADOPT—Loving couple awaits your newborn. Expenses paid. Contact our attorney...

ADOPTION—Dear Birthmother: Professional couple willing to give your newborn love and affection. Expenses paid. Secure future for your child with all the opportunities you'd hoped for. Contact the law firm of...

LOVING ARMS WAITING TO ADOPT...

CHICAGO COUPLE WILLING TO ADOPT YOUR NEWBORN...

WANTED TO LOVE: YOUR NEWBORN...

There were more. Lots more. The requests for babies filled two columns. Chandra felt her knees go weak. She sank into one of Roy's overstuffed leather chairs positioned near the desk and let the breath out of her lungs at the thought of the uphill battle that was before her.

"This is just one paper, from Denver. Ads like this appear in newspapers all over the country. Sterile couples want babies. I have three clients myself who are interested in private adoption. But you know this—it isn't new to you. You worked with kids, and in a hospital."

Of course she knew the facts, but she'd been hiding from them, unwilling to accept the reality that someone else might want her baby. And that was how she'd come to think of J.D.: as hers.

"There's something else you might consider," Roy said, refolding the paper and speaking to her in a kindly voice that reminded her of her own father. "When the judge grants someone custody of the child, he'll probably award that custody to a married couple."

"But—"

Roy held up a flat hand. "I know, I know, single person's rights and all that baloney. But you can argue till you're blue in the face, I'm just tellin' you the facts. A married couple—a *stable* married couple—with a house and a few dollars in the bank to provide security for the baby will have the best shot at adopting B.J."

"J.D.," she corrected automatically. "I think I'd do a damned good job as a mother."

"And a father?"

"Yes, and a father!" she argued. "Look at my job, for crying out loud!"

"Being a father takes more than a job," Roy said calmly, reminding her without words that he and his wife had raised five children. "It's a way of thinking—the male perspective. And there's the most obvious reason for placing a child with a couple."

"Which is?" she asked, knowing and dreading the answer.

"That if one of the parents dies, the kid's got a backup. He won't be orphaned again."

Chandra's shoulders slumped. She couldn't argue against that simple logic, and yet, she told herself, if she gave up now, didn't even fight for custody, she'd always look over her shoulder and wonder if she'd made a mistake. "I don't care what the odds are, Roy," she said, slowly lifting her gaze to meet the questions in his. "I want you to do everything in your power to see that I adopt J.D."

"And you—are you willin' to do the same?"

"Do you even have to ask?"

"Then, if I might make a suggestion," he said, his lips twitching a little, "you might want to find yourself a husband. It'll increase our odds of winnin'."

"Got anyone in mind?" She threw the words back at him, in no mood for jokes.

"That's your department. I'll do my bit—you do yours."

"I won't get married," she said, shoving herself upright.

"No hot prospects?"

Unbidden, a picture of Dallas O'Rourke formed in her mind, a picture she quickly shoved aside. "No," Chandra replied with a wry smile, "no prospects whatsoever."

"Then you'd better start prayin'," Roy advised, "'cause without a little help from the man upstairs, I don't think you've got a ghost of a chance."

"Try, Roy, okay? Just try."

"I'll do my best. You know," he said with an ingratiating grin, "I always aim to please."

Chandra left the attorney's office with her spirits dragging on the concrete sidewalk that flanked the building. She spent the next few hours at the office of Wild West Expeditions planning a day trip for the following weekend. When Rick asked her about her trip with Dr. O'Rourke, she didn't go into much detail, deciding the less said on the subject of Dallas, the better.

For the next few days, Chandra went about her life. She stopped by the hospital on the way to work, then again before she went home. Even the days on which she led a trail ride or guided a rafting excursion, she found time to spend a couple of minutes staring at the baby.

Every day she expected him to be released, but the doctors at the hospital were taking no chances. J.D. had come into the hospital dehydrated and undernourished, as well as jaundiced, and the swelling in his little head was still apparent, though only slightly.

Soon, however, he'd have to leave.

Dallas wanted no part of the baby. Or so he told himself. Getting involved with the infant was as dangerous as falling for Chandra Hill. Yet, even he was intrigued by the infant with the dark eyes, lusty voice and shock of black hair.

No wonder Chandra wanted to adopt him. Had circumstances been different, Dallas would have been interested in the boy himself. But, of course, he had no room for a child in his life—a child or a woman. And this baby, whoever he was, had parents out there somewhere. Sooner or later, they'd show up, either together or alone, but someday a woman would claim to be J.D.'s mother.

"And then what are we going to do?" he asked the baby as he rubbed a large hand over his tiny ribs. The infant stared up at him with those eyes that reached right into Dallas's soul. The doctor knew what it was like to be unwanted and unloved, and he pitied this poor child.

It would be a blessing if Chandra were allowed to adopt him, Dallas thought; at least, then J.D. would know a mother's love. He wrapped the baby back in his blanket, and rather than kiss the downy head, Dallas patted the little bottom. "You're gonna be okay," Dallas assured him, though he wished he could predict the baby's future. As well as his own. He hadn't seen Chandra all day, and he'd made excuses to show up in pediatrics hoping for a glimpse of her.

Deciding he was hopeless, he headed back to the emergency room.

Chandra did everything possible to assure herself the best chances of adopting J.D. She filled out all the appropriate papers and even began interviewing baby-sitters. She wanted all her ducks in line before she talked to Social Services.

In the meantime, Roy Arnette assured her he was doing everything possible to petition the court for guardianship. Aside from having Chandra fill out forms and sign statements, he'd begun collecting personal references from her friends and acquaintances, even checked on her parents in Idaho, since she knew few people in Ranger. In fact, she was beginning to feel that the hospital staff, particularly the nurses on the pediatric floor, were fast becoming the best friends she had in town.

Even Dr. O'Rourke was more than an acquaintance. She'd seen him several times at the hospital, and for the most part he'd been friendly, though professional. Never once had the rafting trip been mentioned between them. And, if O'Rourke remembered the passion that had burned so brightly for a few magical hours, he didn't show it. Once she'd thought he'd been staring at her, but that flicker of interest she'd seen, or hoped to see, in his eyes was quickly replaced by the cool exterior that had earned him the name Dr. Ice.

"No woman has ever gotten through to him," Shannon Pratt had divulged once when she and Chandra were sharing a cup of coffee in the cafeteria. "I remember when he came here, several of the single nurses zeroed in on him." She'd smiled at the memory. "Every one of them struck out. And these gals were big leaguers. He wasn't the least bit interested."

Chandra had stared at the bottom of her cup, wishing she could confide in Shannon, but unable to bring up the rafting trip. What had occurred between Dallas and her had been special. "Surely the man must have dated someone."

"Not that I know of. Rumor has it that he was burned badly by his ex-wife." Shannon had finished her coffee. "Believe me, if there were a way to that man's heart, no one's found it yet. And the best have tried."

Now, two days after Shannon's revelation about Dallas, Chandra stopped by the hospital again. Gathering all her courage, she dropped by Dallas's office, hoping to see him, but his receptionist told her that he wasn't available.

In the pediatrics wing, Leslie Nelson was off duty, but Shannon was stationed at the second-floor desk. She let Chandra hold J.D., and once again Chandra's heart wrapped possessively around this little boy. "It's going to be all right," she whispered into his cap of dark hair. "We're going to work this out."

Eventually, she gave the baby back to Shannon, who suggested Chandra drop by at feeding time so that she could give J.D. his bottle. Chandra asked a few questions, but was told that, as far as Shannon or any of the nursing staff of the hospital knew, no one had yet found the mother.

From the hospital, Chandra called the Sheriff's Department and was eventually connected with Deputy White, who informed her that there was nothing new on the case. No one, it seemed, was missing an infant. All the hospitals in a three-hundred-mile radius had been contacted, and no babies had been stolen from the nurseries. It was as if J.D.'s mother didn't exist.

"Nobody just leaves a baby in a barn," Chandra told herself as she walked through the breezeway connecting the parking lot to the hospital. Of their own accord, her eyes swept the staff lot, but Dr. O'Rourke's truck wasn't tucked into any of the parking spots reserved for hospital physicians, and she chided herself for looking.

* * *

"Oh, for crying out loud!" Chandra felt like cursing when, two hours later, she drove down the lane to her house. A tan station wagon was parked near the back porch, and the driver, sitting and smoking, was Bob Fillmore from the *Banner*. Blast it all, she should've known he wouldn't give up. One little article wasn't enough.

Sam, teeth bared, black lips snarling fiendishly, paced by the vehicle. The hairs on the back of his neck stood on end, and every time Fillmore moved, Sam lunged at the car, barking ferociously.

Just what I need, Chandra thought, bracing herself, though the retriever's antics amused her. Sam yipped excitedly as she parked her rig near the back porch.

Knowing that she couldn't duck the reporters forever, she decided to tell everything she knew to Fillmore, hopefully ending any interest the press could have in her.

"Slow day for news?" she asked, hopping out of the truck and forcing a smile she didn't feel. "Sam, down!" She snapped her fingers and pointed to the ground at her feet. Sam reluctantly trotted over and lay by her side, his steady gaze never leaving the car.

"That animal should be locked up!" Fillmore tossed his cigarette butt onto the gravel as he crawled out of his car, but his eyes never left the retriever. "I thought he was going to tear me limb from limb."

"That's the general idea," Chandra said.

Suddenly, the reporter was all business. "Back to your question—about the news? Seems that most of the news is right in your backyard these days. I didn't get much of an interview at the hospital. And the Sheriff's Department hasn't been overly helpful. I thought you could fill in a few of the holes in my story." As if he read denial forming on her lips, he continued, "Look, you're the only one who knows exactly what happened, and I just want to get this story right. The kid's parents may be looking for him right now. He could've been stolen, right? You might be doing them and the baby a big favor...." He let his sentence trail off, implying that there might be a big reward for finding the child. As if money were the answer.

Her stomach lurched and a bad taste filled her mouth. The dislike she'd felt for Bob Fillmore grew more intense. "I just want to do right by the child," Chandra said in the same confidential tone he'd used with her, "and I don't want to interfere with the investigation by the Sheriff's Department." She said nothing about wanting to become the baby's mother. Right now, a statement to that effect would have the same result as spraying gasoline on a slow-burning fire. Fillmore's interest in the story—and in Chandra herself—would definitely heat up. Time enough for that later.

He smiled easily. "No chance of messing anything up with the police. I just have a few questions. Simple ones. Really. Questions that might help the baby find his mom."

Chandra bit back a hot reply about the woman who had forsaken her son. And as for Fillmore, she didn't trust the reporter for a minute. In Tennessee, her life had been ripped open, the focus of several "in-depth" interviews after Gordy Shore had died and his parents had filed suit against her. All of those reporters had seemed a cut above Fillmore, and they'd made her life a living hell. There was no telling what the reporter from the *Banner* might do.

Yet she couldn't very well hide the truth, could she? She couldn't refuse to talk to the man. She'd only make him think she had something to hide. Frowning, she unlocked the back doors of the Suburban and pulled out two sacks of groceries. Sam followed obediently at her heels and only growled when Fillmore, trying to help, grabbed the handle of a gallon of milk. "I could carry those bags."

"Already got 'em." Balancing the groceries, she unlocked the back door, and Sam streaked inside. The retriever settled on the rug under the table and, with one final growl of disapproval, watched Fillmore enter the cabin.

Chandra stuffed a carton of eggs into the refrigerator. "You know, I thought people usually called ahead for an interview."

"I did. This morning. No answer. I left a message. When you didn't call back, I figured the time and place was okay with you."

"And what if I hadn't shown up?" she asked, waving him into a chair. Casting a glance at her answering machine, she noticed the red light flashing. She had no option but to get this over with.

"I would've waited. Speaking of which—" he checked his watch and scowled "—the photographer should be here by now. He knew about this shoot. Would you mind if I used your phone?" He was already picking up the receiver when Chandra nodded. The man was pushy, no doubt about it. He dialed quickly, then tapped a toe while he waited. "Yeah. It's Fillmore," he said into the mouthpiece. "I'm lookin' for Levine. Should've been here by now. I'm at the Hill place on Flaming Moss Road...yeah, eighteen, twenty miles out...well, tell him to get his butt in gear, okay? We're waiting."

Chandra, only half listening to the reporter, pulled out a couple of sodas from the refrigerator. Her throat was already parched, and at the thought of an interview, her mouth turned as dry as a desert wind. She held one can up silently and Fillmore, still growling orders into the phone, grinned and waved an affirmative. While he was finishing his call, she cracked ice into a couple of tall glasses, not really in the mood to sit down and sip Pepsi with the man from the *Banner.* Her only consolation was that she figured it wouldn't hurt to have the reporter on her side, pretend to go along with him and then, at the first available instant, make some excuse to end the interview early. He'd have a deadline, so he wouldn't be back, and that, thankfully, would be the end of the press camping out on her doorstep. She hoped. If not and he got wind of the fact that she was planning to adopt J.D., so be it. At least he wouldn't be out to smear her. She felt better about offering him the cola.

"Look," she said, once he'd hung up and settled into a chair at the table. She placed one of the dewy glasses in front of him and resisted the urge to press the other to her forehead to ward off a headache. "I just don't want this to get out of hand. No media circus on this, okay?"

"I'm just here to tell a story." After draining half his glass, Fillmore reached into his jacket pocket and pulled out his tape recorder, pen and notepad. "Okay, let's start at the beginning. How did you find the baby?"

Chandra had gone over the same tale so many times that she said the words without much emotion, explaining about discovering the child, calling 911 and driving to meet the ambulance. No, she didn't know to whom the baby belonged. No, she couldn't imagine who would leave a baby alone. Yes, the baby had needed medical attention, but he had seemed strong enough.

They were both about finished with their drinks when Fillmore brought up the baby's future. "What if the mother shows up?"

"Then I guess the court decides if she's a fit parent," Chandra replied, studying the melting ice in her glass. She hoped her face was impassive.

"And where do you fit into it?"

Yes, where? "I don't know," she answered truthfully, just as Sam's ears pricked forward and the dog scrambled to the door with a bark. Chandra glanced out the window and her heart dropped. Dallas's truck slowed to a stop by Fillmore's car. *Great,* she thought, knowing instinctively that Fillmore wouldn't budge if he recognized the doctor who had admitted J.D. into the hospital.

"Well, well, well, the good Dr. O'Rourke," Fillmore drawled, a satisfied smile slithering across his lips. "What's he doing here?"

"I wouldn't know," Chandra said, rising to answer the door. Dallas had, indeed, arrived—all six feet of him greeted her as she swept the door open and invited him in. "Hi," she said, motioning toward Fillmore. "Join the crowd."

Dallas grew rigid and as he walked into the kitchen, the temperature seemed to drop ten degrees. Both men stared at each other for a few agonizing seconds. "Fillmore," Dallas finally said, not bothering to hide his distaste for the man. "What're you doing here?"

"Just checkin' out a story. What about you?" The reporter clicked his pen loudly, and the tape in his machine continued to whir.

"I took an excursion with Ms. Hill over the weekend. She left something in my truck."

"Excursion? You mean a rafting trip?" Fillmore glanced from Dallas to Chandra and back again.

Dallas shrugged. "My brother thought I could use a little R and R." He reached into the pocket of his jeans and pulled out her bandanna, the one she'd used to tie back her hair, clean and pressed.

"So how was the trip? Exciting?"

Dallas turned chilling eyes on the reporter. "Very. Ms. Hill is an excellent guide. In fact, have you ever been on one of those trips down the Rattlesnake at—what was it called?" He looked to Chandra for help, but she had the feeling he knew exactly what he was saying. "Grizzly Loop? I think it's just your speed, Fillmore."

Bob Fillmore smirked, as if he refused to be goaded by Dallas.

"And if Chandra can't help you, maybe the owner can. What's his name—Rick Benson—you remember, the guy you did the piece on a few years back."

The muscles in Chandra's neck tensed. This was no time to intimidate the reporter, for God's sake! What was Dallas doing?

"I'll keep it in mind," Fillmore replied as he scraped his chair back and stood. Chandra hoped fervently that he was finished. "Tell me, Doctor, since I'm writing about the abandoned child, what's his status with the hospital?"

Dallas looked in Chandra's direction. "He's about to be released."

No! So that's why Dallas was here, to break the news and prepare her. Chandra's heart leapt to her throat. "Released to whom?" she asked, trying to keep a calm appearance.

Dallas slanted a glance at the reporter, as if he realized he'd said too much.

"That's right," Fillmore added, "who'll get the kid?"

"I think that's up to Social Services."

Fillmore grinned. "This is getting better by the minute. When, exactly, will he be released?"

"Dr. Williams and Dr. Spangler will decide."

"They the kid's pediatricians?"

"That's right," Dallas said as Sam barked loudly.

A compact Ford, silver-blue in color, roared down the drive, leaving a plume of dust in its wake.

What was this? Chandra wondered. More bad news?

"About time," Fillmore muttered, scooping up his notepad and tape recorder as he scraped his chair back. "It's Sid. He'll want a few pictures of the barn, you know, where the kid was found. And he might have a few questions. Then we'll be outta your hair."

Chandra could hardly wait. They walked outside, and Sid Levine, gathering camera bag, umbrella, light meter and other equipment, unloaded his car. "Hi, fella," he said to Sam as the retriever bared his teeth and galloped toward the newcomer. Sid reached down and scratched Sam behind the ears. "Hey, slow down, I'm not gonna hurt anything."

Growling, Sam sniffed at the proffered hand then, traitor that he was, began wagging his tail so hard that it thumped against the fender of the Ford.

"We were on our way to the barn to get some pictures of the inside," Fillmore said, waving the photographer along as he crossed the yard.

"I'll be there in a minute. Just let me take a few shots out here," Levine said, apparently used to Fillmore's brusque manner.

Inside the barn, Chandra, as she had with the sheriff's deputies, pointed out the stall where she'd found the baby. One of her favorite geldings, Max, a curious buckskin, strolled inside and stood waiting for some oats to be tossed his way. The other horses poked their noses into the barn door and their shadows drifted inside, but they didn't follow the buckskin's lead. Even Cayenne, usually friendly, eyed the intruders, snorted disdainfully and refused to amble inside.

Max draped his head over the top of the stall and eyed Fillmore, who was busy in the end box where the baby was found, then nuzzled Chandra's jacket, looking for a piece of carrot or apple. "Sorry, buddy," she whispered to the horse, who snorted and stamped a foot impatiently.

Dallas had followed her into the barn. He leaned against the ladder to the hayloft while Fillmore asked still more questions and the photographer scurried inside, sending up dust motes and disturbing the cobwebs that draped from the windows. Chandra could feel Dallas's gaze on her back as she petted Max's velvety nose and answered the questions as best she could. Fillmore tried to ignore the doctor, but Chandra couldn't. His presence seemed to charge the air in the musty old barn, and she sensed that some of the reporter's questions were worded more carefully just because Dallas was within earshot.

"This it?" Sid Levine asked, looking around the barn, searching, it appeared, for sources of light. A grimy circular window over the hayloft and a few rectangles of glass at eye level over the stalls gave little natural illumination to the interior.

"In here," Fillmore replied from the stall.

Once again, Chandra pointed out the position of the child. Then, while the reporter asked a few more questions, the photographer took aim and began clicking off shots. Dallas said nothing, just watched the men going through the motions of creating news.

It's almost over, Chandra thought, *it has to be.*

"So...you been a resident of Ranger long?" Fillmore asked.

"A few years," she replied.

"And before that?"

Chandra felt the sweat break out between her shoulder blades. She didn't want her past splayed all over the front page of the *Ranger Banner*. She'd buried her life in Tennessee and hoped that it would stay that way.

"I'm originally from Idaho, up near McCall," she said easily.

"Ahh," Levine said, nodding to himself. "So that's where you get the interest in rafting and trail riding."

"Grew up doing it," she replied. "My father was a real outdoorsman." From the corner of her eye she saw Dallas straighten a little, but Fillmore, evidently satisfied, snapped off his tape recorder and checked his watch. "Thanks for your time. I've gotta shove off if I'm gonna put this story to bed tonight."

The muscles in Chandra's back relaxed a little. If they would just leave, she could find out about J.D. It seemed forever before Fillmore's car was moving down the drive and the afternoon sun was warming her back as she and Dallas watched the reporter take his leave.

Levine was still finishing up in the barn, but Chandra couldn't wait. "What's going to happen to the baby?" she asked, laying a hand on Dallas's arm. She attempted to keep the desperation from her voice, but found it impossible. "What will Social Services do?"

"Probably place the child in a temporary home until a judge decides where he'll be placed permanently."

"Oh, God," she whispered, her throat dry. J.D needed someone who loved him, someone who would care for him. While he was in the hospital, he was being cared for, even loved a bit, by the nurses, and Chandra could see him every day. But now...

To her surprise, Dallas placed a comforting arm around her shoulders. "Don't worry. He'll be fine." Her throat clogged at his tenderness.

"How do you know that?" she demanded, her eyes beginning to burn with unshed tears. She hadn't realized until just then how much she'd thought of the baby as hers. Everyone had been warning her that he could be taken away, but she hadn't listened.

"He'll be placed with someone who'll care for him." Dallas smiled down at her and squeezed her a little. "And I'll make sure that whoever gets him will allow you to see him."

She couldn't believe it. "You can do that?" she asked skeptically.

"I can try." A sliver of uneasiness clouded his features. "But don't get too involved. You don't know what will happen."

"I know, I know," she said, her throat clogging as Dallas offered her the comfort of his arms. She laid her head against his shoulder, drinking in the smell of him, glad for the strong arms that surrounded her. How right it felt to be sheltered by him. For years she'd stood on her own, relied on no one, and now all she could think about was leaning on Dallas. "The mother might show up. Damn that woman, anyway!"

She heard a camera click behind her and jumped. Dallas whirled, his eyes blazing, as Sid Levine lowered his .35 millimeter and snapped the camera back into his case. "All finished," he said, and his eyes held a spark of nastiness that Chandra hadn't seen before.

"I hope I don't see my picture on the front page," Dallas said, and the treachery on the photographer's face was replaced by a glimmer of fear as he slid into his Ford and took off.

"Bastards. Every last one of them," Dallas growled, his eyes narrowing on the silver car as it roared down the lane.

"Just tell me about the baby." Chandra couldn't worry about the reporter or his sidekick. All that mattered was J.D.—her J.D.

Dallas shoved his hands into his pockets of his jeans. "That's why I stopped by," he said, and Chandra felt a jab of disappointment. There was a little part of her that wanted him to have come to visit her on his own. "I talked to Williams, and it's just a matter of days—possibly tomorrow or the day after—whenever Social Services decides to get their act together."

"Oh, God," she whispered, knowing that soon it would all be over. But she hadn't lost. Not yet.

"Maybe it won't be so bad," Dallas said. "As I said, I'll try to arrange it so you can still visit with the baby—"

"Oh, thank you," she said, and, without thinking, she flung her arms around his neck. "Thank you." She felt his arms wrap around her, hold her snug against him for a heartbeat, and for a second she felt as breathless as she had that night by the river. Her heart thundered as his hands moved slowly up her rib cage. But he stopped, pushed her slowly away from him, and when she lifted her eyes to his, she saw his features harden.

He held her at arm's length and dug his fingers into her shoulders. "Look, Chandra, you don't have to thank me, okay? You don't have to do anything to show your appreciation."

"Meaning?"

"Meaning that just because I'm helping you with the baby doesn't mean that there's anything else between us. You're not obligated to show your appreciation."

"Well, that's a relief," she shot back. Did he really think that she would stoop so low as to manipulate him and play with his emotions? "And here I thought I'd have to do something like go to bed with you just to get you on my side."

He sucked in a quick breath at her sarcasm. His eyes flashed, and he looked as if he'd been slapped.

"That is what you were insinuating, wasn't it? Well, let me tell you something, *Doctor*, I *don't* sleep with men to get what I want. Ever."

He lifted a skeptical eyebrow and she couldn't help ramming her point home. "You know, I thought you were different, that you weren't the typical egomaniac M.D. who thinks he's God's gift to women. But it turns out that you're just like all the rest—misconstruing motives, thinking women are coming on to you. All I wanted to do was say thanks."

"Then just say it."

"I did." She shoved her hair from her eyes and planted her hands firmly on her hips. "Now, if you'll excuse me— and even if you won't—I've got work to do." In a cloud of dust and anger, she stormed to the barn, furious with herself and outraged with him.

Once inside, she climbed the loft ladder, kicked down a couple of bales of hay, then hopped to the floor. Finding her pocket knife, she slit the twine, snapped her knife closed and grabbed a pitchfork. She began tossing loose hay into the manger, throwing her back into her work, filling her nostrils with the scent of sweat, horses, dung and dried grass.

Max, snorting expectantly, wandered back to his stall, tentatively nudging his nose into the fresh hay.

A shadow from the open door fell across the floor. Chandra stiffened and turned, facing O'Rourke again. He looked as he did the first night she'd seen him, unapproachable and deadly serious. "I thought you were leaving," she said, throwing another forkful of hay into the manger.

"And I thought we should clear the air."

"About what?"

"Us."

"Us," she threw back at him. "What 'us'? I'm just *using* you, remember?" She plunged her pitchfork into the loose hay again and threw the bleached strands into the next manger. Brandy, a chestnut mare, ambled inside, her white blaze visible as she sniffed the feeding trough.

Before Chandra knew what was happening, Dallas had closed the distance between them. He grabbed her shoulders with hands made of steel. Spinning her around, he forced her to face the conflicting emotions shading his eyes. "I don't think you're purposely trying to *use* me," he said fiercely.

"What a relief," she shot back, her voice dripping sarcasm.

"But what I do think is that, whether you like it or not, you see me as a link to the baby. You're so desperate to be a part of that child's life that you'll manipulate anyone to get what you want."

"And what I see is a man who runs away from his emotions—a man afraid of being spontaneous because it might upset the careful balance in his life!" Breathing hard, she held the pitchfork with one hand. She didn't want to see the anger in his eyes or feel the warm pads of his fingers digging into her skin. Nor did she want the male smell of him to fill her senses.

She ripped herself free. "Look, don't feel *obligated* to do anything, all right? You don't owe me anything, and I can handle my life by myself. And that includes doing what I have to do to be close to the baby. You can walk away from this . . . just turn—" she pointed to the door "—and leave. That's all there is to it."

"I wish." He lifted his hands as if to touch her face, dropped them again, then swore under his breath. "Damn it all to hell, anyway," he muttered before grabbing her again and pulling her roughly against him. Startled, she dropped the pitchfork and it clattered to the dusty concrete floor.

This time his lips crashed down on hers with a possessive savagery that sent one pulsating shock wave after another down her body. He breathed in her breath, his lips moving insistently, his big hands splayed across the gentle slope of her back.

She tried to drag her mouth away, pushed with all her strength, but was unable to break the manacle of his embrace. Instead she was subjected to an elegant torment as his tongue sought entrance to her mouth and his hands moved insistently, rubbing her clothes against her skin.

She moaned softly, her head falling backward, her throat exposed. One of his hands curled in the thick strands of her hair, and he drew her head back farther still, until he could press hot, wet kisses against the curve of her shoulder.

"No . . . please . . . stop . . ." she whispered, hardly believing the words came from her lips.

His touch was electric, his tongue, teeth and lips nipping and creating pulses of desire that swirled deep inside.

"You don't want me to stop," he whispered against her ear, his breath tantalizing and wet.

"Yes . . . no . . . Oh, Dallas, please . . ." With all her might, she coiled her strength, then pushed away from him and found to her mortification that she was panting, her heartbeat thrumming, her pulse pounding in her temples.

Running a trembling hand through her hair, she stepped backward until she ran into a post supporting the hay loft. The splintered wood pressed hard against her back. "For someone who doesn't want to get involved, you're pretty damned persistent," she said, trying to sound haughty, and failing.

"What I want and what seems to keep happening between us aren't necessarily the same." He, too, had trouble finding his breath. He ran a shaking hand over his lips.

"Then I guess the answer is to stay away from each other."

"You think that's possible?" he asked, sliding her a look with his knowing blue eyes.

"Anything's possible if you want it bad enough."

"Is that so?"

"Absolutely."

"I hope you're right, Ms. Hill," he said as he walked to the door. He stopped and looked over his shoulder. "Because if you're not, we've got one helluva problem on our hands."

Chapter Nine

Dallas dragged himself out of the pool, his body heaving from the exertion, his lungs craving more air. He'd swum over a mile in less than forty-five minutes, and he was breathing hard, his heart pumping crazily.

"What're you tryin' to do, kill yourself?" the man in the next lane asked. The other swimmer ripped off his goggles and cap, letting his wet hair fall nearly to his shoulders.

"I was a little keyed up," Dallas replied. He didn't know the man's name, wasn't really interested. He saw him here at the pool a couple of times a week and usually they swam their laps at about the same pace. Not this morning. Dallas had been wound tighter than a clock spring, his muscles tense, his attitude one notch shy of downright surly.

All because of that damned woman. He didn't know whether to hate her or to love her. She'd upset his well-ordered life, and for that, he was angry with her; but she brought out a part of him he'd kept hidden, a part that felt younger and carefree. He supposed, if he didn't love her, at least he owed her one.

He climbed to his feet, grabbed his towel and rubbed the rough terry cloth over his face, neck and shoulders. Seeing her yesterday with the reporter should have been warning enough, but no, he'd hung around and let down his guard enough to allow that louse of a photographer to snap a picture of them together. Not that it really mattered, he supposed. The picture probably wouldn't be printed, and if it was, so what?

Worse yet, he'd let the man goad him into tracking her down in the barn and acting like some horny barbarian. God, what was happening to him?

In the shower room, he ignored the other men who were in various stages of dressing, shaving or blow-drying their hair. They joked and laughed over the whine of hair dryers and electric razors, but Dallas barely noticed. He'd never been part of that club of men who sought camaraderie in the locker room before facing the day.

He washed the chlorine from his skin and hair and, as they had for the past week, his thoughts swirled around Chandra. Chandra the camping guide. Chandra the seductress. Chandra the would-be mother. God, she was crazy for that kid; that much was obvious.

But Dallas wasn't too sure about how she felt about him. Unless her emotions were as jumbled as his. Dunking his head under the shower one final time, he twisted off the knob and tried not to think about last night, how he, after a short shift at the hospital, had gone home and fallen into bed, only to dream about her—her honey-gold hair, her laughing eyes, her luscious pink lips and her breasts, round and full with dark, sweet tips.

Suddenly embarrassed at the swelling that the thought of her always brought to mind, he turned on the faucet again, gave himself a douse of ice-cold water, then muttering obscenities under his breath, wrapped a towel around his hips and walked briskly to his locker. He changed into clothes quickly, shoved his fingers through his hair and, slinging his bag over his shoulder, strode outside.

The day echoed his mood. Gray clouds clustered over the mountaintops, threatening to explode in a deluge of late-summer rain. Well, great, let it pour. Maybe the drops from the dark sky would cool his blood. He hoped so. Ever since he'd met Chandra Hill, it seemed he'd been battling his body, his mind telling him not to get involved, his damned body wanting nothing more than to plunge into her with a fierce possession.

He'd *never* felt this way before. *Never*. Even with Jennifer, there had been an edge of control in their lovemaking, and not once had he discovered that his passion had ruled him. But now, with Chandra, he couldn't stop thinking about making love to her over and over again.

He unlocked his truck and slipped behind the wheel. Jamming his key into the ignition, he decided that he'd be better off not seeing the lady again.

Maybe another woman... He considered the women he knew and, without even realizing the turn of his thoughts, his mind had wandered back to Chandra Hill. Yesterday's kiss... a simmering passion...

Getting to know her more intimately would either be a blessing or a curse, and he strongly suspected the latter. He shoved a tape into the player and, muttering oaths at the other drivers, he eased his truck into the snarl of traffic and turned toward the hospital.

"I have no choice but to release him," Dr. Williams said with a quiet authority that brooked no argument.

Chandra had caught up with him after his rounds, and they were now in his office at the hospital, he seated on one side of a glossy black desk, she on the other. Behind him, through the window, she noticed the dark clouds that hinted of a late-summer thunderstorm. The thunderheads reminded her of Dallas and the storm she often saw gathering in his eyes, but then, just about anything these days caused her to think about Dr. O'Rourke.

Or the baby. And that was why she was here. She hadn't slept a wink last night, worried about the child. She'd spent the night tossing and turning, her mind spinning with schemes to get custody of the boy, and oftentimes, she hated to admit, those schemes also involved Dallas.

Dr. Williams was staring at her, waiting for her to say something.

"I just think it might be best for the child if he stayed here at the hospital a few more days."

"Why? He's healthy."

"But—"

"Really, Miss Hill, the hospital has done everything it can for the child." Williams gave her a soft smile that was barely visible beneath his neatly trimmed red beard. "He'll stay the night, and tomorrow the caseworker from Social Services will come for him."

"And take him where?" Chandra asked, managing not to sound frantic.

"I don't know." Williams sat back in his chair and shook his balding head. "Her name is Marian Sedgewick, and she's coming for the baby at about eleven. I'm sure you could call her and find out more about his placement."

The phone on the corner of his desk rang shrilly, and Chandra rose. "Thanks, Doctor," she said.

"Anytime." But he was already picking up the receiver.

Chandra walked along the hall of the pediatrics wing, refusing to be discouraged. This was to be expected. The baby couldn't stay here forever. But she'd have to move quickly. Near the nurses' station, she stopped and rummaged in her purse for change, then placed a call to Roy Arnette.

"I'm sorry, but Mr. Arnette isn't in right now. Can I take a message?" Chandra left her name and number. Deflated, she walked to the nurses' station, where Shannon Pratt was busy fielding phone calls.

"Go on back," she mouthed, the phone cradled between her shoulder and ear, as she wrote hastily on a clipboard.

Chandra didn't need any more encouragement. She hurried to the nursery and spied J.D., wrapped in a white blanket, his eyes moving slowly as he tried to focus. Her heart squeezed at the sight of his chubby face. Where would he be tomorrow? Who would change him, feed him, kiss him good-night?

An uncomfortable lump filled her throat as Shannon, all smiles, bustled by. "It's been a madhouse this morning," she apologized. "Leslie told me you were coming in to feed him." She motioned toward J.D.'s crib.

"I'd love to."

"Well, we could use the extra hands." Shannon walked into the nursery, still talking. "This is, and I quote, 'highly irregular,' but I talked long and hard and got the okay from my supervisor who, in turn, worked it out with admin. So we're all set." She handed Chandra gloves and a mask. "You can scrub up in the lavatory, and once you've donned all these glamorous accessories—come back. Believe me, your little guy will be hungry...."

Your little guy. If only. Chandra scrubbed her hands and arms and yanked on her gloves. The smell of antiseptic and newborn babies reminded her of her own practice. She'd been happy back then, treating the patients, getting to know their mothers, fitting into the cozy community of Collier, Tennessee and thinking she would put down roots and start her own family.

But Doug had had other ideas....

"Hey, you look like one of us!" Shannon said as Chandra walked out of the washroom. "And look who's waiting...."

"J.D.," Chandra said, grinning behind the paper mask. "How're ya, pumpkin?" She took the little bundle eagerly, held his tiny, wriggling body close to hers. Nurse Pratt handed her a bottle of formula, and the baby, still blinking up at Chandra, began to suckle hungrily. Tiny little noises, grunts of pleasure, accompanied the slurping sound as he tugged on the nipple.

"You've named him?"

Chandra, startled, jumped and the bottle came out of J.D.'s tiny mouth. He let up a wail that could put a patient in cardiac arrest. Quickly, she nudged the nipple back between the baby's tiny lips. "I'm sorry," she said to Shannon, "I was so into this, I forgot you were there. And, yes, I decided he needed a name."

"Well, I think it's a much better name than Baby John Doe." With a twinkle in her eye, she hurried back to the nursery and, with a black marking pen, wrote "J.D." in large letters on the tag of his bassinet.

Chandra smiled. For the first time since she'd moved to Ranger two years before, she felt a part of the community. Living as she did, miles out of town, meeting only a few townspeople at the market or at work, she hadn't cultivated many friends. Most of the people she dealt with were tourists who wanted a thrill before returning to their cities and nine-to-five jobs. A few returned from one year to the next, but her only real contacts with people in town were the men she worked with.

The nurses and staff of the hospital seemed special. She wondered if it was the hospital surroundings. For the first time since she left Collier, she wondered if leaving her profession had been the right choice.

So she was here. Again. Being set up for a fall. Dallas saw Chandra with the baby, this time taking a bottle from him and swaying gently, brushing the top of his downy head with her lips.

Was she out of her mind? Didn't she know she was playing Russian roulette with her emotions? Yet he, too, could feel the tug on his heartstrings, the unlikely and unwanted pull of tenderness for the child. Seeing them together, she cradling the little dark head so close to her breast, the baby nuzzling closer, caused a tightness in his chest and a deep sadness that he would never be a father, never a husband. He'd tried once and failed.

The familiar metallic taste of loathing filled his throat when he remembered his wife and her betrayal. Though he hadn't loved her as he should have, he'd been faithful to her and fair, and he'd cared about her. And she'd driven a knife into his heart, cutting him so deeply, the scar would never heal. He'd never feel free to love someone like Chandra, to father her children....

He coughed loudly. What the hell was he doing even thinking such ludicrous thoughts? It was one thing to fantasize about making love to her, to consider bedding her and having a quick affair that would end as surely as had his own brief marriage. But to consider a lifetime together, marriage and children? What in God's name was wrong with him?

Clearing his throat, he approached her. She turned, and the sight of her hair fanning her face nearly undid all his hard-fought resolutions to keep away from her. Her lips moved slightly, smiling at the sight of him.

"Thank God you're here," she said, and he realized that she'd somehow become dependent upon him.

This very headstrong, independent woman was beginning to trust him, and he thought guiltily of his detective friend digging into her past. He could call off the investigation, but decided it wouldn't hurt to know more about her. She seemed to have brushed their episode in the barn from her mind.

She said breathlessly, "I just talked to Dr. Williams. They're releasing J.D. tomorrow."

"So it's been decided."

"'Morning, Doctor." Shannon emerged from the nursery and turned her attention to Chandra. "Here, let me change him."

"He hasn't burped yet," Chandra protested, drawing her fine eyebrows together.

"That's all right." Nurse Pratt wriggled her nose at the tiny baby. "We'll take care of it, won't we? And I'll take your lovely accessories..." Shannon accepted the baby, bottle, gloves and mask from Chandra, and after a few quick words with Dallas about a peculiarly obstinate patient in CICU, carried J.D. back to the nursery.

Dallas took the crook of Chandra's arm in his broad hand and pulled her gently toward the nurses' station. "I wouldn't worry too much about the baby. He'll be in good hands."

"How do you know?" She stopped short, looking up at him. "*What* do you know?"

"Rumor is that the child will be placed in temporary custody of the Newells."

"The sheriff?"

"He and his wife, Lenore. She's a part-time nurse here and they've done this sort of thing before. Lenore's known for taking in stray dogs, cats and opening their home to runaways or children who are waiting to be placed in more permanent quarters."

Anxiously, Chandra bit her lower lip and Dallas experienced a sudden urge to kiss her and tug on that very lip. "Come here," he said, all thoughts of denying himself long gone. He pulled her around a corner and down a short hallway to a quieter part of the floor. At the end of the hall, in the landing of the emergency stairs, he tugged on her hand, yanking her hard against him. She gasped, and he captured her lips with his. Seeing the startled look on her face, the surprise in her wide, gray-green eyes, he expected her to frantically push away, but she didn't resist.

His mouth moved over hers, and she leaned against him, circling his waist with her arms, her breasts crushed against the hard expanse of his chest. This time she seemed to melt against his body. He twisted his hands in her hair and played with her lower lip, touching it with his tongue before drawing it into his mouth.

Chandra's heart thumped crazily. What was he thinking, kissing her here, in broad daylight, where at any minute— Her senses reeled, her body reacted and a tingling blush suffused her skin. She closed her eyes and let herself get lost in the smell and touch and taste of him. There was the faint odor of chlorine that clung to his skin, the smell of soap. And his hair was still damp. Somewhere, faraway, a metal cart rattled.

"What the hell am I going to do with you?" he muttered into her hair, breathing deeply, his heart drumming so loudly, she could hear the wild beat.

Before she could answer, he kissed her again, long and hard, creating a whirlpool of emotions inside her. She sighed into his open mouth, and his tongue touched hers before he closed his mouth and every muscle in his body tensed. He dropped his hands to his sides then, and she nearly fell over.

"What?" she asked, before seeing that his eyes, now open, were focused on something or someone standing just beyond Chandra's shoulder.

Chandra turned and found herself gazing into the flushed face of Nurse Alma Lindquist. "Excuse me," the big nurse said, obviously embarrassed. "I, uh, well, I'm looking for you, Doctor, and Shannon said she saw you goin' down this hall." She turned her gaze to Chandra. "She didn't mention—"

"What is it?" Dallas was all business, and Chandra felt like crawling into a hole. Caught like a couple of lusty teenagers—by Alma Lindquist, of all people. Alma's eyebrows were arched over her glasses, and a tiny I-got-you grin was barely visible on her face. Chandra was absolutely mortified.

"Dr. Warren isn't in yet, and I need to get into the medications for E.R. However, if you're busy—"

"I'll be right there," Dallas said, his eyes glittering as Alma tried and failed to smother her knowing smile. She sauntered off down the hall, and Chandra's face felt red-hot.

"This was a mistake," Dallas said, jamming his hands through his hair and shaking his head. "Look, I can't get involved with anyone. It just wouldn't work."

"I don't remember asking you," Chandra replied, though his words stung.

"But you haven't exactly been backing off, have you?"

"I've done nothing to encourage you," she reminded him, wounded. "You came on the rafting trip. I didn't invite you."

"My brother—"

"Whatever. It doesn't matter. And you showed up at my house the other night—and barged into my barn. Again without an engraved invitation."

"And you camp out here at the hospital."

"Because of the baby!" she shot back, knowing in her heart what she would never admit to him. "Don't you understand?" she said instead. "J.D. means everything to me!"

"Oh, Chandra..." he said, and a dark emotion flickered in his eyes.

"And don't give me all the reasons I shouldn't try to adopt him, because I'm going to," she replied, embarrassed and angry and frustrated. She tossed her hair over her shoulders.

"You're serious about adopting him?" Dallas asked, obviously skeptical.

She wished she could call back the words, but the damage was done. There was no reason to play coy. "I hope to. I've already told my attorney to draw up the necessary papers. I'll petition the court—"

"And what did your attorney say?"

"Well, after he tried to talk me out of it," she replied, sliding the doctor a glance, "he told me I'd better go about increasing my chances."

"How?"

"By getting married."

Dallas blanched. Rock solid, all-business Dr. Dallas O'Rourke actually lost his color. Good! Chandra had the feeling O'Rourke needed to be shaken up once in a while.

"That's right, Doctor, I guess I'm in the market for a husband." She straightened her blouse. "Seems that the courts will look more kindly on a couple rather than a single woman."

"You're joking!" He was absolutely stricken, and Chandra's heart nosedived.

"Only about being in the marriage market," she said. "But I'm not going to let any prejudice against single women stop me. If I have to fight this through the Supreme Court, I will."

"Or get married?"

"That was a joke, Doctor," she said, and then decided to drop the bomb. "I was married once. It wasn't all it was cracked up to be."

He didn't move, but his eyes didn't leave hers and she silently counted her heartbeats. "Maybe you married the wrong man," he finally said.

"I did," she admitted, quivering at the thought of discussing her short-lived marriage with him. Once the divorce had been finalized, she'd never spoken of Doug or her marriage to anyone. Not even to her family. "But even if I did marry the wrong guy, I'm not sure I would recognize the right one if he landed on my doorstep."

"Oh, Ms. Hill, I think you would."

She lifted a shoulder dismissively. "I'm not going to lose any sleep over it. See you later," she said breezily, as if his passionate kiss and harsh words hadn't bothered her in the least. With a forced smile, she turned and left him there, trying not to notice that the taste of his lips still lingered on hers.

Dallas tried to ignore the fact that he was jealous—of a man whose name he didn't know. Whoever Chandra's ex-husband was, he was a damned fool.

Now, as Dallas folded his arms over his chest, he tried to keep his thoughts on the business at hand, which was his patient. "The nurses say you've been giving them trouble, Mr. Hastings."

"Call me Ned. And don't give me no guff about not takin' those pills. I've lived eighty-five years without takin' pills, and I'm not about to start now."

"Even though you're in intensive care and have had one heart attack already? All the medication does is help regulate your heartbeat."

Ned scratched his head, his mottled scalp showing through thin gray hair. "I know you're just doin' your job, Doc, and I 'preciate it, but I don't need any goldurn pills to keep my ticker from conkin' out."

"I'm not so sure about that."

"And about those nurses of yours. Always fussin' over me. Pokin' and proddin' and cluckin' their tongues. You're lucky I'm still in this hospital."

Dallas swallowed a smile. The old coot was lovable in his own way. But stubborn. "I don't think you're being realistic about your health."

"Hell, I didn't get to my age by lyin' in a hospital, with tubes run through my body and pills bein' stuck in my mouth every hour of the day. I live alone, I'm proud of it, and I don't need no mamby-pamby women stewin' over me."

"I see he's his usual jovial self," Lenore Newell said. She placed the thermometer into a disposable cover, and with a smile, stuck the thermometer under Mr. Hasting's tongue. "This should keep you quiet a while," she said.

He sputtered, but didn't spit the thermometer out as Dallas had expected.

Nurse Newell took the old man's pulse and, while eyeing her watch, added, "Some people would think spending a few days being pampered by women would be heaven."

"Humph," Ned growled around the thermometer. "They're just plain stupid or they haven't been in this damned place," he mumbled.

"Shh," she ordered, winking at the doctor as she waited for the beep and digital readout of her patient's temperature.

"Keep giving him the medication," Dallas said, seeing the glint of fondness in the old man's glare. "And don't take any abuse from this guy."

Hastings's thick eyebrows shot up.

"I'll be back," Dallas promised him. As he left the room, he heard Ned Hastings still growling around the thermometer.

Lenore caught up with Dallas in the staff lounge. "Cantankerous old son of a gun," she said with a ready smile. Behind big glasses, her eyes gleamed with affection.

"He keeps life interesting," Dallas remarked.

"Don't they all?"

Dallas poured himself a cup of coffee while Lenore rummaged through a basket of tea bags. The lounge was nearly empty. Three nurses surrounded a round table by the window, and a couple of residents, who looked as if they'd each pulled thirty-six-hour shifts, were stretched out on the couches, one in scrubs, the other wearing a rumpled lab coat and slacks. Each supported more than a day's growth of beard and bloodshot eyes.

"Been here long?" Dallas ventured.

One of them, the lanky one with long blond hair, shoved a hand through his unruly locks. "Days, weeks, years... I can't remember."

"We came on duty in 1985," his companion joked. He was shorter and thin, with a moustache and eyes that appeared owlish behind thick glasses.

"Time for a break," Dallas suggested.

"Man, I'm gonna sleep for a week," the tall one said.

"Not me. I'm going out for a five-mile jog and set of tennis."

"Yeah, right!" They struggled to their feet and headed out the door.

Dallas stirred his coffee before glancing at Lenore. "I heard you might have another mouth to feed."

She smiled. "Yep. The abandoned baby. Judge Reinecke seems to think that the baby would be best at our house, at least for a while. We've cared for more than our share of orphans."

Dallas stared into his coffee, not knowing whether he should bring up Chandra or not. Maybe she was better off away from the baby. But he remembered her look of desperation at the thought that the child would be taken away from her. Knowing he might be playing with emotional fire, he nonetheless had to do anything in his power to help her. "Look, there's a woman, the woman who brought the baby in, Chandra Hill. I know she'd like to visit the baby fairly often."

Lenore dunked a tea bag into a steaming cup of water. "I've heard about her. Seems she's pretty attached to the boy."

"Well, it wouldn't hurt for her to drop by."

"Of course not. Tell her to stop in anytime."

"Lenore! Hey, what's this I hear about you and the Baby John Doe?" one of the other nurses called over. "You got any room left over there?"

Dallas took his coffee and left as the two other nurses joined into the conversation. He'd done what he could. Now it was up to Chandra.

He spent the rest of the day in the hospital and finally, at five, stopped in at pediatrics for one last look at J.D. Holding the child, he sighed. "What're we gonna do with you?" he wondered aloud. "You're giving the woman who found you fits, y'know."

The baby yawned, as if he were bored to death.

"Okay, okay," Dallas said, smiling down at the child. "We'll see what we can do."

He left the infant with a nurse and walked outside. The storm that had threatened earlier had cleared up and the day was dry and warm, no lingering clouds in the sky. Whistling under his breath, he walked to his truck and stopped when he spied his half brother chewing on a toothpick, one lean hip resting against the fender, his knee bent and the sole of one boot pressed against the front tire. A grimy duffle bag had been dropped on the asphalt near the truck.

"I thought I might have to spend the whole weekend here waiting for you," Brian said as Dallas approached. As usual, Brian's cocky grin was in place, his eyes squinting slightly against a lowering sun. His jeans were so faded, they'd ripped through the knees, and the denim across his butt was frayed, on the point of giving way completely. His shirt was bright orange, faded neon, and said simply, SURF'S UP!! diagonally in purple letters that stretched from his right shoulder to his left hip.

"What's doing?"

Brian grinned, as if he read the caution in Dallas's eyes. He straightened and held out his hands, surrendering to his half brother's suspicion. "Don't worry, I haven't gone through the money yet. I just came by to say I'm shipping out. On my way back to school."

About time. "That's good."

"Right, and I probably won't see you until Christmas. You'll come to Mom's?"

"I'll see. Christmas is a long way off."

"She'd be disappointed if you didn't come."

Well, maybe. From Brian's point of view, their mother loved Dallas as much as she did her other children. But Dallas remembered a time when, after the divorce from his father and her remarriage, Eugena O'Rourke McGee had been so involved with raising a daughter and the twins that she hadn't so much as smiled at him. She'd been tired most of the time from chasing the younger kids.

Dallas, a reminder of her marriage to a military doctor who had never been able to show any emotion, was, for the most part, left on his own. He'd been enrolled in boarding school while his parents were married, and his status didn't change when his mother remarried, even though none of her other children had ever stepped foot in a school away from home until college. Joanna, Brian and Brenda had been raised at home.

Yes, there was the possibility that his mother might miss Dallas at Christmas, but not for the reasons Brian expected. In her later years, she'd developed a fondness for her firstborn, probably born of guilt, but never had Eugena given him the love she'd lavished on her younger children.

Dallas was no longer bitter about that particular lack of love; he just didn't dwell on it.

"Ahh, come one, it'll be fun. And Joanna and Brenda will kill ya if ya don't show up."

That much was true. For all the love he hadn't received from his mother, his sisters had adored him. "I'll think about it."

"See that you do. Well, I'm outta here." Bending down, Brian slung the strap of his duffle over his shoulder and offered his brother one of his killer smiles. "Thanks a lot. For everything. And, oh—did you manage to go on the raft ride?"

Dallas grinned. "An experience of a lifetime."

"What did you think of the lady?"

"She's something else."

"I'll say." Brian's grin turned into a leer. "Strong little bugger. And great legs! Boy, I bet she's a tiger..." His voice faded away when he caught the set of his brother's jaw. "So you noticed?"

"Just that I already knew her."

"A nice piece." When Dallas's lips thinned, Brian laughed. "Of work. Hey! What did you think I meant?" He glanced down at his brother's hands and grinned even more broadly. Dallas realized that he'd instinctively clenched his fists. "Hey, bro', is there something you're not tellin' me?"

Dallas forced himself to relax. This was just Brian going into his macho-man routine. "Nothing. Just that I already know her."

"And you've got the hots for her."

Dallas didn't reply, but just glared at his half brother, wondering if they had anything in common at all.

"Well, go for it, man! I don't blame you. The lady's nice...real nice."

"What do you mean, 'go for it'?"

"Ask her out, spend some time with her, get to know her. For crying out loud, here you are and—pardon me for pointing it out—in the middle of no-friggin'-where, and a woman like that falls into your lap. Take a chance, man. I know you got burned by Jennifer the Jezebel, but not all women are Wicked Witches of the West."

"I should take advice on my love life from you?" Dallas asked, slightly amused.

"Well, you'd better take it from somebody, 'cause the way I see it, your 'love life,' as you so optimistically call it, doesn't exist."

Dallas wanted to smack the smug smile off the younger man's face, but, for once in his life, Brian was right. Instead, Dallas stuck out his arm and shook his brother's hand. "Thanks for the advice."

"Don't thank me. Just do something, man."

"I could give you the same words of wisdom."

Brian's grin was positively wicked. "Not about *my* love life, you couldn't." With a cocksure grin, he strolled over to his car and yanked open the door. Throwing his bag into the back seat, he crawled into the interior, started the engine of the old Pontiac Firebird and took off in a cloud of exhaust that slowly dissipated in the clear mountain air.

Brian's advice hung like a pall over Dallas as he drove to his condominium. This morning he'd wanted to drive Chandra from his life forever. Then he'd seen her in the hospital and could hardly keep his hands off her. No, he'd better face facts, at least for the present. Brian was right; he should kick up his heels a little. He didn't have to fall in love.

That thought hit him like a bucket of ice water. In love? *I guess I'm in the market for a husband.*

Her words ricocheted through his mind. Had she been joking, or had she been hinting? "Quit this, O'Rourke, before you make yourself crazy."

But forget her he couldn't, and before he knew it, he was making plans to see her again. As soon as he walked into his home, he dropped his mail, unopened, on the table, then picked up the phone book. He punched out the number of Wild West Expeditions. Chandra answered, and he couldn't stop the tug of the muscles near the corners of his mouth.

"I thought we should get together after work," he said, feeling the part of a fool, like some creepy lounge lizard. God, he was just no good at this.

"Why?"

"We left on the wrong note. How about I take you to dinner?"

A pause. A thousand heartbeats seemed to pass. "Dinner?" she finally said. "I don't know...."

"Neither do I, but I've been thinking and..." He let out his breath slowly, then decided honesty was the best policy. "Well, I'd like to see you again."

"Even though I'm only interested in a husband or, more precisely, a father for my yet-unadopted child."

There it was—that biting sarcasm that he found so fascinating. No wimp, Ms. Hill. "Even though," he said, smiling despite himself. "Dress up. I've got a surprise for you. I'll pick you up at your place at six-thirty."

"What if I already have plans?" she asked, obviously flirting with him a little. It occurred to him that she was as nervous about this as was he.

"Cancel them." He hung up, feeling a little like a jerk, but looking forward to the evening ahead. This morning he'd tried to drive her from his mind, but now, damn it all to hell, he was going to fulfill a few of his fantasies with the gorgeous Ms. Hill.

After all, it was just a date, not a lifetime commitment.

Chapter Ten

A date? She couldn't believe it. Yet here she was, pawing through her closet of work shirts, jeans and a few old dresses trying to come up with an outfit for Dallas's surprise.

And her heart was pounding as if she were a schoolgirl. *Take it easy, Chandra,* she told herself, knowing that Dallas's mood could change as rapidly as the weather in these mountains.

She settled for a rose-colored skirt and a scooped-neck blouse, and was just brushing her hair when Sam, ever vigilant, began to growl. "Jealous?" Chandra teased, her heart surprisingly light as she patted the dog on his head, and was rewarded with a sloppy lick of his tongue.

Dallas stood on the doorstep, balancing two grocery sacks. "Wait a minute—I thought we were going out," she said as she opened the door and he stepped inside.

"We are." He placed the brown paper bags on the kitchen counter. "Got a picnic basket?"

"You're kidding, right?" she asked, but caught the glint of devilish mischief in his eyes. *This* was the serious Dr. O'Rourke—this man who seemed hell-bent to confuse her? It seemed that he enjoyed keeping her equilibrium off-balance.

"Someone told me I wasn't spontaneous enough, that I needed to get out of my rut," he said with a shrug. "So—the basket?"

"Right. A picnic basket." Wondering what he was up to, she rummaged in the closet under the stairs and came up with a wicker basket covered with dust. She blew across the top and dust motes swirled in a cloud. "Doesn't get much use," she explained, finding a cloth and wiping the woven wicker clean.

"I thought we'd take a ride into the hills."

"Like this?" She eyed his slacks and crisp shirt. "Are you crazy?"

"Just spontaneous."

"Yeah, right," she replied, but wiped out the interior of the basket and lined it with a blanket. Dallas reached into his grocery bag and filled the basket with smaller sacks, a bottle of wine, glasses and a corkscrew. "Did you bring the horses, too, or is that what I'm supposed to provide?"

"The horses and the destination."

"Oh, I get it—you're counting on me to provide you with a free trail ride, is that it?" she teased, feeling her spirits lifting along with the corners of her mouth.

He laughed and the sound filled the cabin, bouncing off the rafters as he snapped the lid of the basket shut. Approaching her slowly, he held her gaze with his. "Are you going to fight me all the way on this?"

"I don't have a side saddle." Oh, Lord, he was so close she could see a small scar near his hairline, obviously old and faded with the passage of time from ruffian boy to man. She had to elevate her chin a fraction to meet his gaze, and her throat caught at the depth of blue in his eyes.

"Improvise," he suggested, his breath tickling her scalp.

"I could change—"

"And leave me overdressed? No way!" His gaze lowered, past her lips and chin, along the column of her throat, to the scooped neck of her blouse and the beginning of the hollow between her breasts, just barely visible. "Besides, you look—" He broke off, his Adam's apple working in his throat. Reaching forward, he touched a strand of her hair and wound its golden length around one finger.

The moment, only seconds, seemed to stretch a lifetime, and as he laid her curl back against her cheek, his finger grazing her skin, her diaphragm pressed so hard against her lungs, she had trouble breathing.

"I think we should go," she said, stepping back from him and feeling clumsy and embarrassed and totally unbalanced. Just being close to him caused her to lose her cool facade. This one enigmatic man had managed, in the span of one week, to create havoc with her emotions. "I—I'll saddle up."

"*I'll* saddle up. You bring the basket." He swung out the door, and Sam, with one look over his shoulder, trotted after him.

"I'm going to change your name to Judas," Chandra warned, swinging the basket from the table and following man and dog to the barn. She was struck by the natural way Dallas strode across the yard, as if he belonged here. Sunlight gleamed in his dark hair and warmed her crown. His dress clothes seemed appropriate somehow, though she could just as easily envision him in faded jeans, a work shirt open and flapping in the breeze as he chopped firewood. And Sam, the turncoat, padded happily behind him, tongue lolling, tail moving slowly with his gait.

Within minutes, Dallas had saddled Max and Brandy, and they were riding along a dusty trail. Chandra had hiked her skirt around her thighs and felt absolutely ridiculous as well as positively euphoric. The sky was a clear cobalt blue, and two hawks circled lazily overhead.

The mountain air was clean, the horses' hooves thudding softly, stirring dust, causing creatures in the brush to scurry through the undergrowth. Once in a while, Sam gave chase, startling the horses as he dashed by, barking wildly at some unseen prey.

After nearly an hour of riding through the forest, the trail forked, and Chandra veered sharply to the right, back-trailing downhill.

"You sure you know where you're going?" Dallas asked.

"Positive." She nudged Brandy in the sides as the pines and blue spruce gave way to a meadow. The game little mare sprinted forward, ears pricked, nostrils flared, her hooves pounding across the field of dry grass and wildflowers in shades of pink, blue and lavender.

Chandra's skirt billowed behind her, and her bare legs held fast to Brandy's sides. Wind streamed through Chandra's hair, and she laughed as she heard Max close to Brandy's heels, his galloping hooves loud against the dry ground.

"Come on, Brandy," Chandra said, leaning over the little mare's shoulders and watching the horse's ears flatten against her head. She picked up speed, but it was too late. Max, black legs flashing in the sun, raced past. Dallas rode low in the saddle, his shoulders hunched forward, the picnic basket propped between the saddle and his chest.

"We should've beaten them," Chandra told the mare as she pulled up. Both horses were sweating and blowing hard. Chandra, too, was having trouble breathing, but Sam wasn't even winded. He saw a squirrel, streaked off across the meadow and splashed through the creek that zigzagged through the grass. Spring water gurgled and rushed over rocks, and the big gold dog bounded through the stream before disappearing into the woods.

"Should we worry about him?" Dallas asked, swinging off Max at a bend in the creek where the water pooled and reflected the intense blue of the sky.

"He'll be back. He's used to it." Chandra hopped to the ground and felt the tickle of grass against her bare ankles. "That's how I found him, you know. He crawled into the yard, ripped from stem to stern by something—bear, raccoon, possum or something else, I suppose—and I had to sew him up. I've had him ever since."

Dallas's eyes narrowed on the forest into which the dog, joyfully yelping and giving chase, had disappeared. "Hasn't learned much."

"He'll be all right," Chandra replied.

While the horses grazed near the stream, Dallas and Chandra unfolded the blanket in the shade of a pine tree. He uncorked the wine and poured them each a glass of Chablis. "What are we drinking to?" she asked, and his blue eyes deepened to a mysterious hue.

"How about to us?"

She laughed, tucking her legs beneath her as she sat on the edge of the blanket, her skirt folded over her knees. He wasn't serious. This was all a lark, a fantasy. "Us? I thought there wasn't any us—that you couldn't get involved or muck up your life with a woman." She took a long swallow of wine and watched the play of emotions across his face.

His jaw slid to one side, and his hair was rumpled by the breeze that blew from the west. "I didn't want any complications."

"Didn't...?"

"Still don't," he admitted, lying on the blanket and leaning back on one elbow while he sipped from his glass. "But sometimes things change. And what you don't want changes with it." He plucked a dry blade of grass and chewed on it. "From the minute I saw you in the emergency room, I knew you were going to be trouble—big trouble." He squinted as a pheasant, wings beating franti-

cally, rose from the grass as Sam leapt and barked in the
frightened bird's wake. "And I thought the only reasonable thing to do, the only sane path to take, was to avoid
you."

She smiled. For the first time since she'd met him, she felt
that Dallas was being honest with her. His eyebrows were
pinched together, and his lips, moving on the straw, pursed
hard, as if he were angry with himself.

"So..." she prodded.

"So I did. And then my brother gave me that damned
coupon."

"But you still weren't convinced that I wasn't trouble,"
she said.

"Hell, no. Then I knew you were more trouble than I'd
even imagined." He laughed again and took a long swallow
of his wine. "And that's when things got really out of
hand." He looked at her directly then, his gaze holding hers.
"I couldn't keep my hands off you, and that's not the way
it usually is with me. In fact," he admitted, glancing away,
as if the admission were embarrassing, "I was starting to
become obsessed."

"With...?" she asked warily.

"You." A muscle in his jaw convulsed, and Chandra realized just how difficult it was for him to bare his soul. They
weren't so different, she decided; they both bore wounds
that wouldn't heal. "Anyway, I wasn't sleeping at night, and
I couldn't think of anything but you. Making love to you."

Chandra nearly dropped her glass. Her hands began to
sweat, and she took a long swallow of wine to avoid those
blue, blue eyes.

"So that's when I decided never to see you again."

She glanced up sharply. "But you're here—"

"Believe it or not, I ran into Brian and he told me I was
crazy to keep avoiding you. He told me I should loosen up,
enjoy life, take a chance or two...." Dallas lifted a shoul-

der and beneath the crisp white fabric, his muscles moved fluidly.

A tight knot formed in the pit of Chandra's stomach. He reached over and refilled her glass before adding more wine to his own.

"So, for the first time in my life, I took Brian's advice. Believe me, it wasn't easy." He studied the label for a second before propping the bottle against the inside of the wicker basket.

Chandra felt as if time were suspended between them. Surely she could think of something clever to say, something that would lighten the mood. But all words escaped her, and she could feel his gaze moving slowly over her, caressing her, causing her skin to tingle under his silent appraisal. "So what is this?" she finally asked, her voice as soft as the wind in the pines. "A seduction?"

"If you want it to be."

"No!" she said quickly, breathlessly. She'd thought of making love to him. But it was one thing to fantasize, another to actually do it. She gulped her wine and glanced his way, hoping that she could see some indication that he was joking, but not a glimmer of humor sparked in his eyes.

"Afraid?"

"Look, Dallas. Maybe you can make all sorts of plans— you know, buy the wine, pick out the right cheese and bread, and just...just map out some way for us to get together. But it doesn't work that way with me. I can't just drink a little wine and say, 'what the hell,' and start stripping off my clothes. It's just not me...." Slowly, she climbed to her feet and dusted her hands. "This isn't going to work." She whistled to the horses, and while Brandy ignored her and continued to pluck grass, Max responded.

She reached for his reins, but Dallas caught up with her and gently grabbed her wrist. "I've been accused of being blunt," he admitted. "Too blunt."

"Well, at least you don't leave me guessing." She tried to pull away, but his grip tightened, and slowly he tugged, forcing her to face him.

"It's just that I want you," he said. "I want you so much, I can't think of anything else. I ache for you at night, embarrass myself during the day when I start to think of you. I've tried to fight it—hell, I had myself convinced that I didn't want, didn't need, a woman. And I was right. I don't need just any woman, Chandra. I need you."

Her heart turned over, and she felt the pads of his fingers, warm and smooth against the inside of her forearm. Her heart nearly stopped as she dropped the reins and stared into eyes the color of a mountain sky.

"You want me, too." He placed the flat of his free hand over her heart, his fingertips skimming her bare skin, his palm resting over the neckline of her blouse, seeming to press against her breast.

Her heartbeat quickened, and her breath, unsteady to begin with, came in quick bursts through her lips.

"W-wanting isn't enough," she said.

"It was enough on the rafting trip." He kissed the side of her neck then, and her throat constricted. Somewhere she heard a dog barking and the jingle of a bridle, but those sounds were in the distance, and now she heard only the rapid tattoo of her heart and the rasp of air through her lungs.

Dallas pulled her blouse down over one shoulder and placed his lips against her skin. An endless ache started at the apex of her legs and moved slowly upward.

The fingers surrounding her wrist pulled gently, insistently, forcing her to follow him to the ground, and she didn't resist, fell willingly against him, their arms and legs entwining, his body wedged between hers and the bent grass.

He moved his mouth over hers, fiercely, possessively, until it seemed that the fever in his blood had ignited all her senses. She felt the pressure of his tongue, the urgency in his hands, the hot, throbbing desire that blossomed inside her.

He pulled her blouse from the waistband of her skirt and slowly ran his hands over her ribs, moving upward, brushing the lace of her bra. She moaned into his mouth as his thumb skimmed against her already taut nipple.

"Dallas," she whispered as he unbuttoned her blouse and the cool mountain air caressed her skin. He shoved the blouse aside, and then with her above him, craned his neck so that his lips touched her bra and the lace-encased nipple. She writhed, and he pulled her downward, one hand splayed against the bare skin of her back, the other tangled in her hair. He kissed and teased her through the lace, his tongue wet and wonderful in delicious ministrations that caused her to convulse.

"Please, please, please . . ." she moaned, and he groaned against her flesh, unhooking the bra and letting her breasts fall free, unbound, above him. He took one eagerly into his waiting mouth, suckling hungrily, his tongue and teeth pulling and tugging, creating a whirlpool of warmth deep within her body.

She found the buttons of his shirt and quickly dispensed with them, pushing the white fabric over corded shoulders that flexed, strong and sinewy against her fingers. She arched against him as the shirt was discarded, and her breasts felt the rough hairs of his chest when he lifted his head to stare up at her eyes.

"Chandra," he whispered, his voice rough and pleading, his hands smoothing her back, exploring the cleft of her spine. "You're so gorgeous," he whispered, moving his gaze from her eyes and past her parted lips to her breasts, white and firm, floating above him, enticing him to delirious heights of sexuality.

Never had he felt so free, so anxious, so aroused. His lust was like a living, breathing creature he couldn't control.

With his hand, he sculpted her, teasing the hard nipples and kneading the warm flesh of her breast. Shockwave after delicious shockwave spread through him, and she responded by throwing her head back, her luxurious mane of golden hair falling over her shoulders and back. He didn't stop. Couldn't. He fastened his mouth over her nipple again and slowly slid his hand beneath the waistband of her skirt, skimming her abdomen and reaching lower still.

Sweat broke out on her body, and though he relieved her of her skirt and panties, a dewy sheen covered her body as he continued to touch her, kiss her, caress her.

She found herself helping him with his jeans, and he kicked them off, then lay under her, wanting to delve into her and never stop. When he firmly grasped one buttock, she pressed herself hard against him.

"Make love to me, Chandra," he whispered into her hair. "For now and forever, make love to me."

She closed her eyes and swallowed as he ran one finger down the hollow of her breasts, down past her navel and farther still, until she bucked above him, and he reacted, capturing her lips in his and rolling her over in one quick motion. As he stared down into her eyes, he parted her legs with his knees and hesitated, seeing the trust in her gaze, knowing that she was envisioning a future together.

"Oh, Chandra," he whispered. "I want you....." And in that moment, he knew that life would never be the same. He'd planned all this, to the very seduction. A man of medicine, he never lost his cool, but with this woman, he could very well lose his equilibrium forever. Trying to stay rational, he reached in the grass for his jeans, dug into the pocket for a condom in his wallet. Muttering in frustration, he held up the packet for her to inspect, as if in so doing, they could stop this madness before it went any further.

But it was too late; the bridge had been crossed. A shadow of doubt crossed her eyes for just one second. "Don't stop," she said, as if certain he would deny her. Quickly, he readied himself. She trembled as he brushed the hair from her eyes, and in that moment when their gazes crossed a chasm of doubt, he entered her, in one swift thrust of warmth and need. A hard, primal sound escaped his throat, and he moved, slowly at first, feeling all of her, still aware of her fingertips feather light against his shoulders, her mouth yielding softly to his.

He couldn't stop and wouldn't. His tempo increased, and through fleeting thoughts of satisfying her, he lost control, plunged deep and hard, whispering her name as a litany until he could hold back no longer and he erupted with a roar.

Chandra convulsed beneath him, arching her hips and receiving him with all the ferocity of his own passion. She dug her fingers deep into his shoulders and cried out, and his name echoed through the hills.

"Dallas, oh, Dallas," she said, her throat working, tears filling the corners of her eyes.

Breathing raggedly, afterglow converging upon him, he saw the silent tracks of her tears. Pain shot through him as he realized he'd pushed himself upon her, forced her through seduction and gentle ministrations to have sex with him. Self-loathing swallowed him. "Oh, God, I'm sorry," he said, his throat rough. He pushed her bangs from her forehead, and self-contempt edged his features. What the hell had he been thinking? "I didn't mean to hurt you—"

"No!" She gasped, drawing in deep breaths. "You didn't. Really. It's...it..." She dashed her tears aside with the back of her hand. "It was wonderful. It's just... well, it's been so long."

"For me, too," he admitted, relieved that she wasn't feeling any remorse. He took her into his arms and kissed her crown. "I'm afraid I lost control."

Softly she sighed, and her skin flushed a beautiful pink. "You weren't the only one."

"You're not mad at me for planning this?"

"I could've stopped it." When he was about to protest, she shook her long blond mane. "Really, I could have. If I'd wanted to. But I didn't."

"No regrets?" he asked, kissing a stray tear that slid from her eye.

"None."

Sam loped over to them. Wet from a romp in the creek, he shook himself so hard that his license and collar rattled. Chandra screeched, and Dallas, laughing, picked her up and carried her toward the pool of spring water.

"You wouldn't," she cried, eyeing the frigid water.

"Something's got to cool us off."

"Dallas, no—"

But he waded into the clear depths and sucking in his breath, plunged them both into the icy pond. Shrieking and laughing, Chandra sputtered upward for air, only to find his smiling face next to hers. "You're horrid!" she cried, but laughed when he tickled her.

"Wicked. I'm wicked. Not horrid."

"Worse than that, I think," she said breathlessly as she struggled for the shore. He caught up with her and wrapping arms around her waist, pulled her tight against him. Wet, cold lips pressed anxiously against hers.

"You can't get away from me," he stated.

"Is that a challenge?" She lifted an eyebrow and eyed the shore, judging how far she would have to run should she want to prove him wrong.

"Don't even think about it!"

That was it. With the flat of her hand, she sprayed water in his face, then, laughing, she stumbled up the creek bank, only to be caught midstride and pulled back into the water. "As I said," he repeated, "you'll never get away from me!" He gathered her against him, sliding her intimately against him, pressing kisses against her nape and neck.

"So who's running?" she asked, and kissed him back. She wondered if she loved him and decided it didn't matter.

She cared about him, felt a special fondness toward him, and the passion between them was enough to satisfy her. She thought fleetingly of the future, but dismissed it. Today, for the first time in her life, she'd live for the moment.

Eventually the cold water was too much to bear and they returned to the meadow, where, after dressing, they finished the wine and ate sourdough bread, cheese, grapes and strawberries. The sun sank lower on the horizon, and shadows played across the dry grass.

Chandra lay on the blanket, picking a few wildflowers and twirling the stems between her fingers. "You said you didn't want to get involved," she ventured, glancing over her shoulder. Stretched out on the other side of the blanket, Dallas seemed content to stare at her.

"I didn't. Probably still don't. But I am."

"What happened? I mean—that made you so afraid?"

"Afraid?" He rolled onto his back and stared at the sky, still blue as the sun sank lower in the west. "I've never thought of it as being afraid. Cautious, maybe. Smart, for sure, but afraid?"

She arched an eyebrow. "That's the way I see it."

Scowling, he sighed. "I don't believe in reliving the past. No point to it."

"Except when it affects the future."

Dallas stood and dusted off his pants. He walked to the edge of the creek, where he bent down, picked up a smooth, flat stone and sent it skimming over the water to plop near the far bank as rippling circles disturbed the surface.

Chandra followed him to the shore, and, with a twinkle in her eye, picked up a flat river rock and skipped it over the water just as easily as he had. "What is it with you?" he asked, his features pulled into a look of puzzlement. "Studying to become a doctor, guiding white-water trips, backpacking and skipping stones?" He raked his gaze down her body. "For a woman with so many obvious feminine attributes, you sure like to perform like a man."

"Compete," she corrected. "I like to compete with men."

"Why?"

She shrugged. "I guess I'm the son my father never had. He taught me how to throw from my shoulder instead of my wrist, how to rock climb, and he gave me the confidence that I could do anything I wanted to, regardless of my sex."

Dallas eyed her. "You were lucky."

"I think so. My sisters were both glad that I was the chosen one and they didn't have to do any of the tomboy stuff. I think they missed out. But we weren't talking about me," she reminded him.

He feigned a smile. "You remembered."

"What happened to you?"

"It was simple, really," he said in an offhand manner that seemed meant to belie the pain. "My folks split up when I was still in boarding school. My dad was career military, very rigid, a physician, and my mother got tired of moving around. I can't say as I blame her, Harrison O'Rourke would've been hell to live with. He's . . . clinical, I guess you'd say. Didn't believe in showing his emotions, not to me or Mom. It's amazing she stayed with him as long as she did."

Dallas reached down and skipped another stone, and Chandra's chest grew tight. Talking about his past was difficult for him; she could see the reluctance in his eyes, the harsh lines near his mouth. "Anyway, she remarried. Happily, I think. And ended up pregnant right away. Joanna was born a year later, and only sixteen months after that the twins came along. You met Brian." Chandra nodded. "He has a twin sister named Brenda—she's, uh, much more rational than he.

"So, Mom had her hands full, and I was old enough to be on my own, anyway. I finished high school and was accepted at UCLA in premed."

To gain your father's approval, she thought, her heart twisting for a boy who felt unwanted.

"I met the girl of my dreams before I graduated," he said, his voice turning sarcastic. "Jennifer Smythe."

A painful jab cut into her heart, though why it mattered, Chandra couldn't fathom. "Why was she the girl of your dreams?"

He snorted. "She was perfect—or at least, I thought so. Beautiful, smart, clever, witty and a graduate student in law. Even though she was a few years older than I was, I thought the right thing to do was get married, so we did."

Chandra studied his profile—so severe with the onslaught of memories.

"The marriage was mistake number one. She passed the bar exam and within a few weeks, was hired at a firm where she'd worked during the summers. It was a respectable firm, and the partners were interested in young women to balance the plethora of old men. She supported me while I finished school. Mistake number two. She always felt I *owed* her something."

Dallas frowned darkly and shook his head. "This is really pretty boring stuff—"

"Not at all," Chandra interjected, surprised that he was letting her see so deeply into his private life.

He shot her a look saying more eloquently than words that he didn't believe her, but he continued, though reluctantly. "What I didn't know was that Jennifer didn't want a kid. Period. Now, she never told me this, but she was the only child of rich parents and couldn't see tying herself down to an infant. She thought that between her career and mine, we had it made." Sam galloped up, and Dallas reached down to scratch his ears. The old dog whined appreciatively, and Dallas had to smile.

"Eventually, I graduated and was hired at a hospital in Orange County. Even though we had a few bills, I thought this was the time to start a family, but Jennifer wasn't interested. I should've let it lie, I suppose, but I wanted kids. Badly." He cast Chandra a rueful grin. "In fact, I was obsessed. A bad trait of mine. I figured my folks didn't do the family bit right, so I was going to be the perfect father. As if I knew the first thing about raising kids!''

His eyes darkened, and any trace of humor disappeared from his features. He shook his head, as if in disbelief at his own naïveté.

Chandra felt a whisper of dread as he continued.

''The kicker was that Jennifer did get pregnant, right about the time we were buying our first house. She never told me, of course, and had the pregnancy terminated. I only found out because of a mutual friend who knew the doctor who performed the abortion.''

Chandra swallowed hard against the outrage that burned her throat. No wonder he was so bitter. A shadow, dark and pained, crossed his eyes, and the skin around his mouth grew taut.

''That was the last straw. I stormed over to her office, and I didn't care who heard the argument. I was furious that she wouldn't at least have talked to me, have worked things out before she took such drastic measures. But Jennifer wasn't the least bit reticent, and she told me then that she would never have children. It was her body, it had nothing to do with me, and as she saw it, I shouldn't get all worked up over it. Besides, she pointed out, I was doing well at the hospital, and I put in long hours. I didn't need the responsibility of children to make demands on my time—not to mention hers. What did upset her was that I embarrassed her by coming into the law firm in a rage.''

Chandra placed a hand on his arm, but he didn't seem to notice. ''So that's it. I couldn't deal with her from that point on. I tried to tell myself that losing the baby was for the best, that being married to a doctor was difficult for any woman, that maybe Jennifer would change her mind and there would be other children. But I was kidding myself. I never forgot.''

He shoved his hands into his pockets and rotated his neck, stretching his shoulder muscles. For a second, Chandra thought he'd finished, but his next words came out in a rush of disgust.

"You'd have to meet Jennifer to understand this, but she assumed everything was A-OK. She was delighted with our new life-style. We had money and social status and interesting careers. She was moving up in the law firm at an incredible pace. Her only real worry was that my position as an emergency-room physician wasn't all that glamorous. She thought I had the brains and skill to become a specialist, a notch up in her estimation. I fought her on that one. I like what I do and couldn't see giving it up."

He rolled his eyes to the sky, now streaked with gold and pink, as if he couldn't believe he'd been so foolish. His shoulders, which had been rigid, began to slump.

"Things got worse, of course. Living in L.A. was a grind. Jennifer and I barely saw each other. When I was offered a position at Riverbend, here in Ranger, I thought maybe we had a chance to start over. But I was wrong. Even though I said I'd set her up in her own practice here, Jennifer wouldn't hear of the move. It was obvious at that point that her job was more important than our marriage and she wasn't about to move to 'some podunk little town in the mountains.' She would be bored stiff in a small town in Colorado, without the nightlife and the glitz.

"Besides," he added bitterly, "she was up for a big promotion. If push came to shove, she'd rather live in L.A. without me than move to Colorado. So we separated. I moved. She stayed. We saw each other a couple of times a month and it was a sham. There was no reason to try to hold the marriage together."

He kicked at the grass. "We agreed on a quick divorce. Three weeks after the divorce was final, Jennifer married her boss, a man twice her age who had grown children and didn't want to start another family. The next time I saw her, she admitted that the baby she'd aborted wasn't even mine."

Chandra thought she might get sick. How could someone use this man—this wonderful man?

"Jennifer had been having an affair with her boss for years—which explained her meteoric rise in the firm of James, Ettinburg, Smith and McHenry," he said, his voice still edged in anger. "And I was the dupe who believed that we still had a chance." He snorted in self-disgust, and Chandra wished for the right words that would ease his pain, but there were none and she had to content herself with touching his arm.

"The irony of it all was that it didn't matter. Sure, I would've wanted my own kid, but I would've brought up Jennifer's baby as if it were my own. But it was too late."

"And that's when you gave up on love and marriage?" Chandra asked, her heart aching, her fingers still gripping his forearm.

He slanted a glance down at her. "I think a man who's so involved with his work has no right to ask a woman to be a part of his life."

"You're wrong," she whispered. "Oh, you're so wrong." Moved by his agony, she threw her arms around him and kissed his lips. "You would make a wonderful husband and a terrific father!" Then, realizing what she'd said, she dropped her arms and swallowed hard.

"Why, Ms. Hill," he drawled, his eyes sparkling, "is that a proposal?"

"I already told you, I'm not interested in getting married," she said quickly, a flood of embarrassment washing crimson up her neck. How could she have done anything so rash? This entire evening had been an exhibition in throwing away her self-control. What was happening to her?

"But *I* should be ready to walk down the aisle again?" He laughed without a trace of mirth, and she realized that the two women in his life who should have loved him, his mother and his wife, had hurt him so badly, he might never trust another woman again.

"You know, Chandra," he was saying, still discussing marriage, "there's a saying that what's good for the gander is good for the goose. Or something like that." He picked a stick from her hair, and she smoothed a wrinkle from his shirt, wondering what marriage to him would be like. Would there be long days of comfortable familiarity or passionate nights of lovemaking and unexplored emotions?

"What about you?" he asked suddenly, and her insides turned to jelly. "I bared my soul. Tell me about your ex-husband."

Chandra wanted to tell him everything, but found the words difficult. "He was a doctor," she finally said, and Dallas froze, his face instantly serious.

"Was he the reason you dropped out of medical school?"

"I, uh, really didn't drop out," she said, then at his look of amazement, shook her head. "I can't talk about it, but Doug was and is a major reason that I decided to give up my practice."

Dallas's hand covered hers. "Whatever happened," he said gently, and Chandra felt tears prick her eyes, "it was a mistake. Whatever he did, it was wrong."

"You don't know—"

"No, but my guess is that you're a helluva doctor."

She blushed, and blinked back tears. "Come on, O'Rourke," she said, eyeing the darkening sky and sensing that they'd said enough for one evening. Someday she'd tell him everything, but not tonight. She didn't want to ruin this night with more bitter memories. "We'd better go while it's still light."

They rode back to her house in relative silence. The forest seemed to close around them, and dusk sent long, purple shadows through the woods. Even Sam seemed to pick up on the mood, and he followed behind Brandy, keeping to the trail, never bounding off into the undergrowth.

By the time they returned to the house, the first stars winked in the sky. The temperature had dropped several degrees with the coming night. Together, Chandra and Dallas took care of the horses, removing the saddles, blankets and bridles, and brushing the animals down. Dallas forked hay into the manger while Chandra filled the water trough and measured out oats.

Max, grinding his ration of grain, nuzzled her chest. "Oh, you think you should get some special favors, do you?" she asked, chuckling, then found apples for each eager set of lips.

Once the horses were cared for, Dallas and Chandra walked across the yard to the house. The moon had risen and offered a silvery light to the shadowed hills.

Chandra asked Dallas in for coffee, and it felt natural to sit with him at the table, cradling cups, watching the steam rise. He was silent, brooding about something, and yet the silence was companionable. An unspoken question lingered between them—just how far would this relationship take them? Was this to be only a one-night stand? An affair? Or a lifetime together?

The coffee was nearly gone when Dallas scraped his chair back. "So where do we go from here?" he asked, his gaze roving through the small rooms and up the stairs to the loft, where her bed was visible through the slats of the railing.

"Do we have to make a plan?" She held her empty cup in a death grip and stared into the stain on the bottom of the earthenware as if she could read the future from the dregs of her coffee. But she knew that they couldn't just let things lie as they were.

Yet, they hardly knew each other. One afternoon of making love hardly seemed enough of a basis to plan a future together.

"You told me once that you were in the market for a husband."

"That was a joke—"

"Kind of a joke," he said, his gaze holding hers. "You were half-serious."

The air seemed to grow cooler yet. Chandra rubbed her arms. The conversation was making turns she hadn't expected, turns she wasn't certain she could deal with. But she had to be honest with him. "Well...actually I'm in the market for a father for J.D. If I adopt him, and I intend to, I'll need a father figure for him, or so my attorney insists. So being a husband would probably be secondary," she admitted, hating the awful truth, but knowing it had to be said.

"That could get messy." He glanced out the window to the night beyond the glass before returning his gaze to her. "J.D.'s dad—whomever you choose—might not like me hanging around."

So he wasn't interested. Of course not. What had she expected? she silently chided herself. A proposal? "I suppose not." She tried to hide the disappointment in her voice and refused to back down. She gambled, wondering if she'd lost every last ounce of her sanity. "You told me that you wanted children. And J.D. does need a father—a father he can depend upon, a father to love him." She rotated the cup in her hands and, gathering all her courage, looked Dallas steadily in the eyes. "This could be an opportunity of a lifetime—for both of you."

"Are you propositioning me?" he asked, but there wasn't a glimmer of humor in his eyes.

Why not? she thought, her palms beginning to sweat. "I—I think that getting married for the sake of the baby wouldn't be such a bad idea," she said. "People marry for much worse reasons. And it—it wouldn't have to be forever. You said that if your wife's baby hadn't been yours, you still would have raised it as your own. Well, J.D. doesn't even have a biological father."

Dallas gazed at her face. "What that boy needs is two parents who love each other, two people who will provide a stable life for him."

"No baby is assured of that," she said boldly.

He rubbed his palms on his pants. He appeared more nervous than usual. "I'll be honest with you. I don't know if I can change, Chandra. I was sure that I'd never marry again, never have children. Hell, until today, I was convinced that I should avoid you."

"And now?" she asked breathlessly, her own hands sweaty around her empty cup.

"And now you've nearly convinced me to take the plunge. I'm on the verge of doing something we might regret for the rest of our lives." He held her gaze for what seemed a lifetime, staring at her as if measuring her. "This is absolute madness."

"I don't think so." Good God, was she actually saying this—trying to convince him to walk down the aisle with her? Why? Just for J.D., or did she feel a pang of guilt for making love with Dallas this afternoon? Or were there deeper reasons still, reasons she couldn't yet confront? She studied the handsome lines of his face and knew in an instant that she wasn't speaking from remorse. No, she liked Dr. O'Rourke and thought living with him wouldn't be unpleasant. He evoked emotions within her she didn't want to analyze, so she justified marrying him by telling herself it was all for the baby.

Dallas shoved his hands into his pockets, but he never stopped staring at her. "I don't know if it would work—hell, I'm half-certain it won't, but I'm willing to marry you—for the sake of the child, to help you win custody. Because I don't think that kid could find a better mother."

Time stood still. The clock by the front door was ticking loudly. Here was her chance. He was offering to marry her for J.D.'s sake. And hers. A thousand doubts, like dark moths, flitted through her mind. She ignored them.

Touched, she swallowed back the tears that formed in the corners of her eyes. "You—you don't have to be so noble."

He snorted, and the muscles of his shoulders bunched. "Noble? I've never done a noble thing in my life."

"But...this..." She shook her head, and he touched the tip of her chin, raising her face with one long, insistent finger.

"There's a benefit for me, too, you know."

She was afraid to ask, but a warning sensation swept through her, chilling her blood.

"I'll be making love to you every night, and that's worth something. In fact, it's worth a lot." He smiled then, softening the blow.

Nonetheless, all of her romantic fantasies turned to dust. He only wanted to sleep with her. Nothing more. And yet there were times when his gentleness nearly broke her heart.

"I just want you to understand," he said softly, "that I'm not going to accept anything in name only. I won't expect you to cook or clean or pamper me, but I'll want you in my bed. And I'll want to know the truth about your past and the baby."

That seemed more than fair—if a little cold. Gathering her courage, Chandra lifted her chin and met his gaze with hers. If he had the right to bargain, so, she reasoned, did she. "Fair enough," she agreed, her voice shaking. She couldn't believe she was discussing *marriage*, for crying out loud. She'd sworn off men and marriage, and here she was bargaining.

Not exactly the silken thread from which romantic dreams were woven. "But, if you marry me, I'll expect you to be faithful."

His lips moved slightly, and he cocked a dubious eyebrow. "A tough request, Ms. Hill," he mocked, "since I've been celibate for three years. It'll be damned hard to give up all that womanizing. Nonetheless, you've got yourself a deal.''

With that, he took her hand and drew her to her feet. Rounding the table, he yanked her toward him, deftly swept her into his arms and carried her up the stairs, sealing their bargain with a kiss.

Chapter Eleven

Marriage. The word rattled around in Chandra's brain until a headache threatened the back of her eyes. And to think how she'd practically gotten down on her knees and begged him to marry her! Good Lord, was she going out of her mind? The idea of marrying him for J.D.'s sake had seemed so right last night. Curled in his arms as she'd tried to sleep, she'd known she'd made the right decision. But this morning, with dawn streaking the hills and the soft call of a morning bird in the distance, she told herself she was crazy. She couldn't marry Dallas. Not even for J.D. Or could she?

She hadn't turned on any lights as she'd crept downstairs to stand at the window, steam from her coffee rolling across her face as she gazed at the sunrise, blazing magenta in the distance. Dallas was now awake and in the shower. A few minutes earlier, he'd leaned over the rail and playfully suggested that she might join him. She'd declined, telling him she had to feed the horses, but glancing up at him and catching a glimpse of his naked, well-muscled torso, corded shoulders, beard-darkened chin and blue eyes, she'd almost given in. "Your loss," he'd said with a flash of white teeth, and she'd believed him.

But she had needed time to sort through everything in her mind. Yes, she wanted the baby. Desperately. But to marry a man who wasn't in love with her? What kind of future would a loveless marriage bring? For herself? For J.D.? For Dallas?

Upstairs, the water was still running, but soon she'd have to face him again. And do what? Say last night was a big mistake? Surely he had misgivings—second thoughts?

She gulped her coffee and it burned the back of her throat. "Come on." She whistled quietly to Sam, then, snagging her denim jacket from a peg by the door, set off across the yard. Her boots crunched in the gravel and made footprints on the frost. The air was clear with the sharp bite of autumn. A few dry leaves blew from the trees and danced across the drive.

She shoved open the barn door, and Max nickered eagerly. "Hungry?" she asked, snapping on the lights as the smell of horses, dung, leather and dry hay greeted her. "Stupid question, eh? When are you *not* famished?"

Max snorted. The horses were anxious, pawing or snorting, liquid brown eyes trained on her. "Breakfast's coming," she promised as Brandy shoved her velvet-soft muzzle over the stall. Cayenne eyed Chandra as well, and the other horses nickered softly. "Yeah, you guys all know I got myself into a lot of trouble yesterday, don't you?"

She climbed the loft and kicked down a couple of bales, only to hear the barn door open. "Chandra?" Dallas asked, and the horses swung their attention toward the noise.

"Up here." She hopped down and pulled out her knife, slashing the twine as Dallas grabbed a pitchfork and began scooping hay into the manger.

"I thought maybe you'd run out on me," he said, his eyes dark in the barn. "I figured you might have come down with a case of cold feet."

No reason to lie. "Second thoughts."

Dallas threw another forkful into Max's manger, and his shoulders moved effortlessly beneath his shirt. Chandra's throat went dry at the thought of touching his arms and running her fingers along the ridge of his spine.

"You don't have to go through with it, you know."

"I just don't want to make a mistake." She found the grain barrel, scooped up oats with an old coffee can and began pouring the grain along the trough.

"It's your decision, Chandra," he said slowly.

"Doubts, Doctor?" she accused as she patted Cayenne's head. The sorrel gelding tossed his mane and dug his nose into the grain.

Dallas lifted a shoulder. "It's one thing to be spontaneous, but I'm not sure we really thought this out last night." As Chandra walked past him toward the grain barrel again, he touched her lightly on the shoulder, forcing her to meet his gaze. "Believe it or not, I think we can make this work, but it is a little premature. So let's take things a little slower—one step at a time. Then if either party changes his or her mind, no big deal. We'll call the whole thing off."

Relief surged through her, and it must have been evident in her face, because he laughed.

"You know, Ms. Hill, this was your idea. I'd be satisfied with a hot and heavy affair."

Her cheeks burned hotly. "But that wouldn't help J.D."

A hint of a darker emotion flickered in his eyes, and his mouth tightened slightly. He dropped his hand and started shoving the rest of the hay into the manger. As he hung the pitchfork on the wall, he spotted a mousetrap, tripped, without a victim. "You need a cat," he observed.

"You have one?"

He shook his head. "Animals complicate life."

"So how're you going to deal with a wife and child?"

"And a dog and a small herd of horses," he added, re-setting the trap and placing a piece of grain on the trip. "That's the hundred-thousand-dollar question, isn't it? Too bad I don't have any answer. What about you, Ms. Hill, how're you going to deal with a husband and a child?"

"The child will be easy," she predicted, his good mood infectious. She couldn't help teasing him a little. "But that husband—he's gonna be trouble. I can feel it in my bones."

His grin widened slowly. "You'd better believe it." Quick as a cat, he grabbed her and yanked her, squealing and laughing, into his arms. "Somehow, I think you'll find a way," he whispered, just before his lips crashed down on hers in a kiss that melted her knees.

When he finally lifted his head, he stared long into her eyes. "Yes," he said, as if answering some questions in his own mind, "this is going to be interesting. Very interesting." He glanced at his watch and groaned. "We'd better get moving. I've got to be at the hospital by eight. And you've got a wedding to plan."

Chandra didn't know whether to laugh or cry.

"You're getting married?" Roy Arnette's jaw dropped open. "What is this, some kind of joke?" Seated behind his desk, he'd been surprised by her visit, and was even more surprised when she'd told him her intentions.

"No joke, Roy," she assured him, declining comment on the fact that Dallas, only three hours earlier, had given her an out, should she want one.

"Hell, Chandra, you *can't* just up and marry someone for that kid."

"Isn't that what you told me to do?"

"But I was *kidding!*" Sitting on his side of his desk, he yanked on his string tie. "You told me you weren't dating anyone."

"I wasn't."

"And what—the bridegroom fairy came in, waved a magic wand and, poof, instant husband and father?" Frowning, he pushed an intercom button and ordered coffee from his secretary. "Well, tell me, who's the lucky guy?"

"Dallas O'Rourke."

"*Doctor* Dallas O'Rourke? You can't be serious! After what happened to you with Doug—he was a doctor, remember? That was part of the problem—so now you're planning to marry an emergency-room physician? Come on!"

"I'm serious," she insisted. "Look, don't blame yourself. This is my decision."

"What do you know about the guy?" he asked, shaking his head. "What?"

A soft tap at the door announced the secretary's arrival. With a smile to Chandra, she placed a tray laden with coffee cups, a plastic carafe, a small basket of doughnuts and a folded newspaper on his desk. "Thanks, Betty," Roy said as the tall woman poured them each a cup of coffee.

Roy offered her a doughnut, but Chandra shook her head and the attorney, too, left the pastries untouched. He took a long sip from his cup and said, "All right, let's start over When are you getting married?"

"We haven't discussed it yet," she admitted. "In fact, we haven't exactly ironed out many details. I'm meeting him tonight at the hospital, and he's taking me over to the Newells'."

"The sheriff? You're going to see the sheriff?"

"J.D. is being released today. The Newells have been granted temporary custody as foster parents." Chandra reached for her cup and caught a glimpse of the folded newspaper. Her heart did a somersault. "Oh, no," she said, snatching up the paper and snapping it open. On the front page in big bold letters the headline read, MYSTERY BABY FOUND IN BARN, and near the article were two pictures, one of the barn, the other of her and Dallas, his arm around her shoulder, his mouth pressed close to her ear.

She quickly read the article, which was more informative than the one single-column report that had appeared the day after the baby was found. She and Dallas were identified, in the caption under the picture, and though nothing was blatantly stated, there was an insinuation that she and he, the woman who had discovered the baby and the physician who had first examined him, were romantically involved. There was a plea, within the text, for the real parents of the child to come forward and claim him.

Her heart wrenched painfully. "No," she whispered to herself. "Not now!"

"What? Not now what?"

She handed the paper to Roy, and he scowled as he skimmed the article. "Well, this isn't too bad. Fillmore isn't known to be overly kind with his pen, so you'd better consider yourself lucky. At least it isn't a hatchet job, and since you and Dallas are planning to tie the knot, I don't see that there's any real harm done."

Perhaps not, but Chandra felt as if someone had just placed a curse on her. That was crazy, of course. She wasn't even the kind of woman who believed in curses or voodoo or omens. And yet, her skin crawled as she stared down at the photo of her and Dallas huddled together, consoling each other . . . and falling in love.

"Bastard!" Dallas slammed the newspaper into the trash basket in the staff lounge, causing more than a few heads to turn and gaze speculatively in his direction. He didn't really give a damn. He didn't blame Fillmore for the article; the baby was news. Big news. But the picture of Chandra and him was hardly necessary.

He'd only been at the hospital half an hour and already he'd noticed a few sidelong glances cast his way, a couple of smirks hidden not quite quickly enough. It had started with

Ed Prescott. As Dallas had locked the door of his truck in the parking lot, Prescott had wheeled his red Porche into his reserved spot.

"Well, O'Rourke, you old dog," he'd said as he climbed out of the sporty little car and caught up with Dallas's impatient strides. "You made the front page."

"What?" Dallas hadn't seen the paper yet as the weekly *Banner* was usually delivered by mail.

"Haven't you seen it?" Laughter had danced in Prescott's keen eyes. "Here, take my copy!" He'd slapped the newspaper into Dallas's hands and walked briskly toward the building. Prescott's chortling laughter had trailed back to Dallas as he'd opened the folded pages and found his life unraveled in, of all places, the *Banner*.

"Stupid idiot son-of-a-bitch," he growled now, wondering if he were leveling the oath at Prescott or himself. And just wait until Fillmore got wind of the fact that he and Chandra were getting married and hoping to adopt J.D. He'd never hear the end of it!

At the elevator, he waited impatiently, pushing the button several times and opening and closing his fists to relieve some tension. "Come on, come on," he muttered as the elevator stopped and three young nurses emerged.

They saw him, and nearly as one, tried to smother grins as they mouthed, "Good morning, Doctor."

It was all he could do to be civil. He climbed in the car and pushed the button for the fourth floor. He'd check his patients in CICU and ICU, then retreat to the emergency room, where he was scheduled for the day. If everything was under control, he'd head up to pediatrics before J.D. was to be released. Then he'd go to his office, return some calls and check his mail. His investigator friend from Denver had called and said a package should arrive—the information about Chandra. Good Lord, what had possessed him to order an investigation?

He wasn't looking forward to scanning the P.I.'s report, and yet, he may as well. After all, he planned to marry the woman; it wouldn't hurt to know what he was in for.

Crossing his arms over his chest, he watched the numbers of the floors light up. Chandra was so enraptured with little J.D., Dallas was concerned for her. Even if he and she were married, there were no guarantees that they would be chosen as the adoptive parents. What then? Dissolve the marriage? Strike two? "Hell, O'Rourke, you've really got yourself in a mess this time!"

The elevator thudded to a halt and the doors opened. Jane Winthrop, a nurse who usually worked in admitting, was waiting for the car. Pushing a medicine cart, she nearly ran into him. "Oh, Doctor," she said with a smile. "Excuse me."

Was there a special gleam in her eye? Of course not. He was just being paranoid. "No problem," he replied, skirting the cart with the tiny cups of pills arranged neatly on the shiny metal surface.

"I saw your picture in the paper today," she said, and he jerked his head up to meet her eyes, but found no malice in her gaze. "I sure hope that Chandra Hill gets to adopt that baby. He belongs with her, you know. That's why he was in that barn. It's God's will."

The doors closed, and Nurse Winthrop, her cart and her wisdom disappeared.

Rubbing the tension building in his neck, Dallas turned toward ICU and knew that it was going to be a long day. He decided to go directly to his office and only stopped by his receptionist's desk to collect his mail.

There it was, along with the letters, advertisements and magazines—a package with a Denver postmark. His heart stopped for just a second, and he felt guilty as hell, but he took the stack of mail and a fresh cup of coffee into his office. He set the coffee on the ink blotter and dropped the correspondence and bills onto the desk, then ripped his letter opener through the package from Denver.

He couldn't believe he was so anxious that his stomach had begun to knot. There was a computer report, a note from Jay and a few copies of newspaper clippings, mainly of a trial in Tennessee, a malpractice suit brought by the parents of Gordy Shore, a boy who had died while in Chandra's care.

Dallas let his coffee grow cold as he continued to read, and he learned more than he wanted to know about his future wife.

"A shoot down the south fork, a trail ride over Phantom Ridge and a day hike along the west bank of the river," Rick said, eyeing his schedule. He tapped his finger on the last expedition. "Chandra, you can handle the day hike. Randy's got the trail ride, and Jake will take our friends from Boston down the river. All right with you?"

"Fine," she agreed as Jake and Randy began packing gear for their expeditions.

"Good, then I'll hold down the fort here."

Chandra eyed the younger men. Jake was tall and strapping with wheat-blond hair, a tan and blue eyes that cut a person right to the quick. Randy was more laid-back, with a moustache, day's growth of beard and red-brown hair a little on the shaggy side. She turned to see Rick staring at her, his expression uncharacteristically serious. These men, who often joked with her, were the only family Chandra had in Ranger.

"Saw your picture in the paper," Randy said as he tucked trail mix and a couple of candy bars into a backpack. The horses were stabled out of town, so he would meet his clients, drive to the stables and start the ride from that point.

"I hope you're not talkin' 'bout that damned *Banner*," Rick growled, frowning.

"'Fraid so. Chandra's big news around this town," Randy teased. "You and the doctor looked pretty chummy to me."

"We are," she said with a shrug.

"And here I thought you'd always had the hots for me, but were just too shy to make the first move."

"If only I'd known," she quipped. These men could tease her and needle her because she knew they cared. Once she'd proved herself on the river, they'd both taken on the roles of brothers.

"I just hope O'Rourke knows what a prize he's found," Jake said forcefully. Jake was always more serious than Randy.

"Dallas O'Rourke?" Rick asked. Still behind the desk, he absently counted out the cash, the "seed money" as he called it, that he kept in the safe at night before replenishing the till each morning.

"The one and only."

"How'd you land that one?" Rick asked.

"Must have been that little sashay you took down Grizzly Loop," Randy teased.

"Get a life, Randy," Chandra said, refusing to be baited.

"And keep that rag that some people consider a newspaper out of my shop," Rick ordered. "I'd just as soon wring Bob Fillmore's neck as say hi."

Chandra spent the next hour stocking the shelves with supplies, then met her group of hikers and drove them to the foothills. They spent most of the day walking the trails that crisscrossed Rattlesnake Canyon. At noon, dusty and hot, they paused to eat at the river, then headed downstream until they'd circled back to the car. Clouds were beginning to form over the hills, and the temperature descended as she dropped her tired party off at the offices of Wild West.

For the next hour, she cleaned up and helped Rick close the shop before driving through town and along the road that led to the hospital. At five-fifteen, she dashed up the stairs to the pediatrics wing and discovered Leslie Nelson at the desk. "Is he still here?" she asked without preamble, but she knew from Leslie's sorry expression that J.D. had already been released. Fear, cold as a night wind, touched her soul. What if things didn't go as planned? What if she never saw J.D. again?

Leslie sighed unhappily. "The caseworker—what's her name—Miss Sedgewick ... She was here earlier with Sheriff Newell, and the baby was placed under his care. You know Lenore, don't you?" Chandra shook her head, and Leslie waved aside her doubts. "Well, she's just about the best person J.D. could be placed with. She *adores* kids, and since hers left home, she's been taking in strays, so to speak, kids with all sorts of problems—drugs, family breakups, abuse or runaways. She's one in a million."

"I guess I should be relieved," Chandra said. But she wasn't. She was used to finding J.D. here, and now things had changed. His little life was on its own path, out of her control....

"I think so, and I'm sure she'd let you visit J.D. as often as you want." Leslie leaned over the desk and motioned Chandra closer, as if to tell her a secret. "Just between you and me," she said confidentially, "it's a good thing he's been moved."

"Why?"

"The press! Ever since that story came out in the *Banner* this morning, the phone's been ringing off the hook. Newspaper reporters from as far away as Chicago and Seattle trying to get more information. We're routing all the calls to Dr. Trent's office—he's the chief administrator—and we're not to talk to anyone about the baby."

So the media circus had begun. Chandra's stomach turned over. "Is Dr. O'Rourke in?"

"He was in earlier—checked on a couple of patients, but I don't know his schedule."

"Thanks, Leslie." Chandra turned to leave as the phone at the nurses' station began ringing insistently. Walking on numb legs toward the wing that held the clinic and doctors' offices, Chandra hoped to find Dallas. She'd known the press would come sniffing around, of course, but she'd hoped the public wouldn't be interested.

Dallas wasn't in his office. The receptionist told her he'd be back within the half hour and that she could wait in the lounge. Chandra tried, but the chairs were too uncomfortable and her thoughts were whirling. What if the reporters started digging into her past? The headlines haunted her...

Local Doctor Accused Of Malpractice
By Young Patient's Parents

"My Boy Could Have Been Saved,"
Gordy Shore's Mother Testifies

Doctor Chandra Hill Pendleton Sued By Shores

The headlines had kept coming. Doug's practice had been mentioned, as well as hers, causing a deeper rift in their marriage. Then some of Doug's patients had requested that their files be sent to other cosmetic surgeons. "This'll all blow over," Doug had said, trying to console her, but he couldn't understand the pain and guilt she felt over losing a beautiful boy and suffering the hate of his parents.

No wonder she'd taken back her maiden name and left Tennessee with all its painful memories. Perhaps leaving Collier had looked like the coward's way out, but there had been nothing left for her in Tennessee: no medical practice, no friends, no husband and certainly no children. No, it had been better to make a clean break. And she was still a physician, though unlicensed in Colorado.

Face it, she silently advised herself as she flipped through a dog-eared women's magazine that didn't hold her interest. *You're a lousy judge of character. You married Doug and became friends with Willa and Ed Shore. They all turned on you.*

And now you're planning on marrying Dallas O'Rourke. Good Lord, Chandra, will you never learn?

Bored with waiting, she watched as the receptionist answered the phone and juggled appointments. When the woman's back was turned, Chandra slipped down the hall and pushed open a door with brass letters that spelled "Dallas O'Rourke, M.D." Fortunately the door was unlocked, and Chandra, feeling just a tingle of guilt, rationalized her behavior by telling herself that she was about to become Mrs. Dallas O'Rourke. She needed a little information on the man.

The room was cluttered. A suede-and-leather jacket had been tossed carelessly over the back of one chair, and a tie dangled from the handle of the window. His desk was piled high with papers, though there did seem to be a few distinct piles, as if there were some semblance of order to the paperwork. Medical journals and encyclopedias filled a bookcase and laminated certificates were mounted over the desk. The view from his window overlooked a parking lot, and the two chairs angled near the front of his desk appeared seldom used.

A stack of mail was opened and strewed over the papers on the desk. As she quickly skimmed the letters and bills, her own name leapt out at her: "INVESTIGATIVE REPORT ON CHANDRA HILL."

Chandra's insides froze and her heart turned to ice. Her throat worked, though she couldn't speak. Surely, she'd read the heading incorrectly! She skimmed the first page and felt sick. Dallas had been checking up on her? The tightness in her chest constricted a notch as she sifted through the pages, obviously already read by Dr. O'Rourke. "Why?" she whispered. Why would he ask her to marry him and then check up on her? Or maybe it was the other way around? She found the postmark on the envelope. No. He'd only received this damned report today.

Her hands shaking, she dropped into a chair and began reading about herself, starting with her date of birth and her parents, and later, as they came along, her sisters. Her history inched its way through the pages, a listing of her accomplishments in elementary and high school, as well as in college and medical school. Even names of her friends were listed and those of a few of the men she'd dated.

Nausea churned in her stomach. Her life reduced to eighteen pages of a computer printout, including copies of the newspaper articles about her, her credit history, her health and her marriage and divorce from Doug.

Her stay in Ranger was tagged on at the end, listing Rick as her boss. The first story in the *Banner* about J.D., which had been published just last week, was the final entry.

"Oh, God," she whispered, dropping her head into her hands. How could she ever face Dallas again? Mortified and furious, she clamped her jaw and bit down hard in order to get control of herself. She couldn't let him reduce her to the rubble she'd once been. Never again would she feel this way! She forced her pain to shift to anger. It wasn't hard. She was beyond furious. If and when she ever set eyes on Dallas again, she'd tear him limb from limb! Who did he think he was, sneaking around behind her back, digging up her life to file it neatly onto some private investigator's computer disk?

The door opened, and she twisted her head to find Dallas striding into the room. His eyes dropped to the report in her hands and he sucked in his breath. "What're you doing in my office?"

Chandra stood slowly, dropping the report and pushing herself upright. He was standing in the doorway, his shoulders nearly touching the frame, his face unreadable.

She didn't care how big or intimidating he was. Rage scorched her blood. How could he—this man she'd planned to marry—do this to her? Inching up her chin, she picked up the horrid pages and waved the report in the air. "And what are you doing checking up on me?"

"You're supposed to wait in the lounge."

"Stupid me! I thought being your fiancé gave me a few privileges."

"Not snooping in my office."

"But it's okay for you to snoop into my life, is that right?" She slapped the damned report onto his desk. "How *dare* you have me investigated like some criminal! Who do you think you are that you can open up my life and check me out? I thought—no, I hoped—you were above that sort of thing!"

A muscle in the corner of Dallas's jaw came to life, but there was no anger in his eyes. "What did you expect, Chandra?"

"Trust!" she shot back, and he winced.

"And I expected the truth, which you seemed to twist around to suit your advantage."

"I did not—"

"You came waltzing in here with a baby whom you claim you've never set eyes on before and a load of medical knowledge. And you ended up turning this hospital upside down—"

"I've done no such thing!"

Dallas snorted, his face a steely mask. "You read the headlines today in the *Banner*?"

"Yes, but—"

"You see the picture?"

"What, exactly, is your point?" she asked, leveling a glacial stare at him.

"I just wanted to know whom I was dealing with."

"Because you thought I might have stolen the baby, then, seeing he needed medical attention, brought him in here?"

"At first, yes, but—"

"Well, you're way off base, Doctor!"

"I know that now." Unbuttoning his lab coat, Dallas dragged one hand through his thick hair. "But I didn't—not in the beginning."

"And you check up on any person you've never met before?"

"Any person I think I might marry."

She stiffened. Marriage? Now? After this damned report? She didn't think so. "When you ordered that investigation, you couldn't have had the faintest idea we might discuss the remote idea of wedded bliss!" She shook her head, disbelieving that their relationship had come to this. She was trembling inside, her breathing erratic, and she went to the window to open it a crack and let in some fresh air. "You really are a bastard, O'Rourke," she said quietly.

A cold smile crept across his lips. "Coming from you, that's quite an indictment. Your résumé—" he motioned to the damning report "—is chock full of deadbeats. Especially your ex-husband."

She felt as if she'd been slapped. "A failing of mine, I guess. I just can't say no when a real jerk asks me to marry him!"

"*You* asked me, lady. Not the other way around." He flung the white jacket over an already crowded spoke of a brass hall tree before glancing at her again.

Chandra felt the color drain from her face. "You arrogant son of a—"

"Don't," he cut in. "Let's not sink to name-calling. *Bastard* and *jerk* were good enough. I got the message."

That was it. She'd had it! She grabbed her purse and started for the door. He reached for her arm, but she spun away from him.

"Chandra, wait!" Her hand was on the doorknob, and she, ignoring him, yanked hard.

With a curse, he slammed the door closed. "Don't go—"

She turned frigid eyes on him. "Don't you have some patients to see or, at the very least, some new person in your life that you can sic a private detective on?"

"There's only one new person in my life," he admitted.

"Meaning me?" she spat. "Well, scratch me off the list. I'm not into the humiliation game, okay? I don't hang out with people who dredge up my dirt." She sighed loudly, trying to rein in her galloping rage. With difficulty, she stared into his cobalt blue eyes—eyes that seemed to see into the darkest corners of her heart. "It's too bad, you know," she said shakily. "Maybe if you'd grown up with a little love, if someone had cared for you, you'd know how to care back, how to treat people, how to—" She stopped suddenly when she saw the raw pain in his eyes. She knew then that she'd hit her mark, that she'd wounded him as deeply as he'd hurt her.

Stonily, he stepped away from the door. "I don't think we have anything more to discuss," he said, his voice flat. He moved to the desk, snatched up the damaging report and held it out to her. "You can have this."

Why did she suddenly feel like a heel? She was in the right, damn it! She snatched the report from his hands, but felt the overwhelming need to apologize. She knew she had a sharp tongue, but she didn't usually try to cut someone she cared for so deeply. "Look, I'm sorry. That crack about your family—was...uncalled-for..."

"Don't worry about it." He sat down in his chair and picked up the telephone receiver, staring at her impatiently, waiting for her to leave.

Sighing, she wadded up the damned report and tossed it into a wastebasket near his desk. "Can't we start this afternoon over?" she said, her fury spent.

"Why?"

"Because there's more to us than what's contained in some investigator's printout."

He dropped the receiver. "Let's not delude ourselves, okay? What we've got is a baby—that's all. He's our one common bond. Unless you want to count sex."

Swallowing hard, she glanced through the window to the traffic moving steadily in and out of the parking lot. He was right, of course. Though she'd like to think that love was involved, it wasn't. Love, as far as Dallas O'Rourke was concerned, didn't exist. She'd have to settle for this man who didn't love her, so that she could become J.D.'s mother.

"Well, as long as we understand each other," she said, managing to keep her voice steady.

"You still want to marry me?" he asked, squinting at her, as if looking for flaws.

"I still need a father for J.D."

Dallas drummed his fingers on his desk and pulled his forehead into a frown of disgust. Chandra felt as if her life were on a balance, slowly wobbling, and she was unable to right it.

"I guess I shouldn't have checked up on you," he finally said. "But I thought, when you first brought J.D. to the emergency room, that you could have stolen him or that you were covering for the real mother—that you had a sister or cousin who was in trouble. Believe it or not, I just wanted to help, and I had to be sure that the story you were giving me wasn't a line."

"And now?"

He slid a glance to the wastebasket. "I think the report's filed in the appropriate slot. All I need to know now is that you're playing straight with me."

"I've never lied to you."

"Except about your practice."

"Well, now you know."

"Not everything, Chandra."

"I—I'll tell you about it," she said nervously, her hands beginning to sweat. "But not now. Trust me on this?"

His jaw slid to one side, and as he stood, he retrieved his leather jacket from the hall tree.

"For God's sake, Dallas, don't you trust anyone?" she asked, hating the silence that was radiating from him. She knew why he had trouble trusting people. God knew that she hadn't been completely honest with him herself, and yet she hoped that he would give her the benefit of the doubt.

He slid his arms into his leather jacket, adjusted the collar and looked at her. His features had lost some of their severity, but he didn't smile. "I'm trying," he admitted, "but it's not easy." He walked to the door and held it open for her. Then, as if to leave the argument behind them in the office, he asked, "Okay, it's confession time, how did you get past the sergeant?"

"The what?"

"Dena—the receptionist. She takes her job seriously."

"I've worked in hospitals," Chandra explained. "And your door was unlocked."

"My mistake," he said, smiling crookedly. "Well, one of my mistakes. I seem to be making more than my share lately." He reached forward and took her hand in his. "Come on," he said with a slow smile. "I think there's someone waiting to see you."

"J.D.?" Her heart soared.

"Mmm." He tugged on her hand and led her out of the office before locking the door. "High crime element in the neighborhood," he explained with a glimmer in his eyes. "You never know who you'll catch prowling around."

"Very funny."

"I thought so." He guided her through the corridors to an exterior exit. "Oh, by the way, I thought we'd get dinner first, then visit your friend. But we have one stop first."

"A stop?"

"City Hall. I think we'd better stop by and apply for a marriage license. Unless you're chickening out."

"Me? Chicken out?" she asked, her heart racing. This was it. Her out. If she only dared take it. She licked her lips nervously as she stared into his incredible blue eyes. "No way."

Chapter Twelve

Lenore Newell couldn't have been more delighted with company, or so it seemed to Chandra. She insisted Chandra drink a glass of iced tea while she held the baby. Lenore prattled on and on about the children she'd cared for over the years. The living room of the Newell home, a quaint two-storied farmhouse flanked by a wide front porch, was filled with pictures of children, dozens of them, some who had only stayed a few weeks, others who had lived with the Newells for years.

Over the fireplace, a family portrait, showing Lenore and Frank some twenty years younger and surrounded by four beaming-faced boys, gave testament to the Newells' strong family ties and the house itself seemed cozy and warm.

The furniture in the living room was upholstered in well-worn floral prints that matched a circular rug. Crocheted cloths covered the end tables, and a cuckoo clock near the chimney chirped the hours.

"He's just as sweet as he can be," Lenore said, touching J.D.'s cheek with her finger. The baby, sleeping in Chandra's arms, yawned, then snuggled closer. "I just can't imagine anyone in her right mind giving him up." She glanced over at Dallas, who was standing near an upright piano littered with more photographs of children and teenagers. "Frank says no one's come in to claim him yet. Can you believe that?"

"Hard to," Dallas drawled.

Lenore sighed. "Well, the child's better off with a family who loves him!" She sat in a chair next to the rocker in which Chandra was holding the baby. "Are you thinking of trying to adopt him?"

The question didn't surprise Chandra. Surely Lenore had guessed how close she felt to the baby. "I hope to."

"Good! This child needs a mother." She turned her gaze back to Dallas, and added with a crafty wink, "He could use a father, as well, you know."

"We're already a couple of steps ahead of you, Lenore," Dallas confided, slouching against the upright.

"Are you?" She arched her eyebrows in anticipation of a little small-town gossip. Dallas didn't give her any more details, but Chandra, sending him a murderous look, decided Lenore had the right to know everything.

"Dallas and I plan to be married."

Lenore's mouth rounded, and she couldn't hide the surprise and ultimate delight in her eyes. "Married!" She turned to Dallas for confirmation, but received only a noncommittal shrug. "Don't tell me Dr. Ice is melting."

"Very funny, Lenore," Dallas observed with a dry smile as the screen door squeaked on rusted hinges and Frank Newell, tall and whip-lean, strode into the foyer.

"In here—we've got company," his wife sang out. "There's beer and iced tea in the fridge."

Frank paused under the arch that separated the living room from the foyer. "Well, Doctor," he said with a widespread grin at the sight of Dallas. He motioned to the glass of iced tea in Dallas's hand. "Can't I buy you anything stronger?"

"This'll do."

"You'll never guess what!" Lenore said, bustling to her feet and heading past her husband toward the kitchen. Her footsteps retreated, but her voice still carried. "Dallas and Chandra are going to get married and adopt the baby! How is that for perfect?"

"Is that so?" Frank asked, frowning and looking suddenly tired.

"That's the plan."

"For you and about six hundred other couples."

"*What?*" Lenore asked. Carrying a tray laden with two bottles of beer, a pitcher of tea, pretzels and cookies, she bustled back to the living room.

Chandra felt icicles form in her heart. "Others?"

"The phones down at the station have been ringing off the hook. Seems the story in the *Banner* got picked up by the news services and now we've got TV and newspaper reporters calling in every damn minute, along with attorneys and people wanting to adopt as faraway as San Francisco. From what I hear, the same thing's going on at Riverbend."

The bottom dropped out of Chandra's world. She felt Dallas's gaze on her as she involuntarily held J.D. more tightly. She couldn't give him up. Wouldn't. Desperation wrenched her heart, and it was all she could do to sit and rock instead of scooping the baby into her arms and fleeing. A lump filled her throat, and she sent up a silent prayer that she be given the privilege of raising this precious child.

Frank twisted open a bottle of beer. "I'm surprised the press hasn't camped out in the front yard, but I suppose it's only a matter of time." He took a long swallow and sighed, his kind eyes resting on Chandra. "You won't be out of this, you know. Bob Fillmore and the *Banner* were just the tip of the iceberg. For the next few weeks, Miss Hill, I'm afraid you'll be hounded.''

''There are laws about trespassing,'' she said.

''And we'll uphold them. But your phone will be ringing non-stop. They've already named this guy, you know.'' He nodded toward the baby. ''Some reporter in Denver got wind of the fact that several couples are trying to bid for him. Our Baby John Doe is now the Million Dollar Baby.''

Chandra's heart turned to stone, and Lenore protested, ''He can't be raffled off like some prize quilt at a county fair!''

''I know. It's just a gimmick. But I don't think this is going to blow over.'' Frank offered Dallas a beer, but the doctor declined. ''And I suppose you'll get your share of the press as well, O'Rourke. Yep—'' he shook his head slowly before draining half his bottle ''—we're all in for a lot of fun.''

Frank Newell was right. By the time Chandra arrived home that night, her answering-machine light was blinking, and the tape was filled with the names and telephone numbers of local reporters as well as a call from a couple in Salt Lake City. Chandra suspected this couple was only the first. Soon there would be a lot of couples desperately calling in hopes of adopting J.D.

''Fat chance,'' she muttered. The only people she telephoned were her parents. They deserved to hear what was going on in her life from her own lips.

Her mother answered and shouted for Chandra's father to pick up the bedroom extension. ''I can understand you wanting the baby,'' her mother rambled on. ''God knows you've wanted a child forever, but what about this doctor fellow? How can you be sure that marrying him won't be a mistake? Oh, well, I don't want to discourage you, honey, it's just that I don't want to see you hurt again.''

"I won't be, Mom," Chandra said, winding the telephone cord around her wrist and leaning against the kitchen counter.

"Of course she won't, Jill," Chandra's father cut in. "Chandra knows what she's doing. I'm behind you one hundred percent, girl."

"Well...well...well, so am I," her mother stuttered. "I just think you can take this slow, you know, make sure. You've got the rest of your life—"

"Not if she wants to adopt that baby—"

"Do whatever you think is best," Jill said, sounding irritated with her husband. "And know you've got our blessing. If you tell us when the wedding's scheduled, we'll be there!"

"With bells on," Chandra's father added.

"That I don't know," Chandra replied. They talked a little longer, about everything and nothing, her father asking about her job, her mother sneaking in questions about Dallas. Finally, with both parents in agreement at last that their daughter was old enough to make her own decisions, they hung up and Chandra turned on the answering machine. Whistling to Sam, she walked outside to the small garden, where a few tomatoes still ripened on the vine and the golden tassels on the corn stirred in the breeze. On the other side of the garden was the orchard where pears and apples littered the ground, beyond which were the forested hills. This small ranch would be a perfect place to raise a child, she thought, her heart tearing at the prospect of losing J.D.

And what about Dallas? What would be the point of marrying him when they had no child to hold them together? *You could have other children, Dallas's children.* If he were willing. And there weren't any guarantees that they would be able to conceive. All the advertisements seeking adoptable children were proof enough of the infertility rate. The thought of carrying Dallas's child nearly brought tears to her eyes. For years, she'd given up on the dream of having her own children, and now, with Dallas, it was possible, and what a wonderful baby they could make together. Her throat was suddenly clogged with unshed tears. Dallas's baby! Oh, God, how perfect! Absently, she rubbed her abdomen. A brother or sister for J.D....

She pulled a weed from the garden and tossed it over the fence. Would she be willing to marry Dallas without the prospect of a child? Without J.D.? She cared for him, perhaps even loved him, but was it enough? She felt confused and frustrated and wanted to do something, *anything* to ensure that the baby would be hers. Sitting around and waiting was killing her. *Calm down,* she told herself. She felt the breath of night as the sun sank below the horizon. Would Dallas ever want her to be a part of his life without the baby?

"Oh, God, what a mess," she said with a sigh as she climbed onto the split-rail fence separating garden from orchard. She sat quietly, watching the sky darken in shades of rose and purple. An owl, hunting early this evening, landed in the gnarled branches of the apple tree.

Then the tranquillity was shattered by the intrusion of headlights flashing brightly on the side of the barn.

Another reporter?

She squared her shoulders and squinted against the coming darkness before she recognized Dallas's rig. Relief swelled through her. Maybe he had good news. Or bad. Her pulse thundered, and she waited until he climbed from the cab of his truck before balancing on the lower rails, waving her hands and calling to him. Sam was already bounding through the pumpkin vines and through the yard, yipping excitedly. Even the old dog had allowed Dallas into his heart.

Dallas paused to scratch Sam's ears, then glanced up, catching Chandra's gaze. His face was grim, his expression sober, and Chandra's heart dropped to her knees. Something was wrong. Horribly wrong! J.D.! She vaulted over the fence and told her racing pulse to slow. Maybe J.D. was fine, but she couldn't quiet the screams of desperation that tore through her heart.

"What is it?" she asked, forcing her voice to stay calm. She couldn't lose control. "Something's wrong. Is it J.D.?"

"The baby's fine," he assured her, but drew her into the warm circle of his arms and held her close to calm her. His breath fanned her hair and she felt the tension in his muscles.

"But there's trouble," she guessed as they stood in the rows of corn, the thick leaves rustling in the breeze.

"There could be." He took her hand and pulled her gently in the direction of the orchard, where they sat on the fence rails and stared across the valley. "My beeper went off as I was heading back here. Dr. Trent, chief of administration, wanted me to stop back by the hospital."

"And?"

"He showed me the first of what appears to be an onslaught of gifts, cards and letters for Baby Doe. One corner of his office was filled, and that's just the start. The hospital fax machine has been working overtime with pleas from barren couples from Colorado, Utah, Arizona and California who want to adopt the baby. Lawyers are calling or showing up in person, and the switchboard has been jammed, which is causing all sorts of problems for the hospital."

Her stomach somersaulted.

"Trent's not too happy about this, to say the least, and he called me in because of the article about you and me. Seems it's already gotten around the hospital that you and I are an item. And I didn't deny it. I told Trent we were getting married and hope to adopt the baby."

Chandra's heart was beating like a drum. "What did he say?"

"'Good luck,' and I quote," Dallas replied, holding one of her hands in both of his. "Trent showed me some of the requests for adoption. You wouldn't believe it. Frank was right. Some people are so desperate that they're offering gifts to the hospital, and we're not just talking peanuts. One physician and his wife from South Dakota are willing to buy some very expensive equipment for the pediatric wing."

"But that's bribery—"

"Another couple—both lawyers—offered free legal services to the hospital."

"I can't believe it."

He slung an arm over her shoulder, and his expression had become sober, his eyes dark with emotion. "I think it's time we thought about this long and hard. There's a good chance that the baby will be adopted by someone we don't know, someone who lives thousands of miles away from here."

So this was it—he was breaking up with her. And they'd lost the baby. Chandra wanted to crumble into a million pieces, but she wouldn't give up without a fight.

"I don't believe all this," she argued heatedly. "I can't believe that the state or the hospital would...would stoop to blackmail!"

"It's not the hospital's decision, anyway. And a good thing. Trent always has his eyes on possible endowments. But his hands are tied. He and the hospital lawyers are just trying to figure out what to do with all the gifts that are coming in—the pediatric wing is already filled with stuffed animals."

"So we still have a chance," Chandra said, unable to calm the fear that rushed through her blood.

"If you're still willing to toss our hat into the ring."

"Absolutely!"

His lips twitched and a glint of admiration twinkled in his eyes. "I had a feeling you wouldn't back down."

"No way. We haven't lost yet."

"Well, then, I don't think we should wait. Forget the marriage license and waiting period. I think we should fly to Las Vegas tonight. The sooner we're married, the sooner we'll be able to fight this as a couple."

"You're serious?" she whispered, touched. She wanted to throw her arms around him and kiss him over and over again.

Dallas reached into his pocket and withdrew two airline tickets. His eyes never left her face. "Well, Ms. Hill, this is it. Do or die. Are we going through with this?"

Her throat closed for a second. Marriage. Just like that. A quick elopement to the tower of glitz in Nevada. So much for moonlight and roses, candlelight and wine. Romance didn't have any part of this transaction . . . well, at least not much. But she couldn't deny the feelings of love that were sprouting in her breast, nor could she voice them. She managed a smile. "Where would we live? What would we do—"

"We can live here—or you can move into my condo."

"No, here," she said, her mind spinning with plans for the future. "The cabin's big enough, and I need to be near the horses, and J.D. would love to live out here in the country—" She gathered in her breath and stopped. "But what do you want?"

He hesitated for a minute and drew his gaze away. "I just want to make you happy," he said, and Chandra could hardly believe her ears. This man who had told her all they had in common was the baby and sex?

"You don't have to pretend to fall in love with me," she said, and watched his eyes cloud. She rushed on. "We both know that this is only for the baby."

"And what happens if we lose him?" Dallas asked.

She sighed and her heart seemed to break into a thousand pieces. "That can't happen."

"What if it does?"

Then I'll set you free. Oh, Lord, would she be able to? Or was she falling hopelessly in love with a man who couldn't learn to give love in return? "You won't have to be obligated to me, Dallas. I'll sign whatever prenuptial agreement your lawyers come up with."

"I think it's a little late for prenuptials—that is, if you still want to get married. Well?" He stared at her so intensely that her breath was lost somewhere in her throat. "What do you say?"

"I'd say we'd better get a move on if we're going to catch our flight." She hopped lithely off the fence, determined to ignore the omnipresent doubts.

Together, they walked through the garden and into the house, where she threw her one good dress and a few essentials into a small bag. Then, making sure that her horses and Sam were fed, she climbed into Dallas's truck, and they headed to Denver where they planned to take a ten o'clock flight to Las Vegas. The way Dallas explained it, they'd be married sometime after midnight, stop long enough to drink a bottle of champagne over an extremely late dinner, then catch an early-morning flight back to Denver.

They'd lose a night's sleep, but not much more as they would go to their respective jobs as Dr. and Mrs. Dallas O'Rourke tomorrow morning. Just like that. Quick and simple. She wondered what she'd tell her parents, who expected to be invited to the wedding, and her sisters, who had both shied away from marriage. Then, of course, how was she going to handle her new role as Dallas's wife? Life was suddenly becoming complicated.

As Dallas drove through the night-shrouded mountains toward Denver, she glanced at him. His profile was strong and handsome, and his eyebrows were pulled low over his eyes as he squinted against the glare of oncoming headlights.

As far as husbands went, she knew, Dallas would be better than most. Good-looking, rugged, definitely male, passionate and, for all intents and purposes, honest. And as far as their lovemaking was concerned, even now she felt goose bumps. Maybe in time he would learn to love her. They could learn together.

But she didn't kid herself. He wouldn't be easy to live with, and he did brood. His temper was as volatile as hers and as many times as she longed to make love to him, she'd just as soon strangle him.

Well, if nothing else, she decided, seeing the lights of Denver glow ethereally against the night black sky, marriage to him would never be dull.

As far as romance went, the ceremony left a lot to be desired. The minister was red eyed and drowsy, and his breath was laced liberally with liquor. He wore a clerical collar, black jacket and slippers.

His little wife, a mere slip of a woman, smiled through her yawns, and his sister, whose floral dress stretched at the seams, played piano.

Chandra, dressed in a simple pink dress, held Dallas's hand as the minister went through the ritual. Dallas seemed amused by the scene. Wearing black slacks and a white shirt, he was dressed more like a patron of the neon-lit casinos than a bridegroom.

No rings were exchanged, but upon the orders of the minister, Dallas swept Chandra into his arms and kissed her long and hard in the little chapel on the outskirts of Las Vegas.

"It doesn't seem real," Chandra observed as they walked back to the rented car, dodging traffic, that rushed by in the early-morning hours.

"We've got a signed certificate. It's legal.'

"But—"

He snorted as he opened the door of the white sedan for her. "The last time I got married, we had a bona fide church, preacher, six attendants, a three-tiered cake and all the trimmings. It didn't make for any guarantees.''

Sighing, she scooted into the interior of the Plymouth. Her first wedding had been complete with a long, white, beaded gown, bridesmaids in lavender silk and ushers in matching tuxedos. A huge reception with flowing champagne, an incredible ice sculpture and hors d'oeuvres hadn't created a perfect marriage. Far from it. Dallas was right. And yet, as she caught a glimpse of her ringless left hand, she wondered if she'd made the biggest mistake of her life.

"My folks will kill me," she said, thinking of the calls she would have to make, the questions that would be hurled at her, the explanations she'd have to repeat over and over again.

"Mine will be relieved." He started the engine and edged the Plymouth into traffic, toward the hotel where they'd registered earlier.

"Will they?"

His grin turned cynical. "Oh, sure. My mother won't have to feel guilty about not paying me enough attention, and my father will probably think now he'll finally get that grandson he thinks he's owed. I'm the last of his line of O'Rourkes."

"He'll get that grandson," she said firmly, eyeing the glitter that was Las Vegas. People spilled out of casinos, music and conversation filled the air, and the night was as bright as day, lit by a trillion watts of neon.

Dallas stopped for a red light, and in the glow, his face turned hard, his lips compressed. "Sorry to shatter your dreams, Chandra, but J.D. won't count. At least not with my father."

"He damned well better," she said, her fists clenching in determination.

"You don't know Harrison O'Rourke. He's from the old school, and J.D. won't be blood kin."

"And therefore worthless?"

"As far as the family tree goes," Dallas said, frowning as the light changed and he stepped on the accelerator. "Nope, Harrison will expect an O'Rourke son—not a daughter, mind you." He slid her a glance and grinned cynically. "So don't go disappointing him."

"Wouldn't dream of it," she said, her temper flaring at Harrison O'Rourke's antiquated ideas. "I'll tell you one thing, if and when I ever get the honor of meeting your ogre of a father, he'd better treat all our children equally—and that includes J.D. and our daughters!"

Dallas shook his head as he turned toward the hotel. "So now we've got daughters?"

"We might!"

"Even if we don't adopt J.D.?" he asked, turning his gaze her way for just a second.

"I—I can't think about not having J.D. Not yet," she said softly. She clutched the handle of her purse in a death grip and tried to think about anything other than the awful fact that little J.D.'s future was out of her hands.

Dallas drove to the rental-car parking lot of the hotel. Twenty stories high, the concrete-and-steel building glowed like the proverbial Christmas tree. A marquee announced a famous comic as the weekend's entertainment, and liveried bellboys and ushers welcomed them.

The lobby was awash with light, and a fountain spraying pink water two stories high was situated in the central foyer. Veined marble and forest green carpet covered the floor.

Chandra could hardly believe that she was actually here, married and about to spend the wee morning hours of her honeymoon in the bridal suite.

With the help of the bell captain, they were whisked to the nineteenth floor and left in a three-room suite complete with complimentary champagne, heart-shaped tub and a round bed covered with silk sheets.

"Don't you think this is overdoing it a little?" she asked, eyeing the bed, beyond which the view of the city, lights winking endlessly, stretched into the desert.

"I thought it was the least I could do. This won't be much of a honeymoon."

She swallowed a smile and arched a coy brow. "You think not?" She glanced meaningfully at the bed. "Somehow, I think you'll find a way to make up for lost opportunities."

"You might be right," he agreed, striding so close to her they were almost touching. Only a breath of air separated their bodies, and Chandra's pulse quickened. Slowly he surrounded her with his arms and lowered his mouth to hers. "Maybe we should open the champagne and toast the bride and groom...."

Her breath was already lost in her lungs. "Later," she whispered.

"You're sure?"

Oh, God, was that her heart thumping so loudly when he hadn't yet touched her? "Yes, Doctor," she whispered breathlessly, "I'm positive."

With a wicked grin, Dallas lifted her off her feet and carried her quickly to the bed. "You know, Mrs. O'Rourke, I like the way you think." He dropped her on the silken coverlet, and his lips found hers, molding intimately over her mouth as his body formed to hers. She welcomed his weight and the gentle probing of his tongue.

His fingers worked on the small buttons of her dress, and the pink fabric parted. Dallas groaned as he shoved the dress off her shoulders and stripped it from her body. He moved his hands easily over the silk of her slip and touched the lace that covered her breasts. "You're so beautiful," he murmured against her hair.

She opened his shirt and touched the fine mat of hair on his chest. He caught his breath, and she watched in wonder as his abdomen sucked in and became rigid. "So are you," she whispered, fascinated by this man.

His lips found hers again, and he made short work of their clothes, kicking them into a pile and never once releasing her. Chandra's skin seared where his fingers touched her body, and her breasts ached for more of his sweet, sweet touch. She arched against him, feeling the magic of his hands, lost in the wonder of his mouth.

He kissed her face, her neck, her hair. She writhed against him, trying to get closer, and when his tongue rimmed the delicate circle of bones at the base of her throat, she cried out. He moved lower still, kissing her breasts and suckling on her nipples while he explored her back and hips with sure hands.

"Dallas," she whispered, her voice rough and low, "Dallas." She traced a path along the curve of his spine, and he held back no longer. Suddenly he was atop her, his knee between hers, his chest heaving.

Their lips locked, and he entered her for the first time as her husband. "I can't wait," he whispered, and began his magical rhythm. Chandra clung to him, moving with him, feeling the sweat collect on her skin. She thought he whispered words of love, but in her fevered state she might have heard her own voice as they exploded together and she cried out.

"Dallas!"

"Oh, love, oh, love," he sighed, collapsing against her, spent.

They held each other for endless minutes as the fog of afterglow surrounded them. Chandra closed her eyes, for she knew she might cry, not from sadness, but from deeper emotions that tore at her heart.

When her heartbeat was finally normal, she opened her eyes and found him staring at her. "You okay?" he asked, and she smiled, shyly and self-consciously, as if she'd been a virgin.

"I'm fine. You?"

He swept back the hair from her face and kissed her forehead. "Well, I'm a helluva lot better than fine. In fact, I think I'm great."

She giggled, and to her mortification he picked her up and carried her, stark naked, into the bathroom. "What're you doing?" she asked as he dropped her into the tub and twisted on the faucets.

"If this is going to be a honeymoon, we've got to make the most of it," he replied, his eyes glinting devilishly as warm water rushed into the tub.

"By bathing?"

"Or whatever." He lit two candles, brought in the champagne and turned out the lights. She couldn't take her eyes off his lean muscles, how they moved so easily under his skin. She was intrigued by all of him—the way his dark hair matted across his chest, the corded strength of his shoulders, the white slash of a smile that flashed crookedly in the light of flickering candles.

He stepped into the tub and gathered her into his arms, and their slick bodies melded together. "This is crazy," she said with a laugh as he positioned her legs around him.

"This is wonderful," he corrected. The water rose to their chests, and he turned off the faucets. In the shadowy light, he gazed at her with eyes that seemed to shine with love.

"Now, Mrs. O'Rourke," he said, tracing a drip from her neck to the hollow of her breast, "let's find a way to stretch out these few hours as long as we can."

Hours later, after sipping champagne in the tub and making love on the round bed until they were both exhausted, they awoke and headed downstairs. Dawn was just sending shafts of light across the desert floor and through the streets of the now-quiet city. The neon lights, so brilliant the night before, were dimmed as Dallas drove toward the airport.

He parked the rental car in the lot near the terminal before they headed inside, ready to return to Ranger and fight for custody of J.D. Chandra was prepared for an uphill battle, but anything as precious as that baby was worth whatever it took. By sheer determination alone, she should be allowed to adopt the child she had saved.

As she walked down the concourse with Dallas at her side, her new role as his wife started to sink in. She felt suddenly secure and worked at convincing herself that she and Dallas would be given custody. No parents would love a child more.

From the corner of her eye, she saw Dallas slow near an airport shop, and she wondered if he was going to buy some souvenir of the trip.

"Goddamned son of a bitch!" he growled, stopping short and fishing in his pocket for change. He dropped several coins onto the counter.

Before the startled cashier could ring up the sale, Dallas grabbed a newspaper and snapped it open. There on page one, in grainy black and white, was a picture of J.D.

Baby Abandoned In Colorado Barn, the headline screamed, and in smaller letters, Mother Still Missing As Hundreds Hope To Adopt The Million Dollar Baby.

Chandra's throat went dry. She curled her fingers over Dallas's arms, seeking strength. "How—how did they get that picture?" she whispered, her eyes skimming the newsprint and her legs threatening to give way when the article revealed that the child was living with Sheriff Newell. "How did they get this information?"

"Ranger's a small town," Dallas replied, tight-lipped, a deep flush staining the back of his neck. Never had she seen him more furious. "Gossip runs rampant."

For the first time, Chandra had to face the fact that the odds against them were insurmountable. They were just a couple—a recently married couple—who would stand in line with hundreds of other couples—every one of them as anxious to adopt the baby as she and Dallas were.

"Come on," Dallas said, his voice sounding strangely faraway. "We've got a flight to catch."

Her throat caught, and tears threatened her eyes. *You're just tired,* she told herself, all of her earlier euphoria long gone.

"We haven't lost yet," Dallas reminded her, and he grabbed hold of her elbow and propelled her toward the boarding gate.

"You're right," she said, then shivered. Inside, she knew she was in for the fight of her life.

Chapter Thirteen

So here they were at home—a married couple. They'd driven directly to the cabin and now, after showering and changing, they were preparing to go into town.

Chandra poured herself a cup of coffee and smiled as she poured another for Dallas. It would be easy, she thought, to get into a routine with him, to wake up every morning in his arms and to read the paper, drink coffee and work around the house and outbuildings.

He planned on moving first his clothes and then his furniture as soon as possible. They'd even talked of expanding the cabin, and Dallas wanted to talk to an architect about the remodeling. Things were moving swiftly, but for the first time in years, Chandra felt comfortable depending upon someone besides herself.

She heard him on the stairs, and glanced up to see his handsome face pulled into a frown as he buttoned his shirt.

"I could help you with that," she offered, and he flashed her a slice of a grin.

"You're on."

When he reached the kitchen, she kissed his chest and slipped each button through its hole.

"If you keep this up, I'll never get to work," he said, his eyes lighting with a passionate flame.

"Uh-uh." She finished the shirt and handed him his coffee cup. "Come on outside, I think we should talk."

"About . . . ?"

She braced herself. "Me and what happened in Tennessee."

"You don't have to—"

"Of course I do," she said as he placed a hand on her shoulder. "We've got to start this marriage with a clean slate—no lies, no misunderstandings, no surprises."

Together they walked outside and Chandra felt the morning sun against her back as they leaned over the rail of the fence and watched the horses picking at the dew-laden grass. Sam trotted behind them only to be distracted by a squirrel.

"What happened?" Dallas finally asked, and Chandra decided to unburden herself.

"Medicine was my life," she admitted, thinking of all those grueling years in med school when she had not only worked for hours on end, but had to endure being the butt of too many jokes. Feeling Dallas's eyes upon her, she forced the words about her past from her throat. "I went to school in Philadelphia, then took a position with a hospital in Collier, Tennessee.

"You know about the patient I lost, a seven-year-old boy. His name was Gordy. It . . . it was messy." Her throat clogged momentarily, but she willed herself to go on, to get over the pain. "You saw the newspaper articles, but they didn't explain exactly what happened. I was sued for malpractice by the parents, though they brought him in much too late. They thought he had the flu, and he just got worse and worse. By the time we rushed him to the hospital . . . well, he died of pneumonia within the hour. The parents blamed me." She swallowed hard, looking not at Dallas but concentrating on a swallow as it flew about the barn roof. "There was an investigation, and I was cleared, but . . . well, I had other personal problems."

"Your marriage."

"Yes," she said with a sigh. "Everything seemed to unravel. So," she finished, trying to force a lightness into her voice, "I ended up here, with a job as a white-water and mountain guide."

"Don't you miss it?" He touched her lightly on the arm, and her heart warmed at the familiarity they'd slipped into.

"What—medicine?"

"The healing."

"Sometimes, but not often. I'm still a doctor," she said. "It wouldn't take much to get licensed here, but I guess I wasn't ready to start practicing again." She felt inexplicably close to tears, and he threw his coffee cup on the ground and took her into his arms.

"Losing a patient is hard, but it happens," he whispered.

"Children shouldn't die."

Gently, he rotated her, forced her to look at him, and Chandra didn't pull away from him as he kissed her lips. "No," he agreed, "no child should ever die, but, unfortunately, it happens. We try our best, and sometimes it isn't good enough." He looked down into her eyes, his own shining in the morning sunlight.

"I couldn't help feeling guilty, that if I would have gotten to him sooner, I could've saved his life."

"How could you have known?"

She shook her head and sighed, resting her cheek against Dallas's chest, feeling his warmth seep into her and hoping some of the old feelings of remorse would disappear. "I was married to Doug at the time, and he couldn't understand why I took it so hard. I wanted out of medicine, at least for a while, and he . . . he objected. We were making good money. He was a plastic surgeon in Memphis, and he didn't want our life-style to change. He told me that if I quit practicing that I would only be proving that I wasn't cut out to be a doctor, that all of his friends in medical school, the ones who had predicted I couldn't make it, would be proved right."

"Wonderful guy," Dallas remarked, his voice steely.

"We had our share of problems."

Dallas kissed her crown. "He was wrong, you know. Wrong about you. My guess is that you were and still are a damned good doctor."

"Have you ever lost a patient?"

"Too many."

"A child?"

"There've been a few. And I know what you went through. Each time, you can't help feeling that somehow you should have performed a miracle and saved his life."

Her throat knotted, and she couldn't swallow. Tears, unwanted, burned behind her eyes. "Yes," she whispered as he pulled her closer, holding her, murmuring into her hair, kissing her cheek. She wouldn't cry! She wouldn't! She'd spent too many years burying the pain and her past. "All those years of school, all those hours of studying, all those nights of no sleep, and I couldn't save one little boy!" Slowly, she disentangled herself and swallowed the lump that seemed determined to lodge in her throat.

"It's over," Dallas promised. "You've got a new start. We've got a new start. So it's time we took the first step and tried to adopt that baby together."

Chandra smiled through her tears and took Dallas's hand.

Cameras flashed, microphones were thrust in their faces and reporters, en masse, had collected around the Newells' house.

"Is it true you're married?" a woman with flaming red hair asked as Chandra tried to duck past the crowd.

"Yes."

"And you met Dr. O'Rourke when you brought the baby in—is that right?" another female voice called.

"No comment," Dallas growled.

"Oh, come on, Doctor, give us a break. Tell us a little about the baby. Where do you think he came from? Have you checked with any of the local clinics and found out if a woman in the third trimester never delivered?"

"No," Dallas said.

"You have no idea where the mother is?"

"None." He helped Chandra up the stairs of the Newells' front porch as reporters fired questions nonstop. To keep the crowd at bay, a deputy was posted near the front door, but he let Chandra and Dallas pass, presumably on orders from the sheriff or his wife.

"Isn't it a madhouse out there?" Lenore asked, her eyes shadowed with worry, her face grim.

"I guess it's to be expected," Chandra replied, anxious to see the baby.

"I suppose." But Lenore's face seemed more lined this morning, her lips pinched into a worried pucker. "I've taken in a lot of children in my day, but I've never seen the likes of this," she admitted, parting the lace curtains and sighing at the group of reporters camped in her yard. "And I've quit answering the phone. Seems everyone in the state is interested in adopting little J.D."

Chandra's heart sank like a stone. Even though she held J.D. and gave him a bottle, she felt as if she were losing him, that the cord that had bound them so closely was being unraveled by unseen hands. As she held the bottle, she stared into his perfect little face. She didn't kid herself. Sooner or later, if the media attention surrounding J.D. kept up at a fever pitch, other would-be mothers would be trying to see him and hold him. They would argue that Chandra, just because the child was discovered in her barn, had no more right to be with him than they did. It wouldn't be long before the courts or the Social Services stepped in, and in the interest of fairness, she might not be allowed to see him.

"Has it been this way for long?" Dallas asked Lenore.

"Since before dawn. And the phone has been ringing since about six last night. Someone must've let it slip that the baby's here because before that there was nothing. I was living a normal life. I don't like this, I tell you."

"Neither do I," Dallas replied, and Chandra bit her lip to keep tears from spilling on the baby who would never be hers.

As Chandra settled into a comfortable life with Dallas, the interest in the baby didn't decrease. While she was busy making closet space for Dallas's things, helping him fill out change-of-address forms and planning the addition to the house, her name and picture appeared in newspapers as far away as Phoenix and Sante Fe. At first she was considered a small-time heroine, the woman who had discovered the baby and rushed him to the hospital. Over the next week, her life was opened up and dissected, and all the old head-lines appeared.

The story of little Gordy Shore and his death was re-vived, and her marriage to Doug Pendleton, subsequent divorce and change of name and life-style in Colorado were hashed and rehashed in the newspapers and on the local news. She'd given two interviews, but quit when the questions became, as they always did, much too personal.

It was known that she was trying to adopt the baby, along with hundreds of other applicants, and it had even been speculated that her marriage to Dallas, at first a seeming fairy-tale romance of two people who meet via an abandoned infant then fall in love, was a fraud, a ploy for custody.

"I don't know what I expected," she admitted to Dallas, upon reading a rather scorching article in the *Denver Free Spirit*. "But it wasn't this."

Dallas, who had been polishing the toes of his shoes, rested one foot on the seat of a chair and leaned across the table to stare more closely at her. "Giving up so soon, Mrs. O'Rourke? And here I thought you liked a battle."

"Not when the stakes are so high," she admitted, her stomach in knots. She hazarded a quick glance at him. "And I'm not giving up. Not yet."

"Not as long as there's an ounce of breath in your body, I'd wager," he said, winking at her.

She rolled her eyes, but giggled. The past few days had been as wonderful as they had been gut wrenching. Though she was worried about adopting J.D., her life with Dallas was complicated, but interesting, and their lovemaking was passionate. She couldn't resist him when he kissed her, and she felt a desperation in their lovemaking, as if they each knew that soon it would be over. If they weren't awarded custody of J.D., they would have no reason to stay together. That thought, too, was depressing. Because each day she was with him, she loved him a little more.

Sam whined to go out, and she slung the strap of her canvas purse over her shoulder. "I guess I'd better get to work," she said. "And I'll talk to my attorney today, see what he's come up with."

"I'll walk you," Dallas offered, holding open the door for her as Sam streaked across the yard. The morning was cool, the sky, usually clear, dark with clouds. Even through her jacket, Chandra shivered.

She reached for the handle of the door of her Suburban, but Dallas caught her hand.

"What's up, Doctor?" she asked, turning to face him and seeing his gaze was as sober as the threatening sky.

"I think I've gone about this marriage thing ass-backward," Dallas admitted.

"We both have."

"Right. But I decided that we need to set things right. So, I hope this is a start." He reached into his pocket and withdrew a small silver ring, obviously old, with a single diamond surrounded by smaller sapphires.

"Where did you get this?" she whispered as he slipped it over her finger, and the ring, a size or two too big, lolled below her knuckle.

"It was my grandmother's. Harrison's mother. I don't remember much about her—except that she was kind and loving, and the one person in the world who would always stand up for me." He cleared his throat suddenly, and Chandra's heart twisted with pain for the man who had once been such a lonely boy. "She died when I was about eight and she left me this—" he motioned to the ring "—and a little money for college and medical school."

Chandra, her throat thick, her eyes heavy with tears of happiness, touched the ring with the fingers of her other hand.

"You can have it sized," he said. "Or if you'd prefer something new—"

"Oh, no! It's...it's perfect! Thank you!" Moved, she threw her arms around his neck and kissed his throat, drawing in deep breaths filled with his special scent. "We're going to make this work, Doctor," she whispered into his ear. "I just know it!"

Opening the door of the Suburban, she saw the ring wink in the little morning light that permeated the clouds. She wondered vaguely if Jennifer had worn this very ring, and a little jab of jealousy cut through her. But she ignored the pain; Jennifer was history. Chandra, now, was Mrs. Dallas O'Rourke.

She pushed all negative thoughts aside as she drove into town and stopped at Roy Arnette's office. The lawyer was waiting for her, his glasses perched on the end of his nose, his mouth tiny and pinched. "Have you talked to the Newells today?" he asked as she sat down.

"It's only nine in the morning."

Roy sighed. "Then you don't know."

"Know what?" she asked, but she read the trouble in his eyes, and her throat seemed to close in on itself.

"There's a woman. Her name is Gayla Vanwyk. She claims to be the baby's mother."

"But she couldn't be—" Chandra whispered, her world spinning wildly, her heart freezing.

"Maybe not. But the police are interested in her."

"But where did she come from? How did she get here? She could be some kook, for crying out loud, someone who read about J.D. in one of these—" She thumped her hand on a newspaper lying open on Roy's desk. "She could just be after publicity or want a child or God only knows what else!"

"Look, Chandra, I'm only telling you what I know, which is that the police are interested in her enough to have some blood work done on her."

"Oh, God—"

"If she's the natural mother . . ."

Tears jammed her throat, and Chandra blinked hard. "If she is, why did she leave him?" she demanded, outraged.

"If she's the natural mother, this complicates things," Roy said. "She'll have rights."

"She gave those up when she left him!"

"Maybe not, Chandra," he said as gently as possible, and Chandra felt as if her entire world were crumbling.

Dallas! She needed to talk to Dallas. He'd know what to do. "I won't lose him, Roy, I won't!" she cried, though a horrible blackness was seeping into her soul. Again she saw how small her chances of becoming J.D.'s mother actually were. Sobs choked her throat, but she didn't let them erupt. "I want to see her," she said with dead calm.

"You can't. The police are still talking to her."

"I'll wait," she insisted, somehow managing to keep the horrid fear of losing the baby at bay. "But at the first opportunity, I want to talk to that woman!"

"She's definitely postpartum," Dallas said quietly. The bottom dropped out of Chandra's world as she sat slumped into a chair in his office, her heart heavy. "Now we're waiting for the lab to check blood types." He looked tired, his blue eyes dark with worry, his hair uncombed. He rubbed his neck, as if to straighten the kinks, and Chandra was reminded of the first time she'd seen him in the emergency room so few weeks before. He'd been weary then, too, but she'd known that this man was different, special. And now he was as sick with worry as she was. Maybe even more so.

"So she's had a baby," Chandra whispered with a stiff lift of her shoulder as she feigned nonchalance. "That doesn't mean she had *this* baby."

"Very recently."

"Does she look like J.D.?"

He shook his head. "Who can tell? She has black hair, dark eyes. And it doesn't matter, anyway. The boy could look like his father—or someone else in the family."

Chandra's hands were shaking. She clasped them together and saw the ring, Dallas's grandmother's ring, her wedding ring, a symbol of a marriage that, perhaps, was never meant to be. Taking in a shuddering breath, she stared past Dallas to the window where the first drops of rain were slanting over the glass. Thunderheads brewed angrily over the mountains, and the sky was dark as pitch. "I can't believe it. Not after all this... She can't just appear and claim the child...."

Dallas rounded his desk and took her hands in his; the stones of the ring pressed into his palm. "Don't tell me you're a quitter after all, Mrs. O'Rourke."

"It seems the odds are against us, aren't they?" Chandra had only to crane her neck to see the newspapers littering Dallas's desk. "That name—the Million Dollar Baby—it's stuck. Did you know that? Some couples are actually in a bidding war to gain custody. What chance do we have?"

Dallas's eyes flickered with sadness. He pressed a kiss against her temple. "We haven't lost yet."

"But it doesn't look good."

"We won't know if she's even possibly the mother until the blood work is analyzed. Even then, we can't be sure. She has no birth certificate—claimed she had him out in the woods near your place. She can't or won't name the father.''

Chandra's shoulders slumped. Even if this woman did prove to be a fraud, she was just the first. Woman after woman could claim to be mother of the baby, and sooner or later the real one might show up. If, God willing, she and Dallas were allowed to adopt J.D....

Her heart ripped, and she bit her lip to fight back tears. Dallas was right about one thing, they hadn't lost yet, even though the odds of adopting the child seemed to be getting slimmer by the minute.

Dallas drew her to her feet and wrapped his arms around her, as if he really cared. Her heart nearly crumbled, and she wanted to lean against him, to sob like a baby, to cling to him for his strength, but she wouldn't break down. Instead, she contented herself with resting her head against his chest and listened to the calming rhythm of his heartbeat. God, how she loved him. If he only knew.... But she couldn't tell him. Not yet. She'd seem like some simpering female, depressed and clinging to a man who had no real ties to her.

Gayla Vanwyk wasn't too happy about being in the hospital, that much was certain from the crease in her brow and the pout of her full lips. Dallas guessed her age at twenty-three, give or take a couple of years. She was a beautiful girl, really, with curling black hair that framed a heart-shaped face filled with near-perfect features. Her exotic eyes were deep brown, rimmed with curling ebony lashes and poised above high cheekbones.

She sat in Dr. Trent's office, smoking a cigarette and staring with obvious distrust at the people in the room. Dallas stood near the window and looked down at the parking lot where, wedged between the cars of doctors, nurses, staff and patients, were double-parked vans and cars. Reporters milled about the parking lot and lobby.

"Shouldn't I have my attorney here or somethin'?" Gayla asked, eyeing the men and women who had dealt with the infant.

Dr. Trent, as always soft-spoken, smiled kindly. "This isn't an inquisition, Miss Vanwyk. These are some of the doctors who examined the child when he came into the hospital, and they'd like to explain his conditions to you." He tried to calm her down, to explain that they were only interested in the health of the baby, but she wasn't buying it.

"Look, I've done all I have to," she said, crushing her cigarette in a glass ashtray Trent had scrounged out of his desk. "I know my rights. I want my baby back."

"As soon as the test results are in, we'll forward them to the police and Social Services," Trent said.

"Good. And how long will that take?" She stood up, ending the interview, and deposited her pack of cigarettes into a well-worn purse.

"A day at most, but Social Services—"

"Screw Social Services, I just want my kid."

"You left him," Dallas said, unable to let the conversation end so abruptly.

"Yeah, I had to. No choice."

"Why not?"

"That's personal," she said, narrowing her eyes on him. "And I don't have to talk to you. You're the doctor who wants to adopt him, aren't you? You're married to the woman who found him."

"I just want to get to the truth."

"Well, you got it." She turned on her heel and left the scent of heavy perfume and smoke wafting after her.

"If that's the mother, I don't envy the kid," Dr. Spangler said, fiddling with the buttons on his watch. "Maternal, she's not."

Dallas shoved his hands into the back pockets of his pants. "I don't buy it," he said, his eyes narrowing a little as he considered the woman's story. Even if she was the baby's mother, she seemed more defensive than concerned about the child.

In his own office, he punched out the number of his friend in Denver, the private investigator. Why not check out Miss Vanwyk? If she proved, indeed, to be J.D.'s mother, and the state saw fit to grant her custody, there wasn't much Dallas could do about it. If, however, she wasn't the baby's mother, or he could prove her unfit, then at least the baby would be placed in a home with loving parents—not necessarily with Chandra and him, but with people who loved him.

And what will you and Chandra do? Call the whole thing off? Divorce? Or start over? Living together not for the sake of a child, but because you love each other.

Love? Did he love her already?

Impossible. Love was out of his realm. Or was it? After all, he had given her the ring, a ring he'd never even shown to Jennifer.

At the realization that he'd fallen all too willing a victim to love again, Dallas flung one leg over the corner of his desk and wondered how he could convince Chandra that, with or without the baby, they belonged together....

"Killingsworth Agency," a female voice cooed over the phone, and Dallas snapped his wandering thoughts back to attention. First, he had to find out about the woman claiming to be the baby's mother; next, he'd deal with his marriage.

Three days later, Chandra was a nervous wreck. Certainly blood tests couldn't take so long...unless they were testing DNA.

She'd begged Dallas for information, but he claimed he, as a prospective adoptive parent, was being kept as much in the dark as she. It was all she could do not to find Miss Vanwyk and demand answers.

"In due time," Dallas told her. "You can't risk talking to her now. It might jeopardize our chances of adopting the baby."

And so she kept away. But the press didn't let up, and Chandra felt as if her life were being examined through a microscope. As was Gayla Vanwyk's. Chandra's life seemed to be a story right out of the most sensational of the tabloids, and she had trouble sleeping at night. Were it not for Dallas's strong arms on which she had come to depend, she doubted she would be getting any rest at all.

As for work, things were slowing down as summer receded into fall. And though Chandra needed to fill her idle days, Rick wouldn't hear any arguments from her. "Listen, you look like you haven't had a decent night's sleep in two weeks, and we're not busy, anyway. Until all this hubbub about that kid dies down, you take some time off. Consider it paid vacation or a honeymoon or whatever, but you take all the time you need to put your life in order. Listen to someone who knows what he's talking about—this is free advice, Chan. If I would've spent more time working things out with Cindy, she'd probably still be here with the kids and I would still be playing Santa Claus instead of getting Christmas cards from St. Louis."

Never, in the years she'd worked with him, had Chandra heard him complain about the split from the woman who'd borne his children. Though he hadn't married anyone else, hardly even dated, Rick just didn't talk about his past.

Chandra grabbed a rag from behind the register and slapped at a cobweb hanging from the wagon-wheel chandelier. "But I can't just sit around the house and stare at Sam all day," she protested, frowning as she spotted another dangling string of dust.

"Why not? It'd do you some good. You haven't taken any time off since you started working here."

Randy breezed through the door and heard the tail end of their argument. "Hey, you may as well take advantage of Rick's good humor," he said, his eyes twinkling. "I am. I'm gonna find me a woman and a kid and get married and take a few months' paid vacation—"

"Get outta here," Rick said, chuckling to himself. "No, not you, Randy. But you, Chan, do yourself a favor. Get to know that husband of yours."

That husband of mine, she thought ruefully. For how long? Snagging her long denim coat from the peg near the door, she hurried outside and shivered in the cold mountain wind. The first snow of the season had dusted the highest peaks, but here, in the lower valley, raindrops danced in the parking lot, creating shallow puddles that she had to dodge as she made her way to her Suburban. The thought of living without little J.D. was crippling, the thought of living without Dallas devastating. In a few short weeks, they'd become so close, and their marriage, though it hadn't been based on love, had provided, in many ways, the happiest moments of her life—though her parents had been shocked when she'd called them with the news.

"You shouldn't have been so hasty!" her mother had warned. "What do you know about this man?"

Chandra's father had come to her rescue. "Oh, hush, Jill. She's old enough to know what she's doing!"

"And that's what you said when she married Doug!"

Now, remembering the telephone conversation, Chandra smiled at her parents' happy bickering. They'd be lost without each other. They depended upon each other, and, yes, they argued with each other, but she never doubted that their love ran as deep as any ocean and their devotion to each other, as well as to their three daughters, was stronger than any force on earth.

She'd hoped for that same kind of love and devotion in her own marriage to Doug, and it hadn't occurred. But this time... if only Dallas could love her....

She wasn't ready to go home, knowing that there would be more messages from reporters on her answering machine. She drove instead to the hospital, hoping that she could share a cup of coffee with Dallas or just talk to him.

In the parking lot, Chandra encountered reporters, hand-held cameras, microphones and tape recorders. A police cruiser was idling near the entrance, and Chandra recognized the flat, frowning face of Deputy Stan Bodine behind the wheel. Chandra waved at him as she drove to a rear parking lot.

She left her Suburban far from the main doors and dashed through the physician's lot to a side entrance. Inside the hospital, she shook the rain from her hair and rubbed her hands from the cold, then hurried to Dallas's office.

He wasn't in. Dena checked his schedule and relayed that Dallas wasn't due back in the hospital until two, at which time he was to report for his shift in ER.

Chandra visited the nurses in the pediatrics wing, then took the elevator to ER. Dallas hadn't signed in yet. There were a few patients in the waiting room as Chandra started for the door. She was near Alma Lindquist's desk when she heard the voice of a distraught mother.

"But he hasn't taken any liquids. I can't get him to drink, and his temp's been at a hundred and four for a couple of days. The pediatrician says it's just the flu, but I'm worried."

"Who's your pediatrician?" Nurse Lindquist inquired.

"Dr. Sands, and I trust him, but Carl is so sick..."

Chandra couldn't help but overhear the conversation, and she looked at the small boy cradled in his mother's arms. His face was pale, and he could barely keep his eyes open. "Has he had any blood work done?" she asked.

"No, I don't think so," the mother replied, her own face pasty with worry.

"You haven't had a white count?"

"Not that I know of." The mother looked perplexed. "Dr. Sands says there's a virus going around...."

Alma rose from her chair. "Mrs. O'Rourke, this isn't..."

But Chandra didn't hear her. As she looked at the little boy, images of another sick child came to mind. She saw

Gordy Shore's listless eyes and pale face, his lethargy palpable.

"Admit this child immediately. Get a white count, and if that's elevated, have his lungs X-rayed." Chandra turned to the mother. "Have there been any other symptoms—vomiting? Diarrhea? Swelling?"

"No, he just barely moves, and he's usually so active," the mother replied, obviously close to tears.

"Don't worry. We'll take care of him."

"Thank God."

"Has Dr. Sands listened to his lungs—"

"Last week," the mother replied.

"Admit this child," Chandra ordered again, but Nurse Lindquist's lips pressed into a stubborn line. Obviously, she wasn't taking any instructions from a woman who held no authority at Riverbend, but Chandra, spying Dallas walking from the stairs, flew past her. "That patient," she said, motioning to the little boy, "is supposed to have the flu, but he hasn't had a white count and..." She rattled off the conversation to Dallas and, thankfully, he listened to her.

"There are other patients," Nurse Lindquist objected as Dallas approached, but he surveyed the waiting room where a few people sat patiently, flipping through ragged magazines.

"Anything life threatening?" he asked.

"No."

"Admit this child—now," he ordered as an ambulance roared to the doors. "And call Dr. Hodges if we need more help." He then led the mother and child back to the examining room.

Pandemonium broke loose as another ambulance, siren screaming, pulled up to the door. Paramedics began wheeling stretchers into the emergency room.

Chandra heard the page calling for every available staff member, and she saw the influx of personnel and equipment. Suddenly, nurses, doctors and volunteers were everywhere as the first of the patients were wheeled into examining rooms.

"Bad accident...truck jackknifed on the freeway..." she heard a paramedic explain to a nurse. "This one needs help, he's lost a lot of blood and his blood pressure has dropped—"

"Put him in room three. Dr. Prescott's on his way."

Chandra didn't even think about the ramifications of what she was doing, but followed Dallas into the examining room, where he was leaning over the boy, a stethoscope to his chest.

"I don't hear anything, but we'll have to see—"

Shannon Pratt stuck her head into the examining room. "Dr. O'Rourke, we need you! Big accident. Multiple victims. We're calling all the staff back to the hospital."

"I can handle this," Chandra said, motioning to the boy, her heart in her throat. "You had blood taken?"

"It's in the lab now."

"I'll take him to X-ray." Chandra met the questions in Dallas's gaze and didn't flinch. A special glimmer passed between them. "They need you out there," she said. Shouts, moans and the sound of rattling equipment and frantic footsteps filtered through the door.

"You're sure about this?" Dallas asked.

"Positive. Come on," she said to the boy as she lifted him into a wheelchair, "let's get some pictures taken...."

The rest of the afternoon passed in a blur. Chandra helped out where she could, but was sent home when the administration caught wind that a doctor not certified in the state was giving advice, if only to other physicians. Though she didn't actually treat anyone, the administration was taking no chances. They didn't even allow her to do volunteer work, for fear that her connection to Dr. O'Rourke, Baby John Doe and Gordy Shore—plus the fact that she was unlicensed—could be grounds for one helluva lawsuit should anything go wrong.

But Chandra was grateful to have been able to help, and she wondered, not for the first time, about becoming licensed in Colorado.

The cabin seemed suddenly lonely and empty. Dallas had told her not to wait up for him, and she felt a despondency she'd never experienced in all the time that she'd lived here.

Several calls had come in while she was out. One had been from a reporter from Los Angeles, another from a married couple from Bend, Oregon, and a third from a lawyer in Des Moines whose clients "would pay big money" for an infant. As if she could or would help them.

Chandra took down the numbers and relayed them to Marian Sedgewick, the social worker, who, to Chandra's dismay, hedged concerning the adoption. She had mentioned that even if Gayla Vanwyk were a fraud, many couples were trying desperately to adopt the child. Though Chandra's petition was given special consideration because of all Chandra's help with the child and obvious love for the baby, there were also good reasons for placing him with someone else.

"Oh, Lord, what a mess." It seemed that the odds of adopting J.D. were impossible. Chandra wanted to cry, but didn't. Even if they couldn't adopt the baby, she and Dallas still had each other. Or did they? Without J.D. would Dallas be willing to try and make this marriage work? She could trick him, of course, by becoming pregnant with his child. He wouldn't divorce her then, not with his feelings on children and family. But could she do it?

No.

She wouldn't base this marriage on lies or trickery, even if it cost her the husband she loved as much as life itself.

Feeling as if the weight of the world rested on her slim shoulders, Chandra walked to the barn and saddled Brandy. The rain had let up a little, and the game little mare was frisky, anxious to stretch her legs as Chandra rode her over the sodden fields surrounding the house. Thoughts of J.D. and Dallas filled her mind, but she refused to be depressed.

And just like the afternoon sun that had begun to peer through the dark clouds, her mood lightened.

The smell of rain-washed ground filled her nostrils, and the cool wind raced through her hair. She thought of life without Dallas or J.D. and decided, while her knees were clamped firmly around her mount's withers, that she'd have to tell Dallas that she loved him. She'd always been truthful with him before, and now, even if it meant his rejection, she had to confront him with the simple fact that she'd fallen in love with him. If he laughed in her face, so be it. If he divorced her on the spot, she'd survive. But life would never be the same, and these past few precious days would surely shine as the brightest in her life.

She rode Brandy back to the barn, groomed all the horses, fed and watered the stock, and when she was finished, snapped out the lights. "You could use a bath yourself," she told Sam. "Maybe tomorrow, since I'm a woman of leisure for the next week or so." That thought, too, was depressing. What if she had no husband, no baby, no job? A lump filled her throat, and she scratched Sam's ears. "Well, buddy, we've still got each other, right?"

The big dog loped to the back door.

Chandra couldn't shake her dark mood. She showered, changed and started cooking a huge pot of stew. As the stew simmered, she baked cornbread and found a frozen container of last year's applesauce. Now, no matter what time Dallas arrived home, she'd have a hot meal ready and waiting. *As if that were enough to tie him to you!* What a fool she'd been! And what a mess she'd gotten herself into!

Once the bread was out of the oven, she turned the stew down and grabbed a paperback thriller she'd been trying to read ever since J.D. and Dallas had slammed into her life. But the story didn't interest her and before long she tossed the damned book aside, sitting near the fire and wishing she could predict the future.

She must've dozed, because before she knew it, Sam was barking his fool head off.

Dallas!

Her heart leapt and she wondered if she had the nerve to tell him that she loved him.

As he opened the door, she flung herself into his arms and held him close. Tears filled her eyes at the thought that she could not only lose J.D., but this man, as well.

"What's this?" he asked with a familiar chuckle that touched her heart.

"I'm just glad to see you," she said, embarrassed and sniffing.

His arms held her tight, and he buried his face in her hair. "And I'm glad to see you." He kissed her cheek and held her at arm's length, surveying her. His face drew into a pensive frown at the sight of her tears.

"The accident victims?"

"Most will pull through," he said, sounding as weary as he looked, "but we lost a couple."

"I'm sorry."

"So am I," he said, holding her and sighing in relief or contentment, she didn't know which. She caught a glimpse of naked fear in his eyes, and she wondered what had happened.

"How about a glass of wine?"

"You got one?"

"In a minute." She pulled out a bottle of chardonnay from the refrigerator, found the corkscrew and poured them each a glass. "What will we toast to?" she asked.

"How about to you?" he suggested, releasing the top button of his shirt. "You're a local hero—make that heroine."

"I am? And all this time I thought that the Bob Fillmores of the world would like to tar and feather me in the press."

"Oh, but that's changed. You vindicated yourself," he said with a twinkle in his tired eyes. "Remember the boy you wanted me to treat this afternoon? The boy with the flu. Well, you were right. He has pneumonia. And I think we treated him in time. We pumped him full of antibiotics, and he's starting to respond. Thanks to you. If he'd had to sit around the waiting room . . ." He shrugged. "Well, it could've been bad."

Chandra felt tears well in her eyes. Vindicated? She hardly thought so. She'd lost Gordy Shore, but this time another life had been spared.

Dallas took a swallow of his wine, then twisted one finger in a lock of her hair, staring at the golden strands as if he were fascinated with her. "You know, even old hard-nosed Trent conceded that Riverbend could use another doctor. If you're interested."

"Another Dr. O'Rourke?" she replied, shaking her head, but smiling nonetheless. "Could the world stand it?"

"Could you?" His voice was low and serious.

"I—I don't know." She blinked hard. Practice medicine again? It had been so long. And, in truth, she'd missed it. But she wasn't sure she was ready. "How would you feel about having a doctor for a wife?"

Dallas grinned crookedly, as if he knew something she didn't. He tossed back his wine and set down the glass. "Personally, I'd go for it. I wouldn't mind seeing you every day. In fact, you would certainly perk up the place, but I'm not the only one we have to consider. I don't know how our son would feel about his mother—"

Her wineglass crashed to the floor, shattering and splashing chardonnay all over the floor. Sam jumped to his feet, growling fiercely.

"Our . . . son?" she repeated hoarsely. Her throat closed, and for a few seconds she could hear nothing save the rush of blood through her head. "The baby—is he . . . ?"

Dallas's face split into a wide grin. He took her hand and led her to the stairs where she sank onto the bottom step. "Gayla Vanwyk was lying. She's not J.D.'s mother. She was hired by a couple who wanted a child so badly that they would do anything, including pay her ten thousand dollars to pose as the mother. It might've worked, too. Her blood type was compatible with the child's and since we didn't know the father, it would be hard to disprove her story.''

Nothing was making much sense. ''Then how—''

''The DNA testing. She balked at that, and Sheriff Newell was already checking her out. I'd already called my friend in Denver—you remember, the private investigator?''

''How could I ever forget?'' Chandra said dryly.

''Well, he worked the pieces of the puzzle out and called Sheriff Newell, who confronted Gayla with the truth. She broke down and confessed. She had a baby a few weeks ago, which she sold to another couple, the Hendersons. This was just a way to make a little more cash. Charges are already being considered against the couple that put her up to it.''

''But I talked to Marian Sedgewick. There are other people who want the baby—''

''I know. Influential people with money. But when push came to shove, Social Services was worried about a scandal if it turns out that any of the couples who have applied for custody of the Million Dollar Baby have done anything the least bit shady.''

''So...?'' she prodded, hardly daring to hope, though her silly spirits were rapidly climbing.

''So, until the mother is located, the baby will be put in a permanent foster-care situation, and hopefully those parents will be able to adopt him.''

''Meaning us?'' she asked. Her breath caught deep in her lungs.

''Meaning us.''

Tears ran down her face. ''Thank God.''

''This means we have to stay married, you know.'' His steady blue gaze assessed her as he leaned over the stairs, his face so close, she could see the lines of worry near his eyes.

''I wouldn't have it any other way.''

''No?''

''Oh, God, Dallas, don't you know how much I love you?'' she asked, the words tumbling out in a rasp. ''Even if we had lost J.D., I would have wanted to stay married to you. I—I . . .'' Words failed her as she realized he might not feel the same.

But Dallas's blue eyes reflected the depth of his emotions, of his love. He gathered her into his arms. "And here I'd been thinking that you'd leave me if it weren't for the baby," he said, his voice cracking with raw emotion.

"Oh, Dallas. Never!" she cried, taking his face in her hands and kissing him long on the lips. "I just spent the last few hours scheming how to keep you married to me if we lost the baby. No matter what happens, Doctor, you're stuck with me."

"Promise?" he asked, hardly daring to believe her as he folded her into his arms.

"Forever!"

"I'm going to hold you to it, Ms. Hill."

"Mrs. O'Rourke," she corrected with a hearty laugh that seemed to spring from her very soul. She wound her arms around his neck and brushed her lips over his. With or without the baby, she knew she would love this man forever, but the fact that they were to become J.D.'s parents only made their future brighter and happier.

"Come on, *Mrs. O'Rourke*," he said, lifting her off her feet and carrying her up the stairs. "Let's celebrate."

Epilogue

Deep in sleep, Chandra heard the cry, a pitiful wail that permeated her subconscious. Sam barked, and she was instantly awake.

Dallas mumbled and turned over. "Some father you turned out to be," she muttered, grinning at him just the same. They'd been married over two months and she still felt like a newlywed as each day brought more happiness.

The baby cried again and Chandra smiled. "Coming," she whispered, sliding her feet into slippers and crawling out from the warmth of the bed. She threw on her robe, padded to the bassinet and picked up the squalling infant. "Shh..." she murmured, kissing the down that was his hair. She carried him downstairs and heated a bottle, all the while rocking slowly back and forth, humming and feeling happier than she ever had in her life..

Outside, snow powdered the ground and moonglow cast the icicles and snow with a silvery sheen. As she sat in the rocker near the dying embers in the fireplace, she placed a bottle in her baby's mouth. J.D. suckled hungrily, and Sam circled three times before dropping onto the rug near the hearth.

"Merry Christmas." She heard the words and looked up to see Dallas, his hair rumpled, his eyes still heavy with sleep, looking not too different from the first time she'd seen him in the hospital emergency room.

"Merry Christmas to you, too. Even though it's only Christmas Eve."

"I know, I know." He shuffled down the stairs, clad only in jeans, and plugged in the lights of the Christmas tree. The red, green, blue and yellow bulbs reflected on the window-panes. "Are you ready for the tribe?" he asked, tossing a mossy length of oak onto the grate before taking J.D. from her arms and feeding his son.

"Your family? Why not?"

"They're loud, opinionated and—"

"I've already met Brian."

"Well, Mom and the girls aren't as bad as he is."

Chandra laughed. "You'll have to put up with mine, too."

"Can you imagine everyone in here?" He looked around the small cabin. The addition wasn't yet finished, and with all the relatives, the room would be cramped. Fortunately, Dallas's family was staying at his condo, as the lease hadn't yet expired, and Chandra's family was going to sleep at the local hotel.

"It'll be perfect."

Dallas, still holding J.D., sat next to the hearth, and Chandra cuddled up next to him. Sam wagged his tail and placed his head in her lap.

"I have an early Christmas present for you," Chandra confided, deciding now was the time to share her secret.

"Can't it wait?"

"Nope. I think you'll want it now."

One dark eyebrow lifted in interest.

"Well, actually, you're not going to receive it until next summer, but it's been ordered."

His face pulled into a frown and she giggled. He must've suspected, for his lips slid into a wide smile. "Don't tell me—"

"That's right, Doctor. We've got a brother or sister for J.D. on the way."

Dallas swallowed hard, and he forgot about the bottle, causing J.D. to cry out.

"Here, let me handle this one," Chandra said, reaching for the baby. "You know, I was worried that someone would come and take this little guy away from us." The baby cuddled close to her breast and yawned.

"Never," Dallas promised. "I don't care how many children we have, J.D. is our first, and I'd walk through hell to keep him with us."

"Would you?" Tears glistened in her eyes.

"You and J.D. and now the new baby are the most important things in my life," he said, his voice husky. He cradled his wife and child close to him. "Nothing will ever change that. And nothing, *nothing,* will ever come between us. I love you, Chandra, and I always will."

The sound of his conviction caused the tears to stream from her eyes. "Come on," he said. "Let's change this guy and put him back to bed."

While the lights of the Christmas tree twinkled and the fire blazed in the grate, Chandra carried J.D. up the stairs. Dallas, holding her, kissed the top of her head. "I've never been this happy in my life," he admitted, and his happiness was the best Christmas present she'd ever received.

*   *   *   *   *

A Note from Kasey Michaels

Dear Reader,

I was delighted to hear that *His Chariot Awaits* had been chosen for inclusion in *The Parent Trap*, as it remains one of my favorite stories. As a matter of fact, I might call it my "story that grew."

While writing *His Chariot Awaits*, I discovered a new character within its pages, and she cried out for her own book. Which she got: *Romeo in the Rain*. From there, the story grew to include another heroine, who lives in *Sydney's Folly*. Lastly, this "family" of books took a wild turn and entered the world of time-travel in *Timely Matrimony*, and in this book everyone from all four books came back to tell me what they'd been up to since I'd last seen them....

Indeed, quite a lot of books from one little idea! And it all began when my husband rented a limousine to take me to dinner on our twenty-fifth wedding anniversary. You see, I got into the back of the limousine, sat down on the plush cushions, looked forward, and saw—a woman driver! By the time we reached the restaurant, the first plot idea was already "cooking" in my brain.

I sincerely hope you enjoy *His Chariot Awaits*. Heaven knows it has taken me for a most lovely, unexpected ride!

Kasey Michaels

HIS CHARIOT AWAITS

Kasey Michaels

To Kathleen Schlosser,
chauffeur *extraordinaire*

Chapter One

"Feel free to kiss me, Sis. You're looking at the genius who just landed us our first contract!"

"We have a contract? Right. *Sure* we do, brother mine. And on the way home a pink and purple pig waved to me as it flew by on the thruway." Josephine Abbott hung Esmeralda's keys on the white ceramic hook just inside the kitchen door of the century-old farmhouse, then plopped her weary body onto the nearest chair. "A contract! If that's supposed to be a joke, it's not funny. Rule number one, Andy— never hit a girl when she's down."

"You do look sorta beat, Joey," Andy remarked with the candor only a loving brother can use. "Esmeralda's not giving you any trouble, is she?" he asked, using his sister's name for the white stretch automobile that made up the entire assets of Abbott's Aristocrat Limousines. "Stay there, and I'll get you something cold to drink."

"Thanks, and no, Esmeralda's fine. Better than I am, actually. I've just spent three hours driving Mr. and Mrs. Reginald Putney III—of the New York and Newport Putneys, *dahling*—and their real estate agent around every blessed construction area within twenty miles. Not that they were too particular, you understand: just a five-bedroom Tudor, separate servant quarters, a six-car garage and a formal dining room large enough to hold *Maman*'s mahogany sideboard—and the Second Fleet, I imagine. And, oh yes, let's not forget the swimming pool and tennis court."

Andy gave a long low whistle. "They found a house like that around here?" he asked incredulously, twisting open a small bottle of orange juice and placing it in front of his sister. "I know we've got some good ones, but that sounds like a pretty tall order."

Joey lifted the bottle, tipped it toward Andy in a gesture of gratitude and then took a long drink of the ice-cold liquid. "That's the house they're going to *build*, Andy," she explained. "They were looking for 'just the correct piece of property' to serve as a setting for their architectural jewel." She slipped off her low-heeled black leather pumps and lifted feet onto the facing seat. "All in all, bunkie, this is not a happy camper you're looking at right now. So no more cracks, okay?"

"Whoops!" Andy had pulled out the chair, not realizing his sister's feet were there, and quickly mumbled an apology as she was sent flying front to brace her hands against the edge of the table so that she wouldn't slide onto the floor.

"I love you, too," Joey grumbled, grimacing as she struggled to sit up straight once more.

"I said I was sorry about that, Sis." Turning the chair around so that he could straddle it, Andy leaned toward her, barely able to contain his excitement. "But I meant what I said when you came in, Josephine. No joke! We *have* got a contract." He spread his arms as if trying to show just how big the fish was that he had landed. "A real, honest-to-God, genuine, signed-on-the-dotted-line contract!"

Joey looked at her brother through narrowed eyes. He'd called her Josephine. Nobody had called her Josephine since she turned ten and developed a great, chin-crushing uppercut. He must be serious. She leaned toward him until they were almost nose to nose across the narrow kitchen table.

"Tell me about it, Andrew," she urged. "I'm all ears. And don't leave anything out, especially the part about how we got a signed-on-the-dotted-line contract—because we don't *own* any such animal. I wouldn't even know what to put in one, more's the pity."

Andy sat back and held out his hands, as if warding off an attack. "All right, all right, I'll start at the beginning. Remember that job I had Thursday, the day after you applied for the loan and came home moaning about not having any bona fide contract clients?"

"I said start at the beginning of the story—not at the beginning of time," Joey cut in as she set down the empty orange juice bottle. "I mean, Esmeralda's a car, but I don't think we need to hear the history of the discovery of the wheel, do we?"

"Yeah, well, I had to start somewhere, didn't I? Are you going to score points off me or listen to my story?"

"Now it's my turn to say I'm sorry," Joey answered sincerely. "Please ignore me, Andy. As I said, it has been a bad day."

"Apology accepted. Anyway, this guy, this Daniel Quinn, he moved here last month but still works in New York—in some humongous building on Sixth Avenue."

"How nice for him," Joey commented dryly, getting up to start dinner. Andy was a sweet kid, really he was, but he could take forever to get to the point, and she was hungry. She had to keep her hands busy, or else she would be tempted to go over and shake the story out of him. "You want frozen Chinese or frozen Italian? Lasagna it is. I'll make a tossed salad to go with it. Go on, I'm listening."

"Jeez, you're a tough audience," Andy said, shaking his head. "Now, where was I? Oh, yeah. This guy, Quinn, travels to New York three days a week and works the rest of the time at home. He's been driving himself back and forth, but he told me he thought he'd try a limousine service at least once to see if it would be worth his while to have someone else drive him. He spent the whole time reading, so I guess he wasn't working—I could see him in the mirror because the glass was down. Anyway, he called here today while you were out showing the Putneys all the local hot spots."

"It's a good thing you want to be a singer and not a stand-up comedian, old chum. By the time you get to the punch line, the audience would have forgotten what the joke was about in the first place."

Her brother stood and turned to leave the room. "You're right, Joey, I'm a lousy storyteller. Never mind, it can wait until after dinner. Go wash your lettuce. I'll just watch television a while."

"Andrew Carlisle Abbott, you get back in here this instant and finish your story!" Joey called after him, laughing. "This Quinn fellow—he's the one who wants a contract with us? For three days a week? For how long? What rate did you quote him?"

Andy grinned and tilted his head to one side so that his dark copper hair fell down over his forehead. "You've heard every word I said, haven't you, Sis? I thought I'd lost you. It's for three days a week—Monday, Wednesday and Friday for six months—and I quoted him our usual weekday business rate, no discounts. He didn't even blink. We start Monday."

"And the contract?" Joey asked, suddenly feeling as if she were about to burst with excitement but wanting to hear the rest of Andy's story before she allowed her emotions to get the best of her.

"I took your car and went over to his place right away, before he could change his mind. He'd already had his legal department draw up a contract and we filled in the blanks together."

"His own contract? I'm not sure I like that. I don't owe him my firstborn or anything, do I?"

"Relax. I'm a partner, right, as well as a college graduate and fairly literate? I *can* negotiate a simple contract. He's taking it back to his lawyers, and we should have it by Friday. We start driving him on Monday. He's a good guy, Joey. I wish I could drive him, at least for the first few times, but I've already got my plane and hotel reservations for tomorrow night, and I don't want to let the guys down. We've been planning this rafting trip for a long time."

"You did tell him about me?"

Joey had come up against male chauvinism more than once since starting the limousine service, so Andy knew immediately why his sister had asked the question. "Sure. Of course I told him," he answered airily, hungrily eyeing the salad makings. "Don't I always?"

Joey wielded the paring knife, neatly beheading a carrot. "How many tired woman-driver jokes did he crack before he finally ran down?"

Andy gingerly reached over her shoulder to steal a thick slice of green pepper. "Not a single one. He knows you're going to be his driver, and it's all right with him. Now, are you going to stand there all day or are you going to put down that potentially lethal weapon and give me a great big kiss for a job well done?"

Joey closed her eyes and let the joy race through her. Andy had done it; he'd really done it! Darn those Putneys for putting her in such a foul mood, and darn herself for being such a pessimist, even for a little while. She hadn't started Abbott's Aristocrat Limousines for the Putneys of the world. She'd done it for herself, and for Andy. And now, they might just get that loan for a second limousine. They were really on their way. Nothing could stop them!

She dropped the paring knife and turned to throw her arms around her brother's waist, hugging him tightly. "Andy, you darling, you're a genius! Three days a week in New York, with nothing to do but go to the museums, and walk in the park, and take in the Wednesday matinees, and—oh, Andy, you doll! How can I ever thank you?"

"You can loan me fifty bucks for that new oar," he suggested boldly, sensing his opportunity. "My old one's really beat, and you don't want your genius brother stranded up the Colorado for three weeks without his paddle, do you?"

"Done!" Joey promised, giving him another kiss before skipping over to the refrigerator and sticking her head inside. "There's got to be a bottle of wine left over from Christmas floating around in here somewhere. Andy, go out to Esmeralda and get the corkscrew from the bar. We've got something to celebrate!"

"Are you *still* working? It's six o'clock. I'm bored out of my skull. There's nothing to do around here."

Daniel Quinn laid the manuscript in his lap and peered over the top of his tortoiseshell reading glasses at the young boy who stood in front of him. His son's chin was hanging somewhere in the vicinity of his knobby knees. "Wow! That bad, huh?" he asked commiseratingly, shaking his head. "Where's Mrs. Hemmings?"

"In the kitchen," Richie Quinn replied, adding, "I was trying to explain how I could convert her recipes to the metric system, but she wasn't interested."

"You're kidding. Imagine that," his father supplied tongue in cheek. "I would have thought she'd be hanging on your every word."

"She threw me out, actually," Richie added, two small spots of angry color staining his pale cheeks.

Daniel's left eyebrow rose speculatively as he looked at his son. Richie's shoulders were slumped, his hands buried deep in the pockets of his plaid shorts, one sneakered foot kicking at a fringed corner of the Oriental rug, his carroty-colored hair drooping over his eyes.

At ten, Richie was tall for his age, but too thin. Too thin and too sad. Daniel couldn't remember the last time he'd seen the child smile or heard him laugh in real amusement. His son was also, at times, too damn smart for his own good. "Gifted," his teachers called it. There were times Daniel thought his son's intelligence was a curse, and his heart ached for him.

He sought to communicate, man to child. "Caught you elbow-deep in the cookie jar?" he ventured, removing his glasses and laying them on top of the manuscript. "That was always the reason I was banned from my grandmother's kitchen."

Richie raised his head and his freckles stood out vividly against his pale, child-of-the-city skin. His voice was weary, as if it was an actual effort to speak. "Mrs. Hemmings doesn't bake homemade cookies, Dad. She buys them at the supermarket. Oatmeal cookies. And some weird-looking things she calls health bars. Do you have any idea of the amount of chemicals and preservatives in that sort of thing? I won't touch them. Besides," he added softly, "I want chocolate chip."

"Hey, don't we all? But oatmeal's good for you," Daniel countered, placing the manuscript to one side unreluctantly—for it wasn't the author's most promising work—and getting to his feet. He refrained from commenting on the health bars because he'd never tried one and never wanted to, no matter how good—or bad—they might be for him. "Besides, it's almost dinnertime, isn't it? You don't want to eat now."

"I'm not hungry anyway. Just bored. I hate this place," Richie said, digging his hands even deeper into his pockets, and finally sounding like the child he was. "There's nothing to do around here. I still don't see why we had to leave New York for this dump. I miss Freddie."

Daniel walked over to a nearby table and lifted the lid of the ice bucket, just to see that Mrs. Hemmings had once again forgotten to fill it. He replaced the lid with a silent sigh. He hadn't really wanted a drink anyway; he'd just wanted something to do with his hands, something that would keep his face hidden from his son while he fought to get his sudden anger under control.

He was only partially successful, as he was unable to keep from remembering that, along with describing Richie as "gifted," his teachers had also mentioned the word *precocious*. "Freddie! Always Freddie," he exploded, losing his temper. "Freddie's the doorman at our old apartment, Rich, for crying out loud. I want you to meet some new friends, some kids your own age."

"Freddie is my best friend," Richie argued to Daniel's back.

"Freddie snuck you into an off-track betting parlor and taught you how to handicap the horses," his father answered tiredly, for it was an old argument. "I'm trying to raise a son, not a racetrack tout. And there are plenty of kids in this neighborhood. I see them riding their bicycles all the time. You just aren't trying, Rich."

"Oh, yeah, sure. Bring that up again. You're just jealous because I won two hundred dollars after picking that long shot mudder at Aqueduct! And it wasn't fair to make me put it all in the bank!" Richie shot back at Daniel. He stomped over to the wing chair his father had vacated and flopped onto it, his long legs spread out in front of him. "Besides, I don't *want* to try. Why can't you understand that, Dad? I just want to go back to New York. This is nothing but a hick town full of boring kids. All the kids around here care about is riding bikes, and soccer—and *baseball*!"

Richie didn't know it, but he had just described his father's own happy, uncomplicated childhood. Daniel turned to look at his son, to look at the reason he had sold his exclusive Park Avenue condominium apartment and uprooted the two of them to Pennsylvania, the reason he had agreed to the grind of commuting to the city three days a week. Had he really expected thanks? The kid was miserable! "You're lonely, Richie, and I'm sorry about that," he began, repeating empty words he knew had already been said too many times. "But it's only been a month. Give it time. Perhaps in the fall, when school starts—"

Richie cut him off. "*School!* I'm not going to be stuck in this place when school starts," he declared hotly. "I'm going back to live in New York, whether you like it or not! And you know I can do it!" He turned and ran toward the staircase in the hallway.

"Rich! Richard Quinn, you come back down here right now! Richie, do you hear me? Oh, damn it," Daniel ended disgustedly as his son disappeared up the wide stairs to the second floor. "What's the use?"

Walking back over to the chair, he sat down, replaced his reading glasses and opened the manuscript once more, only to stare at it without really seeing the words. He had thought this move was such a good idea; getting Richie out of the city and into the open air, where he could experience a normal childhood. But it wasn't working.

"And that's the understatement of the century," he said out loud, closing the manuscript once more. Langley Books must have published a half dozen self-help books for mothers raising children alone, but he couldn't remember a single one directed at fathers raising a child in a motherless home. "Talk about your instant bestsellers," he mused. "I'd be good for a half dozen copies myself."

"What's that you say, Mr. Quinn?" Daniel looked up to see Mrs. Hemmings walking into the room, wiping her hands on her apron. "I've just come to get the ice bucket in case you want a drink, not that I hold with drinking strong spirits, you understand. Herbert, my dear departed husband, drank, and he's been dead a dozen years. There's a lesson there, don't you think?''

Daniel didn't bother answering, as he had quickly learned that Mrs. Hemmings asked a lot of questions, but was never really interested in hearing any answers. Besides, having already experienced the housekeeper's garbled logic firsthand, he decided that her "dear departed" Herbert had probably been run over by a beer truck. "Has Richie been bothering you, Mrs. Hemmings?" he asked instead.

The housekeeper's expression went from grim to grimmer, and she shook her head. "That's one unhappy lad you've got there. You know what I mean?"

"Yes, Mrs. Hemmings," Daniel said on a sigh, knowing that Richie's unhappiness had more to it than the move to Pennsylvania. It also had a lot to do with his Grandfather Langley. "I know exactly what you mean."

Joey strode confidently along the brick sidewalk of the Plexiglas-canopied Hamilton Mall—an ebony-haired bundle of unlimited energy neatly packed into a slim, five-foot-nothing frame. Still humming garbled snatches of a hit song, she approached the broad intersection at Seventh Street and the tall Soldiers and Sailors Monument that stood squarely in the middle of the street.

Stopping on the cement traffic island in the middle of the intersection to wait for the Walk sign to turn green, she jauntily saluted the bronze statues guarding the monument. It was a practice she'd begun in her youth and stubbornly adhered to ever since, no matter how many times the policeman on the corner looked at her as if trying to judge her sobriety. Some things were just traditional.

The knife-sharp creases in her black pleated skirt fanned out around her knees as she resumed her walk, and she quickened her pace as she took a moment to glance at the slim gold watch on her left wrist. Although she was not tall, her legs were long and straight and the black leather heels she wore added almost four inches to her height. The policeman looked at her a second time, his expression openly admiring.

Automatically reaching up to smooth the foaming lace neckcloth that cascaded halfway down the front of the black vest she wore over the crisp white long-sleeved blouse that completed her uniform, she smiled back at the officer.

Her mood was just too good to let anything bother her. It was June, the sun was shining, she had her health, and she had just walked out of the bank after submitting her request for a whopping loan and been given a fairly enthusiastic "we'll see" by the vice president in charge of ambiguous answers. But, as the man's "we'll see" was a lot better than the "you've got to be kidding, Miss Abbott" expressed by the loan officer she'd approached before landing the Quinn contract, she'd immediately decided that Abbott's second limousine was all but an accomplished fact.

It was still difficult for Joey to believe that she was the owner of her own business. She'd come back home to Allentown two years earlier when Andy graduated with honors from Lehigh University in nearby Bethlehem. Within hours of her arrival Joey had discovered that during her nearly two years as a jobless free spirit, her finances had declined almost to the point where she would have to start drawing on her principal.

She had also learned that Andy—with a degree in mechanical engineering in his back pocket—had no plans to take any of the positions he had been offered, but had every intention of becoming Pennsylvania's answer to Bruce Springsteen.

"Baby Andy," now towering over Joey by more than a foot, had obviously been expecting his wandering, carefree big sister to understand how he felt, so his surprise had been very real when she had looked up at him through the bright orange lenses of her oversize wire-rimmed sunglasses and declared flatly, "In your dreams, Sherlock!"

Andy had used every argument he could think of, but to no avail. Joey had been adamant. It was one thing for Andy to want to become a professional singer—but it was a horse of an entirely different color to think that he wouldn't have to find some sort of gainful employment while waiting for his big break to come along.

The inheritance from their father, added to that of their mother, who had died when Andy was only six, had been enough to keep a roof over their heads and pay their college tuition. But the remaining money, along with Joey's own savings and investments from her years with Ransom Computers, wasn't enough to give even one of them a free ride forever.

As much as she wanted to help her brother, Joey had known the two of them would have to find a way to put food on the table—and feeding Andy was no easy task! Joey had taken a deep breath and announced that both she and Andy had to get themselves gainfully employed—fast.

Going back to Ransom Computers had been out of the question. If there was one thing Joey had decided during her two-year hiatus it was that she wanted—needed—to be her own boss. A second decision, one that had taken her all of five seconds to make, was that she never wanted to see another computer spreadsheet or corporate meeting as long as she lived.

Andy, having told her that mechanical engineering wasn't nearly as glamorous as it was cracked up to be, had then suggested that they look around to find something more suited to the lives they wanted to live. "Of course," he had added tongue in cheek, "that might mean you'll be wanting us to drive tractor trailer trucks full of frozen french fries or something, considering that all you've been doing for two years is driving from here to there and back again."

Driving. Joey loved to drive. She loved the feeling she got whenever she was behind the wheel. She loved watching the scenery and the people go by. Since the first time she sat on her father's lap at the age of ten and "helped" him steer their ancient family station wagon along a deserted back-country lane, Joey had been fascinated with driving.

Andy had been nearly knocked off his feet as Joey launched herself into his arms, kissing him soundly on both cheeks. *Driving*. What an absolutely brilliant brother! What an absolutely brilliant idea!

And that, as she had just finished explaining to the vice president in charge of ambiguous answers, was how Abbott's Aristocrat Limousines had been born.

"Abbott's Aristocrat, because we call it AA Limousines for short and that makes us first in all the telephone directories," she had told the vice president with pride. "People have the tendency to begin at the beginning when looking in those books. We were going to call it Abbott American Aristocrat—for AAA, you understand—but we only needed two A's to be first."

Now, Joey thought as she headed left into the parking lot, all we need is *two* limousines. She waved to the parking lot attendant as she walked along the aisle between the rows of cars, then stopped beside her pride and joy, the long, gleaming white limousine she had affectionately dubbed Esmeralda. Opening the door, she picked up her black chauffeur's cap and placed it at a jaunty angle on top of her short, soft black curls before sliding behind the wheel and slipping her seat belt over her shoulder and around her small hips.

She took a moment to run her hands lovingly over the plush maroon velvet of the wide bench seat, then turned to look over her shoulder at the rest of the interior. The smoked-glass partition between the driver and passenger sections was in the lowered position so that she had a clear view of the "club room," as Andy called the area that held two facing velvet seats, a small drinks bar, television set, VCR and combination radio and tape deck. "All the comforts of home and then some," the salesman had said the first time Joey saw it, and she still had to agree.

The limousine was big, a stretch model, but it wasn't gigantic. She hadn't been afraid she couldn't handle a larger vehicle, but she had disliked the feeling that she was driving a bus. Esmeralda handled beautifully, and sat six in the back easily, which was more than enough room for her clients, who ranged from newlyweds to prom goers to society matrons to businessmen. Allentown, indeed the entire area, seemed to have a large appetite for limousines.

That appetite was growing, fed by the construction of Interstate 78, the highway that was rapidly bringing New York City within reasonable commuting distance. Daniel Quinn wasn't the only Saucon Valley resident commuting to the city. A building boom that had begun two years earlier was in full swing, with new housing developments and industrial parks springing up almost overnight and local real estate values climbing into the stratosphere.

Joey couldn't have picked a better time to go into business, and her business was growing right alongside that of the rest of the community.

For herself, Joey didn't intend to get too big—her memories of Ransom were still with her—but she would have been a fool not to take advantage of the opportunity that had somehow dropped into her lap. Andy's music career had begun to progress slowly but had not exactly skyrocketed him to the cover of *Rolling Stone*. So as long as there were two drivers available she couldn't see any reason not to add a second limousine. It only made good sense.

After paying the parking attendant she pulled into the traffic on Sixth Street, a small frown creasing her normally smooth forehead. If only she had something more concrete to show the bank than her past records and a few optimistic projections for increased revenue. She knew the demand for her services was growing; after all, hadn't she lately been turning down an average of three jobs a week? Being a free spirit was one thing, but money was still money!

"But now you *do* have a contract—thanks to Mr. Daniel Quinn, bless his heart—and by this time next week you'll have your loan!" she reminded herself as she slipped a recording into the tape deck and headed back toward Seventh Street and the drive home to nearby Saucon Valley.

Chapter Two

Chapter Two

Early Monday morning Joey Abbott tooled Esmeralda down the narrow, twisting macadam road that only two years earlier had been bordered by a rolling, treed landscape almost devoid of development, admiring the sprawling houses and small estates that had been delicately carved into the countryside.

Every house was a reflection of its owner, whether it was a modern wood-and-glass multistory flight of fancy or an updated re-creation of some bygone era. Each home occupied at least two acres of land, kept as close to natural as possible, with hardly any trees having been sacrificed to open lawns.

Joey slowed the limousine to watch for the left turn she would have to make onto Olde Country Lane, then drove about a half mile before seeing the oversize mailbox with the name Quinn painted on it in black block letters. She turned in the long driveway that curved up the sloping front yard and parked Esmeralda in front of the mellow pink three-story Colonial, silently complimenting her new employer's good taste.

Sneaking a quick look in the rearview mirror, Joey pressed her lips together to smooth her Radiantly Red lipstick as she turned her head this way and that, making sure her hair passed muster. Satisfied that she was as good as she was going to get, she unhooked her seat belt and stepped out onto the driveway.

Hands on hips, she surveyed the area in front of the house, noting that the driveway returned to the street in a semicircle, while also branching off at the end of the house, probably leading to a separate garage. "Poor man," she said out loud, "roughing it like this in the boonies after all those bright lights in the big city."

She debated whether or not to ring the doorbell, checking her watch to make sure she was on time. Some people didn't appreciate having their doorbell rung at six o'clock in the morning, and Joey wasn't eager to meet Mrs. Quinn if she wasn't ready for company. She'd give Mr. Quinn five minutes to show up before searching for him, she decided. She reached into the limousine to pull out a soft white cloth, planning to keep herself busy polishing Esmeralda's already gleaming chrome.

She was squatted in front of Esmeralda's grille, careful to keep her uniform skirt off the ground, when a young male voice pointed out, "You're not Andy Abbott."

Joey turned to see a boy of about twelve sitting on his haunches next to her, glaring into her eyes. "Good point," she acknowledged, flicking the soft cloth lightly against his freckled nose before standing up. "And you're not Mr. Daniel Quinn, unless he's a child prodigy. Are you?"

The boy stood at the same time. He was taller than she was, although Joey silently determined that that wasn't much of a feat. Nearly everybody was taller than she was. The boy tipped his head to one side and asked, "Am I what?

Daniel Quinn, or a child prodigy? Your question lacks direction. Always be specific."

Joey frowned, looking at the boy in consternation. "Oh, great. Everybody's a critic. Is your father home? You are Mr. Quinn's son, aren't you? Take the second question first, if that's all right with you."

"That's better," the boy complimented without cracking a smile. "That was reasonably lucid. Yes, I am my father's son and, yes, he is at home. My name is Richie. Richie Quinn. Now, who are you?"

Joey couldn't believe her ears. It must be all those vitamins kids are taking these days, she thought. She couldn't remember even *knowing* a word like *lucid* when she was twelve years old, let alone being able to use it in a sentence. He was very tall. Maybe he was a little older than she thought. "Richie, is it? How old are you, anyway?" she asked, curiosity getting the better of her.

"I'm ten years old, but everyone thinks I'm a lot older because I'm intellectually gifted," Richie informed her, clearly not intending to brag, but merely stating a fact. "I'm still waiting to hear your name, and what you're doing here instead of Andy."

"I'm Joey. Joey Abbott, Andy Abbott's sister," she answered quickly, realizing she had just been firmly put in her place. "You're tall for ten," she added weakly, almost apologetically.

Richie just shook his head. "Joey? That can't be your real name. A joey is a baby kangaroo. You must really be Josephine."

Fun was fun and all that, but enough was also enough! "And *you* must be mistaken," Joey supplied stonily, her eyes narrowing dangerously as she placed her hands on her hips and glared at him. "You may call me Joey, or Ms. Abbott, or Hey You—but don't you *ever* call me Josephine. Not if you want to live to see eleven."

Richie seemed to consider this for a moment, then brightened. "I don't think it matters what I call you, since I won't be seeing you again. My father won't allow himself to be driven by a woman."

"Wrong again, kiddo," Joey countered. "Your father already knows his chauffeur is a woman. Now, what do you say you run off and find him for me so we can get this show on the road. Not that this hasn't been fun, but I want to beat the traffic through the tunnel."

"Lincoln Tunnel?" Richie asked, his voice carefully uninterested. "I guess the buses go through there too—to the Port Authority."

"Yes, they do," Joey agreed absently as she heard the heavy white front door of the brick house opening, then turned to get her first look at her contract employer. "Oh!" she exclaimed in sudden shock, Richie and his comment quickly fleeing from her mind.

Daniel Quinn was quite a man, even at six-something o'clock in the morning. Tall, about the same height as Andy, he had broad shoulders and a narrow waist, as if he had joined that increasing group of executives who visited health clubs several times a week. His strides were long and confident as he came down the half dozen steps of the wide, curved cement porch, his head held high as his piercing blue eyes shot fiery bolts straight through her, figuratively nailing her black leather pumps to the driveway.

He was sleek and graceful, like a jungle cat, his tanned skin molded cleanly over the strong bones of his face. His double-breasted suit was flawless, midnight-blue with fine pinstripes; his shirt pristinely white; his tie the requisite conservative deep maroon worn by television news commentators and politicians all over the world.

He was, in a word, the corporate world's version of a hunk. *All the good ones are married,* she thought, immediately wondering why she had thought it. Joey swallowed hard and forced herself to walk toward him, her right hand outstretched. "Mr. Quinn, I presume?" she heard herself say, then stood uncomfortably as her hand was ignored.

"Who are you?" Daniel Quinn barked sharply, running his gaze up and down the length of her in obvious disbelief—and dissatisfaction. "You're not Andy."

He has more in common with his son than their last name, Joey thought sarcastically as she silently cursed her absent brother. Andy had said Mr. Quinn knew about her. Obviously there had been a breakdown in communications. "I'm Joey Abbott, Mr. Quinn. Andy's big sister."

"Joey?" Daniel repeated, looking toward the limousine and then back at her. "Joey's a man's name. Andy told me . . . I just assumed . . . that is . . . no! Absolutely not! This is totally out of the question! I hired a chauffeur, not a *chauffeurette.*"

"Told ya," Richie offered in a low, singsong voice as he sidled past Joey to stand next to his father, before continuing. "I informed her that you won't care to be driven by a woman, Dad," he said, his childish voice now deliberately deepened for this man-to-man exchange. "I knew you wouldn't allow a woman to drive you through downtown traffic."

Daniel looked down at his son, feeling vaguely uneasy with this rare show of male togetherness. Usually Richie went out of his way to take the opposite side of any issue. "You don't think I'll be safe with a woman driver?" he asked the boy. His startlingly blue eyes narrowed speculatively. "Or have you just made a quick bet with Mrs. Hemmings that I won't allow it?"

Joey could sense a sudden tension in the air, a tension that had nothing to do with the fact that she had taken her brother's place as Daniel Quinn's chauffeur. "Look, I don't want to butt in here, but if we're going to reach the city before noon we should get on the road now. Give me a shot, Mr. Quinn, just one round trip. I haven't lost a passenger yet. Then, if you don't like me, we can see about making some other arrangements until my brother returns in three weeks. He's on vacation with friends in Colorado," she added, although why she was bothering to explain herself she couldn't quite understand.

Without waiting for an answer, she walked up to Daniel, relieved him of the bulging leather attaché case he was holding and quickly deposited it in the backseat of the limousine. Purposely holding the door open so that Esmeralda's plush maroon interior beckoned invitingly, she prompted, "Mr. Quinn?"

Richie moved closer to Joey, and his father overheard him whisper out of the corner of his mouth, "Nine to five he cans you on the spot."

"You're on, bunkie," Joey whispered back at him, winking. "Fifty cents too steep for you?"

"Hey," Richie said, surprised. "You're not half-bad—for a girl!"

Daniel decided it might be time to teach his son a lesson. "Be right with you, Ms. Abbott. Richie—pay the lady tonight, out of your allowance." He placed his hand firmly on Richie's shoulder and guided the boy out of Joey's earshot. "Put a candle in the window, kid," he whispered, once more reaching out to the boy on a level he hoped would have some effect. "Do you think she sits on a pillow to see over the steering wheel? I'll be back around seven-thirty—if I live that long."

Richie's face was carefully, maddeningly blank. "If you say so, Dad," he answered, shrugging so that Daniel's hand was left suspended in midair. "And if I'm still here, we might even have dinner together."

Daniel opened his mouth to call his son back, but the boy had moved with surprising speed, running up the steps two at a time and disappearing into the foyer. Daniel sighed, suddenly feeling very old and very tired. *Tonight*, he decided silently. *We'll talk tonight, when I get home. This has gone on long enough.*

Walking over to where Joey was standing, still with one hand on the open door, he brushed past her with only a mumbled "thanks," and allowed her to close the door behind him. He reached for his attaché case and randomly pulled out an accounting spreadsheet. Maybe if he kept his attention glued to the pages he could fight off the nearly overwhelming urge to tell Ms. Joey Abbott to move over, and let him drive.

The highway wasn't too congested, with most of the traffic being caused by interstate trucks on their way to New York, but Joey knew that commuter-filled cars would be lined up ten deep at the tollbooth by the time they reached the entrance to the New Jersey Turnpike.

Her passenger had been unusually quiet for a first-time rider; most of her clients seemed eager to make friends with the person who quite literally held their lives in the palms of her hands. Aside from the obvious but harmless jokes about women drivers, clients most often discussed the state of the weather, their reason for hiring a chauffeur in the first place—some of them actually embarrassed to be riding in such luxurious comfort—and wondered out loud how a "little bit of a thing" like Joey could pilot a vehicle the size of Esmeralda.

But Daniel Quinn hadn't said a word, even when Joey lowered the tinted-glass partition to double-check the address of his destination. She'd left the glass in the lowered position for a few minutes, inviting conversation, then raised it, determinedly shoved a Learn Conversational French cassette into the tape deck and practiced saying "Would you kindly direct me to the nearest policeman."

Let him sit back there and read his stupid reports, she thought, glancing in the rearview mirror to see his silhouette outlined through the glass. *It's not like I want to talk to the man anyway, unless it's to ask him how he came to have a son like Richie.* "That kid's something else," she said out loud, missing the opportunity to repeat after the instructor: "I am a lost American. Would you please direct me to—insert the name of your hotel."

Yes, Joey decided, Richie Quinn was quite a character—part boy, part man and part nasty little brat. He was also intelligent, extremely intelligent—that she could tell just from listening to him speak—but he was still a child, and his emotional maturity hadn't quite caught up to his superior intellect. He had the makings of a rare handful, and she didn't envy his parents a bit.

Yet, she thought, conjuring up a mental picture of the boy who had dared to correct her speech, he isn't a happy child, for all his intelligence and material possessions. Joey would have been willing to bet that Richie had every toy known to man—and then some—and probably a computer as well.

It was Richie's paleness that bothered Joey most. Although he looked just like his father, with his bright red hair already showing signs of deepening to the rich chestnut of the older Quinn, Richie definitely lacked his father's outward signs of good health. How could a ten-year-old boy make it to the middle of June without acquiring at least a slight tan? It wasn't normal.

She stole another look into the rearview mirror. Maybe she should ask Mr. Quinn if Richie wanted to join the baseball team. The roster was full but, as one of the coaches, Joey could still find a place for him. The Quinns had only lived in Saucon Valley for a month, according to Andy; maybe they just hadn't had the time to search out an activity for their son.

Before she could talk herself out of it, and before she could remember Andy's warnings about poking her nose into places where it didn't necessarily belong—and might not be particularly wanted—Joey pressed the button that lowered the partition and called back to her passenger, "Has Richie found a team yet, Mr. Quinn?"

Daniel raised his spectacled eyes from the page he had been reading for the third time, wondering how this book from a rival publishing house could have made the best-seller list. It certainly wasn't riveting enough to keep his mind off the fact that he had somehow allowed himself to be torpedoed down a busy turnpike with a half-pint female behind the wheel.

"Team?" he repeated in confusion. "What sort of team are you referring to, Ms. Abbott? Sports? Richie doesn't care for team sports."

Joey took the time to shoot a quick look over her shoulder at her passenger. "Really?" she questioned, as if genuinely astonished, although she had already guessed as much. Richie seemed more like a loner than a joiner. "But aren't there any junior baseball teams in New York—in Central Park or somewhere? After all, with both the Yankees and the Mets in town, I would think every little boy would want to play baseball."

Daniel lifted a hand to adjust his reading glasses, horn-rimmed half-frames that had a tendency to slide to the end of his nose whenever he spoke. "I don't know why you would suppose that, Ms. Abbott," he returned stiffly. "Richie's into horse racing—or at least the odds-making end of it, as numbers fascinate him—but I can't recall his expressing any desire to become a jockey," he pointed out reasonably. "And shouldn't you be keeping your eyes on the road?"

"Well, excuse *me*," Joey muttered beneath her breath, "I guess that puts me firmly in my place." Raising her voice without turning her head, she explained, "I didn't mean to intrude, Mr. Quinn. It's just that I help coach a local team of ten- to twelve-year-old boys and girls whenever I'm free, and I thought it might be a good way for Richie to meet some of the other kids in the neighborhood."

Daniel shook his head in self-disgust, realizing that he had overreacted to Joey Abbott's obviously innocent and well-meaning overture. He was becoming defensive about his son—overly defensive—and was beginning to see criticism even when it wasn't there.

He had Wilbur Langley to thank for that, he knew, as Richie's maternal grandfather had been making the boy his personal project lately, pointing out all the child's supposed problems and offering his own totally unacceptable brand of solutions. Having Richie move in with him was Wilbur's latest brainstorm, and as far as Daniel was concerned, it easily topped the man's long list of unsuitable remedies to Richie's problems.

"Forgive me if I snapped at you, Ms. Abbott," Daniel apologized gruffly. "As a former Little Leaguer myself, I have to admit I was disappointed when Richie decided not to follow in my footsteps. Rich is just not very—um—physical."

"That's a pity," Joey said commiseratingly, silently wondering why the child should suddenly seem so important to her. "With his height he'd make our local basketball coach a very happy man. At this age they don't need to be experts—it's enough to have one tall boy he can camp underneath the basket to wait for rebounds. Oh, well, maybe you and your wife can convince Richie to at least give baseball a try." She peeked into the rearview mirror again, trying to see his expression. "It's worth a shot, isn't it?"

"Richie's mother has been dead for seven years, Ms. Abbott," Daniel informed her, his words clipped and cold even to his own ears. "I'm raising Richie myself, which is why we moved to your area in the first place. It's not easy, raising a child in the city."

Joey was aware of the increased tempo of her heart upon hearing that her new client was a widower. "I'm so sorry," she said automatically, ashamed of her real reaction. Although she felt badly for motherless Richie, there was no denying facts. Daniel Quinn was a very attractive man, and he had appealed to her on sight.

She fell silent, suddenly trying to remember the last time she'd looked at a man and found him interesting, attractive. She couldn't remember. Yes, yes she could. It was a long time ago, during her junior year in college. His name was Pete Williams and he had been a campus jock—majoring in football, willing coeds and, when the spirit moved him, political science.

Joey had been fascinated with Pete, mostly, she thought now, because he had been fascinated with her, but it hadn't lasted beyond the middle of their senior year. Pete had been what she had bitterly described as "a legend in his own mind," and she had eventually tired of the role of adoring handmaiden.

There hadn't been anyone since Pete. Joey had been too busy carving out a niche for herself in the corporate world, and her two years spent traveling the country hadn't lent themselves to forming any lasting romantic attachments. For the past two years she'd been fully occupied building up Abbott's Aristocrat.

Joey frowned. She was twenty-eight years old. The business was still in need of her undivided attention—and there was Andy and his "career" to consider. At the rate she was going, she'd better prepare herself to be an old maid. Shrugging fatalistically, she comforted herself that she had at least not lost the ability to notice an attractive man when he landed in her backseat!

And Daniel Quinn was going to be her regular passenger three days a week until her brother returned from Colorado in three weeks. She smiled. Maybe there was hope for her yet.

Suddenly, a loud noise penetrated the well-engineered silence inside the limousine, a sound reminiscent of a pistol shot. "What the devil—" she exclaimed as the tractor trailer in the process of passing her in the left lane veered toward Esmeralda, forcing the limousine toward the shoulder of the road.

"Hold on, Mr. Quinn!" Joey shouted in warning, clutching the steering wheel with both hands. She shot another quick look to her left. She could see that the truck had lost the right-front tire on its cab, and the driver seemed to be fighting a losing battle with the balky steering and the heavy, shifting load he was hauling behind him.

A look to the right told her that orange-and-white-striped construction barrels lined the shoulder of the road, making the area too narrow and too dangerous for Joey to consider escaping the truck by turning that way. Quickly checking the rearview mirror, she saw a huge fuel truck riding her rear bumper.

She couldn't slam on the brakes, not unless she wanted to have Esmeralda turned into a big white metal pancake. She had been riding behind another large trailer truck, so there was no open space in front of her.

There was simply nowhere to go to get away from the out-of-control truck.

The driver of the truck in front of her, seeing her problem, tooted his horn and accelerated, trying to give her enough room to shoot over into the passing lane, ahead of the swerving tractor trailer.

"Oh, God," Joey breathed, understanding what had to be done.

It might work. If she could accelerate fast enough...if she kept her head and didn't turn the wheel a second too soon—or a moment too late...if the disabled truck didn't sideswipe the limousine first...if she could successfully thread Esmeralda through the very small eye of the needle that was the only patch of open highway left between her and sure disaster...it might just work.

All this and more raced through Joey's mind in a few precious heartbeats as she slammed the gas pedal to the floor—including random thoughts concerning the extent of her medical insurance and the realization that Daniel Quinn was being extremely quiet in the backseat.

Esmeralda responded to Joey's commands beautifully, the sleek limousine powerfully surging ahead of the disabled tractor trailer, then successfully threading the needle to safety with at least two inches to spare between it and the truck in front of it.

Joey watched in her rearview mirror as the disabled truck swerved completely into the lane she had just vacated, then limped to a stop half on the shoulder of the road. Her heart pounding, her mouth uncomfortably dry, she eased her white-handed grip on the steering wheel and beeped her horn in thanks as she passed the trucker whose swift action had given her the room she needed to pull off her evasive maneuver.

"That was—er—that was very *good*, Ms. Abbott," she heard Daniel say, his voice almost normal. "I thought we'd had it for a moment. Congratulations, and thank you. I saw my life passing before my eyes for a second back there, and I realized I have a lot more I want to do before I meet my Maker."

Joey laughed, happy for any excuse to release the tension of the past few moments. "You're welcome, Mr. Quinn, and I feel the same way," she responded happily, remembering it was just what she had been thinking about before the near accident.

"Daniel, Ms. Abbott," he corrected. "Now that we've practically decorated the same highway together, I think we can dispense with the formalities. I'll call you Joey, if I may, and I'll be happy to have you as my chauffeur for the next three weeks and beyond, if our schedules don't conflict. You're a very competent driver. I don't know if I would have reacted nearly so well."

"Well, thanks again—Daniel," Joey responded, smiling at him as she saw his face reflected in the rearview mirror. "I appreciate it—even while I wish I could have proved myself a little less dramatically. We'll be coming up on the tunnel soon," she went on, suddenly uncomfortable with their unexpected relaxation of formality. "You should be at work in another fifteen minutes."

"You know you're to pick me up again at five-thirty?" Daniel asked. "What will you do all day?" He made a face as he heard himself ask the question, wondering why he should care what she did. After all, entertaining his chauffeur wasn't his problem. "Surely you don't drive all the way back to Allentown?"

"Good Lord, no!" Joey answered happily, pulling up to the tollbooth for the Lincoln Tunnel. "But don't worry about me, Daniel. A person who can't find something to do in New York City doesn't deserve your pity. Today I think I'll walk around Forty-second Street and the theater district. Most of the theaters are dark on Mondays so it won't be too crowded."

"Sounds—um—delightful," Daniel remarked, secretly thinking he would be bored out of his mind within twenty minutes. He picked up the book that had slid to the floor during the course of their near accident and once more ignored his driver.

Chapter Three

"Langley Books. How about that!" Joey repeated out loud for the tenth time as she walked away from the security parking garage, her well-traveled purple high-top sneakers cushioning the soles of her feet from the hard New York City pavement. "I wonder what Daniel does there—and it's dollars to doughnuts he isn't the office boy."

Langley Books, she knew, was one of the largest publishing houses in the world, and one of the last still privately owned and not a part of a multi-imprint house or conglomerate. It was also one of the most respected and diversified houses in the industry, publishing everything from self-help and textbooks to romance, sci-fi and thrillers, both in hard cover and paperback.

Joey knew all about Langley Books. Oh, yes, she certainly did. After all, hadn't they turned down her query letter just three weeks ago, without so much as asking to see the manuscript?

One for the Road might have been Joey's baby, an outpouring of her innermost thoughts and personal observations during her years since leaving Ransom Computers, but to Langley Books it was just another rejected idea. "Not suited to our needs at this time," the printed form letter had read, and her brother, Andy, had quickly fashioned an airplane of the paper and launched it toward the wastebasket in the corner of the kitchen.

"Their loss, Joey, their loss," he had told her bracingly. "Just don't give up. It's a great book."

"This from a guy who hasn't read a word of it," Joey had replied, lifting her head from the cradle of her arms as she sat slumped at the table. "But thanks anyway. What bothers me is that they didn't even give me a chance. How are they going to know whether or not the book is good if they refuse to read the thing? This is the third publishing house to turn me down unread. If only I knew somebody with some influence—some clout."

"And now I do," Joey said out loud, not attracting any attention to herself, because hearing people speak out loud to nobody in particular on the streets of New York was as accepted as the never-ending traffic. "I know Daniel Quinn. Heck, I even saved the guy's life—in a manner of speaking. I wonder if he has any real pull at Langley Books. For all I know, he could be the head of the accounting department. The very *handsome* head of the accounting department," she amended, smiling in spite of herself.

"Mr. Quinn," a woman's voice said over the intercom, "I have Courtney Blackmun's agent on line one. He says he won't talk to anybody other than the publisher on this one. Something about Ms. Blackmun wanting a new press kit. Shall I say you're in conference and can't be disturbed?"

Daniel depressed the button and spoke into the small brown box. "It's all right, Mrs. Feather. I'll take it." Picking up the phone, he deliberately smiled, hoping the smile would show in his voice. "Harry! Good to hear from you again. How's the tour going? Did Courtney get the flowers we sent? I caught her kickoff appearance on that talk show last week. She was wonderful, as usual."

Quickly moving the phone away from his ear so that he wouldn't go deaf, Daniel depressed the button that would send Harry's irate shouts bouncing off the walls of the paneled office, then adjusted the volume of the speaker phone.

"How's the tour going?" Harry screamed. "How's the tour going! It's *not* going, damn it! What idiot found it necessary to put the name of Courtney's daughter's boarding school in her press kit? She saw it this morning and damn near took the roof off the hotel. She refuses to go on with the tour until she has a whole new press kit."

Daniel rubbed a hand across his mouth, silently acknowledging that somebody in the publicity department had made a major blunder. Courtney Blackmun deserved a little privacy. She was one of their top money-makers and her fourteen books had been bestsellers both in hard cover and paperback.

But Courtney could also be Langley Books' major pain in the neck. Demanding and autocratic though she was, her fame made her very valuable—while her carefully worded contracts made her impervious to editing—and she must be kept happy at all costs, no matter how it galled Daniel to bow to her sometimes outrageous demands.

"But Harry," Daniel pointed out rationally, "the press kits preceded this tour by a good month. Printing new ones now with her daughter's school name deleted would only call attention to it."

Daniel could hear Harry's world-weary sigh through the speaker box. "*You* know that, Daniel, and *I* know that," the agent said tiredly. "The secret to our keeping Courtney from zooming straight through the ozone layer is in making sure *she* doesn't know that. We only need one, to show to her. See what you can do, all right? We'll be in Chicago on Friday for a cable show. Have a new kit waiting for us when we arrive."

"I'll do that," Daniel answered, glad that Harry was being reasonable. "And tell Courtney I'd be happy to take her out to dinner when she gets back to New York."

The agent laughed, his deep chuckles filling the room. "Good idea. She's always had a soft spot for you, hasn't she, Daniel? Even when you and Veronica—well, I gotta go now, to make nice-nice with the talent. Ten percent is ten percent, right?"

Daniel broke the connection, then leaned back in his high-backed leather swivel chair, the one he had inherited from Wilbur Langley when his father-in-law retired from the company to divide his time between his Park Avenue penthouse and his travels all over the globe. Publishing was a crazy business, he reflected, mentally composing a memo to the publicity department, but he loved it. He had always loved it.

Daniel had been at Langley since leaving college, rapidly rising through the ranks by means of his market-wise instincts and his uncanny ability to discover average writers and mold them into bestselling authors. Now, at the age of thirty-four, he was at the peak of his career. He was publisher of Langley Books, a position he had been destined to occupy—even if he hadn't been married to Wilbur Langley's only child, Veronica.

Veronica. Harry's mention of his late wife's name galled Daniel, for it seemed that even in New York, where there was a scandal a minute, the gossip about his failed marriage refused to fade away.

Thinking about Veronica naturally led Daniel to thinking about their son, Richie. Wilbur Langley hadn't been any more helpful with Richie than he had with Veronica. Wilbur loved Richie, and meant well, but he wasn't above using any method he could to earn his grandson's favor. After a lifetime spent showering his only daughter with lavish gifts and extravagant indulgences, he seemed determined to repeat that destructive history with his only grandson.

"He ruined Veronica with his indulgences," Daniel said aloud, hitting his clenched fist against the desktop. "I'll be damned if I'll let him turn Richie into the same sort of spoiled, willful child!"

Joey was beginning to think the ice cream cone had been a mistake. The double-dipped mint chocolate chip ice cream was coolly delicious, but it was also melting a lot faster in the hot afternoon sun than she could eat it. Shifting the sugar cone from one hand to the other, she licked at her spread fingers, chasing a bright green rivulet of ice cream with her tongue as she stepped down from the curb and headed across Forty-second Street.

It was just past three o'clock, and she still had a little more than two hours to kill before she picked up Daniel Quinn for their return to Saucon Valley. She might as well walk down toward the Port Authority, to see if her friend Bo-Jo still kept his hot dog wagon on the same corner. Bo-Jo Hennessey was one of her favorite New York characters, and she had written about him in her manuscript. Wait until she told him she had an "in" at Langley Books! Besides, Bo-Jo would give her a soda and a clean napkin to wipe off her hands.

Suddenly, her tongue halting in mid-swipe, her light gray eyes widening in disbelief behind her sunglasses, Joey watched a young boy approaching her from the other curb. She blinked twice, doubting what she was seeing, but the vision refused to go away.

It was Richie Quinn, walking across Forty-second Street big as life, wearing a borderline-obscene graphic T-shirt and a pair of neon orange-and-electric-blue-striped shorts. His high-top sneakers barely clung to his sockless feet, the shoelaces undone and slapping against the street with every step he took. There was a huge army-green canvas knapsack strapped to his back and he was wearing a very smug, very self-satisfied grin. He even had a portable tape player strapped to his waist, the earphones stuck in his ears.

He looked totally at home on the busy streets of Manhattan.

"But he *belongs* in a three-story Colonial in safe, quiet Saucon Valley," Joey announced out loud, as if striving to convince herself that she wasn't really witnessing some sort of twisted mirage.

Richie didn't see her standing stock-still in the middle of the intersection, but just kept walking, absently looking to his left as an ambulance went racing by, its siren blaring. He was about to pass within inches of Joey when she reached out her free hand and took hold of his knapsack, hauling him back two paces.

"Park it right here, buster!" she ordered.

"Hey! You nuts or something? Let go! Knock it off!" Richie countered without turning around, struggling to free himself.

"When Michael Jackson sings opera, sweetcakes," Joey responded coldly. "All right, young man—explain yourself."

"You!" Richie exclaimed incredulously, turning his head to look straight into her eyes. His grimace was comically painful. "Of all the stupid, dumb luck! What do you think the odds are for something like this happening? A thousand to one? A million?"

"Oh, I don't know," Joey answered consideringly, eyeing her melting ice cream cone. "I've heard that if you stand on a New York street corner long enough, sooner or later you'll see everyone you've ever met."

The light changed and one of New York's "finest" approached the pair, pleasantly inquiring if they planned to abandon the middle of the intersection any time soon, or if he should just direct the traffic around them.

Joey smiled at the policeman, ignoring his lilting sarcasm, and politely begged his pardon, attempting to drag

Richie back the way he had come, just as Richie tried to move in the other direction.

"She won't let go of me, officer," he told the policeman, his lower lip trembling in a way that immediately had Joey wishing spanking was still fashionable. "She must be some loony. I don't even know who she is. She just grabbed me and started telling me I remind her of her long-lost brother, or something. Don't arrest her or anything. She's harmless. I think she needs help, poor thing."

"Poor thing! Why, you *miserable*, fast-talking little beast, I'll—" Joey growled at the boy before looking up at the policeman, once more smiling brightly as that very tall, very large man stared down at her suspiciously, his fists on his hips. "Um, that is, please don't listen to him, officer," she pleaded quickly, suddenly feeling two feet high. "I work for his father. This boy is running away from home."

"Son?" the policeman questioned, looking at Richie intently.

Richie stood very straight, his arms at his sides, his chin in the air. "I never saw this woman before in my life!" he answered passionately, reminding Joey of every B-movie she had ever seen on the late-late show. She looked at him again, momentarily admiring the way he had somehow conjured up a tear in his left eye.

"Oh, good grief!" she declared, rolling her eyes. "Believe that one, officer, and I've got a great bridge you've just *got* to see. This is Richie Quinn, and his father is Daniel Quinn. Mr. Quinn works at Langley Books on Sixth Avenue. Like I said—I work for him."

"*As* I said—not *like* I said. You really should work on your grammar, you know," Richie corrected facetiously, too quietly for the policeman to overhear him. "She does not work for my father, or else I'd know who she is," he told the officer. "This is obviously a kidnap plot. I know all our employees. Why don't you ask her what she *says* she does for my father?"

"I'm his chauffeur!" Joey proudly announced at once, just before the officer's skeptical expression alerted her to the fact that she had charged headfirst into the neat little trap Richie had set for her.

She was dressed in a white blouse and black skirt—having left her vest and lace jabot in the limousine—and she was wearing orange-lensed sunglasses and bright purple high-top sneakers. Her hair was windblown, she looked young enough to be too young to buy a drink in Manhattan, and she was standing in the middle of the street with light green, chocolate-dotted goop dripping down her hand.

"Sure you are, honey," the policeman said soothingly, just as if she were a recent escapee from the home and apt to become dangerous at any moment, "and I'm the mayor of New York. Now, why don't you and the boy and I just walk on down to the station house on the corner, and I'm sure we can have this whole thing cleared up in no time."

"That's a great idea, sir," Richie complimented grandly, bowing as he backed toward the opposite curb. "But I don't think so. I have to go home now. My mother will be wondering where I am. Just let her go. I won't press charges. And I have your badge number, so my father will be sure to call your superiors to tell them how helpful you've been. Have a nice day, sir, and thank you."

Her upper arm gently but firmly held by the officer, Joey turned her head and watched as Richie Quinn tipped her a jaunty salute and melted into the crowd of pedestrians moving uptown. She yelled after him, "I'll get you for this, Richie Quinn! If it's the last thing I do, you rotten little monster, *I'll get you for this!*"

The policeman's indulgent grin disappeared like the sun behind a storm cloud. "Threats, is it now, missy? And to a nice young boy like that, worrying about his mother. For shame," he growled, his grip tightening on her upper arm. "Attempted kidnapping, and now terrorizing threats against that same child. All right, missy, we'll have it your way. Listen up. You have the right to remain silent—"

"What!" Joey turned to gape wide-eyed at the police officer as he read her her rights under the law. "You've got to be kidding, officer!" Out of the corner of her eye she saw Bo-Jo Hennessey standing beside his portable hot dog cart, practicing a tune on his harmonica. Immediately she shouted to him for help.

Bo-Jo, whom Joey had described in her manuscript as being "magnificently oblivious to the trials and tribulations of mere mortals" waved back at her and yelled, "Yo, Joey! Long time no see. How's the chauffeurin' business goin'?" before returning to his practice.

" . . . you have the right to have an attorney present during questioning—"

Joey knew when she was beaten. "Just great, Bo-Jo," she called out, grinning. "Couldn't be better. Catch you later." Under her breath she added, "In five to ten, I imagine, if I get time off for good behavior."

She was sitting on a worn wooden bench set against the far wall, slightly apart from the noise and confusion in the madhouse that made up the main receiving room of the police station. An elderly, poorly dressed man sat slumped beside her, snoring loudly, his head resting against her shoulder. Her feet were swinging back and forth a good four inches above the floor and she looked not so much angry as she did defeated. Defeated and frightened.

Daniel's heart went out to her. And he had thought walking the streets of New York would be boring. Obviously Joey Abbott had found a way around the problem. Richie had a lot to answer for this time.

He walked across the room, carefully threading his way between the startling array of felons and arresting officers until he was standing directly in front of his chauffeur. She

looked so young, so appealing; he couldn't help himself.
"So," he asked, tongue in cheek, "you come here often?"

Joey stiffened immediately, recognizing Daniel's voice.
Her head went up with a snap, dislodging the grumbling,
drunken man from her shoulder, and she glared at her boss.
"Where is he?" she growled, gritting her teeth. "Where is
that miniature mobster? You can have him when I'm done
with him—but I get first dibs. I'm going to kill him—slowly,
very slowly. And then I'm going to kill him all over again."

"You mean Richie, of course," Daniel answered reasonably, gently easing the still-sleeping man against the wooden
arm of the bench and sitting down. "He's with his grandfather. I believe he made his anonymous phone tip to the
police from there, and then the desk sergeant phoned me at
my office. I've already called his grandfather and told him
to have Richie ready to leave with us within the hour."

Joey gave a toss of her head, sniffing. She was still very
angry. "And you think that makes it all better? Am I supposed to be grateful that he tried to clear my good name—
considering the fact that he was the one who landed me in
this mess in the first place? Maybe you think now I'll only
want to kill him once instead of twice? That kid of yours
should be kept on a strong leash, do you know that? At the
very least he should come equipped with a warning label—
like explosives."

Daniel stared at Joey, noted the high color in her cheeks,
and felt his sense of humor tickled in spite of himself.
"You're angry, aren't you? I have a sort of sixth sense about
these things, you see," he said, silently deciding she looked
pretty explosive herself.

"Angry?" Joey repeated, rising. "Don't be ridiculous.
Why should I be angry? I've been hauled off to jail like a
common criminal—and *fingerprinted*! Look at me, I'm all
blue—and then locked in a holding pen with six of the most
frightening-looking women this side of a horror show—one

of them was named Peaches—and you wonder if I'm angry? No, I'm not angry—I'm homicidal!''

"Lower your voice, for crying out loud," Daniel advised quickly, standing up and looking around to make sure no one had overheard her. "That's how you got in here in the first place. Richie hadn't meant for you to be arrested. He was just frightened, and trying to get away from you. Everything would have worked out if you hadn't threatened him in front of the cop."

Joey put her hands on her hips and glared up at her employer. "You're kidding—right? I mean, you aren't actually *defending* that little monster! You can't be serious!''

And now she was supposed to go along to his grandfather's home and pick up the little darling to transport him back home? Fat chance! As far as Joey was concerned Daniel Quinn and his juvenile delinquent son could hitchhike back to Saucon Valley. She just wanted to forget this entire day had ever happened.

She started for the door, then stopped, her head drooping on her neck. "I forgot. I can't leave. Not until I pay the fine." She turned back to look at Daniel. "I don't suppose I could apply to you for a small loan? They don't seem to want to honor my credit cards."

Daniel was confused. He had arranged for all the charges to be dropped, promising to reprimand his son for his twisting of the truth, convincing the desk sergeant that the boy had meant no harm, that things had just somehow gotten out of hand. "What fine?" he asked, feeling more sorry for Joey by the moment.

Suddenly, after more than two hours of panic that had begun the moment the iron-barred door of the female holding cell closed behind her, the outright ridiculousness of the situation finally hit Joey, and she began to giggle. The giggles soon turned into hearty laughter, bringing tears to her eyes. *"Littering!"* she managed to squeak, holding on to herself as she rocked on her heels. "I got so mad at Richie that I threw my ice cream cone into the street in disgust. Officer O'Malley wrote me up for littering!''

Daniel was laughing along with her, for her laughter was infectious. "What flavor?" he managed to ask.

"Mint chocolate chip," Joey answered as they approached the desk sergeant and Daniel reached into his pocket to pull out his billfold. "My favorite."

"Adding insult to injury, I imagine?" Daniel commented as he waited for a receipt, then took hold of Joey's elbow and gently turned her toward the door. "If I buy you another cone, will you promise not to murder my son? He's no prize, but he's all I've got, and I'm rather attached to him. You understand, don't you?"

Joey took a deep breath of the warm late-afternoon air, feeling the tightness around her heart easing at last. How she had hated being locked inside that dreadful building, away from the light, her freedom gone. "Two scoops?" she asked, allowing Daniel's hand to remain on her elbow, secretly glorying in their slight physical contact.

"Two scoops," Daniel promised fervently as they descended the wide steps and headed for the cabstand on the corner, his smile very warm and very genuine.

A half hour later, after picking up Esmeralda at the parking garage, Daniel and Joey were on their way to Park Avenue and Wilbur Langley's penthouse apartment.

"I'll wait out here," Joey bit out from between clenched teeth, suddenly feeling rumpled and dirty and not up to meeting Wilbur Langley in his luxurious surroundings. She felt herself to be at enough of a disadvantage as it was, without opening herself up to Richie's sure-to-be-cutting remarks about her appearance. All she wanted now was to return to Saucon Valley as quickly as possible and then stand under a shower for at least an hour.

Daniel got out of the backseat and walked to the driver's door, pulling it open without ceremony. "You should keep that locked at all times," he cautioned automatically as he grabbed hold of her arm and half pulled her out onto the pavement. "Now, come with me. Richie's got some tall apologizing to do and I want to get it over with as soon as possible. I can't let him believe he's going to get away scot-free on this one or there'll be no dealing with him in the future."

Joey gave in, seeing that passersby were beginning to look at her. Normally this wouldn't bother her, but she had been the center of attention on one city street today and had learned her lesson. She went along quietly, following Daniel across the lobby to a private elevator he operated with a key he had taken from his billfold.

Thirty-seven floors of stony silence later, the silver metal doors whispered open and they stepped onto a snow-white cloud of carpeting that threatened to swallow Joey's ankles. The room they were in was more than large, it was immense, styled in stark black and white with touches of scarlet in the pillows, vases and a wall-sized painting, which was nothing more than a white background and an overwhelming pair of slightly parted, glistening red female lips. "How New York," Joey said noncommittally, hating the place on sight.

"Wilbur's in his starkly sexual period, or at least that's how he explained it to me," Daniel informed her tightly, and the censure in his voice made her look up at him. A muscle was working in his cheek as his gaze remained deliberately above the many marble statues of lovers embracing each other in a variety of casual to semishocking ways. "Rich!" he called out, obviously in a hurry to remove both his son and himself from the apartment as soon as possible. "Richie! Front and center—now!"

Suddenly, the deep plush of the carpet giving no warning of his entrance, a man appeared inside the room, obviously having been outside the windowed wall that opened onto a large balcony. "Daniel, my boy!" Wilbur Langley cried warmly, briskly walking across the expanse, his hand outstretched in greeting. "And this must be the loyal employee who got turned in to the coppers by my reprobate grandson. You rescued her, of course, just like the white knight you are. My, my, she looks quite the worse for wear, doesn't she?"

Joey looked at Wilbur Langley with mingled interest and anger. He was quite a man, tall, broad shouldered and extremely handsome despite his years. His silver mane topped a deeply tanned face, a face that wore a smile that seemed genuinely welcoming. "Mr. Langley," she responded wonderingly, knowing that she was in danger of succumbing to his smile in spite of herself. "Lovely place you've got here—if you're into 'weird.' "

Wilbur laughed out loud, taking her hand and raising it to his lips. "*Touché*, my dear," he congratulated. "I deserved that, didn't I? You don't like my decorations? I admit to being bored with them myself. They were the result of the decorative talents of one of my recent companions, but it's time her inspirations followed her out of my life. Would you care to be in charge of the renovations? I've been thinking about blue—everything blue."

Joey couldn't fight it any longer. Wilbur Langley was a "character," and she'd always been intrigued by characters. "Blue would be nice—except denim blue. I don't think you could be comfortable in anything resembling a rustic setting. You seem more the midnight-blue-velvet type. What do you think, Daniel?"

The tic in Daniel's cheek was beating like a congo drum. "I think we'd better lasso Richie and get the hell out of here before Wilbur hires you away from me. Wilbur, where have you hidden him?"

The older man stepped back a pace, pressing a hand to his chest. "Hidden him, dear boy? *Moi?* As if I'd ever do such a thing. Whatever makes you think that?"

"Experience," Daniel retorted sharply, brushing past his father-in-law to walk toward the balcony. "Richie! Don't make this any harder than it has to be."

Richie Quinn stepped in front of the open doors, then moved inside the room to face his father. "Sorry, Dad. I didn't hear you the first two times you called me," he explained. Joey stifled a giggle, wondering if Richie realized exactly what he had said. He walked past his father, to stand beside Wilbur. "Miss Abbott," he went on, nodding slightly to Joey while deliberately avoiding her eyes. "Are you all right now? I'm sorry I couldn't stick around earlier, but you know how it is. I had already promised to meet Grandpa at the Plaza for high tea."

"You *knew* he was coming to the city?" Daniel asked his father-in-law. "You knew, and you didn't phone me? Damn it, man—oh, what's the use in talking about it? You're worse than he is."

Wilbur Langley hastened to smooth the ruffled waters and protect his grandson. "I was going to tell you, Daniel. Right after high tea. The Plaza makes the best hot fudge sundaes in town, you know."

"Oh, brother!" Joey exclaimed, suddenly seeing the resemblance between Richie and his grandfather. No wonder Daniel was having so much trouble with his son. The two of them were, separately or together, a real piece of work. It was time she stepped in and fought her own battle with Richie, before her grievances got lost in the shuffle. She walked down the two steps into the living room, not stopping until she was nose to nose with the boy.

"Is there still a problem, Miss Abbott?" Richie asked, his tone no longer so self-assured, for now both she and his father were looking at him strangely.

"*You*'ve got the problem, sonny boy," Joey shot back at him, lightly jabbing a finger against his chest. "I'm not quite as civilized as your father and your grandfather, and I'm more than willing to make a scene. If you don't start apologizing to me in ten seconds—and apologizing hard—I'm going to start raining all over your little parade. You got that, buster?''

The three males in the room, all in various stages of shock, opened their mouths, but it was Richie who spoke. "I'm sorry, Joey. I didn't mean to get you into any trouble! Honest! I won't do it again." he promised, clearly amazed at the sound of his own voice, and just as clearly relieved that Wilbur's housekeeper took that moment to enter the room and announce dinner.

Chapter Four

"Dessert? You've got to be kidding." Joey held out her hand and shook her head. "No, honestly, Wilbur, I couldn't swallow another bite. What? Mississippi Mud Pie? Oh, my *favorite*! It's like eating fudge in pastry. I give up—you've found my weak spot."

Wilbur deftly sliced a piece of the pie and handed the platinum-edged plate to Daniel, who grinned wickedly as he passed it to Joey. "We'll have to get more air in the tires before we head home," he teased, amazed that anyone so little could eat so much. He was liking his lady chauffeur more with each passing minute, and not just because she had succeeded so brilliantly in bringing Richie to heel. Richie's apology an hour earlier had been genuine and he'd been on his best behavior ever since.

"Do you know how much cholesterol there is in chocolate, Joey?" Richie teased now from across the glass-topped dining room table, rolling his eyes. "I can almost hear your arteries clogging."

Joey pointedly took a forkful of the pie and waved it lazily in Richie's direction before putting it into her mouth, her eyes slowly closing in ecstasy as the chocolate seduced her taste buds. "Ah, kiddo, but what a way to go!" she pointed out, sighing.

Richie's mouth worked silently as Joey slid a second piece of pie past her lips, her smile suggesting she had just died and gone to heaven.

Wilbur watched the exchange, measuring the thrusts and parries of the two combatants, then smiled as Richie quietly asked his grandfather to cut a slice of the pie for him. "Only a small one, please, Grandpa," he temporized. "After all, I did eat all my broccoli."

Daniel had also been watching Joey's play with the fork, and he felt a strange, hungry sensation growing in his belly that had nothing to do with Mississippi Mud Pie.

Joey Abbott intrigued him—there was no denying it. She was working in a profession he hadn't considered geared to female participation, yet she was one of the most feminine women he'd ever met. She might be small and perishable looking, but her character and determination seemed rock solid.

She'd handled the harrowing incident on the highway without turning a hair, when he had been sure they were moments away from death.

She'd dared to beard Richie in his protective grandfather's den and come off the rousing victor, capturing Wilbur Langley's admiration as well as Richie's, and Daniel's, respect.

But in those first few moments at the police station, when he had observed her unnoticed, he had seen a frightened, defeated Joey Abbott, a sad, caged canary who had lost the power to sing. He had been given a glimpse behind the lighthearted free spirit to the vulnerable woman beneath the cheerful exterior.

She was, he decided, a complex human being. She was also infinitely appealing.

The question was: what was he going to do about it, if anything? He had enough to deal with finding some way to reach Richie without entertaining thoughts of romancing his chauffeur. *Romancing his chauffeur?* Even the thought was ludicrous!

Wilbur rose at the head of the table, patting his flat stomach as if congratulating it on having received another fine meal. "Well, I guess you three will want to be on the road soon. Are you sure I can't interest you in an after-dinner brandy, Joey? Just a small one? You didn't even touch your wine. It's a long ride back to the wilds of Saucon Valley. Terrible place—I can't imagine life without the Met within strolling distance!"

"I'm driving, Wilbur, remember?" Joey answered, also rising. "I never drink when I'm on duty."

"Grandpa?" Richie interrupted, moving to Wilbur's side as they reentered the living room. "Do I really have to go with them? I just wanted to visit with you for a few days. I miss you so much."

Daniel, who had allowed himself to mellow a bit over dinner, felt his jaws tightening as his son began working his wiles on his grandfather. "Richie, we've been over this and over this," be broke in before Wilbur could respond. "You're never going to learn to live in Saucon Valley if you keep running back to New York every five minutes. You've got to give our new home a chance."

Give me a chance, Joey thought as she stood discreetly to one side, knowing that although Daniel hadn't said as much, it was what he had meant. She felt very sorry for Daniel Quinn. He might rule Langley Books, something she had found out during dinner, but when it came to his son he was totally at sea. It was sad to watch.

"Hey, wait a minute, guys," she broke in, reminding them of the promise she had exacted from Richie before

Wilbur invited them to remain in town for dinner. "This kid has an appointment with me tomorrow, to sign up for baseball. That was the deal we struck before dinner, right?"

The look Richie threw her would have melted mint chocolate chip ice cream at ten paces, but Joey ignored it. She knew Richie was beginning to like her, in spite of himself. "You owe me, kiddo, remember? I'd accept your apology for having me tossed in the pokey if you'd promise to join my baseball team."

Richie pouted at her, trying one more time to wriggle out of his punishment, mostly out of habit. "You tricked me into it," he declared, then added brightly, "besides, the agreement would never stand up in court."

"Then aren't I the lucky one that this case will never see court," Joey observed mildly. "Your father okayed the arrangement, Richie, if you'll remember, and that's good enough for me."

Wilbur, who had admitted he thought Joey's idea of punishment was very amusing "in a droll sort of way" when first he'd heard it, seemed to undergo a change of heart. "Daniel," he said, facing his son-in-law, "don't you think Richie's been punished enough? After all, it was only a harmless prank. Not that Joey's wasn't a delightful suggestion, of course. I think we should all just forget it now."

"Oh, sure, that's easy for you to say. But then *you* didn't have to bunk with Peaches all afternoon," Joey groused, crossing her arms over her chest as Wilbur looked at her in confusion. "Besides, a deal's a deal. And you can turn off the waterworks, Richie—those tears won't cut any mustard with me. I've seen it all before, remember?"

Daniel looked from Richie to Joey, watching as the young woman outstared his son, and wondered why it bothered him that Joey seemed able to reach Richie while he could not. Granted, the two seemed to do nothing but argue, but Joey was winning those arguments, which was more than could be said for his own constant running battles with his son.

Besides, Richie was going to play baseball. Daniel had always wanted his son to play the game. Almost black-mailing him into joining a team wasn't Daniel's idea of the right way of going about the thing, but there were times when the end justified the means. "Richie," he warned in what he hoped was his most fatherly voice.

Richie shrugged his thin shoulders fatalistically. "All right, all right, I give up," he agreed, turning to kiss Wil-bur goodbye. "But baseball's still stupid. I'm only going to do it for Joey."

Seeing the hurt that clouded Daniel's eyes, Joey winced, then hastened to bid her host good-night and hurried toward the elevator. Kids could be so darn cruel, she thought, sighing.

"I don't feel right about this, Joey. Are you sure you should be driving home alone on these country roads this late at night?"

Daniel was standing on the driveway, watching as Joey slipped into the backseat to retrieve the attaché case he had forgotten to take with him as he stepped out of the limou-sine. "Don't worry about me," he heard her say as he tried not to notice how shapely her exposed legs were as she leaned across the velvet seat. "It's only eleven o'clock. I don't turn back into a pumpkin for another hour." She backed out of the car and turned to hand him the case. "There you go, all set!"

Daniel reached out to take the case and their hands col-lided on the handle, each of them pulling back at the same time, as if they'd been stung. The case dropped to the driveway and Daniel bent to pick it up, giving him the time he needed to compose himself.

Joey used that same time to take a deep breath and give her head a small shake. She'd felt the electric current flowing between them in those few short seconds and it had startled her. Joey already knew she found Daniel attractive, but she hadn't counted on such a sharp, physical response at his slightest touch. She must be more desperate for male companionship than she had thought. She really should get out more.

"So," she heard him say as he straightened, "you'll be picking up Richie at three tomorrow afternoon? He'll be ready, if I have to handcuff him. That boy needs a lesson."

"That *boy* needs to be a boy," Joey replied quickly, speaking before she could think. "I—um, that is—I didn't mean—"

"Yes, you did," Daniel said, cutting her off. "And you're absolutely right. Half the time he acts old enough to be my father, and the rest of the time he behaves like a three-year-old. A particularly *backward* three-year-old. I'd like to apologize again for what he did to you today. I should ground him until he's thirty for hopping a bus to New York, but it was Wilbur who sent him the fare. How do I ground a man like Wilbur? He thinks he's Peter Pan—he'd just fly away."

Joey could see the pain in Daniel's eyes, and hear the confusion and sorrow in his voice even as he tried to make a joke. She hastened to assure him that she was none the worse for wear after her short stint in jail. "Hey, I already told you not to worry about it," she responded, deliberately smiling. "Not every girl can brag about being fingerprinted. I just hope I look all right on my mug shot."

"We never did get you another mint chocolate chip ice cream cone," Daniel pointed out, knowing he was keeping her talking just so that he wouldn't have to say good-night and go inside the house. Richie was in the house, waiting to pounce, after sitting silent as a stone beside him in the backseat all the way home. He was sure of it. He also was sure he wasn't up to another confrontation before midnight.

"That's all right, really," Joey told him, suddenly feeling extremely protective of this very large, very self-sufficient male. She wished she could say something that would take that haunted, hurt look from his face. "I'll let you owe me. Well, I guess I should be on my way. Tell Richie to be ready by two-thirty. I want to have time to introduce him to the other kids before practice starts." She turned to leave, then another thought struck her. "He has a glove, doesn't he?"

"Damn!"

"I'll take that as a no," she said, turning to face Daniel once more. "There's a good sporting goods store near the park if you want me to take him there before practice. An outfielder's glove, I imagine, as I have a feeling Richie is a natural-born right fielder."

"That's where we always put the kids who couldn't catch a Ping-Pong ball in a barrel," Daniel remembered, scowling as he spoke. He'd played first base himself, both in high school and college. The thought of having his son, his only hope of immortality, shipped off to right field was very lowering. "Does it have to be right field?"

Joey shrugged. "It's a start," she offered lamely, then turned on her heels once more, wishing she had never started all of this in the first place. She should have sentenced Richie to washing Esmeralda twice a week for a month. She hadn't meant to cause Daniel any more pain than he already had. She wouldn't want to fight a tug-of-war over a child of hers against Wilbur Langley.

"A hundred dollars enough?" he called after her.

"A hundred dollars? Enough for what?" Joey's mind grasped at understanding Daniel's words.

"For a mitt," he explained. "It's been a while since I priced one. I want him to have a good one—oversize, to give him every chance at snagging a fly ball."

Joey shook her head. "For a hundred dollars I can get him a mitt *and* a butterfly net—for the really hard-to-catch balls, you understand."

Daniel blushed and was thankful that Joey couldn't see his painfully flushed cheeks in the dim light radiating from the porch. "Whatever," he said, looking after her as she walked around Esmeralda to get back behind the wheel. She was leaving, and he didn't want her to go—and not just because he wanted to delay his talk with Richie. "Don't forget to lock your door."

"Good night, Daniel. See you Friday."

She had already turned the key in the ignition when Daniel's knuckles tapped at the tinted window, and she lowered it warily, wondering what was wrong.

"What would you say," he began, bending down to lean in the opening, "if I tagged along with you and Rich tomorrow? I mean, I had planned to work at home tomorrow, so it isn't as if I'd be losing time I couldn't make up somewhere else in the day. That is, if you don't think I'd get in the way or anything..."

Now it was Joey's turn to rescue Daniel. "I think that would be just fine," she told him hurriedly before he could feel foolish for begging to share some time with his own son. "We'll see you at two o'clock—so we can stop at the sporting goods store."

"We?"

Joey laughed, then explained. "We, Daniel. As in Esmeralda and me." She patted the steering wheel. "*This* is Esmeralda. We go everywhere together."

As Daniel watched the gleaming white limousine pull out of the driveway onto the narrow macadam road he scratched his head, wondering how Richie was going to take this latest development, then realizing he didn't care if Richie liked it. *He* liked it very much.

* * *

In the end, Joey left Esmeralda at home, opting instead to pick up Daniel and Richie in her five-year-old baby-blue Mercedes convertible, even if that meant she wouldn't be able to take the entire team to the local ice cream shop for a treat after practice.

Esmeralda was too formal for what she wanted to accomplish, for the mood she wanted to set. After all, how could she expect the other kids to take Richie seriously if he arrived in a limousine, with his chauffeur opening the door for him as he stepped out onto the baseball diamond with his brand-new, unbroken-in outfielder's glove? It would be the kiss of death!

Of course, there was another reason for leaving Esmeralda behind in the garage, and that other reason was Daniel Quinn. Joey rather liked the idea of having Daniel riding up front in the passenger seat beside her as they drove to the field. She wanted to know this man better, whether it was professionally correct to do so or not.

Daniel stepped out of the front door of the rambling brick Colonial as Joey pulled into the driveway, and she nearly ran the Mercedes into a rhododendron bush when she saw how he was dressed. Gone was the dark pin-striped suit and sedate tie, and with it the air of a successful businessman. In its place were a broad-shoulder-hugging, kelly-green polo shirt and white cotton duck slacks that accentuated his narrow waist and long, muscular legs. The front of his chestnut hair lifted slightly in the breeze and he was wearing a smile that seemed relaxed, almost boyish.

This man could make a serious dent in my heart, Joey decided, turning off the ignition and stepping out onto the driveway, purposely keeping the Mercedes between her and her very appealing contract client. "Hi," she breathed, unsurprised to find that this single mundane word was suddenly the limit of her vocabulary.

"Hi, yourself," Daniel countered, his white-toothed grin forcing her to clutch the side-view mirror to maintain her footing. What had happened since she picked Daniel up yesterday morning to change her acknowledgment of his attractiveness into a wild, uncontrollable crush?

"Rich will be out in a minute."

Mention of Richie's name effectively wiped the inane smile from Joey's face as reality came crashing back in on her. Richie. The reason for their meeting today. The ten-year-old walking emotional accident, looking for a place to happen. "Is that a promise," she asked, tilting her head to one side, "or just wishful thinking?"

Daniel's expression turned stern. "It's a promise," he said, walking over to lay a hand on the hood of the Mercedes. "Don't look now, but Esmeralda seems to have shrunk—and turned blue. Not that it matters. We won't be needing this today, if you don't mind. We'll take my car, if you just point me in the right direction."

Like many good drivers, Joey hated being relegated to the passenger side of the front seat. If her brother, Andy, had been there he would have given an exaggerated grimace and covered his head with his hands the moment Daniel spoke. But Andy wasn't there, and Joey didn't explode or make the suggestion that Daniel was being slightly chauvinistic. She just reached inside the car, pocketed the keys and said, "Fine by me, Daniel," her expectations for their day together soaring higher and higher.

The sound of the front door of the house slamming closed made them both turn their heads in that direction just in time to see the door open once more and the red-faced Mrs. Hemmings emerge behind Richie, a large wooden spoon in her hand. "I don't care who your grandfather is, young man, you'd better not sass me again, not if you know what's good for you!"

"Oh, yeah," Richie countered, hands on hips, "well, we'll just see about that, won't we? Grandpa says you're just the hired help, and the hired help don't tell the employer what to do. Grandpa says—"

"Richie!" The single word shot through the air like a booming cannonball slamming against a brick wall. Joey winced as Daniel started back up the steps to the covered porch, fire in his eyes. "Apologize to Mrs. Hemmings at once!"

"Dad," Richie remarked, surprised. "I didn't see you out here."

"Obviously. Now, what's going on here?"

Both housekeeper and son began speaking at once, so that Joey only heard the random words "farina" and "make my own bed" and "I've never seen the like before" as Daniel looked from one to the other, his frown deepening into a furious scowl.

So much for romance. Joey let an exasperated sigh escape her lips, then leaned back against the Mercedes to watch the action. Daniel surprised her. She had decided that he was a loving father, but totally inept at handling his son— and maybe even a little afraid of him. If he had been any or all of these things, he was certainly a fast learner at finding ways to correct his previous shortcomings.

"Let me get this straight," Joey heard him say when the complaints finally stopped. "Richie—you don't make up your own bed in the morning? Saunders never said anything—Saunders was our housekeeper in New York, Mrs. Hemmings," he told the woman. "You're nearly eleven, Richie. Beginning tomorrow, you'll make your own bed or sleep in it unmade. Now, what's this about farina?"

"He refuses to eat it, that's what," Mrs. Hemmings said, shaking her head. "My Herbert ate farina every morning of his life, and he still would if he wasn't dead."

"It's probably what killed him," Richie sniped, sticking out his chin, and Joey found herself hiding a smile behind her hand.

"There—he said it again, Mr. Quinn!" Mrs. Hemmings pointed out, waving the spoon in Richie's direction. "In all my born days, I can't remember a child with such an evil tongue. I saw this movie last night—"

"*The Bad Seed?*" Daniel interposed wryly, believing he knew what the housekeeper was trying to say.

Mrs. Hemmings shook her head. "*Mary Poppins*," she corrected. "The one with Julie Andrews in it. Such a pretty girl—and what a lovely voice! Anyway, I have to tell you, Mr. Quinn, I'm no Mary Poppins. She might have been able to handle this boy of yours, but not me! I think I'll have to hand in my notice."

Richie's eyes lit with triumph. Joey saw it, standing twenty feet away. Daniel was closer. He not only saw it—he reacted. "Richie," he said, his tone the one he must normally have reserved for the boardroom, for Joey hadn't heard it before, even in those tense moments in Wilbur's penthouse, "you are to *apologize* at once to Mrs. Hemmings. Furthermore, beginning today you are going to be assigned daily chores in order to *help* Mrs. Hemmings. We'll start with making your own bed, taking out the trash and...and..."

"And clearing the table after meals," Mrs. Hemmings added helpfully, the light that had suddenly died in Richie's eyes now gleefully gleaming in hers.

Joey had to turn away to hide another smile as Richie, once more caught off stride, quietly apologized to the housekeeper before both he and his father left the porch and approached the Mercedes.

"All set?" Daniel asked with a forced smile as he opened the passenger door, forgetting that he had planned to drive his own car. Clearly he was more upset by this latest knowledge about his son than he was willing to reveal to Joey. "Richie," he ordered, "get yourself into the backseat, and keep your mouth shut."

"Hi, Richie," Joey said cheerfully, receiving an unintelligible mutter from the boy in reply. Pulling the car keys from her pocket, she slid behind the wheel and turned the ignition, glad she had opted to put the top down, for the heat emanating from the backseat would have made a closed car feel like an inferno. "First stop, Crazy Louie's discount sporting goods store," she announced, mentally crossing her fingers in the hope the remainder of the afternoon would go smoothly.

"Tuesday, Thursday and Saturday? That's great! I go in to the city Monday, Wednesday and Friday. It couldn't be better. You can count me in!"

Joey overheard Daniel's answer to head coach Steve Mitchum's suggestion that he sign on as the team's first base coach. Her heart did a small flip in her chest as she lifted her eyes to the blue summer sky and whispered a fervent "thank you."

It had been, all things considered, a most wonderful afternoon. For Daniel. Clearly he was in his element on a ball field, shagging balls in the outfield, taking charge of batting practice for a while and even helping instruct the pint-size pitching staff.

He looked years younger than Steve, and much more physically fit, even though both men were about the same age. His chestnut hair tamped down beneath a blue Bulldogs baseball cap, he had even taken a few swings of his own during batting practice, knocking three balls over the center field fence. Running around the bases after the last hit, he laughingly doffed his cap as the team cheered him on, and then, sliding into home plate, he completely ruined his white slacks.

As she sat in the shade beside the cement dugout, Joey allowed her smile to fade as she caught sight of Richie—standing among the ankle-high white-topped dandelions in right field. Obviously this first practice wasn't going as swimmingly for the ten-year-old Quinn.

"There's going to be many a splinter in that boy's bottom before the end of the season if we can't find some way to reach him," she mused, shaking her head as she remembered how painfully inept Richie looked at bat, on the bases and now deep in no-man's-land.

And Richie was hating every minute of it, Joey was sure. She had seen him looking at his father, his expression confused, as that man had patiently helped another child adjust his grip on the bat. Richie's pain had nearly broken her heart. Richie loved his father, just as Daniel loved his son. But getting them both to admit to that love was going to be a problem.

Steve had taken charge of Richie at the beginning of the practice, just as Joey had hoped, but he had admitted to her only a few minutes earlier that the boy did not exactly show signs of being a natural athlete. From her vantage point beside the dugout, Joey had watched Daniel watching Richie, and it was obvious to her that Daniel's opinion coincided with Steve's.

"There has to be something I can do," she declared, her gray eyes narrowed as she rose to her feet, brushing off the seat of her jeans.

"Do about what?" Daniel asked, coming up beside her. Without waiting for her answer, he continued. "This is great, isn't it? You know Steve asked me to help coach the team, don't you? You don't mind, do you? I mean, I'm not stepping on any toes, am I?"

Oh, brother, Joey thought, sighing. *I thought a man had to be older than Daniel is before he entered his second childhood.* "No, I don't mind," she told him honestly as they walked across the first-base line toward the pitching mound. "Steve needs more help, as I can only be here when I'm not on the road with Esmeralda. But I don't know how

Richie is going to take your good news. He doesn't seem exactly thrilled to be here, does he?''

Daniel turned his head to look toward right field. Richie was sitting on the grass, his new fielder's glove stuck on his head to shade his eyes from the late-afternoon sun. ''He looks lost, doesn't he?'' he commented, sighing. ''Poor kid. I would have gone to him, but Steve said dads shouldn't coach their own kids. He told me experience has taught him that we tend to be too hard on our own flesh and blood. How could I be hard on Richie? I could cry for him. He looks like a fish out of water.''

Joey knew Daniel was reaching out to her, asking for her help, and she stubbornly ignored any niggling thoughts that she could be getting in over her head. She sought wildly in her mind, then heard herself saying, ''We've tried him everywhere except on the pitching mound. Do you think we should give him a try?''

The practice had wound down and Steve and most of the team had already gone. Daniel looked around for a moment, then shrugged. ''Why not? It's worth a shot. Hey, Richie! Come here a minute.''

Richie got up slowly, then jogged in to join them on the pitcher's mound. ''I hope you're satisfied,'' he accused coldly, looking directly at Joey, his expression more hurt than angry. ''I looked like a real jerk out there. Everybody was laughing at me.''

Joey ignored him, even as she pitied him. ''Your dad and I want to see if you can pitch,'' she told him, already walking back to the dugout to get a catcher's mask and mitt. ''Daniel,'' she called back over her shoulder, ''you can toss a few in to me to give him the general idea.''

''She's kidding, right?'' Richie asked his father, pulling a face. ''I mean, she really doesn't think I'm going to do this, does she? Dad, help! Get me out of here.''

''She's Joey to you, or Ms. Abbott,'' Daniel answered, slipping his own glove onto his right hand, watching appreciatively as Joey, in jeans and halter top, walked away from them. ''And no, she's not kidding. Now, pay attention. We're both left-handed, so you can just imitate my moves.''

Richie spread his feet and lifted his chin in defiance. He'd had a long afternoon, and clearly he felt he had been pushed as far as he was willing to go. He had begun to like Joey, and now he felt she had betrayed him. ''I won't do it, and you can't make me. I know what you're doing. You don't really care about me. If you want to ask Joey out, go ask her. I don't want her anyway!''

''That's enough! Go to the car—*now*!'' The sound of Daniel's voice raised in anger had Joey looking quickly toward the pitching mound, just in time to see Richie blindly running toward the Mercedes.

She turned to go to the boy, then looked at Daniel and realized that for the moment, he needed her more. He was still standing on the pitching mound, staring at his raised left hand as if it didn't belong to him. She ran to his side, taking his arm. ''Daniel,'' she asked softly, ''what is it? What happened?''

He looked down at her, visibly shaken, his blue eyes bleak. ''I raised my hand to him,'' he said, speaking as if he were slightly dazed. ''I almost slapped my son. I've never laid a finger on him, Joey—*ever*—but just now...'' He pressed a hand to his eyes. ''I had such high hopes for today. I thought he liked you. I thought we could begin to establish a relationship, find some sort of common ground. What a joke! My God, what am I going to do now? Maybe Wilbur's right, and I should let Richie go live with him.''

Joey bit her lip, trying not to succumb to the need to slide her arms around Daniel and lend him her comfort. ''You'd do that?'' she asked, squeezing his forearm, her voice deliberately mocking. ''He's your son, Daniel, not a throwaway soda bottle. You have to make this work, for your sake as well as his.''

Daniel placed his free hand over hers on his arm. He smiled, but his smile was wan, defeated. ''A throwaway soda bottle, Joey? That's an unusual comparison. You're right, however. I've got to go on trying. Richie's been through a lot, you know."

Joey nodded, not really wanting to hear more. She was getting too involved as it was. "Growing up without a mother isn't easy. I know that from my own experience," she offered sympathetically. "But you're a good father, and you and Richie will eventually work things out."

"Eventually," Daniel repeated dourly. "I don't know if I can wait that long."

Joey shrugged, then bent to pick up their gloves and started back to the dugout to gather up the rest of their gear, Daniel tagging along beside her like a stray puppy intent on following her home. How did she always manage to get herself mixed up in everyone else's problems? "We'd better not leave Richie alone too long, Daniel. If that kid of yours is half as smart as I give him credit for, he'll soon get bored waiting for us, hot-wire my car and head for the New Jersey Turnpike."

Daniel nodded, taking the heavy canvas bag full of bats and mitts from her and hefting it onto his shoulder as they walked to the car. "Much as I'm sure you've seen enough of anybody named Quinn to last you a lifetime, Joey, would you go to dinner with me tonight? I'd really like to talk with you some more."

Joey looked up at him. "About Richie, I suppose?" she asked, feeling her heart sink to her toes.

"About Richie," Daniel admitted, then added softly, "and . . . other things."

The "other things" had her heart making a spectacular rebound, repositioning itself somewhere high in her throat. Consigning her feelings of personal protection to a far corner of her mind, Joey smiled up at him, saying, "I hear they make a great version of Mississippi Mud Pie at some new restaurant on Cedar Crest Boulevard. I can't be bought, Daniel—but that doesn't mean I'm not open to bribes."

Chapter Five

The restaurant had been decorated in an upscale, metropolitan decor that blended well with the more personal, homey atmosphere created by the staff. Joey and Daniel had spent more than a half hour sipping their drinks while waiting for their table to open, speaking of generalities and enjoying the people around them.

It was only after they had placed their orders that Daniel took a deep breath and searched his mind for some way to begin explaining the complex bundle of nerves that was his son. It wasn't going to be easy for him, and the sight of Joey sitting across the small round table from him wasn't helping matters at all.

He had known she was pretty, and had already privately acknowledged that he was physically attracted to her. But he'd had no idea of the shattering effect a simple, sophisticated, slim black sheath, a small amount of artfully applied makeup and the soft candlelight flickering against her smooth skin would have on his powers of concentration.

She was sitting quietly, a miniature oasis of calm in his increasingly frenetic world, interestedly observing her surroundings, her moist red lips parted in a slight smile as her intelligent gray eyes sparkled with delight. Was her delight with the evening, or with him? And why did it matter so much to him?

He realized that they had been sitting in silence for almost five minutes. "About Richie—" he began after clearing his throat.

Joey turned her head to face him and she leaned forward slightly, as if encouraging him to confide in her. "You may not believe this, Daniel, but I really do like your son. He may be a handful, but you have to admit—he's never boring."

Daniel averted his eyes and began idly toying with his salad fork. "He's a pretty likable kid. You're probably wondering why I lost my temper with him this afternoon."

Joey smiled, shaking her head. "Actually, using my own brief experience with him as a guide, I'm wondering what took you so long. Surely you must have been tempted long before today."

They both laughed, easing the sudden tension that had sprung up between them with just the mention of Richie's name. Daniel wasn't thrilled that Joey recognized that his son was a problem, but it was a relief to finally have someone agree with him. Richie's teachers in the private school he attended in Manhattan had had nothing but praise for his outstanding academic achievements, and the doting Wilbur Langley refused to listen to a single word against his grandson, believing the child to be perfect in every way.

"My wife, Veronica, died when Richie was three," Daniel began quietly, knowing no other way to start than at the beginning. "After her death, and with Wilbur retiring from the company shortly after the funeral to travel the world, I devoted myself almost exclusively to Langley Books, even more than I had before she died. Richie is now making me pay the price of my neglect of him.''

Joey raised her eyebrows skeptically. ''I'd hardly term Richie a neglected child.''

Daniel shook his head. ''Materially, no, he's not. Wilbur showered him with gifts from abroad for years, then doubled his efforts when he returned to New York three years ago and found that his grandson was now old enough to be a companion of sorts. Richie had always been a quiet child, you understand, so it was easy for me to turn most of his care over to Saunders, and the nurse I hired when he was still a baby. It wasn't until Wilbur reentered our lives that the real trouble started, although I should have been paying more attention to the warning signs.''

''Warning signs?'' Joey prompted when Daniel fell silent.

He nodded. ''Richie knew the alphabet and numbers when he was two, and it was all uphill from there. By the time he was seven I didn't have a clock or radio in the whole apartment that he hadn't taken apart and put back together three times. I enrolled him in gifted classes at the recommendation of his teachers, then left the raising of him to others while I buried myself in my own work.'' He leaned forward, lowering his voice. ''You know, I read somewhere that many gifted children may be able to run rings around other people intellectually, yet not possess the common sense to come in out of the rain.''

Joey laughed out loud. ''Daniel! You're overreacting. Richie has plenty of common sense. I'm sure he'd at least take an umbrella.''

''Really?'' Daniel leaned back once more. ''Did my son display any common sense when he hopped a bus to New York? Have you ever been inside the Port Authority? He's only ten years old. Anything could have happened to him!''

Joey took a sip of her wine. "You have a point there. But it was Wilbur's idea, wasn't it? You can't blame a ten-year-old for listening to his grandfather."

"All roads lead back to Wilbur Langley," Daniel said, sighing. "You know," he told her, his voice filled with yearning, "all I ever wanted was a kid I could play ball with—but somehow, we both seem to have gotten lost along the way."

Joey felt sorry for Daniel, yet was angry with him for kicking himself so hard. "You can't blame yourself for what you think are your failures with Richie. It must have been hard for you—for both of you—when your wife died. It was only natural for you to bury yourself in your work."

Daniel's voice hardened. "Veronica walked out on us when Richie was six months old. He never really knew her, except for the few times she descended out of nowhere to shower gifts on him before flitting off somewhere else. Our marriage had been a mistake from the beginning, and I was just as glad to see her go running off in search of what she called fun. I was sorry she had to die in that plane crash, but I'd be a hypocrite if I said I had still loved her."

Joey sat back while the waiter placed two tossed salads on the table, her expression turning pensive. "I don't know what to say, Daniel. 'I'm sorry' just doesn't seem to cover it. But you have Richie with you now, away from Wilbur and his influence—which I assumed prompted you to move to Saucon Valley in the first place. You'll just have to take it one day at a time. Your relationship will grow, if you both give it a chance."

"Yes," Daniel agreed, giving her the ghost of a smile. "But now there's another complication."

"Another—I don't understand."

Daniel reached across the table and took her hand. "You, Joey. You're the new complication."

"*Me?* What do I have to do with anything?"

"Richie likes you," Daniel explained, ignoring his salad. "I don't think he wanted to, but he does just the same. He wants your approval, which is why I found him in the garage tonight, tossing a baseball against a target he'd painted on the wall. You've reached him, Joey—when I couldn't."

Joey was pleased, but confused. "I'm flattered. But then why did he run away this afternoon, instead of letting us watch him pitch?"

Daniel took a deep breath, then explained. "He doesn't know which Quinn you want for a friend. It's either/or in Richie's mind."

"He doesn't think I'm only pretending to like him in order to get to you, does he?" she asked once the waiter had removed the uneaten appetizers and replaced them with the entrées. *Stupid question, Joey,* she told herself. *Nothing like admitting you find the guy attractive.*

Daniel shook his head at her mistaken impression, hastening into speech. "On the contrary. This afternoon, just before I sent him to the car, Richie accused *me* of using him to get to *you!*"

"Oh." Joey's voice had grown very small. So had she, Daniel observed in private amusement, as she leaned against the high-backed chair, as if drawing herself into a protective shell. Daniel's pulse sped up, believing he had frightened her, but a moment later she recovered her composure and sat forward once more. She propped her elbows on the table, laid her chin in her hands and inquired sweetly: "So, was your own personal *Wunderkind* right, Mr. Quinn? *Are* you trying to 'get to' me?"

Daniel's head snapped back slightly. He had expected questions from Joey, but he hadn't expected her to be quite so direct. "I don't know," he answered truthfully. "Strangers don't exactly come up to you to shove a paper bag over your head, do they? I mean, you are very attractive. I'd have to be blind not to see that."

Joey chewed on a bite of steak, her brow furrowed in thought. "I've decided to take that as a compliment," she told him a moment later. "I'm sure there was one hidden in there somewhere."

Daniel laughed aloud, feeling the tension that had knotted his shoulders draining away, leaving him feeling lighter, and almost carefree. "You're something else, Joey Abbott," he said, reaching across the table to take her hand in his and squeeze it gently. "You remind me of a fresh spring breeze after a long, cold winter. I don't think I can remember the last time I laughed out loud."

"Poor boy," Joey teased, although he could see that his words had touched her. "But I think you made a good choice, moving to Saucon Valley. This is a family-oriented kind of place, a place where you and your son can really come to know each other. Richie will think so too, once he understands that this move is permanent and takes that chip off his shoulder."

"He still hates baseball, even if he's willing to try, just to gain your approval," Daniel pointed out, in case either of them was beginning to feel too confident. "He hates the sport, the boys on the team and the coaches—all of us. Richie has become an equal-opportunity hater."

Joey's chin came up. "I wasn't expecting a miracle today, Daniel. Give him time, he'll come around. And if he can't cut it as a player, we can introduce him to the wonderful world of statistics. Richie seems to be attracted to numbers. There are records kept for everything a player does—except for the most sneezes while at bat in a doubleheader, and there will probably be one for that any day now."

Shaking his head in wonderment at her persistence, as well as her thoughtfulness, Daniel considered her latest idea. "He could enter all the players' statistics into his computer," he mused. "The kids would be all over him, wanting to know their batting averages. Joey, I think you just might have hit on the perfect solution!"

"Good," Joey replied, "although I still don't believe Richie was throwing that ball tonight just to please me. I saw how he was looking at you today while you coached those other boys. Richie loves you, Daniel, never doubt that. Now, let's eat. I have to clean my plate so you'll reward me with a slice of that wonderful pie that got me here in the first place."

"Exactly how much land do you and your brother own, Joey?" Daniel was standing in the middle of the wide gravel driveway, trying with narrowed eyes to pierce the darkness beyond the well-lit barn that served as Esmeralda's garage. "I noticed when I picked you up earlier that you're rather isolated out here. Was this once a working farm? I remember seeing several smaller buildings besides the house and barn."

"Andy and I only own thirty-five acres now, much less than when we actually farmed for a living." Joey was leaning against the side of Daniel's Cadillac, randomly thinking that he looked quite at home in this setting. "Dad sold some acreage right after we bought the place, in order to make improvements on the house and outbuildings—little conveniences, like indoor plumbing—and I sold more to take care of Andy's college expenses after Dad died. But that's the end of it—the rest is ours, no matter how much we're offered for it."

"You've been approached, of course. You're too close to the new highway not to have been." Daniel knew what he had paid for his building lot, and was curious to learn why Joey and her brother had turned down what could only be an enormous profit.

Joey didn't really hear him. She was thinking about the loan manager's advice that she put up part of the farm as collateral for her purchase of a second limousine. The thought still rankled. She'd turned him down flat, of course. No matter how sure she was that Abbott Aristocrat Limousines would be successful, there was no way she was going to put Andy's and her inheritance—their last visible link to their father—on the line. No way.

"Joey?" Daniel leaned against the car next to her, trying to get her attention.

"My dad was an engineer," she began softly, as if speaking to herself. "Not as in a choo-choo, railroad engineer, but an electrical engineer, and a darn good one. He was so good that he was rarely ever home. He was always working, always on call. Andy and I used to call him Uncle Daddy, because we saw him so seldom. Then one day, about a month after our mother died, Dad walked away from his career and put everything he had into this farm." She tilted her head and smiled up into Daniel's eyes. "We didn't have to call him Uncle Daddy anymore. He gave us more than this farm—he gave us himself. Every day of his life, until he died."

Joey's face was luminous with love as she spoke of her father. "Your father must have been a wonderful, caring, unselfish man," Daniel said, sliding an arm around her shoulders and pulling her to his side as they both leaned against the Cadillac. She fit against him perfectly, the top of her head nestling against his chest. "Now I understand why you and your brother turned out so well."

"Thank you," Joey responded, humbled, and a little sad. "Dad was quite a teacher."

"Joey, I—" Daniel began, pushing himself away from the Cadillac to stand in front of her, his hands on her shoulders.

"Yes, Daniel?" Joey prompted helpfully. She was looking up at him, her gray eyes misty with memories he couldn't share.

"Oh, the hell with it." He groaned, lowering his head. "I can't fight it anymore." His lips covered hers, his arms closing more fully around her as her hands slid up his chest to lock behind his neck, wordlessly showing him that he hadn't been wrong to believe she'd accept his touch.

Her mouth was warm and soft beneath his and after a moment he dared to deepen the kiss, astonished at the sudden yearning to possess her that raced through his body. She was so small, yet so strong, so worldly-wise, yet so vulnerable. He felt fiercely protective of her even as his mind raced to find a way to breach all her defenses.

And she was so willing, so giving. He sensed that she trusted him to be gentle with her, to take only what she was willing to give and not press for more. He could feel her trembling beneath his hands as they stood alone in the dark, the sounds of the summer night their only companions, their only censors. Her trust in him brought him back to his senses even as his body cursed him for a fool.

"Oh, Joey," he breathed huskily at last, breaking their kiss to press her head against his chest. "You don't know how lucky you are. That was some first kiss."

"Yes, I do, and yes, it certainly was," she responded shakily, as breathless as he. "As a matter of fact, on a scale of one to ten, I'd rank it a twenty-three."

She could feel his chest move as he chuckled, easing the tension between them that had been growing ever since dinner. "You know," he said, rubbing the side of her head with his hand, mussing her hair with his big fingers, "I've never kissed a chauffeur before. It's quite an experience."

"I can imagine," Joey responded with a laugh, moving away from him slightly, so that she could take his hand and begin walking toward the house. "I've never kissed a client before, if it comes down to that. You do know that, don't you?"

Daniel stopped walking to pull her in front of him and lift her chin with his finger as they stood within the soft yellow glow of the porch light. "I do know that, Joey," he said softly, bending to kiss the tip of her nose. "And I won't kiss you like that again—at least not tonight—so you don't have

to go running for cover. That's what you're so tactfully trying to do, isn't it?''

Joey looked up at him, wiggling her eyebrows comically.
"Not too subtle, huh?" she asked. "Sorry about that. I
guess I was being a bit childish.''

He led her toward the old-fashioned porch swing and they
sat down, still holding hands. "You were being a bit intelligent, and I don't blame you," he admitted wryly. "But
that doesn't mean I'm ready to go home. It's barely midnight. Tell me more about your father."

Joey was more than eager to comply with his request, for
she, too, was reluctant to end the evening. "All right," she
agreed, "what do you want to know?"

Pulling her against his chest once more, only because it
felt so right to have her there, Daniel said, "Oh, I don't
know. Just let your mind roam free, and tell me whatever
occurs to you.''

Joey looked up at the quarter moon and smiled as a
memory took hold of her. " 'Look at that glass of milk,
Joey,' Dad used to tell me," she began slowly. " 'To some
people,' he'd say, 'it's half-empty. You know what it is to
me? It's half-full. You know how the weatherman says it's
partly cloudy? He's wrong, pumpkin. It's partly sunny. It's
the same with everything in life. It's all in the way you look
at it. Always remember that.' "

"That's a good philosophy," Daniel told her, beginning
to understand Joey's optimistic outlook.

"Yes," Joey answered, her voice suddenly sad. "Yes, it
is. It's also all too easy to forget. Unfortunately, I forgot it
myself for a while. After Dad died I threw myself into my
studies at college, commuting so that I could take care of
Andy. After I graduated I was offered a job with Ransom
Computers and I jumped at it, to help with Andy's tuition.
I wanted to keep busy, busy to the point where I didn't have
either the time or the energy to miss Dad, the man who had

meant the world to me. I really believed I would be happier that way."

"I can understand that," Daniel told her. "When Veronica left I buried myself in work, and after she died I did everything but live at the office. If you work hard enough, you don't have any time to think. It wasn't until I realized that I was losing Richie that I woke up to what I was doing, what I was missing."

Joey pushed at the porch floor with her toes, setting the swing into motion. "You were lucky to have Richie," she told him. "I had Andy, but he was older, more independent, and by the time he was a senior in high school I was so involved with climbing the corporate ladder that he was pretty much on his own. After he went off to college I worked even harder, to avoid coming home to an empty house. Besides, the money was good. No, let me amend that. The money was great."

"Let's all hear it for greed," Daniel slid in, laughing at her dogged honesty.

"It sure does make the world go round, doesn't it?" Joey remarked, not looking for an answer, but lost in her own memories. "But it only works so long. Then, some rainy morning, as you sit slumped behind your shiny teak desk in your plush corner office, you casually look into your coffee cup, and decide that it's half-empty."

He could feel the tenseness in her body, hear the pain in her voice. "Your teak desk? Your corner office?" he asked, knowing the answer.

She nodded her head, fighting back sudden tears. "I can still feel how that stupid, random thought stunned me—like a shot to the solar plexus. I stared into that damned cup for a full hour, as the world of Ransom Computers revolved around me, my mind filled with memories of Dad, while I blubbered like a baby."

Daniel didn't know what to say, didn't know how to comfort her, but he shouldn't have worried. Joey scrubbed at her eyes and looked up at him, smiling widely. "And you know what I finally did, Daniel Quinn? At the end of that hour I blew my nose, pushed my sixteen-position chair clear of my teak desk, stood up and walked away. I walked away from my Rolodex, my hefty expense account, my awe-inspiring title of production executive, my rosy lucrative future—and I didn't even bother to look back. I've never looked back!"

If Daniel had been surprised before, now he was astounded. Joey had been an executive—a top executive. He had known she was intelligent, but he'd had no idea just how intelligent. If she had told him she'd had a breakdown from stress, or lost her job due to a takeover—that he could have understood. But to work yourself that far up the ladder, and then just walk away! "You're kidding!" he exclaimed with astonished condemnation, staring at her. "What did you do then?"

Joey was feeling pleased with herself, so pleased that she was finally pouring out her story some other way than by scribbling it onto page after page of her journal.

"Well," she went on, "the first thing I did was check my bank account and make arrangements for Andy's junior and senior year of college. Then, for two years I roamed the country in my trusty baby-blue Mercedes, stopping where I wanted, camping out on a moonlit beach in San Diego or checking into a bed and breakfast in some sleepy Maine town. Driving long country miles with the top down and the wind blowing through my hair—just plain old reveling in the simple joy of being alive, hokey as that sounds."

She had also kept a hit-or-miss journal of her travels—not that she so forgot herself as to reveal this to Daniel—recording her thoughts, her feelings, her reactions to the people and places she had seen. She had soaked up her experiences like a thirsty sponge soaks up water, and promised herself that never again would she be so foolish as to put herself in a box of anyone else's making, no matter how well padded it might be.

"Then, two years ago," she concluded aloud, "when Andy graduated and told me he wanted to be a singer, we hatched the idea of Abbott's Aristocrat Limousines, to keep body and soul together until Andy gets his big break."

"I see," Daniel said, not seeing at all. "And once Andy gets this big break of his—what then? Do you sell the limousine service and use the profits to hit the road once more—like some sort of gypsy—until you run out of money again?"

Joey snuggled down once more. "That's a good point, Daniel. I don't really know how to answer that. I might, if the spirit moves me. I guess I'll just take it one day at a time."

Suddenly she was wildly reaching for the arm of the swing and trying to maintain her balance as Daniel leaped to his feet. "I don't believe it! You're as bad as he is!" he exclaimed, glaring down at her.

"As bad as whom?" she asked, totally confused. What *was* Daniel's problem?

"That's *who*!" Daniel shouted, his motives for correcting her grammar no less childish than his son's had been. "And Wilbur Langley—that's who! And to think I believed you'd be a good influence on Richie. A lady chauffeur with orange sunglasses and purple high-top sneakers! If Wilbur's Peter Pan, then you're Tinker Bell! My God, I ought to have my head examined!"

Joey watched, openmouthed, as Daniel stomped his way across the wooden porch and slammed across the gravel driveway to his car. "That's *woman* chauffeur, you chauvinist!" she shouted after him, throwing herself back against the porch swing and pumping it back and forth furiously. A moment later Daniel and his Cadillac roared off into the night.

Chapter Six

"Hi, Joey! Did you and Dad have a good time last night? Dad overslept this morning, and now he's grumbling through the house like a bull with a sore paw, or at least that's what Mrs. Hemmings says. She's pretty funny, once you get to know her, and she's going to let me help her make some chocolate chip cookies tonight after I give her a hand with the dishes. If you want, we have time to go to the garage for a while. I want to show you something."

Joey blinked twice, disbelieving both what she was hearing and what she was seeing. Richie Quinn was smiling as he came down the front steps and approached the limousine, his tall, too thin body clothed in its usual mismatched, psychedelic mayhem. He was actually smiling, and his enthusiastic voice was light and cheery. What a difference a day could make! Had Mrs. Hemmings slipped something into his cocoa?

"You're pretty chipper for six in the morning, Rich," she said, readily falling into step beside him as they walked around the side of the house to the garage. "What's up? Your horse finish first yesterday at Belmont?"

Richie turned to grin at her. "Dad told you about that, huh? No, it was nothing like that. Billy Simpson came by last night on his bike. It's a ten-speed. I'm going to get one just like it."

"Billy Simpson from the baseball team?" Joey asked weakly, her head reeling.

Richie nodded, then took a small hand control from his back pocket and pointed it at the garage, electronically opening the oversize overhead door. "He lives about a mile away, didn't you know that? Jeez, and you're his coach. Anyway, he came over last night and we hacked around for a while."

"Hacked around?" Joey stepped into the garage, where she could see the large, six-foot-wide blue target Richie had painted on one wall. Now she knew how Alice had felt when she tumbled into Wonderland. She searched the garage with her eyes, looking for the tea party.

Richie picked up his fielder's glove from a small work-bench and bent to retrieve a whiffle ball from the floor. "On the computer, Joey," he supplied helpfully. "Billy has some great games he brought with him. Terrific graphics. You like computer games, Joey?"

"I used to think I did," she replied, smiling wryly, thinking of her years at Ransom, "but I don't play them anymore. What's that?" she asked, pointing to the center of the target, which was painted in the shape of a particularly fearsome, leering face.

"He's Kreppo, the evil king of Wanjung. I guess you haven't played computer games in a while. It's the best game out right now. I painted him there for inspiration. It was Billy's idea, actually, and it really works. I think I'm getting pretty good at hitting him."

Joey looked at the narrowed, slanted eyes, pointy bared teeth and cauliflower ears of King Kreppo. "He's a real incentive giver, I'll say that for him. Okay, let me see what you can do.''

Richie positioned himself behind a strip of tape he had secured to the floor and wound up, delivering the ball straight to King Kreppo's chops. ''All right!'' he shouted, turning to Joey. ''Is that rad, or what?''

''Rad?'' Joey repeated, longing to find Billy Simpson and give him a smacking kiss square on his freckled nose. Almost overnight, Richie Quinn had been turned into a ten-year-old. ''It's *awesome*!''

''It's *late*, Ms. Abbott,'' corrected a frigid voice from the driveway. ''If it wouldn't be too much to ask, might we be on our way?''

Joey looked across to where Daniel was standing, attaché case in hand and condemning scowl on his face, then back to Richie, who was winding up for another pitch, his smile still intact. ''Some mad scientist must have crept in here last night and done a personality transplant on these two,'' Joey muttered under her breath. ''Be right there, Daniel,'' she called more loudly, waving goodbye to Richie as her tight-lipped employer turned on his heels and disappeared around the corner of the house.

''So much for hoping Daniel would have calmed down by this morning. I have a feeling today is going to be terrific. Just peachy-keen terrific from beginning to end,'' she grumbled fatalistically, sliding behind the wheel and twisting the key in the ignition.

Deliberately leaving the glass partition in the down position, she strapped on her seat belt and put Esmeralda in gear, the limousine gliding effortlessly down the curved drive and out onto the narrow macadam road. Sneaking a quick look in the rearview mirror, she saw that Daniel, dressed for success once more in a sedate business suit, was already hard at work in the backseat, a computer spreadsheet opened across his lap. She fought down the nasty urge to turn on the heater, for the chill in the air was a tangible thing on this warm June morning.

Joey didn't know whether to be angry or amused. Not everyone agreed with her life-style—she'd learned that long ago—but she'd never had anyone respond quite so negatively as Daniel had last night. She would have thought she had baldly announced she was a mad killer on temporary leave from the state penitentiary, for the fear she had seen on Daniel's face as he had accused her of being "just like him."

Him. Wilbur Langley. As she merged Esmeralda into the early-morning commuter traffic on the thruway, Joey turned her thoughts to Wilbur, and the facts she had gleaned from Daniel's comments about his father-in-law and late wife. All right, so Wilbur was a feckless, reckless, if somewhat elderly playboy. So what? He'd earned the right to have some fun, hadn't he? After all, he had run Langley Books for a long time.

Granted, she thought, as she put on the turn signal to move into the passing lane, Wilbur had overstepped the role of loving grandparent in his treatment of Richie. Joey could agree with Daniel on that one point at least, if the bus ticket incident was to serve as an example of Wilbur's idea of what constituted a good time. But life with Wilbur Langley would be much like life with the fictional Auntie Mame, and every child should have at least one delicious Auntie Mame in his life.

Joey concluded that Daniel must believe he was seeing history repeating itself with Richie, assuming that Daniel blamed Wilbur for Veronica's lack of maturity. Her gray eyes narrowed as another thought hit her. "Wait a minute, Joey, old girl. Back up a few paces and think about this," she muttered beneath her breath. Did Daniel really believe that *she* was another Veronica? Was it Richie he was protecting, or himself?

"Why, that—" she began, suddenly very angry. How dare he think that! Who did he think he was, anyway? She was *so* responsible! Hadn't she raised Andy single-handedly when her father died? Hadn't she taken care of Andy economically? Hadn't she been a good employee? She had thought Stan Ransom was going to have a spasm when she told him she was quitting her cushy job, for crying out loud! Yes, she had been good. She had been damned good!

And now she was damned good at heading up Abbott's Aristocrat Limousines! Just who did he think he was, this Daniel Quinn, to look down his patrician nose at her lifestyle? "Like he's so simon-pure," she groused, slanting another quick look into the rearview mirror.

Why hadn't she realized all this last night, as she lay awake in her lonely bed, trying to make some sense of Daniel's desertion? She'd been so busy worrying about him, worrying about Richie, that she had forgotten to take care of Numero Uno.

"Tinker Bell, is it?" Joey gritted from between clenched teeth as her knuckles turned white on the steering wheel. How dare he insult her that way, hurt her that way? Well, she wasn't hurt anymore. Now she was angry!

Her foot rode the gas pedal heavily as she continued her garbled train of thought. If she was such a bad influence, just how did Daniel explain the sudden change for the better in his son, Richie? "Yeah," she whispered meanly, "how do you explain that, Mr. Holier-than-thou Quinn? After all, whose idea was it to sign Richie up for baseball? Answer me that, you miserable—" she gritted, pulling into line at the tollbooth for the New Jersey Turnpike.

"It's a good thing you're not in any danger of falling in love with that hypercritical stick," she complimented herself, reaching for a tissue to wipe at her strangely moist eyes. "Well, that's it! I'll hold on until Andy gets back, but then I'm outta here! And if Daniel Quinn doesn't like it, well then, he can darn well take the bus!"

* * *

This is ridiculous! Daniel folded the spreadsheet with more energy than care, stuffing it into his attaché case before flopping back against the seat and crossing his arms over his chest. He glared out the side window for a moment as the limousine stood still in line at the tollbooth, then directed his glare to the back of Joey's cap-covered head. *This is bloody ridiculous!*

Less than twenty-four hours ago they had laughed together across a dinner table. Less than twenty-four hours ago he had held her, kissed her, smelled the perfume of her hair, listened to her dreams—and done a little dreaming of his own. *Now she's talking to herself a mile a minute up there and I'm sitting back here, my spine aching with righteous pride and indignation. It's like a scene out of a bad novel—a very bad novel.*

What a difference a day makes! Oh, God, that's trite! "But true," he remarked quietly as the limousine inched closer to the tollbooth. Would this ride never end? How was he going to keep up this pretense of not caring—twice a day, three days a week, for six months? "It's impossible!" he hissed, shifting uncomfortably in the seat.

And then there was the problem of Richie. Only a fool could be unhappy with the change in Richie, the change that was taking on signs of being nearly miraculous.

Richie liked Joey. Joey was one of the Bulldogs' baseball coaches. Joey was driving him to New York three days a week. Adding Tuesday and Saturday games and Thursday practices, staying away from Joey Abbott—and keeping Richie away from her—would be like trying to remove a fifty-cent wad of chewing gum from the bottom of his shoe.

Couldn't she even take a hint? He had barked at her in the garage, the only words he'd spoken to her since he ran away last night like a spooked teenager, yet she had answered him politely, and with a smile. She hadn't said a word to him since she slipped behind the wheel—not "how are you?" or "did you manage to remove your tail from between your legs yet?" or even "drop dead!" No, she'd just sat up front, with the dividing glass opened, keeping her eyes on the road and her mouth shut—except for the heated conversation she seemed to be holding with herself. It was just like a woman to behave herself, making the man look even more stupid than he already felt!

"Why the hell don't you take off that stupid cap?" he heard himself bark loudly, wishing he had known he was going to say something that ridiculous, so that he could have choked himself first.

He watched as Joey took the ticket from the automated tollbooth but did not step on the gas. Instead, she slowly turned her head to look at him, her expression maddeningly blank. "Why the hell don't I just sprinkle you with pixie dust and make you disappear?" she asked just as the tinted glass divider slid up, cutting off all further hope of conversation until the limousine delivered him to Langley Books.

That night, when he reentered the limousine, the first thing he noticed—after noting Joey's stony expression as she held the door for him—was that the glass divider was still in the raised position. It was a long, silent ride home to Saucon Valley.

Joey wasn't at the Thursday practice, having been hired to drive three women to Philadelphia for the day, so that Daniel had to wait until Friday before seeing her again. By then, he had a plan to permanently remove Joey Abbott from his life, if not from his dreams.

Daniel's solution to his dilemma had a name. As a matter of fact, it had several names, like Roseanne, and Muffy, and Stephanie and, if none of them worked, even the ever lovely Ursula. Yes, he thought meanly, mumbling his grudging thanks as Joey held the door for him as he climbed inside the limousine Friday morning, Ursula would really put the capper on it.

"Please leave the glass down today, Joey," he said as pleasantly as his clenched jaws allowed before the car door could be slammed shut and he lost his chance to speak to her again.

"You're the boss," she replied, smiling brightly, just as if they had never argued. *Not that we actually have,* he reminded himself with a slight sense of shame. *I've acted like an ass, and she let me. But the fact remains. Joey Abbott is poison to me, and the worst sort of influence on someone as susceptible as Richie. I'm doing the right thing. I know I am.*

He watched as Joey gracefully slid behind the steering wheel, looking as fresh and pretty as the proverbial daisy, and even more beautiful this morning than she had seated across the dinner table from him in the restaurant. *But then flighty butterflies are always lovelier than worker bees,* he reminded himself with a strangely unsatisfying smirk.

"Are you free tonight, Joey?" he asked once they were on their way.

Joey's heart did a small flip in her breast. So, Daniel was having second thoughts, was he? Well, never let it be said Joey Abbott was one to hold a grudge. "Yes, Daniel. I'm free this evening," she replied, turning her head to smile at him.

"Good," Daniel declared, nodding his head. "In that case, I'll be bringing someone home with me this evening, to spend the weekend. I'd like you to drive us to dinner— someplace romantic. Roseanne prefers seafood if my memory serves me correctly."

"Roseanne?" Joey whispered under her breath, hoping Daniel didn't notice Esmeralda's slight swerve toward the passing lane. "Seafood, you say?"

"That's right. Seafood. You know—those finny things that live in the ocean. Any suggestions?"

Joey had several suggestions—none of them repeatable. She chanced a quick peek in the rearview mirror and saw the smug look on Daniel's face. Her eyes narrowing, she rapidly debated the consequences of tossing him out on the shoulder of the highway and leaving him there.

The bank manager had called late Thursday afternoon, telling her that her loan was on the way to being approved, thanks to the Quinn contract. She could salvage her pride by tossing Daniel out on his ear, but that would mean she could also wave that second limousine bye-bye at the same time. She might consider herself a free spirit, but she certainly didn't believe in lopping off her own nose to spite Daniel Quinn's smirking face!

She knew what he was doing, of course. He was attracted to her, just as she had been attracted to him. Now he was going to prove to her just how little she meant to him by going out of his way to throw other women in her face. It was pitiful. *Men are such little boys,* she told herself, ordering a smile onto her own face. *Well, two can play at this game!*

"Stokesay Castle in Reading is a lovely restaurant," she heard herself saying politely. "It's about a forty-five-minute ride each way, so it makes for a nice evening out. I take couples there all the time and I've never had a complaint."

Daniel expelled his held breath in defeat. Her hesitation had allowed him to hope he had scored a direct hit with the mention of Roseanne's name. Joey hadn't even flinched. Maybe he was reading too much into a single candlelit dinner and one soul-shattering kiss. But there was still Richie to consider, he reminded himself, refusing to acknowledge the pain Joey's obvious lack of jealousy caused him. If he could make Joey hate him, she'd get out of Richie's life as well.

"Stokesay Castle?" he repeated, deliberately employing a world-weary New Yorker tone of laughing disbelief. "That's a pretty ambitious name for a small town restaurant. What does it have—a prefab turret and a couple of stone fireplaces?"

"Stokesay Castle," Joey began in her most professional voice, "is a 1931 recreation of the original Stokesay Castle built in the thirteenth century and still standing today in Shropshire, England. Mr. George Bear Hiester, obviously a very rich and very besotted gentleman, had it built as a honeymoon cottage for his bride, duplicating the original down to the last hand-hewn beam and leaded window. It sits on top of a high hill just outside the town of Reading, where it commands a delightful thirty-mile view of the countryside."

"You sound like a professional tour guide, but we'll play it your way," Daniel said, wanting to do nothing more than reach into the front seat and strangle her, or kiss her. Compromising, he moved from the wide backseat to the smaller seat located just behind the glass partition. "How did this great castle come to be a restaurant? Did poor old George lose it all in the stock market crash?"

Joey kept her head facing front and her eyes on the road, doing her best to ignore the heady scent of his cologne. "It would appear that George's bride had little taste for castles, even castles with three hundred-amp electrical service and all the modern conveniences," she informed him politely, then added, "Roseanne? Roseanne who?"

"What an ungrateful woman Mrs. Hiester must have been," Daniel answered, allowing his fingers to stray to the nape of Joey's neck, where they lightly teased at the sensitive nerve endings so that she was forced to press her head back against his hand. "Roseanne Philpot. She's a dress designer. She thinks Richie is adorably refreshing and extremely intelligent and usually shows up with an educational toy in tow."

"Bully for Richie," Joey countered, having successfully rid herself of Daniel's teasing fingers. "And bully for Roseanne. I'll call the manager for reservations once we get to New York. We'll probably have to drive straight to Reading, unless you object. I'll have you booked for the Blue Room. It's 'sumptuous.'"

"How efficient of you," Daniel complimented gruffly. Looking around himself in some surprise, he wondered how he had forgotten his good intentions enough to be sitting directly behind Joey, touching her like a servant boy stroking the hem of the queen's robe.

"I have my moments," Joey responded dryly, seeing Daniel's face reflected in the rearview mirror and doing her best not to laugh at his baffled expression. "Now it's up periscope time, before you forget how much you loathe me. Your hand, Daniel?" she prompted smartly as she moved to press the button that would raise the glass partition. "Move it or lose it!"

Still holding open Esmeralda's passenger door, Joey occupied herself with glaring at Daniel's retreating back as he walked toward the double glass doors of the Sixth Avenue office building.

"Once around the park, if you please, Joey darling," she heard a voice say just as a blur of royal blue whizzed past her to enter the backseat of the limousine.

She leaned over the top of the car door to get a good look at her unexpected passenger. "Wilbur Langley!" she exclaimed as he winked at her from the interior of the limousine, waggling the fingers of one hand at her in greeting. She noted his obviously expensive suit. "Congratulations. I see you've officially entered your blue period. Now, what do you think you're doing?"

"Why, Joey, dear," he responded happily, "I thought I was clear enough. I'd like a leisurely spin around the park, of course. Then I thought we'd stop at Tavern on the Green for a spot of liquid refreshment. Unless you'd rather elope with me to Barbados. I'm flexible. Oh!" he exclaimed. "I've just had a lovely thought. Could I possibly ride up front with you? I've never done, you know, and it might be easier to hold a conversation that way. That is, if it isn't against some chauffeuring law, or something.''

"A law like that was made to be broken, Wilbur, if it even exists. Besides, I'm off duty until five-thirty.'' Joey held out her hand to assist Wilbur's exit from the backseat, then walked around the limousine with him to unlock the passenger door and open it with a flourishing bow.

Joey inched Esmeralda back into the heavy Manhattan traffic and headed for the park, her usual good humor resurfacing after the trying silence she'd endured ever since raising the glass partition between herself and her maddening employer. A dose of Wilbur Langley, she decided, might be just what the doctor ordered.

"How's that son-in-law of mine treating you, my dear?'' Wilbur asked after a moment. "Richie was not his usual lucid self on the telephone last night, mumbling and grumbling about his father not allowing him to mention your name in his presence. What did you do—slap his face when he made a pass at you at dinner?''

"How did you know we went out to—oh, Richie told you. You two are worse than a pair of old biddies hanging over a back fence. And no, I didn't slap his face.''

"But he did make a pass,'' Wilbur inserted slyly, folding his hands across his chest in satisfaction. "I always said that boy had a good head on his shoulders.''

"Only until I knock it off,'' Joey responded tightly, turning the limousine into a parking garage. "Let's walk, Wilbur. I've been driving for hours, and I'd like to have my mind entirely free to talk to you. I think it's safer that way, and I don't mean traffic-wise.''

Wilbur scrambled from the car first, to help Joey exit from the driver's side, and she couldn't help noticing the strange look the two of them got from the young parking attendant. "Thank you, kind sir,'' she said, turning back to leave her cap on the front seat and pick up her sunglasses. "Shall we adjourn to the park?"

They walked in companionable silence for some minutes as Joey rethought her decision to consult with Wilbur Langley about Daniel. After all, he was the man's father-in-law—as well as the man Daniel had described as an irresponsible Peter Pan. How could she tell him her problem without letting it slip that Daniel also heartily disapproved of him?

They stopped to listen to a jazz trio who had set up their instruments at one of the entrances to the park, then lingered to watch a magician play tricks on passersby who volunteered to help him with his show. Joey laughed out loud as Wilbur pointed out a huffing, puffing nanny chasing after her charge, who was in the process of making a run for it across the wide lawn.

Finally, Wilbur pulled her over to sit beside him on a bench, as a group of joggers, led by a high-stepping coach, took possession of the pathway. "Such a pointless waste of good energy, don't you think?" Wilbur asked, pointing to the sweating, straining crowd as they jogged past.

"I think it would be easier to just skip dessert," Joey said, agreeing with him. "So, Wilbur, how's Richie? I haven't seen him since Wednesday morning."

Wilbur leaned back against the faded wooden bench, rubbing his hands together. "He's fine, I'm happy to report, although I must tell you that both you and I have dropped a notch on his favorite people list. Some young upstart named Billy Simpson now holds that most coveted spot. I'm quite distraught. I think I'll have to purchase season tickets to the Yankees, perish the thought, just to win my way back into his good graces."

Joey leaned over and kissed the man's cheek. "You old fraud. You don't fool me for a moment. You're glad Richie's found a friend. I don't know why Daniel's so set against—um, that is—"

As Joey's voice trailed off in confusion, Wilbur patted her hand, saying, "That's all right, my dear. It's no great secret that Daniel thinks I'm a bad influence on my grandson. I most probably am, you know."

Joey squeezed his hand in hers. "Well, Wilbur, don't feel like the Lone Ranger. Daniel thinks I'm a bad influence, too."

"On whom? Richie—or Daniel?"

Joey smiled at Wilbur's quick perception. "Does the name Roseanne Philpot ring any bells?" she asked as they rose once more and walked leisurely across the grass, the bright sunlight warming their shoulders.

"Roseanne Philpot? He's pulling her out, is he?" Wilbur marveled, a low whistle hissing through his perfectly capped teeth. "The boy is desperate, isn't he? Funny, I would have thought he'd go for Ursula. She's only half as smart as Roseanne, but she's built like a—well, never mind that. Congratulations, my dear, and welcome to the family. We're sorely in need of an infusion of fresh young blood."

"Whoa, Wilbur!" Joey exclaimed, stopping in her tracks. "Don't you think you're presuming a bit much? I like Daniel, very much. But we hardly even know each other. Not only that, but we're barely speaking. I wouldn't go planning the wedding if I were you. Besides, who says I'd even *want* to get married. I'm quite happy as I am."

"Of course, my dear," Wilbur agreed smoothly, drawing her hand through the crook of his arm. "You're right to be prudent. After all, you're not even thirty, are you? There's plenty of time. I suppose this means I shall have to instruct Richie to cancel the orchestra?"

Chapter Seven

She was very tall, very thin and very, very beautiful. She was dressed from blond head to shapely calf in some redder-than-red flowing thing that defied description and probably cost half as much as Esmeralda. If Roseanne Philpot was to be the competition, Joey thought with a grimace, Daniel believed in pulling out all the stops. Fortunately for Joey, her worry was wasted, and short-lived.

Roseanne, Joey soon learned, considered herself to be a liberated woman. She had clawed her way to the top of the designing world through her own efforts—except for the two million dollars in "seed money" she had acquired thanks to her ex-husband, Phineas "The king of ripple potato chips" Philpot. But, as she considered her marriage to have been comparable to living in a war zone, she comforted herself with the thought that she had earned every penny of that two million dollars.

Being an independent woman, Roseanne obviously admired any woman who took her life into her own hands, broke new ground and dared to go where only men had successfully gone before. Daniel, in his intention to demonstrate to Joey just how little he needed her, had made a serious blunder in forgetting Roseanne's dedication to the feminist movement.

"A woman chauffeur?" Roseanne had exclaimed as she and Daniel walked arm in arm across the wide pavement toward the open limousine door. "How fascinating! Daniel, you didn't tell me your limousine service was broadminded enough to hire women drivers."

"Actually, Ms. Philpot," Joey interjected politely, smiling directly into Daniel's suddenly smoldering eyes, "I'm not just a driver. I am the co-owner of Abbott's Aristocrat Limousines." *Stuff that in your briefcase and tote it,* her eyes told Daniel.

Roseanne dropped Daniel's arm in order to take Joey's right hand in both of hers, pumping it up and down enthusiastically. "That's absolutely wonderful! I applaud you. I can't tell you how much I admire women willing to take charge of their own lives. Please, leave the partition down so that you can tell me all about it on our way to this castle Daniel has told me about."

By the time Esmeralda was tooling down the New Jersey Turnpike, Roseanne and Joey were on a first-name basis, and Daniel was slouched in his seat, sulking. He did come in for some reflected praise at one point, as Roseanne congratulated him for being sure enough of his own masculinity to hire a woman driver, but for the most part he found himself politely, and totally, ignored.

When they arrived at Stokesay Castle, Roseanne asked Joey what she would do to occupy her time while they had dinner, and Joey explained that it was her custom to sit in the kitchen with the cooks. "Sometimes I sample whatever's on the menu, but most of the time I just nibble on some pizza until it's time to go," she told them as Roseanne stood in the cobbled courtyard, marveling at the immensity of the restaurant grounds.

"But that's horrible! Daniel! You'd be a party to this sort of archaic, chauvinistic discrimination?" Roseanne exclaimed, turning on Daniel, who suddenly found himself feeling like Simon Legree sending little Eliza out onto the ice floe.

"Boy oh boy, Daniel," Joey teased in a low voice, moving to stand beside him. "However do you sleep nights, you monster?"

Roseanne wiped her hands briskly against each other, dismissing any such nonsense. "Well, Daniel, I won't have it, do you hear me? Relegating Joey to the kitchens, like some medieval serf? I had thought better of you, Daniel, truly I had."

"Yeah," Joey intoned softly, shaking her head. "We had thought better of you, Daniel."

Daniel spoke to her out of the corner of his mouth. "You're enjoying this, aren't you?" he accused, looking down at her condemningly.

"You got that in one, bunkie," Joey retorted happily as Roseanne took her arm and led her into the castle, leaving Daniel to follow or to stay as he chose.

Joey missed the first game of the Bulldogs' season, as she would miss most of the Saturday games, having leased Esmeralda as the bridal car in a local wedding. She hated missing the games, but weddings were always fun, and brides and bridegrooms were very undemanding passengers, who were always more interested in each other than in telling her how to drive.

Sunday morning, as she used the local car wash's vacuum to remove the last of the confetti and rice from the tufted velvet upholstery of the backseat, Steve Mitchum, the Bulldogs' coach and the owner of the car wash, filled her in on what had happened at the game.

"Billy Simpson held them to a six-hitter, but he walked seven batters, and that really killed us," Steve informed her, yelling so that he could be heard over the sound of the vacuum's motor. "Still, we only lost 10–8 to last year's league champions, so there's hope for us yet. It's a long season."

Keeping her head carefully averted, Joey asked, "I guess the game was too close to let any of the scrubs in for an inning?"

"If you mean did Richie Quinn get in, the answer is no," Steve returned, winking at her, "but he did do a bang-up job keeping the stats. That kid adds faster in his head than I do using a calculator. Not only that, but he has a memory like an elephant."

"In what way?" Joey asked, surprising herself at how her heart had filled with near-maternal pride at Steve's praise of Richie.

"He could remember how many pitches Billy threw, and what pitch he used to strike out their cleanup hitter in the fourth inning—you name it and Richie knew it. Like I told Daniel—that kid's got a home with me any time he wants one!"

"*As* I told Daniel," Joey corrected, too quietly for Steve to hear, proving to herself that Richie had begun to rub off on her as well. "Daniel was there?" she questioned, keeping her voice deliberately light. "I know he has company this weekend, so I didn't think he'd be able to make it."

Steve eyed her closely. "You mean the blonde?" he asked, helping Joey replace the vacuum on the shelf. "He brought her along. She told me the kids' uniforms are all wrong—something about flow, and natural motion being more important than pinstripes. But she did compliment me for having Melissa Hancock playing third base. Strange woman, don't you think? I was surprised to see Daniel with her. He seems more your type."

Joey smiled up at him. "And what type is that, Steve? Really, I'd like to know."

Steve looked at her uncomfortably, then spread his arms. "Jeez, I don't know, Joey. Just more—more *touchable*.

Yeah, that's it. Touchable. And more fun. You're a lot of fun, Joey."

She fished in the pocket of her jeans for her car keys. "That's me all right, Steve. I'm a lot of fun. A real barrel of laughs. But would you want to settle down with me?"

Steve spread his hands in front of him, as if warding off attack. "Hey, Joey! I'm a married man."

"Good morning, Steve." Joey and Steve both turned to see Daniel walking toward them, having turned his car over to one of the attendants. "I thought I'd get my car washed before driving Roseanne back to New York. Good morning, Joey," he added, seemingly as an afterthought.

"Good morning, Daniel," Joey answered with more civility than welcome, sliding behind the wheel. "Well, Steve, I gotta go. I'm picking up a client at the Newark airport at three. Daniel, I'll see you tomorrow morning."

She had turned the key in the ignition before Daniel's knock against the side window caught her attention. She lowered the window in time to hear him say, "Isn't there some way we could combine our efforts? After all, it's only nine o'clock. There would be plenty of time to drop Roseanne on Park Avenue and still get to Newark before three."

Joey tried to hide her smile, and failed miserably. As wars went, it seemed that she had conquered him with ridiculous ease. Clearly this was surrender. Well, never let it be said that Joey Abbott was a poor winner. "That seems reasonable, Daniel," she agreed quickly. "I can be at your house in half an hour."

"Great!" Daniel said, Joey recognizing the tone of victory in his voice too late to do anything about it. "I'll see that Roseanne is ready for you. I'm sure you two still have plenty to say to each other, even if you did talk for three hours over dinner Friday night. Now I'll have the whole afternoon free to take Richie and Billy Simpson to that movie they want to see. Thanks a lot, Joey. Just add the trip to my tab."

That was how Joey got to spend two long, frustrating hours listening to Roseanne Philpot's philosophy of life as they drove to New York City in a sudden pouring rain. And that was how Joey Abbott learned that, when it came to love and war, Daniel Quinn certainly subscribed to the old saying that warned "all is fair."

Monday's trip to the city was, as Joey was to write later in her journal, a complete, undiluted disaster, with a capital *D*. She was still bristling at Daniel's high-handed attitude of the day before, and Daniel, who seemed to be a sudden convert to the feminist movement, treated her more like one of the boys than most boys she knew. He had even slapped her on the back companionably as he climbed into the backseat of the limousine.

The ride to Manhattan had been accomplished in stony silence—which more than pleased Joey, who wasn't feeling all that talkative that morning. But the trip home was one long headache, beginning with the moment the left rear tire blew out just as the limousine pulled onto the New Jersey Turnpike.

She cursed once, softly, under her breath, steered Esmeralda onto the shoulder of the road and got out to inspect the damage. There was no doubt about it. The tire was as flat as three-day-old seltzer. With her hands jammed onto her hips, she allowed another short, unlovely descriptive phrase to pass her lips.

"I may be way out of line here," Daniel interposed silkily, leaning his tall frame against the side of the car, "but I don't think flat tires respond well to having their legitimacy questioned."

Joey turned to look at him, standing at his ease, his hip against the car door, his arms crossed over his chest and an infuriatingly pleased smile on his face. "Oh, shut up!" she exclaimed, kicking the flat tire and bruising herself in the process so that she spent the next few moments hopping about on one foot, rubbing at her abused toes. "If you say one more word, Daniel Quinn, I'll bop you. I swear I will!" she warned tightly as his mouth opened to, she was sure, point out that it was equally useless to try kick-starting the tire back to life.

"I was only going to ask you if you've got a spare in the trunk," Daniel told her, unable to suppress a short laugh at her predicament. "A male driver would have one. A tire jack, too."

Joey shook her head slowly, feeling her blood beginning to boil. "Oh, you'd love it if I didn't have a spare, wouldn't you? You've been just dying to show me up as a poor driver, ever since that first day. Admit it, Daniel. You just hate it that I'm self-sufficient—that I don't need a big, strong man to take care of me."

He pressed a fist against his chest, his expression innocently incredulous. "Me? You'd think that of me? Is that what you and Roseanne decided? Do you really think I'm one of those Neanderthal types who goes out to get the meat, while the little woman keeps the cave warm? Well, you couldn't be more wrong."

"Oh, yeah, sure," Joey grumbled as a large tractor trailer whizzed by, sending up a cloud of dust that drifted over Esmeralda, Daniel and herself like a shroud.

"You don't believe me, do you?" Daniel asked as the dust settled. "How can I convince you? Let's see—you believe that I'm a chauvinist, and I believe I can remember accusing you of being irresponsible. As I see it, we can settle both problems quite easily."

"Really," Joey said, wondering what had been wrong with her brain to ever make her believe she had been in any danger of losing her heart to this man.

"Yes, really," Daniel said, opening the car door. "I can get back into this car right now, proving that I feel you are

my equal, and therefore equally as capable of changing a tire
as any man. And you can change the tire, proving to me that
you're more than a silly, irresponsible little girl, playing at
life. Simple, isn't it?''

Joey's eyes got very wide. "You—you're going to get
back in the car, and let me change this tire by myself?'' she
squeaked in disbelief.

"Can't you handle it?''

"*Of course* I can handle it!'' she shouted above the roar
of late-afternoon rush hour traffic. "With one *hand* tied
behind my back, I can handle it! But I'll be darned if I'm
going to jack up your weight as well as Esmeralda's. Go sit
on the bank until I'm done.''

Daniel smiled and saluted her smartly before walking
around the back of the limousine and seating his long frame
on the grass embankment, fully prepared to watch his
chauffeur change a flat tire.

"Hi, Sis. Miss me?''

Joey had raced into the house to grab the telephone before the caller could hang up, having heard it ringing as she
trudged wearily toward the porch steps. "Andy!'' she exclaimed, her heart leaping at the sound of her brother's
voice. "I just got in. You don't know how good it is to hear
from you!''

"Yeah? Well, you almost didn't hear from me, sister
mine. The phone must have rung at least ten times. I was
just about ready to give up hope. Why didn't you put the
answering machine on before you went out? How are prospective customers supposed to get through to us? Maybe
I'd better hop the next plane home and take charge of
things, before you put us out of business.''

"You take charge? Har-de-har-har, *brother mine*,'' Joey
answered, reaching over to pull a kitchen chair closer to the
telephone so that she could collapse her aching, weary body
onto it. "*You*'re going to take charge? You couldn't possi-

bly mean the same Andy Abbott who once booked us for three weddings on the same day?''

''Why can't you ever forget that, Sis? We pulled it off, didn't we?'' Andy complained, the whine in his voice sounding clearly in her ears. ''So, how are you doing, anyway? Have you heard from the bank?''

Joey glanced down at her grease-covered blouse, dusty skirt and shredded panty hose, then held up her right hand to inspect the three broken fingernails that had been sacrificed while lifting the spare tire into place. ''Me? Hey, I'm doing great. Just fine, honest. Couldn't be better. We'll get the final word from the bank in a few days, but it looks good at this end.''

''Gee, Sis, don't sound so overwhelmed with happiness.'' There was a small silence on the other end of the phone. ''It's Monday, isn't it? You sort of lose track of time on the river, you know. Today's a Quinn day. Is he giving you any trouble?''

Joey felt the beginnings of frustrated tears stinging at the back of her eyes. ''No, Andy, he's not giving me any trouble. You've just caught me at a bad time. I had a blowout with Esmeralda on the way home.''

''Gee, that's tough. Too bad it didn't happen when Mr. Quinn was with you. He would have fixed it for you.''

Immediately Joey bristled. ''You, too!'' she shot back with some heat. ''Just what makes you men think a woman can't change a simple flat tire? It's not like performing brain surgery, for heaven's sake. This is *my* business, and tire blowouts are a part of it. I'm not playing at this job, you know.''

''Uh, sure, Joey. Of course. Sorry about that,'' Andy mumbled, clearly confused. ''Hey, the guys are calling me, Sis. I gotta go now. I'll call you again later in the week, okay?'' Before Joey could answer, her brother had broken the connection.

She replaced the telephone receiver and dropped her head into her hands. "What's the matter with me?" she groaned on a sob. "I've changed a dozen tires in my life. Why does it bother me so much that Daniel didn't help me with this one? What is that man doing to me? Why do I want him to see me as a woman, but treat me like a lady—like someone who's special to him? Why isn't this game we're playing funny anymore?"

That night, just as Joey was about to go to bed, there was a knock at the kitchen door.

"May I come in?" Daniel asked as she peeked at him through the curtains of the glass-topped door. He was dressed casually in slacks and a knit shirt, and he was holding a small bouquet of flowers in front of him, as if for protection.

Her fingers fumbled nervously as she struggled to release the dead bolt and let him in. Clutching the top of her short cotton robe to her breast, she stepped back two paces, her bare toes curling against the cool linoleum floor. "Hello, Daniel," she said in a small voice, hating herself for avoiding contact with his eyes.

Daniel moved inside, still holding the flowers. He was nervous, and he disliked the feeling. Joey looked beautiful, all freshly scrubbed, her nose shiny, her dark hair clinging to her shapely head in soft, damp ringlets. She smelled like soap and shampoo, and something deep inside him twisted into a knot, then squeezed itself tight.

"I would have been here sooner, but it takes longer when you have to kick yourself all the way," he said, holding out the bouquet.

Joey looked up at last, and he could see that her gray eyes were overly bright. "For me?" she said, her voice low and faintly hoarse. She took them gingerly, doing her best not to let their fingers touch. "I'll put them in water."

Daniel followed along behind her as Joey walked toward the dining room in search of a vase. "About this afternoon," he said in a rush, eager to have his apology over and done with as soon as possible. "I don't know what got into me, Joey, honestly I don't. I'd skin Richie alive if he ever treated a woman that way. Please forgive me. I acted like a complete—"

"Yes. Yes, you did," Joey said, cutting him off. "But I accept your apology. There," she said, dropping the flowers into a milk glass vase that had belonged to her mother, "this will do. Now all they need is a nice long drink of water. Excuse me, please."

Daniel frowned for a moment, then stepped to one side, allowing Joey to pass by him back into the kitchen. Once more he found himself following her, like a puppy dog hoping for a treat. "Would you believe I got them at the supermarket? Mrs. Hemmings was right—they sell everything in those places nowadays."

"Mrs. Hemmings is very nice," Joey said, placing the vase in the middle of the kitchen table.

Oh, this is going great, Daniel thought, grimacing. After Joey sat down he sat as well, carefully choosing a chair on the other side of the table. "Do you think we can call a truce, Joey?" he asked, leaning forward to move the vase to one side in order to see her better. "I don't think there can be any winners in our little war. Besides, Richie has been asking about you."

"I haven't seen him since last week," Joey told him, and he noticed that she hadn't said either yes or no to his offer of a truce. "I was disappointed that he wasn't awake when I picked you up this morning."

Daniel nodded, eager to get on to a safer subject, and for once Richie was a safer subject. "He spent last night with Billy Simpson, and they went to Hershey Park today with Billy's parents. He just got home a little while ago."

"Hershey Park is a nice place," Joey commented dully. "The whole town smells like a chocolate bar, and the rides are fun. Richie and Billy seem to be hitting it off very well. I'm glad, for both of you."

Daniel reached across the table to take hold of Joey's hands, stopping her in the midst of shredding a second paper napkin. "They never would have met if you hadn't blackmailed Rich into joining the Bulldogs. If I haven't thanked you for that yet, please let me do it now."

He was left with his empty hands stretched across the table as Joey suddenly sprang to her feet to fill the teakettle and put it on the stove. "I don't want your thanks, Daniel. I would have done the same for any child. You don't owe me anything."

The hem of Joey's bathrobe barely skimmed the top of her thighs as she bent forward to turn on the burner and Daniel swallowed hard, knowing he had to talk before he could act. Yet acting was just what he wanted to do. The memory of Joey's kiss still burned in him, and he had to know if his disgust at her cavalier way of looking at life had been successful in putting out the fire.

As Joey stood with her back to him, waiting for the water to come to a boil, Daniel rose and walked around the table to lay his hands on her shoulders. "I hurt you the other evening, didn't I?"

"Hurt me?" Joey repeated hollowly. "Don't be silly. How could you have hurt me? I'd have to care in order to be hurt. I'm going to have a cup of tea. Do you want tea or coffee?"

"Joey," Daniel whispered huskily, using his hands to turn her around to face him. "You have to understand. If Veronica showed me nothing else, she showed me that I need stability in my life. It's great to see every cup as half-full, every cloudy day as partly sunny. I'll bet you even do crossword puzzles in ink—the eternal optimist. But to work hard for something and then just throw it away on a whim, to take off across the country like some—some—"

"Some irresponsible butterfly? Some overage Tinker Bell? Some footloose, fancy-free gypsy? What's the matter, Daniel? Don't tell me you're suddenly at a loss for words."

"Damn it, Joey, will you just shut up and let me talk!" Daniel fairly shouted, giving her slim shoulders a small shake. "Don't you understand anything? I'm attracted to you. It doesn't take a rocket scientist to know that there's some sort of chemistry going on between us—something that's been going on between us since that first day."

Joey's eyes were liquid smoke as she replied shakily, "Yes, Daniel. I know. But that doesn't change anything. I'm not what you want in a woman. I'm too much like Veronica, too much like Wilbur."

Daniel crushed her against his chest, holding her to him tightly. "You're nothing like Veronica. Veronica cared only for herself. You care about people, Joey, maybe too much. Don't ever say you're like Veronica."

Joey gloried in this new closeness, her hands raised to clutch at Daniel's forearms as she melted against his strength. "That leaves Wilbur," she pointed out honestly, mentally slapping herself for not letting well enough alone. Daniel was here, in her house. She was here, in his arms. When would she ever learn to keep her great, big, stupid mouth shut?

Rubbing his cheek against the top of her head, Daniel closed his eyes and thought about Joey's admission that she wouldn't be opposed to selling the limousine service she had worked so hard to build in order to go out and experience life, in the same way she had done after leaving Ransom Computer. "You were just answering a hypothetical question that night," he reasoned, as much to himself as to her, "and I overreacted. You wouldn't really leave the business.

You had two years to get the wanderlust out of your system."

Joey pushed against him until she stood at arms' reach, glaring up at him, her eyes no longer gray smoke, but gray ice. "Says who—or is that *whom*? Do you think I want to spend the rest of my life chauffeuring other people around?"

Daniel was losing her, and he knew it. "No, of course I don't think that," he hastened to answer, trying without success to draw her back into his arms. "You'll want to marry someday, and have children. If you want to continue working, you'll want to work at something more conventional."

"And who makes you the authority on what's conventional?" she shot back at him. "If your precious Roseanne could hear you now her dark roots would turn white! Here!" she shouted, grabbing the flowers from the vase and handing him the dripping stems. "Take your stupid peace offering and get out of here!"

"With pleasure!" Daniel yelled back at her, holding the sopping flowers as he turned toward the door. He stopped just as his hand touched the knob and turned back to her. "You know, I'm not quite sure what we're arguing about, but I'm damned sure of one thing—*you're crazy!*"

It wasn't until he was halfway home that Daniel realized that he had goofed—again.

Chapter Eight

Tuesday arrived, and with it came a drenching, day-long rain, relieving Joey of the necessity of seeing Daniel at Richie's baseball game. Wednesday brought back the sun, and a surprise that went a long way toward restoring Joey's sense of humor.

Wednesday, Joey learned as she picked up Daniel at his office at five-thirty for another long, silent ride to Saucon Valley, was to bring her sweet, petite Muffy Arnstein.

Muffy was the most female female Joey had ever seen, a woman so appealingly helpless she would have made Roseanne Philpot gag at the sight of her. Dressed in chiffon ruffles and drooping bows that accentuated her full bosom, generous hips and infinitesimal waist, her hair was black as midnight, while her magnolia-pure skin and cherry lips reminded Joey of Hollywood's version of Snow White.

Although they were both pretty much the same height, Muffy made Joey feel as if she had been somehow suddenly catapulted back to pre-puberty. If Daniel sincerely believed that a female's "womanliness" could be measured in direct proportion to her bra size, Joey decided, then Muffy Arnstein was the perfect woman.

Muffy didn't walk. Oh, no. Muffy bounced, her sky-high heels clicking against the pavement as she approached the limousine, hanging on to Daniel's arm as if she could not conceive of crossing such a dangerous stretch of territory without his manly protection.

Joey tore her fascinated gaze away from Muffy's bouncing bosom in order to look at Daniel and gauge his mood. It was infuriatingly smug. He was grinning from ear to ear, just like a little boy who has found all the Christmas presents his parents had hidden in the attic, and she knew that if she'd had something heavy in her hand at that moment, she would have bopped him over the head with it without a second thought.

"This way, Muffy," she heard Daniel saying as he guided the woman toward the curb, and Esmeralda.

"Oh, Danny!" Muffy exclaimed in a high, childlike soprano as Joey opened the back door to allow the seemingly glued-together couple to enter. "Don't tell me this little ol' gal drives this big ol' car for you! I must say, I am impressed. Why, I just shudder to think of my ever being brave enough to even think of doing such a thing. Is she going to be driving us *all the way* to that delicious castle you told me about over lunch?"

"Yes, *Danny*, what is it to be?" Joey asked quietly as Daniel approached the limousine and unstuck his companion long enough for her to slide across the backseat. "Do I take you all the way, or can I drop you somewhere—preferably over the side of the Phillipsburg Bridge into the Delaware River. But not to worry, Danny boy. I have a sneaking suspicion dearest Muffy would float."

Daniel spoke through clenched teeth. "Just cut the cute act and drive. I called ahead, and we have reservations at Stokesay Castle for eight o'clock. And this time," he added meanly, "*you* eat in the kitchen."

"Yes, master," Joey answered, tipping her cap. "Anything you say, master. Oh," she added, just about to turn away, "would you care for a gas mask? Muffy's perfume might just eat up all the oxygen back there."

Daniel didn't answer her, but merely slid onto the backseat and pulled the door shut behind him. His left arm was immediately grabbed by Muffy, who continued to hold on to him with the tenacity of a pit bull until they reached Stokesay Castle more than two hours later. His head was ringing from her constant, inane chatter, and his self-respect was dragging in the mud.

Joey opened the door for them once the limousine had glided to a halt in the courtyard, then took herself off to the kitchen, where she sat perched on a high stool and allowed the chef to feed her delicious samples of all that was offered on that night's menu.

Daniel, however, ate nothing. All he could do was sit across the table from Muffy and think of poor Joey, forced to sit in a steamy kitchen and eat greasy pizza. It was possibly the longest night in his recollection, and he didn't breathe easily until he had released Muffy into Mrs. Hemmings's care and locked the door to his study behind him, intent on pouring himself a double Scotch on the rocks.

"Damn!" he exclaimed into the darkness as he lifted the lid of the ice bucket. "Talk about poetic justice." There was nothing inside the bucket except a small puddle of warm water.

Joey was free to attend the Bulldogs' Thursday practice, but Daniel only dropped Richie off and drove away, Muffy by his side. Joey watched as his car disappeared around the corner, refusing to admit that his defection bothered her personally—it was just that he was letting down the team.

"Hi, Joey," Richie called as he loped across the infield to her, his fielder's glove dangling from his right hand. "Dad says he's sorry he has to skip practice, but he's got to take

Muffy to Philadelphia to visit her brother. Boy, is she an airhead! I think Dad's really lost it this time. I think I liked it better when he worked all the time. Grandpa says he's drowning, but not to worry about it. I hate it when Grandpa's cryptic, but it makes him happy. Are you going to be here for the whole practice? Coach Mitchum is going to give me a few pointers on playing the outfield."

Joey assured Richie that she had the entire afternoon free, then complimented him on how well he was keeping the statistics for the team. "I was just looking over the book, Richie. I've never seen it in such good shape."

"It is stimulating," Richie agreed, shrugging as if to say it wasn't really important, "but I'd rather play right field. Billy's been helping me with my hitting. You know, it's really all basic physics. I mean, there's the force, the action and the opposite reaction. It's just a matter of finding the right combination, the right equation—"

Holding up her hands as if to ward off his explanation, Joey laughed, pleading, "Please, Rich, you're taking all the romance out of the game!" then quickly changed the subject. "So, how is your grandfather? I saw him one day last week in New York, but he could have flown off to Timbuktu since then, knowing Wilbur."

"He's still in New York," Richie told her, waving to Billy as he climbed out of a station wagon and headed onto the ball field. "He wanted me to come for a visit, but I just don't have the time right now. So I invited him to come to Saucon Valley for a visit."

"Do you think he will?" Joey asked, trying but failing to picture Wilbur Langley in the suburbs.

"He says he thinks he might have to get up-to-date on his shots first, but he'll think about it," Richie answered, laughing. "Well," he went on as Steve Mitchum clapped his hands to call the team to order, "here we go again. Joey, do you think you could take me home? Billy's mom said she would, but it's been a long time since I've had a ride in Esmeralda, and—"

"I'd love to," Joey answered, suddenly realizing how much she had missed Richie, and assured that she wouldn't be running into Daniel at the Quinn house, as he would have his hands full with Muffy. She grimaced, silently reworking that last thought in her head.

Once the two-hour practice was over, she and Richie drove to a nearby ice cream parlor to spend some time talking over hot fudge sundaes before heading for home. Richie successfully delayed the trip further by begging Joey to drive him to the local computer store, where he pulled a crumpled wad of bills from his pocket to pay for a new game for his computer. It was nearly supper time before she pulled Esmeralda into the sloping curved driveway in front of the brick Colonial.

The front door opened almost immediately and an irate-looking Daniel Quinn bounded down the steps, yelling, "Where the hell have you two been? Do you have any idea what time it is? I've been to Philadelphia and back, for God's sake! Billy Simpson's been home for over an hour! I was ready to call the police."

Joey's cheeks puffed out as she expelled her breath sharply with the realization that she had managed to look bad in Daniel's eyes once more. How was she to have known that Daniel was going to drive to Philadelphia, drop Muffy on her brother like a hot potato and race home again, just in time to point out, yet again, how flighty and irresponsible she was?

"I'm sorry, Daniel," she said, hastening to get out of the car and save Richie from his father's wrath. "It's my fault entirely. I should have called Mrs. Hemmings to say we'd be late."

"No, you shouldn't have," Daniel interrupted. "That would have been the logical, sensible thing to do. But you're a free spirit, aren't you? Free spirits don't look at clocks, or worry about anything but enjoying the moment."

"It's not Joey's fault, Dad," Richie cut in, stepping in front of her protectively. "I'm the one who wanted to stop at the computer store. Don't be angry with Joey."

Both Daniel and Joey looked at Richie, who was actually volunteering to take the blame when he could just as easily have gotten off the hook, and neither one of them could think of anything to say. Luckily, at that moment, Mrs. Hemmings appeared in the doorway to ask Richie if he thought he could set the dinner table from where he was standing.

Uncomfortable silence reigned on the driveway for several moments after Richie trotted into the house, a silence that Joey finally broke. "There are times I almost believe that the Richie I met on Forty-second Street and the Richie who just ran inside to help Mrs. Hemmings are two entirely different boys. You must be very pleased. Saucon Valley seems to have been just what the doctor ordered. Daniel?" she prompted when he didn't answer her.

"Muffy was a mistake, Joey," Daniel admitted quietly at last, staring down at her intently. "So was Roseanne, when you come right down to it, but Muffy was the worst. The very worst. I had to drive her to Philadelphia fast, before I strangled her with her own hair."

Joey felt a small thrill of triumph race through her body, but quickly stifled it. "She was certainly—um—*different*, I'll say that for her."

Daniel sniffed, shaking his head. "I haven't been called Danny since the third grade. I'd only known her from seeing her at Wilbur's parties. Roseanne, too." He looked directly into Joey's eyes as another thought hit him. "Wilbur's got some strange friends, do you know that?"

"And you haven't even gotten to Ursula," Joey pointed out, remembering Wilbur's mention of that particular name the day they had strolled together through Central Park. "He seemed to think she might be a winner."

"Ursula?" Daniel repeated, his brow furrowing in confusion. "You know about Ursula? When did you talk with Wilbur? Damn that man! Why can't he mind his own business?"

Walking over to lean a hip against Esmeralda's front fender, Joey reasoned, "You and Richie *are* his business, at least in Wilbur's mind. I know I'm overstepping myself saying this, Daniel, but maybe it's time you put the past to rest and worked with the present. Your father-in-law cares about you. You might try working with him, instead of against him. It's stupid to be in competition with him over your son's affection."

Daniel's eyes narrowed for a moment in quick anger, then his expression softened. "You're right, of course. I have been measuring Wilbur against his raising of Veronica, and barely giving him a chance. He may not be a typical gray-haired grandfather, but he wouldn't have been able to gain so much influence over Richie if I had been paying enough attention to my own son." His features hardened again. "But that doesn't give him the right to start meddling in *my* life! That's what he's doing, isn't it—trying his hand at a little matchmaking?"

"If you mean, is he trying to get the two of us together, yes, I think he is," Joey returned just as angrily. "But don't worry, Daniel. I wouldn't have you if you got down on your knees and begged me!"

"And you'd hold your breath a long time before I'd even think of it," Daniel told her, moving away from the limousine. "We're totally incompatible—even more than Roseanne or Muffy."

"Or Ursula?" Joey shot back at him, already heading around to the driver's side of the limousine.

"Especially Ursula!" Daniel shouted. "I don't want any woman in my life right now. I've just found my son, and that's more than enough for me right now. The last thing I need is some idiotic woman to drive me insane. When the hell is your brother getting back?''

Taken slightly off her guard, Joey answered him automatically, ''Andy? Next Tuesday. Why?''

''Then we only have tomorrow and Monday to get through,'' he pointed out, his voice strangely quiet. ''Starting Wednesday morning, I want to see Andy behind the wheel. You got that?''

''In spades!'' Joey yelled, opening the car door. ''Tell Richie I said goodbye,'' she added before starting the engine and sending Esmeralda fishtailing down the drive, the tires spitting out angry bits of gravel in their wake.

By Monday morning Joey was beginning to think of the tinted-glass partition that divided the front seat from the passenger compartment as her own private Berlin Wall, complete with snarling guard dogs.

After dropping Daniel on Sixth Avenue she parked Esmeralda at a local garage and walked to Wilbur's penthouse, using her smile and a carefully folded five dollar bill to bribe the doorman into calling upstairs to see if Daniel's father-in-law was at home. He was, and she rode up on the elevator with her hands wrapped tightly around the flat brown paper bag she had brought with her, wondering just what she thought she was doing.

''Joey, darling!'' Wilbur greeted as the door of the elevator whispered open and she stepped onto the shiny parquet floor that had replaced the ankle-deep white carpeting. He kissed her on both cheeks, then took hold of one hand and held it out in front of her. ''Let me look at you. How difficult it is to imagine you in anything but this ridiculous uniform. You should wear chiffon, my dear. Baby-pink chiffon.''

''Like Muffy?'' Joey asked, grimacing.

"Good Lord, no!" Wilbur responded, dropping her hands. "Never, ever like Muffy. Unfortunate child, I think she was off redoing her lip gloss when the brains were being handed out. Forgive me. I can't imagine what I was thinking, comparing you to Muffy Arnstein. I guess I shall just leave the dressing of you up to your own discretion, although I would hope you'd seriously reconsider the purple sneakers. They just aren't *in* anymore, you know."

Joey looked around the massive living room, nodding her head in appreciation. The room was furnished entirely in the English country style, with plenty of overstuffed blue-and-white-chintz sofas, and a gigantic faded Oriental carpet cushioning her footsteps. "I like this new phase much better, Wilbur," she complimented sincerely. "I believe even Daniel would approve."

Wilbur looked around the room himself, as if seeing it for the first time. "I had an extra room converted into a computer room cum bedroom for Richie. The walls are covered with baseball pennants and pictures of Einstein and some other bearded fellow the boy favors. I think he'll be pleased. Now, sit down. What can I do for you?"

Joey sat down on one corner of the sofa that faced the fireplace, the paper bag now clutched tightly in both hands. "This is crazy," she said, not really speaking to Wilbur. "I really shouldn't be doing this. I'm taking advantage of you. I'm so ashamed of myself."

Wilbur leaned back against the soft cushions, eyeing the flat package. "Let me venture a guess, my dear. You've written a book, and now you want my opinion as to whether or not it's any good."

Joey's head shot up in surprise. "How—how did you know?"

He leaned over to remove the bag from Joey's nerveless fingers. "It's a sixth sense we publishers develop over the course of several decades. What is it—romance? Mystery? Horror?"

Wrinkling her nose, she said, "Fictionalized personal experience—the very worst thing of all to pull off successfully, at least according to everything I've read on the subject. I've already been turned down several times, including a form rejection letter from Langley Books." She tried to take the package back from him. "I really shouldn't be wasting your time with it, Wilbur, but—"

"But you'll force yourself to, right?" he teased, lightly slapping her fingers away before sliding the rubber-band-held sheaf of papers from the bag. "Have you shown this to Daniel?"

She shook her head. "Daniel wouldn't understand," she explained. "I've told him a little bit about it in a way, and he thinks—well, to be perfectly honest, he thinks I'm slightly deranged. He'd never give a book that attempts to justify my life-style an even chance." She made a face. "That sounds a little self-righteous, doesn't it? Daniel's entitled to his own opinion."

"Daniel's entitled to be horsewhipped," Wilbur stated firmly, reaching into his pocket to retrieve a snow-white handkerchief, which he handed to Joey. "Here. Wipe your eyes. I'll read your book."

Joey dried her eyes and smiled at Wilbur. "Only if you promise to be brutally honest."

"Brutal it is," he agreed, laying the manuscript to one side. "Now, dearest Joey, since my son-in-law is too blind to see what's in front of his face, how about I try my hand at monopolizing your time? How does luncheon at the Plaza sound to you?"

"The Plaza sounds absolutely lovely, Wilbur," Joey said honestly, allowing him to help her to her feet. "Thank you."

If Carl Sandburg's Chicago fog tiptoed into town on little cat feet, New York's fog roared in on a Mack truck, thick and fast, and mowing down anything in its path. Traffic inched along the streets of Manhattan, the entire city brought to its knees by the swirling, dense mist.

At five-thirty, after spending the afternoon with Wilbur, Joey carefully nudged Esmeralda into a parking space just outside Daniel's office building. Her eyelids narrowed as she searched the pavement for some sign of him. She hoped he would be on time because, at the rate things were going now, she doubted they would be clear of the city in less than an hour.

The rear passenger door opened and closed before she could register the fact that he had found Esmeralda in the sea of limousines and mist. He knocked sharply against the glass partition, motioning for her to lower it. "How fast can you get to the Allentown-Bethlehem-Easton International Airport, Joey?" he began without preamble.

"To ABE?" she asked, frowning. "Wouldn't Newark Airport be closer? Besides, what planes would be taking off in this pea soup?"

"None," he answered shortly. "That's why Courtney Blackmun's flight from the West Coast is being diverted to the ABE airport. Her plane will be landing there in a little over two hours. I told Harry, her agent, we'd pick her up and take her to my house for the night. Now, if you've no further questions, I suggest we get on with it. Or do you want me to drive?"

"No, I don't want you to drive," Joey sneered back at him. "I don't *have* a death wish." She raised the glass partition and steered Esmeralda out into the swell of private cars and fog.

It was only after thinking about it for a few minutes that she regretted her quick sarcasm, for she really would have liked to learn more about Courtney Blackmun, a novelist whose work she truly enjoyed.

They had only traveled about forty miles when Daniel knocked on the glass partition once more. "It's really slow going, isn't it, Joey?" he commented, leaning his forearms against the top of the rear-facing seat so that his head was close to hers. "Person to person—and not chauvinist to helpless female—would you like me to take over the wheel for a while? Not that you aren't doing beautifully, because you are. As I told you before, you really are an exceptionally good driver."

"Thank you. They let me take off the training wheels a while ago. But I don't mind driving, Daniel," Joey answered honestly, turning her head to give him a quick, forgiving smile, "though it would be nice to have someone to talk to while I try to keep my eyes on the white line in the middle of this mess. This is unusual, a fog this heavy. It wasn't forecast. It reminds me more of the California coast than New Jersey." She hoped her reminder of the West Coast would bring Daniel's mind back to Courtney Blackmun.

Daniel's mind was very obliging. "That's where Courtney's coming from—San Francisco, to be precise. She just finished up the first leg of the publicity tour for her new book. Have you read it yet?"

Joey shook her head. "I've been meaning to get it, but I haven't had time."

"I'll get you a copy. I'm sure I have one at home. Would you like it autographed?" Daniel didn't know why he was going out of his way to be so nice to Joey, but talking about Courtney kept his mind busy, and away from thoughts of asking Joey to pull Esmeralda onto the shoulder of the road so that he could climb into the front seat with her until the fog lifted. Or, he thought, smiling, she could climb into the backseat with him. Surely together they could find some mutually satisfying way to pass the time.

"I'd like that," Joey said, turning on the windshield wipers, for the fog was lifting as it began to rain.

"You'd like what?" Daniel asked vaguely, his attention all centered on the soft curve of Joey's neck.

"An autograph. I'd like a Courtney Blackmun auto-graph," she repeated helpfully.

"Oh, yes. Courtney," Daniel said, remembering his bestselling author. "She'll be staying overnight, and catching a plane to New York tomorrow morning."

"I have the day free, Daniel, if you'd like me to drive her. The airports will be jammed tomorrow after this," Joey offered shakily, feeling his fingers rubbing lightly against her nape and realizing that she was suddenly finding it rather difficult to breathe.

"I guess so," he answered absently. "Joey," he said before he could talk himself out of it, "there's a rest stop just ahead. Pull over."

"Pull over?" Joey swallowed, hard.

"Pull over, Joey," Daniel repeated huskily, his lips softly brushing the delicate skin just beneath her right ear, "*please*."

He was out the passenger door and reinstalled in the wide front seat before she could put the gear lever into the park position, and she was in his arms before either of them could remember that they really weren't speaking to each other.

His hands were hard and demanding as they ranged up and down her back, his lips wildly searching, his body pressed tightly against hers. Her mouth opened beneath his as she welcomed his possession, her eyes tightly closed, her heart pounding loudly in her ears, so loudly that she could not hear her saner self telling her that she was being a fool.

"Oh, Joey," Daniel breathed at last, holding her against his chest, "it's still just as good. Maybe even better. I'm not going to fight it anymore. You can drive Esmeralda to Alaska and back, or climb mountains in Peru, or run for president—I don't care. Just please let Richie and me tag along with you."

Tears filled Joey's eyes. This was surrender, but they were both winners. "I don't want to do any of those things," she told him, suddenly realizing that she was speaking the truth.

"My cup became completely full the moment I met you. There's nowhere else I'd rather be, than to be with you. Nothing else I'd rather do than hold you forever and ever."

He pushed her slightly away from him, looking down into her eyes. "You mean that, don't you? My God, you mean it. Oh, Joey!" he groaned, claiming her lips once more as he pulled her from behind the wheel and onto his lap.

Several minutes later, when the defroster finally cleared the steamed windows, Daniel steered Esmeralda back out onto the highway, Joey sitting close beside him, her head pressed comfortably against his shoulder. "I haven't necked in a car since high school," she told him, rubbing her cheek against his suit coat.

"I should think so. It's damned uncomfortable, if you want my opinion, and way too public. We'll deposit Courtney with Mrs. Hemmings and the two of us can continue on to your place," Daniel told her as they crossed over the bridge at Phillipsburg and entered a fog-free Pennsylvania. "We have a lot to talk about."

Joey lifted her head to smile into his eyes. "Talk about, Daniel?" she asked, pretending to be shocked. "You mean you really want to *talk*?"

Daniel lifted one eyebrow and leered at her. "What do you think?"

Chapter Nine

Joey wasn't quite sure what was going on, hadn't been sure of much of anything ever since Daniel ordered her to pull Esmeralda into the roadside rest stop—but she was more than willing to "go with the flow." As a matter of fact, she was pretty sure she would need to resort to plastic surgery in order to have the inane smile wiped from her face. She was so happy she almost believed she could hear herself purring.

This was what life was all about—what it was really all about. This was what her father and mother had had and taken for granted, what her father had missed so desperately when his wife was gone, the regret he must have carried with him to his grave. This was what he had wanted for his children. Love. Complete, total love. A reason to believe that life was, even in the worst of times, always more than half-full.

She hadn't found this sense of completeness climbing the corporate ladder at Ransom Computers. She hadn't discovered it hiding in the laid-back far West or waiting for her on the warm shores of southern Florida. She hadn't met up with it as she drove Esmeralda everywhere and arrived nowhere, meeting people and learning and growing, but never really discovering anything.

She had been going about it all wrong. Happiness wasn't a place, or an occupation, or the freedom to see a sunrise or eat ice cream for breakfast. Happiness was loving, and being loved.

There was nothing of this sort of love, this complete happiness that was worth any pain, in the manuscript she had given Wilbur. This particular, mind-blowing revelation was a whole other book, a whole other world. A world that just might be too private for her ever to want to share it with anyone else.

Daniel hadn't said he loved her, she realized as, following her directions, he steered the limousine toward the off ramp nearest the airport. She wrinkled her nose. Neither had she, if it came right down to it. *There's plenty of time for hearts and flowers,* she decided, reluctantly moving away from the comfort of his shoulder in order to check her hair in the rearview mirror. *Right now it's enough that he knows he can't live without me.*

"Lord, that's smug!" she exclaimed out loud, running a finger across her kiss-swollen bottom lip.

"What?" Daniel asked, before turning onto the road leading to the terminal. "What's smug?"

"Smug?" Joey repeated in sudden panic. "Did I say smug? I meant *smudged*. It's my lipstick. My lipstick is smudged."

"Your lipstick, my dearest chauffeurette, is *missing*," Daniel informed her with what could only be called a note of triumph in his voice. "Now help me find a parking place for this boat. Courtney's plane should have landed a half hour ago."

"What does she look like?" Joey asked as she raced across the parking lot, taking two steps to each of Daniel's

longer, ground-eating strides. "I mean, I've seen her picture on the back of her book jackets, but those things don't
really tell you anything. Attila the Hun would look good
after three hours of hair and makeup, photographed
through cheesecloth, and with a wind machine running."

Daniel took her hand as he entered the terminal and
stopped for a moment, trying to decide which way to go.
"She'll be easy to recognize, Joey. Courtney will be the one
with a mountain of luggage, and steam coming out her ears.
Maybe her nose, too."

"Temperamental?" Joey asked, adjusting her cap with
her free hand while trying to catch her breath.

"Talented," Daniel corrected, his pace increasing once
more as he spotted his bestselling author sitting cross-legged
on an oversize Gucci suitcase directly beneath a No Smoking sign, a lit cigarette dangling from her long, slim fingers.
He released Joey's hand. "You don't have to hang on to
your cap. We've lucked out. I don't think Mount Saint
Courtney is going to blow her top."

Joey looked across the terminal to the baggage claim area,
immediately knowing that she was looking at Courtney
Blackmun. She would have recognized her even if she had
never seen her picture. Courtney Blackmun *looked* like a
writer, from her designer luggage, to her sleek, sophisticated ivory shantung suit and deep emerald blouse, to her
long, silk-clad legs, to the cloud of cigarette smoke making
a blue-gray halo around her artfully windblown ebony
shoulder-length curls. *"Wow!"* she said, impressed. "She
looks more like one of the heroines in her books than the
heroines in her books."

"Yeah," Daniel said quietly out of the corner of his
mouth as he waved at the writer. "Just don't gush, okay?
Courtney hates gushers. Hello, Courtney!" he said in his
cheeriest voice as he and Joey halted in front of her. "Been
waiting long?"

"I never gush," Joey grumbled, feeling as if she had just been relegated to the role of teenage rock-star groupie. "I wouldn't know how to gush."

"Daniel," Courtney said coolly, rising to her full height, which put her a good half foot above Joey, who first looked up at the woman, then down at her own feet, to gasp in dismay as she discovered that she was still wearing her purple high-tops. "Who's your little friend?"

Go ahead, Daniel, Joey cried inwardly, longing to tug on his sleeve and feed him lines. *Tell her who your little friend is. Tell her that we're late because you spent a half hour necking in a limo on the New Jersey Turnpike. Come on, Danny boy, sock it to her!*

"Joey is my chauffeur, Courtney," Daniel said, stooping to kiss the author on the cheek. "Courtney Blackmun, allow me to introduce you to Joey Abbott. Joey, give me a hand with these bags, will you? Courtney's been waiting here long enough."

Joey watched as Courtney's left eyebrow—one perfectly sculpted brow of a perfectly matching pair—rose a fraction. "Your chauffeur, Daniel?" she questioned, looking at Joey levelly. She held out her right hand, taking Joey's in a firm grip. "How nice to meet you, Joey. You must lead an interesting life."

Courtney's green eyes could see inside and read her soul, Joey was sure of it. The woman had done no more than touch her hand, and she was convinced the writer now knew her entire life's story. Joey retrieved her hand quickly, wanting to find a lead helmet with which to cover her head so that Courtney couldn't use her X-ray eyes to read her mind as well. "Nice—nice meeting you, Ms. Blackmun," she heard herself stammer as she quickly gathered up the two smaller pieces of luggage and headed for the door.

She got as far as the limousine before realizing that Daniel had the keys to the trunk in his pocket. Resisting the urge to throw the cases to the ground and then stomp on them, she laid them down gently and turned to see Courtney and Daniel taking their good sweet time in joining her, Courtney's arm comfortably twined around his as they laughed at some private joke.

"I could be invisible, for all that man cares," Joey told herself, trying but not succeeding in working up a head of steam. She wasn't angry. Not really. She was hurting, badly, and she couldn't understand how Daniel could run so hot and cold—kissing her passionately one moment and treating her like an employee the next. A not very important employee, too.

"It's a good job I didn't tell him I love him," she muttered, leaning against Esmeralda's rear fender. "He might want me, but when itch comes to scratch, I'm still just a freewheeling chauffeur, and not good enough to acknowledge in public. Steamed-up cars and the privacy of my house in the dark—that's all I'm good for. Well, if that's what he thinks, he can just go take a flying leap!"

Daniel deposited the heavy suitcase beside the trunk and produced the key chain, handing it over to Joey. "Sorry about that. I forgot I still had them," he said sheepishly. "Courtney, let me get you settled in the backseat and we'll be on our way in a moment. All in all, you've had a pretty rough day."

"I'll show him a rough day," Joey groused under her breath, hefting the largest suitcase into the trunk. "Courtney Blackmun in full sail will look like a toy boat in the Central Park lake compared to the rough day I'm going to give him!"

"Hey, that's heavy. I would have handled it," Daniel said, coming up behind her, leaning over her to shift the suitcase to one side of the trunk. He lifted the two smaller bags and dropped them beside the suitcase. "You should have waited."

Joey's eyelids were narrowed as she looked up at him. "Really?" she asked, putting her hands on her hips. "And how long would I have to wait to be introduced to Courtney? Or was that never part of the program?"

Daniel was confused, and his expression clearly reflected it. "What do you mean, Joey? I introduced you."

"What do you mean, Joey?" she recited in a singsong voice, her belligerent chin nearly stabbing him in the chest. "I *mean*, Mr. Quinn, when am I going to be introduced as something other than your chauffeur? Admit it! You had another moment of madness back there on the turnpike, and now you've come screeching back to your senses. You don't have to knock me over the head with a brick, you know. I can take a hint."

"What in hell are you talking about?"

"I'm talking about how you're ashamed of me, of how you *really* feel about me."

Daniel's face went dead white, something Joey had already realized happened only when he was very angry. He reached out to take hold of her shoulders. "You idiot!" he accused. "There's a time and a place for everything. And the middle of that terminal wasn't either of them. All I wanted to do was get Courtney out of there before the fire marshal fined her. You want commitment, Joey? You want acknowledgment? I'll give you an introduction that'll knock your socks off. Come with me!"

Before she knew what was happening to her she was standing beside the open door to the passenger compartment and Daniel was announcing in a loud voice that brooked no argument, "Courtney Blackmun, I'd like to introduce you to Joey Abbott."

"Yes, we've already met," Courtney responded sweetly, smiling up at Joey in that Cheshire cat way that Joey had already learned to fear. "Was there something else you neglected to tell me, Daniel?"

"Yes, there is. As Joey just pointed out to me, it seems that I somehow forgot to tell you that Joey Abbott is not only my employee, but also the most infuriating, independent, mind-destroying, *exasperating* female I have ever met—and I'm crazy about her.''

Joey leaned against his side, smiling down at Courtney. "He's crazy about me," she verified simply. "Isn't he cute?"

Courtney reached into her purse and withdrew a slim gold cigarette case. "He's utterly adorable," she said, lifting a cigarette to her lips and lighting it with a jeweled lighter. "If you'd like to kiss the bride, Daniel, please do it quickly. Then, if you're both done with telling me what I already know, and it wouldn't be too much bother, I'd like to go somewhere quiet and take a long, hot bath."

"I think you must have believed Courtney's publicity, Daniel," Joey said two hours later, turning the sizzling hamburgers on the gas grill with a large spatula. "She couldn't have been more sweet."

"That's because she's smoking again," Daniel told her as he sat at his ease in a lawn chair, feeling oddly aroused by Joey's efficient movements as she worked in shorts, tank top and an oversize apron carrying the notice: "It's my kitchen and I'll cook what I damn well please."

"What does smoking have to do with it? And stop leering at me. Richie's here, remember?"

"She's always more mellow when she lapses back into her single vice. The cigarettes also mean that she's ready to get down to work again. According to Courtney, smoking makes writing easier—something to do with stimulating and concentrating the creative brain cells. Between books she quits."

"Which explains why her publicity tours are always such a headache, right? I mean, what with the withdrawal symptoms and all that?" Joey asked, lifting the hamburgers onto already prepared buns. "Well, I just think it's nice that she's in her room writing down ideas for her new book, and you're free to be here with me."

Daniel took the plate she handed him, holding it under his nose and sniffing appreciatively at the charcoal-broiled aroma. "I'm also free to be away from Mrs. Hemmings, who has been giving hourly bulletins on the amount of smoke floating through the upstairs, quoting more statistics than the surgeon general. That's why Richie is with me. She didn't want him exposed to side-steam smoke."

"Umm, I think I like you in shorts," Joey commented, sitting cross-legged on the grass with her hamburger and leaning her back against his bare leg. "You've got great legs, for a man. Straight, and not too fuzzy. And that's side-*stream* smoke, Daniel."

"Not if your name is Mrs. Hemmings," Daniel explained, ruffling her short curls. "Uh-oh. I think we've got company. Behave yourself, woman."

Richie appeared from around the corner of the house just as his father took the first bite of his hamburger. "That's right, don't call me," he complained, not really upset. "Just let me stay in the barn playing with the kittens—and starving to death. Boy, Joey, that smells good," he complimented, grabbing a loaded plate for himself. "Hey, and real homemade potato salad, too. This is really neat. Picnicking. Could you guys see Grandpa eating from a paper plate?"

"Only if it was at the Plaza and a tuxedo-clad waiter was holding it for him," Daniel said, making Joey choke on a bite of potato salad. He pounded her lightly on her back until she stopped coughing. "Joey, didn't you say there was a Phillies game on television tonight?"

The conspiratorial tone of his voice had Joey hiding a smile behind her hand as she answered his question. "Yup. It started ten minutes ago, as a matter of fact. There's a lefty pitching."

"Really?" Richie remarked around a mouthful of hamburger. "I think it's really interesting the way lefties can make the curve ball break left to right as it travels downward across the plate. That's why they're particularly effective against left-handed batters, you know."

"Yes," Joey broke in wryly as she heard Daniel suppressing a laugh, "we know."

"I figure," Richie went on, undaunted, "that if I can just study their motion long enough, and then feed the data into my computer, I can figure out a way to beat 'em. Do you mind if I go inside and watch?"

"Be my guest," Joey answered in a strangled voice as Daniel's leg shifted behind her, so that she fell into the cradle between his knees.

"Thank God! I thought he'd never leave," Daniel said once Richie had gone, taking a second hamburger along with him as he ran up the porch steps, the wooden screen door slamming shut behind him. "If he thinks he can actually beat a good left-hander with a computer, he needs more help than I can give him."

"Oh, yeah?" Joey pushed herself back up to a sitting position and turned to look him in the eye. "I've seen what a computer can do, Daniel, my friend. Five bucks says he goes two for four the next time he's up against a lefty. Put up or shut up. And help me clean up around here before it gets too dark to find everything."

"Pretty cocky, aren't you? And pretty bossy, too. Cocky and bossy," he mused, shaking his head, and not moving another muscle. "That's a bad combination. Maybe I'd better round up Richie and get out of here while the getting's good. What do you think?"

Joey grabbed his hands and pulled him to his feet. "I think he doth protest too much," she told him, growing more sure of herself and his love for her with each passing moment. "Now come here and kiss me. I've been a good girl ever since you got here, dragging your son in tow as protection. You owe me, Daniel Quinn. It's time to pay up."

"Oh, is that right?" he asked teasingly, lifting her at the waist to deposit her on top of one long picnic bench, so that they were at eye level with each other, their bodies pressed tightly together from hip to thigh. Raising her hands, he twined her arms around to the back of his neck, laughing as he added jokingly, "Why don't you try to make me?" Then he felt his muscles tense as he watched her smile slowly leaving her face. "Oh, Joey," he sighed, surrendering yet again to the power this small female held over his heart.

He took her into his arms as the sun set behind the trees, not caring if it ever rose again, if he couldn't face that sunrise with Joey by his side. She was nothing that he had been looking for, if indeed he had been looking for anything, but she was all that he ever wanted. All that he ever needed. She had driven into his life and into his heart. And he would never let her go.

She wasn't as independent as Roseanne, but she was definitely more free. She wasn't as helplessly feminine as Muffy, but she was more than enough female for him to handle. She wasn't as *Ursula* as Ursula, but then no one was—or even should be. She wasn't immensely talented, like Courtney Blackmun, but who wanted the hassle of living with a temperamental writer, anyway? Not him, that was for sure. Never again.

No, Joey wasn't anything like Roseanne, or Muffy, or Ursula, or Courtney. More important, she was light-years away from anything Veronica had been.

She was Joey. Just Joey. Loving, kind and giving Joey. Free-spirited, generous, optimistic Joey, without a single selfish, self-interested bone in her body. She gave without question, and accepted without tying strings around him. And he loved her.

His mouth buried against the curve of her neck, his hands freely roving over previously unexplored territory as she nibbled at his ear, Daniel felt his body rock with shock at his last thought.

He loved her.

Daniel Quinn loved Joey Abbott.

"How about that!" His hands stilled in the act of creeping beneath her loose cotton tank top. Slowly, as a smile slid onto his face, he lifted his head to look deeply into her eyes. "I'm in love with you," he said, and she could hear the laughter in his voice.

"And that's funny?" she asked him, her heart suddenly pounding even faster than it had been ever since he'd lifted her onto the bench. "You have a perverted sense of humor, Daniel. I think you ought to know that."

"Why? I'm a reasonably normal man, respected in my field, who has gone and fallen in love with a half-pint, big-mouthed, baseball-playing, purple sneaker-wearing chauffeur who used to be a computer executive and full-time vagabond. Oh, yes. Did I forget to mention that her brother wants to be a rock star with his own MTV video? All in all, I'd say it's very funny."

"And I've fallen in love with a big-shot New York publisher who only learned to laugh ten minutes ago, and who has a whiz kid son, a kooky housekeeper who keeps bringing her dead husband into the conversation and a father-in-law who thinks he's Peter Pan. You're no bargain, Daniel Quinn. Just remember that. Now, the question remains— what are we going to do about it?"

Daniel kissed the tip of her nose. "About what? Richie? Peter Pan? I refuse to take lifelong responsibility for Mrs. Hemmings, no matter how much my son likes her chocolate chip cookies."

"Forget the cookies. I mean, what are we going to do about the fact that we love each other," Joey reminded him, pressing her forehead against his.

Joey watched, amazed, as Daniel's face rearranged itself into a leer. "Well, I can think of one thing. But we'd have to dump the kid first."

Batting her eyelashes furiously, Joey gasped, asking, "Why *Danny*, whatever do you mean?"

"Hey, you guys!" Richie's voice came booming out at them from beneath the wooden porch roof, so that Joey, startled, nearly tumbled from the bench onto the grass. "I've got it. I know I've got it. I have to get right home and feed it into my computer."

"He's got it," Daniel said quietly as he steadied Joey on the bench.

"Bully for him," Joey commented fatalistically, knowing the mood had been broken. "Let's just hope it's not catching. I think you'd better let go now, Daniel, I'm not going to fall."

Richie ran down the steps onto the lawn, then stopped, suddenly realizing that his father and Joey were locked in each other's arms. "Hey, what are you two guys doing, anyhow?"

"And to think he used to be so articulate," Daniel mused in mock sorrow, releasing Joey reluctantly.

"And much more perceptive," Joey agreed, brushing down her clothes while trying to recover her composure, "not that I think it's going to take him too long to catch on. You'd better help me down before he starts giving us chapter and verse from his last sex education class."

Within ten minutes the three of them had succeeded in clearing up the remnants of their cookout. Richie had run ahead to get in Daniel's car, his father lingering behind only long enough to arrange for Joey to pick up Courtney in the morning and steal one last, unsatisfying kiss.

"I could send him to summer camp," he suggested, not wanting to let her go. "As a matter of fact, I'd even consider sending him to Wilbur for a few weeks. Joey, you're looking at a desperate man!"

She shook her head. "Only if you can send Andy along with him. Remember, he comes home tomorrow. That's two strikes, Daniel—with both of our houses out of the running. You'll have to come up with another idea."

He leaned down for one last kiss. "Give me time. I'll think of something," he promised, and then he was gone.

Joey fell asleep that night with a smile on her face, to dream that her father and mother were in the bedroom with her, silently giving her their blessing.

Joey didn't recognize the Courtney Blackmun that walked out the front door early the next morning, dragging one of her own suitcases behind her. She was wearing well-worn jeans and a thin cotton top that hung down to her thighs, and her glorious black hair was tied back haphazardly in a ponytail. Her face, still beautiful, was free of makeup, and she was wearing bright green high-top sneakers.

"Wilbur would be appalled," Joey said under her breath as she got out of the limousine in order to relieve Courtney of the suitcase. "Good morning, Ms. Blackmun," she called out, moving across the driveway at a near run. "Let me get that for you."

"No need, Joey," the writer responded, hefting the suitcase down the steps. "And please, the name is Courtney. Richie is bringing the other two, if he can tear himself away from Mrs. Hemmings's heavenly blueberry pancakes. I came out ahead of him to have a cigarette. Mrs. Hemmings frowns upon them, you know."

"There have been rumors to that effect," Joey sympathized, opening the trunk. "But where's Daniel? He's usually an early riser." She looked around, expecting him to appear at any moment. Needing him to appear, so that she could look into his eyes and believe that yesterday had been real and not just some wonderful, wishful dream.

Richie came stumbling out the door, nearly lost beneath the weight and bulk of one overnight case and the large Gucci bag. "Dad's on the phone with London, Joey, and says you're to go on without him but come straight back here. Oh, yeah, and you're to drive carefully. Do you want me to kiss you goodbye instead?" he finished, making puckering motions with his mouth.

"You'll do five laps before the game this afternoon for that one, buster," Joey warned him, ruffling his hair as he passed her on the way to the trunk. "And tell your father I *always* drive carefully. Courtney?" she prompted, holding open the door to the backseat.

Courtney shook her head. "I'd much rather ride up front with you, if you don't mind the cigarette smoke. I don't think I'm dressed for all that opulence back there."

The woman was full of surprises, Joey thought, shutting the passenger door and gesturing toward the front of the limousine. "Esmeralda and I would be honored to have you."

Courtney settled herself into the front seat, fastening her lap and shoulder belt and promptly lighting a cigarette. "All right," she said, exhaling a long stream of smoke, "let's have it. How serious is this thing between you and Daniel?"

Her question had surprised Joey, but she answered it honestly. "Very serious, at least on my part. I'm in love with the guy."

"He's been hurt. But you already know that, don't you?"

"Veronica. His late wife," Joey answered solemnly, nodding her head. "Daniel told me about it. It was all very sad."

"It was all very criminal," Courtney declared, "and all because of a book."

"A book?" Joey averted her eyes from the road for a moment to sneak a look in Courtney's direction, trying to understand. "I think I've lost you. Daniel told me she was killed in a plane crash. How could a book have anything to do with that?"

Courtney settled herself more comfortably in her seat and lit another cigarette. "I have to quit these things before they kill me," she said, holding the cigarette in front of her and glaring at it. "I've quit at least a dozen times, only to start again when an idea hits me. I'm going to do a three-generational saga this time, ending with the bombing of Nagasaki."

"Courtney," Joey prompted, not caring that she was being told something the rest of the world wouldn't know for another two years, "you opened this particular can of worms. Now finish it."

The writer stubbed out the cigarette, breaking its length in two in the ashtray. "Filthy habit. All right, Joey, I'll agree that the marriage was doomed from the beginning. Veronica was beautiful, but she was spoiled rotten. Wilbur saw to that, bless his heart. He meant well. Men always *mean* well."

"I like Wilbur," Joey warned stiffly.

"Who doesn't like him?" Courtney countered, popping a breath mint into her mouth. "Wilbur's a pussycat. I really believe Daniel married Veronica because he liked Wilbur so much, even if they have been playing tug-of-war with Richie this past year or so. Daniel didn't need to marry the boss's daughter, you know. He's the best in the business, or I would have jumped ship years ago. In publishing, loyalty is nothing but a seven-letter word meaning 'make me an offer I can't refuse.' "

Joey was silent, trying to remember to concentrate on the traffic as they crossed the Phillipsburg Bridge into New Jersey.

"It could have been a civilized divorce, if it hadn't been for the book. Veronica fancied herself to be a writer, you understand." Courtney turned to look at Joey, shaking her head as she made a face. "Bad," she said, shivering with distaste. "Very, *very* bad."

"But she wanted Daniel to publish it?" Joey questioned, a lump vaguely resembling a rock the size of Gibraltar forming in her stomach.

"Why not? Wilbur had published the first one." Once again, Courtney turned to Joey. "*Badder* than bad," she intoned gravely. "It was Veronica's version of the Civil *Wa-ar, dahling*. Wilbur bought up all the copies and sent them overseas to some needy country that didn't have any books of their own. I think they sent them back. Daniel told her he wouldn't publish her second effort. Veronica, well— Veronica didn't take rejection well."

Joey thought she was going to be sick. "What did she do?"

The jeweled cigarette lighter snapped closed and Courtney expelled another thin white stream of smoke. "She punished him, of course. She took lovers—quite openly. She tried to drive a wedge between Wilbur and Daniel. She neglected her son, bad-mouthed her husband to anyone who would listen and finally got herself killed in that plane crash before Daniel could work up the courage to strangle her. No writer's had a snowball's chance in hell of getting close to him ever since. No female writer, that is. He's a good one, Joey, don't let him get away. I don't believe in gossip, but I like you, which is why I told you all this. Not that you're writing a book, right?"

Joey laughed weakly. "Right!" she said, wanting to crawl off somewhere and die.

Chapter Ten

Joey's mind was racing out of control as she headed back down the New Jersey Turnpike, racing toward Pennsylvania. Why had she ever shown her manuscript to Wilbur? Why hadn't she just kept on submitting the darn thing over the transom, like any other unpublished writer? Why hadn't she just tried to get a literary agent, and let him handle it? Why had she ever written the damn thing in the first place?

Had she sworn Wilbur to secrecy? No, of course she hadn't. That would have been too obvious, too intelligent, too *normal*. No, she had just handed the thing to him, and asked him to give his honest opinion.

An honest opinion? From Wilbur Langley? The man who looked at her and saw her as the answer to all his prayers for making Daniel and Richie into a family again? The same man who had published his daughter's book when it was "badder than bad"?

Whom had she been kidding? Of course, Wilbur was going to like her manuscript. The man liked twelve-foot-long blood-red lips on his walls, for crying out loud! When it

came to women—daughters, prospective daughters-in-law
or pretty women who appealed to him—Wilbur Langley had
about as much objectivity as a three-year-old set loose in a
toy store.

She'd been out to have her ego stroked, that was what
she'd done. Oh, she could have talked herself into believing
that she had only wanted Wilbur's opinion because his approval of her work would also justify her leaving Ransom
Computers and wandering the country for two years like
some gypsy. After all, Daniel had condemned her life-style.
She had been looking for justification of her life, her reason for existing.

"And I wanted to know if I was talented," she admitted
out loud, so that the tolltaker on the Phillipsburg Bridge
looked at her warily as she drove away. "I wanted to have
someone pat me on the back and say I was this decade's answer to J. D. Salinger."

Her foot rode the gas pedal heavily as she tooled Esmeralda down the thruway, hoping against hope that Wilbur's
doorman was wrong, and the retired publisher had not left
town that morning to visit his grandson "in the wilds of
Pennsylvania."

Why had Wilbur decided to visit today, of all days?
Maybe he hadn't had time to read her manuscript. It was
possible. Anything was possible.

Maybe, even if he *had* read it, he wouldn't have shown it
to Daniel. Because, she thought grimly as she pulled Esmeralda into the Quinn driveway, if he ever did show it to
Daniel her world would be over.

Mrs. Hemmings opened the front door for her, shaking
her head as she informed her that Daniel and Richie had already left for the Bulldogs' baseball game, but Mr. Wilbur
was there if she wanted to see him. "A very nice man, Mr.
Wilbur," the housekeeper remarked as she led the way to the
living room, "but he's a bit strange. He kept turning the

lights on and off, saying he didn't know we had such conveniences in Pennsylvania.''

Joey smiled at Mrs. Hemmings's obvious confusion and
relaxed a bit. She had forgotten all about the baseball game.
Maybe there was still time to save herself. ''Just don't forget to take him around back to show him the little house
with the half-moon on the door,'' she advised just as Wilbur came into the foyer, his arms outstretched in greeting.

''Darling Joey!'' he exclaimed, taking hold of both her
hands and bringing them to his lips. ''At last someone has
shown up to greet me. Daniel and my grandson are nowhere to be found. Why didn't you tell me you were so
vastly talented? I wept as I read your brilliant manuscript, I
tell you. Wept and laughed, and sighed deep, satisfied
sighs.''

''You laughed, you cried, it became a part of you,'' Joey
recited dully, not believing him for a minute. ''You didn't
show it to Daniel, did you?''

''Daniel?'' Wilbur repeated, looking puzzled as he sat on
the sofa facing the chair she had dropped into, exhausted.
''Why should I show it to Daniel? You're my coup, not his.
Let him discover his own genius. You're mine. I want to edit
you personally.''

''Edit me?'' Joey repeated, too relieved to fully take in
what Wilbur was saying.

He leaned across the coffee table to pat her hand. ''Did
you think I completely walked away, my dear? I still dabble
in the company occasionally, taking care of my own select
list of authors. One of them is on the bestseller list right
now. I think you might know of her. Courtney Blackmun?''

Joey's eyes nearly popped out of her head. ''You edit
Courtney Blackmun? Wilbur, I'm impressed!''

He leaned back in his seat. ''Don't be, my dear. She only
allows me a bit of comma movement here and there, and an
occasional minor correction of syntax. Courtney's a law

unto herself at Langley Books. But she's not my only author. And now I have you. Congratulations, Joey Abbott, and welcome to my stable. Stable—as if writers were horses."

Joey shook her head, first slowly, and then quickly, vehemently in the negative. "No, Wilbur," she told him fiercely. "I can't, honestly. I can't let Daniel know I've written a book. He'll think I was only using him in order to get published. It's not like I was planning a career as a writer. I just wrote it, that's all. Maybe in a couple of years I'll consider it again, but for now—"

Wilbur's brow furrowed as he considered this new thought. "But that's ridiculous. If you were using him, then why didn't you give the manuscript directly to him, instead of to me?"

She jumped to her feet, spreading her hands. "Because I was using him to get to you, of course!" she blurted, knowing she was in danger of becoming hysterical. "Maybe I was even using Richie in order to get to either one of you. Who knows what he'll think! Courtney says—"

"Courtney?" Wilbur repeated, cutting her off as he rose to put his arm around her. "Lovely girl, Courtney. She told you about Veronica, didn't she? I'm sure she meant well. Courtney is never mean. But I see why you're upset. Have you considered a pen name? *One for the Road* must be put in print. It would be a crime to hide it because you're afraid of what Daniel might think."

"Oh, Wilbur!" Joey groaned, laying her head against his silk-shirted chest. "What a fine mess I've gotten myself into this time!"

Joey went home without seeing Daniel, knowing that Andy had arrived back in town that afternoon and would be wondering why his loving sister hadn't been there to greet him. He'd also be wondering where his dinner was, she thought fatalistically, knowing that there was no problem so big that it couldn't be pushed into the background long enough to satisfy Andy's enormous appetite.

The Mercedes was gone when she pulled into the driveway in front of the house, and a note propped against the salt shaker on the kitchen table told her that Andy had gone to see the Bulldogs play, hoping to find her there. Shrugging her shoulders, she decided to start dinner, knowing he would be home soon, three hotdogs under his belt, and still ravenous. Besides, it would pass the time until Daniel was to pick her up for their prearranged dinner date.

Andy came barreling through the door just as the kitchen timer signaled that the spaghetti noodles were al dente, grabbing his sister in a bear hug that lifted her completely off the floor. "Hi, Sis!" he shouted into her ear. "Boy, that smells good. Miss me?"

"Did Fay Wray miss King Kong? Did Tarzan miss Cheetah? Put me down, you big ape, before the spaghetti gets all mushy. Let me look at you. Is it possible? It looks like you've grown. What did you bring me?"

Andy turned a kitchen chair around and straddled it. "Just like a kid—'what did you bring me, Daddy?' I got you a turquoise necklace from this really neat Indian reservation we visited, but it's still in my suitcase. I'll unpack after dinner, okay?"

"Squash?"

"Squash? I thought we were having spaghetti and meatballs. I hate squash."

Joey pretended to hit him with the colander as she prepared to drain the spaghetti. "Not squash. *Squash*. Is it a squash necklace?"

Andy shrugged, reaching into the salad bowl in the middle of the table to extract a slice of cucumber. "Darned if I know. It's blue. Hey, what's with Mr. Quinn? He used to have a sense of humor."

Pausing in the middle of pouring the spaghetti into the colander, Joey turned her head to correct her brother's mistaken impression. "Daniel's got a wonderful sense of humor. You just can't tell a joke, brother mine. I've told you that before. Just keep practicing on that guitar. It's the only hope you've got."

The telephone rang and Andy hopped up to answer it. He said hello, and then just listened. Hanging it up a few moments later, he straddled the chair once more and said, "That was Mr. Quinn. He says he has to cancel your date for tonight. Something about having his father-in-law in town and having to catch up on some work he's been neglecting. He sounded strange." Andy popped another cucumber slice into his mouth.

Joey looked down at the amount of cooked spaghetti, knowing there wasn't enough for her, as she had thought she was going out for dinner. It didn't matter, because she had suddenly lost her appetite. Numbly, her hands moving automatically, she set the food in front of her brother and then sat down before she fell down.

He couldn't know. It was ridiculous. Wilbur wasn't going to tell him. He was going to leave that up to her. He'd promised, under the pain of forfeiting his lifelong membership at the Metropolitan Museum. It had to have been Andy, ridiculous and horrible as that seemed.

"Andy," she asked carefully as he twirled some spaghetti around his fork and popped it into his mouth, "what made you think Daniel has no sense of humor? What joke did you tell him?"

Waiting until Andy was done chewing and swallowing was almost more than she could bear. "I didn't tell him a joke, Sis," he said at last. "Well, not an *actual* joke. I was talking to him between innings—we won by the way—and I just asked him what he thought of your book."

"You asked him what he thought of my book?" Joey squeaked, closing her eyes, and leaning her forehead on her hand. "Oh, Andy, how could you?"

"What do you mean, how could I? You told me on the phone that he's some sort of publisher. Why shouldn't I ask him? I mean, you're my sister, and I know you. You wouldn't let an opportunity like that pass you by."

"But just in case I had, you were going to do my dirty work for me, right? Go on," she said tightly.

"Yeah, well, there's not much more to tell. I just asked him if he got a good laugh out of your spelling. I may not have read your book, but I do read your trip log. You've got to be the only person in the world who spells New Jersey with a G. Anyway, Daniel didn't think it was funny—the G business, you know. He just looked at me in this goofy way and then went back out to coach first base. Do I drive him tomorrow, or do you?"

Remembering Daniel's earlier order—given in anger, but given just the same—that Andy take over the job of chauffeuring him as soon as he got back from vacation, Joey said, "You do," and then fled from the kitchen before her brother could see the tears she could no longer hide. It was all over. Daniel hated her. He had every right to hate her. She hadn't been honest with him. And now it was too late for anything except regret.

Daniel was unsurprised to see Andy behind the wheel when Esmeralda's gleaming white body pulled up in front of the door the next morning. Wilbur, standing beside him, leaned closer to him and gibed, "Not that I'm the sort to say 'I told you so,' but—I told you so! To use the vernacular, you blew it, buster."

"Thank you for those words of wisdom, Wilbur," Daniel replied tersely. "Now why don't you go crawl into your bed before the sun comes up?"

Wilbur stepped back a pace, clutching a hand to his chest. "Ah! You got me! I'm cut to the quick. But the question remains—what are you going to do about my favorite author?"

"Courtney Blackmun?" Daniel asked, avoiding the question. "What should I do with her? She's tucked up in her Manhattan apartment, puffing and creating. You should be doing handsprings. I know I am."

"Not that favorite author. I mean Joey," Wilbur corrected, unruffled. "What are you going to do about dearest Joey?"

Daniel's head snapped around as he confronted his father-in-law. "Joey's *my* author, if she'll let me within ten feet of her work."

Wilbur smiled and corrected, "On the contrary, old son. I discovered her. Joey's mine."

Andy had apparently heard enough. Letting go of the passenger door he'd been holding open, he approached the men. "Why don't you just cut her in half? Then you can both have some of her."

Wilbur looked down at Andy. "This is the brother, I presume. He's as tall as she's small, isn't he?" He held out his hand. "Andrew? You're the aspiring singer, isn't that correct? If you can sing as well as your sister can write, I may have a theatrical agent for you. I believe he once had something to do with a lad named Spring-something-or-other."

Daniel watched in knowing resignation as Andy, formerly angry for his sister's sake and ready to take on the world to defend her, turned into a smiling tower of jelly at Wilbur's words. "And another one bites the dust," he spit in disgust, heading for the limousine. "Come on, Andy, I've got places to go and people to see."

"You shouldn't be going to the city, Daniel," Wilbur called after him. "You should be crawling over to Joey's house—preferably on your knees."

"I'll handle this my own way, and in my own time, thank you. Goodbye, Wilbur," Daniel called over his shoulder as he bent his tall frame in order to enter the backseat. "Try not to corrupt Mrs. Hemmings while I'm gone."

* * *

"I can't do it."

"Of course you can, Sis. We've got nothing else on for tonight," Andy said, chasing his retreating sister from the kitchen out onto the porch.

She threw herself onto the porch swing and began rocking it back and forth furiously. "All right then, Andy, I *won't* do it. Is that better? And what is he up to, coming back from New York this early in the day?" She glared up at her brother. "Did he bring someone named Ursula with him?" she asked suspiciously.

Andy shook his head. "He was alone. Now look, Joey, it's only a trip to Stokesay Castle. You've made the trip five dozen times. Why not tonight?"

She crossed her arms tightly against her breast and continued to rock the old swing back and forth at a dangerously fast rate. "Because I wouldn't cross the street with Daniel Quinn, that's why. I'm not about to chauffeur him and his latest dinner companion to Reading. I didn't contract out for that."

Leaning against the wooden porch rail, Andy lifted a hand to scratch at a spot just above his left ear, a clear warning sign that he was about to say something she didn't want to hear. The last time he'd scratched that spot he had told her he wanted to be a rock star. "I'm not contracted out for that—am I, Andy?" she asked, jamming her feet against the porch to stop the swing.

"Well, ac-tu-ally—" Andy began warily.

"Andrew Abbott, what have you gotten me into?" she shrieked, remembering that Andy had been the one to sign the contract. Why hadn't she taken the time to read it before gaily delivering it to the loan officer at the bank like a Christmas pudding? "Andrew—speak to me!"

Andy took a deep breath and began talking fast. "The contract says that Daniel has first dibs at our service for the length of the contract. It says that he is to have the driver of his choice, and that the contract is null and void if we fail to deliver without adequate explanation of our inability to perform. So that's why we have to transport Daniel to Stokesay Castle tonight for his dinner date, and that's why you have to drive him. If we don't, we blow the contract. You said the guy from the bank called today to say we have the loan, so we can't lose Daniel now or else we'll lose the whole ball game. Right?" he ended, lifting his hands as if to ward off physical attack.

Joey's next words were spoken very slowly. "I think I'm going to be ill. Seriously ill."

Andy lowered his hands. "But you'll do it?"

"I'll do it," she answered, rising to her feet with all the dignity of a French aristocrat about to face the guillotine. "But he's going to regret it. *Boy*, is he going to regret it!"

"He's a nice guy, Sis. Why do you hate him?" Andy asked as Joey headed for the kitchen door.

"Because it's easier than the alternative," she replied, her answer totally lost on Andy, who wasn't a woman in love, and couldn't understand.

Stokesay Castle was always beautiful, but this warm summer night it was exquisite, sitting atop its own slice of the mountain, its turrets catching the last lingering rays of the setting sun, its gray stone walls and mullioned windows looking warm and inviting. It was a place constructed out of love, and with a loving eye to detail, from the large, dark wood-paneled entranceway to the dining rooms hung with full-size portraits and heavy tapestries.

No matter how many times Joey made the trip, bringing lovers here for the perfect setting for "popping the question" over specially prepared dinners, and happily married couples celebrating their anniversaries, the castle remained special to Joey.

That was why she had regretted telling Daniel about it in the first place, for he had brought Roseanne here, and

Muffy, but never her. And that was why she was dying by
inches now as she tooled Esmeralda along the twisting
roadway that led to the restaurant.

It had been a silent drive, with Daniel sitting alone in the
back of the limousine, looking perfectly wonderful in his
dark suit, and completely remote, with his hands crossed
against his chest. He had been waiting for her when she
pulled into the drive, and helped himself into the backseat,
a single curt nod of his head motioning her to proceed to
Reading.

It took forty-five minutes to reach the castle, long, heartbreaking minutes during which Joey's mood rocketed back
and forth between anger and the faint, wild glimmerings of
hope. After all, he was alone. Was he meeting someone?
Was this to be the moment he would unveil the famous Ursula? Or was he sitting back there struggling with his con-
science, trying to find some way to make up for breaking her
heart?

Surely he knew her heart was broken. It didn't take a
computer whiz to figure out that he had learned about *One
for the Road* and immediately jumped to all the wrong con-
clusions.

No, she decided at least three times between Kutztown
and the outskirts of Reading, *he isn't planning some cute,
silly, romantic way to apologize. He's doing this deliberately, riding in splendor while I sit up front, my stupid cap
on my stupid head, his paid lackey. He's just putting me
back in my place—firmly. I could kill him! I love him so
much!*

"Your driving wasn't quite as smooth as usual, Joey,"
Daniel remarked blandly as he exited the limousine, having
waited almost a full five minutes for her to climb out of the
front seat and stomp around to the other side to open his
door.

"Be happy I didn't run you off the cliff," she answered
from between compressed lips, watching as he entered the

restaurant without looking at her. She waited until the door closed behind him, standing at attention until she was sure it was safe to release her pent-up breath. "And now, Mr. Daniel Quinn, I hope you enjoy your dinner. I hope you enjoy it because it's going to be a long walk back to Saucon Valley!"

She was just about to strap on her seat belt, her fingers fumbling with the need to be away from the restaurant before she could change her mind, when one of the waitresses knocked on the windshield. "Hi, Joey," she said, motioning for her to lower the window. "Come on inside. I have something to show you."

"Not tonight, Ginny," Joey pleaded. "I really have to be going. Some other—"

"But it's the neatest thing! You've got to see it, Joey. It's up on the roof—on top of the tower. Come on. It'll just take a minute."

Joey sighed, removing the key from the ignition. "What is it, Ginny?" she asked, following the waitress into the restaurant. "Have you finally figured out where Elvis has been hiding himself all these years? Has he taken up residence in the secret room in the tower? Have you looked in the dungeon lately—maybe Buddy Holly is down there."

Ginny, a devoted rock and roll fan, laughed nervously. "Don't be silly," she admonished, taking Joey's hand and leading her up the winding staircase that led to the top of the tower. "The owners have decided to fix up an outdoor eating area for young lovers up here and I knew you'd want to see it so you could tell your clients about it. Hey, Joey, you remember that couple you brought down last year—the guy who had me put the engagement ring in his girlfriend's champagne glass? They were back last week for their first anniversary. She's going to have a baby just before Christmas! Isn't that sweet?"

"Adorable," Joey agreed, wondering why fate had chosen a nice girl like Ginny to drive a stake through her heart.

She tried to change the subject. "How will you get the food all the way up here before it gets cold?"

"A dumbwaiter, dummy," Ginny answered with a smile, opening the door at the top of the stairs and then standing back to motion for Joey to precede her.

Joey took two steps onto the flat, parapet-ringed roof before the door slammed shut behind her. She whirled about, calling out to Ginny, then froze as a male voice said, "I thought you'd never get here. Come over here and sit down. Your onion soup is getting cold."

She didn't turn around, but only stared at the closed door. "Daniel," she said, closing her eyes, trying desperately not to betray herself by breaking down.

"One and the same," he acknowledged, walking over to place his hands on her shoulders. "It was a juvenile idea, but the best one I could come up with to get you alone."

"I suppose there's really a table set for dinner up here for us?" she asked, still refusing to turn around.

"There is," he told her, rubbing his hands up and down her arms. "I've ordered filet mignon for you. I'm having a large serving of humble pie for my main course."

"Because you were angry when Andy told you I'd written a book?"

"No, my darling Joey. Because I was *stupid* when Andy told me you'd written a book. Stupid, and temporarily insane. You'd never try to use me to get a book published. You're entirely too honest to do something like that. I should have known that immediately. Especially not to publish a book like *One for the Road*."

Now she did turn around. It was the "darling" that did it. The "darling" and the way his voice had softened when he mentioned the title of her book. "You read it?" She looked up at him, her gray eyes wide with the unspoken question: Did you like it?

His hands tightening on her shoulders, he smiled and nodded that he had. "It's a curiously naive, yet comforting look at the people of this country through the eyes of someone just discovering life. Youth and innocence shine through every word, Joey. Your youth, your innocence."

She swallowed down hard on the sudden lump in her throat. "You laughed, you cried, it became a part of you," she joked feebly, her bottom lip trembling as tears threatened to spill down her cheeks.

"I'm tossing Wilbur for the chance to edit it—and all the books you're going to write. Best two out of three falls wins," Daniel told her as his finger came up to gently wipe away one traitorous tear. "If you'll let me?"

"Just try to weasel your way out of it, buster!" she warned, putting her hands against his chest, just to be sure he was real. And he was real, real and solid, and more wonderful than ever.

His next words proved it. "I love you, Josephine Abbott. Please, for my sake, and Richie's sake, and even, God help me, Wilbur's sake, will you marry me, Josephine?"

She answered him with her kiss, never even noticing that he had called her Josephine.

* * * * *

> "Motherhood is full of love, laughter and sweet surprises. Silhouette's collection is every bit as much fun!"
> —Bestselling author **Ann Major**

This May, treat yourself to...

WANTED:
MOTHER

Silhouette's annual tribute to motherhood takes a new twist in '96 as three sexy single men prepare for fatherhood—and saying "I Do!" This collection makes the perfect gift, not just for moms but for all romance fiction lovers! Written by these captivating authors:

Annette Broadrick
Ginna Gray
Raye Morgan

> "The Mother's Day anthology from Silhouette is the highlight of any romance lover's spring!"
> —Award-winning author **Dallas Schulze**

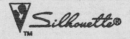

by
Cathryn Clare

The Cotter brothers—two private detectives and an
FBI agent—go wherever danger leads them...except
in matters of the heart!

But now they've just gotten the toughest assignments of
their lives....

Wiley Cotter has...
THE WEDDING ASSIGNMENT: March 1996
Intimate Moments #702

Sam Cotter takes on...
THE HONEYMOON ASSIGNMENT: May 1996
Intimate Moments #714

Jack Cotter is surprised by...
THE BABY ASSIGNMENT: July 1996
Intimate Moments #726

From Cathryn Clare—and only where
Silhouette Books are sold!

CCAR1

STEP INTO THE

WINNER'S CIRCLE

A collection of award-winning books
by award-winning authors!
From Harlequin and Silhouette.

Available this May

A Human Touch
by *Glenda Sanders*

VOTED BEST SHORT CONTEMPORARY ROMANCE—*RITA AWARD WINNER*

When dire circumstances force together a single mother with an adorable one-month-old baby and an arrogant lawyer, emotions start to get out of control as *A Human Touch* proves to have a powerful effect on their lives.

"Glenda Sanders weaves a masterful spell..."

—*Inside Romance*

Available this May wherever Harlequin books are sold.

What do women really want to know?

Trust the world's largest publisher of
women's fiction to tell you.

HARLEQUIN ULTIMATE GUIDES™

I CAN FIX THAT

A Guide For Women
Who Want To Do It Themselves

This is the only guide a self-reliant
woman will ever need to deal
with those pesky items that
break, wear out or just don't work
anymore. Chock-full of friendly
advice and straightforward,
step-by-step solutions to the
trials of everyday life in our
gadget-oriented world! So, don't
just sit there wondering how to
fix the VCR—run to your
nearest bookstore for your copy now!

Available this May, at your favorite retail outlet.

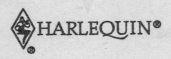

HARLEQUIN®

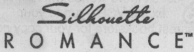